AMID THE SAVAGERY OF WAR, THERE IS A THIN LINE BETWEEN MAN AND BEAST . . .

WIKTOR: In the heart of the forest, the old man filled Michael Gallatin's head with Shakespeare—and taught him to hunt on four legs. He left his pupil with one command, "Live free," and one unanswerable question, "What is the werewolf, in the eye of God?"

CHESNA VAN DORNE: Known to the Allies as Echo, she was Germany's Golden Girl, a propaganda film star who sipped champagne with the Nazi top echelon. Posing as her fiancé, Gallatin discovered a woman of rare, glorious passion—and found a precious clue to Iron Fist that put them both in the path of death . . .

HARRY SANDLER: An American big-game hunter, openly sadistic, he kept a pet hawk so bloodthirsty even his Nazi pals dared not cross him. Gallatin had an old score to settle with Sandler—and he would take his vengeance as a man, not a wolf . . .

COLONEL JEREK BLOK: Mastermind of Iron Fist, former commander of Falkenhousen concentration camp, and gleeful member of the Brimstone Club, he kept a vicious bodyguard everyone called "Boots." Blok liked to think of himself as Chesna's fond uncle—and he didn't approve of her new beau, Gallatin . . .

MOUSE: A deserter from the German Army, he met Gallatin while picking pockets on the streets of Paris. Desperate to return to his homeland, the little man agreed to help the Allies—and learned a devastating lesson about true courage . . .

Books by Robert R. McCammon

Baal
Bethany's Sin
The Night Boat
Stinger
Swan Song
They Thirst
The Wolf's Hour

Published by POCKET BOOKS

THE WOLF'S HOUR

ROBERT R. McCAMMON

POCKET BOOKS

New York   London   Toronto   Sydney   Tokyo

Dedicated to John Sanders.

Thanks also to John Hoomes
for the technical research assistance.

An *Original* Publication of POCKET BOOKS

POCKET BOOKS, a division of Simon & Schuster Inc.
1230 Avenue of the Americas, New York, NY 10020

ISBN: 0-671-66485-9

First Pocket Books printing March 1989

10 9 8 7 6 5 4 3 2

POCKET and colophon are trademarks of
Simon & Schuster Inc.

Printed in the U.S.A.

Prologue

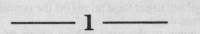

1

The war went on.

By February 1941, it had leaped like a firestorm from Europe to the shores of northwest Africa, where Hitler's commander of German troops, a competent officer named Erwin Rommel, arrived in Tripoli in support of the Italians and began to drive the British force back to the Nile.

Along the coastal road from Benghazi through El Aghelia, Agedabia, and Mechili, the Panzer Army Africa's tanks and soldiers continued to press across a land of torturous heat, sandstorms, gullies that had forgotten the taste of rain, and sheer cliffs that dropped hundreds of feet to flat plains of nothing. The mass of men, anti-armor guns, trucks, and tanks marched east, taking the fortress of Tobruk from the British on June 20, 1942, and advancing toward the glittering prize Hitler so desired: the Suez Canal. With control of that vital waterway, Nazi Germany would be able to choke off Allied shipping and continue the eastward march, driving into the soft underbelly of Russia.

The British Eighth Army, most of the soldiers exhausted, staggered toward a railway stop called El Alamein in the last scorching days of June 1942. In their wake the engineers frantically laid down intricate patterns of mine fields, hoping to delay the oncoming Panzers. There was rumor that Rommel was low on petrol and ammunition, but in their foxholes dug in the hard white earth the soldiers could feel the ground shake with the vibrations of Nazi tanks. And as the sun beat down and the vultures circled, columns of dust rose on the western horizon. Rommel had come to El Alamein, and he was not to be denied his dinner in Cairo.

The sun set, blood red in a milky sky. The shadows of

3

June 30 crept across the desert. The soldiers of the Eighth Army waited, while their officers studied sweat-stained maps in tents and engineer teams continued to fortify the mine fields between them and the German lines. The stars came out, brilliant in a moonless sky. Sergeants checked ammunition reserves and barked at men to clean up their foxholes—anything to get their minds off the carnage that would surely start at dawn.

Several miles to the west, where recon riders on sand-scarred BMW motorcycles and troopers in armored scout cars rumbled through the dark on the edge of the mine fields, a small sand-colored Storch airplane landed with a snarl and flurry of prop wash on a strip bordered by blue flares. Black Nazi swastikas were painted on the aircraft's wings.

As soon as the Storch's wheels stopped turning, an open-roofed command car drove up from the northwest, its headlights visored. A German *oberstleutnant*, wearing the dusty pale brown uniform of the Africa Corps and goggles against the swirling grit, got out of the aircraft. He carried a battered brown satchel that was handcuffed to his right wrist, and he was smartly saluted by the car's driver, who held the door for him. The Storch's pilot waited in the cockpit, following the officer's orders. Then the command car rumbled off the way it had come, and as soon as it was out of sight the pilot sipped from his canteen and tried to get a little sleep.

The command car climbed a small ridge, its tires spitting out sand and sharp-edged stones. On the ridge's other side stood the tents and vehicles of a forward reconnaissance battalion, everything dark but for the meager glow of lanterns inside the tents and an occasional glint of shielded headlights as a motorcycle or armored car moved on some errand. The command car pulled to a halt before the largest and most central of the tents, and the *oberstleutnant* waited for his door to be opened before he got out. As he strode toward the tent's entrance, he heard the rattle of cans and saw several skinny dogs rooting in the trash. One of them came toward him, its ribs showing and its eyes hollowed with hunger. He kicked at the animal before it reached him. His boot hit the dog's side, driving it back, but the creature made no noise. The officer knew the nasty things had lice,

4

and with water at such a premium he didn't relish scrubbing his flesh with sand. The dog turned away, its hide bruised with other boot marks, its death by starvation already decided.

The officer stopped just short of the tent flap.

Something else was out there, he realized. Just beyond the edge of the true dark, past where the dogs were searching through the garbage for scraps of beef.

He could see its eyes. They glinted green, picking up a shard of light from a tent's lantern. They watched him without blinking, and in them there was no cowering or begging. Another damned tribesman's dog, the officer thought, though he could see nothing but its eyes. The dogs followed the camps, and it was said they would lick piss off a plate if you offered it to them. He didn't like the way that bastard watched him; those eyes were cunning and cold, and he was tempted to reach for his Luger and dispatch another canine to Muslim heaven. Those eyes stirred ants of unease in his belly, because there was no fear in them.

"Lieutenant Colonel Voigt. We've been expecting you. Please, come in."

The tent flap had been drawn back. Major Stummer, a rugged-faced man with close-cropped reddish hair and round eyeglasses, saluted, and Voigt nodded a greeting. Inside the tent were three more officers, standing around a table covered with maps. Lantern light spilled over the chiseled, sun-browned Germanic faces, which were turned expectantly toward Voigt. The lieutenant colonel paused at the tent's threshold; his gaze wandered to the right, past the skinny, starving dogs.

The green eyes were gone.

"Sir?" Stummer inquired. "Is anything wrong?"

"No." His answer was too quick. It was stupid to be upset by a dog, he told himself. He had personally ordered an "88" gun to destroy four British tanks with more composure than he felt at this moment. Where had the dog gone? Out into the desert, of course. But why had it not come in to nose amid the cans like the others? Well, it was ridiculous to waste time thinking about. Rommel had sent him here for information and that's what he planned to take back to

5

Panzer Army headquarters. "Nothing's wrong except I have stomach ulcers, a heat rash on my neck, and I long to see snow before I go mad," Voigt said as he stepped into the tent and the flap fell shut behind him.

Voigt stood at the table with Stummer, Major Klinhurst, and the other two battalion officers. His flinty blue eyes scanned the maps. They showed the cruel, gulley-slashed desert between Point 169, the small ridge he'd passed over, and the British fortifications. Inked-in red circles indicated mine fields, and blue squares stood for the many defensive boxes, studded with barbed wire and machine guns, that would have to be overcome on the drive eastward. The maps also showed, in black lines and squares, where the German troops and tanks were positioned. On each map was the recon battalion's official rubber stamp.

Voigt took off his flat-brimmed cap, wiped the sweat from his face with a well-used handkerchief, and studied the maps. He was a big, broad-shouldered man whose fair skin had hardened to burnished leather. He had blond hair with swirls of gray at the temples, his thick eyebrows almost completely gray. "I assume these are up-to-the-minute?" he asked.

"Yes, sir. The last patrol came in twenty minutes ago."

Voigt grunted noncommittally, sensing that Stummer was waiting for a compliment on his battalion's thorough reconnaissance of the mine fields. "I don't have much time. Field Marshal Rommel is waiting. What are your recommendations?"

Stummer was disappointed that his battalion's work wasn't recognized. It had been hard and heavy the past two days and nights, searching for a hole in the British fortifications. He and his men might have been on the edge of the world, for all the desolation around them. "Here." He picked up a pencil and tapped one of the maps. "We believe the easiest way through would be in this area, just south of Ruweisat Ridge. The mine fields are light, and you can see there's a gap in the field of fire between these two boxes." He touched two blue squares. "A concentrated effort might easily punch a hole through."

"Major," Voigt said wearily, "nothing in this damned

desert is easy. If we don't get the petrol and ammunition we need, we're going to be on foot throwing rocks before the week's over. Fold the maps for me.''

One of the junior officers began to do so. Voigt unzipped his satchel and put the maps in them. Then he zipped up the satchel, wiped the sweat off his face, and put on his cap. Now for the flight back to Rommel's command post, and for the rest of the night there would be discussions, briefings, and a movement of troops, tanks, and supplies to the areas Rommel had decided to attack. Without these maps the field marshal's decision would be nothing more than a toss of the dice.

The satchel now had a satisfying weight. "I'm sure the field marshal would want me to say that you've done a remarkable job, Major," Voigt finally said. Stummer looked pleased. "We'll all toast the success of Panzer Army Africa on the banks of the Nile. Heil Hitler." Voigt raised his hand quickly, and the others—all except Klinhurst, who made no bones about his distaste for the party—responded in kind. Then the meeting was over, and Voigt turned away from the table and walked briskly out of the tent toward the waiting car. The driver was already there to open the door, and Major Stummer came out to see Voigt off.

Voigt was a few strides from the car when he caught a quick movement to his right.

His head swiveled in that direction, and at once his legs turned to jelly.

Less than an arm's length away was a black dog with green eyes. It had evidently darted around from the tent's other side and had come up on him so fast that neither the driver nor Stummer had time to react. The black beast was not like the other starving wild dogs; it was as big as a bull mastiff, almost two and a half feet tall at the shoulder, and muscles, like bunches of piano wires, rippled along its back and haunches. Its ears were laid flat along its sleek-haired skull, and its eyes were as bright as green signal lamps. They stared up forcefully into Voigt's face, and in them the German officer recognized a killer's intelligence.

It was not a dog, Voigt realized.

It was a wolf.

7

"Mein Gott," Voigt said, with a rush of air as if he'd been punched in his ulcerated stomach. The muscular monster of a wolf was right on him, its mouth opening to show white fangs and scarlet gums. He felt its hot breath on the back of his handcuffed wrist, and as he realized with a flare of horror what it was about to do, his left hand went to the grip of his holstered Luger.

The wolf's jaws snapped shut on Voigt's wrist, and with a savage twist of its head it broke the bones.

A splintered nub tore through Voigt's flesh, along with a spouting arc of scarlet that spattered the command car's side. Voigt screamed, unable to get the holster's flap unsnapped and the Luger freed. He tried to pull away but the wolf planted its claws in the ground and wouldn't budge. The car's driver was frozen with shock, and Stummer was shouting for help from the other soldiers who'd just returned from their patrol. Voigt's burnished face had taken on a yellow cast. The wolf's jaws were working; the teeth starting to meet through the broken bones and bloody flesh. The green eyes stared defiantly at him. Voigt screamed, "Help me! Help me!" and the wolf rewarded him with a shake of its head that shivered agony through every nerve of his body and all but severed the hand.

On the verge of fainting, Voigt tore the Luger out of his holster just as the driver cocked his own Walther pistol and aimed at the wolf's skull. Voigt pointed his gun into the thing's blood-smeared muzzle.

But as the two fingers tightened on their triggers, the wolf suddenly hurled its body to one side, still clenching Voigt's wrist, and Voigt was thrown directly into the path of the Walther's barrel. The driver's pistol went off with a strident *crack!* at the same time as the Luger fired into the ground. The Walther's bullet passed through Voigt's back, punching a red-edged hole through his chest as it emerged. As Voigt crumpled, the wolf ripped his hand away from the wrist. The handcuff slipped off and fell, still attached to the satchel. With a quick snap of its head, the wolf flung the quivering hand out of its blood-smeared jaws. It fell amid the starving dogs, and they pounced on the new piece of garbage.

The driver fired again, his face a rictus of terror and his

gun hand shaking. A gout of earth kicked up to the wolf's left as it leaped aside. Three soldiers were running from another tent, all of them carrying Schmeisser submachine guns. Stummer shrieked, "Kill it!" and Klinhurst came out of the headquarters tent with his pistol in hand. But the black animal darted forward, over Voigt's body. Its teeth found the metal cuff, and locked around it. As the driver fired a third time the bullet went through the satchel and whined off the ground. Klinhurst took aim—but before he could squeeze the trigger the wolf zigzagged its body and raced off into the darkness to the east.

The driver fired the rest of his clip, but there was no howl of pain. More soldiers were coming from their tents, and there were shouts of alarm all over the camp. Stummer ran to Voigt's body, rolled him over, and recoiled from all the gore. He swallowed thickly, his mind reeling at how fast it all had happened. And then he realized the crux of the matter: the wolf had taken the satchel full of reconnaissance maps, and was heading east.

East. Toward the British lines.

Those maps also showed the position of Rommel's troops, and if the British got them . . .

"Mount up!" he screamed, coming to his feet as if an iron bar had been thrust up his spine. "Hurry, for God's sake! *Hurry!* We've got to stop that beast!" He raced past the command car to another vehicle not far away: a yellow armored car with a heavy machine gun fixed to its windshield. The driver followed him, and now other soldiers ran to their BMW motorcycles and sidecars, which also were armed with machine guns. Stummer slid into the passenger seat, the driver started the engine and turned on the headlights, the motorcycle engines muttered and roared and their lamps burned yellow, and Stummer shouted, *"Go!"* to his driver through a throat that could already feel an executioner's noose.

The armored car shot forward, throwing plumes of dust from its tires, and four motorcycles veered around it, accelerated, and roared past.

A quarter mile ahead, the wolf was running. Its body was an engine designed for speed and distance. Its eyes narrowed to slits and its jaws clamped firmly around the handcuff. The satchel bumped against the ground in a steady rhythm, and the wolf's breathing was a low, powerful rumbling. The racing figure angled a few degrees to the right, went up a rocky hillock and down again as if following a predetermined course. Sand flew from beneath its paws, and ahead of the beast scorpions and lizards darted for cover.

Its ears twitched. A growling noise was coming up fast on the left. The wolf's pace quickened, its paws thrumming against hard-packed sand. The growling was closer . . . much closer . . . and now it was almost directly to the left. A spotlight swept past the animal, came back, and fixed on the running shape. The soldier in the motorcycle's sidecar shouted, "There it is!" and pulled the safety mechanism off the machine gun. He twisted the barrel toward the animal and opened fire.

The wolf skidded to a stop in a flurry of dust, and the bullets ripped a fiery pattern across the earth in front of it. The motorcycle zoomed past, its driver fighting the brake and handlebars. And then the wolf changed course and started running again at full speed, still heading east, still gripping the handcuff.

The machine gun kept chattering. Tracer bullets carved orange lines through the dark and ricocheted off stones like spent cigarette butts. But the wolf zigzagged back and forth, its body hugging the earth, and as the tracers whined around, the animal went over another hillock and out of the spotlight's range.

"Over there!" the gunner shouted against the wind. "It went over that hill!" The driver turned the bulky motorcycle and headed after it, white dust whirling through the headlight's beam. He gave the engine full power, and it responded with a throaty roar of German machinery. They topped the hill and started down—and the headlamp showed an eight-foot-deep gulley just beneath it, waiting like a jagged grin.

The motorcycle crashed into it, turned end over end, and the machine gun went off, spraying bullets in a wild arc that ricocheted off the sides of the gulley and slammed through the bodies of the driver and gunner. The motorcycle crumpled, and its gas tank exploded.

On the other side of the gulley, which the wolf had cleared with a single spring of its hind legs, the animal kept going, dodging pieces of hot metal that clattered down around it.

Through the echoes of the blast came the noise of another predator, this time coming from the right. The wolf's head ticked to the side, sighting the sidecar's spotlight. The machine gun began to fire, bullets thudding around the wolf's legs and whistling past its body as it ran in quick, desperate circles and angles. But the motorcycle was closing the distance between them, and the bullets were getting nearer to their target. One tracer flashed so close that the wolf could smell the bitter scent of a man's sweat on the cartridge. And then it made another quick turn, leaped high in the air as bullets danced underneath its legs, and scrambled into a gulley that cut across the desert toward the southeast.

The motorcycle prowled along the gulley's rim, its sidecar occupant searching the bottom with the small attached spotlight. "I hit it!" he vowed. "I know I saw the bullets hit—" He felt the hair on the back of his neck crawl. As he twisted the spotlight around, the huge black wolf that was running behind the motorcycle leaped forward, coming up over the sidecar and slamming its body against the driver. Two of the man's ribs broke like rotted timbers, and as he was knocked out of his seat the wolf seemed to stand up on its hind legs and lunge over the windshield as a man might jump. The tail slapped the gunner disdainfully in the face; he scrambled madly out, and the motorcycle went about another fifteen feet before it reeled over the edge and crashed down to the bottom. The black wolf ran on, coming back to a due easterly course.

Now the network of gullies and hillocks ended, and the desert was flat and rocky under the blazing stars. Still the wolf raced on, its heart beginning to beat harder and its lungs pumping the clean smell of freedom, like the perfume of life, into its nostrils. It snapped its head quickly to the left, released the handcuff, and gripped the satchel's leather handle so the bag no longer bumped the ground. It fought and defeated the urge to spit the handle out, because it held the foul taste of a man's palm.

And then, from behind, another guttural growl, this one lower-pitched than the voices of the other two predators. The wolf glanced back, saw a pair of yellow moons speeding across the desert, following the animal's tracks. Machine-gun fire erupted—a red burst above the double moons—and bullets shot up sand less than three feet to the wolf's side. It jinked and spun, checked its speed, and darted forward again, and the next long burst of tracers singed the hairs along its backbone.

"Faster!" Stummer shouted to his driver. "Don't lose it!" He got off another burst, and saw sand kick up as the wolf angled sharply to the left. "Damn it!" he said. "Hold it steady!" The animal still had Voigt's satchel, and was heading directly toward the British lines. What kind of beast was it, that would steal a case full of maps instead of scraps from the garbage heap? The damned monster had to be stopped. Stummer's palms were sweating, and he struggled to line the thing up in the gun's sights, but it kept dodging, cutting, and then picking up its speed as if it . . .

Yes, Stummer thought. As if it could think like a man.

"Steady!" he bellowed. But the car hit a bump, and again his aim was knocked off. He had to spray the ground ahead of the thing and hope the beast ran into the bullets. He braced himself for the gun's recoil and squeezed the trigger.

Nothing. The gun was hot as the midday sun, and it had either jammed or run dry.

The wolf glanced back, marking that the machine was closing fast. And then it returned its attention to the distance ahead—but too late. A barbed-wire fence stood just ahead, less than six feet away. The wolf's hind legs tensed, and its body left the ground. But the fence was too close to avoid completely; the wolf's chest was sliced by barbed knots, and as its body went over, its right hind leg caught in the coils.

"Now!" Stummer shouted. "Run it down!"

The wolf thrashed, muscles rippling along its body. It clawed the earth with its forelegs, to no avail. Stummer was standing up, the wind rushing into his face, and the driver pressed the accelerator to the floorboard. The armored car was about five seconds away from smashing the wolf beneath its stubbled tires.

What Stummer saw in those five seconds he might never have believed, had he not witnessed it. The wolf twisted its body, and with its front claws grasped the barbed-wire that trapped its leg. Those claws parted the wire, and held them apart as it wrenched its leg loose. Then it was on all fours again and darting away. The armored car ground the wire under its bulk, but the wolf was no longer there.

But the headlights still held it, and Stummer could see that the animal was bounding instead of running, leaping right and left, sometimes touching a single hind leg to the earth before it leaped and twisted again in another direction.

Stummer's heart slammed in his chest.

It knows, he realized. That animal knows. . . .

He whispered, "We're in a mine fi—"

And then the left front tire hit a mine, and the blast blew Major Stummer out of the car like a bloody pinwheel. The left rear tire detonated the next mine, and the shredded mass of the right front wheel hit the third one. The armored car buckled, its gasoline ignited and tore the seams apart, and in the next second it rolled into yet another mine and there was nothing left but a center of red fire and scorched metal flying heavenward.

Sixty yards ahead, the wolf stopped and looked back. It watched the fire for a moment, its green eyes aglow with destruction, and then it abruptly turned away and continued threading through the mine field toward the safety of the east.

2

He would soon be here. The countess felt as excited as a schoolgirl on a first date. It had been more than a year since she'd seen him. Where he'd been in that time, and what he'd done, she didn't know. Nor did she care. That was not her business. All she'd been told was that he needed a sanctuary, and that the service had been using him for a dangerous assignment. More than that, it was not safe to know. She sat before the oval mirror in her lavender-hued dressing room, the golden lights of Cairo glittering through the French doors that led to the terrace, and carefully applied her lipstick. On the night breeze she could smell cinnamon and mace, and palm fronds whispered politely in the courtyard below. She realized she was trembling, so she put her lipstick down before she made a mess of her mouth. I'm not a dewy-eyed virgin, she told herself, with some regret. But perhaps that was part of his magic, too; he had certainly made her feel, on his last visit here, that she was a first-grader in the school of love. Perhaps, she mused, she was so excited because in all this time—and through a procession of so-called lovers—she had not felt a touch such as his, and she longed for it.

She realized she was the kind of woman her mother had once told her to stay away from, back in Germany before that insane maniac had brainwashed the country. But that was part of this life, too, and the danger invigorated her. Better to live than exist, she thought. Who had told her that? Oh, yes. He had.

She ran an ivory brush through her hair, which was blond and styled like Rita Hayworth's, full and falling gently over her shoulders. She had been blessed with a fine bone structure, high cheekbones, light brown eyes, and a slim build. It wasn't hard to keep her figure here, because she didn't care much for the Egyptian cuisine. She was twenty-seven years old, had been thrice married—each husband more wealthy than the first—and she owned a major share in Cairo's daily English newspaper. Lately she'd been reading her paper with more interest as Rommel advanced on the Nile and the British fought valiantly to stem the Nazi tide. Yesterday's headline had been ROMMEL HELD TO A STANDSTILL. The war would go on, but it appeared that, at least this month, Hitler would not be saluted east of El Alamein.

She heard the soft purr of the Rolls-Royce Silver Shadow's engine as the limousine pulled to the front door, and her heart jumped. She'd sent the chauffeur to pick him up, following the instructions she'd been given, at the Shepheard's Hotel. He was not staying there, but had attended a meeting of some kind—a "debriefing," she understood it was called. The Shepheard's Hotel, with its well-known lobby of wicker chairs and Oriental rugs, was full of war-weary British officers, drunken journalists, Muslim cut-throats, and, of course, Nazi eyes and ears. Her mansion, on the eastern outskirts of the city, was a safer place for him than a public hotel. And eminently more civilized.

The Countess Margritta stood up from her dressing table. Behind her was a screen decorated with blue and golden peacocks, and she took the pale sea-green dress that was hanging over it, stepped into it, and buttoned it up. One more look at her hair and makeup, a quick misting spray of Chanel's new fragrance over her white throat, and she was ready to go. But no, not quite. She decided to undo a strategic button so the swell of her breasts was unconfined. Then she slid her feet into her sandals and waited for Alexander to come up to the dressing room.

He did, in about three more minutes. The butler rapped quietly on the door, and she said, "Yes?"

"Mr. Gallatin has arrived, Countess." Alexander's voice was stiffly British.

"Tell him I'll be down shortly." She listened to Alexander's footsteps moving along the teak-floored corridor. She was not so eager to see him that she would go downstairs without making him wait; that was part of the game between ladies and gentlemen. So she gave it another three or four minutes, and then taking a deep breath, she left the dressing room at an unhurried pace.

She walked along a corridor lined with suits of armor, spears, swords, and other medieval weapons. They belonged to the former owner of the house, a Hitler sympathizer, who'd fled the country when the Italians had been knocked around by O'Connor back in 1940. She didn't care much for weapons, but the knights seemed to go with the teak and oak of the house, and anyway they were valuable and made her feel as if she were being guarded around the clock. She reached the wide staircase with its banisters of carved oak and descended to the first floor. The living room doors were closed; that's where she'd instructed Alexander to take him. She took a few seconds to compose herself, held her palm up against her mouth to get a quick hint of her breath—

spearminty, thank God—and then she opened the doors with a nervous flourish.

Silver lamps burned on low, polished tables. A small fire flickered in the hearth, because after midnight the desert breeze would turn chilly. Crystal glasses and bottles of vodka and Scotch caught the light and gleamed on a decanter against the stucco wall. The carpet was a blaze of intertwined orange and gray figures, and on the mantel a clock ticked toward nine.

And there he was, sitting in a wicker chair, his legs crossed at the ankles and his body in repose, as if he owned the area he occupied and would warrant no intrusion. He was staring thoughtfully at the mounted trophy on the wall above the mantel.

But suddenly his eyes found her, and he stood from the chair with smooth grace. "Margritta," he said, and offered her the red roses he held in his hands.

"Oh . . . Michael, they're lovely!" Her voice was smoky, with the regal lilt of the north German plains. She walked toward him—not too fast! she cautioned herself. "Where did you find roses in Cairo this time of year?"

He smiled slightly, and she could see his white, strong teeth. "Your neighbor's garden," he answered, and she could hear a trace of the Russian accent that mystified her so much. What was a Russian-born gentleman doing working with the British Secret Service in North Africa? And why was his name not Russian?

Margritta laughed as she took the roses from him. Of course he was joking; Peter Van Gynt's garden did indeed have an immaculate rosebed, but the wall separating their properties was six feet tall. Michael Gallatin couldn't possibly have gotten over it, and anyway his khaki suit was spotless. He wore a light blue shirt and a necktie with muted gray and brown stripes, and he had a burnished desert tan. She smelled one of the roses; they were still dewy.

"You look beautiful," he said. "You've done your hair differently."

"Yes. It's the new style. Do you like it?"

He reached out to touch a lock of her hair. His fingers caressed it, and slowly his hand moved to her cheek, a gentle touch grazing the flesh and goose bumps rose on Margritta's arms. "You're cold," he said. "You should stand closer to the fire." His hand moved along the line of her chin, the fingers brushing her lips, then pulled away. He stepped closer to her and put an arm around her waist. She didn't back away. Her breath caught. His face was right there in front of hers, and his green eyes caught a red glint from the hearth as if flames had sparked within them. His mouth descended. She felt an ache throb through her body. And then his lips stopped, less than two inches from hers, and he said, "I'm starving."

She blinked, not knowing what to say.

"I haven't eaten since breakfast," he went on. "Powdered eggs and dried beef. No wonder the Eighth Army's fighting so hard; they want to go home and get something edible."

"Food," she said. "Oh. Yes. Food. I've had the cook make dinner for you. Mutton. That's your favorite, isn't it?"

"I'm pleased you remembered." He kissed her lightly on the lips, and then he briefly nuzzled her neck with a softness that made the chill bumps burst up along her spine. He released her, his nostrils flared with the scent of Chanel and her own pungent woman-aroma.

Margritta took his hand. The palm was as rough as if he'd been laying bricks. She led him to the door, and they were almost there when he said, "Who killed the wolf?"

She stopped. "Pardon me?"

"The wolf." He motioned toward the gray-furred timber wolf mounted above the fireplace. "Who killed it?"

"Oh. You've heard of Harry Sandler before, haven't you?"

He shook his head.

"Harry Sandler. The American big-game hunter. He was in all the papers two years ago, when he shot a white leopard atop Mount Kilimanjaro." Still there was no recognition in Michael's eyes. "We've become . . . good friends. He sent me the wolf from Canada. It's a beautiful creature, isn't it?"

Michael grunted softly. He glanced at the other mounted trophies Sandler had given Margritta—the heads of an African water buffalo, a magnificent stag, a spotted leopard, and

17

a black panther—but his gaze returned to the wolf. "Canada," he said. "Where in Canada?"

"I don't know exactly. I think Harry said up in Saskatchewan." She shrugged. "Well, a wolf's a wolf, isn't it?"

He didn't answer. Then he looked at her, his eyes piercing, and smiled. "I'll have to meet Mr. Harry Sandler someday," he said.

"Too bad you weren't here a week ago. Harry passed through Cairo on his way to Nairobi." She gave a playful tug at his arm to pull his attention off the trophy. "Come on, before your food gets cold."

In the dining room, Michael Gallatin ate his medallions of mutton at a long table under a crystal chandelier. Margritta picked at a hearts-of-palm salad and drank a glass of Chablis, and they made small talk about what was happening in London—the current popular plays, the fashions, the novels and music: all things Margritta missed. Michael said he'd enjoyed Hemingway's latest work, and that the man had a clear eye. And as they spoke, Margritta studied Michael's face and realized, here under the brighter light of the chandelier, that he'd changed in the year and five weeks since their last meeting. The changes were subtle, but there nonetheless: there were more lines around his eyes, and perhaps more flecks of gray in the sleek, close-trimmed black hair as well. His age was another mystery; he might be anywhere from thirty to thirty-four. Still, his movements had the sinuosity of youth, and there was impressive strength in his shoulders and arms. His hands were an enigma; they were sinewy, long-fingered, and artistic—the hands of a pianist—but the backs of them were dappled with fine dark hairs. They were a workman's hands, too, used to rough labor, but they managed the sterling knife and fork with surprising grace.

Michael Gallatin was a large man, maybe six-feet-two, with a broad chest, narrow hips, and long, lean legs. Margritta had wondered at their first meeting if he'd ever been a track-and-field athlete, but his response had been that he "sometimes ran for pleasure."

She sipped at her Chablis and glanced at him over the rim. Who was he, really? What did he do for the service? Where had he come from and where was he bound? He had a sharp nose, and Margritta had noticed that he smelled all food and drink before he consumed it. His face was darkly handsome, clean-shaven and rugged, and when he smiled it was like a flare of light—but he didn't let her see that smile very often. In repose his face seemed to become darker still, and as the wattage of those green eyes fell their somber hue made Margritta think of the color in the deep shadow of a primeval forest, a place of secrets best left unexplored. And, perhaps, a place also of great dangers.

He reached for his goblet of water, disregarding the Chablis, and Margritta said, "I've sent the servants away for the evening."

He sipped at the water and put the goblet aside. Pressed his fork into another piece of meat. "How long has Alexander worked for you?" he asked.

The question was totally unexpected. "Almost eight months. The consulate recommended him. Why?"

"He has . . ." Michael paused, considering his words. *An untrustworthy smell,* he'd almost said. "A German accent," he finished.

Margritta didn't know which one of them was crazy, because if Alexander was anymore British he'd be wearing a Union Jack for underdrawers.

"He hides it well," Michael continued. He sniffed at the mutton before he ate it, and chewed before he spoke. "But not well enough. The British accent is a masquerade."

"Alexander cleared the security checks. You know how stringent those are. I can tell you his life history, if you want to hear it. He was born in Stratford-on-Avon."

Michael nodded. "An actor's town, if there ever was one. That's got the *Abwehr*'s fingerprints all over it." The *Abwehr,* as Margritta knew, was Hitler's intelligence bureau. "A car will be coming for me at oh-seven-hundred. I think you should go, too."

"Go? Go *where?*"

"Away. Out of Egypt, if possible. Maybe to London. I don't think it's safe for you here anymore."

"Impossible. I've got too many obligations. My God, I

19

own the newspaper! I can't just clear out on a moment's notice!''

"All right, stay at the consulate. But I think you should leave North Africa as soon as you can."

"My ship hasn't sprung a leak," Margritta insisted. "You're wrong about Alexander."

Michael said nothing. He ate another piece of mutton and dabbed at his mouth with a napkin.

"Are we winning?" she asked him after another moment.

"We're holding," he answered. "By our teeth and finger-nails. Rommel's supply network has broken down, and his panzers are running out of petrol. Hitler's attention is fixed on the Soviet Union. Stalin's calling for an Allied attack from the west. No country, even one as strong as Germany, can wage war on two fronts. So, if we can hold Rommel until his ammunition and petrol dries up, we can force him back to Tobruk. And past that, if we're lucky."

"I didn't know you believed in luck." She arched a pale blond eyebrow.

"It's a subjective term. Where I come from, 'luck' and 'brute strength' are one and the same."

She pounced on the opportunity. "Where *do* you come from, Michael?"

"A place far from here," he replied, and the way he said it told her that there would be no more discussion of his personal life.

"We have dessert," she said when he'd finished his meal and pushed the plate away. "A chocolate torte, in the kitchen. I'll make us some coffee, too." She stood up, but he was faster. He was at her side before she could take two steps, and he said, "Later for the torte and coffee. I had another dessert in mind." Taking her hand, he kissed it, slowly, finger by finger.

She put her arms around his neck, her heart hammering. He picked her up, effortlessly, in his arms, and then plucked a single rose from where they were arranged in a blue vase at the table's center.

He took her up the staircase, along the hall of armor, to her bedroom with its four-poster bed and its view of the Cairo hills.

They undressed each other by candlelight. She remembered how hairy his arms and chest were, but now she saw that he'd been injured; his chest was crisscrossed with adhesive bandages. "What happened to you?" she asked as her fingers grazed his hard brown flesh.

"Just a little something I got tangled up in." He watched as her lace slip floated to her ankles, and then he picked her up out of her clothes and slid her against the cool white sheet.

He was naked now as well, and seemed larger still for the knots of muscle exposed to the candlelight. He eased his body down beside hers, and she smelled another odor under his faint lime cologne. It was a musky aroma, and again she thought of green forests and cold winds blowing across the wilderness. His fingers traced slow circles around her nipples, and then his mouth was on hers and their heat connected, flowed into each other, and she trembled to her soul.

Something else replaced his fingers: the velvet rose, fluttering around her risen nipples, teasing her breasts like kisses. He drew the rose down along the line of her belly, stopped there to circle her navel, then down again into the fullness of golden hair, still circling and teasing with a gentle touch that made her body arch and yearn. The rose moved along the damp center of her desire, fluttering between her taunt thighs, and then his tongue was there, too, and she gripped his hair and moaned as her hips undulated to meet him.

He paused, holding her back from the edge, and began again, the tongue and the rose, working in counterpoint like fingers on a fine golden instrument. Margritta made music, whispering and moaning as the warm waves built inside her and crashed through her senses.

And then there it was, the white-hot explosion that lifted her off the bed and made her cry out his name. She settled back like an autumn leaf, full of color and wilted at the edges.

He entered her, heat against heat, and she clung to his back and held on like a rider in the storm; his hips moved with deliberation, not frantic lust, and just as she thought she could accept no more of him, her body opened and she sought to take him into the place where they would be one creature with two names and pounding hearts, and then even the hard spheres of his manhood would enter her, too, instead of being simply pressed against the moistness. She wanted all of him, every inch, and all the liquid he could give her. But even in the midst of the maelstrom she sensed him holding himself apart, as if there were something in himself that even he could not get to. In their cell of passion she thought she heard him growl, but the noise was muffled against her throat and she could not be sure it wasn't her own voice.

The bed's joints spoke. It had spoken for many men, but never so eloquently.

And then his body convulsed—once, twice, a third time. Five times. He shivered, his fingers twisting the tangled sheet. She locked her legs around his back, urging him to stay. Her lips found his mouth, and she tasted the salt of his effort.

They rested awhile, talking again, but this time in whispered voices, and the subject was not London or the war but the art of passion. And then she took the rose from where it lay on the bedside table, and she followed the trail down to his restirring hardness. It was a beautiful machine, and she lavished it with love.

Rose petals lay on the sheets. The candle had burned low. Michael Gallatin lay on his back, sleeping, with Margritta's head on his shoulder. He breathed with a faint, husky rumbling noise, like a well-kept engine.

Still later, she awakened and kissed him on the lips. He was sleeping soundly, and did not respond. Her body was a pleasant ache; she felt stretched, re-formed into his shape. She looked at his face for a moment, assigning the craggy features to memory. It was too late for her to feel real love, she thought. There had been too many bodies, too many ships passing in the night; she knew she was useful to the service as a refuge and liaison for agents who needed sanctuary, and that was all. Of course she decided who she would sleep with, and when, but there had been many. The faces blended together—but his stayed apart. He was not like the others. And not like any man she'd ever known. So call it schoolgirl infatuation and leave it at that, she thought. He had his destination, and she had her own, and they were not likely to be the same port.

She got out of bed, carefully so as not to awaken him, and went naked into the large walk-through closet that separated her bedroom from the dressing room. She switched on the light, chose a white silk gown, shrugged into it, then took a brown terrycloth robe—a man's robe—off a hanger and draped it around a female-shaped dress dummy in the bedroom. A thought: perhaps a spray of perfume between her breasts and a brush of her hair before true sleep. The car might be coming at seven in the morning, but she recalled that he liked to be up by five-thirty.

Margritta walked, the well-used rose in hand, into the dressing room. A small Tiffany lamp still burned on the table. She sniffed the rose, smelled their mingled scents, and put it into a vase. That one would have to be pressed between silk. She drew a contented breath, then picked up her brush and looked into the mirror.

The man was standing behind the screen. She could see his face above it, and in the second of calm recognition before terror she realized it was a perfect killer's face: devoid of emotion, pale, and quite unremarkable. It was the kind of face that blends easily into crowds, and you do not remember a moment after seeing.

She opened her mouth to call for Michael.

3

There was a polite cough, and a peacock's eye winked fire. The bullet hit Margritta in the back of the skull, precisely where the assassin had aimed. Her blood, bone, and brains splattered onto the glass, and her head thunked down amid the vials of beauty.

He came out, snake-quick, dressed in tight-fitting black,

the small pistol with its silencer gripped in a black-gloved hand. He glanced at the little rubber-coated grapple hook that clung to the terrace's railing; the rope trailed down to the courtyard. She was dead and the job was done, but he knew that a British agent was here as well. He looked at his wristwatch. Almost ten minutes before the car would meet him beyond the gate. Time enough to send the swine to hell.

He cocked the pistol and started through the closet. And there was the bitch's bedroom, a low candle flickering, a shape in the sheets. He aimed the pistol at its head and steadied his wrist with his other arm: a gunman's pose. The silencer coughed—once, then again. The shape jumped with the force of the bullets.

And then, like a good artist who must see the results of his craft, he pulled the sheets away from the corpse.

Except it was not a corpse.

It was a dress dummy, with two bullet holes in its blank white forehead.

A movement, to his right. Someone fast. The killer panicked and twisted to get off a shot, but a chair slammed against his back and ribs and he lost the gun before his finger could squeeze. It went into the folds of the sheet and out of sight.

He was a big man, six-three and two hundred and thirty pounds, all beef-bred muscle; the breath left his mouth with the roar of a locomotive bursting from a tunnel, and the chair's swing staggered him but didn't put him down. The killer tore the chair out of his combatant's grip before it could be used again, and kicked out, his boot hitting the man's stomach. The kick drew a satisfying grunt of pain, and the British agent, a man in a brown robe, crashed back against the wall holding his gut.

The assassin flung the chair. Michael saw it coming in the flex of the man's hands, and as he dodged, the chair broke to pieces against the wall. Then the man was on him, fingers clenching around his throat, digging savagely into his windpipe. Black motes spun across Michael's vision; in his nostrils was the iron odor of blood and brains—the scent of Margritta's death he'd smelled a second after he'd heard the silencer's deadly whisper.

This man was a professional, Michael knew. It was man against man, and only one would be alive in a matter of minutes.

So be it.

Michael quickly brought his hands up, breaking the killer's grip, and smashed the palm of his right hand into the man's nose. He intended to drive the bones into the brain, but the killer was fast and turned his head to deflect the strike. Still, the nose crumpled and exploded and the man's eyes were wet with pain. He staggered back two steps, and Michael hit him in the jaw with a quick left and right. The killer's lower lip split open, but he grasped the collar of Michael's robe, lifted him off his feet, and hurled him through the bedroom door.

Michael crashed into the hallway and into one of the suits of armor. It fell off its stand in a clatter. The Nazi assassin came through the door, his mouth streaming blood, and as Michael tried to scramble up, a kick caught him in the shoulder and flung him another eight feet along the hall.

The killer looked around, his eyes glinting at the sight of armor and weapons; for an instant his face had a shine of reverence, as if he had stumbled into a holy shrine of violence. He picked up a mace—a wooden handle with a three-foot-long chain attached to an iron ball of jagged spikes—and whirled it gleefully over his head. He advanced on Michael Gallatin.

The medieval weapon shrieked as it swung for Michael's skull, but he ducked its arc and backpedaled out of range. The mace swung back the other way before he could get his balance, and the iron spikes bit brown terrycloth, but Michael leaped back, colliding with another suit of armor. As it fell, he grasped a metal shield and whirled around, catching the mace's next blow as it came at his legs. Sparks flew off the polished metal, the vibration thrumming up Michael's arm to his bruised shoulder. And then the killer lifted the mace over his head to crush Michael's skull—and Gallatin threw the shield, its edge hitting the other man's knees, chopping his legs out from under him. As the killer pitched down, Michael started to kick him in the face but checked himself: a broken foot would not help his agility.

The killer was getting to his feet, the mace still in hand. Michael darted to the wall and pulled a broadsword off its hooks, and then he turned to face the next attack.

The German warily regarded the sword and picked up a battle-ax, casting the shorter weapon aside. They faced each other for a few seconds, each looking for an opening, and then Michael feinted with a thrust and the battle-ax clanged it aside. The killer lunged in, avoided a swing of the sword, the battle-ax upraised. But Michael's sword was there to deflect it; the ax hit the sword's hilt in a burst of blue sparks, snapped off the blade, and left Gallatin standing with a nub of nothing. The killer swung the ax at his prey's face, his body braced for the pleasure of collision.

Michael had, in a split second, judged the fine angles and dimensions of impact. He realized that a step backward would lose him his head, as would a step to either side. So he moved in, crowding the killer, and since blows to the face seemed to do no good, he drove his fist into the exposed hollow of the armpit, his knuckles gouging for the pressure point of veins and arteries.

The killer cried out in pain, and as his arm went dead he lost control of the ax. It left his hand and thunked two inches deep into the oak-paneled wall. Michael hit him in the ruined nose, snapping his head back, and followed with a blow to the point of the chin. The German grunted, spewed blood, and fell back against the second-floor railing. Michael followed him, drew his arm back to strike at the throat—but suddenly the assassin's arms streaked out, the fleshy hands closing on his neck once more and lifting him off his feet.

Michael thrashed, but he had no traction. The killer was holding him almost at arm's length, and in another few seconds the idea would come to throw Michael over the railing to the tiled floor below. There was an oak beam two feet above Michael's head, but it was smooth and polished and there was nothing to hold on to. The blood roared in his brain, oily sweat surfaced from his pores—and deep within, something else stretched and began to awaken from a sleep of shadows.

The fingers pressed into his arteries, interrupting the flow of blood. The killer shook him, partly in disdain and partly to secure a tighter grip. The end was near; the German could see the other man's eyes beginning to bulge.

Michael's arms reached up, fingers grazing the oak. His body trembled violently, a movement that the assassin interpreted as the nearing of death.

For him, it was.

Michael Gallatin's right hand began to twist and contort. Beads of sweat ran down his face, and utter agony played across his features. The black hair on the back of his hand rippled, the sinews shifting. There were little popping noises of cracking bones. The hand gnarled, the knuckles swelled, the flesh turning mottled and thick, the black hair beginning to spread.

"Die, you son of a bitch!" the killer said, speaking in German. He squeezed his eyes shut, all concentration on strangling the man to death. Very soon now . . . very soon.

Something moved under his hands. Like scurrying ants. The body was getting heavier. Thickening. There was a pungent, animal smell.

The killer opened his eyes and looked up at his victim.

He was holding something that was no longer a man.

With a scream, he tried to throw the thing over the railing—but two pairs of claws dug into the oak beam and latched there, and the monster brought up a still-human kneecap and hit him in the chin with a power that all but knocked him senseless. He released the thing and, still screaming, but now in a high, thin drone, scrambled away from it. He fell over scattered armor, crawled toward the bedroom door, looked back, and saw the monster's claws wrench free of the beam. The thing fell to the floor, hitching and convulsing, and thrashed out of its brown terrycloth robe.

And now the assassin, one of the best of his breed, knew the full meaning of horror.

The monster righted itself, crawling toward him. It was not yet fully formed, but its green eyes caught and held him, promising agony.

The killer's hand closed on a spear. He jabbed at the thing, and it leaped aside, but the spear tip caught it on the malformed left cheek and drew a scarlet line against the black. He kicked desperately at it, trying to pull himself through the bedroom door and get to the terrace railing—and then he felt fangs snap shut on his ankle, a crushing power that broke the bones like matchsticks. The jaws opened and snapped on the other leg at the calf. Again, bones broke, and the assassin was crippled.

He screamed for God, but there was no answer. There was only the steady rumbling of the monster's lungs.

He threw up his hands to ward it off, but human hands were of no consequence. The beast jumped upon him, its wet snout and staring, terrible eyes right in his face. And then the snout winnowed toward his chest, the fangs gleaming. There was a hammer blow to his breastbone, followed by another that almost split him in two. Claws were at work, the nails throwing up a red spray. The killer writhed and fought as best he could, but his best was nothing. The beast's claws entered his lungs, ripped away the heaving tissue, drove down into the man's core; and then the snout and the teeth found the pulsing prize, and with two twists of the head the heart was torn from its vine like an overripe, dripping fruit.

The heart was crushed between the fangs, and the mouth accepted its juices. The killer's eyes were still open, and his body twitched, but all his blood was flooding out and there was none left to keep his brain alive. He gave a shuddering, terrible moan—and the monster threw its head back and echoed the cry in a voice that rang through the house like a death knell.

And then, nosing into the gaping hole, the beast began its feeding, tearing with rampant rage at the inner mysteries of a man.

Afterward, as the lights of Cairo dimmed and the first violet light of the sun began to come up over the pyramids, something caught between animal and man spasmed and retched in the mansion of the Countess Margritta. From its mouth flowed grisly lumps and fragments, a creeping red sea that went under the banister and over the edge to the tiled floor below. The naked retching thing curled itself into a fetal shape, shivering uncontrollably, and in that house of the dead no one heard it weep.

ONE

Rite of Spring

a solidified Nazi hold on Western Europe, perhaps an immense
allied effort against the Russian troops and a saving battle for
that territory between Berlin and Moscow. Though their
ranks had been thinned, the Nazis were still the best organized killers in the world. They could still deliver the
bio-toxic experiments and, time and again, thwart the capture of
Soviet Union.

—————— **1** ——————

Again the dream awakened him, and he lay in the dark while
the gusts bellowed at the windows and an errant shutter
flapped. He had dreamed he was a wolf who dreamed he
was a man who dreamed he was a wolf who dreamed. And
in that maze of dreams there had been bits and pieces of
memory, flying like the fragments of an exploded jigsaw
puzzle: the sepia-toned faces of his father, mother, and older
sister, faces as if from a burned-edge photograph; a palace
of broken white stones, surrounded by thick, primeval forest
where the howls of wolves spoke to the moon; a passing
steam train, headlight blazing, and a young boy racing along
the tracks beside it, faster and faster, toward the entrance of
the tunnel that lay ahead.

And from the puzzle of memory, an old, leathery, white-
bearded face, the lips opening to whisper: *Live free*.

He sat up on his haunches and realized then that he had
been lying not in his bed but on the cold stone floor before
the fireplace. A few embers drowsed in the darkness, waiting
to be stirred. He stood up, his body naked and muscular,
and walked to the high bay windows that overlooked the
wild hills of northern Wales. The March wind was raging
beyond the glass, and scattershots of rain and sleet struck
the windows before his face. He stared from darkness into
darkness, and he knew they were coming.

They had let him alone too long. The Nazis were being
forced toward Berlin by a vengeful Soviet tide, but Western
Europe—the Atlantic Wall—was still in Hitler's grip. Now,
in this year of 1944, great events were in motion, events with
great potential for victory or terrible risks of defeat. And he
knew full well what the aftermath of that defeat would mean:

a solidified Nazi hold on Western Europe, perhaps an intensified effort against the Russian troops and a savage battle for territory between Berlin and Moscow. Though their ranks had been thinned, the Nazis were still the best-disciplined killers in the world. They could still deflect the Russian juggernaut and surge again toward the capital of the Soviet Union.

Mikhail Gallatinov's motherland.

But he was Michael Gallatin now, and he lived in a different land. He spoke English, thought in Russian, and contemplated in a language more ancient than either of those human tongues.

They were coming. He could feel them getting nearer, as surely as he sensed the wind whirling through the forest sixty yards away. The world's tumult was bringing them closer, to his house on this rocky coast that most men shunned. They were coming for one reason.

They needed him.

Live free, he thought, and his mouth curled with the hint of a smile. There was some bitterness in it. Freedom was an illusion, in the shelter of his own house on this stormy land, where the nearest village, Endore's Rill, lay more than fifteen miles to the south. For him, a great part of freedom was isolation, and he had come to realize more and more, as he monitored the shortwave broadcasts between London and the Continent, listening to the voices speak in codes through the blizzards of static, that the bonds of humanity had chained him.

So he would not refuse them entrance when they arrived, because he was a man and they would also be men. He would listen to what they had to say, might even consider it briefly before he refused. They had come a long way, over rough roads, and he might possibly offer them shelter for the night. But his service to his adopted homeland was done, and now it was up to young soldiers with mud-grimed faces and nervous fingers on carbine triggers. The generals and commanders might bark orders, but it was the young who died carrying them out; that was the way it had been throughout the ages, and in that respect, the future of warfare would never change. Men being what they were.

Well, there was no keeping them away from his door. He could lock the gate, way up at the end of the road, but they would find a way over it, or cut the barbed-wire fence and walk in. The British had a lot of experience in snipping barbed-wire. So it was best just to leave the gate unlocked, and wait for them. It might be tomorrow, or the day after that, or next week. Whenever; he would still be here.

Michael listened to the song of the wild for a moment, his head cocked slightly to one side. Then he returned to the flagstone floor in front of the fireplace, lay down and curled his arms around his knees, and tried to rest.

2

"He picked a damn lonely place to live, didn't he?" Major Shackleton lit a cigar and cranked down the glossy black Ford's rear window on his side to let the smoke seep out. The cigar tip glowed red in the gloomy twilight of late afternoon. "You Brits like this kind of weather, huh?"

"I fear we have no choice but to like it," Captain Humes-Talbot answered. He smiled as politely as he could, his aristocratic nostrils flared. "Or at least accept it."

"Right." Shackleton, a United States Army officer with a face like the business end of a battle-ax, peered out at the gray, low clouds and the nasty drizzle. He hadn't seen the sun for more than two weeks, and the chill was making his bones ache. The elderly, stiff-backed British army driver, separated from his passengers by a glass window, was taking them along a narrow pebbled road that wound between dark, cloud-shrouded crags and stands of thick pine forest. The last village they'd passed, Houlett, was twelve miles behind them. "That's why you people are so pale," he went on, like a bulldozer through a tea party. "Everybody looks like a ghost over here. You ever come to Arkansas, I'll show you a springtime sun."

"I'm not sure my schedule will allow it," Humes-Talbot

said, and cranked down his window a turn and a half. He was wan and thin, a twenty-eight-year-old staff officer whose closest brush with death had been diving into a Portsmouth ditch as a Messerschmitt fighter screamed past seventy feet overhead. But that had been in August of 1940, and now no Luftwaffe aircraft dared to cross the Channel.

"So Gallatin served with distinction in North Africa?" Shackleton's teeth were clenched around the cigar, and the stub was wet with saliva. "That was two years ago. If he's been out of service since then, what makes your people think he can handle the job?"

Humes-Talbot stared at him blankly with his bespectacled blue eyes. "Because," he said, *"Major* Gallatin is a professional."

"So am I, sonny." Shackleton was ten years the British captain's senior. "That doesn't make me able to parachute into France, does it? And I haven't been sittin' on my tailbone for the last twenty-four months, I'll guaran-damn-tee you that."

"Yes sir," the other man agreed, simply because he felt he should. "But your . . . uh . . . people asked for help in this matter, and since it's of benefit to both of us, my superiors felt—"

"Yeah, yeah, that's yesterday's news." Shackleton waved the man quiet with an impatient hand. "I've told my people I'm not sold on Gallatin's—excuse me, *Major* Gallatin's— record. His lack of field experience, I ought to say, but I'm supposed to make a judgment based on a personal meeting. Which isn't the way we work in the States. We go by the record over there."

"We go by the character over here," Humes-Talbot said, with a bite of frost. "Sir."

Shackleton smiled faintly. Well, at last he'd gotten a rise out of this stiff-necked kid. "Your secret service might have recommended Gallatin, but that doesn't swing a shovelful of shit as far as I'm concerned. Pardon my French." He snorted smoke from his nostrils, his eyes catching a gleam of red. "I understand Gallatin's not his real name. It used to be Mikhail Gallatinov. He's a Russian. Right?"

"He was born in St. Petersburg in 1910," came the careful reply. "In 1934 he became a citizen of Great Britain."

"Yeah, but Russia's in his blood. You can't trust Russians. They drink too much vodka." He tapped ashes into the ashtray on the back of the driver's seat, but his aim was off and most of the ash fell on his spit-shined shoes. "So why'd he leave Russia? Maybe he was wanted for a crime over there?"

"Major Gallatin's father was an army general and a friend of Czar Nicholas the Second," Humes-Talbot said as he watched the road unreel in the yellow gleam of the headlights. "In May of 1918, General Fyodor Gallatinov, his wife, and twelve-year-old daughter were executed by Soviet party extremists. The young Gallatinov escaped."

"And?" Shackleton prodded. "Who brought him to England?"

"He came by himself, working aboard a freighter," the captain said. "In 1932."

Shackleton smoked his cigar and thought about it. "Hold on," he said quietly. "You're sayin' he hid from the murder squads in Russia from the time he was eight to when he was twenty-two years old? How'd he do that?"

"I don't know," Humes-Talbot admitted.

"You don't *know?* Hell, I thought you boys were supposed to know everything about Gallatinov. Or whatever. Haven't you got his records verified?"

"There's a gap in his records." The younger man saw the dim glow of lights ahead, through the pines. The road was curving, taking them toward the sparkle of lanterns. "The information is classified, for the top echelon of the secret service only."

"Yeah? Well, that's enough to tell me I don't want him on the job."

"I presume Major Gallatin named those individuals who remained loyal to the memory of the royal circle and helped him survive. To expose those names would be . . . shall we say, less than prudent?" The small houses and clustered-together structures of a village were coming out of the drizzle. A little white sign on a post said ENDORE'S RILL. "I will pass on a bit of rumor, if I may," Humes-Talbot said, wanting to throw a smoking grenade back at the ugly American. "I understand that the mad monk Rasputin was in Saint Petersburg and enjoyed . . . liaisons with several ladies of breeding in 1909 and 1910. One of those ladies, dare I say, was Elana Gallatinov." He looked into Shackleton's face. "Rasputin may have been Michael Gallatin's real father."

A small cough of cigar smoke came from Shackleton's throat.

There was a tapping noise. Mallory, the driver, rapped his knuckles on the glass and put his foot to the Ford's brake. The car was slowing, the windshield wipers slapping away the sleet and rain. Humes-Talbot rolled the glass barrier down, and Mallory said with a crisp Oxford accent, "Beg your pardon, sir, but I think we should stop for directions. That might be the place." He pointed at a lantern-lit tavern coming up on the right.

"Indeed it is," the young man agreed, and rolled the glass back up as Mallory cruised the big car to a stop in front of the tavern's door. "I'll be back in a minute," Humes-Talbot said as he pulled the collar of his coat up around his neck and opened the door.

"Wait for me," Shackleton told him. "I could use a drink of whiskey to get my blood warm again."

They left Mallory in the car and went up a set of stone steps. A sign creaked on chains above the doorway, and Shackleton glanced up at it to see a painted sheep and the words THE MUTTON CHOP. Inside, a cast-iron stove burned with the sweet musk of bog peat and oil lamps hung from pegs on the wooden walls. Three men who were sitting at a back table talking quietly and drinking ale looked up from their conversation at the uniformed military officers.

"Welcome, gentlemen," an attractive black-haired woman behind the bar said with a heavy Welsh accent. Her eyes were bright blue, and they quickly examined the two visitors with a thoroughness that seemed casual. "What may I do for you?"

"Whiskey, babe," Shackleton said, grinning around his cigar. "Best poison you've got."

She uncorked a jug and poured him a murky shot glass full. "Only poison we've got, if you don't count the ale and

36

bitters.'' She smiled faintly, a sultry smile with a challenge in it.

"Nothing for me, but I would like some information." Humes-Talbot warmed his hands before the stove. "We're looking for a man who lives around here. His name is Michael Gallatin. Do you—"

"Oh, yes," she said, and her eyes glinted. "I do know Michael."

"Where does he live?" Shackleton took a whiff of the whiskey and thought his eyebrows had been singed.

"Around. He doesn't entertain visitors." She stroked a cloth across the jug. "Much."

"He's expectin' us, babe. Official business."

She considered that for a moment, looking at the shine of their buttons. "Take the road that runs through the Rill. It goes on for eight miles and then it turns into dirt, or mud, as the case may be. It splits into two. The road on the left is the rougher one. It goes to his gate. Whether it'll be open or not is up to him."

"We'll open it if it's not," Shackleton said. He took the cigar out of his mouth and, with a grin at the bartender, swallowed the local whiskey.

"Bottoms up," she told him.

His knees buckled as the whiskey seared down his throat like a trail of lava. He thought for a second that he'd swallowed crushed glass, or bits of razor blade. He felt sweat boil out of his pores, and he squeezed a cough down in his chest because the bartender was watching him, smiling knowingly, and he was damned if he'd fall on his ass in front of a woman.

"How do you like it, babe?" she asked, all innocence.

He feared returning the cigar to his mouth, in case the smoke caught fire and blew his head off. Tears burned his eyes, but he clenched his teeth and slammed the shot glass down on the bar. "It . . . needs . . . agin'," he managed to croak, and his face flamed when he heard the men laugh at the back table.

"That it does," she agreed, and her soft laughter was like the rustle of a silk curtain. Shackleton started to reach for his wallet, but she said, "It's on the house. You're a good sport."

He smiled, more sickly than sporty, and Humes-Talbot cleared his throat and said, "We thank you for the information and hospitality, madam. Shall we go, Major?" Shackleford made something that might have been a grunt of assent, and followed Humes-Talbot to the door on leaden legs.

"Major, dear?" the bartender called before he went out. He looked back, wanting to get out of this suffocating heat. "You can thank Michael for the drink when you see him. That's his private stock. Nobody else'll touch the stuff."

Shackleton went out the door of The Mutton Chop feeling like chopped mutton.

Full dark had fallen as Mallory drove them away from Endore's Rill, between the wind-lashed woods and mountains carved by the fingers of time. Shackleton, his face tinged the shade of tallow, forced himself to finish the cigar and then thumped it away out the window. It blew a trail of sparks, like a falling comet.

Mallory turned off the main road—a mud-puddled wagon track—and onto the rougher one on the left. The axles groaned as the Ford's tires plowed through potholes, and the seat springs yowled like pressured steam vents as Shackleton was thrown and jostled. The young British captain was used to uncomfortable roadways, and he clenched the hand grip over his door's window and lifted his rear an inch or two off the leather.

"Man . . . don't wanna . . . be located," was all Shackleton could say as the Ford shook harder than any tank he'd ever driven. Lord have mercy on my achin' tailbone! he thought. The road went on, a path of tortures, through the dense green woods. Finally, after two or three more brutal miles, the headlights found a high iron gate. It was wide open, and the Ford continued through.

The muddy road smoothed a bit, but not by much. Every so often they hit a bump and Shackleton's teeth cracked together with a force that he knew would cut his tongue off if he didn't keep it rolled up in his head. The wind swirled through the forest on both sides of the road, the sleet pelted down, and suddenly Shackleton felt a long way from Arkansas.

Mallory stepped on the brake. "Here! What's that!" Humes-Talbot said, looking along the cone of the headlights. Three large dogs were standing in the road, the wind ruffling their fur. "My God!" Humes-Talbot took off his glasses, hurriedly wiped the lenses, and put them back on. "I believe those are wolves!"

"Hell, lock the damned doors!" Shackleton hollered.

The Ford slowed to a crawl. As Shackleton's fist hammered down the lock on his side, the three animals lifted their muzzles to the scent of hot metal and engine oil and vanished into the dark wall of trees on the left. The Ford picked up speed again, Mallory's age-spotted hands steady on the wheel, and they took a long curve through the forest and emerged onto a driveway paved with fieldstones.

And there stood the house of Michael Gallatin.

It looked like a church, made of dark red stones chinked together with white mortar. Shackleton realized that it must have been a church at one time, because it had a narrow tower topped with a white spire and a walkway around it. But the truly amazing thing about the structure was that it had electricity. Light streamed from the windows on the first floor, and up in the church's tower panes of stained glass gleamed dark blue and crimson. Off to the right was a smaller stone building, possibly a workshed or garage.

The driveway made a circle in front of the house, and Mallory stopped the Ford and pulled up the handbrake. He tapped on the window, and when Humes-Talbot had lowered it, Mallory asked, a little uneasily, "Shall I wait here, sir?"

"Yes, for now." Humes-Talbot was aware the old chauffeur had been supplied from the secret service's pool of drivers, but there was no need to let him know more than was absolutely necessary. Mallory nodded, an obedient servant, and cut the engine and headlamps. "Major?" Humes-Talbot motioned toward the house.

The two officers walked from the car through the biting sleet, their shoulders hunched in their overcoats. At the top of three stone steps was a scarred oak door with a green bronze knocker: an animal of some kind, with a bone clenched in its teeth. Humes-Talbot lifted the bone and the beast's fanged lower jaw rose with it. He knocked against the door and waited, beginning to shiver.

A bolt scraped back. Shackleton felt his gut bubble from the witch's brew in the Mutton Chop. And then the door opened on oiled hinges, and a dark-haired man stood outlined in light. "Come in," Michael Gallatin said.

3

The house was warm. It had oiled oak floors, and in a high-roofed, timber-beamed den a fire blazed in a hearth of rough white rock. After Captain Humes-Talbot had given Michael the letter of introduction signed by Colonel Valentine Vivian of the "London Passport Control Office," Shackleton walked directly to the fireplace to warm his ruddy hands.

"Hell of a time gettin' here," Shackleton growled, working his fingers. "You couldn't have picked a more desolate place, could you?"

"I couldn't find one," Michael said quietly, reading the letter. "If I'd wanted to entertain unannounced visitors, I'd have bought a house in London."

Shackleton got the blood stinging in his hands again and turned to get a better examination of the man he'd come so far to meet.

Michael Gallatin was wearing a black sweater, the sleeves pushed up on his forearms, and faded, well-used khaki trousers. On his feet were scuffed brown loafers. His thick black hair, streaked with gray at the temples, was shorn in a military style, short on the sides and back. On his face was the dark grizzle of perhaps two or three days without a razor's touch. There was a scar on his left cheek that started just under the eye and continued back into the hairline. A blade scar, Shackleton thought. Close call, too. Well, so Gallatin had had some experience in hand-to-hand combat. So what? Shackleton guessed the man's height at around six-two, maybe a quarter of an inch more or less, and his weight at around one-ninety or one-ninety-five. Gallatin looked fit, a broad-shouldered athletic type, maybe a football player, or rugby or whatever the limeys called it. There was a quiet power about the man, like a heavy spring that had been crushed down and was on the edge of explosion. Still, that didn't make him ready for a mission into Nazi-occupied France. Gallatin needed sun; he had the pallor of hibernation about him, probably hadn't seen a bright sun in six months. Hell, there probably hadn't *been* anything but murky gloom in this damned country all winter. But winter was on its last legs now, and the spring equinox—March 21—was only two days away.

"Do you know you've got wolves on your land?" Shackleton asked him.

"Yes," Michael said, and folded the letter up when he'd finished. It had been a long time since he'd had a communication from Colonel Vivian. This must be important.

"I wouldn't go out walkin' if I were you," Shackleton went on. He reached into the inside pocket of his coat, brought out a cigar, and cut its end with a small clipper. Then he struck a match on the white stones of the hearth. "Those big bastards like meat."

"They're bitches." Michael slipped the letter into his pocket.

"Whatever." Shackleton lit the cigar, drew deeply on it, and plumed out blue smoke. "You want to have a little action, you ought to get yourself a rifle and go wolf huntin'. You *do* know how to use a rifle, don't—"

He stopped speaking, because suddenly Michael Gallatin was right there in his face, and the man's pale green eyes froze him to the bone.

Michael's hand came up, grasped the cigar, and pulled it from between the other man's teeth. He broke it in half and tossed it into the fire. "Major Shackleton," he said, with the trace of a Russian accent softened by cool British gentility, "this is my home. You'll ask my permission to smoke here. And when you ask, I'll say no. Do we understand each other?"

Shackleton sputtered, his face reddening. "That was . . . that was a *fifty*-cent cigar!"

"It puts out half-cent fumes," Michael told him, stared into the man's eyes for a few seconds longer to make certain his message was clear, and then turned his attention to the young captain. "I'm retired. That's my answer."

"But . . . sir . . . you haven't heard what we came to say yet!"

"I can guess." Michael walked to the bay windows and looked out at the dark line of the woods. He had smelled his reserve stock of old whiskey wafting from Shackleton's skin, and smiled slightly, knowing how the American—used to bland liquor—must have reacted. Good for Maureen at the Mutton Chop. "There's a cooperative venture under way between the alliances. If this wasn't important to the Americans, the major wouldn't be here. I've been listening to the cross-Channel radio traffic on my shortwave. All those codes, things about flowers for Rudy and violins needing to be tuned. I can't understand all the messages, but I understand the sounds of the voices: great excitement, and a lot of fear. I say that adds up to an imminent invasion of the Atlantic Wall." He looked at Humes-Talbot, who hadn't moved or taken off his wet overcoat. "Within three to four months, I'd guess. When summer smooths the Channel. I'm sure neither Mr. Churchill nor Mr. Roosevelt cares to land an army of seasick soldiers on Hitler's beaches. So sometime in June or July would be correct. August would be too late; the Americans would have to fight eastward during the worst of the winter. If they take their landing zones in June, they'll be able to construct their supply lines and dig into their defensive positions on the border of Germany by the first snowfall." He lifted his eyebrows. "Am I close?"

Shackleton let the breath hiss from between his teeth. "You sure this guy's on *our* side?" he asked Humes-Talbot.

"Let me conjecture a bit further," Michael said, his gaze ticking toward the young captain and then back to Shackleton. "To be successful, a cross-Channel invasion would have to be preceded by a disruption of German communications, detonation of ammunition and fuel dumps, and a general atmosphere of hell on earth. But a quiet hell, with cool flames. I expect the networks of partisans will have a busy night blowing up railroad tracks, and maybe there's a place in the scheme for the Americans, too. A paratroop assault would sow the kind of discord behind the lines that might keep the Germans running in a dozen directions at the same time." Michael walked to the fireplace, beside the major, and offered his palms to the heat. "I expect that what you want me to do has a bearing on the invasion. Of course I don't know where it'll be, or exactly when, and I don't want that information. Another thing you must realize is that the Nazi high command certainly suspects an invasion attempt within the next five months. With the Soviets fighting in from the east, the Germans know the time is ripe—at least from the alliance point of view—for an attack from the west." He rubbed his hands together. "I hope my conclusions aren't too much off the mark?"

"No sir," Humes-Talbot admitted. "They hit the bull's-eye."

Michael nodded, and Shackleton said, "Do you have somebody spyin' for you in London?"

"I have my eyes, my ears, and my brain. That's all I need."

"Sir?" Humes-Talbot had been standing almost at attention, and now he let his back loosen and took a step forward. "Can we . . . at least brief you on what the mission involves?"

"You'd be wasting your time and the major's. As I said, I'm retired."

"Retired? After one lousy field assignment in North Africa?" Shackleton made an unpleasant noise with his lips. "So you were a hero during the battle for El Alamein, right?" He'd read Gallatin's service record during his trip from Washington. "You got into a Nazi commander's HQ and stole deployment maps? Big damned squat! Unless you've missed the point, *major*, the war's still going on. And if we don't get a foothold in Europe in the summer of forty-four, we might find our asses washed out to sea for a long time before we can make another try."

"Major Shackleton?" Michael turned toward him, and the intensity of his glare made the major think he was peering into the green-tinted windows of a blast furnace. "You won't mention North Africa again," he said quietly, but with dangerous meaning. "I . . . failed a friend." He blinked; the blast-furnace glare dimmed for a second, then came back full force. "North Africa is a closed subject."

Damn the man! Shackleton thought. If he could, he'd stomp Gallatin into the floor. "I just meant—"

"I don't care what you meant." Michael looked at Humes-Talbot, the captain eager to get on with the briefing, and then Michael sighed and said, "All right. Let's hear it."

"Yes, sir. May I?" He paused, about to shrug off his overcoat. Michael motioned for him to go ahead, and as the two officers took off their coats Michael walked to a high-backed black leather chair and sat down facing the flames.

"It's a security problem, really," Humes-Talbot said, coming around so he could gauge Major Gallatin's expression. It was one of profound disinterest. "Of course you're correct; it does involve the invasion plans. We and the Americans are trying to clean up all the loose ends before the first of June. Getting agents out of France and Holland, for instance, whose security might be compromised. There's an American agent in Paris—"

"Adam's his code name," Shackleton interrupted.

"Paris is no longer a garden of Eden," Michael said, lacing his fingers together. "Not with all those Nazi serpents crawling around in it."

"Right," the major went on, taking the reins. "Anyway, your intelligence boys got a coded message from Adam a little more than two weeks ago. He said there's something big in the works, something he didn't have all the details on yet. But he said that whatever it is, it's under multilayered security. He got wind of it from an artist in Berlin, a guy named Theo von Frankewitz."

"Wait." Michael leaned forward, and Humes-Talbot saw the glint of concentration in his eyes, like the shine of sword metal. "An artist? Why an artist?"

"I don't know. We can't dig up any information on Von Frankewitz. So anyway, Adam sent another message eight days ago. It was only a couple of lines long. He said he was bein' watched, and he had information that had to be brought out of France by personal courier. He had to end the transmission before he could go into detail.''

"The Gestapo?'' Michael glanced at Humes-Talbot.

"Our informants don't indicate that the Gestapo has Adam,'' the younger man said. "We think they know he's one of ours, and have him under constant surveillance. They're probably hoping he'll lead them to other agents.''

"So no one else can find out what this information is and bring it out?''

"No sir. Someone from the outside has to go in.''

"And they're monitoring his radio set, of course. Or maybe they found it and smashed it.'' Michael frowned, watching the oakwood burn. "Why an artist?'' he asked again. "What would an artist know about military secrets?''

"We have no idea,'' Humes-Talbot said. "You see our predicament.''

"We've got to find out what the hell's going on,'' Shackleton spoke up. "The first wave of the invasion will be almost two hundred thousand soldiers. By ninety days after D day, we're plannin' on having more than one million boys over there to kick Hitler's ass. We're riskin' the whole shootin' match on one day—one turn of a card—and we'd sure better know what's in the Nazis' hand.''

"Death,'' Michael said, and neither of the other two men spoke.

The flames crackled and spat sparks. Michael Gallatin waited for the rest of it.

"You'd be flown over France and go in by parachute, near the village of Bazancourt about sixty miles northwest of Paris,'' Humes-Talbot said. "One of our people will be at the drop point to meet you. From there, you'll be taken to Paris and given all the help you need to reach Adam. This is a high-priority assignment, Major Gallatin, and if the invasion's going to have any chance at all, we've got to know what we're up against.''

Michael watched the fire burn. He said, "I'm sorry. Find someone else.''

"But, sir . . . please don't make a hasty—''

"I said I've retired. That ends it.''

"Well, that's just peachy!'' Shackleton burst out. "We

broke our butts gettin' here, because we were told by some jackass that you were the best in your business, and you say you're 'retired.' '' He slurred the word. "Where I come from that's just another way of sayin' a man's lost his nerve."

Michael smiled thinly, which served to infuriate Shackleton even more, but didn't respond.

"Major, sir?" Humes-Talbot tried again. "Please don't give us your final word now. Won't you at least think about the assignment? Perhaps we might stay overnight, and we can discuss it again in the morning?"

Michael listened to the noise of sleet against the windows. Shackleton thought of the long road home, and his tailbone throbbed. "You can stay the night," Michael agreed, "but I won't go to Paris."

Humes-Talbot started to speak again, but he decided to let it rest. Shackleton muttered, "Hellfire and damnation!" but Michael only pondered the fires of his own making.

"We brought along a driver," Humes-Talbot said. "Is there a possibility you might find some room for him?"

"I'll put a cot in front of the fire." He got up and went to get the cot from his storage room, and Humes-Talbot left the house to call Mallory in.

While the two men were gone, Shackleton nosed around the den. He found an antique rosewood Victrola, a record on the turntable. Its title was *The Rite of Spring,* by somebody named Stravinsky. Well, count on a Russian to like Russian music. Probably a bunch of Slavic jabberwocky. He could use a bright Bing Crosby tune on a night like this. Gallatin liked books, that was for sure. Volumes like *Man from Beast, Carnivores, A History of Gregorian Chants, Shakespeare's World,* and other books with Russian, German, and French titles filled the bookcases.

"Do you like my house?"

Shackleton jumped. Michael had come up behind him, silent as mist. He was carrying a folding cot, which he unfolded and placed before the hearth. "The house was a Lutheran church in the eighteen-forties. Survivors of a shipwreck built it; the sea cliffs are only a hundred yards from here. They built a village on this site, too, but bubonic plague wiped them out eight years later."

"Oh," Shackleton said, and wiped his hands on his trouser legs.

"The ruins were still sturdy. I decided to try to put it back together again. It took me all of four years, and I still have a lot to do. In case you're wondering, I've got a generator that runs on petrol out back."

"I figured you didn't have power lines way out here."

"No. Not way out here. You'll be sleeping in the tower room where the pastor died. It's not a very large room, but the bed's big enough for two." The door opened and closed, and Michael glanced back at Humes-Talbot and the chauffeur. Michael stared for a few seconds, unblinking, as the old man took off his hat and topcoat. "You can sleep here," Michael said, with a gesture toward the cot. "The kitchen's through that door, if you want coffee or anything to eat," he told all three of them. "I keep hours you might find odd. If you hear me up in the middle of the night . . . stay in your room," he said, with a glance that made the back of Shackleton's neck crawl.

"I'm going up to rest." Michael started up the stairs. He paused and selected a book. "Oh . . . the bathroom and shower are behind the house. I hope you don't mind cold water. Good night, gentlemen." He ascended the steps, and in another moment they heard a door softly close.

"Damn weird," Shackleton muttered, and he trudged into the kitchen for something to chew on.

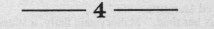

4

Michael sat up in bed and lit an oil lamp. He hadn't been sleeping, only waiting. He picked up his wristwatch from the small table beside his bed, though his sense of time told him it was after three. It was three-oh-seven.

He sniffed the air, and his eyes narrowed. A smell of

47

tobacco smoke. Burley and latakia, a potent blend. He knew that aroma, and it called him.

He was still dressed, in his khakis and black sweater. He slipped on his loafers, picked up the lamp, and followed its yellow glow down the circular staircase.

A couple of fresh logs had been added to the hearth, and a polite fire burned. Michael saw a haze of pipe smoke drifting above the high-backed leather chair that faced the flames. The cot was empty.

"Let's talk, Michael," the man who called himself Mallory said.

"Yes sir." He drew up a chair and sat down with the lamp on a table between them.

Mallory—not his real name, but one of many—laughed quietly, the pipe's bit clenched between his teeth. Firelight glinted in his eyes, and now he didn't appear nearly as old and unsteady as he'd been when he first entered the house. " 'Stay in your room,' " he said, and laughed again. His real voice, unmasked, had a gravelly edge. "That was good, Michael. You scared the balls off that poor Yank."

"Does he have any?"

"Oh, he's quite a capable officer. Don't let the bluff and bluster fool you; Major Shackleton knows his job." Mallory's penetrating gaze slid toward the other man. "And you do, too." Michael didn't answer. Mallory smoked his pipe in silence for a moment, then said, "What happened to Margritta Phillipe in Egypt wasn't your fault, Michael. She knew the risks, and she did her job bravely and well. You killed her assassin and exposed Harry Sandler as an agent for the Nazis. You also did your job bravely and well."

"Not well enough." This still made the sick sensation of grief gnaw at his insides. "If I'd been alert that night, I might have saved Margritta's life."

"It was her time," Mallory said flatly, a statement from a professional in the arena of life and death. "And your time of brooding over Margritta should end now."

"When I find Sandler." Michael's face was tight, and heat rose in his cheeks. "I knew he was a German agent as soon as Margritta showed me the wolf he said he'd sent her from Canada. To me it was perfectly clear it was a Balkan wolf, not Canadian. And the only way Sandler could've killed a Balkan wolf was to go on a hunting trip with his Nazi friends." Harry Sandler, the big-game hunter from America who'd been written about in *Life* magazine, had vanished after Margritta's murder, and left no tracks. "I should have made Margritta leave the house that night. Immediately. Instead I . . ." He clenched his hands on the chair's armrests. "She trusted me," he said, in a hushed voice.

"Michael," Mallory said, "I want you to go to Paris."

"Is it that vital that you be involved with this?"

"Yes. That vital." He puffed smoke and removed the pipe from his mouth. "We'll have one chance, and one chance only, for the invasion to be successful. The time frame, as of now, is the first week of June. That's subject to change, according to the weather and the tides. We have to make sure all potential disasters are dealt with, and I can tell you that watching these commanders hash things out leaves a lot of room for the damnedest mistakes you could imagine." He grunted, and smiled thinly. "We have to do our part to give them a clean house when they move in. If the Gestapo's watching Adam so closely, you can be certain he has information they don't want getting out. We have to learn what it is. With your . . . uh . . . special talents, there's a possibility you can get in and out under the nose of the Gestapo."

Michael watched the fire. The man sitting in the chair next to him was one of three people in the world who knew he was a lycanthrope.

"There's another facet to this you should consider," Mallory said. "Four days ago we received a coded message from our agent Echo, in Berlin. She's seen Harry Sandler."

Michael looked into the other man's face. "Sandler was in the company of a Nazi colonel named Jerek Blok, an SS officer, who used to be commandant of Falkenhausen concentration camp near Berlin. So Sandler's moving in some high circles."

"Is Sandler still in Berlin?"

"We haven't had word from Echo to indicate otherwise. She's keeping watch on him for us."

Michael grunted softly. He had no idea who Echo was, but he remembered Sandler's ruddy-cheeked face from a

Life magazine photograph, grinning as he rested one booted foot on a dead lion on the Kenya grassland.

"We can get you dossiers on Sandler and Blok, of course," Mallory ventured on. "We don't know what their connection might be. Echo would contact you in Berlin. What you might decide to do from there is up to your own discretion."

My discretion, Michael thought. That was a polite way of saying that if he chose to kill Harry Sandler, he would be on his own.

"Your first mission, however, is to find out what Adam knows." Mallory let a trail of smoke trickle from his mouth. "That's imperative. You can relay the information through your French contact."

"What about Adam? Don't you want him out of Paris?"

"If possible."

Michael mulled that over. The man who, in this instance, called himself Mallory was as infamous for what he left unsaid as for what he spelled out.

"We want to tie up all the loose ends," Mallory said after a moment's silence. "I'm intrigued by the same thing you are, Michael: why is an artist involved in this? Von Frankewitz is a nobody, a hack who does sidewalk portraits in Berlin. How is he involved with secrets of state?" Mallory's eyes found Michael. "Will you do the job?"

Nyet, he thought. But he felt a pressure in his veins like the power of a steam furnace building heat. In two years he had not gone one day without thinking of how his friend, the Countess Margritta, had died while he slumbered in the embrace of spent passions. Finding Harry Sandler might wipe the slate clean. Probably not, but there would be satisfaction in hunting the hunter. And the situation with Adam and the impending invasion was a vital issue on its own. How might Adam's information affect D day, and the lives of the thousands of soldiers who would storm ashore on a fateful morning in June?

"Yes," Michael said, tension in his throat.

"I knew I could count on you at the eleventh hour," Mallory said with a faint smile. "The wolf's hour, isn't it?"

"I have one request to make. My parachute training's rusty. I'd like to go over by submarine."

Mallory considered it briefly, then shook his head. "I'm sorry. Too risky with German patrol boats and mines in the Channel. A small transport plane is the safest alternative. We'll whisk you to a place where you can sharpen your skills, do a few practice jumps. Piece of cake, as the Yanks say."

Michael's palms were wet, and he closed his fists. Only two things frightened him: confinement and heights. He couldn't stand the roar and sputter of airplanes, and with his feet off the earth he felt diminished and weak. But there was no choice; he would have to bear it and forge ahead, though the parachute training would be sheer torture. "All right."

"Splendid." Mallory's tone of voice said he'd known all along Michael Gallatin would accept the task. "You're doing well, aren't you, Michael? Getting enough sleep? Eating balanced meals? Not too much meat, I hope."

"Not too much." The forest was stocked with a large herd of deer and stags, plus wild boar and hares.

"I worry about you sometimes. You need a wife."

Michael laughed, in spite of Mallory's well-intentioned seriousness.

"Well," Mallory amended, "perhaps not."

They talked for a while longer, about the war, of course, because that was their crossroads of interest, and as the fire gnawed quietly on oak logs and the wind keened before dawn, the lycanthrope in service to the king stood up and ascended the stairs to his bedroom. Mallory slept in his chair before the hearth, his face in repose again that of an elderly chauffeur.

Dawn came gray and stormy as yesterday's dusk. At six o'clock orchestral music roused Major Shackleton and Captain Humes-Talbot, whose backbones popped and moaned as they pried themselves out of the narrow and wholly uncomfortable dead pastor's bed. They had slept clothed, to ward off the chill that sneaked in around the stained-glass window, and they went downstairs marked with unmilitary wrinkles.

Sleet slashed at the windows, and Shackleton thought he might scream. "Good morning," Michael Gallatin said, sitting in the black leather chair before a newly built fire, a mug of hot Twinings Earl Grey tea in his hand. He wore a dark blue flannel robe and no shoes. "There's coffee and tea in the kitchen. Also some scrambled eggs and local sausage, if you want any breakfast."

"If that sausage is as strong as the local whiskey, I think I'll pass," Shackleton said, with a frown of distaste.

"No, it's very mild. Help yourselves."

"Where's Mallory?" Humes-Talbot asked, looking around.

"Oh, he had his breakfast and went out to change the oil in the car. I let him use the garage."

"What's that racket?" Shackleton thought the music sounded like armies of demons clashing in hell. He walked to the Victrola and saw the record spinning around.

"Stravinsky, isn't it?" Humes-Talbot inquired.

"Yes. *The Rite of Spring*. It's my favorite composition. This is the part, Major Shackleton, where the village elders stand in a circle and watch a young girl dance herself to death in a pagan ritual of sacrifice." Michael closed his eyes for a few seconds, seeing the dark purple and crimson of the leaping, frenzied notes. He opened them again, and stared at the major. "Sacrifice seems to be a particularly popular topic these days."

"I wouldn't know." Gallatin's eyes made Shackleton nervous; they were steady and piercing, and they held a power that made the major feel as boneless as a washrag. "I'm a Benny Goodman fan."

"Oh yes, I know his work." Michael listened to the thunderous, pounding music for another moment; in it was the image of a world at war, fighting against its own barbarity and the barbarity clearly winning. Then he stood up, lifted the needle without scratching the 78 rpm disk and let the Victrola wind down. "I accept the mission, gentlemen," he said. "I'll find out what you want to know."

"You *will?* I mean . . ." Humes-Talbot stumbled over his words. "I thought you'd made up your mind already."

"I had. I changed it."

"Oh, I see." He didn't really, but he wasn't going to question the man's motives any further. "Well, that's good to hear, sir. Very good. We'll put you in a week of training, of course. Give you a few practice parachute jumps and some linguistic work, though I doubt you'll need it. And we'll put together all the information you'll need as soon as we get back to London."

"Yes, you do that." The thought of the flight over the Channel into France made the skin crawl at the back of his neck, but that would have to be dealt with at the proper time. He drew a deep breath, glad now that his decision was final. "If you'll excuse me, I'm going for my morning run."

"I knew you were a runner!" Shackleton said. "I am, too. How far do you go?"

"Five miles, more or less."

"I've gone seven miles before. Loaded down with field gear. Listen, if you've got an extra warm-up suit and a sweater, I'll go with you. I wouldn't mind gettin' the blood movin' again." Especially after trying to sleep in that torture rack, he thought.

"I don't wear a warm-up suit," Michael told him, and removed his robe. He was naked underneath. He folded the robe over the chairback. "It's almost springtime. And thank you, Major, but I always run alone." He walked past Shackleton and Humes-Talbot, who were both too shocked to move or speak, and went out the door and into the cold, sleety morning light.

Shackleton caught the door before it closed. He watched, incredulous, as the naked man began to run with long, purposeful strides down the driveway, then across the grassy field toward the woods. "Hey!" he shouted. "What about the wolves?" Michael Gallatin didn't look back, and in another moment he vanished into the line of trees.

"He's an odd chap, don't you think?" Humes-Talbot asked, peering over the other man's shoulder.

"Odd or not," Shackleton said, "I believe Major Gallatin can get the job done." Sleet dashed him in the face, and he shivered in spite of his uniform and shut the door against the wind.

6

"Martin? Come here and look at this!"

The man whose name had been called stood up from his desk immediately and walked into the inner office, his shoes clacking on the concrete floor. He was heavyset and broad-shouldered, and he wore an expensive brown suit, a spotless white shirt, and black necktie. His graying hair was combed back from his forehead. He had the soft, fleshy features of a child's favorite uncle, a man who liked to tell bedtime stories.

The walls of the inner office were covered with maps, marked with red arrows and circles. Some of the arrows had been scratched out, drawn and redrawn, and many of the circles had been crossed out with angry lines. More maps lay on the office's large desk, along with piles of papers that needed signatures. A small metal box had been opened, and in it were carefully organized vials of watercolors and horse-hair brushes of various sizes. The man behind the desk had pulled his stiff-backed chair to an easel in the corner of the windowless room, and on that easel was a painting in progress: a watercolor of a white farmhouse and behind it the purple rise of jagged mountain peaks. On the floor around the artist's feet were other paintings of houses and the countryside, all of them put aside before they were finished.

"Here. Right here. Do you see it?" The artist wore glasses, and he tapped his paintbrush against a smeared shadow at the farmhouse's edge.

"I see . . . a shadow," Martin answered.

"In the shadow. Right there!" He tapped it again, harder. "Look close!" He picked up the painting, getting watercolors on his fingers, and thrust it in Martin's face.

Martin swallowed thickly. He saw a shadow, and only that. This seemed to be important, and should be handled carefully. "Yes," he answered. "I think . . . I do see it."

"Ah!" the other man said, smiling. "Ah! So there it is!" He spoke German with a heavy—some might think clumsy— Austrian accent. "The wolf, right there in the shadow!" He pointed the brush's wooden end at a dark scrawl that Martin couldn't make heads or tails of. "The wolf on the prowl. And look here!" He picked up another painting, badly done, of a winding mountain stream. "See it? Behind that rock?"

"Yes, *mein Führer,*" Martin Bormann said, staring at a rock and a misshapen line or two.

"And here, in this one!" Hitler offered a third painting, of a field of white eidelweiss. He pointed his crimson-smeared finger at two dark dots amid the sunny flowers. "The eyes of the wolf! You see, he's creeping closer! You know what that means, don't you?"

Martin hesitated, then slowly shook his head.

"The wolf is my lucky symbol!" Hitler said, with a hint of agitation. "Everyone knows that! And here's the wolf, appearing in my paintings with a will of its own! Do you need a clearer portent than *that?*"

Here we go, Hitler's secretary thought. Now we descend into the maelstrom of signs and symbols.

"I'm the wolf, don't you understand?" Hitler took off his glasses, which few but the inner circle ever saw him wearing,

snapped them shut, and slid them into their leather case. "This is a portent of the future. My future." His intense blue eyes blinked. "The future of the Reich, I should say of course. This only tells me again what I already know to be true."

Martin waited without speaking, staring at the farmhouse picture with its unintelligible scribble in the shadows.

"We're going to smash the Slavs and drive them back into their rat holes," Hitler went on. "Leningrad, Moscow, Stalingrad, Kursk . . . names on a map." He grasped a map, leaving red fingerprints on it, and pushed it disdainfully off the desk. "Frederick the Great never considered defeat. Never *considered* it! He had loyal generals, yes. He had a staff who obeyed orders. Never in my life have I seen such willful disobedience! If they want to hurt me, why don't they just put a gun to my head?"

Martin said nothing. Hitler's cheeks were growing red and his eyes looked yellow and moist, a bad sign. "I said we need larger tanks," the *Führer* continued, "and you know what I heard in return? Larger tanks use more fuel. That's their excuse. They think of every possible way to hobble me. Larger tanks use more fuel. Well, what is the whole of Russia but a vast pit of petroleum? And my officers tumble back from the Slavs in terror and refuse to fight for the lifeblood of Germany! How can we hope to hold the Slavs back without fuel? Not to speak of the air raids destroying the ball-bearing plants! You know what they say to that? *Mein Führer*—they always say *mein Führer* in those voices that make you sick as if you'd eaten too much sugar—our anti-aircraft guns need more shells. Our trucks that haul the anti-aircraft guns need more fuel. You see how their minds work?" He blinked again, and the other man saw the understanding settle back in like cold light. "Oh, yes. You were with us at the meeting this afternoon, weren't you?"

"Yes, *mein* . . . Yes," he answered. "Yesterday afternoon." He glanced at his pocket watch. "It's almost one-thirty."

Hitler nodded absently. He wore his brocaded cashmere robe, a gift from Mussolini, and leather slippers, and he and Bormann were alone in the administrative wing of his Berlin headquarters. He stared at his handiwork, at the houses built of unsteady lines and the landscapes with false perspectives, and he dipped his brush into a cupful of water and let the colors bleed out. "It's a portent," he said, "that I'm drawing a wolf without even knowing it. That means victory, Martin. The utter and total destruction of the Reich's enemies. From without and within," he said, with a meaningful glance at his secretary.

"You should know by now, *mein Führer,* that no one can defy your will."

Hitler didn't seem to hear. He was busy returning all his paints and brushes to the metal box, which he kept locked in his safe. "What's my schedule for today, Martin?"

"At eight o'clock, a breakfast meeting with Colonel Blok and Dr. Hildebrand. Then a staff meeting from nine o'clock to ten-thirty. Field Marshal Rommel is due in at one o'clock for a briefing on the Atlantic Wall fortifications."

"Ah." Hitler's eyes lit up again. "Rommel. Now there's a man with a good mind. I forgave him for North Africa. Everything's fine now."

"Yes, sir. At seven-forty this evening, we'll be accompanying the field marshal by plane to the coast of Normandy," Bormann continued. "Then on to Rotterdam."

"Rotterdam." Hitler nodded, putting his box of paints into the safe. "I trust that work is going on schedule? That's vital."

"Yes sir. After a day in Rotterdam, we'll be flying back to the Berghof for a week."

"The Berghof! Yes, I'd forgotten!" Hitler smiled, dark circles under his eyes. The Berghof, Hitler's mansion in the Bavarian Alps above the village of Berchtesgaden, had been his only true home since the summer of 1928. It was a place of bracing wind, vistas that would have stunned the sight of Odin, and memories that lay easy on the mind. Except for Geli, of course. He'd met Geli Raubal there, his one true love. Geli, dear Geli with blond hair and laughing eyes. Why did dear Geli burst her heart with a single shot? I loved you, Geli, he thought. Wasn't that enough? Eva would be waiting for him at the Berghof, and sometimes when the light was just so and Eva's hair was brushed back, Hitler could squint his eyes and see the face of Geli, his lost love and niece, twenty-three years old when she committed suicide in 1931.

His head hurt. He looked at the calendar, the days of March, on his desk amid the clutter.

"It's springtime," Hitler realized.

From beyond the walls, out over the blacked-out city of Berlin, came a howling. The wolf! Hitler thought, his mouth opening in a gasp. No, no . . . an air-raid siren.

The noise built and moaned, felt more than heard behind the walls of the Reich Chancellery. In the distance there was the sound of a bomb exploding, a crunching noise like the smashing of a heavy ax against a tree trunk. Then another bomb, two more, a fifth and sixth in rapid succession. "Call someone!" Hitler commanded, cold sweat sparkling on his cheeks.

Martin picked up the desk telephone and dialed a number.

More bombs fell, the noise of destruction swelling and waning. Hitler's fingers gripped the desk's edge. The bombs were falling to the south, he believed. Down near Tempelhof airport. Not close enough to fear, but still . . .

The crack and boom of distant explosions ceased. Now there was only the wolf howl of the air-raid siren and more answering around the city.

"A nuisance raid," Martin said after he'd spoken with the chief of Berlin security. "A few craters on the airfield and some row houses on fire. The bombers have gone."

"Damn the swine!" Hitler stood up, trembling. "Damn them to hell! Where are the Luftwaffe night fighters when we need them? Isn't anyone awake?" He strode to one of the maps that showed the defensive fortifications, the mine fields and concrete bunkers, on the Normandy coast. "Thank the fates that Rommel is. Churchill and that Jew Roosevelt are going to come to France, sooner or later. They'll find a warm reception, won't they?"

Martin agreed that they would.

"And when they send their cannon fodder, they'll be sitting in London at their polished desks drinking English tea and eating those . . . what do they call those biscuit things?"

"Crumpets," Martin said.

"Drinking tea and eating crumpets!" Hitler steamrolled on. "But we'll give them something special to chew on, won't we, Martin?"

"Yes, *mein Führer*," Martin said.

Hitler grunted and moved to another map. This one was of more immediate concern; it showed the route of the Slavic wave threatening to burst the banks of Russia and flood their filth into German-occupied Poland and Romania. Small red circles showed pockets of trapped German divisions, each fifteen thousand men, slowly dwindling away.

"I want two more armored divisions right here." Hitler touched one of the pressure points, where at this moment, hundreds of miles away, German soldiers fought for their lives against the Russian onslaught. "I want them ready to fight within twenty-four hours."

"Yes, *mein Führer*." Thirty thousand men and almost three hundred tanks, Martin thought. Where would they come from? The generals in the west would bellow if they lost any more of their troops, and those in the east were too busy for additional paperwork. Well, the men and tanks would be found. It was the *Führer's* will. Period.

"I'm tired," Hitler said. "I think I can sleep now. Lock up, will you?" He trudged out of the office and down the long hallway outside, a small man in a bathrobe.

Martin was tired, too; it had been a long day. All of them were. Before he turned out the desk lamp, he went around and picked up the farmhouse painting with its dark smear of shadow. He looked long and hard into that darkness. Maybe . . . just maybe . . . that *was* a wolf, creeping around the farmhouse's corner. Yes, Martin could see it now. It was right there, where the *Führer* had said it was. A portent. Martin put the painting back on its easel. Hitler would probably never touch it again, and who knew where all these pictures would end up?

The wolf was there. The more Martin looked, the clearer it became.

The *Führer* always saw these portents first, and that of course was part of his magic.

59

Martin Bormann switched off the lamp, locked the office door, and walked down the long corridor to his apartment. In the bedroom, his wife Gerda slept soundly, a picture of Hitler on the wall above her head.

7

"Major Gallatin?" the dark-haired copilot said over the muffled roar of the propellers. "Six minutes to the drop zone!"

Michael nodded and stood up, grim-lipped. He hooked his ripcord's clamp around the brace that ran overhead the length of the transport aircraft's spine and walked to the closed door. Above it was a dim red warning light, suffusing the plane's interior with crimson.

It was the twenty-sixth of March, and the time on Michael's wristwatch was nineteen minutes after two. He closed his mind to the lurch and sway of the C-47 and began to inspect the parachute pack's straps, making sure they were hooked with equal pressure on either side of his groin. A strap tightening across the testicles almost a thousand feet in the air would not be his idea of a pleasant experience.

He checked the buckles of the chest straps and then the top fold of the pack itself, making sure nothing would foul the lines as the chute billowed out. It was supposed to be a black chute, because there was a half-moon.

"Three minutes, Major," the polite copilot, a kid from New Jersey, said.

"Thank you." Michael felt the airplane veer slightly to starboard, the pilot correcting course either to avoid searchlights or an anti-aircraft emplacement. Michael breathed slowly and deeply, watching the red bulb above the doorway. His heart was beating hard, and sweat had dampened the inside of his dark green jumpsuit. He wore a black knit cap and his face was daubed with black and green camouflage paint. He hoped it would wash off easily, because it might

draw a bit of unwanted attention on the Avenue des Champs
Élysées.

Strapped to his body was a short shovel with a folding
blade, a knife with a serrated edge, a .45 automatic, and a
pack of bullets. Also a little box, zipped into his jacket, that
contained two chocolate bars and some salted beef jerky.
He figured the heat of his body would have melted the
chocolate bars by now.

"One minute." The red light went out. The New Jersey
kid pulled a latch and the C-47's doorway slid open, letting
in a scream of wind. Michael immediately stepped into
position, his boot tips on the edge and his arms braced
against the doorway's sides. Below him was a black plain
that just as well could have been dense forest or fathomless
ocean. "Thirty seconds!" the copilot shouted against the
wind and props noise.

Something glinted, far below. Michael's breath snagged.
Another glint: a finger of light, rising from the earth, searching the sky.

"Oh Jeez," the other man said.

The searchlight angled upward. They've heard our engines, Michael realized. Now they're hunting. The light
swung around, and its beam knifed through the dark less
than a hundred feet below Michael's boots. He stood steady,
but his gut twisted. There was a burst of red off to the left of
the searchlight, followed by a thunderous boom and a white
flash about five or six hundred feet over the C-47. The plane
trembled from the shock wave, but stayed on course. A
second anti-aircraft shell exploded higher up and more to
the right, but the searchlight was coming around again for
another sweep. The New Jersey kid, his face pallid, grasped
Michael's shoulder. "Major, we're screwed!" he shouted.
"You want to scrub the drop?"

The aircraft was picking up speed, about to make a violent
turn away from the drop zone. Michael knew there was no
time for deliberation. "I'm going," he answered, and he
jumped through the doorway with sweat on his face.

He fell into darkness, his heart swelling and his stomach
rising up in his abdomen. He clenched his teeth, his arms
crossed and gripping his elbows. He heard the high whine of

61

the plane passing on and then there was a bone-wrenching shock as the rip cord pulled and the chute trailed out of its pack with a soft, almost gentle *pop*.

As the parachute bloomed, Michael Gallatin's hurtling descent was braked. He felt as if his internal organs, muscles, and bones were in brutal collision, his kneecaps jerking up so high they almost smashed into his chin. Then he got his legs straightened out and he grasped the chute's guidelines, his heart still racing from the impact with air. He heard another blast from the anti-aircraft cannon, but it was high and to the right and he was in no danger of being shredded by shrapnel. The searchlight veered toward him, stopped, and began to rotate in the other direction again, hunting the intruder. Michael gazed around at the dark earth below, looking for the sign he'd been told to expect. It should be from the east, he remembered. The half-moon was over his left shoulder. He turned slowly under the expanded silk and searched the ground.

There! A green light. A blinker, flashing out a quick tattoo.

Then darkness again.

He guided the chute toward the light and looked up to make sure the lines were all clear.

The parachute was white.

Damn it! he thought. Trust the supply service to screw things up! If a German soldier on the ground saw the white chute, there was going to be hell to pay. The searchlight crew had probably already radioed for a scout car or motorcycle team. Now not only was he in danger, but so was the person with the green blinker. Whoever that might be.

The anti-aircraft cannon spoke again, a knell of distant thunder. But the C-47 was long gone, heading back across the Channel to England. Michael wished the two Americans good luck, and turned his attention to his own difficulties. There was nothing to do at the moment but fall. When he touched ground, he'd be ready for action, but right now he was dangling at the mercy of a white parachute.

Michael looked up, listening to the wind hiss in the silk folds. It stirred a memory. So long ago . . . a world and a lifetime . . . so long ago, when he knew innocence.

And suddenly, in a flash of memory, the sky was bright

blue and there was not a white parachute over his head, but instead a white silk kite, unreeling from his hand to catch the breeze of Russia.

"Mikhail! Mikhail!" a woman's voice called, over a field full of yellow flowers.

And Mikhail Gallatinov, all of eight years old and still fully human, smiled with the May sun on his face.

TWO

The White Palace

─────────── **1** ───────────

"Mikhail!" the woman called, across time and distance. "Mikhail, where are you?" In another moment Elana Gallatinov saw the kite, and then her green-eyed gaze found her son, standing out at the far edge of the field almost to the deep woods. On this day, the twenty-first of May in the year 1918, the breeze blew from the east, and brought with it a faint smell of gunpowder.

"Come home!" she told the little boy, and watched as he waved and began to reel the kite's line in. The kite dipped like a white fish. Behind the tall, black-haired woman whose skin was the shade of porcelain stood the Gallatinov manor, a two-storied house of brown Russian stones with a red, sharply angled roof and chimneys. Large sunflowers grew around the house, and there was a gravel driveway that went from the house through the iron gates and connected with the dirt road to the nearest village, Moroc, six miles to the south. The closest town of any size was Minsk, over fifty miles north on bad roads.

Russia was a huge country, and the house of General Fyodor Gallatinov was a mote of dust on the head of a pin. But the fourteen acres of meadow and woods was the Gallatinov world, and had been so since Czar Nicholas II had abdicated his throne on March 2, 1917. And with the Czar's final words in his signed statement of abdication—"May the Lord God help Russia!"—the motherland had turned into a killer of her children.

But the young Mikhail knew nothing of politics, of Red Russians fighting White Russians and cold-minded men named Lenin and Trotsky. He knew nothing, mercifully, of whole villages razed to the ground by rival factions less than a hundred miles from where he stood reeling in a silken kite; he knew nothing of famine, and women and children twitching as they were hanged from trees, and pistol barrels splattered with brains. He knew his father was a hero in a war, that his mother was beautiful, that his sister sometimes pinched his cheeks and called him a ragamuffin, and that today was the day of a long-anticipated picnic. He got the kite down, wrestling with the wind, and then he clasped it gently in his arms and ran across the field toward his mother.

Elana, though, knew the things that her son did not. She was thirty-seven years old, wearing a long white dress of springtime linen, and gray had begun to creep back from her forehead and at her temples. Lines had etched deeply around her eyes and at the corners of her mouth; not age lines, but the lines of constant inner turmoil. Fyodor had been away at war too long, and gravely wounded at a marshy slaughter hole called Kowel. Gone were the operas and brightly lit festivals of St. Petersburg; gone were the noisy street markets of Moscow; gone were the banquets and royal garden parties of Czar Nicholas and Czarina Alexandra, and left in their shadows were the skeletons of the future.

"I flew it, Mother!" Mikhail shouted when he got closer. "Did you see how high?"

"Oh, that was your kite?" she asked, with feigned surprise. "I thought it was a cloud tied to a string!"

He saw she was teasing him. "It was my kite!" he insisted, and she took his hand and said, "You'd better come down to earth now, my little cloud. We have a picnic to go on." She squeezed his hand—he was as excited as a candle flame—and led him toward the house. In the driveway the hired man Dimitri had brought the carriage and two horses from the barn, and twelve-year-old Alizia was carrying one of the wicker baskets for their picnic from the front door. The maid and Elana's sewing companion Sophie brought the other basket out, and helped Alizia pack them into the back of the carriage.

And then Fyodor emerged from the house, carrying a brown blanket rolled up under one arm and the other hand steadying himself on his eagle-crested cane. His right leg, mauled by machine-gun bullets, was stiff and noticeably thinner than the left leg; but he had learned to move with grace, and as he brought the blanket to the rear of the carriage he lifted his gray-bearded face to the sun.

Elana, after all these years, could still feel her heartbeat quicken as she looked at him. He was tall and lean, with the figure of a swordsman, and though he was forty-six years old and his body bore the scars of rapier and bullet wounds, he yet had a youthful quality, a curiosity and power of life that sometimes made her feel ancient. His face, with its long slender nose, square jaw, and deep-set brown eyes, used to be hard and bitter, the face of a man who has crashed into the ceiling of his limitations. Now, though, it had softened with the reality of his situation: he was retired from the service of the motherland, and would live out the rest of his years here, on this plot of land far from the center of tumult. His forced retirement, after the abdication of the czar, had not been an easy pill to swallow, but now that it was dissolved he felt numb, like an amputated relic.

"What a beautiful day," he said, and watched the wind blowing through the trees. He wore his brown, carefully ironed uniform with its chestful of medals and ribbons, and on his head was his black-visored cap, still bearing the seal of Czar Nicholas II.

"I flew the kite!" Mikhail said eagerly to his father. "I got it up almost to the sky!"

"Good for you," Gallatinov answered, and reached out to Alizia. "My golden angel. Help me inside, will you?"

Elana watched as Alizia helped her father into the carriage while Mikhail stood with his kite in his arms. She touched her son's shoulder. "Come on, Mikhail. Let's make sure everything's packed."

They put the kite into the back of the carriage, too, and Dimitri closed and latched the trunk's lid. Then Elana and Mikhail sat across from Fyodor and Alizia in the red velvet interior, and they waved goodbye to Sophie as Dimitri popped the reins and the two chestnut horses began their journey.

Mikhail looked out the oval window as Alizia drew a

picture and their mother and father talked about things that he barely remembered: the spring festival in St. Petersburg, the estate where they'd lived when he was born, people whose names were familiar only because he'd heard them before. He watched the gently rolling land give way to forests of towering oaks and evergreens, listened to the creak of the wheels and the crisp jingling of the horses' traces. The sweet scent of wildflowers drifted into the carriage as they passed a blossoming meadow, and Alizia perked up from her drawing when Mikhail sighted a herd of deer on the edge of the woods. He'd been cooped up in the house from the middle of October until the end of April, patiently doing the schoolwork lessons that Magda, his and Alizia's tutor, taught him. Now, Mikhail's senses rioted under the heady onslaught of springtime. Winter's pewter had been banished from the land, for a time at least, and Mikhail's world wore fine green robes.

Their May picnic was an annual excursion, a ritual that connected them to their lives in St. Petersburg. This year Dimitri had found a good place for them, on the shore of a lake about an hour's leisurely drive from the Gallatinov house.

The lake was blue and wind-rippled, and as Dimitri pulled the carriage into a meadow Mikhail heard the cawing of crows atop a huge, gnarled oak. Forest circled the lake, the emerald wilderness unbroken by village or habitation for a hundred miles to the north, south and west. Dimitri stopped the carriage and chocked the wheels, then let the horses drink lake water as the Gallatinovs unloaded their picnic baskets and spread the blanket down overlooking the blue pool.

They ate their meal of baked ham, fried potatoes, dark wheat bread, and ginger cake with sugar frosting. One of the horses nickered and jumped around nervously for a moment, but Dimitri got the mare settled down and Fyodor sat facing the woods. "She smells something wild," he told Elana as he poured them both a glass of red wine. "Children!" he warned. "Don't stray too far from us!"

"Yes, Father," Alizia said, but she was already taking off

her shoes and lifting up the hem of her pink dress to go wading.

Mikhail went down to the lake with her and hunted for pretty stones while she walked in the shallows. Dimitri stayed nearby, sitting on a fallen tree and watching the clouds glide past, a rifle at his side.

The enchanted afternoon moved on. His pockets full of stones, Mikhail reclined in the sunny meadow and watched his father and mother sit together on the picnic blanket and talk. Alizia lay beside her father, sleeping, and every so often his hand would move out to touch her arm or shoulder. Mikhail realized, quite suddenly, that his father's hand had never touched him. He didn't know why, nor did he understand why his father's eyes took on a January chill when they met his own. Sometimes he felt like a small thing that lived beneath a rock, and other times he didn't care, but there was no time when there wasn't a hurting deep in his heart.

After a while, his mother laid her head on his father's shoulder, and they slept in the sun. Mikhail watched a raven circling overhead, the light glinting blue black off its wings, and then he stood up and walked to the carriage to get his kite. He ran back and forth, letting the string unwind from his fingers, and a breeze caught the silk, expanded it, and the kite sailed smoothly up into the air.

He started to shout to his parents, but they were both asleep. Alizia was sleeping as well, her back pressed against their father's side. Dimitri sat on his fallen tree, deep in thought, the rifle resting across his knees.

The kite floated higher. The string continued to unreel. Mikhail shifted his fingers to get a better grip. The breeze was fierce beyond the treetops. It grasped the kite, hurled it right and left and made the string thrum like a mandolin. Still the kite ascended—too high, he decided momentarily. He started to reel it back. And then the wind hit the kite from a strange angle, lifted it and turned it at the same time, and the string tightened, strained, and snapped about six feet below the balsawood crossbar.

Oh no! he almost cried out. The kite had been a present from his mother on his eighth birthday, the seventh of

March. And now it was flying away at the mercy of the wind, going over the treetops toward the deep woods. Oh no! He looked at Dimitri and started to shout for help. But Dimitri had his hands pressed to his face, as if in some private agony. The rest of his family slumbered on, and Mikhail thought of how his father hated to be awakened from a nap. In another moment the kite would be over the forest, and the decision had to be made now whether to stand here and watch it go or follow and hope it would fall when the breeze slackened.

Children! he remembered his father saying. *Don't stray too far from us!*

But this was his kite, and if it were lost, his mother's heart would be broken. He glanced again at Dimitri; the man hadn't moved. Precious seconds were ticking past.

Mikhail decided. He ran across the meadow, and into the woods.

Looking up, he could see the kite through the green leaves and tangle of branches. As he followed its erratic progress, he dug a handful of smooth stones from his pocket and dropped them at his feet to mark a trail back. The kite went on, and so did the boy.

Less than two minutes after Mikhail had left the meadow, three men on horseback came down to the lake from the main road. They all wore dark, patched peasant clothing. One of them carried a rifle slung around his shoulder, and the other two were armed with pistols in cartridge belts. They continued to where the Gallatinov family slept in the sun, and as one of the horses snorted and whinnied Dimitri looked around and stood up, pinpricks of sweat sparkling on his face.

2

Fyodor Gallatinov awakened as three shadows fell across him. He blinked, saw the horses and riders, and as he sat up Elana awakened, too. Alizia looked up, rubbing her eyes.

"Good afternoon, General Gallatinov," the lead rider, a man with a long thin face and bushy red eyebrows, said. "I haven't seen you since Kowel."

"Kowel? Who . . . who are you?"

"I *was* Lieutenant Sergei Schedrin. The Guards Army. You may not remember me, but surely you remember Kowel."

"Of course I do. Every day of my life." Gallatinov struggled to his feet, balancing on his cane. His face had become mottled with angry red. "What's the meaning of this, Lieutenant Schedrin?"

"Oh, no." The other man extended a finger and wagged it back and forth. "I'm simply Comrade Schedrin now. My friends Anton and Danalov were also at Kowel." Gallatinov's gaze flickered to the two faces; Anton's was broad and heavy-jowled, and Danalov's bore a bayonet scar from his left eyebrow up to his hairline. Their eyes were cold and only slightly curious, as if they were examining an insect under a magnifying glass. "We've brought the rest of our company with us as well," Schedrin said.

"The rest of your company?" Gallatinov shook his head, not comprehending.

"Listen!" Schedrin cocked his head as the breeze keened through the woods. "There they are, whispering. Listen to what they say: 'Justice. Justice.' Do you hear them, General?"

"We're having a picnic," Gallatinov said firmly. "I'd like for you gentlemen to leave."

"Yes," Schedrin said. "I'm sure you would. What a lovely family you have."

73

"Dimitri!" the general shouted. "Dimitri, fire a warning shot above their—" He turned toward Dimitri, and what he saw closed an iron claw around his heart.

Dimitri stood about fifteen yards away, and hadn't even cocked the rifle or lifted it to a firing position. He stared at the ground, his shoulders stooped. "Dimitri!" Gallatinov shouted again, but he knew he would not be answered. His throat was dry, and he grasped Elana's chilly hand.

"Thank you for bringing them here, Comrade Dimitri," Schedrin told him. "Your service will be noted and rewarded."

Mikhail, moving swiftly through the forest in pursuit of his kite, thought he heard his father shouting. His heart hammered; his father had probably awakened and was calling for him. There was going to be a switching in Mikhail's immediate future. But the kite was falling now, the string snagging in the top of an oak tree. Then the wind kicked it loose, and the kite rose again. Mikhail pushed through dense brush, soft spongy masses of dead leaves and moss, and kept following. Ten more feet; twenty more; thirty more. Thorns grabbed his hair; he pulled free, ducked his head under the thorn branches, and dropped another stone to the ground to mark his way back.

The kite dipped, fell into the arms of an evergreen, and teasingly floated free once more. Then it was rising sharply into the blue sky, and as Mikhail watched it go his face was dappled with sun and shadow.

Something moved in the underbrush, less than a dozen feet to Mikhail's left.

He stood very still as the kite picked up speed and floated away. Whatever had moved was silent now. Waiting.

There was another movement, to the boy's right. The soft crackle of weight settling on dry leaves.

Mikhail swallowed. He started to call for his mother, but she was too far away to hear him, and he wanted no loud noises.

Silence, but for the wind hissing in the trees.

Mikhail smelled the aroma of an animal: a rank, bestial smell, the odor of a creature that had decayed meat on its breath. He felt something—two somethings—watching him from opposite sides, and he thought that if he ran they would leap on him from behind. His impulse was to scream and turn and flee headlong through the woods, but he struck it down; he could not get away by running. No, no. A Gallatinov never runs, his father had once told him. Mikhail felt a droplet of sweat trickling down the center of his back. The beasts were waiting for his decision, and they were very close.

He turned, his legs trembling, and began to walk slowly back, following the trail of lakeshore stones.

A Gallatinov never runs, Fyodor thought. His gaze swept the meadow. Mikhail. Where was Mikhail?

"Our company was slaughtered at Kowel." Schedrin leaned forward, hands clenching the saddle horn. "Slaughtered," he repeated. "We were commanded to run headlong across a swamp into a nest of barbed wire and machine guns. Of course you remember that."

"I remember a war," Gallatinov answered. "I remember one tragedy tripping on the heels of another."

"For you, tragedy. For us, slaughter. Of course we obeyed orders. We were good soldiers of the czar. How could we not obey?"

"We all obeyed the same orders that day."

"Yes, we did," Schedrin agreed. "But some obeyed them with the blood of innocent men. Your hands are still red, General. I can see the blood dripping off them."

"Look closer." Gallatinov stepped defiantly toward the man, though Elana tried to hold him back. "My own blood is on there, too!"

"Ah." Schedrin nodded. "So it is. But not enough, I think."

Elana gasped. Anton had withdrawn his pistol from his holster and cocked it. "Make them go away!" Alizia said, tears in her eyes. "Please make them go away!" Danalov pulled his pistol out and eased the hammer back.

Gallatinov stepped in front of his wife and daughter, his eyes black with fury. "How *dare* you raise a gun to me and my family!" He lifted his cane. "Damn you to hell. Put down those pistols!"

"We have a proclamation to read," Schedrin said, undaunted. He removed a rolled-up piece of paper from his saddlebag and opened it. "To General Fyodor Gallatinov, in service to Czar Nicholas the Second, hero"—he smiled thinly—"of Kowel and commander of the Guards Army. From the survivors of the Guards Army, who suffered and were slaughtered by the ineptitude of Czar Nicholas and his imperial court. Since we cannot have the czar, we will have you. And so the case will be closed to our satisfaction."

An execution squad, Gallatinov realized. God only knew how long they'd been tracking him. He glanced quickly around; no way out. Mikhail. Where was the boy? His heart was beating hard, and his palms were sweating. Alizia began to sob, but Elana was silent. Gallatinov looked at the guns and the eyes of the men who aimed them. There was no way out. "You'll let my family go," he demanded.

"No Gallatinov will leave this place alive," Schedrin replied. "We understand the importance of a task well done, Comrade. Consider this . . . your private Kowel." He unstrapped his rifle and pulled back the bolt to chamber a shell.

"You goddamned dogs!" General Gallatinov said, and stepped forward to strike the man's face with his cane.

Anton shot him in the chest before the cane was swung. The pistol's *crack* made Elana and her daughter jump, and the noise echoed across the meadow like strange thunder. A brooding of ravens leaped from a treetop and winged for safety.

Gallatinov was hurled backward by the force of the bullet, and fell to his knees in the grass. Crimson was spreading across the front of his uniform. He gasped, could not find the strength to stand. Elana screamed and fell down beside her husband, her arms around him as if she could protect him from the next bullet. Alizia turned, began to run toward the lake, and Danalov shot her twice in the back before she'd gotten ten feet away. She tumbled, a sack of bloody flesh and broken bones.

"No!" Gallatinov said, and got his good leg under him.

Blood was creeping from his mouth, and his eyes glinted with terror. He started to rise, Elana still clinging to him.

Schedrin pulled the rifle's trigger, and the bullet hit Gallatinov in the face. Bits of bone and brain splattered over Elana's dress. The jittering body fell backward, carrying Elana with it, and they fell over the picnic baskets, bottles of wine and crumb-flecked platters. Danalov shot Gallatinov in the stomach, and Anton fired two more bullets into the man's head as Elana continued to shriek.

"Oh dear God," Dimitri said, choking, and he ran down to the lake's edge to be violently sick.

Mikhail heard a series of high cracking noises, followed by a scream. He stopped, and the beasts that were tracking him also halted. His mother's voice, he realized. His face tightened with fear, and he began to run through the forest heedless of the danger at his back.

Vines gripped his shirt and tried to trip him. He followed the trail of stones through the underbrush, his boots slipping on moss-covered rocks and sinking into ankle-deep pools of dead leaves. And then he burst out of the forest into the meadow and saw three men on horseback and bodies lying sprawled. Red gleamed on green grass. His stomach knotted, his knees seized up, and he saw one of the men pull back the bolt of his rifle and aim at his . . .

"Mother!" he shouted, his voice echoing horror across the meadow.

Anton and Danalov looked toward the boy. Elana Gallatinov, on her knees with her white dress dripping blood, saw him standing there, and she screamed, "Run, Mikhail! Ru—"

The rifle bullet hit her below the hairline. Mikhail saw his mother's head explode.

"Get the boy!" Schedrin commanded, and Anton lifted his smoking pistol.

He stared, transfixed, at the black eye of the gun barrel. A Gallatinov never runs, he thought. He saw the man's finger twitch on the trigger. A gout of fire leaped from the black-eyed barrel, and he heard a waspish whine and felt heat on his left cheek. A branch snapped beyond his shoulder.

"Kill him, damn it!" Schedrin yelled as he chambered another bullet into his rifle and wheeled his horse around. Danalov was taking aim at Mikhail, and Anton was about to squeeze off a second shot.

A Gallatinov ran.

He twisted around, his mother's scream ringing in his mind, and fled into the forest as a bullet thunked into a tree to his right and showered his hair with splinters. He tripped over a vine, staggered, and almost fell. There was the hoarser *crack* of a rifle shot, and the bullet passed over Mikhail's skull as he struggled for balance.

Then he was picking up speed, tearing into the underbrush, sliding on dead leaves, and fighting through tangles of thorns. He toppled into a gulley, got up, and scrambled out, heading deeper into the wilderness.

"Come on!" Schedrin told the others. "We can't let the little bastard get away!" He dug his heels into his mount's flanks and entered the forest with Anton and Danalov riding just behind him.

Mikhail heard the thunder of hooves. He clambered up a rocky hillside and half ran, half slid down the descending side. "Over there!" he heard one of the men shout. "I saw him! This way!"

Thorns whipped Mikhail in the face and tore across his shirt. He blinked back tears, his legs pumping. A shot rang out, and hit a tree trunk five feet away. "Save your bullets, idiot!" Schedrin commanded, getting a quick glimpse of the boy's back before the branches covered his flight.

Mikhail ran on, his shoulders hunched against the expected impact of a lead slug. His lungs were burning, his heart hammering through his chest. He dared to glance back. The horses and men raced after him, dead leaves flying up in their wake. He looked ahead again, angled to the left, and ran into thick green undergrowth laced with creepers.

Anton's horse stepped into a gopher hole. The animal bellowed and fell, and Anton's right knee burst open like an overripe fruit as he landed on a sharp-edged rock. He screamed in agony, the horse writhing and trying to get up, but both Schedrin and Danalov kept up their pursuit.

Mikhail fought through the undergrowth, slanting down into a valley cloaked with green. He knew full well what would happen if the killers caught him, and fear gave him wings. His feet slipped out from beneath him on a bed of pine needles, and he slid through a place where the shadows had grown crimson mushrooms. Then he was up and running again, and behind him he heard a horse's whinny and a man shouting, "He's over here! Going downhill!"

Ahead was dense forest, close-packed evergreens and thick coils of thorn bushes and stands of wild red berries. He headed for the thickest of it, hoping to leap into the coils and fight his way to the bottom, to a place where the horsemen couldn't follow. He reached out, parted the emerald growth with bleeding hands—and came face to muzzle with the beast.

It was a wolf, with dark brown eyes and sleek russet fur. Mikhail fell backward, his mouth open but the scream shocked out of him.

The wolf leaped.

Its jaws opened, and the teeth gouged furrows across Mikhail's left shoulder as it slammed him to the earth. The breath was knocked out of him, as was all sense. The wolf's teeth clamped on his shoulder, about to tear through the flesh and crush the bones; and then the horse bearing Sergei Schedrin burst through the brush and reared, its eyes flaring with terror. Schedrin lost his rifle, and he cried out, clinging to the horse's neck as he saw the wolf beneath his boots.

The animal released Mikhail's shoulder, spun around in a smooth, graceful motion, and bit deeply into the horse's stomach. The horse made a strangled moan, kicked wildly, and fell onto its side, trapping Schedrin's legs beneath.

"Holy Jesus!" Danalov shouted, reining in his horse on the hillside. Two seconds after he'd spoken, the large gray wolf that had been tracking him leaped onto the horse's flank, clawed up over it into the saddle, and clamped its fangs into the back of Danalov's neck. It shook Danalov like a rag doll, snapping his spine and driving him out of the saddle to the ground. The horse thrashed and tumbled, rolling down the hillside in a flurry of dead leaves and pine needles.

A third wolf, this one blond with ice-blue eyes, darted in and grasped Danalov's flailing right arm. With a savage twist, the beast broke it at the elbow and the splintered bones tore through the man's flesh. Danalov's body jerked and writhed. The gray wolf that had knocked him out of the saddle closed its jaws on Danalov's throat and crushed the windpipe with a casual squeeze.

As Schedrin struggled to free his legs the russet wolf finished tearing the horse's stomach open. Coils of steaming intestines slid from the gaping wound, and the horse shrieked. Another beast, pale brown streaked with gray, leaped from the brush and landed on the horse's throat, tearing it open with teeth and claws. Schedrin was screaming—a high, thin scream—and digging his fingers into the earth to try to pull loose. Only a few feet away Mikhail sat up, stunned and half conscious, with blood and wolf saliva drooling from the wounds in his shoulder.

Over the hilltop Anton heard the sounds of violence and gripped his ruined knee. He tried to crawl through the thicket, his horse struggling to rise on a broken ankle. He crawled perhaps eight feet—far enough to drive agony through every nerve of his body—when two smaller wolves, one dark brown and the other a dusky red, came together from the underbrush and each clenched a wrist, breaking the bones with quick snaps of their heads. Anton cried out for God, but in this wilderness God had fangs.

The two wolves, working in concert, broke Anton's shoulders and rib cage. Then the red one seized Anton's throat while the dark brown beast clamped its jaws to the sides of the man's head. As Anton trembled and moaned, reduced to a mindless husk, the animals crushed his throat and broke open his skull like a clay pot.

Schedrin, his hands clawing the earth, had pulled himself partway free from the shuddering weight atop him. Tears of terror streamed from his eyes, and he grasped hold of a small sapling and kept pulling. The sapling cracked. He smelled the coppery reek of blood, felt sickening heat wash across his face, and he looked around into the maw of the pale brown beast.

Blood dripped from its mouth. It stared into his eyes for maybe three terrible seconds, and Schedrin sobbed, *"Please . . ."*

The wolf lunged forward, gripped the flesh of his face between its fangs, and ripped it off the skull, as if peeling away a mask. Raw red muscles danced underneath, and the grinning skull's teeth chattered. The wolf planted its paws on Schedrin's shoulders and gulped the man's shredded face down with a shiver of excitement. Schedrin's lidless eyes stared from the bloody skull. The gray wolf, large-shouldered and rippling with muscle, came in and broke Schedrin's neck. The russet animal snapped Schedrin's lower jaw away and tore the hanging tongue out. Then the pale brown beast seized the dead man's skull, cracked it open, and began to feast.

Mikhail moaned softly, fighting to stay conscious, his senses brutalized.

The russet wolf that had bitten his shoulder turned toward him, and began to advance.

It got within four feet and halted, sniffing the air to catch Mikhail's scent. Its dark eyes stared into Mikhail's face and held his gaze. Seconds passed. Mikhail, near fainting, stared back, and in his delirium of pain and shock he thought the beast was asking him a question, and that question might have been: *Do you want to die?*

Mikhail, holding the animal's penetrating stare, reached out to one side and picked up a piece of branch. He lifted it, his hand trembling, to strike the wolf's skull when it lunged.

The wolf paused. Motionless, its eyes like fathomless dark whirlpools.

And then the gray animal roughly nudged the other wolf's ribs, and the death trance broke. The russet wolf blinked, gave a snorted *whuff*—a sound of acknowledgment—and turned away to continue its feast on the ruins of Sergei Schedrin. The gray one shattered Schedrin's breastbone and gnawed in after the heart.

Mikhail held the stick with a white-knuckled grip. Over the hilltop one of the animals feasting on Anton's corpse gave a low howl that rapidly built in intensity, echoing through the forest and scaring birds out of the trees. The blond, blue-eyed wolf paused in its chewing of Danalov's shredded torso and lifted its head to the breeze, replying with a howl that made a shiver course up Mikhail's spine and cleared the misty pain from his head. The pale brown animal began to howl, then the russet wolf, singing in eerie harmony with blood-smeared muzzles. Finally the gray wolf lifted its head and sang a wailing, discordant note that silenced the others. The note wavered, grew in power and volume, changed pitch, and slid upward. Then the gray wolf abruptly ceased its singing, and all the wolves returned to their horsemeat and human flesh.

From the distance came a howling that lasted maybe fifteen seconds, faded, and died.

Dark motes spun across Mikhail's vision. He pressed his hand to his shoulder. In the wounds muscle tissue showed bright pink. He almost shouted for his mother and father, but then the images of corpses and murder slammed into his brain again and knocked him witless.

Not witless enough, however, to realize that sooner or later the wolf pack would tear him to pieces.

This was not a game. This was not a fairy tale told to him by his mother in the golden glow of lamplight. This was not Hans Christian Andersen or Aesop's fables; this was life and death.

He shook his head to force back the twilight. Run, he thought. A Gallatinov never runs. Got to run . . . got to . . .

The pale brown, gray-streaked wolf and the blond one snapped at each other over the red chunks of Danalov's liver. Then the blond beast backed off, allowing the dominant animal to gobble up the bits of meat. The large-shouldered gray wolf was ripping pieces out of the horse's flanks.

Mikhail crawled away from them, pushing himself backward with his boots. He kept watching them, expecting an attack; the blond wolf stared at him for a second, blue eyes glittering, then began to feed on the horse's entrails. Mikhail pushed himself into the thicket, the breath rasping from his lungs, and at the center of thorns and green creepers he lost consciousness and fell into night.

The afternoon passed. The sun began to sink. Blue shadows laced the forest, and chill pockets formed. The corpses shrank, being whittled down to their foundations. Bones cracked, the ghosts of pistol shots, and the red marrow lay exposed.

The wolves ate their fill, then lodged chunks of meat in their gullets to be regurgitated. Their bellies swollen, they began to drift off into the gathering shadows.

Except for one. The large gray wolf sniffed the air and stood near the little boy's body. It nosed around the oozing wounds on Mikhail's shoulder, and smelled the tang of blood mingled with wolf saliva. The beast stood staring down into Mikhail's face for a long time without moving, as if in solemn contemplation.

It sighed.

The sun was almost gone. Faint specks of stars appeared over the forest in the darkening east. A crescent moon hung above Russia.

The wolf leaned forward, pushing the boy over on his stomach with its blood-caked muzzle. Mikhail groaned softly, stirred, then lapsed again into unconsciousness. The wolf clamped its jaws gently but firmly around the back of the child's neck, lifting the limp body off the ground with muscular ease. The beast began to stride through the forest, its amber-eyed gaze ticking to right and left, its senses questing for the enemy. Behind it, the child's boots dragged on the ground, and plowed furrows in the leaves.

3

Sometime, somewhere, he heard a chorus of howls. They rang out through the darkness, over the forest and hills, over the lake and the meadow where corpses lay amid the dandelions. The wolf song soared, breaking into discordant notes and returning to harmony again. And Mikhail heard himself moan, in crude emulation of the howling, as pain racked his body. He felt sweat on his face, a savage burning in his wounds. He tried to open his eyes, but the lids were gummed shut by dried tears. In his nostrils was the odor of blood and meat, and he felt hot breath on his face. Something rumbled nearby, like a steady bellows.

The merciful darkness closed around him once more, and he slipped away in its velvet folds.

The high, sweet trilling of birds awakened him. He knew he was conscious, but he wondered for a moment if he were in heaven. If so, God hadn't healed his shoulder, nor had the angels kiss the sticky tears from his eyes. He had to almost rip the lids open.

Sunlight and shadow. Cold stones and the smell of ancient clay. He sat up, his shoulder shrieking.

No, not heaven, he realized. It was still the hell he'd fallen into yesterday. Or he thought a day must've passed, at least. This was a golden morning sun, glinting brightly in the tangle of trees and vines he could see through a large, glassless oval window. The vines had entered the window, and latched on to the wall where a mosaic of figures bearing candles had faded to shades.

He looked up, his neck muscles stiff and aching. Above him was a high ceiling, crossed with wooden beams. He was sitting on the stone floor of a huge room, sunlight streaming through a series of windows, some of which still held fragments of dark red glass. Vines, drunk with the springtime sun, festooned the walls and dangled from the ceiling. The branch of an oak tree had entered one of the windows, and pigeons cooed in the rafters.

It occurred to him, quite simply, that he was a long way from home.

Mother, he thought. Father. Alizia. His heart stuttered, and fresh tears ran down his cheeks. His eyes felt burned, as if scorched by sight. All dead. All gone. He rocked himself, staring at nothing. All dead. All gone. Bye-bye.

He sniffled once, and his nose drooled. And then he sat up straight again, his mind flaming with fear.

The wolves. Where were the wolves?

He could sit here in this place, he decided. Sit right here

until someone came for him. It wouldn't be long. Someone would surely come. Wouldn't they?

He caught a metallic whiff, and looked to his right. On the mossy stone next to him was a piece of bloody meat that might have been a liver. Beside it lay a dozen or so blueberries.

Mikhail felt his lungs freeze. A scream hung in his bruised throat. He scrambled away from the gruesome offering, making an animalish moaning noise, and he found a corner and wedged himself into it. He shivered and retched, losing the remnants of his picnic lunch.

No one was going to come, he thought. Ever. He shook and moaned. The wolves had been here, and they might be back very soon. If he was going to live, he would have to find his way out of this place. He sat, huddled up and shivering, until he could force himself to stand. His legs were unsteady, and threatened to collapse. But then he got himself all the way up, one hand clamped to the throbbing fang wounds at his shoulder, and he lurched out of the room into a long corridor lined with more mosaics and moss-draped statues without heads or arms.

Mikhail saw an exit to his left and went through the portal. He found himself in what might have been, years—decades—ago, a garden. It was overgrown and choked with dead leaves and goldenrod, but here and there a sturdy flower had sprung from the soil. More statues stood about, gesturing like silent sentinels. In the midst of intersecting paths was a white stone fountain, full of rainwater. Mikhail paused at it, cupped his hands into the water, and drank. Then he splashed it on his face and over the shoulder wounds; the raw flesh burned, and made tears creep down his cheeks. But he bit his lower lip and hung on, then looked around to see exactly where he was.

The sun threw light and shadows upon the walls and turrets of a white palace. Its stones were the hue of bleached bone, and the roofs of its minarets and onion domes were the pale green of ancient bronze. The palace's turrets stretched up into the treetops. Stone stairways wound upward to observation platforms. Most of the windows had been broken, smashed by invading oak branches, but some of them remained; they were made of multipaned, multicolored glass, some dark red, others blue, emerald, ocher, and violet. The palace, a deserted kingdom, cast walls of white stone around the garden but had failed to keep out the forest. Oaks had burst upward through geometric walkways, shattering man's order with the brutal fist of nature. Vines had snaked through cracks in the walls, displacing hundred-pound stones. A thicket of black thorns had pushed out of the earth under the feet of a statue, thrown it over, and broken its neck, then embraced its victim. Mikhail walked through the green desolation and saw a crooked bronze gate ahead. He staggered to the gate and used all his strength to pull the heavy, ornate metal open. The hinges squealed. He faced another wall, this one formed of dense forest. In this wall there was no gate. No trails showed the way home. There was nothing but the woods, and Mikhail realized at once that it might go on for many miles and in each mile he might meet his death.

The birds sang, stupidly happy. Mikhail heard another sound as well; a fluttering noise, oddly familiar. He looked back at the palace, lifting his gaze toward the treetops. And there he saw it.

His kite's string had wrapped itself around the thin spire atop an onion dome. The kite fluttered in the breeze like a white flag.

Something moved, down on the ground, to his right.

Mikhail gasped, took a backward step, and hit the wall.

A girl in a tawny robe stood about thirty feet away, on the far side of the fountain.

She was older than Alizia had been, probably fifteen or sixteen. Her long blond hair hung over her shoulders, and she stared at Mikhail with ice-blue eyes for a few seconds; then, without speaking, she glided to the fountain's rim, bent down, and pressed her mouth to the water. Mikhail heard her tongue lapping. She glanced up again, warily, before she resumed her drinking. Then she wiped her mouth with her forearm, swept her golden tresses out of her face, and straightened up from the fountain. She turned away and began walking back to the portal Mikhail had come through.

"Wait!" he called. She didn't. She disappeared into the white palace.

Mikhail was alone again. He must still be asleep, he thought. A dream had just walked through his field of vision and returned into slumber. But the throbbing pain at his shoulder was real enough, and so was the deep ache of other bruises. His memories—those, too, were terribly real. And so, he decided, must be the girl.

He crossed the overgrown garden, careful step by step, and went back into the palace.

The girl was nowhere to be seen. "Hello!" he called, standing in a long corridor. "Where are you?" No answer. He walked away from the room in which he'd awakened. He found other rooms, high-ceiling vaults, most of them without furniture, some with crudely fashioned wooden tables and benches. One chamber seemed to be a huge dining hall, but lizards scampered over pewter plates and goblets that had lain long unused. "Hello!" he kept calling, his voice becoming feeble as his strength quickly gave out. "I won't hurt you!" he promised.

He turned into another hallway, this one dark and narrow, lying toward the center of the palace. Water dripped from the damp stones, and green moss had caught hold on the walls, floor, and ceiling. "Hello!" Mikhail shouted; his voice cracked. "Where are you?"

"Right here," came the reply, from behind him.

He whirled around, his heart slamming, and pressed himself against the wall.

The speaker was a slender man with pale brown, gray-streaked hair and a scraggly beard. He wore the same kind of tawny robe the blond girl had worn; an animal skin, scrubbed of its hair. "What's all this noise about?" the man asked, with a hint of irritation.

"I . . . I don't know . . . where . . . I am."

"You're with us," he answered, as if that explained everything.

Someone came up behind the man and touched his shoulder. "This is the new child, Franco," a woman said. "Be gentle."

"It was your choice. *You* be gentle. How can a person

87

sleep with this mewling racket?'' Franco belched, and then he abruptly turned and walked away, leaving Mikhail facing a short, round-bodied woman with long reddish-brown hair. She was older than his mother, Mikhail decided. Her face was cut and lined with deep networks of wrinkles. And her stocky, peasant's body with its hefty arms and legs was vastly different from his mother's svelte figure. This woman had the memory of field dirt under her fingernails. She, also, wore a similar animal-skin robe.

"My name," the woman said, "is Renati. What's yours?"

Mikhail couldn't answer. He pressed against the mossy wall, afraid to move.

"I won't bite you," Renati said. Her languid, brown-eyed gaze flickered quickly to the wounds in the child's shoulder, then back to his face. "How old are you?"

"Sev—" No, that wasn't right. "Eight," he remembered.

"Eight." She repeated it. "And what name would I use, if I were to sing you a birthday song?"

"Mikhail," he said. And lifted his chin slightly. "Mikhail Gallatinov."

"Oh, you're a proud little bastard, aren't you?" She smiled, showing uneven but very white teeth; her smile was reserved, though not unfriendly. "Well, Mikhail, someone wants to see you."

"Who?"

"Someone who'll answer your questions. You do want to know where you are, don't you?"

"Am I . . . in heaven?" he managed to ask.

"I fear not." She stretched out her arm. "Come, child, let's walk together."

Mikhail hesitated. Her hand waited for his. The wolves! he thought. Where are the wolves? And then he slid his hand into hers, and her rough palm gripped him. She led him deeper into the palace.

They came to a set of descending stone stairs, illuminated by rays of light through a glassless window. "Watch your step," Renati told him, and they went down. Below was a smoky gloom, a warren of corridors and rooms that smelled of grave dirt. Here and there a little pile of pine cones burned, marking a trail through the catacombs. Vaults stood on either side, the names of those entombed and the dates of birth and death blurred by time. And then the boy and woman came out from the catacombs into a larger chamber, where a fire of pinewood logs spat in a grate and its bitter smoke wafted through the air in search of vents.

"Here he is, Wiktor," Renati announced.

Figures were huddled on the earth around the fire, all of them wearing what appeared to be deerskin robes. They shifted, looked toward the archway, and Mikhail saw their eyes glint.

"Bring him closer," said a man in a chair, sitting at the edge of the firelight.

Renati felt the child shiver. "Be brave," she whispered, and guided him forward.

4

The man named Wiktor sat, watching impassively, as the boy was brought into the ruddy light. Wiktor was draped in a deerskin cloak, the high collar sewn from the fur of snow hares. He wore deerskin sandals, and around his throat was a necklace of small, linked bones. Renati stopped, one hand on Mikhail's unwounded shoulder. "His name is Mikhail," she said. "His family name is—"

"We don't care about family names here," Wiktor interrupted, and the tone of his voice said he was used to being obeyed. His amber eyes glinted with reflected fire as he examined Mikhail from dirty boots to tousled black hair. Mikhail, at the same time, was inspecting what appeared to be a majesty of the underworld. Wiktor was a large man, with broad shoulders and a bull neck. His acorn-shaped skull was bald, and he had a gray beard that grew over his stocky chest to his lap. Mikhail saw that under the cloak the man wore no clothing. Wiktor's face was composed of bony ridges and hard lines, his nose sharp and the nostrils flared. His deep-set eyes stared at Mikhail without blinking.

"He's too little, Renati," someone else said. "Throw him back." There was jabbing laughter, and Mikhail looked at the other figures. The man who'd spoken—a boy himself, only about nineteen or twenty years old—had dusky red hair smoothed back from his youthful face, his hair allowed to grow long around his shoulders. He had no room to talk, because he was small-boned and fragile looking, almost swallowed up by his cloak. Beside him sat a thin young woman about the same age, with waves of dark brown hair and steady, iron-gray eyes. The blond-haired girl sat across the fire, watching Mikhail. Not far away crouched another man, this one perhaps in his late thirties or early forties, dark-haired and with the sharp, Asiatic features of a Mongol. Beyond the fire, a figure lay huddled under a shroud of robes.

Wiktor leaned forward. "Tell us, Mikhail," he said, "who those men were, and how you came to be in our forest."

Our forest, Mikhail thought. That was a strange thing to say. "My . . . mother and father," he whispered. "My sister. All of them . . . are . . ."

"Dead," Wiktor said flatly. "Murdered, from the looks of it. Do you have relatives? People who'll come searching for you?"

Dimitri, was his first thought. No, Dimitri had been there on the lakeshore, rifle in hand, and hadn't raised it against the killers. Therefore he must be a killer, too, though a silent one. Sophie? She wouldn't come here alone. Would Dimitri kill her, too, or was she also a silent murderess? "I don't . . ." His voice broke, but he steeled himself. "I don't think so, sir," he answered.

"Sir," the red-haired boy mocked, and laughed again.

Wiktor's gaze darted to one side, his eyes glinting like copper coins, and the laughter ceased. "Tell your story, Mikhail," Wiktor invited.

"We . . ." This was a hard thing to do. The memories were as sharp as razors, and they slashed deep. "We . . . came on a picnic," he began. Then he told the tale of a drifting kite, gunshots, his flight into the forest, and the ravaging wolves. Tears trickled down his cheeks, and his empty stomach churned. "I woke up here," he said. "And . . . next to me . . . was something all bloody. . . . I think it came out of one of those men."

"Damn it!" Wiktor scowled. "Belyi, I told you to cook it!"

"I've forgotten how," the red-haired young man replied with a helpless shrug.

"You pass it over a fire until it burns! It keeps the blood from running! Must I do everything myself?" Wiktor regarded Mikhail again. "But you ate the berries, yes?"

The blueberries, Mikhail remembered. That was another strange thing; he hadn't mentioned the berries. How did Wiktor know about them, unless . . .

"You didn't touch them, did you?" The man lifted his thick gray brows. "Well, perhaps I don't blame you. Belyi here is a complete fool. But you must eat something, Mikhail. Eating is very important, for your strength."

Mikhail thought he gasped; maybe not.

"Take off your shirt," Wiktor commanded.

Before Mikhail's numbed fingers could find the little wooden buttons, Renati stepped forward and unhooked them. She gently drew the cloth away from the furrows in his shoulder and removed the shirt. Then she lifted the grimy garment to her nostrils and inhaled.

Wiktor stood up from his chair. He was tall, almost six feet two, and he came toward Mikhail like a giant. Mikhail took a retreating step, but Renati clasped his arm and held him in place. Wiktor grasped the wounded shoulder, none too easily, and looked at the blood-crusted, oozing slashes.

"Nasty," Wiktor said to the woman. "Going to be some infection. A little deeper and he would've lost the use of his arm. Did you know what you were doing?"

"No," she admitted. "He just looked good to eat."

"In that case, your aim is atrocious." He pressed the flesh, and Mikhail clenched his teeth to stifle a moan. Wiktor's eyes sparkled. "Look at him. He doesn't make a noise." Again he pressed the wounds, and thick fluid spooled out. It smelled wild and rank. Mikhail blinked away tears. "So you don't mind a little pain, do you?" Wiktor asked. "That's a good thing." He released the boy's shoulder. "If you make friends with pain, you have a friend for life."

"Yes sir," Mikhail said hoarsely. He stared up at the man, and wavered on his feet. "When . . . when can I go home, please?"

Wiktor ignored the question. "I want you to meet the others, Mikhail. You know our fool, Belyi. Next to him is his sister Pauli." He nodded toward the thin young girl. "That's Nikita." The Mongol. "Across the fire is Alekza. Your teeth are showing, my dear." The blond girl smiled slightly, a hungry smile. "I think you've probably already met Franco. He prefers to sleep upstairs. You know Renati, and you know me." There was a hollow coughing, and Wiktor motioned to the figure lying under the cloaks. "Andrei isn't feeling well today. Something he ate." The sick coughing continued, and both Nikita and Pauli went over to kneel beside the figure.

"I'd like to go home now, sir," Mikhail persisted.

"Ah, yes." Wiktor nodded, and Mikhail saw his gaze cloud over. "The matter of home." He walked back to the fire, where he knelt down and offered his palms to the heat. "Mikhail," he said quietly as Andrei's coughing faded, "very soon you're going to be . . ." He paused, searching for the correct words. "In need of comfort," was what he supplied. "In need of . . . shall we say . . . family."

"I . . . have a . . ." He trailed off. His family lay dead, out in the meadow. His shoulder wounds throbbed again.

Wiktor reached into the fire and pulled out a bit of fiery branch, holding it where the flames had not yet charred. "Truth is like fire, Mikhail," he said. "It either heals or it destroys. But it never—*never*—leaves what it touches unchanged." His head slowly swiveled, and he stared at the boy. "Can you stand the flames of truth, Mikhail?"

Mikhail didn't—couldn't—answer.

"I think you can," Wiktor said. "If not . . . then you were already dead."

He dropped the branch into the flames and stood up. He

took off his sandals and drew his muscular arms out of the cloak to let it rest on his shoulders. He closed his eyes.

"Stand back." Renati pulled at Mikhail, tension in her voice. "Give him room."

Across the fire Alekza sat up on her haunches, the fine blond down on her legs glinting like spun gold. Nikita and Pauli watched, kneeling on either side of Andrei. Belyi rubbed his hand across his lips, his pale face flushed and anxious.

Wiktor's eyes opened. They were dreamy, fixed on a far distance—a wilderness, perhaps, of the mind. Sweat sparkled on his face and chest, as if he were straining at some inner effort.

Mikhail said, "Wha—" but Renati quickly shushed him.

Wiktor closed his eyes once more. The muscles of his shoulders quivered, and the tawny robe with its snow-hare collar slid off to the floor. Then he bent his body forward, his spine bowing, and his fingertips touched the earth. He sighed deeply, followed by a quick intake of breath. His beard hung to the ground.

June one year ago, Mikhail and his sister had gone by train with their parents to see a circus in Minsk. There had been a performer whose bizarre talent had stayed with Mikhail. The Rubber Man had leaned over in the same position that Wiktor now assumed, and the Rubber Man's spine had stretched with brittle cracking noises like sticks being stepped on. Those sounds now came from Wiktor's backbone, but it was clear in another few seconds that instead of lengthening, his torso was compressing. Bands of muscle stood out around Wiktor's rib cage and ran down along his thighs like quivering bundles of piano wires. Sweat gleamed on the man's back and shoulders, and a darkness of fine hairs suddenly began to spread over the slick flesh like clouds moving across a summer field. His shoulders bowed forward, muscles straining upward under the skin. Bones popped, merry little sounds, and there was the noise of sinews bending and re-forming like squealing hinges.

Mikhail stepped backward, colliding with Renati. She held

his arm, and he stood watching a demon from Hades struggle with the flesh of a man.

Short gray hairs emerged from Wiktor's scalp, from the back of his neck, from his arms and buttocks, thighs and calves. His cheeks and forehead rippled with hair, and his beard had clutched hold of his throat and chest like a phantasmagoric vine. Beads of sweat dripped from Wiktor's nose; it cracked, bringing a grunt from him, and began to change its shape. He lifted his hands to his face, and Mikhail saw the flesh writhe beneath his gray-haired fingers.

Mikhail tried to turn and run, but Renati said, "No!" and held him tighter. He couldn't bear to watch any more of this; he felt as if his brain were about to burst open in his head, and what would ooze out would be black as swamp slime. He lifted his hand, put his fingers over his eyes—but he left himself a narrow crack, and through it he watched Wiktor's shadow contort on the wall in the leaping firelight.

The shadow was still that of a man, but it was rapidly becoming both more and less. Mikhail couldn't shut his ears; the cracking of bones and squealing of sinews were about to drive him mad, and the smoky air smelled of rank wildness, like the inside of a beast's cage. He saw the contorted shadow lift its arms, as if in supplication.

There was a fast, shallow breathing. Mikhail closed the gap between his fingers. The breathing began to slow and deepen, becoming a husky rasp. Then, finally, a smooth bellows rumble.

"Look at him," Renati said.

Tears of terror streaked from his eyes. He whispered, "No . . . please . . . don't make me!"

"I won't make you." Renati released his arm. "Look if you choose. If not . . . then not."

Mikhail kept his hand over his eyes. The bellows breath neared him. Heat brushed his fingers. Then the noise of breathing faded as the thing backed away. Mikhail shuddered, choking down a sob. Truth is like fire, he thought. Already he felt like a pile of ashes, burned beyond all recognition of what had been before.

"I told you he was too small." Belyi sneered from across the chamber.

The sound of that mocking voice caused a flame to spark at the center of ashes. There was still something left, after all, to burn. Mikhail drew a deep breath and held it, his body trembling. Then he released it, and dropped his hand from his face.

Not ten feet away, the amber-eyed wolf with sleek gray fur sat on its haunches, watching him with intense attention.

"*Oh,*" Mikhail whispered, and his knees buckled. He fell to the floor, his head spinning. Renati started to help him up, but the wolf made a low grunt deep in its throat and she retreated.

Mikhail was left to stand on his own. The wolf watched, head cocked slightly to one side, as Mikhail struggled up to his knees, and that was as far as he could get for now. His shoulder was a mass of pain, and his mind spun like a kite seeking a balancing tether.

"Look at him!" Belyi said. "He doesn't know whether to scream or shit."

The wolf spun toward Belyi and snapped its jaws shut about two inches in front of the young man's nose. Belyi's sardonic grin fractured.

Mikhail stood up.

Wiktor turned back to him and advanced. Mikhail took a single step in retreat, then halted. If he was going to die, he would join his parents and sister in heaven, a long way from here. He waited for what was to be.

Wiktor came on toward him, stopped—and sniffed Mikhail's hand. Mikhail dared not move. Then, satisfied with what he smelled, the wolf lifted his hind leg and sprayed a stream of urine onto Mikhail's left boot. The warm, acidic-odored liquid got on Mikhail's trousers and soaked through to his skin.

The wolf finished its task and stepped back. He opened his mouth wide, fangs gleaming, and lifted his head toward the ceiling.

Mikhail, fighting on the edge of another faint, felt Renati's strong hand grip his arm. "Come on," she urged. "He wants you to eat something. We'll try the berries first."

Mikhail allowed her to guide him out of the chamber, his legs wooden. "It's going to be fine now," she said, sounding relieved. "He's marked you. That means you're under his protection."

Before they got very far beyond the archway, Mikhail looked back. On the wall he saw a fire-scrawled shadow, lurching to its feet.

Renati took his hand, and they ascended the stone stairs.

THREE

Grand Entrance

Stone stairs, Michael thought. Just the thing to break an ankle on. He blinked, and returned from his inner journey.

Darkness all around. Above his head an open white parachute, hissing as the wind strummed the taut lines. He looked down and to all sides; there was no sign of the green blinker.

A broken ankle wouldn't be pleasant, and certainly not the way to begin his mission. What was he descending onto? A marshy field? A forest? Hard, tilled earth that would twist his knees like bits of taffy? He had the sensation of the ground coming up fast now, and he grasped the chute's lines and angled his body slightly, bending his knees for the impact.

Now, he thought, and braced himself.

His boots smashed into a surface that gave way under his weight like mildewed cardboard. And then he slammed down against a harder surface that shook and creaked but held him from falling any farther. The harness tightened under his arms, the chute snagged on something above. He looked up and could see a jagged-edged hole in which stars sparkled.

A roof, he realized. He was sitting on his knees under a roof of rotten wood. Somewhere out in the night, two dogs barked. Working quickly, Michael unsnapped the harness straps and shrugged out of the parachute. He narrowed his eyes, could make out heaps of material around him; he grasped a handful. Hay. He had crashed down into a barn hayloft.

He stood up, began to get the chute unsnagged, and drew it in through the hole. Faster! he told himself. He was in

Nazi-occupied France now, sixty miles northwest of Paris.
The German sentries on their motorcycles and in their
armored cars would be all over the place, and the radio
messages might be crackling: Attention! Parachute spotted
near Bazancourt! Patrol all nearby farmland and villages!
Things might get hot very soon.

He got the chute into the loft, then began to bury the silk
and pack in a large pile of hay.

Four seconds later he heard the scrape of a latch drawing
back. He tensed, becoming motionless. There came the soft
squeaking of hinges below. A reddish glow invaded the barn.
Michael slowly, silently slid his knife from its sheath, and
saw by the lantern light that he was balanced near the loft's
edge. A few more inches and he would've gone over.

The lantern probed around, spreading light. Then: *"Monsieur? Où êtes-vous?"*

It was a woman's smoky voice, asking where he was.
Michael didn't move, nor did he lay aside the knife.

"Pourquoi est-ce que vous ne me parlez pas?" she went
on, demanding that he speak to her. She lifted the lantern
high, and said, again in the crisp country lilt of Normandy
French, "I was told to expect you, but I didn't know you'd
drop on my head."

Michael gave it a few seconds more before he leaned his
face over the loft's edge. She was dark-haired, wearing a
gray woolen sweater and black slacks. "I'm here," he said
quietly, and she jumped back and probed the light up at him.
"Not in my eyes," he warned. She dropped the lantern a
few inches. He glimpsed her face: a square jaw, deep-cut
cheekbones, unplucked dark brows over eyes the color of
sapphires. She had a wiry body and looked as if she could
move fast when the situation demanded it. "How far are we
from Bazancourt?" he asked.

She'd seen the hole in the roof about three feet over the
man's head. "Take a look for yourself."

Michael did, pulling his head up through the hole.

Less than a hundred yards away a few lamps burned in
the windows of thatch-roofed houses, clustered together
around what appeared to be a large plot of rolling farmland.

Michael thought he'd have to congratulate the C-47's pilot for his good aim when he got out of this.

"Come on!" the girl urged tersely. "We have to get you to a safe place!"

Michael was about to ease down to the loft again when he heard the rough muttering of engines, coming from the southwest. His heart seized up. Three sets of headlights were quickly approaching, tires boiling up dust from the country road. Scout cars, he reasoned. Probably loaded with soldiers. And there was a fourth vehicle bringing up the rear, moving slower and carrying much more weight. He heard the clank of treads and realized with a cold twist of his insides that the Nazis were taking no chances; they'd brought along a light *panzerkampfwagen:* a tank.

"Too late," Michael said. He watched the scout cars fanning out, surrounding Bazancourt to the west, north, and south. He heard a commander yelling "Dismount!" in German, and dark figures leaped from the cars even before the wheels had stopped turning. The tank came clanking toward the barn, guarding the village's eastern side. He'd seen enough to know he was trapped. He lowered himself to the loft. "What's your name?" he asked the French girl.

"Gabrielle," she said. "Gaby."

"All right, Gaby. I don't know how much experience you have at this, but you're going to need it all. Are any of the people here pro-Nazi?"

"No. They hate the swine."

Michael heard a grinding noise: the tank's turret was swiveling as the machine neared the rear of the barn. "I'll hide as best I can up here. If—when—the fireworks start, stay out of the way." He unholstered his .45 and popped a clip of bullets into it. "Good luck," he told her—but the lamplight was gone, and so was she. The barn-door latch scraped shut. Michael peered through a crack in the boards, saw soldiers with flashlights kicking open the doors of houses. One of the soldiers threw down an incandescent flare, which lit up the entire village with dazzling white light. Then the Nazis began to herd the villagers at gunpoint out of their houses, lining them together around the flare. A tall, lean figure in an officer's cap walked back and forth before them, and at his side was a second figure, this one huge, with thick shoulders and treetrunk legs.

The tank treads halted. Michael looked out a knothole toward the rear of the barn. The tank had stopped less than fifteen feet away, and its crew of three men had emerged and lit up cigarettes. One of the men had a submachine gun strapped around his shoulder.

"Attention!" Michael heard the German officer shout, in French, at the villagers. He returned to the crack, moving silently, so he could see what was happening. The officer was standing before them, the large figure a few steps behind. The flare light illuminated uplifted pistols, rifles, and submachine guns, ringing the villagers. "We knew a kite flier fell down in this arena!" the officer went on, mangling the French language as he spoke. "We shall now wish to grasp that intruder in our gloves! I ask you, humans of Bazancourt, where is the man we wish to cage?"

Like hell you will, Michael thought, and cocked the .45.

He went back to the knothole. The tank crew was lounging around their machine, talking and laughing boisterously: a boys' night out. Could he take them? Michael wondered. He could shoot the ones with the submachine guns first, then the one nearest the hatch so the bastard wouldn't jump down it and slam—

He heard the low growl of another engine and more clanking treads. The tank crew shouted and waved, and Michael watched as a second tank stopped on the dusty road. Two men came out of the hatch and started a conversation about the parachutist that had been reported on the radio. "We'll make a quick sausage out of him," promised one of the men on the first tank, waving his cigarette like a saber.

The barn-door latch scraped. Michael crouched where he was, against the hayloft's rear wall, as the door swung open and the beams of two or three flashlights probed around. "You go first!" he heard one of the soldiers say. Another voice: "Quiet, you ass!" The men came into the barn, following their lights. Michael stayed still, a dark form in shadow, his finger resting lightly on the automatic's trigger.

In another few seconds Michael realized that they didn't

know if he was hiding here or not. Out in the village square the officer was shouting, "There will be severe penetrations for all those cohabitating with the enemy!" The three soldiers were looking around beneath the hayloft, kicking cans and equipment over to prove they were really doing a thorough job. Then one of them stopped and lifted his flashlight toward the loft.

Michael felt his shoulder prickle as the light grazed it and swung to the right. Toward the hold in the roof.

He smelled scared sweat, and didn't know if it was the Germans' or his own.

The beam hit the roof, began to move steadily toward the hole.

Closer. Closer.

"My God!" one of the others said. "Look at this, Rudy!"

The flashlight stopped, less than three feet from the hole's edge.

"What is it?"

"Here." There was the noise of bottles clinking. "Calvados! Somebody's stocked the stuff away in here!"

"Probably some damned officer. The pigs!" The flashlight beam moved, this time away from the hole; it grazed Michael's knees, but Rudy was already walking toward the bottles of apple brandy the other man had uncovered from their hiding place. "Don't let Harzer see you taking them!" warned the third soldier, a frightened and boyish voice. Couldn't be more than seventeen, Michael thought. "No telling what that damned Boots would do to you!"

"Right. Let's get out of here." The second soldier speaking again. Bottles clinked. "Wait. Got to finish it up before we leave."

A bolt drew back; not the door this time, but the mechanism of a submachine gun.

Michael squeezed his body against the wall, cold sweat on his face.

The weapon fired, chattering holes through the wall below the hayloft. Then a second gun spoke in a surly rasp, sending slugs up through the hayloft floor. Hay and bits of wood spun into the air. The third soldier fired up into the hayloft, too, zigzagging a spray of bullets that knocked chunks out of the boards two feet to Michael's right.

"Hey, you idiots!" shouted one of the tank crewmen when the noise of firing had died. "Stop that target practice through the barn! We've got gasoline tins out here!"

"Screw those SS bastards," Rudy said, in a quiet voice, and then he and the other two soldiers left the barn with their booty of Calvados bottles. The barn door remained ajar.

"Who's the mayor here?" the officer—Harzer?—was shouting, his voice edgy and enraged. "Who's in charge? Step forward immediately!"

Michael checked the knothole once more, searching for a way out. He caugh a whiff of gasoline; one of the men on the second tank, parked in the road, was pouring fuel from a can into the gasoline portal. Two more cans stood ready for use.

"Now we can converse," someone said, from beneath the hayloft.

Michael silently turned, crouched down, and waited. Lamplight filled the barn.

"My title is Captain Harzer," the voice said. "This is my companion, Boots. You'll notice he's well clothed to the name."

"Yes, sir," an old man answered fearfully.

Michael brushed hay away from bullet holes in the floor and peered down.

Five Germans and an elderly, white-haired Frenchman had entered the barn. Three of the Germans were troopers, wearing field-gray uniforms and their coal-scuttle helmets; they stood near the door, and all of them carried deadly black Schmeisser submachine guns. Harzer was a lean man who held himself in that strict rigidity that Michael associated with devout Nazism: as if the man had an iron bar up his ass all the way to his shoulder blades. Near him stood the man called Boots—the hulking, thick-legged figure Michael had seen in the flare light. Boots was perhaps six-three, and weighed in the neighborhood of two hundred sixty or seventy pounds. He wore an aide's uniform, a gray cap on his sandy-stubbled scalp, and on his feet were polished black leather boots with soles at least two inches thick. In the ruddy glow of the lamps two of the troopers held, the broad, square face of Boots was serene and confident: the face of a killer who enjoys his work.

"Now we're solitary, Monsieur Gervaise. You don't have to fear any of the others. We'll take care of them." Hay crunched as Harzer paced the floor, continuing to mangle his French. "We know the kite flier fell down near here. We believe someone in your village must be his touch . . . uh . . . agent. Monsieur Gervaise, who might that someone be?"

"Please, sir . . . I don't . . . I can't tell you anything."

"Oh, don't be so absolute. What's your Christian name?"

"Hen . . . Henri." The old man was trembling; Michael could hear his teeth clicking.

"Henri," Harzer repeated. "I want you to think before you answer, Henri: do you know where the kite flier fell down, and who here is helping him?"

"No. Please, Captain. I swear I don't!"

"Oh, my." Harzer sighed, and Michael saw him jerk a finger at Boots.

The big man took one step forward, and kicked Gervaise in the left kneecap. Bones crunched, and the Frenchman screamed as he fell into the hay. Michael saw metal cleats glint on the killer's boot soles.

Gervaise clutched his broken knee and moaned. Harzer leaned down. "You didn't think, did you?" He tapped the white-haired skull. "Use the brain! Where did the kite flier fall down?"

"I can't . . . oh my God . . . I can't . . ."

Harzer said, "Shit," and stepped back.

Boots slammed his foot down on the old man's right knee. The bones broke with pistolshot cracks, and Gervaise howled in agony.

"Are we teaching you how to think yet?" Harzer inquired.

Michael smelled urine. The old man's bladder had let go. The smell of pain was in the air, too, like the bitter tang before a brutal thunderstorm. He felt his muscles moving and bunching under his flesh, and a sheen of sweat had begun to slick his body under his camouflage clothes. The change would be on him, if he wanted it. But he stopped himself on the wild edge; what good would it do? The Schmeissers would cut a wolf to pieces as easily as a human, and the way those troopers were spaced apart there would be no way to get all three of them and the tanks. No, no; there were some things a man was better at dealing with, and one of them was knowing his limits. He eased back from the change, felt it move over and away from him like a mist of needles.

The old man was sobbing and begging for mercy. Harzer said, "We've suspected for some time that Bazancourt is a center of spies. My job is ferreting them out. You understand that this is my job?"

"Please . . . don't hurt me anymore," Gervaise whispered.

"We're going to kill you." It was a statement of fact, without emotion. "We're going to drag your corpse out to show the others. Then we'll ask our questions again. You see, your death will actually be saving lives, because someone will speak up. If no one speaks, we'll burn your village to the ground." Harzer shrugged. "You won't care, anyway." He nodded at Boots.

Michael tensed—but he knew there was nothing he could do.

The old man's mouth opened in a cry of terror, and he tried to crawl away on his shattered legs. Boots kicked him in the ribs; there was a noise like a barrel caving in, and Gervaise whined and clutched the splintered bones that had burst from his flesh. The next kick, with a cleated boot, caught the old man's collarbone and snapped it. Gervaise writhed like a speared fish. Boots began to kick and stomp the old Frenchman to death, working slowly and with careful precision—a kick to the stomach to burst the organs, a stomp to the hand to smash the fingers, a kick to the jaw to snap its joints and send teeth flying like yellow dice.

"This is my job," Harzer told the bleeding, mangled face. "This is what I'm paid for, you see?"

Boots kicked the old man in the throat and crushed his windpipe. Gervaise began strangling. Michael saw the sweat of effort glisten on Boots's face; the man was unsmiling, his features like carved stone, but his pale blue eyes spoke of pleasure. Michael kept his gaze fixed on Boots's face. He wanted to burn it into his brain.

Gervaise, with a final frenzied attempt, tried to crawl to the door. He left blood on the hay. Boots let him crawl for a few seconds, and then he stomped his right foot down on the center of the old man's back and broke his spine like a broomstick.

"Bring him out." Harzer turned and strode quickly toward the other villagers and soldiers.

"I found a silver one!" A soldier held up a tooth. "Does he have any more?"

Boots kicked the jittering body in the side of the head, and a few more teeth flew out. The soldiers bent down, searching for silver in the hay. Then Boots followed Harzer, and two of the soldiers picked up Gervaise's ankles and dragged the corpse out of the barn.

Michael was left in darkness, the smell of blood and terror filled his nostrils. He shivered; the hair had risen on the back of his neck. "Attention!" he heard Harzer shout. "Your mayor has departed this life and left you all alone! I'm going to ask you two questions, and I want you to think carefully before you answer. . . ."

Enough, Michael thought. It was time to ask his own questions. He stood up, went to the knothole. The gasoline smell was thicker. The man on the second tank was pouring in the last of the cans. Michael saw what had to be done, and he knew it had to be done now. He walked underneath the hole, pulled himself up onto the roof, and crouched there.

"Where did the kite flier fall down?" Harzer was asking. "And who is helping him?"

Michael took aim and fired.

The bullet smashed into the gasoline can the crewman was holding. Two things happened at once: gasoline sloshed out of the can onto the man's clothes, and sparks jumped off the edges of the bullet hole. Harzer's shouting ceased.

The gasoline can exploded, and the crewman went up like a torch.

As the man danced and writhed and the fire burned blue

107

in the puddle of fuel around the gas portal, Michael turned his attention to the three crewmen on the tank just below the barn roof. One of them had seen the automatic muzzle flash and was lifting his submachine gun. Michael shot him through the throat, and the submachine gun fired a pinwheel of tracers into the sky. Another man was about to shove himself headlong down the hatch. Michael fired, but the bullet clanged off metal; he shot again, and this time the man cried out and clutched his back, rolling off the tank's side to the ground. Michael registered the fact that three bullets were left in the Colt's magazine. The other crewman fled, running for cover. Michael jumped off the roof.

He landed on the tank near the main hatch with a shock that thrummed up his legs. He heard Harzer shouting for a machine gunner, and telling the soldiers to surround the barn. The hatch was still open, its rim smeared with German blood. Michael caught a movement to his right, almost behind him, and spun around as a soldier fired his rifle. The bullet passed between his knees and ricocheted off the hatch's lid. Michael had no time to aim; he didn't have to, because in the next instant a blast of bullets hit the German in the chest and lifted him off his feet before slamming him to the ground.

"Get in!" Gaby shouted, holding the smoking Schmeisser she'd picked up from the first man Michael had shot. "Hurry!" She reached up, grasped an iron handle, and pulled herself onto the tank. Michael stood stunned for a heartbeat. "Don't you understand French?" Gaby demanded, her eyes full of fire and fury. A rifle spoke; two bullets whanged off the tank's armor, and Michael needed no further persuasion. He jumped into the hatch, down into a cramped compartment where a small red bulb burned. Gaby followed him, reached up, and slammed the hatch shut, then dogged it tight.

"Down there!" Gaby shoved him deeper into the tank's innards, and he slid onto an uncomfortable leather seat. In front of him was a panel of instrument gauges, what looked like a hand brake and a number of shift levers. On the floor were various pedals and before his face was a narrow view slit; to right and left were also view slits, and through the left one he saw the crewman burning on the ground beside the second tank, another man popping up from the tank's hatch to shout, "Turret swivel right sixty-six degrees!"

The tank's turret and stubby cannon began to crank around. Michael pressed his automatic's muzzle against the view slit and squeezed the trigger, blasting a chunk out of the man's shoulder. The German slid back into the tank, but the turret continued to swivel.

"Start us up!" Gaby shouted, an edge of terror in her voice. "Ram him!"

Bullets were knocking against the tank's armored sides like the impatient fists of a mob. Michael had seen this type of German tank in North Africa, and he knew how it was steered—by the levers, which regulated the gears and speed of the treads—but he'd never driven a tank before. He searched in vain for a way to start it; then Gaby's hand slid down in front of his face, turned a key in an ignition switch, and there was a grinding, clattering roar followed by the hollow *boom* of a backfire. The tank was shuddering, its engine running. Michael pressed his foot down on what he hoped was the clutch and battled with the gearshift. A Jaguar touring sedan this was not; the gears ground together, finally meshed with the speed of fresh tar. The tank jerked forward, slamming Michael's skull back against the padded headrest. Up above him, in the gun loader's compartment, Gaby saw figures leaping up onto the tank through her own view slit; she thrust the Schmeisser's barrel through it and raked bullets across two pairs of German legs.

Michael pressed the accelerator to the floor and wrenched on one of the levers. The tread on the right stopped and the left one kept going, turning the tank to the right; that wasn't the direction Michael wanted to go, so he tried another of the levers and this time the left tread stopped and the right tread lunged forward, turning the tank sharply to the left and toward the enemy. The tank vibrated, but it obeyed Allied as well as Axis hands. Michael saw the second tank's turret about to reach the sixty-six-degree mark.

He jammed on the brake. The second tank's cannon spat fire.

There was a banshee scream, and a wave of oven heat hit

Michael's face through the view slit. He had an instant of total confusion, not knowing whether he'd been blown to a million bits or not—and then there came the explosion, out in the farmland maybe three hundred yards beyond Bazancourt.

He had no time for shock, and certainly none for panic. He hit the accelerator again, and the tank continued its sharp left turn. The treads flung up yards of earth. And then the second tank filled the view slit before him, its turret cannon still flickering fire.

"That box behind you!" Gaby shouted. "Reach into it!" Machine-gun bullets whined off the turret, making Gaby duck instinctively.

Michael reached into the box and came up with a steel-jacketed projectile. Gaby pulled a lever, twisted another one, and there was the sound of metal sliding open. "Put it here!" she said, and helped him fit the shell into the cannon breech. She slammed the breech shut, prickles of sweat on her face. "Keep us going straight!" she told him, and she pulled another lever. Something whined, beginning to charge up.

The second tank began to back away, its turret turning again to get off another shot. Michael manipulated the levers and held a steady course, heading right at the monster. A man's head emerged from the hatch, shouting something that Michael couldn't hear above the engine's roar. But he could guess what the order was: Turret turn to ninety-eight degrees. That would give them a killing shot.

The cannon swiveled, seeking its target.

Michael started to hit the brake again, but stopped himself. They might expect him to halt this time. He kept pressing the accelerator, and a stray bullet hit the view slit's edge to his right and knocked sparks all around him.

"Hang on!" Gaby warned, and pulled a red trigger marked *Feuern*.

Michael thought that two things had happened concurrently: his eardrums had been blown out of his head and his bones had wrenched out of their sockets. He instantly knew, however, that his discomfort was mild compared to what befell the second tank's crew.

In the rioting red glare of explosion and flames, Michael saw the entire turret sliced off the other tank like a scalpeled wart. Its cannon fired into the sky as the turret lifted up, spun twice around, and smashed into the dust. Two human torches leaped out of the monster's body and, screaming, ran in search of death.

Michael smelled cordite and seared flesh. Another explosion erupted from the other tank, sending pieces of metal banging down. Michael hit the brake and steered violently to the right to sweep past the gutted carcass.

German soldiers shouted and fled from the tank's path. Michael saw two figures through the view slit: "Fire! Fire!" Harzer was shouting, Luger in hand, but all order was gone. A few paces behind him, Boots watched impassively.

"There's the sonofabitch!" Gaby said. She reached up, unlocked the hatch, and threw it open before Michael could stop her. She lifted her head and shoulders out, took aim with the Schmeisser, and blew most of Harzer's head away. His body took three steps backward before it crumpled, and Boots threw himself flat on the ground.

The tank roared past. Michael grasped Gaby's ankle and pulled her back in. She slammed the hatch shut, blue smoke curling from the Schmeisser's muzzle. "Across the field!" Gaby told him, and he drove straight ahead as fast as the tank could go.

Michael smiled tightly. He was sure Captain Harzer would understand that it had only been Gaby's job.

Its treads boiling up thick yellow dust, the tank rumbled on across the field, away from the village and the erratic flashes of gunfire. "They'll track us with the scout cars," Gaby said. "They're probably already calling for help. We'd better get out while we can."

Michael had no argument. He pulled another cannon shell out of the wooden box behind his seat and wedged it against the accelerator pedal. Gaby climbed up through the hatch, waited for Michael to join her, then tossed her Schmeisser over and jumped. He leaped off a couple of seconds later, and finally landed on the chalky soil of France.

For a moment he couldn't find her in the dust. He saw movement to his left, and she gasped, startled, when he came up silently beside her and grasped her arm. She had the submachine gun, and she motioned ahead. "The woods are that way. Are you ready to run?"

"Always," he answered. They started sprinting toward the line of trees about thirty yards away. Michael restrained his pace so he wouldn't get ahead of her.

They made the woods with no difficulty. Standing amid the trees, Michael and Gaby watched two of the scout cars pass, following the tank at a respectful distance. The tank would lead them several miles, at least.

"Welcome to France," Gaby said. "You believe in grand entrances, don't you?"

"Any entrance I survive is grand."

"Don't congratulate yourself just yet. We've got a long way to go." She put the Schmeisser's strap around her shoulder and cinched it. "I hope you've got a good strong heart; I travel fast."

"I'll try to keep up," he promised.

She turned away, all business and deadly purpose, and began to move quietly through the underbrush. Michael stayed about twelve feet behind, listening for the sounds of anyone or anything coming after them. They weren't being followed; with Harzer dead, all initiative had broken down and no soldiers were combing the woods. He thought of the man with the polished, cleated boots. Killing an old man was easy; he wondered how Boots might do against a ferocious opponent.

Well, life was full of possibilities.

Michael followed the French girl, and the forest sheltered them.

2

After more than an hour of fast walking in a southwesterly direction, crossing a few fields and roads with Gaby's Schmeisser cocked and ready and Michael's ears pricked for sounds, she said, "We wait here."

They were in a stand of trees at the edge of a clearing, and Michael could see a single stone farmhouse ahead. The house was a ruin, its roof collapsed; destroyed, perhaps, by an errant Allied bomb, a mortar shell, or German SS troopers hunting partisans. Even the earth around the house had been charred by fire, and a few blackened stubs of trees were all that remained of an orchard.

"You sure you have the right place?" Michael asked her; a pointless question, and her chilly gaze told him so.

"We're ahead of schedule," she explained, kneeling down with the Schmeisser across her lap. "We won't be able to go in for . . ." She paused while she checked the luminous hands on her wristwatch. "Twelve minutes."

Michael knelt beside her, impressed by her directional skills. How had she navigated? By the stars, of course, or else she simply knew the route by heart. But though they were apparently where they were supposed to be by a given time, there was nothing in the area but the single destroyed farmhouse. "You must've had some experience with tanks," he said.

"Not really. I had a German lover who was the commander of a tank crew. I learned everything from him."

Michael lifted his brows. "Everything?"

She glanced quickly at him, then away again; his eyes seemed to glow like the hands of her watch, and they held steady. "It was necessary that I . . . do my duty for the benefit of my country," she said, a little shakily. "The man had information about a truck convoy." She felt him watching her. "I did what I was supposed to do. That's all."

113

He nodded. *The man,* she'd said. No name, no emotion. This war was as clean as a slashed throat. "I'm sorry about what happened at the village. I—"

"Forget it," she interrupted. "You're not to blame."

"I watched the old man die," he went on. He'd seen death before, of course. Many times. But the cold precision of Boots's kicks and stomps still made his insides writhe. "Who was the man who killed him? Harzer called him Boots."

"Boots is—was—Harzer's bodyguard. An SS-trained killer. Now that Harzer's dead, they'll probably assign Boots to some other officer, perhaps on the Eastern Front." Gaby paused, staring at a fragile glint of moonlight on the Schmeisser's barrel. "The old man—Gervaise—was my uncle. He was my last blood relative. My mother, father, and two brothers were killed by the Nazis in 1940." It was stated as hard fact, without any hint of emotion. The emotion, Michael thought, had been burned out of her as surely as the life in that orchard.

"If I'd known that," Michael said, "I would have—"

"No, you wouldn't have," she told him sharply. "You would have done just as you did, or your mission would be over and you'd be dead. My village would be burned to the ground anyway, and all the people there executed. My uncle knew the risks. He was the man who brought me into the underground." Her gaze met his. "Your mission is the important thing. One life, ten lives, a village lost—it doesn't matter. We have a greater purpose." She looked away from his gleaming, penetrating eyes. If she could tell herself that over and over, it might make death more than senseless, she thought. But deep down in her charred soul, she doubted it.

"It's time to go in," Gaby said when she checked her watch again.

They crossed the clearing, Gaby ready with the Schmeisser and Michael sniffing the air. He smelled hay, burned grass, the apple-wine fragrance of Gaby's hair, but no odor of sweating skin that might've meant soldiers hiding in ambush. As Michael followed Gaby into the ruined farmhouse, he caught just a hint of a strange oily smell; a metallic odor, he thought. Oil on metal? She led him through the tangle of broken timbers and stones to a heap of ashes. He found the oily metal smell again, around this ash pile. Gaby knelt down and inserted her hand into the ashes; Michael heard the hinges of a little compartment open. The ashes were not all entirely ashes, but a cleverly painted and arranged mass of camouflaged rubber. Gaby's fingers found an oiled flywheel, which she turned to the right several revolutions. Then she drew her hand out, and Michael heard the noise of latches being unbolted under the farmhouse floor. Gaby stood up. A hatch smoothly lifted, the rubber ashes piled on top of it. Oil gleamed on metal hinges and gears, and there were wooden steps descending into the earth.

"*Entrez,*" a dark-haired, sallow young Frenchman said, and motioned Michael down the stairs into, literally, the underground.

Michael entered the hatch, with Gaby following right behind him. Another man, this one older, with a grizzled gray beard, was standing in the passageway ahead, holding a lantern. The first man closed the hatch and spun the flywheel shut from the inside, then threw three latches. The corridor was narrow and low-ceilinged, and Michael had to crouch as he followed the man with the lantern.

Then they came to another descending stairway, this one made of stone. The earthen walls were chunks of rough, ancient rock. At the bottom of the steps was a large chamber and a series of corridors snaking off in different directions. Some kind of medieval fortress, Michael assumed. Light bulbs hung from cables overhead and gave off a dim glow. From somewhere else came whirring noises, like sewing machines at work. On a large table in the chamber, laid out under the light bulbs, was a map; Michael approached it, and saw the streets of Paris. Voices swelled, people talking in another room. A typewriter or coding machine clacked. An attractive older woman came into the chamber with a file folder, which she deposited in one of several filing cabinets. She glanced quickly at Michael, nodded at Gaby, and went back to her business.

"Well, laddie," someone said in English, a voice like the rasp of a handsaw, "you ain't a Scotsman, but you'll have to do."

Michael had heard heavy footsteps a few seconds before the voice, so he wasn't startled. He turned, and faced a red-bearded giant in a kilt.

"Pearly McCarren, at your service," the man said, with a rolling Scots burr that made spittle and steam fly out of his mouth into the chilly underground air. "King of Scottish France. Which is from that wall to the one yonder," he added, and brayed with laughter. "Hey, André!" he said to the man who'd carried the lantern. "How about breakin' out a good glass o' wine for me and me guest, eh?" The man left the room through one of the corridors. "That's not really his name," McCarren told Michael, holding his hand to his mouth as if he were confiding a secret, "but I canna pronounce most of their monickers, so I call 'em all André, eh?"

"I see," Michael said, and had to smile.

"You had a little problem, didn't ya?" McCarren turned his attention to Gaby. "Bastards been chewin' up the radio for the last hour. They almost clip your tails?"

"Almost," she answered in English. "Uncle Gervaise is dead." She didn't wait for an expression of sympathy. "So is Harzer, and quite a few other Nazis. Our associate is a good shot. We also took out a tank: a *panzerkampfwagen* two, bearing the organizational symbol of the Twelfth SS Panzer Division."

"Good work." He scribbled a note on a pad, tore off the page, and pressed a little bell beside his chair at the map table. "We'd best let our friends know the SS Panzer boys are prowlin' around. Those Mark Twos are old machines; they must be scrapin' the barrel's bottom." He handed the note to the woman who'd brought the file folder, and she hurried off again. "Sorry about your uncle," McCarren said. "He did a helluva fine job. You get Boots?"

She shook her head. "Harzer was the important target."

"Right you are. Still, it hurts my soul to know that big son of a bitch is alive and kickin'. As the sayin' goes." His pale blue eyes, set in a moon-shaped, jowly face the color of Dover chalk, fixed on Michael. "Come over here and take a look at the noose you're gonna be stickin' your neck into."

Michael walked around the table and stood beside Mc-

116

Carren, who towered at least three inches over him and seemed as broad as a barn door. McCarren wore a brown sweater with patches on the elbows, and a dark blue and green kilt: the colors of the Black Watch regiment. His hair was a few shades darker than his unruly beard, which was the orange hue of flint sparks. "Our friend Adam lives here." McCarren jabbed a thick finger down on the maze of boulevards, avenues, and winding side streets. "A gray stone buildin' on the Rue Tobas. Hell, they're all gray stone, ain't they? Anyway, he lives in apartment number eight, on the corner. Adam's a filin' clerk, works on the staff of a minor German officer who processes supplies for the Nazis in France—food, clothes, writin' paper, fuel, and bullets. You can learn a lot about troops from what the high command's supplyin' 'em with." He tapped the street maze. "Adam walks to work every day, along this route." Michael watched as the finger traced the Rue Tobas, turned onto the Rue St. Fargeau and then ended on the Avenue Gambetta. "The buildin's here, surrounded by a high fence with barbed wire on top of it."

"Adam's still working?" Michael asked. "Even though the Gestapo knows he's a spy?"

"Right. I doubt they're givin' him anythin' but busy work to do, though. Look here." McCarren picked up a folder lying beside the map and flipped it open. Inside were grainy, blown-up black-and-white photographs, which he handed to Michael. They were pictures of two men, one wearing a suit and tie, the other in a light jacket and beret. "These Gestapo men follow Adam everywhere. If not those in particular, then others. They've got an apartment in the buildin' across from his, and they watch his place all the time. We've also got to assume they have the phone lines fixed so they can listen in on his calls." McCarren's gaze met Michael's. "They're waitin', ya see."

Michael nodded. "Waiting to take two birds with one stone."

"Right. And maybe from those two birds they hope to find the whole nest, which would put us out of business at a crucial time. Anyway, they got wind Adam knows somethin', and they sure don't want that information gettin' out."

"Do you know anything about what it might be?"

"No. And neither does anybody in the underground. As soon as the Gestapo found out he knew whatever it is, they started ridin' him like ticks on a terrier."

The gray-bearded Frenchman McCarren had called André brought a dusty bottle of Burgundy and three glasses. He set them on the table next to the map of Paris, and then left them while McCarren poured a glass of wine for Michael, Gaby, and then himself. "To killing Nazis," McCarren said, lifting his glass. "And to the memory of Henri Gervaise." Michael and Gaby joined him in the toast. McCarren swallowed the wine quickly. "So you see your problem, man?" McCarren inquired. "The Gestapo's got Adam in an invisible cage."

Michael sipped the harsh, strong wine and studied the map. "Adam goes to work and comes back along this same route every day?" he asked.

"Yes. I can give you a timetable if you need it."

"I will." Michael's gaze followed the path of intersecting streets. "We must reach Adam while he's walking either to work or to his apartment," he decided.

"Forget it." McCarren sloshed a little more wine into his glass. "We've thought of that already. We were plannin' on pullin' up in a car, shootin' the Gestapo bastards down, and gettin' him the hell out of there, but—"

"But," Michael interrupted, "you realized Adam would be shot first if any other Gestapo men besides these two were trailing him, and you'd never get him out of Paris alive even if he did survive the pickup. In addition, whoever was in that car would most likely be riddled with bullets or captured by the Gestapo, which would not be very good for the underground. Correct?"

"More or less," McCarren said, with a shrug of his massive shoulders.

"So how can Adam be contacted on the street?" Gaby asked. "Anyone who even stops him for a few seconds would be picked up immediately."

"I don't know," Michael admitted. "But it seems to me we've got to do this in two steps. First we must alert Adam that someone's come to help him. The second step is getting him out, which may be . . ." he grunted softly. "Tricky."

"Right-o," McCarren said. He had dismissed his glass and was swigging the Burgundy from the bottle. "That's what me and me mates in the Black Watch regiment said at Dunkirk four years ago, when the Nazis backed us up against the coast. We said it'd be a trick to get out, but we were gonna do it, by God." He smiled bitterly. "Well, most of 'em are lyin' six feet under, and I'm still in France." He swigged again, then thunked the bottle back down on the table. "We've pondered this thing over a lot of different ways, my friend. Anybody who goes after Adam is gonna get nabbed by the Gestapo. Period."

"You have a picture of him, of course," Michael said. Gaby opened another file folder and presented him with black-and-white photographs—front face and profile shots, the kind of pictures on identity cards—of an unsmiling, slender blond man in his midforties, with a wan, washed-out appearance and round wire-framed spectacles. Adam was the type of man who blended into white wallpaper, no distinguishing marks, no personality in his expression, nothing but a face you would usually forget after seeing it. An accountant, Michael thought. Or a bank teller. Michael scanned the typed dossier, written in French, of the agent code-named Adam. Five feet ten inches tall. A hundred and thirty-six pounds. Ambidextrous. Interests include collecting stamps, gardening, and opera. Relatives in Berlin. One sister in . . .

Michael glanced back at one word: *opera.* "Adam attends the Paris opera?" he asked.

"All the time," McCarren answered. "He doesn't have a lot of money, but he spends most of it on that caterwaulin' nonsense."

"He shares a box at the opera house with two other men," Gaby said, beginning to see what Michael was driving toward. "We can find the exact box, if you like."

"Could we get a message to either of Adam's friends?"

She thought about that for a moment, then shook her head. "No. Too risky. As far as we know, they're not his friends, just civil service employees who rent the box with him. Either one of them might be working for the Gestapo."

Michael returned his attention to the photographs of Adam and made sure he knew every inch of that bland, expressionless face. Behind it, he thought, something very important was locked away. He could smell that now, as surely as he could smell the Burgundy on Pearly McCarren's breath and the musky scent of gunsmoke on Gaby's skin. "I'll find a way to get to him," Michael said.

"In broad daylight?" McCarren lifted his shaggy, flame-colored eyebrows. "With the Nazis watchin'?"

"Yes," Michael answered, with authority. He held McCarren's gaze for a few seconds, and the Scotsman grunted and looked away. How he was going to fulfill his mission, Michael didn't know yet, but there had to be a way. He hadn't jumped out of a damned airplane, he reasoned, to call it quits just because the situation appeared impossible. "I'll need an identity card and the proper road passes," he said. "I don't want to be picked up before I get to Paris."

"Follow me." McCarren motioned him through a corridor into another room, where a camera was set up on a tripod and a couple of men were working at a table, carefully inking in the last touches on forged Nazi passes and ID cards. "You'll get your picture taken and we'll make your cards look well used," McCarren explained. "The boys here are old hands at this. Come on, through here." He went on into the next chamber, where Michael saw racks of various Nazi uniforms, bolts of field-gray and green cloth, caps and helmets and boots. Three women were busy at sewing machines, stitching on buttons and insignias. "You'll be a communications officer, in charge of keepin' the phone lines workin'. By the time you leave here, you'll know everythin' about the Germans' wire systems, and you'll be able to recite your units and their locations in your sleep. That'll be two days of intensive study. Also time for the Jerries to settle down upstairs. You'll go to Paris with a driver. One of my Andrés. We've got a nice shiny staff car hidden not too far from here. The big chief says you know your German, so startin' at oh-eight-hundred hours that's all you'll be speakin'." He dug out a pocket watch and flipped it open.

"Which gives you about four hours to wash up and get some sleep. I expect you'll need it."

Michael nodded. Four hours was more than enough sleep for him, and he wanted to get the war paint and dust off his face. "You've got a shower down here?"

"Not quite." McCarren smiled faintly and glanced at Gaby, who had followed them in. "This place was built by the Romans, back when Caesar was a big chief. They liked their baths. Gaby, will you take charge of our friend?"

"This way," Gaby said, and started out of the chamber with Michael a few paces behind.

"Gaby?" McCarren waited until she'd stopped and looked at him. "You did a damned fine job out there."

"*Merci*," she answered, with no hint of pleasure at being praised. Her sapphire-blue eyes, stunning in her dusty, chiseled face, focused on Michael Gallatin. They regarded him with nothing but cool, professional respect. One killer to another, Michael thought. He was glad they were both fighting on the same side. "Follow me," she told him, and he did, through the chilly underground corridors.

3

"There's your tub," Gaby told him, and Michael stood looking at a stone vat about fifteen feet across and four feet deep, full of water in which a few dead leaves and grass floated. "Here's your soap," she said, and tossed him a hard white brick from a wooden rack on which were also several ratty-looking but clean towels. "We just put the water in a couple of days ago." She motioned toward a large stone spout that emerged from the wall over the vat. "I hope you don't mind bathing in water that's already been used."

He put on the best smile he could manage. "As long as that's all it's been used for."

"No, we've got somewhere else for that."

"The comforts of home," Michael said, and suddenly

Gaby pulled off her dusty sweater and began to unbutton her blouse. He watched her undress, not knowing how to respond, and she looked at him as she took her blouse off and her bra was exposed. "I hope you don't mind," she said, without pausing as she reached back and unhooked her bra. "I've got to wash, too." The bra fell away, and her breasts were in full view.

"Oh no," Michael said. "I don't mind at all."

"I'm glad. Even if you did, it wouldn't matter. Some men are . . . you know . . . shy about bathing with women." She took off her boots and socks, and began to unzip her slacks.

"I can't imagine," Michael answered, more to himself than her. He took off his cap and unbuttoned his jumpsuit. Without hesitating, Gaby removed the last of her underwear and, totally naked, walked to a set of stone steps leading down into the water. She descended them, and Michael heard her catch her breath as the water crept up her thighs and reached her stomach. Spring water, he thought. Drawn through an ancient Roman system of pipes into what served as a communal bath, possibly in a temple of some kind. Gaby took the last step, the water just over her breasts, and finally released the air she'd been hoarding. It was chilly enough down here without wet skin, but he didn't care to go to Paris without bathing for the next two days. He stepped out of his underwear and walked down the steps. The cold water shocked first his ankles, then his knees, then . . . well, it was an experience he was not likely to forget.

"Bracing," Michael said, with gritted teeth.

"I'm impressed. You must be used to cold baths, yes?" Before he could answer, she walked to the center of the pool and ducked her head under. She came up quickly, and pushed her thick black hair back from her face. "The soap, please?" She caught it when he tossed it to her, and began to lather her hair. The soap smelled of tallow and oatmeal, definitely not a brand bought in a Parisian boutique. "You thought fast back at Bazancourt," she told him.

"Not particularly. I just took advantage of an opportunity." He ducked down to his neck in the water, trying to get accustomed to the chill.

"Do you do that often?" she asked, her hair dripping suds. "Take advantage of opportunities?"

"It's the only way I know." The wolf's way, he thought. One took what was offered.

Gaby soaped her arms, shoulders, and breasts, her movements fast and efficient instead of slowly seductive. Nothing was being offered here, Michael thought. Gaby was simply getting a job done. She seemed to be totally unconcerned about the fact that her tight, supple body was less than seven feet away from him, and that lack of concern—her confidence that she could deal with whatever problem that arose—intrigued him. But the chill water permitted only twitches, no arousal. Michael watched as she soaped as much of her back as she could reach; she didn't ask him to do the rest. Then she lathered her face, ducked underwater again, and came up rosy-cheeked. She tossed him the soap. "Your turn."

Michael scrubbed the camouflage paint off his face. The harsh soap stung his skin. "The lights," he said, and nodded toward the two bulbs that hung on wires at the wall. "How do you get electricity down here?"

"We've spliced into the lines that feed a chateau about two miles away," Gaby said. She smiled faintly, suds still in her hair. "The Nazis are using it as a command post." She rinsed her hair once more, getting the rest of the soap out; the suds floated around her like garlands of lace. "We don't use the electricity except between midnight and five A.M., and we don't drain enough for them to notice."

"Too bad you don't have a water heater." Michael doused his head under and wet his hair, then soaped it and washed the grit out of it. He scrubbed his chest, arms, and face again, rinsed himself off, and caught Gaby staring at his uncamouflaged features.

"You're not an Englishman," she decided, after a few seconds of studying him without war paint.

"I'm a British citizen."

"Perhaps you are . . . but you're not English." She stepped closer to him. He smelled the natural fragrance of her clean flesh, and he thought of an apple orchard blooming white under a springtime sun. "I saw a lot of Englishmen,

123

caught by the Germans in 1940. You don't look like they did.''

"And how was that?"

She shrugged. Came a foot or two nearer. His green eyes could mesmerize her if she let them, so she stared at his mouth. "I don't know. Maybe . . . as if they were children playing a game. They didn't realize what they were up against when they tried to fight the Nazis. You look . . .'' She paused, the cold water on her breasts. She tried to articulate what it was she was thinking. "You look as if you've been fighting for a very long time.''

"I was in North Africa," he said.

"No. That's not what I mean. You look . . . as if your war is here." Gaby pressed her fingers over her heart. "Your battle is inside, yes?''

Now it was his turn to look away from her, because she saw too deeply. "Isn't everyone's?" he asked, and began walking through the water toward the steps. It was time to dry off and direct his mind to his mission.

The light bulbs flickered. Once, then again. They dimmed to brown and went out, and Michael stood in darkness with the chill water lapping at his waist. "Air raid," Gaby said; he heard a tremor in her voice, and he realized she didn't like the dark. "The Germans have shut the power down.''

There was a distant, muffled noise like a hammer whacking a pillow. Either a bomb exploding or a large-caliber cannon going off, Michael thought. It was followed by other blasts, more felt than heard, and the stones shivered beneath Michael's feet. "This may be a bad one," Gaby said, and this time she couldn't hide the fear in her voice. "Hang on, everybody!" someone shouted in French from another chamber. There was a boom and shudder and Michael heard the roof crack like a pistol shot. Bits of stone splashed into the water. Either bombs were falling close overhead or a battery of anti-aircraft cannons was filling the sky with explosions. Roman dust wafted into Michael's nostrils, and the next blast felt as if it landed within fifty yards of his skull.

A warm, shivering body pressed against him. Gaby clung to his shoulders, and Michael put his arms around her.

Fragments of stone were splashing on either side of them. Six or seven pebble-sized pieces fell onto Michael's back. Another explosion made Gaby press closer into him, her fingers gripping at his flesh, and in a lull of silence between blasts he heard her gasp and moan in expectation of the next bomb fall. He stood, his muscles tensed, and stroked Gaby's wet hair as the bombs fell to earth and the anti-aircraft guns thundered.

Then, a minute later, there was nothing but the sound of their breathing. Their hearts were slamming, and Michael felt Gaby's body quake with the violence of her pulse. Someone was coughing in another chamber, and a voice— McCarren's—shouted, "Anyone hurt?" Other voices answered, saying that there were no injuries. "Gaby?" McCarren called. "You and the Brit all right?"

She tried to answer, but she had dust in her nostrils and throat and she felt as if she might pass out. She hated the dark, the sense of confinement, and the hammering blasts that brought back a terrifying moment four years ago when she'd hidden in a basement with her family while Luftwaffe airplanes bombed her village to rubble.

"Gaby?" McCarren shouted, sounding a little frantic.

"We're all right," Michael told him calmly. "Just shaken up a bit."

The Scotsman whuffed a sigh of relief and went on to check another area.

Gaby couldn't stop shaking. It was the cold water and her own chilled blood. She had her head against the man's shoulder, and it suddenly occurred to her that she didn't know—and shouldn't know—his real name. That was one of the rules of the game. But she smelled his flesh through the musty aroma of wafting dust, and she thought for an instant—but no, of course that couldn't be—that his skin had the faintest wild scent about it, like an animal's odor. It was not unpleasant, just . . . different, in a way she couldn't pinpoint.

The light bulbs flickered again. Off and on, off and on as someone—a German hand—threw the switches that regulated the power flow. And then they came on and stayed on, though muted to a dim brownish cast. "All clear," Michael said, and Gaby looked up into his face. His eyes seemed to be slightly luminous, as if they were absorbing all the available light, and the sight frightened her, though she wasn't exactly sure why. This man was different; something about him, something indefinable. She met his stare, as time was measured in heartbeats, and she thought she saw a glimpse of something—a leaping, elemental thing—behind those green eyes like flames behind icy glass. She was aware of the heat of his body, steam beginning to drift from his pores, and she started to speak—to say what, she didn't know, but she did know that when her voice came out it would tremble.

Michael spoke first, with his body. He turned away from her, walked up the steps to the towel rack, took one for himself and one for her. "You'll catch your death," he told Gaby, offering her the towel as an inducement to leave the chilly water. She came out, and Michael felt his body respond as the water crept down from her breasts, down her flat stomach and her glistening thighs. And then she was standing in front of him, dripping, her black hair wet and sleek, and Michael gently folded the towel around her. His throat was tight, but he got the words out anyway. "I'd better get some rest," he said, staring into her eyes. "I've had an exciting night."

"Yes," Gaby agreed. "Me, too." She clutched the towel around her and left wet footprints on the stones as she went to her clothes and gathered them up. "Your room is down that corridor." She motioned toward it. "It's through the second archway on the right. I hope you don't mind a cot, but the blanket's good and thick."

"It sounds fine." He could sleep in the mud when he was tired, and he knew he'd be asleep within two minutes of hitting that cot.

"I'll come for you when it's time to get up," she told him.

"I hope so," he answered as he dried his hair. He heard her footsteps as she left the chamber, and when he lowered the towel, Gaby was gone. Then he dried his body off, picked up his clothes, and went along the corridor she'd indicated. There was a candle in a brass holder and a box of matches on the floor outside the second archway, and Michael paused to light the wick. He followed the flame into his room, which was a musty, damp-walled chamber that held a narrow, decidedly uncomfortable-looking cot and a metal rod on the wall with a few clothes hangers dangling from it. Michael hung his clothes up; they smelled of sweat, dust, and German-tank engine exhaust, with a hint of scorched flesh. Michael thought that after the war was over he might go into the business of renting his sense of smell, maybe to a maker of perfumes. Once, on a street in London, he'd found a woman's white glove, and in that glove he'd smelled the scents of brass keys, tea and lemons, Chanel perfume, the sweet earthy fragrance of an expensive white wine, the odors of more than one man's perspiration, a distant hint of an ancient rose, and of course the rubber smell of the Dunlop tire that had run across it as it lay on the street. He had learned over the years and by virtue of practice, that scents were almost as powerful to him as vision. His ability was stronger when he was under the change, of course, but much of it had seeped into his life as a human.

Michael pulled the cot's blanket back and got into bed. The springs stabbed his back, but he'd been stabbed by sharper blades. He got himself situated under the blanket, and then he blew out the candle, put the candle holder on the stones beside the cot, and lay his head back on a pillow stuffed with goose down. His body was tired, but his mind wanted to roam, like a beast pacing behind bars. He stared into the darkness, and he listened to the sound of water dripping slowly down a wall.

Your battle is inside, Gaby had said. *Yes?*

Yes, Michael thought. And it came to him, something he pondered every day and every night since he was a child in the Russian forest: I'm not human. I'm not an animal. What am I?

Lycanthrope. A word coined by a psychiatrist, a man who studied jibbering patients in mental wards, their eyes glassy in the glare of the full moon. The peasants of Russia, Romania, Germany, Austria, Hungary, Yugoslavia, Spain, and Greece all had different words for it, but those words converged on the same meaning: werewolf.

Not human. Not an animal, Michael thought. What am I, in the eye of God?

Ah, but there was another bend in the thicket of thought. Often Michael imagined God as a huge white wolf, striding across a snowfield under a sky ablaze with stars, and God's eyes were golden and very clear, and God's white fangs were very, very sharp. God could smell lies and treachery across the firmament, and he tore the hearts out of the disloyal and ate them bleeding. There was no escape from the cold judgment of God, the King of Wolves.

But how, then, did men's God view the lycanthrope? As a pestilence or a miracle? Michael, of course, could only speculate, but he knew one thing for certain: there were very few times when he didn't wish he might be a beast for all of his life, and run free and wild in the green halls of God. Two legs fettered him; four legs let him fly.

It was time to sleep now, to gather his strength for the morning and the job ahead. Much to learn, much to beware of. Paris was a beautiful trap with jagged jaws, and it could break a man's or wolf's neck with equal ease. Michael closed his eyes, trading outer darkness for the darkness within. He listened to the water drip . . . drip . . . drip. He drew a long lungful of breath, let it go in a whisper, and he left this world.

FOUR

The Change

—————— **1** ——————

He sat up, and heard water dripping down a wall of ancient
stones. His vision was fogged by sleep and brain fever, but
a small fire of pine branches smoldered in the center of the
chamber and by its ruddy glow Mikhail could see the figure
of a man standing over him. He said the first thing that came
to him: "Father?"

"I'm not your father, boy." It was the voice of Wiktor,
speaking with a hint of rough agitation. "You'll not call me
that again."

"My . . . father." Mikhail blinked, trying to focus. Wiktor
towered over him, clad in his deerskin robe with its snow-
hare collar, his gray beard trailing down his chest. "Where's
. . . my mother?"

"Dead. All of them are dead. You already know that; why
do you persist in calling to ghosts?"

The little boy pressed his hand against his face. He was
sweating, but his insides felt cold, as if he were July on the
skin and January in the blood. His bones were throbbing,
like a dull axblade chopping an ironwood tree. Where was
he? he wondered. His father, mother, and sister . . . where
were they? It began to come back to him, through the murk
of memory: the picnic, the shootings in the meadow, the
bodies lying on scarlet-spattered grass. And the men after
him, the crash of horse hooves through the underbrush. The
wolves. The wolves. Here his mind sheared away, and the
memories fled like children past a graveyard. But deep down
he knew where he was—the depths of the white palace—and
he knew the man standing before him like a barbarian king
was both more and less than human.

"You've been with us for six days," Wiktor said. "You're

not eating anything, not even the berries. Do you want to die?"

"I want to go home," Mikhail answered, his voice weak. "I want to be with my mother and father."

"You *are* home," Wiktor said. Someone coughed violently, and Wiktor glanced over with his keen amber eyes to where the shape of Andrei lay under a cover of cloaks. The coughing turned into a choking noise, and Andrei's body lurched. When the sound of mortal illness faded away, Wiktor returned his attention to the little boy. "Listen to me," he commanded, and squatted down on his haunches before Mikhail. "You're going to be sick soon. Very soon. You'll need your strength, if you're going to live through it."

Mikhail held his stomach, which felt hot and swollen. "I'm sick now."

"Not nearly like you're going to be." Wiktor's eyes shone like copper coins in the low red light. "You're a thin whelp," he decided. "Didn't your parents feed you any meat?" He didn't wait for an answer, but grasped Mikhail's chin with his gnarled fingers and lifted the boy's face so it caught most of the fire's glow. "Pale as milk pudding," Wiktor said. "You won't be able to stand it. I can tell."

"Stand what, sir?"

"Stand the change. The sickness that's going to come over you." Wiktor released his chin. "Don't eat, then. It would be a waste of good food. You're finished, aren't you?"

"I don't know, sir," Mikhail admitted, and shivered as a chill passed through his bones.

"*I* know. I've learned to recognize strong reeds and weak ones. A lot of weak reeds lie in our garden." Wiktor motioned outward, beyond the chamber, and Andrei suffered another spasm of coughing. "All of us are born weak," Wiktor told the boy. "We have to learn to be strong, or we perish. A simple fact of life and death."

Mikhail was tired. He thought of a mop he'd once watched Dimitri use to swab the carriage, and he felt the way that wet old mop had looked. He lay down again, on a pallet of grass and pine straw.

"Boy?" Wiktor asked. "Do you know anything about what's happening to you?"

"No sir." Mikhail closed his eyes and squeezed them tight. His face felt as if it were made of the candle wax he used to dip his finger in and watch harden.

"They never do," Wiktor said, mostly to himself. "Do you know anything about germs?" He was addressing the boy again.

"Germs, sir?"

"Germs. Bacteria. Virus. You know what those things are?" Again, he didn't wait for a response. "Look at this." Wiktor spat in his hand, and put the spittle-pooled palm in front of Mikhail's face. The boy looked at it obediently, saw nothing but spit. "It's in there," Wiktor said. "The pestilence and the miracle. It's right there, in my hand." He pulled his hand away, and Mikhail watched him lick the saliva back into his mouth. "I'm full of it," Wiktor said. "In my blood and my insides. My heart and lungs, my guts, my brain." He tapped his bald skull. "I'm infested with it," he said, and he stared forcefully at Mikhail. "Just as you are, right now."

Mikhail wasn't sure he understood what the man was talking about. He sat up again, his head pounding. Chills and fever played through his body, malicious partners in torment.

"It was in Renati's spit." Wiktor touched Mikhail's shoulder, where a bandage of leaves and some kind of brown herbal paste Renati had mixed was pressed to the inflamed, pus-edged wound. It was no more than a glancing touch, but the pain made Mikhail wince and draw a breath. "It's in you now, and it's either going to kill you or . . ." He paused and shrugged. "Teach you the truth."

"The truth?" Mikhail shook his head, puzzled and hazy in the brain. "About what?"

"Life," Wiktor said. His breath wafted into the boy's face, and it smelled of blood and raw meat. Mikhail saw flecks of something red in his beard, which also held bits of leaves and grass. "A life beyond dreams—or nightmares—depending on your point of view. Some might call it an affliction, a disease, a curse." He had sneered that last word. "I call it nobility, and I would only live one other life, if I could be reborn: I would know the wolf's way from birth, and be ignorant of that beast called a human being. Do you understand what I'm saying, boy?"

One thought was paramount in Mikhail's mind. "I want to go home now," he said.

"My God, we've brought a simpleton into the pack!" Wiktor almost shouted. He stood up. "There is no home for you now but here, with us!" He nudged with his sandal an uneaten piece of meat that lay on the floor near the boy's pallet; it was rabbit flesh, and though Renati had passed it over a flame a few times, it still oozed a little blood. "Don't eat!" Wiktor thundered. "In fact, I command you not to eat! The sooner you die, the sooner we can tear you to pieces and eat *you!*" That sent a shiver of pure terror through Mikhail, but his face, glistening with sweat, remained impassive. "So you leave this alone, do you hear me?" He kicked the piece of rabbit meat a few inches closer to Mikhail's side. "We want you to get weak and die!" The coughing of Andrei broke his tirade. Wiktor turned away from the boy to go across the chamber, and he knelt at Andrei's side and lifted the blanket. Mikhail heard the breath hiss between Wiktor's teeth, and Wiktor grunted and said, "My poor Andrei," in a quiet, subdued voice. Then, abruptly, Wiktor stood up, shot a dark glance at Mikhail, and stalked out of the chamber.

Mikhail lay very still, listening to the sound of Wiktor's sandals scrape on the stairs going up. The little fire popped and spat sparks, and Andrei's breathing was like a rumble of freight cars on a distant track. Mikhail shivered, full of frost, and stared at the bloody piece of rabbit meat.

I command you not to eat, Wiktor had said. Mikhail stared at the meat, and watched a fly buzz slowly around it. The fly landed on the meat and crawled happily over it, as if searching for a tender place from which to draw the first sip of juice. *I command you not to eat.*

Mikhail looked away. Andrei coughed raggedly, twitched, and then lay still again. What was wrong with him? Mikhail wondered. Why was he so sick? His gaze slid back to the rabbit flesh. He thought of wolf fangs, distended and dripping, and in his mind's eye he saw a big pile of bones licked clean and white as October snow. His stomach mewled like a kitten. He looked away from the meat again. It was so bloody, so . . . *awful*. Such a raw thing would never be found on the gilded plates of the Gallatinov dining table. When was he going home, and where were his mother and father? Oh, yes. Dead. All dead. Something gripped tight in his mind, like a fist around a secret, and he couldn't think about his parents or his sister anymore. He stared at the rabbit flesh, and his mouth watered.

One taste, he thought. Just one. Would it be so bad?

Mikhail reached out and touched the flesh. The fly, startled, buzzed around his head until he swatted it away. Mikhail drew his fingers back and looked at the faint smears of scarlet on the fingertips. He sniffed them. The odor of metal, a memory of his father oiling a silver sword. Then Mikhail licked his fingers, and tasted blood. It was not a bad taste, nor a particularly good one. It was faintly smoky, and a little bitter. But even so, it made his stomach growl louder and his mouth water more. If he died, the wolves—and Wiktor was one of them—would rip him to pieces. So he had to live; that was a simple truth. And if he wanted to live, he would have to force down the bloody meat. He waved the persistent fly away again and picked up the rabbit flesh. It felt slick and slightly oily between his fingers. Maybe there was a little bit of fur on it, too, but he didn't look too closely. He squeezed his eyes shut, opened his mouth. His stomach lurched, but it needed to be filled before it could be emptied. He pushed the flesh into his mouth and bit down.

Juices flooded over his tongue; they were sweet and gamy, a taste of wildness. Mikhail's head pounded and his spine ached, but his teeth worked as if they were the masters and everything else was servant to them. He tore hunks of flesh off and chewed them; it was a tough old rabbit, thickly muscled, and it didn't want to be swallowed without a struggle. Blood and juice trickled over his chin as he ate, and Mikhail Gallatinov—six days and a world away from the boy he used to be—tore the flesh between his teeth and swallowed it with famished relish. When he came to the bones, he scraped them clean and tried to crack them open to get at the marrow. One of the smaller bones burst apart, red marrow exposed. He thrust his tongue into the broken bone and dug out the congealed blood. He ate as if it were the grandest meal ever served on a gold plate.

Sometime later, the hollowed-out bones fell from his bloody fingers, and Mikhail sat on his haunches over the little pile and licked his lips.

It hit him with a frightening force: he'd liked the bloody meat. He'd liked it very much. And that was not all. He wanted more.

Andrei suffered another fit of coughing that ended on a strangled note. The body stirred, and Andrei called out weakly: "Wiktor? Wiktor?"

"He's gone," Mikhail said, but Andrei kept calling for Wiktor in a voice that rose and fell. There was terror in that voice, and an awful weariness, too. Mikhail crawled across the stones to Andrei's side. There was a bad smell over here, a sour and decayed odor. "Wiktor?" Andrei whispered, his face hidden in the folds of the cloaks, only his pale brown, sweat-damp hair showing. "Wiktor . . . please . . . help me."

Mikhail reached down and pulled the cloak away from Andrei's face.

Andrei was perhaps eighteen or nineteen years old, and his face—gleaming with sweat—was as gray as a well-used dishrag. He looked up at Mikhail with sunken brown eyes and gripped Mikhail's arm with skinny fingers. "Wiktor," Andrei whispered. He tried to lift his head, but his neck wasn't strong enough. "Wiktor . . . don't let me die."

"Wiktor's not here." Mikhail tried to pull away, but the fingers clenched tighter.

"Don't let me die. Don't let me die," the young man pleaded, his eyes glassy. He coughed once, softly, and Mikhail saw his thin, sallow chest lurch. The next cough was stronger, and the one after that made Andrei's body shake. Andrei's coughing turned into strangling, and Mikhail tried to work his arm loose but Andrei wouldn't let him go. There was a terrible rattling deep in Andrei's chest, a wet, thick, sliding noise. Andrei's mouth opened wide, and he coughed violently with tears streaming from his eyes.

Something oozed out of Andrei's mouth. Something long and white and wriggling.

Mikhail blinked, and felt the blood drain out of his face as he watched the worm writhe on the stones beside Andrei's head.

Andrei coughed once more, and there was a sound of a heavy mass breaking apart in his lungs. And then they flooded out of his mouth. The white worms tangled and entwined around each other, the first hundred or so clean and ghost white, but then the next ones dappled with crimson lung blood. Andrei shivered and retched, his eyes staring at the shock-frozen boy, but he couldn't open his mouth wide enough for all the worms to get out. They began to ooze through his nostrils as well, and Andrei strangled and choked as his body expelled its cargo. And still they surged out, now dark scarlet and sluggish, and as they spilled onto the stones Mikhail screamed and wrenched his arm loose, leaving bits of his skin under Andrei's fingernails. Mikhail tried to rise, stumbled over his own feet and fell backward to the floor, landing hard on the base of his spine. Andrei reached for him, trying to find his hand, and lifting up out of his bed of cloaks, with blood-black worms frothing from his mouth. Mikhail began to choke, too, and as he scuttled away across the stones he felt the rabbit meat rising; he swallowed it down again, thinking of wolf fangs tearing him to shreds. Andrei got to his knees, and then with a terrible lung-ripping cough he expelled a black knot of worms the size of a man's fist. They streamed from his mouth and down his chest, and were followed by dark ribbons of pure blood. Andrei fell onto his face. He was naked, his body already the yellowish-gray of a corpse. His wiry muscles jittered, his flesh rippling and seething under a sheen of sweat. Mikhail saw darkness spreading across Andrei's back: brown hairs, bursting from the pores. In a matter of seconds hairs covered Andrei's back and shoulders and were creeping down his buttocks and thighs, darkening his arms, bursting from his hands and fingers. Andrei lifted his face, and Mikhail saw it caught in the change, blood still drooling over the lengthening jaw. His eyes had retreated further under a protruding brow, his scalp hair sleek and shining, his throat banded with dark hair. Andrei shivered as his spine began to crack and contort, and he opened his fanged mouth to shriek—a hideous commingling of animal and human anguish.

A hand gripped Mikhail by the scruff of the neck and lifted him off the floor. Another hand—the fingers rough and purposeful—twisted his face away from the grisly spectacle. He was pressed into a shoulder, and he smelled the musky odor of deerskin. "Don't look." It was Renati's voice. "Don't look, little one," she said, and put her hand firmly against the back of his head.

He could still hear, and that was bad enough. The half-human, half-wolf shrieking went on, coupled with the noise of bones popping. Someone else entered the chamber, and Renati shouted, "Get out!" Whoever it was quickly retreated. The shrieking turned into a high, thin howling that made Mikhail's skin crawl and drove him to the edge of madness, and he squeezed his eyes shut as Renati gripped the back of his skull. Mikhail realized then that he had put his arms around her neck. The agonized howling echoed through the chamber.

And then there was a choking whine, like a machine losing power and dying down. A last few fits of raspy breathing, and silence.

Renati put Mikhail down. He kept his face averted as she walked to the corpse's side and knelt down. Nikita, the almond-eyed Mongol with coal-black hair, came into the chamber, glanced quickly at Mikhail and then at the woman. "Andrei's dead," he said, a statement of fact.

Renati nodded. "Where's Wiktor?"

"Gone hunting. For him." He jerked a thumb at Mikhail.

"Just as well, then." Renati reached down, scooped up a handful of bloody worms and tossed them on the fire. They writhed and crisped. "Wiktor didn't want to watch him die." Nikita came forward to stand beside Renati, and as they talked—something about a garden—Mikhail's curiosity pulled him across the chamber. He stood between Nikita and Renati and peered down at Andrei's corpse.

It was the carcass of a wolf with brown fur and dark, sightless eyes. Its tongue lolled in a little pool of blood. Its right leg was the leg of a human being, and at the end of its wiry forelegs were two human hands, the fingers gripping at the stones of the floor as if trying to wrench them apart. Instead of horror, Mikhail felt a stab of pain in his heart. The fingers were pale and skinny, and they were the same fingers that only a few moments ago had been clutching his arm. The absolute power of death hit him with full force, somewhere between the chin and the crown of his head. But it was a blow that cleared his vision, and he saw at that instant that his mother, father, and sister were gone forever, and so were his days of dreaming on the end of a kite.

Renati looked at him and snapped, "Get back!" Mikhail obeyed, and only then did he realize he'd been standing on worms.

Nikita and Renati wrapped the carcass in a deerskin cloak, lifted it between them, and took it away, into a part of the white palace where shadows reigned. Mikhail sat on his haunches next to the fire, his blood moving in his veins like ice-clogged rivers. He stared at Andrei's dark blood on the stone. Mikhail shivered and held his palms toward the fire glow. *You're going to be sick soon*, he remembered Wiktor saying. *Very soon*.

Mikhail couldn't get warm. He sat closer to the fire, but even its heat on his face didn't thaw his bones. There was a tickling in his chest, and he coughed, the noise as explosive as a gunshot between the damp stone walls.

2

The days merged, one into the other, and in the chamber there was neither sunlight nor moonlight, just the fire's glow and spark as someone—Renati, Franco, Nikita, Pauli, Belyi, or Alekza—fed pine branches to the flames. Wiktor never tended the fire, as if it were understood such a menial task was beneath him. Mikhail felt heavy, and slept most of the time, but when he awakened there was usually a piece of barely cooked meat, berries, and a little water cupped in a hollowed stone beside him. He ate without question or hesitation, but the stone was too heavy to lift so he had to bend over it and lap the water up. Another thing he noticed: whoever was cooking the meat was gradually letting it remain bloodier. And it wasn't all flesh meat, either. Now and again it was something that was red and purplish, as if torn from a creature's innards. Mikhail at first refused to touch those grisly tidbits, but nothing new was placed beside him until he ate what was there, and soon he learned not to let anything—no matter how raw or horrid—sit there too long or the flies would come. He also learned that throwing up was futile; no one cleaned it up after him.

Once he awakened, shivering cold on the outside and burning beneath the skin, to a chorus of wolf howls somewhere in the distance. They terrified him at first. He had a few seconds of mad panic when he wanted to get up and claw his way out of the chamber, run through the woods and back to where his parents lay dead so he might find a gun and blow his brains out; but then the panic passed like a shade, and he sat listening to what he heard as music, the notes soaring up into the sky and entwining around each other like summer-passioned vines. He thought even that for a short time he could understand the language of that howling—a strange sensation, as if he'd suddenly learned to think in bits and pieces of Chinese. It was a language of mingled joy and yearning, like the sigh of someone who stands in a field of yellow flowers with the blue sky limitless in all directions and holds a broken string where a kite used to be. It was the language of wanting to live forever, and knowing that life was a cruel beauty. The howling brought tears to Mikhail's eyes and made him feel small, a fleck of dust floating on a wind current over a land of cliffs and chasms.

Once he awakened and found the maw of a blond-furred wolf over his face, the ice-blue eyes steady and piercing as they stared at him. He lay very still, his heart pounding, as the wolf began to sniff his body. He smelled the wolf, too; a musky, sweet scent of rain-washed hair and breath that held the memory of fresh blood. He shivered, lying as if bound, as the blond wolf sniffed slowly over his chest and throat. Then, with a shake of its skull, the wolf opened its mouth and dropped eleven uncrushed blackberries onto the stones beside Mikhail's head. The wolf retreated to the edge of the firelight, sat on its haunches, and watched as Mikhail ate the berries and lapped at the hollow, water-filled rock.

A dull, throbbing pain began to build and spread through his bones. Moving—even breathing—became an exercise in agony. And still the pain built, hour after hour, day after day, and someone cleaned him when he voided and someone else folded the deerskin cloaks around him like an infant. He shivered with cold, and the shivering fired the pain that raced through his nerves and made him moan and weep. Through the hazy twilight, he heard voices. Franco's: "Too small, I tell you. The small ones don't live. Renati, did you want a child so badly?" And Renati, angered: "I don't ask a fool for his opinions. You keep to yourself and leave us alone!" Then the voice of Wiktor, slow and precise: "His color's bad. Do you think he has worms? Feed him something and see if he'll take it." A piece of bloody meat was pressed to Mikhail's lips; Mikhail, adrift in a sea of pain, thought, *Don't eat. I command you not to eat,* and he felt defiance rachet his jaws open. Fresh agony seared him, made the tears stream down his cheeks, but he accepted the food and gripped it with his teeth lest it be snatched away. Nikita's voice drifted to him, and in it was a hint of admiration: "He's stronger than he looks. Watch out he doesn't snap your fingers off!"

Mikhail ate whatever was given to him. His tongue began to crave the blood and fluids, and he could tell what he was eating—rabbit, deer, wild boar, or squirrel, sometimes even the fleshy musk of a rat—and if it was a fresh kill or dead for hours. His mind ceased to revolt from the thought of consuming blood-drenched meat; he ate because he was hungry, and because there was nothing else. Sometimes he was fed only berries or some kind of coarse grass, but it all went down without complaint.

His vision blurred, everything going gray around the edges. His eyeballs pounded with pain, and even the low firelight tortured them. Then, and he wasn't sure exactly when it was because time was twisted, the darkness closed in and he was blind.

The pain never left him; it increased to a new level, and

his muscles stiffened and cracked like the boards of a house about to burst apart from inner pressure. He couldn't get his mouth open enough to eat flesh, and soon he was aware of fingers pushing into his mouth meat that had already been chewed. A freezing-cold hand touched his forehead, and even the light pressure on his skin made him gasp. "I want you to live." It was Renati's voice, whispering in his ear. "I want you to fight death, do you hear me? I want you to fight to hold on. If you live through this, little one, you'll know wonders."

"How is he?" Franco's voice, and in it a measure of true concern. "He's gotten thinner."

"He's not a skeleton yet," she replied testily, and then Mikhail heard her voice soften. "He's going to live. I know he is. He's a fighter, Franco; look how he grits his teeth. Yes. He's going to live."

"He has a long path to travel," Franco said. "The worst is ahead."

"I know." She was silent for a long while, and Mikhail felt her fingers gently combing his sweat-damp hair. "How many have there been who didn't live as long as him? I'd need ten hands to count them all. But look at him, Franco! Look how he strains and fights!"

"That's not fighting," Franco observed. "I think he's about to shit."

"Well, his insides are still working! That's a good sign! It's when they stop and they swell up that you know they're going to die! No, this one's got iron in his soul, Franco. I can tell these things."

"I hope you can," he said. "And I hope you're right about him." He took a few steps, then spoke again. "If he dies . . . it's not on your hands. It's just . . . nature's way. You understand that?"

Renati made a muffled sound of agreement. Then, sometime later, as Renati stroked his hair and ran her fingers over his forehead, Mikhail heard her sing a whispered song: a Russian lullaby, about the bluebird searching for a home and finding rest when the springtime sun melted winter's ice. She sang the tune in a sweet, lilting voice, a whisper meant only for him. He remembered someone else singing such a song to him, but it seemed so long ago. His mother. Yes. His mother, who lay sleeping in a meadow. Renati sang on, and for a few moments Mikhail listened and felt no pain.

A skip of time, a darkness of days. Agony. Agony. Mikhail had never known such agony, and if ever in his young life he might have thought he'd know such torment, he would have crushed himself into a corner and screamed for God's hand to grasp him. He thought he felt his teeth move in his jaws, grinding together in raw, bleeding sockets. He felt broken at the joints, a living rag doll pierced with needles. His pulse was a drumbeat for the damned, and Mikhail tried to open his mouth to scream but his jaw muscles tensed and scraped like barbed wire. Agony building, ebbing, building again to a new crescendo. He was one moment a furnace and the next a house of ice. He was aware of his body jerking, contorting, bending itself into a new shape. His bones arched and twisted, as if they were the consistency of sugar sticks. He had no control over these contortions; his body had become a strange machine, seemingly intent on self-destruction. Blind, unable to speak or scream, hardly able to draw a breath for the anguish in his lungs and his pounding heart, Mikhail felt his spine begin to warp. His muscles went mad; they shot his torso upright, threw his arms backward, twisted his neck, and squeezed his face as if caught between iron clamps. He slammed down on his back as his muscles relaxed, then was lifted upright again as they drew tight as sun-dried leather. At the center of the maelstrom of pain, the core of Mikhail Gallatinov fought against losing the will to live. As his body thrashed and his muscles stretched he thought of the Rubber Man, and that when this was over he might join the circus and be the greatest Rubber Man who'd ever been. And then the pain bit into him again, seized him by the guts, and shook him. Mikhail felt his backbone swell and lengthen with a shriek of shocked nerves. Voices floated to him from the land of ghosts: "Hold him! Hold him! He'll break his neck!"

". . . burning up with fever . . ."

"Never last through it . . . too weak . . ."

"Open his mouth! He'll bite through his tongue!"

The voices moved away in a whirl of noise. Mikhail felt

143

but was powerless to stop his body's contortions, his knees rising toward his chest as he lay on his side. His spine was the center of the agony, his skull a boiling kettle. His knees touched his chin and jammed tight. His teeth gritted together, and in his brain he heard a wailing like the rising of a storm wind, tearing at the foundations of all that had been before. The storm wind rose to a roar, a sound that blanked out all but itself, and its force doubled and tripled. Mikhail saw himself, in his mind's eye, running across the field of yellow flowers as black banners of clouds hurtled toward the Gallatinov house. Mikhail stopped, turned, shouted, "Mother! Father! Alizia!" but there was no answer from the house, and the clouds were hungry. Mikhail turned and ran on, his heart hammering; he heard a crash, looked back, and saw the house flying into fragments before the wind. And then the clouds were coming after him, about to engulf him. He ran, but he couldn't run fast enough. Faster. Faster. The storm roaring on his heels. Faster. His heart, pounding. A banshee scream in his ears. Faster . . .

And a change exploded out of him. Dark hairs burst from his hands and arms. He felt his spine contort, bowing his shoulders. His hands—no longer hands—touched the earth. He ran faster, his body whipsawing, and he began to rip from his clothes. The storm clouds took them, and spewed them to heaven. Mikhail kicked his shoes away, his toes spiraling earth and flowers behind him. The storm reached for him, but he was running on all fours now, racing from the past into the future. Rain swept over him: cold, cleansing rain, and he lifted his face toward the sky and—awakened.

Dark upon dark. His eyelids, sealed by tears. He worked them open, and a faint glimmer of crimson sneaked in. The little fire was still burning, and the chamber smelled strongly of pine ashes. Mikhail got to his haunches, every movement an exercise in pain. His muscles still throbbed, as if they'd been stretched taut and re-formed. His brain, his back, his tailbone all ached. He tried to stand, but his spine shrieked. He craved fresh air, the scent of the wind through the forest; it was a physical hunger in him, and it drove him on. He crawled, naked, across the rough stones, away from the fire.

Several times he tried to stand up, but his bones weren't

ready for it. He crawled on hands and knees to the stairway and ascended them like an animal. At the top he crawled along a moss-draped corridor, and gave a pile of deer skeletons only a passing glance. Soon he saw light ahead: a ruddy light, the light of either dawn or dusk. It came through the glassless windows and painted the walls and ceiling, and where it touched, the moss had not leeched. Mikhail smelled fresh air, but the scent made something in his brain click and whir like the wheels of a pocket watch. It was no longer the pungent, flowery aroma of late spring. It carried a different smell, a dry aroma with a chill center: fire at war with frost. It was the smell of dying summer.

Time had passed. That much was clear to him. He sat, stunned by his senses, and his hand drifted to his left shoulder. The fingers found ridges of pink flesh, and a few flakes of scabs drifted from the skin and settled to the floor. His knees were hurting him now, and it seemed important to him that he stand up before he went any farther. He tried. If bones had nerves, they were aflame. He could almost hear his muscles bending, like the squeaking hinges of old doors long unopened. Sweat was on his face, chest, and shoulders, but he didn't give up, nor did he cry out. His skeleton felt unfamiliar. Whose bones were these, lodged like broken splinters in his flesh? Stand up, he told himself. Stand up and walk . . . like a man.

He stood.

The first step was like a baby's: halting, uncertain. The second wasn't much better. But the third and fourth told him he still knew how to walk, and he went through the corridor into a high-ceilinged room where sunlight turned the rafters orange and pigeons softly cooed overhead.

Something moved, over in the shadows on the floor to Mikhail's right. He heard the noise of leaves crunching. Two bodies lay there, entwined and slowly heaving. Where one began and the other stopped was difficult to tell. Mikhail blinked the last of sleep's mist from his eyes. One of the figures on the floor moaned—a female's moan—and Mikhail saw human skin banded with animal hair that rose and rippled, then disappeared again into the damp flesh.

A pair of ice-blue eyes stared fixedly at him from the

gloom. Alekza grasped a shoulder on which pale brown hairs rose and fell like river tides. Franco's head turned, and he saw the boy standing there at the crossing of sun and shadow.

"My God!" Franco whispered, in a shocked voice. "He's made it through!" Franco pulled away from Alekza, with a moist parting sound, and sprang to his feet. "Wiktor!" he shouted. "Renati!" His shouts echoed through the corridors and chambers of the white palace. "Someone! Come quick!"

Mikhail stared at Alekza's nude body. She made no movement to cover herself. A light sheen of moisture glowed on her flesh. "Wiktor! Renati!" Franco kept shouting. "He's alive! He's alive!"

3

"Follow me," Wiktor said, on a morning in late September, and Mikhail walked in his shadow. They left the chambers of sunlight behind, and went down into a place in the white palace where the air was chill. Mikhail wore the deerskin robe that Renati had made for him, and he drew it tighter around his shoulders as he and Wiktor continued into the depths. Mikhail had realized over the past few weeks that his eyes quickly grew accustomed to darkness, and in the daylight he seemed to be able to see with razor clarity, even able to count the red leaves in an oak tree at a distance of a hundred yards. Still, Wiktor had something he wanted the boy to see, down here in the dark, and he paused to light a torch of boar fat and rags in the embers of a small fire he'd previously arranged. The torch flickered, and the smell of the burning fat made Mikhail's mouth water.

They descended into an area where the murals of robed and hooded monks on the walls still held their colors. A narrow passageway led through an arch, past open iron gates and into a huge chamber. Mikhail looked up, but couldn't see the ceiling. Wiktor said, "This is it. Stand where you are." Mikhail did, and Wiktor began to walk around the room. The torchlight revealed stone shelves packed with thick, leatherbound books: hundreds of them. No, more than hundreds, Mikhail thought. The books filled every available space and were piled up in stacks on the floor.

"This," Wiktor said quietly, "is what the monks who lived here a hundred years ago labored on: copying and storing manuscripts. There are three thousand four hundred and thirty-nine volumes in here." He said it with pride, as if discussing favored children. "Theology, history, architecture, engineering, mathematics, languages, philosophy . . . all here." He made a sweeping gesture with his torch. He smiled slightly. "The monks, as you can see, didn't have much of a social life. Show me your hands."

"My . . . hands?"

"Yes. You know. Those two things on the ends of your arms. Show them to me."

Mikhail lifted his hands toward the torchlight.

Wiktor studied them. He grunted and nodded. "You have the hands of a scholar," he said. "You've lived a privileged life, haven't you?"

Mikhail shrugged, not understanding.

"You've been well taken care of," Wiktor went on. "Born into an aristocratic family." He'd already seen the clothes Mikhail's mother, father, and sister had worn; they were of high quality. Good torch rags, now. He held up one of his own slender-fingered hands and turned it in the light. "I was a professor at the University of Kiev, a long time ago," he said. There was no wistfulness in his voice, only memory. "I taught languages: German, English, and French." A hard glint passed over his eyes. "I learned in three different tongues how to beg for money to feed my wife and son. Russia does not put a premium on the human mind."

Wiktor walked on, shining the torch at the books. "Unless, of course, you can devise a more economical method of killing," he added. "But I imagine all governments are more or less the same: all greedy, all shortsighted. It's the curse of man to have a mind and not have the sense to use it." He paused to gently remove a volume from a shelf. The back cover was gone, and the sheepskin pages hung from the spine. "Plato's *Republic*," Wiktor said. "In Russian, thank God. I don't know Greek." He sniffed at the binding as if inhaling a luxuriant perfume, then returned the book to its place. The chronicles of Julius Caesar, the theories of Copernicus, Dante's *Inferno*, the travels of Marco Polo . . . all around us, the doors to three thousand worlds." He moved the torch in a delicate circle and lifted a finger to his lips. "Shhhh," he whispered. "Be very quiet, and you can hear the sounds of keys turning, down here in the dark."

Mikhail listened. He heard a tentative scratching noise— not a key in a lock, but a rat somewhere in the huge chamber.

"Ah, well." Wiktor shrugged and continued his inspection of the books. "They belong to me now." Again, that hint of a smile. "I can honestly say I have the largest library of any lycanthrope in the world."

"Your wife and son," Mikhail said. "Where are they?"

"Dead. And dead." Wiktor stopped to break cobwebs away from a few volumes. "Both of them starved to death, after I lost my position. It was a political situation, you see. My ideas made someone angry. We were wanderers for a while. Beggars, too." He stared at the torchlight, and Mikhail saw his amber eyes glint with fire. "I was not a very good beggar," he said quietly. "After they died, I struck out on my own. I decided to get out of Russia, perhaps go to England. They have educated men in England. I took a road that led me through these woods . . . and a wolf bit me. His name was Gustav; he was my teacher." He moved the torch so its light fell on Mikhail. "My son had dark hair, like yours. He was older, though. Eleven years old. He was a very fine boy." The torch shifted, and Wiktor followed it around the chamber. "You've come a long way, Mikhail. But you have a long way yet to go. You've heard tales of wolfmen, yes? Every child is scared to bed at least once by such stories."

"Yes, sir," Mikhail answered. His father had told him and Alizia tales of cursed men who became wolves and tore lambs to pieces.

"They're lies," Wiktor said. "The full moon has nothing to do with it. Nor does night. We can go through the change whenever we please . . . but learning to control it takes time and patience. You have the first; you'll learn the second. Some of us change selectively. Do you know what that means?''

"No, sir."

"We can control which part changes first. The hands into claws, for instance. Or the facial bones and the teeth. The task is mastery of the mind and body, Mikhail. It is abhorrent for a wolf—or a man—to lose control over himself. As I say, this is something you'll have to learn. And it's not a simple task, by any means; it'll take years before you master it, if ever.''

Mikhail felt split; he was listening with one half of his mind to what Wiktor was saying, but the other half listened to the rat scratching in the darkness.

"Have you ever read anything on anatomy?'' Wiktor took a thick book from a shelf. Mikhail looked blankly at him. "Anatomy: the study of the human body,'' Wiktor translated. "This one is written in German, and it gives illustrations of the brain. I've thought a lot about the virus in our bodies, and why we can go through the change while ordinary men cannot. I think the virus affects something deep in the brain. Something long buried, and meant to be forgotten.'' His voice was getting excited, as if he were on a university podium again. "This book here''—he returned the anatomy volume and removed another book near it—"is a philosophy of the mind, from a medieval manuscript. It proposes that man's brain is multilayered. At the center of the brain is the animal instinct; the beast's nature, if you will—''

Mikhail was distracted. The rat: *scratch, scratch.* A peal of hunger rang in his stomach like a hollow bell.

"—and that portion of the brain is what the virus liberates. How little we know about the magnificent engine in our skulls, Mikhail! Do you see what I mean?''

Mikhail didn't, really. All this talk of beasts and brains made no impression on him. He looked around, his senses questing: *scratch, scratch.*

"You can have three thousand worlds, if you want them,'' Wiktor said. "I'll be your key, if you choose to learn.''

"Learn?" He tore his attention away from his hunger. "Learn what?"

Wiktor came to the end of his patience. "You're not a half-wit! Stop acting like one! *Listen* to what I'm saying: I want to teach you what's in these books! And what I know about the world, too! The languages: French, English, German. Plus history, mathematics, and—"

"Why?" Mikhail interrupted. Renati had told him the white palace and this forest would be his home for the rest of his life, just as it was for the others of the pack. "What use would I have for those things, if I'm going to stay here forever?"

"What use!" Wiktor mocked him, and snorted angrily. "What use, he says!" He strode forward, brandishing the torch, and stopped just short of Mikhail. "Being a wolf is a wonderful thing. A miracle. But we were born humans, and we can't let go of our humanity—even though the word 'human' shames us to our core sometimes. Do you know why I'm not a wolf *all* the time? Why I don't just run in the forest day and night?" Mikhail shook his head. "Because when we take the form of wolves we age as wolves, too. If we were to spend one year as wolves, we would be seven years older when we returned to human form. And as much as I love the freedom, the aromas, and . . . the fine *wonder* of it, I love life more. I want to live as long as I can, and I want to *know*. My brain hurts for knowledge. I say learn to run as a wolf, yes; but learn to *think* like a man, too." He tapped his bald skull. "If you don't, you squander the miracle."

Mikhail looked at the books he could see by the torchlight. They appeared very thick and very dusty. How could anyone ever read one book that thick, much less all of them?

"I'm a teacher," Wiktor said. "Let me teach."

Mikhail considered it. Those books frightened him, in a way; they were massive and forbidding. His father used to have a library, though the books were thinner and they had gilded titles on their spines. He remembered his and Alizia's tutor, Magda, a large gray-haired woman who used to come to their house in a buggy. It was important to know the world, Magda had always said, so you could find your place in it if you were ever lost. Mikhail had never felt more lost in his life. He shrugged, still wary; he'd never liked homework. "All right," he agreed, after another moment.

"Good! Oh, if the linen-shirted regents could see their professor now!" He grunted. "I'd tear out their hearts and show them how they beat!" He listened to the scratchings of the clawed intruder. "The first lesson isn't in a book. Your stomach's growling, and I'm hungry, too. Find the rat and we'll have our meal." He clubbed the torch on the floor, and sparks flew until the flames were beaten out.

The chamber was in darkness. Mikhail tried to listen, but his heartbeat was a thunderous distraction. A rat could be a good, juicy meal if it was large enough; this one sounded large enough for two meals. He'd eaten the rats Renati had brought him. They tasted like stringy chicken, and their brains were sweet. He looked slowly right and left in the dark, his head tilted to catch the sound. The rat scratched on, but it was hard to pinpoint its location.

"Down on the rat's level," Wiktor advised. "Think like a rat."

Mikhail got down on his haunches. Then on his belly. Ah, yes; now the scratching led him to his right. The far wall, he thought. Maybe in a corner. He began crawling in that direction. The rat abruptly stopped scratching.

"He hears you," Wiktor said. "He reads your mind."

Mikhail crawled forward. His shoulder bumped something: a pile of books. They slithered to the floor, and he heard the rat's claws click on the stones as it scuttled along the far wall. Going from right to left, Mikhail thought. He hoped. His stomach growled, an alarmingly loud noise, and he heard Wiktor laugh. The rat stopped, and remained silent. Mikhail lay on his belly, his head cocked. A sharp, acidic odor came to him. The rat was terrified; it had just urinated. The smell was as clear a pathway as a lantern's beam, but exactly why that was Mikhail didn't yet fully understand. His vision detected more piles of books around him, all outlined in a faintly luminous gray. Still he couldn't see the rat, but he could make out the volumes and shelves on the far wall. If I were a rat, he thought, I would squeeze into a corner. Someplace where my back was protected. Mikhail crawled forward, slowly . . . slowly. . . .

He could hear a muffled, steady *thump* about thirty feet behind him; Wiktor's heartbeat, he realized. His own pulse was all but deafening, and he stayed where he was until it had calmed. He angled his head from side to side, listening.

There. A quick *tick* . . . *tick* . . . *tick* like a small watch. To Mikhail's right, perhaps another twenty feet or so ahead. In the corner, of course. Behind an untidy heap of luminous-edged books. Mikhail crawled toward the corner, his movements silent and sinuous.

He heard the rat's heartbeat increase. A rat had the sixth sense; it could smell him, and in another moment Mikhail smelled the dusty hair of the rat, too. He knew exactly where it was. The rat was motionless, but its heartbeat indicated it was about to burst from its cover and run along the wall. Mikhail kept going, inch after inch. He heard the rat's claws click—and then it darted forward, a blurred luminescence, as it tried to flee across the chamber to the far corner.

All Mikhail knew was that he was hungry and he wanted the rat, but his mind worked instinctively, calculating the rat's angle and speed with an animal's cold logic. Mikhail lunged to the left. The rat squeaked and darted away from his hand. As the rat swerved and shot past him—a streak of gray fire—Mikhail instantly turned to the right, reached out, and gripped the rodent behind the head.

The rat thrashed, trying to get its teeth in Mikhail's flesh. It was a large rat, and it was strong. In another few seconds it was going to fight free. Mikhail decided the issue.

He opened his mouth, put the rat's head between his teeth and bit down on the tough little neck.

His teeth worked; there was no rage or anger in this, just hunger. He heard the bones crunch, and then warm blood filled his mouth. He ripped a last piece of flesh loose. The rat's head rolled over his tongue. The body's legs kicked a few times, but with dwindling strength. And that was the end of a very unequal contest.

"Bravo," Wiktor said. But his voice regained its sternness. "Two more inches and you would've lost it. That rat was as slow as a muffin-stuffed grandmother."

Mikhail spat the severed head onto his palm. He watched as Wiktor approached him, outlined in luminescence. It was good manners to offer the best portion of any meal to Wiktor, and Mikhail lifted his palm.

"It's yours," Wiktor told him, and took the warm dead carcass.

Mikhail worked the skull between his teeth, finally breaking it open. The brains reminded him of a sweet-potato pie he'd eaten, in another world.

Wiktor ripped the carcass open from stub of neck to tail. He inhaled the heady fragrance of blood and fresh meat, and then scooped the intestines out with his fingers and pulled pieces of fat and flesh away from the bones. He offered a portion to Mikhail, who took his share gratefully.

The man and boy ate their rat in the dark chamber, with the echoes of civilized minds in the shelves all around them.

4

The golden weave of days became tinged with silver. Frost gleamed in the forest, and the hardwoods stood naked before the bitter wind. It was going to be a bad winter, Renati had said as she watched the bark thicken on the trees. The first snow fell in early October, and covered the white palace with white.

As the winds of November shrieked and the snow blew like scattershot, the pack huddled together in the depths of the palace, around a fire that was never allowed to burn too high or completely extinguish. Mikhail's body felt sluggish, and he wanted to sleep a lot, though Wiktor kept his head filled with questions from the books; Mikhail had never known there were so many questions, and even in his sleep he dreamed of question marks. Before very long, he began to dream in foreign languages: German and English, in which

Wiktor drilled him with merciless repetition. But Mikhail's mind had sharpened, as well as his instincts, and he was learning.

Alekza's stomach swelled. She stayed curled up a lot, and the others always gave her extra portions of the kill. They never changed within sight of Mikhail; they always went up the stairway and into the corridors on two legs before they left the white palace to hunt on four. Sometimes they brought back fresh, dripping meat, sometimes they returned sullen and empty-handed. But there were a lot of rats around, drawn to the heat of the fire, and those were easily caught. Mikhail knew he was one of the pack now, and accepted as such, but he still felt like what he was: a cold, often miserably uncomfortable human boy. His bones and brain still sometimes ached with a ferocity that almost drove him to tears. Almost. He sniffled in pain a few times, and the stares he received from Wiktor and Renati told him, crying was not tolerated from someone who didn't suffer gut worms.

But the change remained a mystery to him. It was one thing to live with the pack, and quite something else to fully join them. How did they change? Mikhail wondered, adding to his burden of questions. Did they take a deep breath, as if about to leap into dark and icy water? Did they stretch their bodies until the human skin split open and the wolves burst free? How did they *do* it? No one offered to tell him, and Mikhail—the runt of the pack—was too skittish to ask. He only knew that when he heard them howl after a kill, their voices echoing over the snowy woods, there was a burning in his blood.

A blizzard swept down from the north. As it raged beyond the walls Pauli sang in a high, frail voice a folk song about a bird who flew amid the stars, while her brother, red-haired Belyi, kept time with the clicking of sticks. The blizzard settled in, and roared its own music day after day. The fire lost its heat, and the food was gnawed away. Stomachs began to sing. Wiktor, Nikita, and Belyi had to go out into the blizzard to hunt. They were gone for three days and nights, and when Wiktor and Nikita returned, they brought back the half-frozen carcass of a stag. Belyi did not return;

he'd gone after a caribou, and the last Wiktor and Nikita had seen of him he'd been zigzagging through the storm after his prey.

Pauli cried for a while, and the others left her alone. She didn't cry so much, though, that she didn't eat. She accepted the bloody meat with the same hunger as the others, including Mikhail. And Mikhail learned a new lesson: whatever tragedy might happen, whatever torment should befall, life went on.

Mikhail awakened one morning and listened to silence. The storm had ceased. He followed the others up the stairway and through the chambers, where snow lay in drifts on the stones and ice-covered tree limbs stretched overhead. The sun was shining outside, the sky azure over a world of dazzling white. Wiktor, Nikita, and Franco burrowed a path through the snow into the palace courtyard, and Mikhail walked outside with the others to feast on fresh, frosty air.

He breathed deeply until his lungs burned. The sun was fierce, but it made not a dent in the smooth snow. Mikhail was thoroughly enraptured by the beauty of the winter forest by the time a snowball blasted against the side of his head.

"Good shot!" Wiktor shouted. "Give him another one!" Nikita was smiling, already cupping more snow. Nikita reared his arm back to throw it, but at the last second he whirled and flung it into the face of Franco, standing about twenty feet away.

"You ass!" Franco yelled as he dug for a snowball. Renati flung one that grazed Nikita's head, and Pauli threw a snowball with deadly accuracy into Alekza's face. Alekza, laughing and sputtering snow, went down on her rear end, her hands pressed to her pregnant belly.

"You want a war?" Nikita hollered, grinning at Renati. "I'll give you a war!" He threw a snowball that clipped Renati's shoulder, and then Mikhail stood in Renati's shadow and threw one that burst between Franco's eyes and staggered him back. "You . . . little . . . *beast*!" Franco shouted, and Wiktor smiled and calmly dodged a snowball that sailed over his head. Renati was hit by two at once, from Franco and Pauli. Mikhail plunged his numb hands into the snow for another barrage. Nikita ducked Renati's salvo and scrambled to a place where the snow was fresh and unmarked. He dug both hands deeply into it for double snowballs.

And he came up with something quite different. Something frozen, red, and mangled.

Renati's laughter ended on a strangled note. A last snowball thrown by Franco exploded off her shoulder, but she stared at what Nikita held. Mikhail let the snow slither to the ground. Pauli gasped, her face and hair dripping.

Nikita had brought a severed, mutilated hand up from the snow. It was as blue as polished marble, and two fingers had been torn away. The thumb and forefinger were shrunken and curved inward—the last vestiges of a paw—and fine red hair covered the back of the hand.

Pauli took a step forward. Then another, up to her knees in snow. She blinked, stunned, and then moaned the name: "*Belyi* . . ."

"Take her inside," Wiktor said to Renati. Instantly she took Pauli's arm and tried to guide her back to the palace, but Pauli jerked free. "Go *inside*," Wiktor told her, stepping in front of her so she couldn't see what Nikita and Franco were uncovering from the drift. "*Now*."

Pauli wavered on her feet. Alekza caught her other arm, and between them she and Renati led Pauli into the palace like a hollow-eyed sleepwalker.

Mikhail started to follow them, but Wiktor's voice lashed him: "Where do you think you're going? Come here and help us with this!" Wiktor knelt down to push aside the snow with Nikita and Franco, and Mikhail came over to add his shivering strength.

It was a mass of crimson, blood-crusted bones. Most of the meat had been ripped off, but a few shreds of muscle remained. Some of the bones were human and some were wolf, Wiktor quickly saw; Belyi's body, in death, had warred between its poles. "Look at this," Franco said, and held up part of a shoulder blade. Across it were deep scrapes.

Wiktor nodded. "Fangs." There was more evidence of powerful jaws at work: furrows on an arm bone, the jagged edges of the broken spine.

And then, at last, Nikita brushed away some hard-crusted snow and found the head.

The scalp was gone, the skull crushed and the brains scooped out, but Belyi's face remained. Minus the lower jaw, which had been torn away. The tongue, too, had been wrenched from its roots. Belyi's eyes were open, and the red hairs covered his cheeks and forehead. The eyes were directed for a few seconds right at Mikhail, until Nikita moved the head again, and in them Mikhail saw a glassy shine of pure terror. He looked away, shivering but not with the cold this time, and retreated a few paces. Franco picked up a leg bone that still held a few fragments of frozen red muscle, and examined the bone's splintered edges. "Great strength in the bite," Franco said quietly. "The leg was broken with a single crunch."

"So were both the arms," Nikita said. He sat on his haunches, looking at the bones arranged around him in the snow. A patchwork of shadows and sunlight lay on Belyi's face, and the ice in the single remaining eyelid was beginning to melt. Mikhail watched with dreadful fascination as a drop of water trickled down Belyi's blue cheek like a tear.

Wiktor stood up, his eyes blazing, and slowly turned his gaze through all points of the compass. His fists clenched at his sides. Mikhail knew what he must be thinking: they were no longer the only killers in the forest. Something had been watching them, and knew where their den was. It had crushed Belyi's bones, torn out his tongue, and scooped the brains from his skull. Then it had brought the broken skeleton back here like a taunt. Or a challenge.

"Wrap him in this." Wiktor removed his deerskin cloak and gave it to Franco. "Don't let Pauli see him." He began to walk, naked and with a purposeful stride, away from the white palace.

"Where're you going?" Nikita asked him.

"Tracking," Wiktor answered, his feet crunching in the snow. Then he began to run, casting a long shadow. Mikhail watched him weave through the tangle of surrounding trees and spiky undergrowth; he saw gray hair ripple across Wiktor's broad white back, saw his spine start to contort, and then Wiktor vanished into the forest.

Nikita and Franco put Belyi's bones in the robe. The head, with its silent jawless shriek, was the last to go in. Franco stood up, the folded robe clutched in his arms and his face gaunt and gray. He looked at Mikhail, and his lip curled. "You carry them, rabbit," he said in a tone of derision, and he put the sack of remains in Mikhail's arms. Their weight instantly dropped the boy to his knees.

Nikita started to help him, but Franco caught the Mongol's arm. "Let the rabbit do it alone, if he wants to be one of us so much!"

Mikhail stared into Franco's eyes; they laughed at him, and wanted him to fail. He felt a spark leap inside him. It exploded into incandescent fire, and the heat of anger made Mikhail strain to stand with the sack of bones in his arms. He got halfway up before his feet slipped out from under him. Franco walked on a few paces. "Come on!" he said impatiently, and Nikita reluctantly followed. Mikhail struggled, his teeth gritted and his arms aching. But he had known pain before, and this was nothing. He would not let Franco see him beaten; he would let no one see him beaten, not ever. He got all the way up, and then walked with unsteady steps, his arms full of what used to be Belyi.

"A good rabbit always does as he's told," Franco said. Nikita reached out to carry the bones the rest of the way, but Mikhail said, "*No,*" and carried his burden toward the white palace. He smelled the coppery aroma of icy blood from Belyi's remains. The deerskin had its own smell—higher, sweeter—and Wiktor's sweat smelled of salt and musk. But there was another odor in the chill air, and it drifted past Mikhail's nostrils as he reached the doorway. This odor was wild and rank, a smell of brutality and cunning. The smell of an animal, and as different from the odors of Mikhail's pack as black differs from red. It was wafting, he realized, from Belyi's bones: the spoor of the beast that had slaughtered him. The same odor that Wiktor was now tracking across the smooth, blizzard-sculpted snow.

The promise of violence hung in the air. Mikhail felt it like the slide of claws down his spine. Franco and Nikita felt it, too, as they gazed around through the forest, their senses questing, collecting, evaluating with a speed that was now their second nature. Belyi had not been the strongest of the pack, but he'd been very quick and smart. Whatever had torn him to pieces had been quicker and smarter. It was out there now, somewhere in the forest, waiting and watching to see what would be the response to its gift of death.

Mikhail staggered across the threshold into the palace and saw Pauli standing there with Renati and Alekza, her mouth gasping wordlessly as she stared at the folded robe in his arms. Renati quickly stepped forward and took the robe from him, carrying it away.

The sun went down. The stars emerged, shimmering against the blackness. A small fire crackled in the depths of the white palace as Mikhail and the rest of his pack huddled in the circle of its heat. They waited as the wind began to rise outside and shrill through the corridors. And waited. But Wiktor did not come home.

FIVE

The Mouse Trap

At six o'clock on the morning of March 29, Michael Gallatin dressed in a field-gray German uniform, with jackboots, a cap bearing a communications-company insignia, and the proper service medals—Norway, the Leningrad Front, and Stalingrad—on his chest. He shrugged into a field-gray overcoat. On his person were papers—an expert job had been done in acid aging the new photograph and yellowing the documentation, Michael noted—identifying him as an *oberst*—a colonel—in charge of coordinating the signal lines and relays between Paris and the units scattered along the coast of Normandy. He had been born in a village in southern Austria called Braugdonau. He had a wife named Lana and two sons. His politics were adamantly pro-Hitler, and he was loyal to the Reich's service, if not necessarily in awe of Nazism. He had been wounded once, by a fragment of shrapnel from a grenade thrown by a Russian partisan in 1942, and he had the scar under his eye to prove it. Under his coat he wore a leather holster with a well-used but perfectly clean Luger in it, and two extra clips of bullets in his pocket, near his heart. He carried a silver Swiss pocket watch, engraved with figures of hunters shooting stags, and nothing—not even his socks—had a trace of British wool. The rest of what he needed to know was in his head: the roads in and out of Paris, the maze of streets around Adam's apartment and the building where Adam worked, and Adam's nondescript, accountant's face. He had a hearty breakfast of bacon and eggs with Pearly McCarren, washed down with strong black French coffee, and it was time to go.

McCarren, a craggy mountain in a Black Watch kilt, and a young dark-haired Frenchman Pearly referred to as André led Michael through a long, damp corridor. His jackboots, the footwear of a dead German officer, clattered on the stones. McCarren talked quietly as they went along the corridor, filling in last-minute details; the Scotsman's voice was nervous, and Michael listened intently but said nothing. The details were already in his head, and he was satisfied that everything was planned. From here on, it was a walk on the razor's edge.

The silver pocket watch was an interesting invention. Two clicks on the winding stem popped open the false back, and inside was a little compartment that held a single gray capsule. The capsule was small to be so deadly, but cyanide was a potent and fast-acting poison. Michael had agreed to carry the poison capsule simply because it was one of the unwritten regulations of the secret service, but he never intended the Gestapo to take him alive. Still, his carrying it seemed to make McCarren feel better. Actually, Michael and McCarren had become good companions in the last two days; McCarren was a tough poker player, and when he wasn't drilling Michael on the details of his new identity, he was winning hand after hand of five-card draw. Michael was disappointed in one thing, though; he hadn't seen Gaby today, and because McCarren hadn't mentioned her he assumed she had gone back to an assignment in the field. *Au revoir*, he thought. And good luck to you.

The Scotsman and the young French partisan led Michael up a set of stone steps, and into a small cave lit by green-shaded lamps. The illumination gleamed on a long, black, hard-topped Mercedes-Benz touring car. It was a beautiful machine, and Michael couldn't even tell where the bullet holes had been patched and repainted. "Fine machine, eh?" McCarren asked, reading Michael's mind as Michael ran a gloved hand across a fender. "The Germans know how to build 'em, that's for sure. Well, the bastards have got cogs and gears in their heads instead of brains anyway, so what can you expect." He motioned toward the driver's seat, where a uniformed figure sat behind the wheel. "André there's a good driver. He knows Paris about as well as anybody, seein' as he was born there." He tapped on the glass, and the driver nodded and started the engine; it responded with a low, throaty growl. McCarren opened the rear door for Michael as the young Frenchman unlatched two doors that covered the cave entrance. The doors were thrown open, letting in a glare of morning sunlight, and then the young Frenchman began to quickly clear brush away from in front of the Mercedes.

McCarren held out his hand, and Michael gripped it. "You take care of yourself, laddie," the Scotsman said. "Give 'em hell out there for the Black Watch, eh?"

"*Jawohl.*" Michael eased into the backseat, a luxury of black leather, and the driver released the hand brake and drove through the cave entrance. As soon as the car was clear, the brush was put back into place, the green-and-brown-camouflage-painted doors were sealed, and it looked like a rugged hillside again. The Mercedes wound through a patch of dense woods, met a rutted country road, and turned left on it.

Michael sniffed the air: leather and new paint, the faint whiff of gunpowder, engine oil, and an apple-wine fragrance. Ah, yes, he thought, and smiled faintly. He looked out through a window, studying the blue sky full of lacy, billowing clouds. "Does McCarren know?" he asked Gaby.

She glanced at him in the rearview mirror. Her black hair was pinned up under her German staff driver's cap, and she wore a shapeless coat over her uniform. His gaze, that piercing glare of green, met hers. "No," she said. "He thinks I went back to the field last night."

"Why didn't you?"

She thought about it for a moment as she jockeyed the car over a rough section of road. "My assignment was to get you where you want to go," she answered.

"Your assignment ended when you got me to McCarren."

"Your interpretation. Not mine."

"McCarren had a driver for me. What happened to him?"

Gaby shrugged. "He decided . . . the job was too dangerous."

"Do you know Paris?"

"Well enough. What I didn't know I learned from the map." Another glance in the rearview mirror; his eyes were still on her. "I haven't spent *all* my life in the country."

165

"What'll the Germans think if we run into a roadblock?" he asked her. "I imagine a beautiful girl driving a staff car isn't a common sight."

"Many of the officers have female drivers." She concentrated her attention back on the road. "Either secretaries or mistresses. French girls, too. You'll get more respect with a female driver."

He wondered when she'd decided to do this. She certainly didn't need to; her part of the mission was over. Had it been the night of their chilly bath? Or later, as Michael and Gaby had shared a stale loaf of bread and some musky red wine? Well, she was a professional; she knew what kind of dangers lay ahead, and what would happen to her if she were captured. He looked out the window, at the greening country-side, and wondered where her cyanide capsule was hidden.

Gaby reached an intersection, where the rutted dirt road connected with a road of tarred gravel: the route to the City of Light. She turned right and passed a field where farmers stood baling hay. The Frenchmen stopped their work, lean-ing on their pitchforks as they watched the black German car glide past. Gaby was a good driver. She kept a constant speed, her gaze darting to the rearview mirror and then back to the road again. She was driving as if the German colonel in the backseat had somewhere to go, but was in no hurry to get there.

"I'm not beautiful," she said quietly, about six or seven minutes later.

Michael smiled behind his gloved hand, and he settled back into his seat to enjoy the journey.

They went on in silence, the Mercedes's engine a polite, well-oiled purr. Gaby glanced back at him occasionally, trying to figure out what it was about him that had made her want to—no, no, *need* to be with him. Yes, that ought to be admitted. Not to him, of course, but in the chapel of secrets. It was most probably, she reasoned, that the action against the Nazi tank had fired her blood and passions in a way she hadn't been flamed in a long while. Oh, there had been other cinders, but this was a bonfire. It was just the nearness of a man who craved action, she thought. A man who was good at his job. A man . . . who was good. She hadn't lived so long to be a poor judge of character; the man in the backseat was special. Something about him was cruel and . . . beastly, perhaps. That was part of the nature of his occupation. But she'd seen kindness in his eyes, there in the chilly water. A sense of grace, a purpose. He was a gentleman, she thought, if there were indeed any of those left on this earth. Anyway, he needed her help. She could get him in and out of Paris, and that was the important thing. Wasn't it?

She glanced in the sideview mirror, and her heart stuttered.

Coming up behind them, very quickly, was a German BMW motorcycle and sidecar.

Her hands tightened on the wheel, and the motion made the Mercedes swerve slightly.

Michael sat upright with the jerk of the car, and caught the high whine of the motorcycle's engine: a familiar noise, last heard in the desert of North Africa. "Behind us," Gaby said tautly, but Michael had already glanced back and seen the vehicle overtaking them. His hand went to the Luger. No, not yet, he decided. Stay calm.

Gaby didn't slow down, nor did she speed up. She kept her speed steady, an admirable accomplishment when her pulse was beating so fast. She could see the tinted goggles of the helmeted driver and the sidecar's passenger. They seemed to be fixed on her with murderous intent. On the floorboard at her feet was a loaded Luger. She could pick it up and fire out the window in an instant, if need be.

Michael said, "Keep driving." He settled back in his seat again, waiting.

The motorcycle and sidecar pulled up behind them, perhaps six feet from their bumper. Gaby looked in the rearview mirror and saw the sidecar's passenger motioning them over. "They're telling us to pull off," she said. "Shall I?"

Michael paused only a few seconds. "Yes." If it wasn't the right decision, he'd know very soon.

Gaby slowed the Mercedes. The motorcycle and sidecar slowed as well. Then Gaby pulled the heavy car off the road, and the motorcycle came abreast with them before its driver cut the engine. Michael said, "Say nothing," and furiously rolled down his window. The sidecar's passenger, a lieutenant from the markings on his dusty uniform, was already pulling his long legs out of the vehicle and standing up. Michael stuck his head out the rolled-down window and shouted in German, "What the hell are you trying to do, you idiot? Run us off the road?"

The lieutenant froze. "No, sir. I'm sorry, sir," the man babbled as he recognized a colonel's insignia.

"Well, don't just stand there! What do you want?" Michael's hand rested on the Luger's grip.

"I apologize, sir. Heil Hitler." He made a weak Nazi salute that Michael didn't even bother to return. "Where are you going, sir?"

"Who wants to know? Lieutenant, are you wishing a tour with a ditch-digging battalion?"

"No, sir!" The young man's face was gaunt and chalky under a mask of dust. The dark goggles gave his eyes a bulging, insectlike appearance. "I'm sorry to interrupt you, sir, but I thought it my duty—"

"Your *duty?* To what? Act like an ass?" Michael was looking for guns. The young lieutenant didn't have a holster. His weapon was probably in the sidecar. The motorcycle's driver had no visible weapon, either. So much the better.

"No, sir." The young man trembled a bit, and Michael felt a little pang of pity for him. "To warn you that there were air attacks on the road to Amiens before dawn. I didn't know if you'd heard or not."

"I've heard," Michael said, deciding to chance it.

"They got a few supply trucks. Nothing vital," the young lieutenant went on. "But the word's out: with this weather so clear, there are bound to be more air attacks. Your car . . . well, it's very shiny, sir. A very nice target."

"Shall I throw mud on it? Or pig shit?" He kept his tone icy.

"No, sir. I don't mean to be out of line, sir, but . . . those American fighter planes . . . they swoop down very fast."

Michael stared at him for a moment. The young man stood rigid, like a commoner in the presence of royalty. The boy couldn't be more than twenty years old, Michael figured. Damn bastards were robbing the cradles now for their cannon fodder. He removed his hand from the Luger. "Yes, you're right, of course. I appreciate your concern, Lieutenant . . . ?" He let it hang.

"Krabell, sir!" the young man—so close to death, without knowing it—said proudly.

"Thank you, Lieutenant Krabell. I'll remember the name." It would wind up scrawled on a wooden cross, stuck on a mound of French earth after the invasion swept through, he thought.

"Yes, sir. Good day, sir." The young man saluted again— the salute of a puppet—then returned to his sidecar. The motorcycle driver started the engine, and the vehicle pulled away. "Wait," Michael said to Gaby. He let the motorcycle get out of sight, and then he touched Gaby's shoulder. "All right, let's go."

She started off again, driving at the same steady speed, frequently checking not only the mirrors but also the sky for a hint of silver that would be diving upon them, machine guns blazing. The Allied fighters commonly strafed the roads, supply dumps, and any troops they could find; on a clear day such as this, it was reasonable to believe the fighters were prowling for targets—including shiny black German staff cars. Tension knotted her stomach and made her feel slightly sick. They swept past a group of hay wagons, farmers at work, and saw the first sign that pointed to Paris. About four miles east of that sign they came around a curve and found themselves confronted with a roadblock.

"Easy," Michael said quietly. "Don't slow down too soon." He saw perhaps eight or nine soldiers with rifles and a couple of security officers with machine guns. Again, his hand was on the Luger. He rolled down his window once more and prepared to act indignant.

His acting wasn't necessary. The two security officers looked at his insignia and the sleek black car and were sufficiently impressed; even more so when they looked at Gaby behind the wheel. A formality, the man in charge said with an apologetic shrug of his shoulders. Of course the colonel knew about the partisan activity in this sector. What could be done about it except to exterminate the rats? If we might see your papers, the security man said, we'll check you through as quickly as possible. Michael grumbled about being delayed for a meeting in Paris and handed his papers over. The two security men looked at them, more as a demonstration that they were doing something than with true attention. If those men worked for the Allies, Michael thought, I'd have them thrown in prison. Perhaps thirty seconds elapsed, and then the papers were returned to him with crisp salutes and he and the pretty *fräulein* were bidden a good journey to Paris. Gaby drove on as the soldiers moved the wooden barricades aside, and Michael heard her release the breath she'd been holding.

"They're looking for someone," Michael said when they'd gotten away from the roadblock, "but they don't know who. They figure whoever parachuted in might want to get to Paris, so they've got their watchdogs out. If they're all like those two, they might escort us to Adam's door."

"I wouldn't count on that." Gaby again checked the sky; no trace of silver. Yet. The road was clear, too, the countryside slightly rolling and dotted with apple orchards and stands of hardwood trees. Napoleon's country, she thought idly. Her heart wasn't beating so hard now; getting through the roadblock had been a lot easier then she'd expected. "What about Adam?" she asked. "What do you think it is he's trying to get out?"

"I haven't thought."

"Oh yes you have." Their eyes met in the mirror. "I'm sure you've thought about it quite a bit, just as I have. Yes?"

This line of conversation was indelicate, and both of them knew it. Shared knowledge was shared pain, if they landed in the hands of the Gestapo. But Gaby was waiting for an answer, and Michael said, "Yes." That alone wouldn't do; Gaby was silent, still waiting. He folded his gloved hands together. "I think Adam's found something he obviously feels is important enough to risk a lot of lives to get out. My superior thinks so, too, or I wouldn't be here. And needless to say, your uncle wouldn't be dead." He saw her flinch just a fraction; she was tough, but not iron-cased. "Adam's a professional. He knows his business. He also knows that some information is worth dying for, if it means winning this war. Or losing it. Movements of troops and supply convoys we can get anytime, by the radio codes from a dozen agents all over France. This is something that only Adam knows about, and that the Gestapo's clamped the lid on. Which means it's a hell of a lot more important than the usual messages we get. Or at least Adam thinks it is, or he wouldn't be calling for help.''

"What about you?" Gaby asked. He lifted his eyebrows, not understanding. "What would *you* die for?" Gaby glanced at him again in the mirror, then quickly away.

"I hope I won't have to find out." He gave her a hint of a smile, but the question had lodged inside him like a thorn. He was prepared to die for the mission, yes; that was already understood. But that was the reaction of a trained machine, not a man. What, as a man—or half man, half animal—was he prepared to lay down his life for? The human-woven net of politics? Some narrow vision of freedom? Love? Triumph? He explored the question, and found no easy answer.

And suddenly his nerves let go of their chill alarms and he heard Gaby say softly, *"Oh,"* because there in front of them on the long straight route to Paris was a roadblock with a dozen armed soldiers, an armored car with a cannon-snout showing, and a black Citröen that could only be a Gestapo vehicle.

A soldier with a submachine gun was waving them down. All faces turned toward them. A man in a dark hat and a long beige overcoat stepped into the road, waiting. Gaby hit the brakes, a little too hard. "Steady," Michael said, and as the Mercedes slowed he peeled off his gloves.

––––––– 2 –––––––

The man who peered in through the rolled-down window at Michael Gallatin had blue eyes so pale they were almost without color, his face chiseled and handsome in the way of a Nordic athlete—a skier, Michael thought. Perhaps a javelin thrower, or a long-distance runner. There were fine lines around his eyes, and his blond sideburns were going gray.

He wore a dark leather hat with a jaunty red feather in its band. "Good morning, Colonel," he said. "A small inconvenience, I fear. May I see your papers?"

"I *hope* the inconvenience is small," Michael answered icily. The other man's face kept its thin, polite smile. As Michael reached into his coat for his packet of papers, he saw a soldier take up a position directly on the other side of the car. The soldier's submachine gun barrel wandered slightly toward the window, and Michael felt a knot of tension clench in his throat. The soldier was staking out his lane of fire; there was no way Michael could pull the Luger from his holster without being shot to tatters.

Gaby kept her hands on the wheel. The Gestapo agent took Michael's papers and glanced in at Gaby. "Your papers also, please?"

"She's my secretary," Michael said.

"Of course. But I must see her papers." He shrugged. "Regulations, you know."

Gaby reached into her coat. She brought out a packet of papers that had been made for her yesterday, when she'd decided to go to Paris with him. She handed them over with a crisp nod.

"Thank you." The Gestapo agent began to inspect the photographs and documents. Michael watched the man's face. It was a cold face, and it was stamped with a cunning intelligence; this man was no fool, and he'd seen all the tricks. Michael glanced toward the roadside, and saw Lieutenant Krabell and his driver there. The driver was checking the engine as Krabell's papers were being laboriously examined by another Gestapo agent.

"What's the problem?" Michael asked.

"Haven't you heard?" The blond-haired man looked up from his reading, his eyes quizzical.

"If I had, would I be asking?"

"For a communications officer, you're certainly out of touch." A brief smile, a hint of square white predator's teeth. "But of course you know there was a parachute drop in this sector three nights ago. The partisans in a village called Bazancourt helped the man escape. There was also a woman involved." His gaze slid toward Gaby. "Do you speak German, my dear?" he asked her in French.

"A little," she answered. Her voice was cool, and Michael admired her courage. She looked the man straight in the eyes and didn't waver. "What do you want me to say?"

"Your papers speak for you." He continued his inspection, taking his time about it.

"What's your name?" Michael decided to take the offensive. "I'd like to know who to lodge my complaint against when we get to Paris."

"Johlmann. Heinz, middle initial R for Richter." The man kept reading, not intimidated in the least. "Colonel, who's your superior commander?"

"Adolf Hitler," Michael said.

"Ah, yes. Of course." Again, that brief show of teeth. They looked like they were good at tearing meat. "I mean your immediate superior in the field."

Michael's palms were damp, but his heart had stopped pounding. He was in control of himself, and he would not be rushed. He glanced quickly at the soldier on the other side of the car, still holding the submachine gun ready, his finger on the trigger guard. "I report to Major General Friedrich Bohm, Fourteenth Sector Communications, headquarters in Abbeville. Our radio code is 'Tophat.' "

"Thank you. I can get through to Major General Bohm in about ten minutes on our radio equipment." He motioned toward the armored car.

"Be my guest. I'm sure he'd like to hear why I'm being interrogated." Michael stared up at Johlmann. Their eyes met, and locked. The moment stretched, and in it Gaby felt a scream pressing behind her teeth.

Johlmann smiled and looked away. He studied the photographs of the colonel and his secretary. "Ah!" he said speaking to Michael, his cold eyes brightening. "You're an Austrian! From Braugdonau, yes?"

"That's right."

"Well, that's amazing! I know Braugdonau!"

Gaby felt as if she'd just taken a punch to the stomach. Her Luger. So close. Could she get to it before the soldier sprayed her with bullets? She feared she couldn't, so she didn't move.

"I have a cousin in Essen!" Johlmann said, still smiling. "Just west of your hometown. I've been through Braugdonau several times. They have a very fine winter carnival."

"Yes, they do." A skier, he decided.

"Good snow on those mountains. Hard-packed. You don't have to worry about avalanches so much. Thank you, my dear." He returned Gaby's papers to her. She took them and put them away, noting that a couple of other soldiers had wandered closer to have a glimpse of her. Johlmann carefully folded Michael's papers. "I remember the fountain in Braugdonau. You know. Where the statues of the Ice King and Queen are." His teeth flashed. "Yes?"

"I'm afraid you're mistaken." Michael held out his hand for his papers. "There is no fountain in Braugdonau, Herr Johlmann. I think it's time for us to be on our way now."

"Well," Johlmann said with a shrug, "I suppose I am mistaken, after all." He slid the packet into Michael's hand, and Michael was very glad he'd listened to all the details McCarren had given him about the layout and history of Braugdonau. Michael's fingers closed around the papers, but Johlmann wouldn't let the documents go. "I don't have a cousin in Essen, Colonel," he said. "A white lie, and I hope you'll pardon my presumption. But you know, I have been skiing in that area before. Beautiful place. That very famous run about twenty kilometers north of Essen." His smile came back, and it was a horrible happiness. "Surely you know it. The Grandfather. Yes?"

He knows, Michael thought. He smells the British in my skin. Michael felt poised on the edge of a precipice, and beneath him were slavering jaws. Damn it, why hadn't he slid the Luger next to him on the seat? Johlmann was waiting for his answer, his head cocked slightly to one side, the red feather stirring in the breeze.

"Herr Johlmann?" the soldier with the submachine gun said. His voice was nervous. "Herr Johlmann, you'd better—"

"Yes," Michael said. His stomach clenched. "The Grandfather."

Johlmann's smile flicked off. "Oh, no. I'm afraid I meant the Grand*mother*."

"Herr Johlmann!" the soldier shouted. Two other soldiers yelled out, and ran for the trees. The armored car's engine started with a roar. Johlmann looked up. "What the hell is going—" And then he heard the high whine just as Michael did, and he twisted around to see the glint of silver diving toward the roadblock.

Fighter plane, Michael realized. Coming down fast. The soldier with the submachine gun shouted, "Take cover!" and ran for the roadside. Johlmann, sputtering with anger, called, "Wait! Wait, you!" But the soldiers were running for the trees and the armored car was scrambling like an iron roach for cover, and Johlmann cursed and dug into his coat for his pistol as he whirled back to face the false colonel.

But Michael's hand had grown a Luger. As Johlmann's pistol rose, Michael thrust the Luger's barrel into Johlmann's face and pulled the trigger.

There was a *whoosh* like an oncoming avalanche, a chatter of machine-gun bullets from an aircraft's wing guns, and in that instant the sound of the Luger going off was silenced by the larger weapons. Two columns of bullets marched alongside the road, straddling the Mercedes and sending sparks flying, and Heinz Richter Johlmann, ex-Gestapo, staggered back with a single smoking hole in the center of his forehead, just below his jaunty hat. Michael had his papers gripped in his other hand, and as the fighter plane's shadow swept across the earth Johlmann fell to his knees with blood beginning to run down his shock-frozen face. His head sagged forward. His hat, full of gray brains, fell off, and the fighter plane's fierce hot breeze blew the red feather before it like a bloody exclamation mark.

"Krabell!" Michael shouted. The young lieutenant had been about to run for the trees, his driver unable to get the motorcycle's engine started. He turned toward the Mercedes. "This man's been hit!" Michael said. "Get a medic—but first move that damned barricade!"

Krabell and the driver hesitated, wanting to run for cover before the fighter came back for another strafing pass. "Do as I say!" Michael commanded, and the two Germans scrambled to the wooden barricade. They moved it aside, Krabell searching the sky with his goggled eyes, and then Michael heard the deadly whine of the plane coming down for a second attack. "Go!" he told Gaby. She pressed her foot to the floorboard, and the car lunged forward, passing Krabell and the motorcyclist and roaring through the opened barricade. Then the two Germans fled for the trees, beneath which the others had thrown themselves to the ground. As Gaby raced them along the road, Michael glanced back and saw the bright glint of sun on the plane's wings. It was an American aircraft, a P-47 Thunderbolt, and it looked to be headed right for the Mercedes. He saw the fireflash of the machine guns, bullets marching along the road and throwing up gravel. Gaby swerved the car violently to the left, its tires going off the road into grass. There was a *wham!* that Michael felt at the base of his spine, and Gaby fought to keep control of the wheel. We're hit! she thought, but the engine was still roaring, so she kept the speed up. Dust boiled into the car, blinding Michael for a few seconds. When it cleared, Michael saw two shafts of sunlight entering the roof through jagged holes in the metal, and a chunk of the rear windshield the size of his fist had been blown away. Fragments of glass were scattered all over the seat beside him and glittered in the folds of his coat. Gaby saw the glint of sun along the Thunderbolt's wings as the aircraft turned in a tight circle. "Coming back again!" she shouted.

He had not come all this distance to be killed by an American fighter pilot. "There!" he said, grasping Gaby's shoulder and pointing toward an apple orchard on the right.

Gaby spun the wheel, veering the Mercedes across the road and into a flimsy wooden fence that banged the front fender but burst apart to give them passage. She drove past an abandoned hay wagon into the shadows of the orchard, and three seconds later the Thunderbolt zoomed overhead, its bullets chopping branches and white buds from the trees but none of them hitting the Mercedes. Gaby stopped the car and put on the hand brake. Her heart was hammering, her throat scratchy with dust. She looked at the bullet holes in the roof, their exits marked by a hole in the passenger seat and another hole in the floorboard. She felt a vague, dreamy sensation that she thought might be the first cat-feet creepings of shock. Then she closed her eyes and leaned her forehead against the steering wheel.

The plane screamed above them again. No guns were fired this time, and Michael's muscles untensed. He watched the Thunderbolt turn west and dart toward another target, possibly a movement of soldiers or the armored car. The Thunderbolt dove, its guns firing, then it quickly gained altitude and zoomed away, heading west toward the coast.

3

"He's gone," Michael said at last, when he was certain of it. He took a few deep breaths to calm himself, and smelled dust, his own sweat, and sweet apple buds. White blossoms lay all over the car and were still floating down. Gaby coughed, and Michael leaned forward, grasped her shoulder, and pulled her back from the wheel. "Are you all right?" His voice was strained with tension. Gaby nodded, her eyes glazed and watery, and Michael sighed with relief; he'd feared that a bullet had hit her, and if that had happened, the mission was in dire jeopardy. "Yes," she said, regaining some of her strength. "I'm all right. Just dust down my throat." She coughed a few more times to clear it out. What had terrified her most about the encounter was the fact that she'd been at the mercy of God, and unable to shoot back.

"We'd better go. It won't be long before they find out Johlmann was shot by a Luger instead of a machine gun."

Gaby pulled herself together, a simple matter of willpower over scorched nerves. She took the brake off and backed the Mercedes along its path of plowed grass to the road again. She got up on the gravel and drove east. The radiator was making a little tinkling noise but all the gauges indicating that gas, oil, and water were okay. Michael watched the sky with a wolf's undivided attention, but no more planes swept out of the blue. Neither were they being followed, and he assumed—hoped, really—that the soldiers and the second Gestapo man were still in shock themselves. The road unwound beneath the Mercedes's tires, and abruptly the gravel turned to pavement and a sign announced that Paris was eight kilometers ahead. There were no more roadblocks, which relieved both of them, but they passed several truckloads of soldiers going in and out of the city.

And then the road was lined with tall, graceful trees and it widened into an avenue. They passed the last wooden farmhouse and saw the first of many brick and stone houses, then met gray buildings decorated with white statuary like sugar frosting on a cake. Paris gleamed in the sunlight before them, the towers of its cathedrals and monuments glowing like golden needles. Its ornate buildings crowded together much as the structures of any metropolis, but these with the dignity of centuries. The Eiffel Tower stood against a background of drifting clouds as fragile as French lace, and the vaulted roofs of Montmartre were the varied, burnished reds and browns of an artist's palette. The Mercedes crossed the pale green waters of the Seine over a bridge decorated with stone cherubs, and Michael smelled moss and mud-stranded fish. The flow of traffic was heavier once they crossed the Boulevard Berthier, one of the grand avenues that circled the City of Light and was named for Napoleon's marshals, but Gaby was undaunted. She merged into the contest of Citröens, horse wagons, bicyclists, and pedestrians, and most of them gave way before the imposing black staff car.

As Gaby drove through the streets of Paris, one hand on the wheel and the other motioning other vehicles and people out of their path, Michael smelled the aromas of the city: a commingling, heady festival of a thousand scents, from a whiff of smoky perfume through the croissants and coffee of a sidewalk café to the grassy manure being raked by a street cleaner. Michael was near being overwhelmed by scents, as he was when he visited any city. The smells of life, of human activity, were sharp and startling here, none of those damp, foggy odors he associated with London. He saw many people talking, but few smiling. Fewer still were laughing. And that was because there were German soldiers on the streets, carrying rifles, and German officers drinking espresso in the cafés. They reclined in their chairs with the relaxed postures of conquerors. Nazi banners flew from many of the buildings, unfurled in the breeze over the upraised arms and imploring faces of marble, French-carved statues. German soldiers directed traffic, and some streets were blocked by barricades with signs marked ACHTUNG! EINTRITT VERBOTEN! Adding insult to injury by not using the native language, Michael thought. No wonder so many faces scowled at the Mercedes as it swept past.

Compounding the traffic problems were many laboring, swastika-emblazoned trucks, creeping along and backfiring in the midst of bicyclists like bomb blasts. Michael saw several troop trucks, loaded with soldiers, and even a couple of tanks pulled over to the side, their crews sunning themselves and smoking cigarettes. The whole picture said that the Germans believed they were here to stay, and while the French could go about their daily lives it was the conquerors who kept the reins tight. He saw a group of young soldiers flirting with girls, a stiff-backed officer getting his boots shined by a little boy, another officer shouting in German at a waiter who frantically mopped up a carafe of spilled white wine. Michael sat back in his seat, drawing in all the sights, sounds, and aromas, and he felt a heavy shadow over the City of Light. The Mercedes slowed, and Gaby hit the horn to hurry a few bicycling citizens out of the way. Michael smelled horseflesh, and he looked to his left at a military policeman astride a horse that wore blinders with Nazi symbols on them. The man saluted.

Michael nodded absently and wished he had that bastard alone in the forest for one minute.

Gaby drove east on the Boulevard des Batignolles, through an area crowded with apartment buildings and rococo houses. They stayed on that boulevard, crossing the Avenue de Clinchy and then turning north. Gaby turned right onto the Rue Quenton, and they entered a district where the streets were made of rough brown paving stones and clothes hung on lines across windows. The buildings here were painted in faded pastels, some of their façades cracked and the ancient clay bricks exposed like yellow ribs.

Here the bicyclists were fewer, there were no sidewalk cafés or street-corner Van Goghs. The structures seemed to lean drunkenly against each other, as if in forlorn support, and even the air smelled to Michael of bitter wine. Shadows held figures who watched the black car glide past, their eyes dead as counterfeit coins. The Mercedes's breeze stirred old newspapers from the gutters, and their yellowed pages drifted over the littered sidewalks.

Gaby drove fast through these streets, hardly pausing at the blind intersections. She turned left, then right, then left again a few blocks ahead. Michael saw a crooked sign: RUE LAFARGE. "We've arrived," Gaby said, and she slowed down and blinked the headlights.

Two men, both middle-aged, unlatched a doorway and threw it open. It led into a cobblestoned alley just a few inches wider than the Mercedes, and Michael braced for a scrape but Gaby entered the alley with clearance on either side. The two men closed the doorway behind them. Gaby continued up the alley and into a green garage with a sagging roof. Then she said, "Get out," and cut the engine. Michael did. A man with a brown, seamed face and white hair strode into the garage. "Follow me, please," he said in French, and began to walk rapidly away. Michael followed, and glanced back to see Gaby unlocking the Mercedes's trunk and removing a brown suitcase. She closed the trunk, then the garage door, and one of the first two men locked a chain and padlock and pocketed the key.

"Hurry, please," the white-haired man urged Michael, his voice pleasant but firm. Michael's jackboots clattered loudly on the cobblestones, the noise echoing in the silence. Around him, the windows of the crooked buildings remained shuttered. The white-haired man, who had the thick shoulders and arms of a heavy laborer, unlatched an iron gate with spear tips on the top, and Michael followed him across a small rose garden into the back door of a building as blue as a robin's egg. A narrow corridor stretched before them, and a set of rickety stairs. They went up to the second floor. Another door was opened, and the white-haired man motioned him in. Michael entered a room that had a carpet of intertwined, multicolored rags and smelled strongly of fresh bread and boiled onions.

"Welcome to our home," someone said, and Michael found himself looking at a small, frail old woman with snowy hair pulled back into a long braid. She wore a faded blue dress and a red-checked apron. Behind her round glasses she had dark brown eyes that took in all and revealed nothing. She smiled, her heart-shaped face folding into a mass of wrinkles and her teeth the color of weak tea. "Take off your clothes, please."

"My . . . clothes?"

"Yes. That disgusting uniform. Please remove it."

Gaby came in, escorted by the man who'd locked the garage. The old woman glanced at her, and Michael saw the woman's face tighten. "We were told to expect two men."

"She's all right," Michael said. "McCarren—"

"No names," the old woman interrupted crisply. "We were told to expect two men. A driver and a passenger. Why is it not so?" Her eyes, as dark as pistol barrels, returned to Gaby.

"A change in plans," Gaby told her. "I decided to—"

"Changed plans are flawed plans. Who are *you* to decide such things?"

"I said she's all right," Michael told the old woman, and this time he took the power of her stare. The two men had positioned themselves behind him, and Michael felt sure they had guns. One on the left, one on the right; an elbow in each of their faces if the guns came out. "I'll vouch for her," Michael said.

"Then who's to vouch for you, Green Eyes?" the old woman asked. "This is not the professional way." She looked back and forth from Michael to Gaby, and her gaze lingered on the girl. "Ah!" she decided with a nod. "You love him, eh?"

"Certainly not!" Gaby's face flushed crimson.

"Well, maybe it's called something else these days, then." She smiled again, but thinly. "Love has always been a four-letter word. Green Eyes, I told you to take off that uniform."

"If I'm going to be shot, I'd rather it be done while my pants are on."

The old woman laughed huskily. "I think you're the type of man who does most of his shooting with his pants *off*." She waved a hand at him. "Just do it. No one's going to be killing anybody. Not today, at least."

Michael removed his overcoat, and one of the men accepted it and began to rip the lining out. The other man took Gaby's suitcase, put it on a table, and unlatched it. He started rummaging through the civilian clothes she'd brought along. The old woman snatched the Stalingrad medal off Michael's chest and examined it as she held it beneath a lamp. "This trash wouldn't fool a blind tinsmith!" she said with a sharp laugh.

"It's a real medal," Gaby answered coolly.

"Oh? And how do you know that, my little valentine?"

"I know," Gaby said, "because I took it off the corpse after I slit his throat."

"Good for you." The old woman put the medal aside. "Bad for him. You take off your uniform, too, valentine. Hurry, I'm not getting any younger."

Michael went ahead with it. He stripped down to his underwear, and Gaby undressed as well. "You're a hairy bastard," the old woman observed. "What kind of beast was your father?" She said to one of the other men, "Bring him his new clothes and shoes." He went away into another room, and the old woman picked up Michael's Luger and sniffed the barrel. She wrinkled her nose, finding the odor of a recent shot. "You have any trouble on the road?"

"A small inconvenience," Michael said.

"I don't think I want to hear any more." She picked up the silver pocket watch, clicked the winding stem twice, and looked at the cyanide capsule when the back popped open. She grunted softly, closed the watch, and returned it to him. "You might want to keep that. Knowing the time is very important these days."

The white-haired man returned with a bundle of clothes and a pair of scuffed black shoes. "We got your sizes over the radio," the woman said. "But we were expecting two men." She motioned toward the contents of Gaby's suitcase.

"You brought your own clothes, then? That's good. We don't have civilian papers for you. Too easily traced in the city. If either of you are captured . . ." She looked at Michael, her eyes hard. "I expect you to know what time it is." She waited until Michael nodded his understanding. "You won't see your uniforms or the car again. You'll be supplied with bicycles. If you feel you must have a car, we'll talk about it. We don't have a lot of money here, but we have a fortune in friends. You'll call me Camille, and you will talk only to me. You're not to address either of these two gentlemen." She motioned toward the Frenchmen, who were gathering up the German uniforms and putting them in a basket with a lid. "Keep your pistol," she told Michael. "Those are hard to come by." She stared at Gaby for a few seconds, as if evaluating her, then at Michael. "I'm sure you both have had experience in this. I don't care anything about who you are, or what you've done; the important thing is that a lot of lives depend on your being smart—and *careful*—while you're in Paris. We'll help you as much as we can, but if you're captured we don't know you. Is that clear?"

"Perfectly," Michael answered.

"Good. If you'd like to rest awhile, your room is through there." Camille nodded toward a corridor and a doorway. "I was just making some onion soup, if you'd like a taste."

Michael picked up the shoes and bundle of clothes from the table where they'd been set, and Gaby closed her suitcase and hefted it. Camille said, "You children behave yourselves," and then she turned away and walked into a small kitchen where a pot boiled on a cast-iron stove.

"After you," Michael said, and followed Gaby along the corridor to their new quarters. The door creaked on its hinges as Gaby pushed it open. Inside was a four-poster bed with a white quilt and a more somber cot with a green blanket. The room was cramped but clean, with a skylight and a window that looked out over the drunken pastel buildings.

Gaby put her suitcase down on the four-poster bed with solid authority. Michael looked at the cot, and he thought he heard his back groan. He went to the window and slid it open, getting a lungful of Paris air. He was still in his underwear, and so was Gaby, but there seemed no need to hurry about anything, including getting dressed—or undressed, as the case might be. Gaby lay down on the bed and covered herself with a crisp linen sheet. She watched him, framed against the window; she let her gaze play over his muscles, his sleek back, and long, dark-haired legs. "I'm going to rest for a while," she announced, the sheet up to her chin.

"Be my guest."

"There's not room for two in this bed," she said.

"Of course there isn't," he agreed. He glanced quickly at her, saw her long black hair, unpinned now that it was out from under the cap, splayed across the goosedown pillow like an intricate fan.

"Not even if I squeezed over," Gaby continued. "So you'll have to sleep on the cot."

"Yes, I will."

She shifted her position, the goosedown mattress settling beneath her. The sheets were cool and smelled faintly of cloves: an aroma Michael had detected as soon as they entered the room. Gaby hadn't realized how tired she was; she'd been up at five o'clock, and her sleep had been restless at best. Why had she come with this man? she asked herself. She hardly knew him. *Didn't* know him, really. Who was he to her? Her eyes had drifted shut; now she opened them and found him standing over the bed, staring down at her. So close it made her skin tingle.

Her bare leg had slipped out from under the sheet. Michael ran his fingers along her ankle, raising chill bumps. Then he gently grasped her ankle and slid her leg back under the fragrant linen. She thought for an instant that his fingers had burned their impressions on her flesh. "Sleep well," he said, and he put on a pair of brown pants that had patches on both knees. He started to go out, and Gaby sat up with the sheet clutched to her breasts. "Where are you going?"

"To get a bowl of soup," Michael answered. "I'm hungry." And then he turned and left, shutting the door quietly behind him.

Gaby lay back down, but now she couldn't sleep. A heat

pulsed at her center, and her nerves were jangled. It was the remainder of their encounter with the fighter plane, she decided. Who wouldn't be unable to rest after something like that? They were lucky to be alive, and tomorrow . . .

Well, tomorrow would take care of itself. Like all tomorrows did.

She reached down, beside the bed, and pulled the cot a few inches closer. He'd never know. Then, satisfied and growing drowsy in the embrace of goose down, Gaby closed her eyes. A few minutes passed, in which the shadows of airplanes and the sounds of gunfire played through her mind. Those things faded, like bad dreams in daylight.

She slept.

—— 4 ——

Michael dismounted, and the springs mewled softly. He leaned the rusted Peugeot bicycle against a street lamp at the intersection of the Rue de Belleville and the Rue des Pyrenees, and he checked his pocket watch in the yellow glow. Nine-forty-three. Camille had said the curfew began at eleven o'clock sharp. After that time the German military police—the rough, hard-nosed bastards—roamed the streets. He kept his head down, studying his watch, as Gaby slowly pedaled past him, going southeast on the Pyrenees. The darkness took her.

Apartment buildings, most of them once elegant homes decorated with statuary, stood around him, furtive lights gleaming in some of their windows. The avenue was quiet but for a few velo taxis and a horse-drawn carriage or two. On their ride from Montmartre through the twisting streets, Michael and Gaby had seen many German soldiers, strolling the boulevards in rowdy groups or sitting in sidewalk cafés like drunken lords. They'd seen, as well, a number of troop transport trucks and armored cars scuttling busily over the paved stones. But Michael and Gaby, in their new disguises, attracted no attention. Michael wore his patched pants, a blue shirt, and a dark brown corduroy coat that had seen better days; on his feet were the scuffed black shoes, and on his head a brown cap. Gaby wore black slacks, a yellow blouse, and a bulky gray sweater that hid the bulge of her Luger. They wore the outfits of regular, struggling Paris citizens, whose main concern was getting food on the table rather than the dictates of European fashion.

Michael gave her a moment or two more, then he got on his bicycle and pedaled after her, between the aged and sad stone beauties. Much of the statuary was broken, he saw. Some of it had been wrestled up from its moorings and stolen away, probably to grace Nazi dwellings. Michael pedaled at a slow, steady pace. A carriage went past, heading in the opposite direction, the horse's hooves clopping on the pavement. Michael came to the sign marking the Rue Tobas, and he swung the bicycle to the right.

The buildings here were crowded close, and there were few lights. This district, once wealthy, had the air of decay and dissolution. Some of the windows were broken and mended with tape, and much of the carved masonry had either collapsed or been removed. Michael thought of a ballet dancer whose legs had become bloated and thick with veins. Headless statues stood in a fountain that held bits of trash and old newspapers instead of water. A stone wall screamed a black Nazi swastika and the painted words DEUTSCHLAND SIEGT AN ALLEN FRONTEN—"Germany Victorious on all Fronts." We'll soon see, Michael thought as he pedaled past.

He knew this street, had studied it well on the map. Coming up on the right was a gray building—once a stately home—with broken stone steps sweeping up from the curb. He knew this building, too. He kept pedaling and quickly glanced up. On the second floor light crept through the blinds of a corner window. Apartment number eight. Adam was in that room. And Michael didn't look, but he was aware of the gray stone building across the street, too, where the Gestapo had their watchmen. No pedestrians were on the street, and Gaby had already pedaled on ahead to wait for him. Michael moved past Adam's building, sensing he was being watched.

Possibly from the roof of the building opposite Adam's. Possibly from a darkened window. This was a mouse trap, Michael thought. Adam was the cheese, and the cats were licking their whiskers.

He stopped pedaling and let the bicycle coast across the cracked pavement. His peripheral vision caught a flare of light to his left. Someone standing in a doorway, holding a match to a cigarette. The match went out, and smoke plumed. Meow, Michael thought. He kept going, head down, and he saw an alley coming up on his right. He guided the bike toward the alley, turned into it, pedaled about twenty feet farther, and then stopped. He leaned the Peugeot against a wall of gray bricks and walked back to the alley entrance, facing the Rue Tobas, then crouched down on his haunches beside a group of garbage cans and stared across the street at the doorway where the Gestapo man stood smoking his cigarette. A tiny red circle waxed and waned in the night. Michael saw the man, clad in a dark overcoat and hat, outlined in a faint blue haze. Seven or eight minutes crept by. A crack of light drew Michael's attention, and he looked up at a window on the third floor. Someone had just drawn aside a black curtain perhaps three or four inches; the curtain was held open for only a few seconds, then fell back into place again and the light was gone.

Michael reasoned that several teams of Gestapo men kept Adam's apartment under watch all hours of the day and night. From that third-floor surveillance post they had a clear view of the Rue Tobas, and could see anyone going in or coming out of Adam's building. They probably had listening devices in Adam's apartment as well, and certainly had his telephone tapped. So the contact would have to get a message to Adam along his walk to work; but how was that going to be possible with the Gestapo dogging his trail?

Michael stood up and stepped back into the alley, still watching the cigarette smoker. The man didn't see him; his attention drifted back and forth along the street in a relaxed, even bored, vigilance. And then Michael took two more backward steps, and he smelled it.

Frightened sweat.

Someone was behind him. Someone very quiet, but now Michael could hear a faint, raspy breathing.

And suddenly a knife blade was jabbed against his spine. "Give me your money," a man's voice said in French with a thick German accent.

A thief, Michael thought. An alley prowler. He had no wallet to surrender, and any struggle would certainly crash the garbage cans over and cause the Gestapo man to take interest. He decided what to do in the passing of an instant. He drew himself up to full height and said softly in German, "Do you want to die?"

There was a pause. Then: "I said . . . give me your . . ." The voice cracked. The thief was scared to death.

"Take the knife away from my back," Michael said calmly, "or in three seconds I'll kill you."

One second passed. Two. Michael tensed, ready to whirl around.

The knife's pressure against his spine was gone.

He heard the thief running, back along the alley toward its other entrance on the Rue de la Chine. His first thought was to let the man go, but an idea sparked in his mind and grew incandescent. He turned and ran after the thief; the man was fast, but not fast enough. Before the thief could get to the Rue de la Chine, Michael reached out, grabbed the tail of his flagging, dirty overcoat and almost yanked him out of his shoes. The man—all five feet two inches of him—spun around with a muffled curse and swung the knife without aiming. The edge of Michael's hand cracked against his wrist, knocking the blade out of his spasming fingers. Then he picked the little man up and slammed him against the gray brick wall.

The thief's eyes bulged, pale blue under a mop of dirty brown hair. Michael held his collar and clamped a hand over the man's mouth and grizzled chin. "Silence," he whispered. Off in the alley somewhere, a cat screeched and ran for cover. "Don't struggle," Michael said, still speaking German. "You're not going anywhere. I want to ask you some questions, and I want to hear the truth from you. Do you understand?"

The thief, terrified and shivering, nodded.

"All right, I'm going to take my hand away from your mouth. You shout once, and I'll break your neck." He shook the man hard, for emphasis, then dropped the hand away. The thief made a soft moaning sound. "You're German?" Michael asked. The thief nodded. "A deserter?" A pause; then a nod. "How long have you been in Paris?"

"Six months. Please . . . please let me go. I didn't stick you, did I?"

He'd been able to hide in Paris, surrounded by Germans, for six months. A good sign, Michael thought. "Don't whine. What else do you do besides try to stick people? You steal bread from markets, maybe a few pieces of fruit here and there, a pie or two off a shelf?"

"Yes, yes. All that. Please . . . I'm no good as a soldier. I've got weak nerves. Please, just let me go. All right?"

"No. Do you pick pockets?"

"Some. When I have to." The thief's eyes narrowed. "Wait. Who are you? Not military police. What's your game, huh?"

Michael ignored him. "Are you any good at picking pockets?"

The thief grinned, a false show of toughness. Under his grizzle and all that street grime, he was perhaps in his mid to late forties. The Germans were indeed scraping the bottom of the barrel for soldiers. "I'm still alive, aren't I? Now who the hell are *you?*" His eyes glittered with a thought. "Ah! Of course. The underground, yes?"

"I'll ask the questions. Are you a Nazi?"

The man laughed harshly. He spat a wad of phlegm onto the alley stones. "Are you a corpse fucker?"

Michael gave a faint smile. Maybe he and the thief weren't on the same side, but they shared sentiments. He lowered the man to his feet, but kept his hand clenched in the grimy collar. Up at the Rue de la Chine side of the alley, Gaby turned in on her bicycle. "Hey!" she whispered urgently. "What's wrong?"

"I've met someone," Michael said, "who may be useful to us."

"Me? Useful to the underground? Ha!" The little man

pushed at Michael's hand, and Michael unclenched his fingers. "You two can rot in hell, for all I care!"

"If I were you, I'd keep my voice down." Michael motioned back toward the Rue Tobas. "A Gestapo man is standing across the street over there. There might be a whole nest of them in that building. I don't think you'd want their attention, would you?"

"Neither would you!" the man retorted. "So where does that leave us?"

"I have a job for a pickpocket," Michael said.

"*What?*" Gaby had gotten off her bicycle. "What are you talking about?"

"I need some nimble fingers," Michael went on. He stared forcefully at the thief. "Not to pick a pocket, but to put something *into* a pocket."

"You're crazy!" the thief said, with a sneer that made his ugly, heavy-browed face even uglier. "Maybe I ought to call for the Gestapo myself, and be done with you!"

"Be my guest," Michael offered.

The thief scowled, looked from Michael to Gaby and back again. His shoulders slumped. "Oh, to hell with it," he said.

"When's the last time you ate?"

"I don't know. Yesterday, I guess. Why? Are you serving up beer and sausages?"

"No. Onion soup." Michael heard Gaby gasp as she realized what he was about to propose. "Are you on foot?"

"My bike's around the corner." He motioned with a thumb toward the Rue de la Chine. "I work the alleys around here."

"You're going to take a trip with us. We'll be riding on either side of you, and if you call to a soldier or otherwise make any difficulties we'll kill you."

"Why should I go anywhere with you? You'll probably kill me anyway."

"Maybe we will," Michael said, "and maybe we won't. But at least you'll die with some food in your belly. Besides . . . we might be able to work out a financial arrangement." He saw the interest flare in the man's sunken eyes, and he knew he'd tripped the right switch. "What's your name?"

The thief paused, still wary. He looked up and down the

alley, as if fearful of being overheard. Then: "Mausenfeld. Arno Mausenfeld. Ex–field kitchen cook."

Maus, Michael thought. The German word for . . . "I'll call you Mouse," he decided. "Let's get on our way before curfew."

───────────── **5** ─────────────

Enraged, Camille no longer resembled a sweet, elderly lady. Her eyes glinted with red, and her face was inflamed from the roots of her snowy hair to the point of her chin. "Bringing a *German* to my home!" she shrieked, in the throes of a fit. "I'll have you executed as a traitor for this!" She glared at Michael, and looked at Arno Mausenfeld as if he were something that she'd just scraped off the sole of her shoe. "You! Get out! I'm not running a shelter for Nazi bums!"

"Madam, I'm not a Nazi," Mouse replied, with stern dignity. He drew himself up as tall as he could, but he was still three inches shorter than Camille. "Neither am I a bum."

"Get out! Get out before I—" Camille whirled away, ran to a dresser, and opened it. Her hand came out with an old, heavy Lebel revolver. "I'll blow your dirty brains out!" she hollered, all her Gallic graciousness gone, and she aimed the pistol at Mouse's head.

Michael caught her wrist, tilted the pistol up, and scooped it from her grip. "None of that, now," he scolded. "You'll blow your own hand off with this antique."

"You *deliberately* brought this Nazi to my home!" Camille raged, showing her teeth. "You've compromised our security! *Why?*"

"Because he can help me do my job," Michael told her. Mouse wandered into the kitchen, his clothes even more wretched and filthy in the light. "I need someone to get a message to the man I'm after. It needs to be done fast, without attracting a lot of attention. I need a pickpocket—and there he is." He nodded toward the German.

"You're out of your mind!" Camille said. "Utterly insane! Oh my God, I've got a madman under my roof!"

"I am not!" Mouse replied. He stared at Camille, his heavily lined face dark with dirt. "The doctors said I definitely am not a madman." He picked up the soup-pot lid and inhaled. "Nice," he said. "But bland. If you have paprika, I could spice it up for you."

"Doctors?" Gaby asked, frowning. "What doctors?"

"The doctors at the nuthouse," Mouse went on. He pushed his hair out of his eyes with dirty fingers and then dipped those same fingers into the pot. He took a taste of onion soup. "Oh, yes," he said. "This could use some paprika. Possibly a touch of garlic, too."

"What *nuthouse?*" Camille's voice was shrill, and it quavered like an out-of-tune flute.

"The one I escaped from six months ago," Mouse said. He picked up a ladle and scooped out some soup, then slurped noisily. The others were silent, still watching him; Camille's mouth was open, as if she were about to let loose a dish-rattling scream. "It was a place over on the west side of the city," Mouse said. "For crack-ups and people who'd shot themselves in the foot. I told them when they signed me up that I had weak nerves. Did they listen?" Another noisy slurp of soup, and the liquid ran down his chin to his shirt. "No, they didn't listen. They said I'd be in a field kitchen, and that I wouldn't see any action. But did the bastards say anything about the air raids? No! Not a word!" He took a mouthful of soup and sloshed it around between his cheeks. "You know Hitler paints that mustache on, don't you?" he asked. "It's the truth! That cockless bastard can't grow a mustache. He wears women's clothes at night, too. Ask anybody."

"Oh, God save us! A Nazi lunatic!" Camille moaned softly, her face now matching the color of her hair. She staggered back, and Gaby caught her before she fell.

"This could stand a whole clove of garlic," Mouse said, and smacked his lips. "It would be a masterpiece!"

"Now what are you going to do?" Gaby asked Michael.

"You'll have to get rid of him." She glanced quickly at the revolver he held.

For one of the few times in his life Michael Gallatin felt like a fool. He'd grasped at a straw, he realized, and he'd come up with a bent twig. Mouse was happily drinking soup from the ladle and looking around the kitchen—obviously familiar territory to him. A bomb-shocked German escapee from a mental hospital was a fragile lever on which to move closer to Adam; but what else did he have? Damn it! Michael thought. Why didn't I let this madman go? There was no telling what might happen if—

"You said something about a financial arrangement, I believe," Mouse said, and put the ladle down into the pot. "What might you have in mind?"

"Coins on your eyes when we float your body down the Seine!" Camille shouted, but Gaby shushed her.

Michael hesitated. Was the man useless, or not? Maybe no one but a lunatic would dare try what he was about to propose. But they'd only get one chance, and if Mouse made a mistake they might all pay with their lives. "I work for the British Secret Service," he said quietly. Mouse kept poking around the kitchen, but Camille gasped and almost swooned again. "The Gestapo is watching an agent of ours. I have to get a message to him."

"The Gestapo," Mouse repeated. "Mean bastards. They're everywhere, you know."

"Yes, I do know. That's why I need your help."

Mouse looked at him, and blinked. "I'm *German*."

"I know that, too. But you're not a Nazi, and you don't want to go back to the hospital, do you?"

"No. Of course not." He inspected a pan and tapped its bottom. "The food there is atrocious."

"And I don't think you want to continue your life as a thief, either," Michael went on. "What I'd like for you to do will take maybe two seconds—if you're any good as a pickpocket. If not, the Gestapo will pick you up right on the street. And if that happens, I'll have to kill you."

Mouse stared at Michael, his eyes startlingly blue against his grimy, seamed face. He put the pan aside.

"I'll give you a piece of folded paper," Michael said.

"That paper should be placed in the coat pocket of a man I'll describe to you and point out to you on the street. It'll have to be done fast and appear as if you simply bumped against him. Two seconds; no longer. There'll be a team of Gestapo men following our agent, possibly watching him along the route he walks. Anything that looks slightly suspicious is going to draw them down on you. My friend"—he nodded at Gaby—"and I will be close by. If things go wrong, we'll try to help you. But my first loyalty is to our agent. If that means I have to shoot you along with the Gestapo, I won't hesitate."

"Of that I'm certain," Mouse said, and plucked an apple from a clay bowl. He examined it for worms, then bit into it. "You're from Britain, uh?" he asked between crunches. "My congratulations. Your German is very good." He glanced around the tidy kitchen. "This isn't what I expected the underground to be. I thought it was a bunch of Frenchmen hiding in sewers."

"We leave the sewers for your kind!" Camille shot back, still feisty.

"*My* kind," Mouse repeated, and shook his head. "Oh, we've lived in the sewers since 1938, madam. We've been force-fed shit so long we began to enjoy the taste. I've been in the army for two years, four months, and eleven days. A great patriotic duty, they said! A chance to expand the Reich and create a new world for all right-thinking Germans! Only the pure of heart and the strong of blood . . . well, you know the rest." He grimaced; he'd bitten into a sour spot. "Not all Germans are Nazis," he said quietly. "But the Nazis have got the loudest voices and the biggest clubs, and they've succeeded in beating the sense out of my country. So yes, I *do* know the sewers, madam. I know them very well indeed." His eyes looked scorched by inner heat, and he tossed the apple core into a basket. His gaze returned to Michael. "But I'm still a German, sir. Maybe I *am* insane, but I love my homeland—perhaps I love a memory of my homeland, instead of the reality. So why should I help you do anything that might kill my countrymen?"

"I'm asking you to help me prevent *my* countrymen from

being killed. Possibly by the thousands, if I can't reach the man I'm after."

"Oh, yes." Mouse nodded. "Of course this has to do with the invasion."

"God strike us all!" Camille moaned. "We're ruined!"

"Every soldier knows the invasion is coming," Mouse said. "It's no secret. Only no one knows—yet—when it will be, or where. But it's inevitable, and even us dumb field kitchen cooks know that. One thing's for sure: once the Brits and the Americans start marching over the coast, no damned Atlantic Wall's going to stop them. They'll keep going all the way to Berlin; I just pray to God they'll get there before the damned Russians do!"

Michael let that comment pass. The Russians, of course, had been savagely fighting their way west since 1943.

"My wife and two children are in Berlin." Mouse sighed softly and ran a hand across his face. "My eldest son . . . was nineteen when he went to war. On the Eastern Front, no less. They couldn't even scrape enough of him up to send back in a box. They sent me his medal. I put it on the wall, where it shines very pretty." His eyes had become moist; now they hardened again. "If the Russians get to Berlin, my wife and children . . . well, that won't happen. The Russians will be stopped, long before they get to Germany." The way he said that made it clear he didn't believe his own conviction.

"You might help to shorten this war by doing what I ask," Michael told him. "There's a lot of territory between the coast and Berlin."

Mouse said nothing; he just stood staring into space, his hands hanging at his sides.

"How much money do you want?" Michael prodded.

Mouse was silent. Then he said softly, "I want to go home."

"All right. How much money do you need for that?"

"No. Not money." He looked at Michael. "I want you to get me to Berlin. To my wife and children. I've been trying to find a way out of Paris ever since I escaped from the hospital. I couldn't get two miles out of the city before a security patrol picked me up. You need a pickpocket, and I need an escort. That's what I'll agree to."

"Impossible!" Gaby spoke up. "It's out of the question!"

"Wait." Michael's voice was firm. He had been planning on finding a route to Berlin anyway, to contact agent Echo and find the big-game hunter who'd had the Countess Margritta murdered. The photograph of Harry Sandler, smiling as he stood atop the carcass of a lion, had never been very far from Michael's mind. "How would I get you there?"

"That's your job," Mouse said. "Mine is putting a piece of paper in a man's pocket. I'll do it—and I'll do it with no mistakes—but I want to go to Berlin."

Now it was Michael's turn for silent deliberation. Getting himself to Berlin was one thing; escorting an escapee from a lunatic asylum was quite another. His instincts told him to say no, and they were rarely wrong. But this was a matter of fate, and Michael had little choice. "Agreed," he said.

"You're mad, too!" Camille wailed. "As mad as he is!" But her voice wasn't as stricken as it had been before, because she recognized the method in his madness.

"We go tomorrow morning," Michael said. "Our agent leaves his building at thirty-two minutes after eight. It takes him approximately ten minutes to walk his route. I'll work out on the map where I want the job done; in the meantime, you'll stay here tonight."

Camille started to roar with indignation again, but there was no point in it. "He'll sleep on the floor!" she snapped. "He won't dirty my linens!"

"I'll sleep right here." Mouse motioned to the kitchen floor. "I might get hungry tonight, anyway."

Camille took the revolver back from Michael. "If I hear any noise in here, I'll shoot to kill!"

"In that case, madam," Mouse said, "it's best to tell you that I snore."

It was time to get some sleep. They all had a busy day tomorrow. Michael started for the bedroom, but Mouse said, "Hey! Hold on! Which coat pocket do you want the paper in? Outside or inside?"

"Outside will do. Inside would be better."

"Inside it is, then." Mouse took another apple from the

bowl and crunched into it. He glanced at Camille. "Anyone going to offer me some soup, or must I starve to death before morning?"

She made a noise that might've been a snarl, threw open a cupboard, and got a bowl for him.

In the bedroom Michael took off his cap and shirt and sat on the edge of the bed, studying a map of Paris by the light of a white candle. Another candle was lighted on the other side of the bed, and Michael looked up at Gaby's shadow as she undressed. He smelled the apple-wine fragrance of her hair as she brushed it back. It should be done equidistantly between Adam's building and his office, he decided as he studied the map again. He found the spot he was looking for, and he marked it with his fingernail. Then he looked up once more, at the woman's shadow.

He felt the fine down of hair stir from the back of his neck along his spine. Tomorrow was going to be a walk on the edge of danger; perhaps an encounter with death. His heart was beating harder. He watched Gaby's shadow as she peeled off her slacks. Tomorrow might bring death and destruction, but tonight they were alive, and . . .

He smelled the faint aroma of cloves as Gaby drew back the sheet and slipped into bed. He folded the map of Paris and put it aside.

Michael turned and looked at her. Candlelight glittered in her sapphire eyes, and her black hair lay over the pillow, the sheet barely up over her breasts. She looked back at him and felt her heart flutter; then she lowered the sheet, just a fraction of an inch, and Michael saw and recognized the invitation.

He leaned over her, and he kissed her. Lightly at first, on the corners of her lips. And then her lips parted and he kissed her deeply, flame to flame. As their kiss went on, moist and hot, he could almost hear the steam drifting from their pores. Her lips tried to keep him, but he pulled away and stared at her. "You don't know anything about me," he said softly. "After tomorrow we might never see each other again."

"I know . . . I want to be yours tonight," Gaby said. "And tonight I want you to be mine."

She drew him to her, and he pulled the sheet aside. She was naked underneath, her body taut with anticipation. Her arms went around his neck, and they kissed while he reached down, unbuckled his belt, and undressed. As the candles threw their shadows large upon the walls, their bodies pressed together, embraced in the goosedown mattress. She felt his tongue flick across her throat, a touch that was so delicate yet so intense it made her gasp, and then his head slid downward and his tongue swirled between her breasts. She gripped his hair as his tongue moved in slow, precise circles. A fiery pulse beat inside her, growing hotter and stronger. Michael felt her tremble, the taste of her sweet flesh in his mouth, and he grazed his lips down her stomach, down to the dark curls between her thighs.

His tongue in that place, moving as it did, made Gaby arch her body and clench her teeth to stifle a moan. He opened her like a pink flower, his fingers gentle. His tongue slowly traveled up and down the route Gaby had led him to. She gasped as he caressed her, starting to whisper his name, but realized she didn't know it and never would. But this moment, this sensation, this joy; these things were enough. Her eyes were moist, and so was her yearning center. Michael kissed the hollow of her throat with burning lips; he shifted his position and eased himself smoothly into her.

He was large, but her body made room for him. He filled her with velvet heat, and her hands on his shoulders felt the muscles move beneath the skin. Michael balanced on his palms and toes above her, and thrust himself deep within, his hips moving to a slow rhythm that made Gaby gasp and moan. Their bodies entwined and thrust together, pulled apart and pressed together once again; Michael's sinuous, strong movements molded Gaby's body like hot clay, and she yielded her bones to his muscles. His nerves, his flesh, his blood sang with a symphony of sensations, aromas, and textures. The scent of cloves drifted up from the tangled sheet, and Gaby's body breathed the heady, pungent aroma of passion. Her hair was damp, beads of moisture glistening between her breasts. Her eyes were dreamy, fixed on an inner focus, and her legs clasped around his hips to hold him deep inside as he rocked her, gently. Then he was on his back and she above him, her body poised on his hardness, her eyes closed, her black hair cascading around her shoulders like a waterfall. He lifted his hips off the bed, and her body with him, and she leaned forward against his chest and whispered three soft words that had no meaning but the ecstasy of the moment.

Michael cupped his body around hers, and she threw her hands back to grip the iron bedframe as they first strained against each other, then moved in a delicate unison. It became a dance of passion, a ballet of silk and iron, and at its zenith Gaby cried out, heedless of who might hear, and Michael let his control go. His spine arched, his body held in her pulsing grip, and the pressure flooded out of him in several bursts that left him dazed.

Gaby was drifting, a white ship with billowing sails and a strong hand on the wheel. She relaxed into his embrace, and they lay together, breathing as one, as a distant cathedral chimed the midnight hour.

Sometime before dawn, Michael brushed the hair away from her face and kissed her forehead. He stood up, careful so as not to awaken her, and he walked to the window. He looked out over Paris, as the sun showed a faint edge of pink against night's dark blue. It was already light over Stalin's land, and the sun's burning eye rose over Hitler's territory. This was the beginning of the day he'd come from Wales for; within twenty-four hours he would have the information or he would be dead. He breathed the morning air and smelled the scent of Gaby's flesh on him.

Live free, he thought. A last command from a dead king.

The cool, brisk air reminded him of a forest and a white palace, a long time ago. The memories stirred a fever that would never be quenched; not by a woman, not by love, not by any city built by the hand of man.

His skin prickled, as if by hundreds of needles. The wildness was on him, fast and powerful. Black hair rose across his back in bands, ran down the backs of his thighs, and streaked his calves. He smelled the odor of the wolf, wafting from his flesh. Bands of black hair, some of it mingled with gray, ran across his arms, burst from the backs of his hands, and quivered, sleek and alive. He lifted his right hand and watched it change, finger by finger; the black hair rippled across it, circling his wrist, tendrils of hair running up his forearm. His hand was changing shape, the fingers drawing inward with little cracklings of bone and cartilage that shot pain through his nerves and brought a sheen of sweat on his face. Two fingers almost disappeared, and where they'd been were hooked, dark-nailed claws. His spine began to bow, with small clicking sounds and the pressure of squeezed vertebrae.

"What is it?"

Michael dropped his hand to his side, pinning his arm there. His heart jumped. He turned toward her. Gaby had sat up in bed, her eyes puffy with sleep and the aftermath of passion. "What's wrong?" she asked, her voice groggy but carrying a note of tension.

"Nothing," he said. His own voice was a raspy whisper. "It's all right. Go back to sleep." She blinked at him and lay back down, the sheet around her legs. The bands of black hair on Michael's back and thighs faded, returning to the pliant, damp flesh. Gaby said, "Please hold me. All right?"

He waited another few seconds. Then he lifted his right hand. The fingers were human again; the last of the wolf's hair was rippling from his wrist along his forearm, vanishing into his skin with needle jabs. He drew another deep breath, and felt his backbone unkinking. He stood at his full height again, and the hunger for the change left him. "Of course," he told her as he slipped into bed and put his right arm—fully human once more—around Gaby's neck. She nestled her head against his shoulder and said drowsily, "I smell a wet dog."

He smiled slightly as Gaby's breathing deepened and she returned to sleep.

A cock crowed. The night was passing, and the day of reckoning was upon him.

6

"Are you sure you can trust him?" Gaby asked as she and Michael slowly pedaled their bikes south along the Avenue des Pyrenees. They watched Mouse, a little man in a filthy overcoat, pedaling a beat-up bicycle past them, heading north to the intersection of the Rue de Menilmontant, where he would swing to the east and the Avenue Gambetta.

"No," Michael answered, "but we'll soon find out." He touched the Luger beneath his coat and turned into an alley with Gaby right behind him. The dawn had been false; clouds the color of pewter had rolled across the sun, and a chilly breeze swept through the streets. Michael checked his poisoned pocket watch: twenty-nine minutes after eight. Adam would be emerging from his building, following his daily schedule, in three minutes. He would begin his walk from the Rue Tobas to the Avenue Gambetta, where he would turn to the northeast on his way to the gray stone building that flew Nazi flags over the Rue de Belleville. As Adam approached the intersection of the Avenue Gambetta and the Rue St. Fargeau, Mouse would have to be in position.

Michael had awakened Mouse at five-thirty, Camille had begrudgingly fed them all breakfast, and Michael had described Adam to him and drilled him on it until he was sure—or as sure as he could be—that Mouse could pick Adam out on the street. At this time of the morning the streets were still drowsy. Only a few other bicyclists and pedestrians were heading to work. In Mouse's pocket was a folded note that read: *Your box. L'Opéra. Third Act tonight.*

They came out of the alley onto the Rue de la Chine—and Michael narrowly missed hitting two German soldiers walking together. Gaby swerved past them, and one of the soldiers hollered and whistled at her. She felt the damp memory of last night between her thighs, and she nonchalantly stood up in her seat and patted her rear as an invitation

201

for the German to kiss her there. The two soldiers both laughed and made smacking noises. She followed Michael along the street, their bicycle tires jarring over the stones, and then Michael turned into the alley in which he'd encountered Mouse the night before. Gaby kept going south along the Rue de la Chine, in accordance with their plan.

Michael stopped his bike and waited. He stared at the alley entrance, facing the Rue Tobas, about thirty-five feet ahead. A man walked by—dark-haired, stoop-shouldered, and heading in the wrong direction. Definitely not Adam. He checked his watch: thirty-one minutes after eight. A woman and man walked past the alley entrance talking animatedly. Lovers, Michael thought. The man had a dark beard. Not Adam. A horse-drawn carriage went past, the clopping of the horse's hooves echoing along the street. A few bicyclists, pedaling slowly, in no hurry. A milk wagon, its husky driver calling for customers.

And then a man in a long dark brown overcoat, his hands in his pockets, strolled past the alley entrance in the direction of the Avenue Gambetta. The man's silhouette was chiseled, his nose a hawklike beak. It was not Adam, but the man wore a black leather hat that had a feather in its band, as had the Gestapo agent on the road, Michael recalled. The man suddenly stopped, right at the alley's edge. Michael pressed his back against the wall, hiding behind a pile of broken crates. The man looked around, his back to Michael; he gave the alley a cursory glance that told Michael he'd done this too many times. Then the man took off his hat and brushed an imaginary spot of dust from the brim. He returned the hat to his head and strolled on toward the Avenue Gambetta. A signal, Michael realized. Probably to someone else farther up the street.

He had no more time for speculation. In another few seconds a slim, blond-haired man in a gray overcoat, carrying a black valise and wearing wire-rimmed eyeglasses, walked past the alley. Michael's heart pounded; Adam was on time.

He waited. Perhaps thirty seconds after Adam had passed, two more men crossed the entrance, one walking about eight or nine paces in front of the second. One wore a brown suit and a fedora, the second wore a beige jacket, corduroy trousers, and a tan beret. He carried a newspaper, and Michael knew there had to be a gun in it. Michael gave them a few more seconds; then he took a deep breath and pedaled out of the alley onto the Rue Tobas. He turned to the right, heading toward the Avenue Gambetta, and saw the whole picture: the leather-hatted man walking far ahead at a brisk pace on the left-hand side of the street, Adam on the right side and spaced out behind him the man in the suit and the newspaper reader.

A nice, efficient little parade, Michael thought. There were probably other Gestapo men, waiting ahead on the Avenue Gambetta. They had performed this ritual at least twice a day since they'd zeroed in on Adam, and maybe the sameness of the ritual had dulled their reflexes. Maybe. Michael wouldn't count on it. He pedaled past the newspaper reader, keeping his pace steady. Another bicyclist zoomed around him, giving an angry beep of his horn. Michael pedaled past the man in the suit. Even now Gaby would be about a hundred yards or so behind Michael, positioned there as a backup in case things went wrong. Adam was coming to the intersection of the Rue Tobas and the Avenue Gambetta; he looked both ways, paused for a truck to chug past, then crossed the street and walked northeast. Michael followed him, and immediately saw the leather-hatted man step into a doorway and another Gestapo agent in a dark gray suit and two-tone shoes emerge from the same doorway. This new man walked on ahead, his gaze sliding slowly back and forth across the street. Way up at the junction of the Rue de Belleville and the Avenue Gambetta, Nazi flags whipped in the breeze.

Michael put on some speed and pedaled by Adam. A figure on a beat-up bicycle was approaching, the front wheel wobbling. Michael waited until he was almost abreast of Mouse, and then gave a brief nod. He saw Mouse's eyes: glittering and moist with fear. But there was no time to stop the plan, and it was now or never. Michael pedaled past Mouse, and left it up to him.

On seeing the man's nod, Mouse felt a spear of pure terror pierce his guts. Why he'd agreed to something like this, he'd never know. No, that was wrong; he knew fully well why he'd agreed. He wanted to get home, to his wife and children, and if this was the only way to do it . . .

He saw a man with two-tone shoes glance sharply at him, then away. And walking perhaps twenty feet behind the two-tones was the blond-haired man with round eyeglasses whose description had been drilled into his head. He saw the dark-haired woman approaching, slowly pedaling her bicycle. She'd made enough noise last night to give the dead hard-ons. God, how he missed his wife! The blond man, wearing a gray overcoat and carrying a black valise, was nearing the intersection of the Rue St. Fargeau. Mouse pedaled a little faster, trying to get into position. His heart was hammering, and a gust of wind almost threw him off balance. He had the piece of paper clenched in his right hand. The blond man stepped off the curb, began to cross the Rue St. Fargeau. God help me! Mouse thought, his face tight with fear. A velo taxi swept past him, upsetting his aim. His front wheel wobbled violently, and Mouse thought for a terrible instant that it was going to leap off its spokes. And then the blond man was almost up on the opposite curb, and that was when Mouse gritted his teeth and swerved to the right. He threw himself over, the tires skidding out from under him on the edge of the curb, and his shoulder brushed the blond man's arm as Mouse fell. He reached out with both hands, seemingly fighting the air for a grip. His right hand darted into the coat's folds; he felt patched wool lining and the rim of a pocket. His fingers opened. Then the bicycle and his body crashed down over the curb, the impact whooshing the breath out of him. His right hand, the palm sweating, was empty.

The blond-haired man had gone on three paces. He turned, looked back at the fallen, raggedy figure in the gutter, and stopped. "Are you all right?" he asked in French, and Mouse smiled stupidly and waved.

And as the blond-haired man turned away again and kept walking, Mouse saw a gust of wind swirl the folds of his overcoat—and a small piece of paper spun out of them and took flight.

Mouse gasped with horror. The paper spun like a treacherous butterfly, and Mouse reached out for it but the thing whirled past. It landed on the sidewalk, and was scooted along a few more inches. Mouse reached for it again, sweat on the back of his neck. A dark brown, polished shoe stepped on his fingers, and crunched down.

Mouse looked up, still smiling stupidly. The man who stood over him wore a dark brown suit and a fedora. He was smiling, too. Except his face was gaunt and his eyes were cold, and his thin-lipped mouth was not shaped for a smile. The man plucked the piece of paper off the pavement and unfolded it.

Less than thirty feet away Gaby slowed to a crawl and put her hand on the Luger beneath her sweater.

The man in the brown suit looked at the writing on the piece of paper. Gaby started to pull the Luger from her waistband, aware that the Gestapo man in the beret was walking faster toward his companion and he was holding his newspaper with both hands.

"Give me some money, please sir," Mouse said, in his best French. His voice shook.

"You dirty bastard." The brown-suited man crumpled the paper in his fist. "I'll give you a kick in the balls. Watch where you're riding that wreck." He tossed the paper into the gutter, shook his head at his companion, and both of them strode on after the blond-haired man. Mouse felt sick. Gaby was stunned, and she took her hand off the Luger and swerved her bicycle onto the Rue St. Fargeau.

Mouse picked up the crumpled paper from the gutter with his left hand and opened it, his fingers palsied. He blinked and read what was written there in French.

Blue suit, middle button missing. White shirts, light starch. Colored shirts, no starch. Extra collar stays.

It was a laundry list. Mouse realized it must have been in the blond man's inside coat pocket, and it had been knocked out when Mouse's fingers had deposited the note.

He laughed; it was a strangled sound. A flex of his right hand told him the fingers weren't broken, though two of the nails were already turning violet.

I did it! Mouse thought, and felt tears pressing at his eyes. By God, I did it!

"On your feet. Hurry!" Michael had circled back, and now paused astride his bicycle, a few feet from Mouse. "Come on, get up!" He looked down the Avenue Gambetta, watching Adam and his Gestapo guards nearing the Rue de Belleville and the Nazi building.

"I did it!" Mouse said excitedly. "I really did—"

"Get on your bike and follow me. *Now*." Michael pedaled away, heading toward their rendezvous point—the scrawled sign that proclaimed GERMANY VICTORIOUS ON ALL FRONTS. Mouse pulled himself up from the gutter, got on the wobbly-wheeled bike, and followed. He was shivering, and perhaps he was a traitor and deserved to be hanged, but the image of home bloomed in his mind like a spring flower and suddenly he felt very victorious indeed.

7

Tosca, the tale of doomed lovers, was the presentation at the opera. The gargantuan building seemed to rise before Michael and Gaby like a sculpted stone monolith as they approached it along the Avenue de l'Opéra in a battered blue Citröen. Mouse was at the wheel, considerably cleaner since he'd bathed and shaved this evening. Still, his eyes were hollow and his face deeply lined, and though his hair was slicked back with pomade and he wore fresh clothes—courtesy of Camille—there was no mistaking him for a purebred gentleman. Michael, wearing a gray suit, sat in the backseat next to Gaby, who wore a dark blue dress she'd bought that afternoon on the Boulevard de la Chapelle. Its color matched her eyes, and Michael thought she was as beautiful as any woman he'd ever known.

The sky had cleared, and the stars were out. In the polite glow of the succession of street lamps along the avenue, the Opera House—a majesty of columns, finials, and intricate carvings, the stone frontage shaded from pale gray to sea green—stood defiant of time and circumstance. Beneath its domed roof, on which stood statues of Pegasus at either end and a huge figure of Apollo with a lyre at its apex, music was the ruler instead of Hitler. Cars and carriages halted at the cavernous main entrance, debarking their passengers. Michael said, "Stop here," and Mouse slid the Citröen to the curb with only a small grinding of gears. "You know what time to pick us up." He looked at his pocket watch and couldn't help but think of the capsule within.

"Yes," Mouse said. Camille had checked with the ticket office to find out precisely what time the third act would begin. At that time Mouse would have the car waiting in front of the opera.

It had occurred to both Michael and Gaby that Mouse could take the car and go anywhere he pleased, and Gaby had had some bad moments about this but Michael had calmed her. Mouse would be there on time, he'd told her, because Mouse wanted to get to Berlin, and what he'd done for them already was enough to condemn him to a nice torture session with the Gestapo. So, German or not, Mouse was on their side from here on out. On the other hand, if there was really any madness in Mouse, there was no telling how and when it might show itself.

Michael got out, came around the car, and opened the door for Gaby. He said, "Be here," and Mouse nodded and drove away. Then Michael offered Gaby his arm, and they strolled past a German soldier on horseback just like any French couple out for a night at the Opéra. Except Michael wore a Luger in a holster that Camille had supplied, the pistol lying just under his left armpit, and Gaby had a very small, very sharp knife in her shiny black clutch purse. Arm in arm, they crossed the Avenue de l'Opéra to the Opera House itself. In the huge vestibule, where gilded lamps cast a golden glow on statues of Handel, Lully, Gluck, and Rameau, Michael saw several Nazi officers with their lady friends among the crowd. He guided Gaby through the throng, up ten steps of green Swedish marble, to a second vestibule where the tickets were sold.

They bought their tickets, two seats on the aisle near the back of the house, and continued through the building. Michael had never seen such an assembly of statues, multihued marble columns, gilt-edged mirrors, and chandeliers in his life; the grand staircase, a gracefully massive thing with marble balustrades, swept them up to the auditorium. Everywhere he looked there were more staircases, corridors, statues, and chandeliers. He hoped Gaby knew her way here, because in this place of art run riot even his wolf's sense of direction was stunned. At last they entered the auditorium, another marvel of space and proportion which was rapidly filling, and they were shown to their seats by an elderly attendant.

The odors of conflicting perfumes stung Michael's nose. He noted it was chilly in the huge auditorium; due to fuel rationing, the building's boilers had been turned off. Gaby glanced casually around, noting where perhaps a dozen German officers sat with their female companions. Her gaze went up to the third of the four tiers of loges, stacked atop each other and connected by gilded balconies and fluted columns like the layers of a massive and rather gaudy cake. She found Adam's loge. It was empty.

Michael had already seen it. "Patience," he said quietly. If Adam had found the note, he'd be here. If not . . . then not. He took Gaby's hand and squeezed it. "You look beautiful," he told her.

She shrugged, uneasy with compliments. "I don't dress this way very often."

"Neither do I." He wore a crisp white shirt along with his gray suit, a muted gray-and-scarlet-striped necktie, and a pearl stickpin that Camille had given him "for luck." He glanced up at the third tier; Adam still hadn't arrived, and the orchestra was tuning. A hundred things could have gone wrong, he thought. The Gestapo could have searched his coat when he got to work. The note could have fallen out. Adam simply could have hung the coat up and not even looked in the pocket. No, no, he told himself. Just wait, and watch.

The houselights dimmed. The heavy red curtains parted, and Puccini's tale of Floria Tosca began.

As the desperate Tosca murdered her brutal tormentor with a knife at the end of Act II, Michael was aware of the pressure of Gaby's grip on his hand. He glanced again at the third tier. No Adam. Damn it! he thought. Well, Adam knew that he was being watched. Maybe he chose, for whatever reason, not to appear tonight. Act III began, a prison scene. The minutes ticked past. Gaby cast a quick look at Adam's loge—and Michael felt her fingers crunch his hand.

He knew. Adam was there.

"A man's standing in the loge," she whispered, her face close to his. He smelled the delicious apple-wine scent of her hair. "I can't tell what he looks like."

Michael gave it another moment. Then he glanced up and saw the sitting figure. The footlights, dimmed to a moody cast as Tosca visited her imprisoned lover Cavaradossi, glinted on the lenses of eyeglasses. "I'm going upstairs," Michael whispered. "Wait here."

"No. I'm coming with you."

"Shhhhh!" the man behind them hissed.

"Wait *here*," Michael repeated. "I'll be back as soon as I can. If anything happens, I want you to get out." Before Gaby could protest again, he leaned forward and kissed her lips. An electricity passed between them, a tingling of the nerves that connected them for a few seconds like raw wires. Then Michael stood up, walked purposefully up the aisle, and left the auditorium. Gaby stared at the stage, seeing nothing and hearing nothing, all her attention fixed on the deadly drama that was yet to be played out.

Michael ascended a series of wide staircases. An attendant, a young man in a white jacket, black trousers, and white gloves, stood on duty on the third tier. "May I help you, please?" he asked as Michael approached.

"No, thank you. I'm meeting a friend." Michael walked past him, found the rosewood door of loge number six, and rapped quietly on it. He waited. A latch was slid back. The door opened on brass hinges.

And there was the man called Adam, his eyes wide with terror behind his glasses. "I was followed," he said, his voice reedy and trembling. "They're all over the place."

Michael entered the loge and closed the door behind him. He slid the latch shut. "We don't have much time. What's your message?"

"Wait. Just wait." He held up a pale, long-fingered hand.

"How do I know . . . you're not one of *them?* How do I know you're not trying to trick me?"

"I could recite the names of people you know back in London, if that would help. I don't think it will. You'll have to trust me. If you don't, we might as well forget this and I'll swim home across the Channel."

"I'm sorry. It's just that . . . I don't trust anyone. Not anyone."

"You'll have to start right now," Michael said.

Adam sank down in a red-cushioned chair. He leaned forward and ran a shaking hand across his face. He looked emaciated, about to pass out. Onstage, Cavaradossi was being escorted from his cell to face a firing squad. "Oh, God," Adam whispered. He blinked, his glasses reflecting the dank gray light. He looked up at Michael and drew a deep breath. "Theo von Frankewitz," Adam began. "Do you know who that is?"

"A sidewalk artist in Berlin."

"Yes. He's . . . a friend of mine. Back in February . . . he was called to do a special job. By an SS colonel named Jerek Blok, who used to be the commandant of—"

"Falkenhausen concentration camp, from May to December of 1943," Michael interrupted. "I've read Blok's dossier." As little as there was of it. Mallory had gotten him the dossier on Blok; it had told him only that Jerek Blok was forty-seven years old, born into a military and aristocratic German family, and that he was a Nazi party fanatic. There had been no photograph. But now Michael felt like a raw nerve: Blok had been seen in Berlin with Harry Sandler. What was their connection, and how did the big-game hunter figure in this? "Go on."

"Theo . . . was taken to an airstrip, blindfolded and flown west. He thinks that was the direction, because of how the sun felt on his face. Perhaps an artist would remember such things. Anyway, Blok was with him, and there were other SS men, too. When they landed, Theo could smell the sea. He was taken to a warehouse. They kept Theo there for over two weeks, while he painted."

"*Painted?*" Michael stood toward the rear of the loge,

positioning himself so he couldn't be seen from the auditorium. "Painted what?"

"Bullet holes." Adam's hands were white-knuckled on the armrests. "For more than two weeks he painted bullet holes on sections of metal. The sections were obviously part of a larger structure; they still had rivets in them. And someone had already painted the metal olive green." He looked quickly at Michael, then back to the stage. The orchestra was playing a funeral march as Cavaradossi refused a blindfold. "They had pieces of glass for Theo to paint, too. They wanted bullet holes in precise patterns, and what would look like cracks in the glass. Blok wasn't satisfied when Theo finished, and he made Theo do the glass all over again. Then they flew Theo back to Berlin, paid him a fee, and that was it."

"All right. So your friend painted some metal and glass. What's it mean?"

"I don't know, but it worries me." He ran the back of his hand across his mouth. "The Germans know the invasion's coming soon. Why are they spending time painting bullet holes on green metal? And there's this, too: another man came to visit the warehouse, and Blok showed him the work Theo was doing. Blok called this man Dr. Hildebrand. Do you know that name?"

Michael shook his head. Onstage, the soldiers of the firing squad were loading their muskets.

"Hildebrand's father created the chemical gases used by the Germans in the Great War," Adam said. "Like father, like son: Hildebrand owns a chemical manufacturing company, and he's the Reich's most vocal proponent of chemical and germ warfare. If Hildebrand's working on something . . . it could be used against the invasion."

"I see." Michael's stomach had knotted. If chemical gas shells were dropped on the Allies during the invasion, thousands of soldiers would die. And adding to that tragedy was the stark fact that, once repulsed, the invasion of Europe might be delayed for years—time for Hitler to fortify the Atlantic Wall and create a new generation of weapons. "But I don't understand where Frankewitz fits in."

"I don't either. Once the Gestapo found my radio and

destroyed it, I was cut off from all information. But this is something that *must* be followed up. If not . . ." He let the sentence hang, because Michael fully understood. "Theo overheard Blok and Hildebrand talking. They mentioned a phrase twice: *Eisen Faust.*"

"Iron Fist," Michael translated.

A fist of flesh knocked at the loge's door. Adam jumped in his chair. Onstage, the firing squad lifted their rifles, and the orchestra played a dirge as Cavaradossi prepared to die.

"Monsieur?" It was the voice of the white-jacketed attendant. "A message for you."

Michael heard the tension in the young man's voice; the attendant was not alone. Michael knew what the message would be: an invitation from the Gestapo for a lesson in screaming. "Stand up," Michael told Adam.

Adam did—and at that instant the rosewood door was broken open by a man's husky shoulder as the muskets fired onstage. Cavaradossi sagged to the stage. The noise of the gunfire had masked the sound of the door splintering. Two men, both in the dark leather overcoats of the Gestapo, were shouldering their way into the loge. The man in front had a Mauser pistol in his hand, and he was the one Michael went for first.

Michael picked up the red-cushioned chair and smashed it across the man's head. The chair burst to pieces, and the man's face bleached white as blood spewed from his broken nose. He staggered, the gun coming up, and his finger twitched on the trigger. The bullet whined over Michael's shoulder, the noise obscured by the soprano wailing of Ninon Vallin's Tosca as she fell at Cavaradossi's corpse. Michael reached out, grasped the man's wrist and the front of his overcoat, twisted sharply, and lifted the man over his shoulder. He took a lunging step toward the gilded balcony and threw the gunman into space.

The man shrieked, louder than Tosca had ever dreamed, as he fell fifty-two feet to the auditorium floor. For a second their voices blended in eerie harmony; then there were other screams, and the screaming spread like a contagion across the audience. The orchestra stopped in a shatter of broken notes. Onstage, valiant Ninon Vallin was desperately trying to continue her role, so close to the dramatic finale.

But Michael was determined it was not going to be his own swan song. The second man reached into his coat; before the gun could come out, Michael slammed his fist into the man's face and followed it with a blow to the throat. Strangling around a crushed windpipe, the man fell backward and crashed against the wall. But the loge's splintered doorway filled with a new figure: a third man in a pin-striped suit, a Luger in his right hand. Behind him was a soldier with a rifle. Michael shouted to Adam, "Grab on to my back!" and Adam did, putting his arms under Michael's shoulders and locking his fingers together. Adam was light, a hundred and thirty pounds if that; Michael saw the third man's eyes widen as he realized what was about to happen, and the Luger rose for a shot.

Michael leaped to his right and bounded over the balcony with Adam clinging to his back.

——— 8 ———

He had no intention of following the first Gestapo agent's descent to the auditorium's floor; his fingers gripped the fluted finials of the gilded column that rose beside Adam's loge, and the muscles of his shoulders strained as he pulled himself and Adam up toward the topmost tier. A new chorus of screams and shrieks swept across the audience. Even Ninon Vallin cried out, whether in fear for a human life or rage at being upstaged, Michael couldn't tell. He hoisted them up, grabbing whatever handholds he could find. His heart pounded and the blood roared through his veins, but his brain was cool; whatever the future held, it was to be decided very quickly.

And so it was. He heard the vicious *crack!* of a gunshot— a Luger being fired at an upward angle. He felt Adam's body shudder and stiffen. The man's arms, already tightly

213

clamped around him, in an instant became as rigid as iron bars. Warm wetness trickled through the back of Michael's hair and down his neck, drenching his suit jacket; he realized the bullet had just blown away a large portion of Adam's skull, and the muscles of the corpse had frozen in the sudden paralysis of severed nerves. He clambered up the column, a dead man locked on his back and blood trickling over the finials. He pulled himself over the balcony of the uppermost loge as a second bullet flayed away a shower of gold paint four inches from his right elbow.

"Up the stairs!" he heard the Gestapo agent shout. "Hurry!"

The loge Michael found himself in was unoccupied. He spent a few seconds trying to unlock Adam's fingers from where they were clenched together at his chest; he broke two of them like dry twigs, but the others resisted him. There was no time to fight a dead man's grip. Michael staggered through the door into the crimson-carpeted hallway outside and faced a warren of lamplit corridors and staircases. "This way!" he heard a man shout, from somewhere to his left. Michael turned to the right and staggered down a corridor lined with paintings of medieval hunting scenes. The corpse hung to his back, its shoe tips dragging furrows in the carpet. Behind them, Michael realized, was also a trail of blood. He stopped to thrash against the body; but all he did was burn up priceless energy, and the corpse remained latched to him like a lifeless Siamese twin.

A shot rang out. Just over Michael's shoulder, a lamp held by a statue of Diana exploded. He saw two soldiers coming after him, both armed with rifles. He tried to reach his Luger but couldn't get to it because of the corpse's grip. He turned and ran into another corridor, this one curving to the left. The voices of his pursuers shouted directions to each other, their Germanic snarls like the baying of hounds. Now the corpse's one hundred and thirty pounds seemed an eternal weight. He forced himself on, the corpse leaving smears of blood in the halls of beauty.

An ascending staircase was ahead of him, cherubs with lyres mounted on its balustrades. Michael started toward it—and smelled the bitter scent of a stranger's sweat. A

German soldier with a pistol stepped from a shadowed archway on his left. "Your hands," the soldier said. "Up." He motioned with the gun.

In the second that the barrel was uptilted, Michael kicked him in the right kneecap and heard the bones break. The pistol fired, its bullet thunking into the ceiling. The German, his face twisted with pain, staggered against the wall but didn't let go of the gun; he began to take aim, and Michael leaped at him as Adam dragged on his shoulders. He caught the German's wrist. Again the gun fired, but the bullet passed Michael's cheek and smashed something on the other side of the corridor. The German gouged at Michael's eyes with hooked fingers and screamed, "I've got him! Help me! I've got him!"

Even with a broken knee, the soldier was strong. They fought in the hallway, grappling for the gun. The soldier struck Michael in the jaw with a blow that stunned him and made him see double for a few seconds, but he held on to the gun hand. Michael delivered a punch that hit the German in the mouth and knocked two teeth down his throat, strangling his screams for help. The German brought a knee up into Michael's stomach, driving the breath out of him, and the corpse's weight pulled Michael off balance. He fell backward, hitting the wall with a force that cracked Adam's ruined skull against the marble. The soldier, balancing desperately on one leg, raised his Luger to shoot Michael at point-blank range.

Behind the German Michael saw a whirl of dark blue, like a tornado unfurling. A knife glittered with chandelier light. Its blade plunged down into the back of the soldier's neck. The man choked and staggered, dropping his pistol to clutch his throat. Gaby wrenched at the knife, but it had gone in too deeply. She let it go, and the soldier made a terrible moaning noise and crashed face down.

Gaby blinked, stunned at the sight before her: Michael, his hair bloody and gore spattered over one side of his face, and clutched to his back an openmouthed corpse that had a pulpy mess where the right temple had been. Her stomach churned. She picked up the gun, her knife hand smeared with scarlet, as Michael found his balance again.

"Geissen!" a man shouted from down the corridor. "Where the hell are you?"

Gaby helped Michael try to unlock the corpse's fingers, but they could hear the noise of more soldiers approaching. The only route available to them was the ascending staircase. They started up it, Michael's legs beginning to cramp under Adam's weight. The staircase curved and took them to a latched door. As Gaby threw back the latch and pulled the door open, the night wind of Paris rushed into their faces. They had reached the roof of the Opera House.

The tips of Adam's polished black shoes scraped the tarred stones as Michael followed Gaby across the Opéra's huge roof. Gaby looked back and saw figures emerging from the doorway they'd come through. She knew there had to be other ways down, but how long would it take the Germans to cover all the exits? She hurried on, but had to wait for Michael; his strength was ebbing, his back beginning to bow. "Go on!" he snapped. "Don't wait for me!"

She waited, her heart pounding, as she watched for the figures coming after them. When Michael had caught up with her again, she turned and started off. They neared the front of the roof, with the sprawling, glittering city spread around them in all directions. The massive statue of Apollo rose from the roof's apex, and pigeons took flight as Michael and Gaby approached. Michael felt his legs weakening; he was holding Gaby back. He stopped, supporting himself and Adam's weight against the base of Apollo. "Keep going," he told Gaby when she paused again. "Find a way down."

"I'm not leaving you," she said, staring at him with her sapphire eyes.

"Don't be a fool! This isn't the time or place for argument." He heard the men shouting back and forth to each other, coming closer. He got his hand into his coat—and touched not his own Luger, which was trapped in its holster, but the poisoned pocket watch. His fingers gripped it, but he couldn't make himself bring it out. "Go!" he told her.

"I'm not leaving," Gaby said. "I love you."

"No, you don't. You love the memory of a moment. You don't know anything about me—and you wouldn't want to." He glanced at the figures, approaching cautiously about thirty yards away. They hadn't yet seen him or Gaby underneath the statue. The pocket watch was ticking, and time was running out. "Don't throw your life away," he said. "Not for me. Not for anybody."

She hesitated, and Michael could see the strain on her face. She glanced at the oncoming Germans, then back to Michael. Maybe she did only love the memory of a moment—but what was life, if not simply the memory of moments? He pulled the pocket watch free and popped it open. The cyanide capsule awaited his choice. "You've done what you can," he told her. "Now go." And he shook the capsule into his mouth. She saw his throat convulse as he swallowed the pill. He grimaced.

"Over here! Here they are!" one of the men shouted. A pistol fired, and the bullet knocked sparks off Apollo's thigh. Michael Gallatin shivered and fell to his knees, with Adam's weight atop him. He looked up at Gaby, his face sparkling with sweat.

She couldn't stand to watch him die. Another shot was fired, and it zipped by close enough to unthaw her legs. She turned away from Michael Gallatin, tears streaming down her cheeks, and she ran. About fifty feet from where Michael lay dying, Gaby's shoe hit the hand grip of a trapdoor. She pulled it open and looked down at a ladder. Then another glance toward Michael; the figures were surrounding him, victors of the hunt. It was all Gaby could do to keep from firing into their midst, but they'd surely shoot her to pieces. She went down the ladder, and the trapdoor closed over her head.

Six German soldiers and three Gestapo men stood around Michael. The man who'd blown Adam's head open sneered. "Now we've got you, you bastard."

Michael spat out the pill he'd been holding in his mouth. Under Adam's corpse, his body shivered. Prickles of pain shot through his nerves. The Gestapo agent was reaching down for him, and Michael surrendered himself to the change.

It was like stepping from a secure shelter into a maelstrom of wild winds—a conscious choice, and once decided, difficult to reverse. He felt the primeval shriek in his bones as his spine bowed, and with a thunder that boomed in his head, his skull and face began to alter their shape. He shivered, and moaned uncontrollably.

The Gestapo agent's hand froze in midair. One of the soldiers laughed. "He's begging for mercy!" the man said.

"Get up!" The Gestapo man stepped back. "Get up, you swine!"

The moaning changed pitch. It lost its human element and turned bestial.

"Bring a light!" the Gestapo agent shouted. He didn't know what was wrong with the man who crouched before him, but he didn't care to stand any closer. "Somebody get a light on h—"

There was the noise of ripping cloth, and cracking sounds of bones being broken. The soldiers stepped back, and the one who'd laughed now wore a fractured grin. One of the soldiers produced a hand torch, and the Gestapo agent fumbled to switch it on. Before him something heaved, laboring under the stiff corpse at his feet. His hands shook; he couldn't get the balky switch clicked. "Damn it to Hell!" he shouted—and then the switch moved, and the light came on.

He saw what was there, and his breath froze.

Hell had shining green eyes and a sleek, muscular body covered with gray-streaked, black hair. Hell had white fangs, and hell moved on all fours.

The beast shook violently, a powerful motion that broke the corpse's arms like matchsticks and threw the body aside. It cast off, as well, the last of its human masquerade: a blood-covered gray suit, white shirt with the tie still knotted in the ripped collar, underwear, socks, and shoes. Amid the debris was a holster that held a Luger; the beast had deadlier weapons.

"Oh . . . my . . ." The Gestapo agent never got to call on his deity; Hitler was absent, and God knew the meaning of justice. The beast sprang, its jaws gaping, and as it hit the Gestapo agent its teeth were already sinking into the throat and ripping away flesh and arteries in a crimson shower of carnage.

All but two of the soldiers and one of the other Gestapo

agents shrieked and fled for their lives. A German soldier ran the wrong way—not toward the doorway but toward the street. He ended there, on a crushed note. The second Gestapo man, a heroic fool, lifted his Mauser pistol to fire at the beast as it whirled toward him; the fierce green glare of its eyes hypnotized him for perhaps a half second, and that was much too long. The beast leaped upon him, claws making a bloody tatters of the man's face, and the man's strangled, lipless scream shocked the two soldiers from their trances. They ran, too, one of them falling and tangling the second in his legs.

Michael Gallatin raged. He snapped the air, his jaws cracking together. Blood was dripping from his muzzle, its hot perfume heightening his abandon. A human mind calculated in the skull of the wolf, and his eyes saw not the darkness of night but a gray-hazed twilight in which blue-edged figures ran for the doorway, their screams like the high squeals of hunted rats. Michael could hear the panicked beating of their hearts—a military drum corps hammering at an insane speed. The smell of their sweat had sausage and schnapps in it. He bounded forward, his muscles and sinews moving like the fine gears of a killing machine, and he turned on the soldier who was trying to struggle to his feet; Michael looked into the German's face, and in a split second judged him a youth, no more than seventeen. An innocent corrupted by a rifle and a book called *Mein Kampf*. Michael seized the boy's left hand in his jaws and crushed the fingers without breaking the skin, removing the possibility of further corruption by rifle. Then, as the boy screamed and flailed at him, Michael turned away and bounded across the roof after the others.

One of the soldiers stopped to fire his pistol; the bullet ricocheted off the stones to Michael's left, but did not slow him. As the soldier spun around to flee, Michael jumped up and slammed into the man's back, knocking him aside like a scarecrow. Then Michael landed nimbly, and kept going in a blur of motion. He saw the others barreling into the door that led down the staircase, and in another few seconds they would be throwing the latch. The last man was about to squeeze through; the door was already closing, and the

Germans were hollering and trying to pull him in. Michael lowered his head and propelled himself forward.

He leaped, skewing his body in midair, and crashed against the door. It flew open, knocking the Germans down the stairs in a tangle of arms and legs. He landed amid them, clawing and tearing with fevered indiscrimination; then he left them behind, bloody and broken, as he raced down the stairs and through the corridors still marked with the furrows of Adam's shoe tips.

As he came down the sweeping staircase from the main auditorium, he met the crowd that milled in confusion and shouted for refunds. As Michael bounded down the stairs, the shouting ceased; the silence, however, didn't last long. A fresh wave of shrieks crashed against the Opéra's marbled walls, and men and women in their elegant attire jumped over the balustrades like swabbies off the sides of a torpedoed battleship. Michael leaped down the last six steps, his paws skidding across the green marble as he landed, and a bearded aristocrat with an ivory cane blanched and stumbled backward, a wet spot spreading across the front of his trousers.

Michael ran, the power and exhilaration singing in his blood. His heart pumped steadily, his lungs bellowed, his sinews worked like iron springs. He snapped left and right, scaring back those who were too dumbfounded to move. Then he was streaking through the final vestibule, clearing a path of screams, and onto the street. He raced under the belly of a carriage horse, which reared and danced madly. Michael glanced back, over his shoulder; a few people had run out after him, but the panicked horse was in their midst and they scattered away from the pounding hooves.

There was a fresh shriek: worn brakes, and tires clenching stones. Michael looked ahead and saw a pair of lights rushing at him. Without a hesitation, he bounded off the ground and up over the car's front fender and hood. He had an instant to see two shocked faces behind the windshield, and then Michael scrambled up over the top of the car, down the other side, and raced away across the Avenue de l'Opéra.

"My God!" Mouse gasped as the Citröen shuddered to a stop. He looked at Gaby. "What was that?"

"I don't know." She was stunned, and her mind seemed to be full of rusted gears. She saw people coming out of the Opera House, among them several German officers, and she said, *"Go!"*

Mouse hit the accelerator, swerved the car around, and tore away from the Opéra, leaving a backfire and a poot of blue smoke as his last salute.

9

It was after two o'clock in the morning when Camille heard a knock at her door. She sat up in her bed, instantly alert, reached under her pillow, and pulled out the deadly Walther pistol. She listened; the knock came again, more insistently. Not the Gestapo, she reasoned; they knocked with axes, not knuckles. But she took the pistol with her as she lit an oil lamp and went to the door in her long white gown. She almost bumped into Mouse, the little man standing wide-eyed and frightened in the hallway. She put a finger to her lips as he started to speak, and then she walked past him to the door. What a damnable mess! she thought angrily. She'd barely gotten the sorrow-racked girl to sleep twenty minutes before, the fool Brit had gotten both himself and Adam killed, and now she was stuck with a Nazi lunatic! Only a miracle could save this situation, and Joan of Arc was dust.

"Who is it?" Camille asked, making herself sound sleepy. Her heart pounded, and her finger hugged the trigger.

"Green Eyes," said the man on the other side.

No hand in Paris had ever moved faster to unlock a door.

Michael stood there, hollow-eyed, his jaw and chin in need of a shave. He wore a pair of brown corduroy trousers that were two sizes too small, and a white shirt meant for a fat man. On his feet he wore dark blue socks, but no shoes. He stepped into the apartment, past Camille, who stood openmouthed. Mouse made a choking sound. Michael closed the door gently behind him and locked it. "Mission," he said, "accomplished."

"Oh," someone said: a rush of breath. Gaby stood in the bedroom doorway, her face pale and her eyes rimmed with red. She still wore her new blue dress, now misshapen and full of wrinkles. "You . . . died. I watched you . . . take the pill."

"It didn't work," Michael said. He walked past them, his muscles sore and stretched, and his head throbbing with a dull ache: all aftereffects of the change. He went to a bowl of water in the kitchen and splashed his face, then took an apple and crunched into it. Camille, Gaby and Mouse followed him like three shadows. "I got the information," he said as his teeth whittled the apple down to its core; it also served to clean his teeth and get out the last of the crusted blood. "But it wasn't enough." He looked at Camille, his green eyes shining in the lamp glow. "I promised Mouse I'd take him to Berlin. I have my own reasons for going there as well. Will you help us?"

"The girl said she saw you surrounded by Nazis," Camille told him. "If the cyanide pill didn't work, how did you get away from them?" Her eyes had narrowed: it was impossible that this man was standing here. Impossible!

He stared at her, unblinking. "I was faster than they were."

She started to speak again, but she wasn't sure what to say. Where were the clothes he'd left here in? She looked at his stolen trousers and shirt. "I needed a change," he said, in a calm and soothing voice. "The Germans were after me. I took clothes hanging on a line."

"I don't . . ." She glanced at his shoeless feet. He finished the apple, tossed the stripped core into a trash basket, and reached for another. "I don't understand."

Gaby just watched him, her senses still wrecked. Mouse said, "Hey! We heard it on the radio! They said a dog got loose in the Opera House and raised hell! We saw it, too! Right up on our car! Didn't we?" he prodded Gaby.

"Yes," she answered. "We did."

"The information I got tonight," Michael said to Camille,

"has to be followed up. It's vital we get to Berlin as soon as we can. You can help us get there, by arranging the route."

"This . . . is such short notice. I'm not sure I can—"

"You can," he said. "We'll need new clothes. Identity cards if you can get them. And it'll have to be arranged for Echo to meet me in Berlin."

"I don't have the authority to—"

"I'm giving you the authority. Mouse and I are going to Berlin, as soon as possible. Check with whoever you want to. Do whatever has to be done. But get us there. Understood?" He smiled slightly, showing his teeth.

His smile chilled her. "Yes," she said. "Understood."

"Wait. What about me?" Gaby finally shook off her shock. She came forward and touched Michael's shoulder to make sure he was real. He was; her hand gripped his arm. "I'm going to Berlin with you."

He looked into her beautiful eyes, and his smile softened. "No," he said gently. "You're going west, back where you know your job and you do a damned fine one." She started to protest, but Michael put a finger to her lips. "You've done your best for me. But you wouldn't survive east of Paris, and I can't be your guardian." He realized the nail of the finger pressed against Gaby's mouth had blood crusted under it; he took it quickly away. "The only reason I'm taking *him* with me is because I made a bargain."

"Yes, you sure did!" Mouse piped up.

"And I'll honor it. But I work best alone. Do you see?" he asked Gaby.

Of course she didn't. Not yet. But she would see, in the fullness of time; when this war was over, and she was an older woman with children and her own vineyard where German tank treads once tore the earth, she'd see. And be glad that Michael Gallatin had given her a future.

"When can we leave?" Michael turned his attention to Camille, whose brain was already working feverishly on the possible routes from Paris to the diseased heart of the Reich.

"A week. That's the soonest I can get you out."

"Four days," he told her, and he waited until she sighed and nodded.

Home! Mouse thought, giddy with excitement. I'm going home!

Damnedest mess I've ever been in in my life, Camille thought. Gaby was split; she yearned for the man who stood before her—returned miraculously from death—but she loved her country more. Michael had two thoughts. One was of Berlin, and the other was a phrase, a key to a mystery: *Iron Fist*.

In the bedroom, as the candles burned low, Gaby lay on the goosedown mattress. Michael leaned over her, and kissed her lips. They sealed to each other with moist heat for a moment—and then Michael chose the cot, and lay down to ponder the future.

Gaby reached for his hand, and he took hers.

The night went on, and dawn broke with crimson fire.

SIX

Berserker

1

My hand! Mikhail thought, panicked, as he sat up on his bed of hay. What's wrong with my hand?

In the gloom of the white palace's depths, he could feel his right hand throb and burn, as if liquid fire ran through the veins instead of blood. The pain that had awakened him grew, running up his arm to his shoulder. His fingers were twisting, contorting, and Mikhail clenched his teeth to hold back a scream. He gripped his wrist as his fingers spasmed open and clenched closed; he heard little frail popping sounds, and each one drove a new dagger of agony into him. His face began to sweat. He dared not cry out, for the others would mock him. In another few torturous seconds his hand became gnarled and deformed, a freakish dark thing on the end of his white, pulsing wrist. He ached to shriek, but all his throat would allow was a whimper. Bands of black hair rose from his flesh, and they entwined around Mikhail's wrist and forearm like sleek ribbons. His fingers were retreating into their sockets, with crunching noises as the knuckles changed shape. Mikhail gasped, near fainting; his hand was covered with black hair, and where his fingers had been there were curved talons and soft, pink pads. The tide of black hair flowed up his forearm, lapped over his elbow, and Mikhail knew that in another instant he must get up and run screaming for Renati.

But the instant passed, and he didn't move. The black hair rippled, began to draw back into flesh with raw, needling pain, and his fingers cracked again and lengthened. The curved talons drew into his skin, leaving the remains of human fingernails. The hand resurfaced, moon pale, and his

227

fingers hung like strange pieces of meat. The pain ebbed, then went away. All of it had lasted perhaps fifteen seconds.

Mikhail drew a breath, and almost sobbed.

"The change," Wiktor said, sitting on his haunches about seven feet to the boy's left. "It's coming on you." Two large hares, oozing blood, lay on the stones beside him.

Mikhail jumped, startled. Wiktor's voice instantly awakened Nikita, Franco, and Alekza, who'd been curled up nearby. Pauli, her wits still sluggish from Belyi's death, stirred on her hay pallet and opened her eyes. Behind Wiktor stood Renati, who had been watching faithfully for him for three days, ever since he'd gone on the track of whatever had killed Pauli's brother. Wiktor stood up, regal in his snow-crusted robes, the weathered lines and cracks in his bearded face glistening with melted snow. The fire had burned very low, and was chewing on the last of the pine knots. "While you sleep," he told them, "death is in the forest."

Wiktor circled them, his breath ghosting in the chilly air. The hares' blood was already growing frost. "A berserker," he said.

"A *what?*" Franco stood up, reluctantly parting from Alekza's pregnant warmth.

"A berserker," Wiktor repeated. "A wolf that kills for the love of killing. That's what slaughtered Belyi." He glanced at Pauli with his amber eyes; she was still drugged with sorrow, and quite useless. "A wolf who kills for the love of killing," he said. "I found his tracks, about two miles north of here. He's a big bastard, weighs maybe a hundred and eighty pounds. He was going north at a steady pace, so I followed him." Wiktor knelt down by the feeble fire and warmed his hands. His face was washed with flickering crimson. "He's a smart one. Somehow he picked up my scent, and I was careful to keep the wind in my face, too. He wasn't about to let me find his den; he led me through a swamp—and I almost fell through a place where he'd cracked the ice to go out from under me." He smiled faintly, watching the fire. "If I hadn't smelled his piss on the ice, I'd be dead by now. I know he's a red one; I found some of his hair snagged on thorns. That's as close as I got." He rubbed his hands together, massaging the bruised knuckles, and stood up. "His hunting ground's getting thin. He wants ours. He knows he'll have to kill us to get it." He swept his gaze around the circle of his pack. "From now on, no one goes out alone. Not even for a handful of snow. We'll hunt in pairs, and we'll make damned certain we stay in sight of each other. Understood?" He waited until Nikita, Renati, Franco, and Alekza had nodded. Pauli was still dazed, her long brown hair full of bits of hay. Wiktor looked at Mikhail. "Understood?" he repeated.

"Yes, sir," Mikhail quickly answered.

Time, a dream of days and nights, passed. As Alekza's belly swelled, Wiktor taught Mikhail from the dusty books in the lower chamber. Mikhail had no problem with Latin and German, but the English stuck in his throat. It, truly, was a foreign tongue. "Enunciate!" Wiktor thundered. "That's an 'ing'! Speak it!" The English language was a jungle of thorns, but slowly Mikhail began to cut his way through. "We're going to read some of this," Wiktor said one day as he opened a huge, illustrated manuscript written in an English that looked like scrolled woodcarvings. "Listen," Wiktor said, and began to read:

"Methinks I am a prophet new
And thus, expiring, do foretell of him:
His rash fierce blaze of riot cannot last,
For violent fires soon burn out themselves;
Small showers last long, but sudden storms are short;
He tires betimes that spurs too fast betimes;
With eager feeding food doth choke the feeder."

He looked up. "Do you know who wrote that?" Mikhail shook his head, and Wiktor told him the name. "Now repeat it," Wiktor said.

"Shak . . . Shaka . . . Shakaspir."

"Shakespeare," Wiktor enunciated. He read a few more lines, his voice reverent:

"This happy breed of men, this little world;
This precious stone set in the silver sea,
Which serves it in the office of a wall,
Or as a moat defensive to a house,
Against the envy of less happier lands;
This blessed plot, this earth, this realm, this
England."

He looked into Mikhail's face. "Now there's a country where they don't execute their teachers," he said. "At least not yet. I always wanted to see England; a man can live free there." His eyes had taken on the shiny glint of distant lights. "They don't burn your books in England, and they don't kill for the love of it." He brought himself abruptly back. "Well, I'll never see it. But you might. If you ever leave this place, go to England. You find out if it's such a blessed plot. All right?"

"Yes, sir," Mikhail agreed, without fully understanding what he was agreeing to.

And after the gray shadow of one last blizzard had swept across the forest, spring came to Russia; first a torrent of rain, then a green blaze. Mikhail's dreams became bizarre: he was running on all fours, his body hurtling through a dark realm. When he awakened from them, he was shivering and covered with sweat. Sometimes he caught a brief glimpse of black hair, rippling across his arms, chest, or legs. His bones throbbed, as if they had been broken and rejointed. When he heard the beautiful, echoing calls of Wiktor, Nikita, or Renati out on the hunt, his throat convulsed and his heart ached. The change was coming on him; slowly and surely, the change was taking him over.

On a night in early May, Alekza contorted and screamed while Pauli and Nikita held her, the firelight capering, and Renati's bloody hands delivered two babies. Mikhail saw them, before Renati whispered to Wiktor and wrapped the bodies in rags; one of the limp things, a small human form, was missing its left arm and leg and was covered with bites. The second corpse, strangled by a gray cord, had claws and fangs. Renati tied the rags tightly around the dead things, before Franco or Alekza could see them. Alekza lifted her head, sweat glistening on her face, and whispered, "Are they boys? Are they boys?"

Mikhail got away before Renati told her. Alekza's wail rushed past him, and he almost bumped into Franco in the corridor; the man shoved him roughly aside as he hurried by.

When the sun came up, they took the swaddled infants to a place a half mile to the south of the white palace: the Garden, Renati told Mikhail when he asked. The Garden, she said, where all the little ones lay.

It was a place surrounded by towering birches, and arrangements of stones lay on the soft, leaf-covered earth to mark the bodies. Franco and Alekza got on their knees, and together began to dig the graves with their hands as Wiktor held the corpses. At first Mikhail thought this was a cruel thing, because Alekza sobbed and the tears trickled down her face as she dug—but in another few moments her crying was finished, and she worked harder. He realized it was the pack's way of burying their dead: tears gave way to muscle, and fingers dug resolutely at the earth. Franco and Alekza were allowed to dig as deeply as they wished, and then Wiktor placed the corpses in the graves and they were covered over again with dirt and leaves.

Mikhail looked around at all the small squares of stone. All infants in this section of the Garden; farther away, in the deeper shade, were larger squares. He knew Andrei lay over there, as well as members of the pack who'd died before Mikhail had been bitten. He saw how many infants had died: more than thirty of them. It occurred to him that the pack kept trying to have children, but the babies died. Could there ever be a baby who was part human and part wolf? he wondered as the warm breeze stirred the branches. He didn't see how an infant's body could bear the pain; if any baby did survive that torment, it would have to be a very strong soul.

Franco and Alekza found stones and placed them around the graves. Wiktor offered no words, either to them or to God; when the work was finished, he turned and walked away, his sandals crunching in the underbrush. Mikhail saw Alekza reach for Franco's hand, but he pulled quickly away and walked on without her. She stood there for a moment looking after him, sunlight gleaming in her long golden hair. Mikhail saw her lips shiver, and he thought she was going to cry again. But then she stood up a little straighter, her eyes narrowed with cold disdain. He saw there was no love between her and Franco; with the babies buried, so was all affection. Or perhaps Franco thought less of her now. He watched her as she seemed to grow before his eyes. And then her head turned, and her ice-blue gaze locked on him. He stared at her without moving.

Alekza said, "I'll have a boy. I will."

"Your body's tired," Renati told her, standing behind Mikhail. He realized Alekza's stare was fixed on Renati. "Wait another year."

"I'll have a boy," she repeated firmly. Her gaze went to Mikhail, and lingered. He felt himself tremble, in a deep place. And then she abruptly turned and left the Garden, following Nikita and Pauli.

Renati stood over the fresh graves. She shook her head. "Little ones," she said softly. "Oh, little ones. I hope you'll be better brothers in heaven." She glanced back at Mikhail. "Do you hate me?" she asked.

"Hate you?" The question had shocked him. "No."

"I would understand if you did," she said. "After all, I brought you into this life. I hated the one who bit me. She lies over there, right at the edge." Renati nodded toward the shadows. "I was married to a shoemaker. We were on our way to my sister's wedding. I told Tiomki he'd taken a wrong turn; did he listen? Of course not." She motioned toward a larger square of stones. "Tiomki died during the change. That was . . . oh, twelve springs ago, I think. He was not a well man, anyway; he would've made a pitiful wolf. But I loved him." She smiled, but the smile wouldn't stick. "All these graves have their stories, but some of them are even before Wiktor's time. So I guess they're silent riddles, eh?"

"How long . . . has the pack been here?" Mikhail asked.

"Oh, I don't know. Wiktor says the old man who died the year after I joined had been here for over twenty years, and the old man knew of others going back twenty years more. Who knows?'' She shrugged.

"Has anybody ever been born here? And lived?"

"Wiktor says he's heard of seven or eight who were born and survived. They all died over the years, of course. But most of the babies are either born dead or they die within a few weeks. Pauli gave up trying. So did I. Alekza's still young enough to be stubborn, and she's buried so many babies her heart must look like one of these stones by now. Well, I pity her." Renati looked around the Garden and up at the towering birches where the sun shone through. "I know your next question," she said, before Mikhail could ask it. "The answer is: no. No one of the pack has ever left these woods. This is our home; it will always be our home."

Mikhail, still wearing the tatters of last year's clothes, nodded. Already the world that used to be—the human world—seemed hazy, like a distant memory. He heard birds singing in the trees, and he watched a few of them fluttering from branch to branch. They were beautiful birds, and Mikhail wondered if they were good to eat.

"Come on, let's get back." The ceremony—such as it was—had ended. Renati started walking in the direction of the white palace, and Mikhail followed. They hadn't gone very far when Mikhail heard a faraway, high-pitched whistle. Perhaps a mile to the southeast, he gauged it. He stopped, listening to the sound. Not a bird, but—

"Ah," Renati said. "That's a sign of summer. The train's running. The tracks go through the woods not too far from here." She walked on, then paused when Mikhail hadn't moved. The whistle blew again, a short and shrill note. "Must be deer on the tracks," Renati observed. "Sometimes you can find a dead one there. It's not too bad if the sun and the vultures haven't worked on it." The train's whistle faded away. "Mikhail?" she urged.

He listened still; the whistle had made something yearn inside him, but he wasn't sure what it might be. Renati was waiting for him, and the berserker stalked the forest. It was time to go. Mikhail looked back once at the Garden, with its squares of stones, and he followed Renati home.

2

On the afternoon of the second day after the babies had been buried, Franco grasped Mikhail's arm as Mikhail was on his knees outside the white palace, searching in the soft dirt for grubs. Franco pulled him up. "Come on," he said. "We've got somewhere to go."

They started off, heading south through the woods. Franco glanced back. No one had seen them; that was good. "Where are we going?" Mikhail asked him as Franco pulled him along.

"The Garden," he answered. "I want to see my children."

Mikhail tried to pull free of Franco's grip, but Franco held his arm tighter. He thought of crying out, for no particular reason other than he didn't care for Franco, but the pack wouldn't like that. Wiktor wouldn't like it; it was up to him to fight his own battles. "What do you need me for?"

"To dig," Franco said. "Now shut your mouth and walk faster."

As they left the white palace behind and the forest closed its green gates behind them, Mikhail realized Franco wasn't supposed to be doing this. Maybe the pack's laws didn't want the graves opened after the babies were buried; maybe the father was forbidden to see the dead infants. He wasn't sure why, but he knew Franco was using him to do something that Wiktor wouldn't like. He dragged his feet across the earth, but Franco wrenched his arm and pulled him on.

Keeping up with Franco was difficult; the man had a stride that soon made the breath rasp in Mikhail's lungs. "You're weak as water!" Franco growled at him. "Walk faster, I said!"

Mikhail stumbled over a root and fell to his knees. Franco yanked him up, and they kept going. There was a ferocity in Franco's pallid, brown-eyed face; even in his human mask, the wolf's face shone through. Maybe digging up the graves was bad luck, Mikhail thought. That's why the Garden was laid so far from the white palace. But Franco's humanity had taken over; like any human father, he burned to see the results of his seed. "Come on, come on!" he told Mikhail, both of them now racing through the woods.

In another few minutes they burst into the clearing where the squares of stones were, and Franco suddenly stopped dead in his tracks. Mikhail bumped into him, but the collision didn't jar Franco. The man gave a soft, strengthless gasp.

"Dear God," Franco whispered.

Mikhail saw it: the Garden's graves had been torn open, and bones were scattered across the ground. Skulls small and large, some human, some bestial, and some a commingling of both, lay broken around Mikhail's feet. Franco walked deeper into the Garden, his hands curled into claws at his sides. Almost all of the graves had been dug up, their contents pulled out, broken to pieces and wildly strewn. Mikhail stared down at a grinning skull, its teeth sharpened into fangs and gray streamers of hair on its scalp. Nearby lay the bones of a hand, and over there an arm bone. A small, twisted spinal cord caught Mikhail's gaze, then an infant's skull that had been crunched with tremendous force. Franco walked on, drawn toward the place where the fresh corpses had been buried. He stepped over old bones and stepped on a skull whose lower jaw snapped off like a piece of yellowed wood. He stopped, wavering on his feet, and stared at the gouged holes where the infants had been laid two days before. A ripped rag lay on the ground. Franco picked it up—and something torn and red and swarming with flies oozed out and fell into the leaves.

The infant had been cleaved in half. Franco could see the marks of the large fangs. The top half, including the head and the brains, was gone. Flies spun around Franco's face, and with them the coppery aroma of blood and decay. He looked to his right, at another smear of red in the dirt. A small leg, covered with fine brown hair. He made a soft,

235

terrible moaning sound, and old bones crunched under his feet as he stepped back from the crimson remains.

"The berserker," Mikhail heard him whisper. The birds sang in the treetops, happy and unaware. All around were uncovered graves and fragments of skeletons, both infant and adult, human and wolf. Franco spun toward Mikhail, and the boy saw his face—the flesh drawn tight around the bones, the eyes glassy and bulging. The pungent reek of rot wafted past Mikhail's nostrils. "The berserker," Franco repeated, his voice thin and quavering. The man looked around, his nostrils flared and sweat gleaming on his face. *"Where are you?"* Franco shouted; the bird song instantly ceased. *"Where are you, you bastard?"* He took a step in one direction, then a step in another; his legs seemed to want to pull him in two halves. *"Come out!"* he shrieked, his teeth bared and his chest heaving. *"I'll fight you!"* He picked up a wolf's skull and hurled it against a tree trunk, where it shattered with a noise like a gunshot. *"God damn you to hell, come out!"*

Flies battered into Mikhail's face and spun away, disturbed by Franco's turbulence. The man seethed, bright spots of red in his sallow cheeks and his body trembling like a taut and dangerous spring. He screamed, *"Come out and fight!"* and his voice sent the birds flying from their branches.

Nothing responded to Franco's challenge. The grinning skulls lay like mute witnesses to a massacre, and the dark curtains of flies closed over the red infant flesh. Before Mikhail could move to defend himself, Franco rushed him. The man lifted him up off his feet and shoved his back against a tree so hard the breath whooshed from Mikhail's lungs. "You're nothing!" Franco raged. "Do you hear me?" He shook Mikhail. "You're nothing!"

There were tears of pain in Mikhail's eyes, but he didn't let them fall. Franco wanted to destroy something, as the berserker had destroyed the bodies of his children. He shoved Mikhail's back against the tree again, harder. "We don't need you!" he shouted. "You little piece of weak-willed shi—"

It happened very fast. Mikhail wasn't sure exactly when

236

it happened, because it was a blur. A pit of flame opened within him, and seared his insides; there was a second of blinding pain, and then Mikhail's right hand—a wolf's claw covered with sleek black hair that entwined his arm almost to the elbow—streaked up and across Franco's cheek. The man's head snapped back, bloody furrows where the nails had slashed. Franco was stunned, and his eyes glinted with fear. He released Mikhail and jerked back, the blood trickling in crimson lines down his face. Mikhail settled to his feet, his heart slamming; he was as surprised as Franco, and he stared at his wolf's claw, bright red blood and bits of Franco's skin on the tips of the white nails. The black hair advanced past his elbow, and he felt pressure in his bones as they began to change their shape. There was a hollow *pop!* as the elbow went out of joint, and his arm shortened, the bones thickening under the moist, black-haired flesh. The hair advanced up his arm, toward his shoulder, and shone with dark blue highlights where the sun touched it. Mikhail felt throbbing pain in his jaws and forehead, as if an iron vise had begun to tighten around his skull. The tears broke from his eyes and ran down his cheeks. His left hand was changing now, the fingers snapping and shortening, growing hair and young white claws. Something was happening to his teeth; they crowded his tongue, and his gums felt ripped. He tasted blood in his mouth. He was terrified, and he looked desperately at Franco for help; Franco just stared at him, glassy-eyed, the blood dripping from his chin. It smelled to Mikhail like the red wine he remembered his father and mother drinking from crystal goblets, in another life. His muscles tensed and shivered, thickening across his shoulders and down his back. Black hair burst wild at his groin, under his dirty clothes.

"No," Mikhail heard himself groan, the harsh rasping of a frightened animal. "Please . . . no." He didn't want this; he couldn't stand it, not yet, and he fell to his knees in the leaves as the bending bones and thickening muscles freighted him down.

An instant later the black hair that had coiled over his right shoulder began to reverse itself, receding back down his arm. The claws of his fingers cracked and lengthened into fingers once more. His bones straightened, and his muscles thinned to those of a human boy again. His jaw and facial bones made little popping noises as they rearranged. He felt his teeth slide back into their sockets, and that was perhaps the worst of the pain. And less than forty seconds after the change had begun, it had completely reversed; Mikhail blinked, tears burning his eyes, and looked at his human, hairless hands. Blood was oozing from beneath the fingernails. The unaccustomed heaviness of new muscle was gone. His tongue felt human teeth, and blood tanged his saliva.

It was over.

"You little bastard," Franco said, but most of the steam had gone out of him. He looked deflated. "Couldn't do it, could you?" He touched his furrowed cheek and stared at his red-smeared palm. "I ought to kill you," he said. "You marked me. I ought to tear you to pieces, you little shit."

Mikhail struggled to rise. His legs were weak, and wouldn't allow it.

"You're not even worth killing," Franco decided. "You're still too much of a human. I ought to leave you out here, and you'd never even find your way back, would you?" He wiped blood from his oozing wounds and looked at his palm again. "Shit!" he said, disgusted.

"Why . . . do you hate me so much?" Mikhail managed to ask. "I've never done anything to you."

Franco didn't reply for a moment, and Mikhail thought he wasn't going to. Then Franco said, his voice acidic, "Wiktor thinks you're *special*." He slurred the word, as if it were something nasty. "He says he's never seen anyone fight to live as much as you did. Oh, he has high hopes for you." He snorted bitterly. "*I* say you're a weak whelp, but I'll give you this: you're lucky. Wiktor never hunted for anyone else before. He does it for you, because he says you're not ready for the change. *I* say either you become one of the pack, all the way, or we eat you. And I'll be the one who cracks open your skull and chews your brains. What do you think about that?"

"I . . . think . . ." Mikhail tried to stand again. Sweat was on his face. He started up, on willpower and bruised mus-

238

cles. His legs almost went out from under him again, but then he was up, breathing raggedly, and he faced Franco. "I think . . . someday . . . I'll have to kill you," he said.

Franco gaped at him. The silence stretched; distant crows called to each other. And then Franco laughed—more of a grunt, actually—and the laugh made him wince and press his fingers against his slashed cheek. *"You?* Kill *me?"* He laughed again, winced again. His eyes were cold, and they promised cruelty. "I'm going to let you live today," he said, as if from the grace of his heart; Mikhail guessed that it was because he feared Wiktor. "Like I said, you're lucky." He looked around, his eyes narrowed and his senses questing. There was no sign of the berserker except the uncovered graves and the broken bones: the scarred dirt and masses of leaves showed no tracks, there were no hanks of hair caught in the underbrush, and the berserker had rolled in the rotting flesh to mask his scent. This sacrilege against the pack had been done perhaps six or seven hours ago, Franco thought. The berserker was long gone. Franco walked away a few feet, bent down, and brushed flies away. He picked up a small, ripped arm, the hand still attached, and rose to his full height. He gently touched the fingers, exploring them like the petals of a strange flower. "This was mine," Mikhail heard him say in a quiet voice.

Franco bent down again, scooped away a handful of earth, put the chewed arm into it, and carefully replaced the dirt. He patted it down and covered it over with brown leaves. He sat on his haunches for a long time as flies buzzed around his head in search of the lost flesh. Several of them landed on Franco's bleeding cheek and feasted there, but he didn't move. He stared, motionlessly, at the patchwork of earth and leaves before him.

And then, abruptly, he stood up. He turned his back on the ruined Garden, and quickly strode away into the forest without glancing at Mikhail.

Mikhail let him go; he knew the way home. Anyway, if he lost his bearings he could follow the smell of Franco's blood. His strength was coming back, and his skull and heart had stopped pounding. He looked at the garden of scattered skeletons, wondering exactly where his own bones would lie, and who would cover them. He turned away, shunting those thoughts aside, and trailed Franco by following his tracks on the bruised earth.

3

Three more springs came and passed, and the summer of Mikhail's twelfth year scorched the forest. During that time, Renati had almost died with worms from an infected boar. Wiktor himself had nursed her to health and hunted for her, showing that granite could be tender. Pauli had given birth to a girl baby that Franco had sired; the baby had died in the night, her body contorting and rippling with light brown hair, when she was two months old. Nikita had seeded a child in Alekza's belly, but the growth passed away in a rush of blood and tissue when it was less than four months along.

Mikhail wore a deerskin robe and sandals that Renati had made for him, his old clothes much too small and tattered. He was growing, getting gangly, his thick black hair hanging around his shoulders and down his back. His mind was growing, too, from the food of Wiktor's books: mathematics, Russian history, the languages, classical literature—all were the feast that Wiktor offered. Sometimes it went down easily, other times Mikhail all but choked on it, but Wiktor's thundering voice in the fire-lit chamber commanded his attention. Mikhail even enjoyed Shakespeare, particularly the gruesomeness and ghosts of *Hamlet*.

His senses grew as well. There was no longer any true darkness for him; the deepest night was a gray twilight, with flesh-and-blood forms outlined in an eerie pale blue. When he truly concentrated, cutting off all distractions, he could find any of the pack in the white palace by trailing the distinctive rhythm of their heartbeats: Alekza's, for instance, always beat fast, like a little snare drum, while Wiktor's beat with slow and stately precision, a finely tuned instrument. Colors, sounds, aromas intensifed. In daylight he could see a deer running through the dense forest at a distance of a hundred yards. Mikhail learned the importance of speed: he caught rats, squirrels, and hares with ease, and added to the pack's food supply in a small way, but larger game eluded him. He often awakened from sleep to find an arm or leg covered with black hair and contorting into wolfish form, but the totality of the change still terrified him. Though his body may have been ready for it, his mind certainly was not. He marveled at how the others could slip back and forth between worlds, almost as if by wishing it. The fastest of them was Wiktor, of course; it took him less than forty seconds to complete the change from human flesh to gray wolf hide. The next quickest was Nikita, who made the transformation in a little over forty-five seconds. Alekza had the prettiest pelt, and Franco the loudest wail. Pauli was the shyest, and Renati the most merciful; she often let the smallest, most defenseless prey escape even when she'd run it to exhaustion. Wiktor scolded her for this frivolity, and Franco scowled at her, but she did as she pleased.

After the destruction of the Garden, a coldly furious Wiktor had taken Nikita and Franco out on a long, fruitless hunt for the berserker's den. In the three years since, the berserker had made himself known by leaving little piles of excrement around the white palace, and once the pack had heard him wailing in the night: a deep, hoarse taunt that changed direction as the berserker deftly shifted his position. It was a challenge to battle, but Wiktor declined; he chose not to run into the berserker's trap. Pauli had sworn she'd seen the berserker on a snowy night in early November, when she'd been running at Nikita's side on the trail of caribou. The red beast had come out of the snow at her, close enough for her to smell his rank madness, and his eyes had been cold black pits of hatred. He had opened slavering jaws to crush her throat—but then Nikita had swerved toward her, and the berserker disappeared into the snowfall. Pauli swore this, but Pauli sometimes mixed nightmares with reality, and Nikita didn't remember seeing anything but night and whirling flakes.

On a night in mid-July, there were no snowflakes, only the

whirl of golden fireflies rising from the forest floor as Mikhail and Nikita, in human form, ran silently through the woods. The herds had been thinned by the drought weather, and hunting had been poor for the last month. Wiktor had ordered Mikhail and Nikita to bring back something—any-thing—and now Mikhail followed the older man as best he could, Nikita running about twenty feet ahead and breaking a trail. They were heading south at a steady pace, and in a short while Nikita slowed to a brisk walk.

"Where are we going?" Mikhail asked in a whisper. He glanced around through the night's twilight, looking for anything alive. Not even a squirrel's eyes glinted with star-light.

"The railroad tracks," Nikita answered. "We'll see if we can't make this an easy hunt." Often the pack was able to find a dead deer, caribou, or smaller animal that had been hit by the train, which passed through the forest twice a day between May and August, going east in daylight and west at night.

Where the forest was stubbled with large boulders and cliffs fell off to the south, the tracks emerged from a rough-hewn tunnel, curved downhill along the bottom of a wooded gulley for at least six hundred yards, and then entered another tunnel to the west. Mikhail followed Nikita down the embankment, and they walked along the tracks, their eyes searching for the dark shape of a carcass and their nostrils sniffing the warm air for fresh blood. Tonight, no kills lay on the rails. They continued to the eastern tunnel—and then Nikita suddenly said, *"Listen."*

Mikhail did, and he heard it, too: a soft rumble of thunder. Except the sky was clear, the stars sparkling behind a gauze of hazy heat. The train was coming.

Nikita bent down, placing his hand against the iron. He could feel it vibrate as the train gathered power, heading into its long downhill run. In another moment it would burst out of the tunnel only a few yards distant.

"We'd better go," Mikhail told him.

Nikita stayed where he was, his hand on the rail. He stared at the tunnel's rocky opening, and then Mikhail saw him look toward the western tunnel's entrance, far away. "I used to come here alone," Nikita said quietly. "I used to watch the train roar past. That was before the berserker, damn him to hell. But I've seen the train go past many times. On its way to Minsk, I think. It comes out of that tunnel"— he nodded toward it—"and goes into that one there. Some nights, if the engineer's in a hurry to get home, it takes less than thirty seconds to make the distance. If he's drunk and riding the brake, it takes around thirty-five seconds from one tunnel to the next. I know; I've counted them off."

"Why?" Mikhail asked. The train's thunder—a traveling storm—was getting closer.

"Because someday I'm going to beat it." Nikita stood up. "Do you know what, for me, the grandest thing in the world would be?" His almond-shaped, Mongol eyes stared through the darkness at Mikhail. The boy shook his head. "To be *fast,*" Nikita went on, excitement mounting in his voice. "The fastest of all the pack. The fastest who ever lived. To will the change between the time the train comes out of the first tunnel and reaches the second. Do you see?"

Mikhail shook his head.

"Then watch," Nikita told him. The western tunnel had begun to lighten, and the rails were throbbing with a steam engine's mighty pulse. Nikita threw off his robe and stood naked to the world. And then, quite suddenly, the train burst from the tunnel like a snorting, black-mawed behemoth with a single yellow, cyclopean eyeball. Mikhail leaped backward as its hot breath enfolded him. Nikita, standing right at the edge of the tracks, didn't move a muscle. Freight cars rumbled past, red cinders spinning in the turbulence. Mikhail saw Nikita's body tense, saw his flesh ripple and begin to grow its sheen of fine black hair—and then Nikita started running along the tracks, his back and legs banded with wolf hair. He ran toward the eastern tunnel, his spine contorting in an instant, his legs and arms shivering and beginning to draw themselves upward into the torso. Mikhail saw the black hair cover Nikita's buttocks, a dark wartlike thing grew and burst at the base of the spine and the wolf's tail uncurled, twitching like a rudder. Nikita's backbone racheted down, and he ran low to the ground, his forearms thickening and his hands starting to twist into claws. He caught up with the engine, racing alongside it toward the mouth of the eastern tunnel. The engineer was riding the brake, but the furnace was still spouting sparks. Grinding wheels thundered two feet away from Nikita's legs. As he ran, his heart hammering, his feet contorted and threw him off balance, and he lost precious seconds as he struggled to right himself. The train's engine left him behind, black smoke and sparks swirling around him. He breathed the corruption of man, and his lungs felt poisoned. Mikhail lost sight of Nikita in the black maelstrom.

The train roared into the eastern tunnel, and continued its journey to Minsk. A single red lamp swung back and forth on the railing of its last freight car.

The smoke that had settled along the gulley had the sour tang of burned green timber. Mikhail walked into it, following the tracks, and he could feel the heat of the train's passage. Cinders still spun to earth, a night of dying stars. "Nikita!" he called. "Where are—"

A dark, powerful form leaped at him.

The black wolf planted its paws on Mikhail's shoulders and drove him down to the earth. Then the wolf stood astride his chest, its slanted eyes staring fixedly into his face, and its jaws opened to show clean white fangs.

"Stop it," Mikhail said. He grasped Nikita's muzzle and pushed the wolf's head astride. The wolf snarled, snapping at his face. "Will you *stop* it?" Mikhail demanded. "You're about to squash me!"

The wolf showed its fangs again, right in front of Mikhail's nose, and then a wet pink tongue came out and licked across Mikhail's face. Mikhail yelped and tried to shove the beast off, but Nikita's weight was solid. Finally, Nikita stepped off Mikhail's chest, and the boy sat up knowing he would find paw bruises on his flesh the next morning. Nikita ran in a circle, snapping at his tail just for the fun of it, and then he leaped into the high weeds on the gulley's side and rolled in them. "You're crazy!" Mikhail said, getting to his feet.

As Nikita rolled in the weeds, his body began to change again. There was a cracking sound of sinews lengthening, of bones being rejointed. Nikita gave a small mutter of pain, and Mikhail walked away a few yards to give him privacy.

In another thirty seconds or so, Mikhail heard Nikita say quietly, "Damn."

The Mongol walked past Mikhail, on his way uphill toward his cast-off robe. "I tripped over my own damned feet," he said. "They always get in the way."

Mikhail got in pace beside him. The black smoke was rising out of the gulley now, and the scorched iron smell of civilization was going with it. "I don't understand," he said. "What were you trying to do?"

"I told you. To be *fast*." He glanced back, in the direction the train had gone. "It'll be back, tomorrow night. And the night after that. I'll try again." He reached his robe, picked it up, and put it around his shoulders. Mikhail was watching him blankly, still not fully comprehending. "Wiktor will tell you a story, if you ask," Nikita said. "He says the old man who led the pack when Wiktor came in remembered someone who could will the change in twenty-four seconds. Can you imagine that? From human to wolf in twenty-four seconds? Wiktor himself can't beat half a minute! And I—well, I'm pathetic."

"No, you're not. You're fast."

"Not fast *enough*," Nikita said forcefully. "I'm not the quickest, I'm not the strongest, I'm not the smartest. And all my life, even when I was a boy your age breaking my ass in a coal mine, I wanted to be something special. You work at the bottom of a mine shaft long enough, you dream of being a bird. Maybe I still have that dream—only I want my legs to be wings."

"What does it matter, whether you're the quickest or—"

"It matters to me," he interrupted. "It gives me a purpose. Do you see?" He went on without waiting for the boy to respond. "I come here during the summer, but only at night. I don't want the engineer to see me. I *am* getting faster; it's just that my legs haven't figured out how to fly yet." He motioned down the tracks toward the distant eastern tunnel. "Some night I'm going to beat the train. I'm going to start right here, as a man, and before the train reaches the other tunnel I'm going to cross the tracks in front of the engine as a wolf."

"Cross the *tracks?*"

"Yes. On all fours," Nikita said. "Now we'd better find something for the pack to eat, or we'll be looking all night." He started walking away, downhill toward the east, and Mikhail followed him. A little more than a half mile from where Nikita had chased the train, they found a crushed rabbit lying on the tracks. It was a fresh kill, its eyes bulging as if still mesmerized by the glowing yellow orb of the monster that had passed over it. The rabbit was a small find, but it was a beginning. Nikita picked it up by the ears and carried it at his side, swinging it like a broken toy as they continued their search.

The smell of the rabbit's blood made Mikhail's mouth water. He could almost feel a bestial growl strain to leave his throat. He was becoming more like the pack every passing day. The change was waiting for him, like a dark friend. All he had to do was reach out for it, and embrace it; it was that close, and it was eager. But he didn't know how to control it. He had no idea how to "will the change," as the others seemed to. Was it like a command, or a dream? He feared losing the last of being a human; the full change would take him to a place where he dared not go. Not yet; not just yet.

He was salivating. There was a growl; not his throat, but his stomach. He was still more boy than wolf, after all.

On many nights during that long, drought-plagued summer, Mikhail hunted with Nikita along the railroad tracks. Once, in early August, they found a small deer suffering, two of its legs severed by the train's wheels. Nikita had bent down and looked into that deer's shock-silvered eyes, and Mikhail had watched him reach gentle hands out to stroke the animal's flanks. Nikita had spoken quietly to the deer, trying to calm it—and then he placed his hands on the deer's skull and gave it a sharp, violent twist. The deer had slumped, its neck broken, all suffering ended. And that, Nikita told him, was the meaning of mercy.

The train kept to its schedule. Some nights it roared down the hill, from tunnel to tunnel; other nights its brakes screamed and hurled sparks. Mikhail sat on the embankment, in the shelter of the pines, and watched as Nikita raced it along the rails, his body twisting, fighting for balance as the change swept over him. It always seemed to be his legs, the earth-rooted wings, that refused to let him fly. Nikita was getting faster, but never fast enough; the train invariably outpaced him, and left him in its smoke as it thundered into the eastern tunnel.

August ended, and the summer's final train rumbled away toward Minsk, its red lantern swinging on the last car like a scarlet grin. Nikita, his shoulders slumped, trotted back to where he'd left his robe, and Mikhail watched his body shed its glossy black hair. Nikita, man-shaped again, put on his robe and breathed the smoke's bitter odor as if breathing the sweat of a fierce and respected enemy. "Well," he said at last, "summer will come again."

They went home, walking toward autumn.

--------- 4 ---------

Winter, the cruel white lady, closed her fist around the forest, and sealed it in ice. Cold cracked trees, ponds were white slabs, and the sky glowered with low clouds and mist. For day upon day, the sun remained a stranger, and the whole world was a sea of snow and black, leafless trees. Even the crows, those ebony-gowned diplomats, froze where they perched, or fought to reach the sun on freezing wings. Only the snow hares scurried in the blank silence of the forest, and as the winds swept down from Siberia even the hares shivered in their burrows.

So, too, the pack shivered in the depths of the white palace. They crowded together, ghost-breathed, around the pine-knot flames. Mikhail's education, however, went on; Wiktor was a hard taskmaster, and he and the boy huddled close as Mikhail recited Shakespeare, the works of Dante, mathematics problems, and European history.

On a day in January, Pauli and Nikita went outside to find more firewood. Wiktor told them to stay close to the white palace and within sight of each other. The mist had descended, making visibility difficult, but the fire had to be tended. And not half an hour had passed before Nikita came back into the den, moving like a numb sleepwalker, his eyebrows and hair silvered with ice. He carried an armload of sticks, which fell to his feet as he continued on into the circle of the fire. His eyes were dazed. Wiktor stood up and said, "Where's Pauli?"

She had been within twenty feet of him, Nikita said. Twenty feet. They had been talking, trying to warm each other with words. And then, quite suddenly, Pauli simply hadn't answered. There had been no cry for help, no sounds of a struggle in the mist. One moment Pauli had been there, the next . . .

Nikita took Wiktor and Franco up to show them. They found bright gouts of blood on the snow, less than forty yards from the ice-domed palace. Pauli's robe was nearby, also splattered with gore. On the ground lay a few sticks, like bleached bones. Pauli's footprints ended where the paw prints of the berserker came out of a thicket of thorns. In the snow was the furrow of a body being dragged, over a hillock and down into dense woods. They found some of Pauli's insides, purple as bruises on the snow. The berserker's tracks and the furrow of Pauli's dragged body went on, through the forest. Wiktor, Franco, and Nikita threw aside their robes and, shivering, changed shapes in the clinging mist. Three wolves—one gray, one pale brown, one black—loped through the drifts on the berserker's trail. A mile to the east, they found one of Pauli's arms, blue as marble, wedged between two rocks. It had been ripped loose from the shoulder. They came to a place of cliffs, where the wind had swept the jagged rocks clean of snow, and the berserker's tracks ended as did all traces of Pauli's corpse.

For the next few hours, the trio of wolves searched in widening circles that took them farther and farther away from the white palace. Once Franco thought he saw a huge red shape standing on an outcropping of rock above them, but the blowing snow obscured his sight for a few seconds and when he could see clearly again the shape was gone. Nikita picked up Pauli's scent—a musky summer-grass smell—in the crosscurrent of wind, and they tracked it another half mile to the north before they found her head lying at the bottom of a ravine, her skull gnawed open and her brains gone.

The berserker's tracks led them to the edge of a rocky chasm, then they vanished on the stones. Caves pocked the chasm's sides; it would be a treacherous climb down, but it could be done. Any of those caves might be the berserker's den. But if not, Wiktor, Nikita, and Franco might break their necks for naught. It was snowing harder; the iron smell of a blizzard grayed the air. Wiktor signaled with a snort and toss of his head, and they turned back for the long journey home.

All this Wiktor related as the pack crouched around the fire. When he finished he moved away, sitting in a corner by himself. He chewed on a warthog's bones and stared at the empty pallet where Pauli used to lie, his eyes burning in the cold gloom.

"I say we go out and hunt the bastard down!" Franco shouted as the blizzard roared beyond the walls. "We can't just sit here, like . . . like . . ."

"Like human beings?" Wiktor asked quietly. He picked up a small twig from the fire and watched it burn.

"Like *cowards!*" Franco said. "First Belyi, then the Garden ransacked, now Pauli gone! It won't stop until it kills all of us!"

"We can't go out in this storm," Nikita observed, sitting on his haunches. "The berserker can't either."

"We've got to find it and kill it!" Franco paced in front of the fire, almost stepping on Mikhail. "If I could just get my claws in its damned throat, I'd—"

Renati snorted derisively. "You'd be its breakfast."

"You shut up, you old hag! Who asked you to speak?"

Renati was on her feet in an instant. She stepped toward him, and he whirled toward her. Russet hair rose and rippled on the backs of Renati's hands, her fingers starting to curve into claws.

"Stop it," Wiktor said. Renati glanced at him, her facial bones already beginning to warp. "Renati, please stop it," he repeated.

"Let her kill him," Alekza said, her ice-blue eyes cold in her beautiful face. "He deserves to die."

"Renati?" Wiktor stood up. Renati's spine had begun to bow over.

"Come on, come on!" Franco sneered. He held up his right hand, which was covered with light brown hair and had already grown talons. "I'm ready for you!"

"Stop it!" Wiktor shouted, and the sound of his voice made Mikhail jump; it was his schoolmaster's thunder. The voice echoed between the walls. "If we kill each other, the berserker wins. He can come right in here and take our den if we're lying dead. So stop it, both of you. We've got to think like humans, not act like beasts."

Renati blinked, her mouth and jaw misshapen. A little ooze of saliva trickled over her lower lip, down her russet-haired chin, and hung for a second before it dripped off. And then her face began to return to its human side again, the muscles writhing under the flesh, the fangs retreating with wet clicking sounds. The wolf hair dissolved to a stubble and went away. Renati scratched the backs of her hands as the last of the hair irritated her flesh. "You little bastard," she said, her stare still directed at Franco. "You show me respect, do you understand?"

Franco grunted and gave her a chilly smile. He motioned disdainfully at her with his right hand, now human and pale once more, and he walked away from the fire's heat. The musky smell of enraged animals lingered in the chamber.

Wiktor stood between Renati and Franco; he waited until their tempers had cooled, and then he said, "We're a family, not enemies. The berserker would like for us to turn on each other; it would make his task so much easier." He tossed the burning twig into the fire. "But Franco's right. We've got to find the berserker and kill it. If we don't, it'll kill us, one by one."

"You see?" Franco said to Renati. "He agrees with me!"

"I agree with the law of logic," Wiktor corrected. "Which, unfortunately, you don't always obey." He paused for a moment, listening to the high wail of the storm through the broken windows on the level above. "I think the berserker lives in one of those caves we found," he went on.

"Nikita's right: the berserker won't go out in this storm. But *we* could."

"You can't see your hand in front of your face out there!" Renati said. "Listen to that wind!"

"I hear it." Wiktor circled the fire, rubbing his hands together. "When the storm breaks, the berserker will go out on the hunt again. We don't know his patterns, and once he smells us in his cave he'll find another den. But . . . what if we found his cave, and him in it, while the storm's still blowing?"

"It can't be done!" Nikita shook his head. "You saw that chasm. We'd kill ourselves trying to get down in there."

"The berserker can do it. If he can, so can we." Wiktor paused to let that point sink in. "The greatest problem would be finding his cave. If I were he, I would've marked every one of them with my scent. But maybe he hasn't; maybe, once we get down into that chasm, we can pick up his scent and follow it right to him. He might be sleeping; that's what I'd do, if I had a full belly and I thought I was safe."

"Yes, that's it!" Franco said excitedly. "Kill the bastard in his sleep!"

"No. The berserker's big and very strong, and none of us would do so well against it claw to claw. First we find the berserker's cave, and then we seal him in with rocks. We make it good and tight, so he can't dig himself out. If we're fast, we can get the cave sealed before he knows what's happening."

"And provided he doesn't have a back way out," Renati said.

"I didn't say the plan was foolproof. No plan ever is. But the berserker's insane; he doesn't think like an ordinary wolf. Why should he worry about running when he thinks he can destroy anything on four legs or two? I'd say he's found a nice warm cave with no back door, where he can curl up, chew on bones, and brood about how to kill the next one of us. I believe it's worth the risk."

"*I* don't," Renati told him. Her brow furrowed. "The storm's too strong. It would be hard enough getting from here to there, much less finding the right cave. No. The risk is too high."

"And what's the alternative, then?" Wiktor asked. "Wait for the storm to pass and the berserker to hunt us again? We should take advantage of the fact that he's just had a feast; he'll be sluggish, with all that meat in his belly. I say we go now, or we risk the destruction of the pack."

"Yes!" Franco agreed. "Hunt him now, while he thinks he's safe!"

"I've decided. I'm going." Wiktor looked around at the others. His gaze lingered for a few seconds on Mikhail, then moved away. "Franco, will you go with me?"

"Me?" His eyes had widened. "Yes. Of course I will." His voice was unsteady. "I just hope I . . . don't hold you up."

"Hold me up? How?"

"Well . . . I didn't mention it before. It's nothing, of course, but . . . I have a stone bruise on my foot. You see?" He slipped off his deerskin sandal and showed the blue bruise. "My ankle's a little swollen, too. I'm not sure when it happened, exactly." He pressed the bruise, and winced a fraction too much. "But I can still go," he said. "I won't be as fast as usual, but you can count on me."

"To be an utter ass," Renati finished for him. "Forget Franco and his poor feet. I'll go with you."

"I need you to stay here. To take care of Mikhail and Alekza."

"They can take care of themselves!"

Wiktor had already dismissed her. He looked at Nikita. "Any stone bruises on your feet?"

"Dozens," Nikita said, and stood up. "When do we go?"

"It's my ankle that's giving me the trouble!" Franco protested. "See? It's swollen! I must've stepped down wrong when we were—"

"I understand," Wiktor told him, and Franco was silent. "Nikita and I will go. You can stay here, if that's what you want." Franco started to speak again, but he thought better of it and closed his mouth. "The sooner we go, the sooner we can get back," Wiktor said to Nikita. "I'm ready now." Nikita nodded, and Wiktor turned his attention to Renati. "If we're able to find the berserker's cave, and seal him in, we'll want to stay long enough to make certain he doesn't dig out. We'll try to be back within forty-eight hours. If the storm gets too bad, we'll find a place to sleep. You'll take care of everything, yes?"

"Yes," Renati said glumly.

"And you and Franco will stay away from each other's throats." It was a command. Wiktor looked at Mikhail. "You'll keep them from killing each other, won't you?"

"Yes, sir," Mikhail answered, though what he could do if Renati and Franco clashed he didn't know.

"When I get back, I want you to have finished the lesson we started yesterday." It was a reading about the destruction of the Roman Empire. "I'll ask you questions about it."

Mikhail nodded. Wiktor stripped off his robe and removed his sandals, and Nikita did the same. The two men stood naked, their breath coming out in misty plumes. Nikita began to change first, the black hair twining over his flesh like strange vines. Wiktor's eyes glinted in the low light as he stared at Renati. "Listen to me," he said. "If for any reason . . . we don't come back after three days, you'll be in charge of the pack."

"A *woman?*" Franco yelped. "In charge of *me?*"

"In charge of the pack," Wiktor repeated. A gray tide of wolf hair was sliding over his shoulders and streaking down his arms. His flesh looked slick and oily, and sweat glistened on his forehead as his eyebrows merged. Steam wafted around his body. "Do you have any objection to that?" His voice was getting hoarse, and his facial bones were shifting. Fangs pushed out between his lips.

"No," Franco answered quickly. "No objection."

"Wish us luck." The voice was a guttural rasp. Wiktor's flesh shivered, growing its thick, gray-haired hide. Most of Nikita's head and face had already changed, the snout spewing a blast of steam as it lengthened with popping sounds that Mikhail had once thought hideous. Now the sounds of transformation were as beautiful as music played on exotic instruments. The two bodies contorted, flesh giving way to wolf hair, fingers and toes to claws, teeth to fangs, noses to long black muzzles; all accompanied by the music of bones, sinews, and muscles changing shape, rearranging themselves into canine form, and an occasional grunt from

253

either Wiktor or Nikita. And then Wiktor gave a harsh *whuff* and he loped out of the chamber toward the stairway, with Nikita a few strides behind. Within seconds, the two wolves were gone.

"My ankle *is* swollen!" Franco showed Renati again. "See? I couldn't get very far on it, could I?"

She ignored him. "We'll need some fresh water, I think." She picked up a clay bowl that had been left by the monks; the water, filmed with dirty ice, was almost gone. "Mikhail, will you and Alekza get us some more snow, please?" She handed the bowl to Mikhail. All they would have to do was climb the stairs and scoop up snow that was blowing in the windows. "Franco, will you take the first watch, or shall I?"

"You're in charge," he said. "Do as you please."

"All right. You take the first watch. I'll relieve you when it's time." Renati sat down before the fire, newly regal.

Franco muttered a curse under his breath; it wouldn't be pleasant to go up into the tower, with all those glassless windows and the cold whirling in, but keeping watch was an important duty that everyone shared. He stalked away, Mikhail and Alekza went to scoop up a bowlful of snow, and Renati rested her chin on her hand to worry about the man she loved.

5

Sometime during the night, the storm snapped. It passed on, leaving the forest covered with drifts eight feet high, the trees bent under arctic ice. A bone-throbbing cold followed the blizzard, and the day dawned white, the sun hidden behind clouds the color of wet cotton.

It was breakfast time. "God, it's cold!" Franco said as he and Mikhail struggled across a white desert where green thicket used to be. Mikhail didn't answer; it used up too much energy to speak, and his jaws felt frozen. He glanced back, about fifty yards, at the white palace; it was almost invisible against the blankness. "I curse this place!" Franco said. "Damn the whole country! Damn Wiktor, and damn Nikita, damn Alekza, and damn that damned Renati. Who does she think she is, ordering me around like a servant boy?"

"We'll never find anything," Mikhail told him quietly, "if you make all that noise."

"Hell, there's nothing alive out here! How are we supposed to find food? *Create* it? I'm not God, that's for sure!" He stopped, sniffing the air; his nose stung with cold, and his ability to smell was hampered. "If Renati's in charge, why doesn't *she* find us food? Answer me that!"

There was no need to answer. They had drawn lots—the shortest twigs from the fire—for the task of finding breakfast. Actually Mikhail had drawn the shortest twig, and Franco the next shortest. "Anything alive out here," Franco went on, "is buried in its hole, keeping warm. Like we ought to be doing. Smell the air. You see? Nothing."

As if to prove Franco wrong, a hare with gray-tipped fur suddenly shot across the snow in front of them, heading for a stand of half-buried trees. "There!" Mikhail said. "Look!"

"My eyes are freezing."

Mikhail stopped and turned toward Franco. "Aren't you going to change? You can catch it if you change."

"To hell with it!" Franco's cheeks had grown red splotches. "It's too cold to change. My balls would freeze off, if they haven't already." He reached down and checked himself.

"If you don't change, we won't catch anything," Mikhail reminded him. "How hard would it be for you to chase down that rabbit if—"

"Oh, now *you're* giving orders, is that it?" Franco scowled at him. "You listen to me, you little shit: *you* drew the shortest twig. You change and catch us something. It's about time you pulled your weight around here!"

The question stung Mikhail, because he knew there was truth in it. He walked on ahead, his arms clasped around himself for warmth and his sandals crunching through the ice-crusted snow.

"Well, why don't you change, then?" Franco jabbed him, sensing blood. He strode after the boy. "Why don't you change so you can chase down rabbits and howl at the damned moon like a maniac?"

Mikhail didn't answer; he didn't know what to say. He looked for the hare, but it had disappeared in the whiteness. He glanced back at the white palace, which seemed to float like a distant mirage between earth and sky, all of them the same hue. Large flakes began to fall again, and if Mikhail hadn't felt so cold, miserable, and useless, he might have thought they were beautiful.

Franco stopped a few yards away from him and blew into his cupped hands. Snowflakes drifted into his hair and laced his eyelashes. "Maybe Wiktor enjoys this life," he said grimly, "and maybe Nikita does, too, but what were they to begin with? My father was a rich man, and I was a rich man's son." He shook his head, the snowflakes sliding down his ruddy face. "We were on our way by carriage, to visit my grandparents. A storm caught us; a storm very much like the one yesterday. My mother froze to death first. But my father, my little brother, and I found a cabin, not far from here. Well, it's gone now; the snow broke it down years ago." Franco looked up, searching for the sun. He couldn't find it. "My little brother died weeping," he said. "At the end he couldn't even open his eyes; the lids were frozen together. My father knew we couldn't stay there. If we were going to live, we had to find a village. So we started walking. I remember . . . we both wore our fur-lined coats and our expensive boots. My shirt had a monogram on it. My father wore a cashmere scarf. But none of it kept us warm enough, not with that wind shrieking into our faces. We found a hollow and tried to make a fire, but all the wood was icy." He looked at Mikhail. "Do you know what we burned? All the money in my father's wallet. It burned very bright, but it gave off no heat. What we would've given for three lumps of coal! My father froze to death, sitting upright. I was a seventeen-year-old orphan, and I knew I was going to die if I didn't find shelter. So I started walking, wearing two coats. I didn't get very far before the wolves found me." He blew into his hands again and worked his knuckles. "One of them bit me, on the arm. I kicked him in the muzzle so hard I knocked three of his teeth out. That bastard—Josef was his name—was never right in the head after that. They tore my father to pieces and ate him. They probably ate my mother and little brother, too. I never asked." Franco surveyed the blank sky once more and watched the snow falling. "They took me into the pack to be a breeder. The same reason we took you in."

"A . . . *breeder?*"

"To make babies," Franco explained. "The pack needs cubs, or it's going to die. But the babies don't live." He shrugged. "Maybe God knows what He's doing, after all." He looked toward the trees, where the snow hare hid. "You listen to Wiktor, and he'll go on about how noble this life is, and how we ought to be proud of what we are. I don't find anything noble in having hair on your ass and gnawing on bloody bones. Damn this life." He gathered saliva in his mouth and spat in the snow. "You change," he told Mikhail. "You go run on all fours and piss against a tree. I was born a man, by God, and that's what I am." He turned away and began trudging the seventy yards or so back to the walls of the white palace.

"Wait!" Mikhail called. "Franco, wait!" But Franco didn't wait.

He looked back over his shoulder at Mikhail. "Bring us back a nice juicy rabbit," he said acidly. "Or if you're lucky, maybe you can dig us up some fat grubs. I'm going back in and try to get wa—"

Franco didn't finish his sentence, for in the next instant what had appeared to be a mound of snow a few feet to his right burst open, and the huge red wolf lunged out, snapping its jaws shut on Franco's leg.

The bones broke like pistol shots as the berserker wrenched Franco off his feet, and its fangs tore the flesh into crimson ribbons. Franco opened his mouth to scream, but only a choke came out. Mikhail stood stunned, his brain reeling. The berserker had either been lying in wait under the snow, just its nostrils lifted up to catch air, or else it had burrowed beneath the drifts to ambush them. There was no time to wonder what had happened to Wiktor and Nikita; there was only the reality of the berserker ripping Franco's leg apart, and blood steaming in the snow.

Mikhail started to shout for help, but by the time Renati and Alekza got here—if they even heard him—Franco would be dead. The berserker released Franco's tattered leg, and closed its jaws on his shoulder as Franco desperately fought to keep the fangs away from his throat. Franco's face had gone death white, his eyes bulging with terror.

Mikhail looked up. A tree branch, coated with ice, was about three feet over his head. He leaped up for it, grasped the branch, and it cracked off in his hands. The berserker paid him no attention, its teeth deep in the muscle of Franco's shoulder. And then Mikhail sprang forward, dug his heels into the snow, and drove the stick's sharp end into one of the berserker's gray eyeballs.

The stick gouged the berserker's eye out, and the wolf released Franco's shoulder with a roar of pain and rage. As the berserker staggered back and shook its head to clear the agony, Franco tried to crawl away. He got about six feet before he shuddered and passed out, his leg and shoulder mangled. The berserker snapped wantonly at the air, and its remaining eye found Mikhail Gallatinov.

Something passed between them: Mikhail could feel it, as strongly as the pounding of his heart and the blood rushing through his veins. Maybe it was a communion of hatred, or a primal recognition of impending violence; whatever it was, Mikhail understood it fully, and he gripped the sharp stick like a spear as the berserker hurtled toward him across the snow.

The red wolf's jaws gaped open for him, its powerful legs preparing to leap. Mikhail stood his ground, his nerves tingling, every human instinct urging him to run but the wolf inside him waiting with cold judgment. The berserker made a feinting move to the left that Mikhail instantly saw was false, and then it left the ground and came at him.

Mikhail fell to his knees, under the big body and the flailing claws, and he drove the stick upward. It pierced the berserker's white-haired stomach as the beast went over him; the stick cracked in two, its point deep in the berserker's belly, and the wolf contorted in midair, one of its forelegs slamming across Mikhail's back and two talons ripping through the deerskin cloak. Mikhail felt as if a hammer had struck him; he was knocked onto his face in the snow, and he heard the berserker grunt as it landed on its stomach a few yards away. Mikhail twisted his body, his lungs seizing cold air, and he faced the berserker before it could leap onto his back. The one-eyed beast was on its feet, the spear driven so deep in its gut that it had almost disappeared. Mikhail stood up, his chest heaving, and he felt hot blood trickling down his back. The berserker danced to the right, positioning himself between Mikhail and the white palace. The stick clenched in Mikhail's right fist was about seven inches long, the length of a kitchen knife. The berserker snorted steam, feinted in and then out again, blocking Mikhail from fleeing home. "Help us!" he shouted toward the white palace. His voice was muffled by the snowfall. "Renati! Help—"

The beast lunged forward, and Mikhail stabbed at its other eye with the stick. But the berserker stopped and whirled aside, spraying snow up from under its paws, and the stick jabbed empty air. The berserker twisted its body, darting around to Mikhail's unprotected side, and it leaped at him before he could stab with the stick again.

The berserker hit him. Mikhail had the image of the freight train, one eye blazing, as it roared on the downhill tracks. He was knocked off his feet like a rag doll, and would have broken his back if not for the snow. His breath whooshed out of him, and his brain was stunned by the impact. He smelled blood and animal saliva. A brutal weight crushed down on his shoulder, pinning his hand and the stick. He blinked, and in the haze of pain saw the berserker's maw above him, its fangs opening to seize his face and strip it away from the skull like flimsy cloth. His shoulder was trapped, the bones about to burst from their sockets. The berserker leaned forward, the muscles bunching along its flanks, and Mikhail smelled Franco's blood on its breath. The jaws stretched open to crush his skull.

Two human hands, streaked with brown hair, caught the berserker's jaws. Franco had roused himself and leaped atop the red beast. His brown-stubbled face a rictus of pain, Franco gasped, *"Run,"* as he twisted the berserker's head with all his strength.

The berserker thrashed against him, but Franco held tight. The jaws snapped together, and teeth pierced Franco's palms. The weight was off Mikhail's shoulder; he lifted his arm, the bones throbbing, and drove the sharp stick up into the berserker's throat. It plunged in three inches before it met an obstruction and broke again. The berserker howled and shivered with agony, snorting a crimson mist, and Mikhail pushed himself out from under the wolf as it reared up and tried to throw Franco off its back. "Run!" Franco shouted, hanging on by his bloody fingernails.

Mikhail got up, snow all over him. He began running, the last few inches of the broken stick falling from his hand. Snowflakes whirled around him, like dancing angels. His shoulder throbbed, the muscles deeply bruised. He looked back, saw the berserker shake itself in a violent frenzy. Franco lost his grip and was flung off. The berserker tensed to leap on Franco's body and finish him, but Mikhail stopped. "Hey!" he shouted, and the berserker's head angled toward him, its single eye blazing.

Something blazed within Mikhail as well. He felt it, like a fire that had opened at his center, and to save Franco's life—and his own—he would have to reach into those white-hot flames, and grasp what had been forged.

I want it, he thought, and he fixed on the image of his hand twisting into a claw, the picture of it radiant in his mind. He thought he heard an inner wail, like wild winds unleashed. Pinpricks of pain swept up his spine. *I want it.* Steam drifted from his pores. He shivered, pressure squeezing his organs. His heart pounded. He felt pain in the muscles of his arms and legs, a terrible clenching pain around his skull. Something cracked in his jaw, and he heard himself moan.

The berserker watched him, transfixed by the sight, its jaws still open and ready to break Franco's neck.

Mikhail lifted his right hand. It was covered with sleek black hair, and the fingers had retracted into white claws. *I want it.* The black hair raced up his arm. His left hand was changing. His head felt as if it were caught in an iron vise, and his jaw was lengthening with brittle cracking sounds. *I want it.* There was no turning back now, no denying the change. Mikhail threw his deerskin cloak off, and it slithered to the snow. He fumbled with his sandals, barely got them off before his feet began to contort. He fell, off balance, and went down on his rump.

The berserker sniffed the air. It made a grunting noise, and watched the thing take shape.

Black hair scurried over Mikhail's chest and shoulders. It entwined his throat and covered his face. His jaw and nose were lengthening into a muzzle, and his fangs burst free with such force they slashed the inside of his mouth and made blood and saliva drool. His backbone bent, with stunning pain. His legs and arms shortened, grew thick with muscle. Sinews and cartilage popped and cracked. Mikhail shuddered, his body thrashing as if getting rid of the last human elements. His tail, slick with fluids, had thrust from the dark growth at the base of his spine, and now it twitched in the air as Mikhail got on all fours. His muscles continued to quiver like harp strings, his nerves aflame. Musky-smelling fluids oozed over his pelt. His testicles had drawn up like hard stones, and were covered with coarse hair. His right ear rippled with hair and began to change into a triangular cup, but the left ear malfunctioned; it simply remained the ear of a human boy. The pain intensified, bordering on the edge of pleasure, and then rapidly subsided. Mikhail started to call to Franco, to tell him to crawl away; he opened his mouth, and the high yip that came out scared him.

He thanked God he couldn't see himself, but the shock in the berserker's eye told him enough. He had willed the change, and it was on him.

Mikhail's bladder let go, streaking yellow across the white. He saw the berserker dismiss him, and start to lean over Franco again. Franco had passed out, was unable to defend himself. Mikhail bounded forward, got his forelegs and hind legs tangled up, and he went down on his belly. He got up once more, shaky as a newborn. He shouted at the berserker; it emerged as a thin growl that didn't even snag the red wolf's attention. Mikhail leaped clumsily over the

261

snow, lost his footing, and fell again, but then he was right beside the wolf and he did it without thinking: he opened his jaws, and sank his fangs into the berserker's ear. As the animal roared and twisted away, Mikhail tore the ear off to its fleshy roots.

The berserker staggered, stunned by the fresh pain. Mikhail had the ear between his teeth; his throat convulsed, blood in his mouth, and he swallowed the wolf's ear. The berserker spun in a mad circle, snapping at the air. Mikhail turned, the twitching of his tail almost throwing him off his paws again, and he ran.

His legs betrayed him. The ground was right in his face, and all perspective was bizarre. He stumbled, slid over the snow on his stomach, scrambled up, and tried to flee, but matching the movement of four legs was a mystery. He heard the berserker's rumbled breath right behind him, and he knew it was about to leap; he feinted to the left and swerved to the right, skidding off balance once more. The berserker jumped past him, digging up a flurry of snow as it fought to change direction. Mikhail struggled up, the hair bristling along his back; he swerved violently again, his spine amazingly supple. He heard the click of fangs as the berserker's jaws narrowly missed his flank. And then Mikhail, his legs trembling, turned to face the red beast, snow whirling into the air between them. The berserker rushed at him, snorting steam and blood. Mikhail planted his paws, his legs splayed and his heart seemingly about to explode. The berserker, expecting his enemy to dodge to either side, suddenly checked his speed and dug his paws into the snow, and Mikhail reared up on his hind legs like a human being and lunged forward.

His jaws opened, an instinctual movement that Mikhail couldn't remember triggering. He clamped them on the berserker's muzzle and crunched his fangs down through hair and flesh into cartilage and bone. As he bit deeply, he brought his left claw up in a savage arc and raked the talons across the berserker's remaining eye.

The beast howled, blinded, and twisted his body to throw the small wolf off, but Mikhail held tight. The berserker lifted up, hesitated for only an instant, and then smashed down on Mikhail. He felt a rib snap, a crushing pain jabbing through him, but the snow again saved his spine. The berserker lifted up again, and as the beast rose to his full height Mikhail released his grip on the bleeding muzzle and scrambled away, the pain of his broken rib almost stealing his breath.

The berserker clawed the air with blind fury. He raced in a circle, trying to find Mikhail, and slammed his red skull against the trunk of an oak tree. Dazed, the beast whirled around, fangs snapping at nothing. Mikhail backed away from him, to give the thing plenty of room, and he stood near Franco, his shoulders slumped to ease the pain in his rib cage. The berserker gave an enraged series of grunts, snorting blood, and then he spun to right and left, the crushed nose seeking a scent.

A russet shape shot across the snow and crashed headlong into the berserker's side. Renati's claws flailed ribbons of red hair and flesh, and the berserker was thrown into a tangle of thorns. Before the berserker could grasp her, Renati darted away again and circled warily. Another wolf—this one blond, with ice-blue eyes—leaped in from the berserker's other side, and Alekza raked a claw along the berserker's flank. As he turned to snap at her, Alekza bounded away and Renati darted in to seize one of the berserker's hind legs between her teeth. Her head twisted, and the berserker's leg snapped. Then Renati scrambled away as the red wolf staggered on three legs. Alekza lunged forward, grasped the beast's remaining ear, and ripped it away. She danced back as the berserker clawed at her, but his movements were getting sluggish. He went a few paces in one direction, stopped and turned in another, and behind him he left bright splotches of crimson on the snow.

But he was strong. Mikhail stood back and watched as Renati and Alekza wore him down, the death of a thousand bites and scratches. The berserker at last tried to run, dragging the broken leg behind him. Renati slammed into his side, knocking him to the ground, and crushed a foreleg between her jaws as Alekza gripped his tail. The berserker struggled to rise, and Renati drove her talons into his belly and ripped him open with a grace that was almost beautiful.

263

The berserker shivered, and lay writhing on the bloody white. Renati leaned forward, seizing the red wolf's unprotected throat between her fangs. The berserker made no effort to fight back. Mikhail saw Renati's sleek muscles tense—and then she released the throat and stepped away. She and Alekza both looked at Mikhail.

He didn't understand at first. Why hadn't Renati torn the throat out? But then it dawned on him as the two wolves stared impassively: they were offering the kill to him.

"Go on," Franco said, a raspy whisper. He was sitting up, his torn hands clenched to his shoulder. Mikhail was amazed on a new level; he'd understood the human voice as clearly as ever. "Take the kill," Franco told him. "It's yours."

Renati and Alekza waited as the snowflakes drifted to earth. Mikhail saw it in their eyes: this was expected of him. He walked forward, his legs slipping and ungainly, and he stood over the conquered red wolf.

The berserker was more than twice his size. He was an old wolf, some of his hair gone gray. His muscles were thick, carved from struggle. The red skull lifted, as if listening to Mikhail's heartbeat. Blood oozed from the holes where the eyes had been, and a crushed paw feebly scarred the snow.

He's asking for death, Mikhail realized. He's lying there, pleading for it.

The berserker made a deep groaning noise, the sound of a caged soul. Mikhail felt it leap within him: not savagery, but mercy.

He leaned his head down, sank his fangs into the throat, and bit deep. The berserker didn't move. And then Mikhail braced his paws against the berserker's body, and ripped upward. He didn't know his own strength; the throat tore open like a Christmas package, and its bright gift spilled out. The berserker shuddered and clawed the air, perhaps fighting not death, but life. Mikhail stumbled back, flesh between his teeth and his eyes glazed with shock. He had seen the others tear the throats of prey, but never until this moment had he understood its sensation of supreme power.

Renati lifted her head to the sky, and sang. Alekza added her higher, younger voice in harmony, and the music soared over the snow. Mikhail thought he knew what the song was about: an enemy had been killed, the pack was victorious, and a new wolf had been born. He spat the berserker's flesh from his mouth, but the taste of blood had ignited his senses. Everything was so much clearer: all colors, all sounds, all aromas were heightened to an intensity that both thrilled and scared him. He realized that up until the moment of his change he had been living only a shadow life; now he felt real, gorged with strength, and this form of black hair and muscle must be his true body, not that weak pale husk of a human boy.

Dazed with the blood fever, Mikhail danced and capered as the two wolves sang their arias. And then he, too, lifted his head and opened his jaws; what came out was more of a croak than music, but he had time to learn to sing. All the time in the world. And then the song faded, its last notes echoed away, and Renati began to change back to human form. It took her perhaps forty-five seconds to alter from a sleek wolf to a naked woman with sagging breasts, and then she knelt down beside Franco. Alekza changed as well, and Mikhail watched her, fascinated. Her limbs lengthened, the blond fur re-formed into the long blond hair on her head and the golden down between her legs and on her forearms and thighs, and then she stood up, naked and glorious, her nipples hardened by the cold. She went to Franco's side, too, and Mikhail stood on all fours, aware that something had grown hard at his groin.

Renati inspected Franco's mangled leg and scowled. "Not good, is it?" Franco asked her, his voice groggy, and Renati said, "Quiet." She shivered, her bare flesh covered with goose bumps; they were going to have to get Franco inside before all of them froze. She looked at Mikhail, the wolf. "Change back," she told him. "Now we need hands more than teeth."

Change *back?* he thought. Now that he was here, he had to go back *there?*

"Help me lift him," Renati said to Alekza, and they struggled to get Franco up. "Come on, help us!" she told Mikhail.

He didn't want to change. He dreaded going back, to that

265

weak, hairless body. But he knew it had to be, and even as the knowledge sank into him he felt the change taking him in the other direction, away from the wolf toward the boy again. The change, he realized, always began first in the mind. He saw his skin, smooth and white, his hands ending in fingers instead of claws, his body supported upright on long stalks. And so it began to happen, just as the images were held in his mind, and his black hair, claws, and fangs left him. There was a moment of searing pain that drove him to his knees; his broken rib was returning to the rib of a boy, but it remained broken, and for an instant the jagged edges ground against each other. Mikhail grasped his white side with human fingers, and when the pain had cleared, he stood up. His legs were shaky, threatening collapse. His jawbones clicked back into their sockets, the last of the dark hair itched fiercely as it retreated into the pores, and Mikhail stood in a mist of steam.

He heard Alekza laugh.

He looked down, and saw that neither pain nor cold had unstiffened him. He covered himself, his face reddening. Renati said, "No time for that. Help us!" She and Alekza were trying to cradle Franco between them, and Mikhail stumbled forward to add his dwindling strength.

They carried Franco to the white palace, and on the way Mikhail retrieved his robe and hurriedly put it around himself. Renati and Alekza's robes lay on the snow, just outside the palace wall. They let them lie until they'd gotten Franco down the stairs, a treacherous trip, and had put him down near the fire. Then Renati went up to get the cloaks, and while she was gone Franco opened his bloodshot eyes and gripped the front of Mikhail's robe. He drew the boy's face close.

"Thank you," Franco said. His hand slipped away, and he'd passed out again. Which was fortunate, because his leg had been all but severed.

Mikhail sensed a movement behind him. He smelled her, fresh as morning. He looked back, over his shoulder, and found his face almost pressed into the golden hair between Alekza's thighs.

She stared down at him, her eyes glinting in the ruddy light. "Do you like what you see?" she asked him quietly.

"I . . ." Again, his groin brittled. "I . . . don't know."

She nodded, and gave him a hint of a smile. "You'll know, soon enough. When you do, I'll be waiting."

"Oh, get out of the boy's face, Alekza!" Renati came into the chamber. "He's still a child!" She threw Alekza her robe.

"No," Alekza answered, still staring down at him. "No, he's not." She slid her cloak on, a sensuous movement, but she didn't draw its folds together. Mikhail looked at her eyes and then, his face flaming, looked to the other place again.

"In my youth you'd be burned at the stake for what you're thinking," Renati told the girl. Then she pushed Mikhail aside and bent over Franco again, pressing a handful of snow against his shattered leg bones. Alekza drew her cloak shut with nimble fingers, and then she touched the two bloody furrows on Mikhail's back; she regarded the smear of red on her fingertips before she licked it off.

Almost four hours later Wiktor and Nikita came home. They had intended to tell the others how their search had failed, because the berserker had marked every one of the caves with his spoor and Wiktor and Nikita had been caught by the winds on a narrow ledge overnight. They'd intended to tell them this, until they saw the huge red wolf lying dead in the snow and the crimson carnage all around. Wiktor listened intently as Renati told him how she and Alekza had heard the berserker howl and had gone out to find Mikhail locked in combat. Wiktor said nothing, but his eyes shone with pride, and from that day on he no longer looked at Mikhail and saw a helpless boy.

In the firelight Franco offered his right leg to the sharp edge of a piece of flint. The bones were already broken, so it was only a matter of cutting through torn muscle and a few tatters of flesh. His body oozing sweat, Franco gripped Renati's hands and clenched a stick between his teeth as Wiktor did the work. Mikhail helped hold Franco down. The leg came off, and lay on the stones. The pack sat around it, deliberating, as the smell of blood perfumed the chamber.

The wind had begun to scream outside again. Another

blizzard was sweeping across Russia, the land of winter. Wiktor drew his knees up to his chin, and he said softly, "What is the lycanthrope, in the eye of God?"

No one answered. No one could.

After a while, Mikhail got up and, pressing his hand against his wounded side, went up the stairs. He stood in a large chamber and let the wind flail him as it shrieked through the broken windows. Snow whitened his hair and gathered on his shoulders, making him appear aged in a matter of seconds. He looked up at the ceiling, where faded angels dwelled, and wiped blood from his lips.

SEVEN

The Brimstone Club

1

Germany was Satan's country: of that, Michael Gallatin was certain.

As he and Mouse rode in their hay wagon, their clothes filthy and their skin even more so, their faces obscured by over two weeks' beard growth, Michael watched prisoners of war chopping down trees on either side of the roadway. Most of the men were emaciated, and they looked like old men, but war had a way of making teenagers look ancient. They wore baggy gray fatigues, and swung their axes like tired machines. Standing guard over them was a truckload of Nazi soldiers, armed to the teeth with submachine guns and rifles. The soldiers were smoking and talking as the prisoners labored, and off in the far distance something was on fire, a pall of black smoke hanging against the gray eastern horizon. Bomb strike, Michael figured. The Allies were increasing their bombing raids as the invasion drew closer.

"Halt!" A soldier stepped into the road in front of them, and the wagon driver—a wiry German member of the Resistance named Gunther—pulled in the horse's reins. "Get these loafers out!" the soldier shouted; he was a young lieutenant, overeager, with red cheeks as fat as dumplings. "We've got work for them here!"

"They're volunteers," Gunther explained, with an air of dignity, though he wore the faded clothes of a farmer. "I'm taking them to Berlin for assignment."

"I'm assigning them to road work," the lieutenant countered. "Come on, get them out! *Now!*"

"Oh, shit," Mouse whispered under his scraggly, dirty brown beard. Michael reclined in the hay beside him, and next to Michael were Dietz and Friedrich, two other German Resistance fighters who'd been escorting them since they'd reached the village of Sulingen four days before. Beneath the hay were hidden three submachine guns, two Lugers, a half-dozen potato-masher hand grenades and a *panzerfaust*-tank killing weapon with an explosive projectile.

Gunther started to protest, but the lieutenant stalked around to the back of the wagon and shouted, "Out! All of you, out! Come on, move your lazy asses!" Friedrich and Dietz, realizing it was better to comply than argue with a young Hitler, got out of the wagon. Michael followed them, and last out was Mouse. The lieutenant said to Gunther, "Now, you, too! Get that shit wagon off the road and follow me!" Gunther swatted the horse's flanks with the reins and steered the wagon under a stand of pine trees. The lieutenant herded Michael, Mouse, Gunther, and the other two men over to the truck, where they were given axes. Michael glanced around, counting thirteen German soldiers in addition to the young lieutenant. There were more than thirty prisoners of war, hacking the pines down. "All right!" the lieutenant barked, a clean-shaven schnauzer. "You two over there!" He motioned Michael and Mouse to the right. "The rest of you that way!" To the left for Gunther, Dietz, and Friedrich.

"Uh . . . excuse me, sir?" Mouse said timidly "Uh . . . just what are we supposed to be doing?"

"Clearing trees, of course!" The lieutenant narrowed his eyes and looked at the five-foot-two-inch, brown-bearded, and dirty Mouse. "Are you blind as well as stupid?"

"No, sir. I only wondered why—"

"You just obey orders! Go on and get to work!"

"Yes, sir." Mouse, clasping his ax, trudged past the officer, and Michael followed him. The others went to the opposite side of the road. "Hey!" the lieutenant shouted. "Runt!" Mouse paused, inwardly quailing. "The only way the German army can use you is to put you into an artillery cannon and shoot you out!" Some of the other soldiers laughed, as if they considered this a fine joke. "Yes, sir," Mouse answered, and went on into the thinned woods.

Michael chose a place between two prisoners, then started swinging the ax. The prisoners didn't pause in their work or otherwise acknowledge him. Wood chips flew in the chilly morning air, and the smell of pine sap mingled with the odors of sweat and effort. Michael noted that many of the prisoners wore yellow Stars of David pinned to their fatigues. All the prisoners were male, all of them dirty, and all wore the same gaunt, glassy-eyed expression. They had disappeared, at least for the moment, into their memories, and the axes swung with a mechanical rhythm. Michael felled a thin tree and stepped back to wipe his face with his forearm. "No slacking, there!" another soldier said, standing behind him.

"I'm not a prisoner," Michael told him. "I'm a citizen of the Reich. I expect to be treated with respect . . . *boy,*" he added, since the soldier was at the most nineteen years old.

The soldier glowered at him; there was a moment of silence, broken only by the thud of the axes, and then the soldier grunted and moved on along the line of workmen, his arms cradling a Schmeisser submachine gun.

Michael returned to work, the axblade a blur of silver. Beneath his beard, his teeth were gritted. It was the twenty-second of April, eighteen days since he and Mouse had left Paris and started along the route Camille and the French Resistance had set up for them. During those eighteen days, they had traveled by wagon, ox cart, freight train, on foot, and by rowboat across Hitler's domain. They had slept in cellars, attics, caves, the forest, and hiding places in walls, and they had lived on a diet of whatever their helpers could spare. In some cases they would have starved had Michael not found a way to slip off, remove his clothes, and hunt for small game. Still, both Michael and Mouse had each lost almost ten pounds, and they were hollow-eyed and hungry looking. But then again, so were most of the civilians Michael had seen: the rations were going to the soldiers stationed in Norway, Holland, France, Poland, Greece, Italy, and of course fighting for their lives in Russia, and the people of Germany were dying a little more every day. Hitler might be proud of his iron will, but it was his iron heart that was destroying his country.

And what about the Iron Fist? Michael wondered, as his axblade hurled chips into the air. He'd mentioned that phrase to several of the agents between Paris and Sulingen, but none of them had the faintest idea what it might mean. They agreed, though, that as a code name it fit Hitler's style; as well as his will and heart, his brain must have some iron in it.

Whatever Iron Fist was, Michael had to find out. With June approaching and the invasion imminent, it would be suicide for the Allies to storm the beaches without fully knowing what they'd face. He hacked another tree down. Berlin lay a little less than thirty miles to the east. They'd come this far, across a land cratered and ablaze at night with bomb blasts, evading SS patrols, armored cars, and suspicious villagers, to be nabbed by a green lieutenant interested in chopping down pines. Echo was supposed to contact Michael in Berlin—again, arranged by Camille—and at this point any delay was critical. Less than thirty miles, and the axes kept swinging.

Mouse cut through his first tree and watched as it toppled. On either side of him, prisoners worked steadily. The air was full of stinging bits of wood. Mouse rested on his ax, his shoulders already tightening. Off in the deep forest, a woodpecker stuttered, mocking the axes. "Go on, get to work!" A soldier with a rifle came up beside Mouse.

"I'm resting for a minute. I—"

The soldier kicked him in the calf of his right leg—not hard enough to knock him off his feet, but with enough force to break a bruise. Mouse winced, and saw his friend—the man he knew only as Green Eyes—stop working and watch them.

"I said get to work!" the soldier commanded, not seeming to care that Mouse was a German or not.

"All right, all right." Mouse picked up his ax again and limped a little deeper into the woods. The soldier was right behind him, looking for another excuse to kick the little man. Pine needles scraped Mouse's face, and he pushed the branches aside to get in at the trunk.

And that was when he saw two dark gray, mummified feet hanging in front of his face.

He looked up, stunned. His heart gave a lurch.

Hanging from a branch was a dead man, gray as Jonah's

beard, the rope noosed around his broken neck and his mouth gaping. His wrists were tied behind him, and he wore clothes that had faded to the color of April mud. What age the man had been when he died was hard to tell, though he had curly reddish hair: the hair of a young man. His eyes were gone, taken by the crows, and pieces of his cheeks had been torn away, too. He was a skinny, dried-up husk, and around his neck was a wire that held a placard with the faded words: I DESERTED MY UNIT. Below that, someone had scrawled with a black pen: *And went home to the Devil.*

Mouse heard someone making a choking sound. It was his own throat, he realized. He felt the squeeze of the noose around it.

"Well? Don't stand there gawking. Get him down."

Mouse glanced back at the soldier. "Me? No . . . please . . . I can't . . ."

"Go on, runt. Make yourself useful."

"Please . . . I'll be sick . . ."

The soldier tensed, eager for another kick. "I said to get him down. I won't tell you again, you little—"

He was shoved aside, and he staggered over a pine stump and went down on his butt. Michael reached up, grasped the corpse's ankles, and gave a strong yank. Most of the rotten rope parted, fortunately before the corpse's head came off. Michael yanked again, and the rope broke. The corpse fell, and lay like a piece of shiny leather at Mouse's feet.

"Damn you!" The soldier leaped up, red-faced, thumbed the safety off on his Karabiner, and thrust the barrel into Michael's chest. His finger lodged on the trigger.

Michael didn't move. He stared into the other man's eyes, saw the indignant child in them, and he said, "Save your bullet for the Russians," in his best Bavarian accent, since his new papers identified him as a Bavarian pig farmer.

The soldier blinked, but his finger remained on the trigger.

"Mannerheim!" the lieutenant bawled, striding forward. "Put down that gun, you damned fool! They're Germans, not Slavs!"

The soldier obeyed at once. He thumbed the safety off again, but he still stared sullenly at Michael. The lieutenant stepped between them. "Go on, watch them over there," he

told Mannerheim, motioning toward another group of prisoners. Mannerheim trudged away, and the dumpling-cheeked
officer turned his attention to Michael. "You don't touch my
men. Understand? I could've let him shoot you, and I'd be
within my rights."

"We're both on the same side," Michael reminded him,
his gaze steady. "Aren't we?"

The lieutenant paused. Too long. Had he heard something
false in the accent? Michael wondered. His blood felt icy.
"Let me see your travel permit," the lieutenant said.

Michael reached into his mud-streaked brown coat and
gave the man his papers. The lieutenant unfolded them, and
studied the typewritten words. There was an official seal on
the lower right-hand corner, just beneath the permit admin-
istrator's signature. "Pig farmer," the German muttered
quietly, and shook his head. "My God, has it come to *this?*"

"I can fight," Michael said.

"I'm sure. You may have to, if the Russian Front breaks
open. Dirty bastards won't stop until they get to Berlin.
What service are you volunteering for?"

"Butchering," Michael replied.

"I imagine you've had some experience at that, haven't
you?" The lieutenant looked distastefully at Michael's dirty
clothes. "Ever fire a rifle?"

"No, sir."

"And why haven't you volunteered before now?"

"I was raising my pigs." A movement caught Michael's
eye; over the lieutenant's shoulder he saw a soldier walking
toward Gunther's hay wagon, where the weapons were hidden. He heard Mouse cough, and knew Mouse had seen,
too.

"Hell," the lieutenant said, "you're almost as old as my
father."

Michael watched the soldier approach the hay wagon. The
skin crawled at the nape of his neck. And then the soldier
hoisted himself up into the back of the wagon and lay down
in the hay to sleep. Several others catcalled and hooted at
him, but he laughed and took his helmet off, cradling his
head with his hands. Michael saw three soldiers sitting in
the rear of the truck, and the others were spread out amid

the prisoners. He glanced at Gunther, across the road. Gunther had stopped chopping a tree, and was staring at the soldier who lay unwittingly atop an arsenal.

"You look fit enough. I don't think the butchering service would mind if you cleared trees with my detail for a few days." The lieutenant folded Michael's papers and gave them back to him. "We're going to widen this road for the tanks. So you see? You'll be doing your service for the Reich and you don't even have to get your hands bloody."

A few days, Michael thought grimly. No, that wouldn't do at all.

"Both of you get back to work," the lieutenant ordered. "When the job's finished, we'll send you on your way."

Michael saw the soldier in the hay wagon shift his position, trying to get comfortable. The man smoothed the hay down, and if he felt any of the weapons underneath it . . .

There was no time to wait and see if the soldier discovered the guns or not. The lieutenant was striding back to the truck, confident in his powers of persuasion. Michael grasped Mouse's elbow and pulled him along, toward the road. "Keep your mouth shut," Michael warned him.

"Hey, you!" one of the other soldiers called. "Who told you to quit?"

"We're thirsty," Michael explained as the lieutenant listened. "We've got a canteen in our wagon. Surely we can have a drink of water before we continue?"

The lieutenant waved them on and swung himself up into the truck bed to rest his legs. Michael and Mouse walked on across the road as the prisoners kept on chopping and pine trees cracked as they fell. Gunther glanced at Michael, his eyes large and frightened, and Michael saw the soldier in the wagon winnow his hand into the hay for whatever was disturbing his recumbent posture.

Mouse whispered urgently, "He's found the—"

"Ah-ha!" the soldier cried out as his fingers found the object and he pulled it free. "Look what these dogs are hiding from us, Lieutenant Zeller!" He held it up, showing the half-full bottle of schnapps he'd discovered.

"Trust farmers to bury their secrets," Zeller said. He

stood up. The other soldiers looked on anxiously. "Are more bottles in there?"

"Wait, I'll see." The soldier began burrowing through the hay.

Michael had reached the wagon, leaving Mouse about six paces behind. He dropped the ax, reached deeply into the hay, and his hands closed on an object that he knew was there. He said, "Here's something for your thirst," as he drew out the submachine gun and clicked off the safety.

The soldier gaped at him, the young man's eyes blue as a Nordic fjord.

Michael shot him without hesitation, the bullets stitching across the soldier's chest and making the body dance like a marionette. As soon as the initial burst was released, Michael whirled around, took aim at the soldiers in the back of the truck, and opened fire. The axes ceased chopping; for an instant both the prisoners and German soldiers stood as motionless as painted statues.

And then pandemonium broke loose.

The three soldiers in the truck went down, their bodies punctured. Lieutenant Zeller threw himself to the floorboards, bullets whining all around him, and reached for his holstered pistol. A soldier standing near Gunther leveled his rifle to fire at Michael, and Gunther sank his ax between the man's shoulder blades. The other two Resistance fighters lifted their axes to strike two more soldiers; Dietz's ax all but took a man's head off, but Friedrich was shot at point-blank range through the heart before he could deliver the blow.

"Get down!" Michael shouted at Mouse, who stood dazed in the line of fire. His bulging blue eyes stared at the dead German in the hay. Mouse didn't move. Michael stepped forward and punched him in the stomach with the submachine gun's butt, the only thing he could think to do, and Mouse doubled over and fell to his knees. A pistol bullet knocked a shard of wood out of the wagon beside Michael, its path grazing the horse's flank and making the animal shriek and rear up. Michael knelt down and fired a long burst at the truck, popping its tires and shattering both rear and front windshields, but Zeller hugged the truck bed's floor-boards.

Gunther chopped down with his ax again, cleaving the arm of a soldier who'd been about to blast him with a Schmeisser. As the soldier fell, writhing in agony, Gunther picked up the weapon and sprayed bullets at two other soldiers who were running for cover in the trees. Both of them staggered and fell. A pistol bullet whined past Michael's head, but Zeller was firing without aiming. Michael reached over the edge of the wagon, his hand searching in the hay. Another bullet knocked a storm of wood splinters into his face, one of them driving into the flesh less than an inch beside his left eye. But Michael had what he was after; he pulled it out, ducked down, and wrenched the pin loose on the potato-masher hand grenade. Zeller shouted to any-one who could still hear him: "Kill the man at the wagon! Kill the son of a—"

Michael threw the grenade. It hit the ground short of the truck, bounced, and rolled up underneath it. Then he flung himself over Mouse's body and covered his own head with his arms.

The grenade exploded with a hollow *whump!* and the blast lifted the truck up off its flattened tires. Orange and purple flames roared, their violence hurling the truck to one side on a pillar of fire. It crashed over, the rending of metal followed by a second blast as the gasoline and oil ignited. A column of black smoke with a red center rose into the sky. Zeller didn't fire again. A rain of burning cloth and scorched metal fell, and the wagon horse jerked its reins free from the branch Gunther had tied them to, then fled madly down the road.

Gunther and Dietz, who'd scooped up a dead man's rifle, were kneeling amid the pine stumps, shooting at the four soldiers who'd escaped the first blaze of bullets. One of the men panicked, got up from the ground, and ran, and Dietz shot him in the head before he'd taken three strides. And then two prisoners rushed forward, into the midst of the remaining soldiers, and their axes began a merry work. Both men were shot before they could finish, but three more prisoners took their places. The axes rose and fell, the blades smeared with scarlet. A final shot rang out, fired into the air from a falling hand. There was a last shriek, and the axes stopped.

Michael stood up, retrieving the submachine gun he'd thrown aside. It was still warm, like a comforting oven. Gunther and Dietz got up from their shelter and quickly began to inspect the bodies. Gunshots flared as they dispatched the wounded. Michael reached down and pulled at Mouse's shoulder. "Are you all right?"

Mouse sat up, his eyes watering and still stunned. "You hit me," he gasped. "Why'd you hit me?"

"Better a tap than a bullet. Can you stand?"

"I don't know."

"You can," Michael said, and hauled him to his feet. Mouse still held his ax, his knuckles bleached white around the handle. "We'd better get out of here before any more Germans come along," Michael told him; he looked around, expecting to see the prisoners disappearing into the woods, but most of them simply sat on the ground, as if awaiting the next truckload of Nazis. Michael crossed the road, with Mouse a few paces behind, and he approached a thin, dark-bearded man who'd been among the chopping party. "What's wrong?" Michael asked. "You're free now. You can go, if you like."

The man, his face stretched like brown leather over the jutting bones, smiled faintly. "Free," he whispered in a thick Ukrainian accent. "Free. No." He shook his head. "I don't think so."

"There are the woods. Why don't you go?"

"Go?" Another man, even thinner than the first, stood up. He had a long-jawed face, and was shaven almost bald. His accent was of northern Russia. "Go *where?*"

"I don't know. Just . . . away from here."

"Why?" the dark-bearded man inquired. He lifted his thick brows. "The Nazis are everywhere. This is their country. Where are we to go that the Nazis wouldn't hunt us down again?"

Michael couldn't fathom this; it was utterly against his nature that anyone whose chains had been broken wouldn't try to keep them from being forged again. These men had been prisoners for a very long time, he realized. They had forgotten the meaning of freedom. "Don't you think there's any chance you might be able to—"

"No," the bald prisoner interrupted, his eyes black and remote. "No chance at all."

As Michael talked to the men, Mouse leaned against a pine tree nearby. He felt sick, and he thought he might faint from the smell of blood. He wasn't a fighter. God help me get home, he prayed. Just help me get ho—

One of the dead Germans suddenly sat up, about eight feet from where Mouse stood. The man had been shot through the side, his face ashen. Mouse saw who it was: Mannerheim. And he also saw Mannerheim reach for a pistol lying beside him, pick it up, and point it at Green Eyes' back.

Mouse started to scream, but his voice croaked, unable to summon enough power. Mannerheim's finger was on the trigger. His gun hand wavered; he steadied it with his other hand, which was covered with crimson.

Mannerheim was a German. Green Eyes was . . . whoever he was. Germany was Mouse's country. I DESERTED MY UNIT. Runt. *And went home to the Devil.*

All these things whirled through Mouse's mind in an instant. Mannerheim's finger began to squeeze the trigger. Green Eyes was still talking. Why wouldn't he turn? Why wouldn't he . . .

Time had run out.

Mouse heard himself shout—the cry of an animal—and he strode forward and smashed the ax blade down into Mannerheim's brown-haired skull.

The gun hand jerked, and the pistol went off.

Michael heard the whine of a wasp past his head. Up in the trees, a branch cracked and fell to earth. He turned, and saw Mouse holding the handle of his ax, the blade buried in Mannerheim's head. The man's body slumped forward, and Mouse released the ax as if he'd been scalded. Then Mouse fell to his knees in the dirt; he stayed there, his mouth half open and a little thread of saliva hanging over his chin, until Michael helped him to his feet.

"My God," Mouse whispered. He blinked, his eyes

281

bloodshot. "I killed a man." Tears welled up and ran down his cheeks.

"You can still get away," Michael told the dark-bearded prisoner as Mouse's weight leaned against him.

"I don't feel like running today," was the answer. The man gazed up at the pewter sky. "Maybe tomorrow. You go on. We'll tell them . . ." He paused; it came to him. "We'll tell them the Allies have landed," he said, and smiled dreamily.

Michael, Mouse, Gunther, and Dietz left the prisoners behind. They continued along the road, keeping to the woods, and found the hay wagon about a half mile ahead. The horse was calmly chomping grass in a dewy field.

They got away as quickly as they could, black smoke like banners of destruction now hazing the western horizon as well as the eastern. Mouse sat staring into space, his mouth working but making no sounds, and Michael looked ahead, trying to shake the image of the young soldier's face just before he had slaughtered him. The bottle of schnapps, unbroken in the gunfire, had been sipped from by all and deposited under the hay. In these times liquor was a price-less commodity.

They went on, and every turn of the wheels took them closer to Berlin.

2

Michael had seen Paris in sunshine; he saw Berlin in gray gloom.

It was a huge, sprawling city. It smelled musty and earthy, like a cellar long sealed from light. It looked ancient as well, its stocky buildings the same shade of gray. Michael thought of tombstones in a damp graveyard where deadly mush-rooms thrived.

They crossed the Havel River in the Spandau district, and on the other side were immediately forced off the road by a column of Kubelwagens and troop trucks heading west. A chill wind blew off the Havel, making faded Nazi flags snap from their lampposts. The pavement was cracked with tank treads. Across the cityscape spouts of dark smoke rose from chimneys, and the wind curled them into question marks. The stone walls of rowhouses were adorned with battered posters and proclamations, such as REMEMBER THE HEROES OF STALINGRAD, ONWARD TO MOSCOW, GERMANY VICTORIOUS TODAY, GERMANY VICTORIOUS TOMORROW. Epitaphs on gravestones, Michael thought; Berlin was a cemetery, full of ghosts. Of course there were people on the streets, and in cars, and flower shops, and cinemas, and tailorshops, but there was no vitality. Berlin was not a city of smiles, and Michael noticed that people kept glancing over their shoulders, fearful of what was approaching from the east.

Gunther took them through the elegant streets of the Charlottenburg district, where dwellings styled like ginger-bread castles housed equally fanciful dukes and barons, toward the war-worn inner city. Row houses crowded together, grim-looking structures with blackout curtains: these were streets where dukes and barons held no power. Michael noticed something strange: there were only elderly people and children about, no young men except for the soldiers who swept past in trucks and on motorcycles, and those men had young faces but old eyes. Berlin was in mourning, because its youth was dead.

"We have to take my friend home," Michael said to Gunther. "I promised him."

"I was ordered to take you to a safe house. That's where I'm going."

"Please." Mouse spoke up; his voice quavered. "Please . . . my house isn't far from here. It's in the Tempelhof district, near the airport. I'll show you the way."

"I'm sorry," Gunther said. "My orders were—"

Michael clamped a hand around the back of his neck. Gunther had been a good companion, but Michael didn't care to argue. "I'm changing your orders. We can go to the safe house after we get my friend home. Either do it or give me the reins."

"You don't know what a risk you're taking!" Dietz

snapped. "And us, too! We just lost a friend because of you!"

"Then get off and walk," Michael told him. "Go on. Get off."

Dietz hesitated. He, too, was a stranger in Berlin. Gunther quietly said, "Shit," and popped the reins. "All right. Where in Tempelhof?"

Mouse eagerly gave him the address, and Michael released Gunther's neck.

Not too much farther, they began to see bombed buildings. The heavy B-17 and B-24 American bombers had delivered their freight, and rubble choked the streets. Some of the buildings were unrecognizable, heaps of stones and timbers. Others had split open and collapsed from the force of the bombs. A haze of smoke lay close to the street. Here the gloom was even thicker, and in the twilight the red centers of smoldering heaps of rubble glowed like Hades.

They passed an area where civilians, their clothes and faces grimy, were searching through a building's wreckage. Tongues of flame licked along fallen timbers, and an elderly woman sobbed as an old man tried to comfort her. Bodies under sheets were laid out, with precise German geometry, along the fissured sidewalk. "Killers!" the elderly woman shouted, and whether she was looking at the sky or toward Hitler's chancellery at the heart of Berlin, Michael couldn't tell. "God curse you, you killers!" she shrieked, and then she sobbed again with her hands over her face, unable to bear the sight of ruin.

Ahead of the wagon stretched a landscape of destruction. On both sides of the street, buildings had exploded, burned, and collapsed. Smoke hung in layers, too heavy for even the wind to tatter. Factory chimneys jutted up, but the factory had been crushed like a caterpillar under a steel-soled boot. The rubble was so high that it clogged the street, forcing Gunther to find another route south into the Tempelhof. Off to the west, a large fire raged, spitting up whirling red flames. Bombs must have fallen last night, Michael thought. Mouse was sitting slumped over, his eyes glassy. Michael started to touch the little man's shoulder, but then he drew his hand back. Nothing could be said.

Gunther found Mouse's street and in another moment stopped the wagon at the address Mouse had given him.

The row house had been made of red stones. There was no fire; the ashes were cool, and they spun in the wind past Mouse's face as he got out of the wagon and stood on what remained of the front steps.

"This isn't it!" Mouse said to Gunther. His face was slick with cold sweat. "This is the wrong address!"

Gunther didn't answer.

Mouse stared at what used to be his home. Two walls had collapsed and most of the floors. The central staircase, badly scorched, ran up into the building like a warped spine. A sign near the jagged, burnt hole where the front door had been warned DANGER! ENTRANCE FORBIDDEN! It was stamped with the seal of the Nazi party's inspector of housing. Mouse had a terrible desire to laugh. My God! he thought. I've come all this way, and they won't let me into my own house! He saw the broken shards of a blue vase in the wreckage, and he remembered that they'd once held roses. Tears burned his eyes. "Louisa!" he shouted, and the sound of that awful cry made Michael's soul shrivel. "Louisa! Answer me!"

A window opened in a fire-scorched building across the street, and an old man peered out. "Hey!" he called. "Who're you looking for?"

"Louisa Mausenfeld! Do you know where she and the children are?"

"They took all the bodies away," the old man said with a shrug. Mouse had never seen him before; a young couple used to live in that apartment. "It was a terrible fire. See how it burned these bricks?" He patted one for emphasis.

"Louisa . . . the two little girls . . ." Mouse wavered; the world, a brutal hell, was spinning around him.

"The husband died, too, in France," the old man continued. "That's what I heard, at least. Are you a relative?"

Mouse didn't answer, but he did speak: a cry of anguish that echoed between the remaining walls. And then, before Michael could leap out of the wagon and stop him, Mouse started running up the spindly staircase, the burned risers cracking under his weight. At once Michael was going after him, into a realm of ashes and darkness, and he heard the old man shout, "You can't go in there!" before the window slid shut.

Mouse kept climbing the steps. His left foot smashed through a flimsy stair; he pulled it loose and kept going, gripping the blackened railing and pulling himself along. "Stop!" Michael called, but Mouse didn't. The staircase shook, a section of the railing suddenly breaking and tumbling down into a pit of debris. Mouse balanced on the edge for an instant, then grasped the railing on the other side and continued up. He reached a floor, about fifty feet above the ground, and stumbled over a pile of burned timbers, the weakened floorboards shrieking under him. "Louisa!" Mouse shouted. "It's me! I've come home, Louisa!" He went on into a warren of rooms that had been sliced open by the destruction, revealing the possessions of a dead family: a soot-coated oven; shattered crockery, and an occasional dish or cup that had miraculously survived the concussions; what had once been a pine-plank table, now burned down to its legs; the frame of a chair, springs rusting like coiled guts; the remnants of wallpaper on the walls as yellow as patches of leprosy, and against them the lighter squares where pictures used to hang. Mouse went through the small rooms, calling for Louisa, Carla, and Lucilla. Michael couldn't stop him, and there was no use in trying. He simply followed Mouse from room to room, close enough to grab him if the little man fell through the floor. Mouse entered what had been the parlor; there were holes in the floorboards where burning debris from above had settled and gone through. The couch where Louisa and the girls liked to sit was a burned tangle of springs. And the piano, their wedding gift from Louisa's grandparents, was a horror of keys and wires. But there was the fireplace of white bricks that had warmed Mouse and his family on so many frigid nights. And there was a bookcase, though few books remained. Even his favorite rocking chair had survived, though badly scorched. It was still there, just as he'd left it. And then Mouse looked at the wall, next to the fireplace, and Michael heard him gasp.

Mouse didn't move for a moment; then, slowly, he crossed

the creaking floor and went to the framed Cross of Iron: his son's medal.

The frame's glass was cracked. Other than that, the Cross of Iron was unmarred. Mouse lifted the frame off the wall, his touch reverent, and read the inscription of his son's name and date of death. His body shook; his eyes glinted with madness. Two bright spots of crimson rose in his pale cheeks above the dirty beard.

Mouse hurled the framed Cross of Iron against the wall, and fragments of glass exploded across the room. The medal made a tinkling sound as it fell to the floor. At once he rushed forward, scooped the medal off the floor, and turned—his face swollen with rage—to throw it through a broken window.

Michael's hand clamped on Mouse's fist, and sealed it tight. "No," he said firmly. "Don't throw it away."

Mouse stared at him incredulously; he blinked slowly, his brain gears slipping on the grease of despair. He made a moaning sound, like the wind through the ruins of his home. And then Mouse lifted his other hand, balled it into a fist, and struck Michael as hard as he could across the jaw. Michael's head snapped back, but he didn't release Mouse, nor did he try to defend himself. Mouse hit him again, and a third time. Michael just stared at him, green eyes aflame and a drop of blood oozing from a cut on his lower lip. Mouse pulled his fist back to strike him a fourth time, and the little man saw Michael's jaw tense, preparing for the blow. All the strength suddenly drained out of Mouse's shoulder; his muscles went limp, and his hand opened. He slapped the face of Green Eyes, a weak slap. And then his arm fell to his side, his eyes stinging with tears, and his knees sagged. He started to fall, but Michael held him up.

"I want to die," Mouse whispered. "I want to die, I want to die, oh God please let me . . ."

"Stand up," Michael told him. "Come on, stand up."

Mouse's legs had no bones. He wanted to fall to this floor and lie there until Thor's hammer destroyed the earth. He smelled gunsmoke on the other man's clothes, and that bitter aroma brought back every horrifying second of the battle in the pine forest. Mouse wrenched away from Michael, and staggered back. "You stay away from me!" he shouted. "Damn you to hell, stay away!"

Michael said nothing. The storm was coming, and it would have to whirl its course.

"You're a *killer!*" Mouse shrieked. "A *beast!* I saw your face, there in the woods. I saw it, as you killed those men! Germans! *My* people! You shot that boy to pieces, and you never even flinched!"

"There wasn't time for flinching," Michael said.

"You enjoyed it!" Mouse raged on. "You *liked* the killing, didn't you?"

"No. I didn't."

"Oh God . . . Jesus . . . you've made me into a killer, too." Mouse's face contorted. He felt as if he were being wrenched apart by inner tides. "That young man . . . I murdered him. I killed him. Killed a German. Oh my God." He looked around the decimated room, and he thought he could hear the screams of his wife and two daughters as the bombs blew them to heaven. Where had he been, he wondered, when the Allied bombers had dropped death onto his loved ones? He didn't even have a picture of them; all his papers, his wallet, and photographs had been taken from him in Paris. This was the cruelty that drove him to his knees. He scrabbled onto a pile of burned rubble and began to search desperately for a picture of Louisa and the children.

Michael wiped the blood from his lower lip with the back of his hand. Mouse flung bits of wreckage to either side, but he kept the Iron Cross in his fist. "What are you going to do?" Michael asked.

"You did this. You. The Allies. Their bombers. Their hatred of Germany. Hitler was right. The world fears and hates Germany. I thought he was mad, but he was right." Mouse dug deeper into the debris; there were no pictures, only ashes. He scrambled to burned books and searched for the photographs that used to be on the shelves. "I'll turn you in. That's what I'll do. I'll turn you in, and then I'll go to church and beg forgiveness. My God . . . I murdered a German. I murdered a German, with my own hands." He sobbed and tears ran down his face. "Where are the pictures? Where are the pictures?"

Michael knelt down a few feet away from him. "You can't stay here."

"This is my *home!*" Mouse shouted, with a force that made the empty window frames shake. His eyes were bloodshot and sunken into his head. "This is where I live," he said, but this time it was a whisper from his raw throat.

"No one lives here." Michael stood up. "Gunther's waiting. It's time to go."

"Go? Go *where?*" He was echoing the Russian prisoner who'd seen no purpose in flight. "You're a British spy, and I'm a citizen of Germany. My God . . . why I let you talk me into this; my soul's burning. Oh Christ, forgive me!"

"Hitler brought down the bombs that killed your family," Michael said. "You think no one grieved over the dead when Nazi planes bombed London? You think your wife and children were the only bodies ever taken out of a blasted building? If you do, you're a fool." He spoke calmly and quietly, but his green gaze pierced Mouse. "Warsaw, Narvik, Rotterdam, Sedan, Dunkirk, Crete, Leningrad, Stalingrad: Hitler strewed corpses as far north, south, east, and west as he could reach. Hundreds of thousands to grieve over, and you cry in the wreckage of a single room." He shook his head, feeling a mixture of pity and disgust. "Your country is dying. Hitler's killing it, but before he finishes the job he's going to destroy as many as he can. Your son, wife, and daughters: what are they to Hitler? Did they matter? I don't think so."

"You shut your mouth!" Tears glittered, false diamonds, in Mouse's beard.

"I'm sorry the bombs fell here," Michael continued. "I'm sorry they fell in London. But when the Nazis took power, and Hitler started this war, the bombs had to fall somewhere."

Mouse didn't reply. He couldn't find any photographs in the debris, and he sat on the burned floor rocking himself.

"Do you have relatives here?" Michael asked.

Mouse hesitated; then he shook his head.

"Anywhere you can go?"

Another shake of the head. Mouse sniffled and wiped his oozing nose.

"I have to finish my mission. You can go to the safe house with me, if you like. From there Gunther might be able to get you out of the country."

"This is my home," Mouse said.

"Is it?" Michael let the question hang; there was no answer. "If you want to live in a cemetery, that's up to you. If you want to stand up and go with me, come on. I'm leaving." Michael turned his back on Mouse, went through the flame-scarred rooms to the stairway, and descended to the street. Gunther and Dietz were drinking from the bottle of schnapps; the wind had grown bitter. Michael waited, near the row house's scorched entrance. He would give Mouse two minutes, he decided. If the man didn't come out, then Michael would decide what to do next. It was an unhappy situation; Mouse knew too much.

A minute passed. Michael watched two children digging through a pile of blackened bricks. They discovered a pair of boots, and one of the children chased the other from them. Then Michael heard the staircase creak, and he felt his muscles relax. Mouse walked out of the building, into the somber gray light. He looked up at the sky, and around at the other buildings, as if seeing things for the first time. "All right," he said, his voice weary and emotionless. His eyes were red-rimmed and swollen. "I'll go with you."

Once Michael and Mouse were back in the wagon, Gunther snapped the reins and the spavined farm horse started off. Dietz offered Michael the schnapps, and Michael drank from it, then held the bottle out for Mouse. The little man shook his head; he stared at his open right palm. In it was the Cross of Iron.

Michael didn't know what he would've done if Mouse hadn't come out. Kill him? Possibly. He didn't care to think about that. He was a professional, in a dirty business, and first and foremost was the mission at hand. Iron Fist. Frankewitz. Blok. Dr. Hildebrand, and gas warfare. And, of course, Harry Sandler. How did they all fit together, and what was the meaning of painted bullet holes on green metal?

He would have to find out. If he failed, so might the Allied invasion of Europe.

He settled back, against the wagon's side, and felt the outline of a submachine gun in the hay next to him. Mouse stared at the Iron Cross, mesmerized that such a small cold thing should be the last item that held any meaning in his life. And then he closed his hand around the medal and slipped it into his pocket.

3

The safe house was in the Neukolln district of Berlin, an area of grimy factories and row houses crowded along the railroad tracks. Gunther knocked at the door of a row house, and it was opened by a thin young man with close-cropped brown hair and a long-jawed face that looked as if it had never worn a smile. Dietz and Gunther escorted their charges into the building and up a staircase to the second floor, where Michael and Mouse were taken to a parlor and left alone. A middle-aged woman with curly gray hair came in about ten minutes later, bearing a tray of two cups of tea and slices of rye bread. She asked no questions, and Michael asked none of her. He and Mouse wolfed down the tea and bread.

The parlor windows were covered with blackout curtains. Perhaps half an hour after the tea and bread had been served, Michael heard the sound of a car stopping outside. He went to the window, pushed the curtain aside, and peered out. Night was falling, and there were no lamps along the street. The buildings were dark against the darkness. But Michael saw a black Mercedes parked at the curb, and he watched as the driver got out, walked around, and opened the door for the passenger. A woman's shapely leg came out first, then the rest of her. She glanced up at the crack of yellow lamplight that spilled around the blackout curtain's edge. She had no face. And then the driver closed the door, and Michael let the curtain fall back into place.

He heard voices from downstairs: Gunther's, and a woman's. An elegant German accent, very refined. There was aristocracy in its syllables, but it held a strangeness, too, something that Michael couldn't quite define. He heard someone ascending the stairs, heard the woman reach the closed parlor door.

The knob turned, the door opened, and the woman without a face walked in.

She wore a black hat, and a veil that obscured her features. She carried a black valise in her ebony-gloved hands, and she wore a black velvet cloak over a dark gray pinstriped dress. But golden curls escaped the hat, the thick blond hair falling in ringlets around her shoulders. She was a slim, tall woman, perhaps five feet ten, and Michael could see the glint of her eyes behind the veil as her gaze fixed on him, went to Mouse, then returned to him again. She closed the door behind her. Michael smelled her perfume: the faint aromas of cinnamon and leather.

"You're the man," she said in blue-blooded German. It was a statement, directed at Michael.

He nodded. Something strange about her accent. What was it?

"I'm Echo," she said. She put the black valise on a table and unzipped it. "Your companion is a German soldier. What's to be done with him?"

"I'm not a soldier!" Mouse protested. "I'm a cook! Was a cook, I mean."

Echo stared at Michael, her features impassive behind the veil. "What's to be done with him?" she repeated.

Michael knew what she was asking. "He can be trusted."

"The last man who believed anyone can be trusted is dead. You've brought along a dangerous liability."

"Mouse . . . my friend . . . wants to get out of the country. Can that be arran—"

"No," Echo interrupted. "I won't risk any of my friends to help yours. This . . ." She glanced quickly at the little man, and Michael could almost feel her cringe. "This *Mouse* is your responsibility. Will you take care of him, or shall I?"

It was a polite way of asking if Michael would kill Mouse, or if one of her agents should do the job. "You're right," Michael agreed. "Mouse *is* my responsibility, and I'll take care of him." The woman nodded. "He goes with me," Michael said.

She was silent for a moment: an icy silence. Then: "Impossible."

"No, it's not. Back in Paris I depended on Mouse and he came through for me. As far as I'm concerned, he's proven himself."

"Not to me. And for that matter, neither have you. If you refuse to do your duty, I refuse to work with you." She zipped up the valise and started toward the door.

"I'll work without you, then," Michael said. And then the answer to her accent's mystery came to him: "I don't need a Yank's help, anyway."

She stopped, her black gloved hand on the doorknob. "What?"

"A Yank's help. I don't need it," he repeated. "You *are* an American, aren't you? It's in your accent. The Germans around here must have lead ears not to hear it."

This seemed to touch a nerve. Echo said frostily, "For your information, *Brit,* the Germans know I was born in the United States. I'm a citizen of Berlin now. Does that satisfy you?"

"It answers my question, but it hardly satisfies me." Michael gave her a thin smile. "I imagine our mutual friend in London gave you some of my background." Except the part about his affinity for running on all fours, he knew. "I'm good at what I do. As I say, if you refuse to help me, I'll get the job done on my own—"

"You'll die trying," Echo interrupted.

"Maybe. But our mutual friend must have told you I can be trusted. I didn't live through North Africa being stupid. If I say I'll be responsible for Mouse, I mean it. I'll take care of him."

"And who'll take care of you?"

"That's a question I've never had to answer," Michael said.

"Wait a minute!" Mouse scowled, his eyes still swollen from tears. "Don't I have anything to say about this? Maybe I don't want you to take care of me! Who the hell asked you, anyway? I swear to God, I was better off in the loony bin! Those nuts made sense when they talked!"

"Quiet!" Michael snapped; Mouse was a breath away from an executioner's bullet. The little man cursed under his breath, and Michael returned his attention to the veiled woman. "Mouse has helped me before. He can help me again." Echo grunted with derision. "I didn't come to Berlin to murder a man who risked his life for me," Michael plowed on.

"Uh . . . *murder?*" Mouse gasped as he got the whole picture.

"Mouse goes with me." Michael stared into the veil. "I'll take care of him. And when the mission's over, you help us both get out of Germany."

Echo didn't respond. Her fingers tapped on the black valise as the wheels went round in her mind.

"Well?" Michael prompted.

"If our mutual friend were here, he'd say you're being very stupid," she tried once more, but she could tell that the dirty, bearded green-eyed man standing before her had chosen his position and would not be moved. She sighed, shook her head, and returned the valise to the table.

"What's happening?" Mouse asked fearfully. "Am I going to be murdered?"

"No," Michael told him. "You've just joined the British Secret Service."

Mouse choked, as if he'd gotten a chicken bone stuck in his throat.

"You have a new identity." Echo unzipped the valise, reached into it, and brought out a dossier. She offered it to him, but when Michael stepped forward to take it, Echo held her other hand to her nose. "My God, what a smell!"

Michael took the dossier and opened it. Inside were type-written sheets of paper, in German, outlining the history of a Baron Frederick von Fange. Michael couldn't help but smile. "Who suggested this?"

"Our mutual friend."

Of course, he thought. This bore the rather wicked fingerprints of the man he'd last seen as a chauffeur named Mallory. "From a pig farmer to a baron in one day. That's not bad, even for a country where money buys royal titles."

"The family is real enough. They're in the German social registry. But even though you may have a title," Echo said, "you still smell like a pig farmer. Here's the other information you requested." She gave him another dossier. Michael looked over the typewritten pages. Camille had radioed coded inquiries ahead to Echo, and Echo had done an excellent job in putting together background material on SS Colonel Jerek Blok, Dr. Gustav Hildebrand, and Hildebrand Industries. There were black-and-white photographs, blurred but serviceable, of the two men. She also provided a typewritten page on Harry Sandler, and a photograph of the big-game hunter sitting at a table surrounded by Nazi officers, a dark-haired woman on his lap. A hooded hawk gripped its talons to his forearm.

"You've been very thorough," Michael complimented her. Looking at Sandler's cruel, smiling face made his gut clench. "Is Sandler still in Berlin?"

She nodded.

"Where?"

"Our primary assignment," she reminded him, "doesn't involve Harry Sandler. It's enough for you to know that Sandler won't be leaving Berlin anytime soon."

Of course she was right: first Iron Fist, then Sandler. "What about Frankewitz?" he asked.

That, too, had been among Camille's inquiries. "I know his address. He lives near Victoria Park, on Katzbachstrasse."

"And you'll take me to him?"

"Tomorrow. Tonight I think you should read that information and do your homework." She motioned toward the Von Fange biography. "And for God's sake, get yourself shaved and cleaned up. There are no bohemian barons in the Reich."

"What about me?" Mouse looked stricken. "What the hell am *I* supposed to do?"

"What, indeed?" Echo asked, and Michael could feel her staring at him.

He quickly skimmed the biography of the Baron von Fange: land holdings in Austria and Italy, a family castle on the Saarbrucken River, a stable of thoroughbred horses, fast cars, expensively tailored clothes: the usual bounty of the privileged. Michael looked up from his reading. "I'll need a valet," he said.

"A *what?*" Mouse squeaked.

"A valet. Someone to hang up the expensive clothes I'm supposed to have." He turned his attention to Echo. "Incidentally, where *are* these clothes? I'm sure you don't expect me to play a baron's role with pig shit on my shirt."

"They'll take care of you here. And your 'valet,' too." She might have offered a hint of a smile; the veil made it difficult to tell. "My car will be here for you at oh-nine-hundred. My driver's name is Wilhelm." She zippered the valise and held it close to her side. "I think that concludes our business for now. Yes?" Without waiting for an answer, she strode to the door on her long, elegant legs.

"One minute," Michael said. She paused. "How do you know Sandler's planning on staying in Berlin?"

"Knowing such things, Baron von Fange, is why I'm here. Jerek Blok's also in Berlin. It's no mystery: Blok and Sandler are both members of the Brimstone Club."

"The Brimstone Club? What's that?"

"Oh," Echo said softly, "you'll find out. Good night, gentlemen." She opened the door and closed it behind her, and Michael listened to the sound of her footsteps as she descended the stairs.

"A valet?" Mouse sputtered. "What the hell do I know about being a damned valet? I've only owned three suits in my life!"

"Valets are seen and not heard. You do your part and we might get out of Berlin with our skins still on. I meant what I said about your joining the service. As long as you're with me—and I'm protecting you—I expect you to do what I say. Understood?"

"Hell, no! What do I have to do to get my ass out of this crack?"

"Well, that's simple enough." Michael heard the Mercedes's engine growl. He went to the window, pulled the curtain aside slightly, and watched the car move away into the night. "Echo wants to kill you. I imagine she could do it with one bullet."

Mouse was silent.

"You think about it tonight," Michael told him. "If you do as I say, you can get out of this corpse of a country before the Russians swarm in. If not . . ." He shrugged. "It's your decision."

"Some choice! Either I get a bullet in my head or a Gestapo branding iron burning my balls off!"

"I'll try my best to make sure that doesn't happen," Michael said, knowing that if the Gestapo caught them, a red-hot iron to the testicles would be the least of the inflictions.

The gray-haired woman came to the parlor and escorted Michael and Mouse down the stairs, through a door at the back of the building, and then down more steps into a cobwebbed basement. Oil lamps flickered in a rat's nest of rooms, most of them empty or piled with broken furniture and other junk. They came to a wine cellar, where two other men waited; these two men moved aside a large rack of wine bottles, exposing a square hole cut in the bricks. Michael and Mouse followed the woman through a tunnel, into the basement of another row house—and there the rooms were well lit and clean, and held boxes of hand grenades, submachine gun and pistol ammunition, explosive detonator caps, fuses, and the like. The gray-haired woman led Michael and Mouse to a large chamber where several men and women were working at sewing machines. Racks of clothes—most of them German uniforms—stood around the room. Tape measures were produced, suits and shirts were chosen and marked for size, and a crate of shoes was brought out for the baron and his valet to go through. The women who took Mouse's measurements clucked and fretted, knowing it was going to be a long night of shortening trousers, shirt and coat sleeves. A man with hair clippers and a razor appeared.

Someone else brought in buckets of hot water and cakes of coarse white soap that could scrub the warts off a frog. Under the strokes of clippers, razor, and soap, Michael Gallatin—who was no stranger to transformation—began to merge with his new identity. But as he changed, he recalled the aromas of cinnamon and leather, and he found himself wondering whose face lay behind the veil.

4

The black Mercedes arrived promptly at nine in the morning. It was another moody day, the sun hidden behind the thick gray clouds. The Nazi high command rejoiced at such weather: the Allied bombers scrubbed their missions when the clouds closed in.

The two men who emerged from the row house on the edge of the railroad tracks were vastly changed from those who'd entered it the evening before. The Baron von Fange was clean-shaven, his black hair neatly trimmed and the weariness slept out of his eyes; he wore a gray suit and vest, a pale blue shirt with a thin gray-striped tie and a silver stickpin. On his feet were polished black shoes, and a beige camel-hair topcoat was draped over his shoulders. Black kid gloves completed his attire. One might have guessed the clothes were tailor-made. His valet, a short stocky man, was similarly clean-shaven and had a fresh haircut that did nothing for his large, unsightly ears. Mouse wore a dark blue suit, and a plain black bow tie. He was utterly miserable; the shirt's collar was starched to the point of strangulation, and his new, glossy black shoes pinched his feet like iron vises. He'd also learned one of the duties of a valet: manhandling the calf-skin luggage, full of clothes for both the baron and himself. But, as Mouse hefted the luggage from the row house to the trunk of the Mercedes, he had to give the tailors credit for their attention to detail: all the baron's shirts were monogrammed, and even a scrolled FVF had been worked into the suitcases.

Michael had already said his goodbyes to Gunther, Dietz, and the others. He settled himself into the backseat of the Mercedes. When Mouse started to climb into the back, Wilhelm—a big-shouldered man with a waxed gray mustache—said, "A servant rides in the front seat," and firmly shut the rear passenger's door in Mouse's face. Mouse, grumbling under his breath, took his place in the front. Michael heard the Cross of Iron jingle in the little man's pocket. Then Wilhelm started the engine, and the Mercedes slid smoothly away from the curb.

A partition of glass separated the front and rear seats. Michael smelled Echo's aroma in the car, a heady scent. The car was perfectly clean: no handkerchiefs, no pieces of paper, nothing to give a clue to Echo's identity. Or so Michael thought, until he opened the shining metal ashtray on the back of the driver's seat; in it there was not a trace of ashes, but instead a green ticket stub. Michael looked closely at the lettering on it: *KinoElektra*. The Cinema Elektra. He returned the stub to its resting place and closed the ashtray. Then he opened a little hinged rubber flap between himself and Wilhelm. "Where are we going?"

"We have two destinations, sir. The first is to visit an artist."

"And the second?"

"Your lodgings while you enjoy Berlin."

"Will the lady be joining us?"

"A possibility, sir," Wilhelm said, and that was all.

Michael closed the flap. He glanced at Mouse, who was busy trying to stretch his shirt collar with a forefinger. Last night, while they'd slept in the same room, Michael had heard Mouse sobbing. Mouse had gotten out of his bed and stood at the window in the darkness for a long time. Michael listened to the soft *clink* of the Iron Cross as Mouse had turned it over and over in his hand. Then, sometime later, Mouse had sighed deeply, snuffled his nose on his sleeve, and crawled back into his bed. The tinkling noise of the Iron Cross had ceased, and Mouse slept with the medal clenched in his fist. For now, at least, his crisis of the soul had passed.

Wilhelm was an expert driver, which was good because the streets of Berlin were nightmares of horse-drawn wagons, army trucks, tanks, and streetcars, not to mention the areas that were clogged with smoldering rubble. As they drove toward the address of Theo von Frankewitz and a light rain began to patter down on the windshield, Michael mentally reviewed what he'd learned from the dossiers.

There was no new information about Jerek Blok; the man was a Hitler fanatic and a loyal Nazi party member whose activities since leaving his command of Falkenhausen concentration camp were shrouded in secrecy. Dr. Gustav Hildebrand, son of a German pioneer in the field of gas warfare, had a home near Bonn, where Hildebrand Industries was located. But there was a new item of interest: Hildebrand also maintained a residence and lab on the island of Skarpa, about thirty miles south of Bergen, Norway. As a summer home, that would be quite a journey from Bonn. And as a winter retreat . . . well, the winters were very long and very arctic that far north. So why did Hildebrand work in such an isolated place? Surely he could have found a more idyllic location. It was a point that merited looking into.

Wilhelm drove slowly along Victoria Park, as rain slashed through the budding trees. It was another area of row houses and small shops, and pedestrians hurried along under umbrellas.

Michael opened the flap once more. "Are we expected?"

"No, sir. Herr von Frankewitz was home at midnight; we'll find out if he's still in." Wilhelm was just creeping the Mercedes along the street. Looking for a signal, Michael thought. He saw a woman cutting roses in the window of a flower shop, and a man standing in a doorway trying to get an uncooperative umbrella open. The woman put her roses in a glass vase and set them in the window, and the man got his umbrella open and walked away. Wilhelm said, "Herr Frankewitz is in, sir. That's his apartment building." He motioned to a structure of gray bricks on the right. "It's apartment five, on the second floor." He braked the Mercedes. "I'll be driving around the block. Good luck, sir."

Michael got out, his coat collar up against the rain. Mouse started to get out, too, but Wilhelm grasped his arm. "The baron goes alone," he said, and Mouse started to pull angrily away but Michael told him, "It's all right. Stay in the car," and then he strode to the curb and into the building Wilhelm had indicated. The Mercedes drove on.

The building's interior smelled like a damp tomb. Nazi slogans and epithets had been painted on the walls. Michael saw something slink past in the gloom. Whether it was a cat or a very large rodent, he couldn't tell for sure. He went up the staircase, and found the tarnished number "5."

He knocked on the door. Down the hallway, an infant squalled. Voices, a man and woman's, raised and tangled in argument. He knocked again on the door, aware of the small two-shot derringer in its special pocket of his vest: a gift from his hosts. No answer. He balled his fist to knock a third time, beginning to wonder if Wilhelm had gotten his signals crossed.

"Go away," a man's voice said from the other side of the door. "I don't have any money."

It was a tired gasp of a voice. The voice of someone whose breathing wasn't right. Michael said, "Herr von Frankewitz? I have to talk to you, please."

A silence. Then: "I can't talk. Go away."

"It's very important."

"I said I have no money. Please . . . don't bother me. I'm a sick man."

Michael heard footsteps shuffling away. He said, "I'm a friend of your friend in Paris. The opera lover."

The footsteps stopped.

Michael waited.

"I don't know who you're talking about," Frankewitz rasped, standing close to the door.

"He told me you'd done some painting recently. Some metal work. I'd like to discuss it with you, if I may."

Another silence stretched. Von Frankewitz was either a very careful man or a very frightened one. And then Michael heard the clicking of locks disengaging. A bolt was thrown back, and the door opened about two inches. A slice of a white-fleshed face appeared in the crack, like the visage of a ghost emerging from a crypt. "Who are you?" Frankewitz whispered.

"I've traveled a long way to see you," Michael said. "May I come in?"

Frankewitz hesitated, his pallid face hanging in the darkness like a quarter moon. Michael saw a gray eye, bloodshot, and a thicket of oily brown hair tumbling over a high, white forehead. The gray eye blinked. Frankewitz opened the door and stepped back, allowing Michael to enter.

The apartment was a close, dark place with narrow windows filmed by the soot of Berlin's factories. A threadbare black and gold Oriental carpet covered the wooden floor, which felt none too sturdy under Michael's shoes. The furniture was heavy and ornate, the kind of things kept in dusty museum basements. Everywhere there were throw pillows, and the arms of a sea-green sofa were protected with lace coverlets. The apartment odors assailed Michael's nostrils: the smoke of cheap cigarettes, a sweet floral cologne, oil paints and turpentine, and the bitter scent of sickness. In a corner of the room, near one of the slender windows, was a chair, an easel, and a canvas with a landscape in progress: a red sky above a city whose buildings were made of bones.

"Sit here. It's the most comfortable." Frankewitz swept a pile of dirty clothes off the sea-green sofa, and Michael sat down. A spring stabbed his spine.

Frankewitz, a skinny man wearing a blue silk robe and slippers, circled the room straightening crooked lamp shades, pictures, and a bunch of wilted flowers in a copper vase. Then the artist sat down in a high-backed black chair, crossed his thin white legs, and reached for a pack of cigarettes and an ebony cigarette holder. He screwed a cigarette in with nervous fingers. "You've seen Werner, then? How is he?"

Michael realized Frankewitz was talking about Adam. "He's dead. The Gestapo killed him."

The other man's mouth opened, and a small gasp came out. His fingers fumbled with a pack of matches. The first match was damp, shooting a tiny spark before it went out. He got the cigarette lit with the second match, and he drew deeply from the ebony holder. A smoky cough welled up from his lungs, followed by a second, third, and then a flurry of coughs. His lungs rattled wetly, but when the fit of coughing was over, the artist puffed on his cigarette holder again, his sunken gray eyes damp. "I'm sorry to hear that. Werner was . . . a gentleman."

It was time to take the leap. Michael said, "Did you know that your friend worked for the British Secret Service?"

Frankewitz smoked his cigarette in silence, the little red circle glinting in the gloom. "I did," he answered at last. "Werner told me. I'm not a Nazi. What the Nazis have done to this country—and to my friends . . . well, I have no love for the Nazis."

"You told Werner about taking a trip to a warehouse, and painting bullet holes on green metal. I'd like to know how you came to do that work. Who employed you?"

"A man." Frankewitz's thin shoulders shrugged beneath the blue silk. "I never knew his name." He pulled on the cigarette, exhaled smoke, and coughed harshly again. "Forgive me," he said. "I'm sick, you see."

Michael had already noticed the crusted sores on Frankewitz's legs. They looked like rat bites. "How did this man know you could do the job?"

"Art is my life," Frankewitz said, as if that explained everything. But then he stood up, moving like an old man though he couldn't be more than thirty-three, and he went over to the easel. Leaning against the wall near it was a stack of paintings. Frankewitz knelt down and began to go through them, his long white fingers as tentative as if having to prod sleeping children awake. "I used to paint, in a café not too far from here. I'd moved indoors for the winter. This man came in for coffee. He watched me working. Later he came in again, and several more times. Ah, here you are!" He was addressing a painting. "This is what I was working on." He pulled the canvas out and showed it to Michael. It was a self-portrait, of Frankewitz's face in what appeared to be a cracked mirror. The cracks looked so real Michael imagined slicing a finger on one of the jagged edges. "He brought another man in to see it: a Nazi officer. I later found out the second man's name was Blok. Then, maybe two weeks later, the first man came to the café and asked me if I'd like to make some money." Frankewitz smiled faintly, a chilling smile on that frail white face. "I can always use money. Even Nazi money." He regarded the self-portrait for a moment; the face in the picture was a fantasy of self-flattery. Then he returned the canvas to the stack and stood up. Rain was slashing against the windows, and Frankewitz watched the drops run trails across the grimy glass. "They picked me up one night, and we drove to the airfield. Blok was there, and several more men. They blindfolded me before we took off."

"So you have no idea where you landed?"

Frankewitz returned to his chair and pushed the cigarette holder between his teeth again. He watched the rain falling, blue smoke drifting from his mouth and his lungs rasping as he breathed. "It was a long flight. We landed once, for refueling. I could smell the fuel. And I felt the sun on my face, so I knew we were flying west. When we landed, I could smell the sea. They led me into a place where they took off my blindfold. It was a warehouse, without windows. The doors were locked." A blue haze of smoke whirled slowly around Frankewitz's head. "They had all the paint and tools I needed, arranged very neatly. They had a little room for me to live in: a chair and cot, a few books and magazines, a Victrola. Again, no windows. Colonel Blok took me to a large room where the pieces of metal and glass were laid out, and he told me what he wanted done. Bullet holes, he said; cracks in the glass, just as I'd done the cracked mirror in my painting. He said he wanted patterns of holes painted on the metal, and he marked them with a piece of chalk. I did the work. When I finished, they blindfolded me and led me out to an airplane again. Another long flight, and then they paid me and drove me home." He tilted his head to one side, listening to the music of the rain. "That's all."

Hardly, Michael thought. "And how did Ad—Werner find out about this?"

"I told him. I'd met Werner last summer. I was in Paris, with another friend. As I said, Werner was a gentleman. A dear gentleman. Ah, well." He made a despondent motion with his cigarette holder, and then terror flickered across his face. "The Gestapo . . . they didn't . . . I mean, Werner didn't tell them about *me*, did he?"

"No, he didn't."

Frankewitz sighed with relief. Another cough gurgled up, and he suffered another spasm. "Thank God," he said when he could speak again. "Thank God. The Gestapo . . . they do terrible things to people."

"You said they led you from the airplane to the warehouse. They didn't drive you?"

"No. It was maybe thirty paces, no more than that."

Then the warehouse had been part of the airfield, Michael thought. "What else was stored in the warehouse?"

"I didn't get much of a chance to look around. There was always a guard nearby. I did see some barrels and crates. Oil drums, I think they were, and some machinery. Gears and things."

"And you overheard the term 'Iron Fist'? Is that right?"

"Yes. Colonel Blok was talking to a man who came to visit. He called the man Dr. Hildebrand. Blok used that name several times."

Here was a point that needed clarification. Michael said, "Why did Blok and Hildebrand let you overhear them talking if the security was so tight? You had to be in the same room with them, yes?"

"Of course I was. But I was working, so maybe they thought I wasn't listening." Frankewitz blew a plume of smoke toward the ceiling. "Anyway, it wasn't such a secret. I had to paint them."

"Paint them? Paint what?"

"The words. Iron Fist. I had to paint them on a piece of metal. Blok showed me how to make the letters, because I don't read English."

Michael paused as that sank in. "English? You painted—"

" 'Iron Fist' in English letters," Frankewitz said. "On the green metal. Olive green to be exact. Very drab. And underneath that I painted the picture."

"The picture?" Michael shook his head. "I don't understand."

"I'll show you." Frankewitz went to the easel, sat down

305

in the chair, and arranged a pad of drawing paper in front of him. He picked up a charcoal pencil as Michael came up to stand behind him. Frankewitz spent a moment in silent deliberation, then began to sketch. "This is very rough, you understand. My hand hasn't been doing what I've asked of it lately. It's the weather, I think. This apartment's always damp in the springtime."

Michael watched the drawing take shape. It was a large, disembodied fist, covered with armor plate. The fist was squeezing a figure that had yet to be defined.

"Blok stood and watched over my shoulder, just as you are," Frankewitz said. The pencil drew skinny legs dangling down from the iron fist. "I had to do the rough sketch five times before he was satisfied with it. Then I painted it on the metal, beneath the lettering. I graduated in the upper third of my class at art school. The professors said I had 'promise.' " He smiled wanly, his hand working as if with a mind of its own. "The bill collectors bother me all the time. I thought you were one of them." He was drawing a pair of limp arms. "I do my best work in the summer," he said. "When I can get out in the park, in the sunshine."

Frankewitz had finished the figure's body: a cartoonish form, caught in the fist. He started on the head and facial features. "I had a painting in an exhibition once. Before the war. It was a picture of two goldfish swimming in a green pond. I've always liked fish; they seem so peaceful." He drew in a pair of wide, bulging eyeballs and an uptilted slash of a nose. "Do you know who bought that painting? One of Goebbels's secretaries. Yes. Goebbels himself! That picture might be hanging in the Reich Chancellery, for all I know!" He sketched a sweep of dark hair hanging down over the forehead. "My signature, in the Reich Chancellery. Well, the world is a strange place, isn't it?" He completed the face with a black square of a mustache, and lifted the pencil. "There. That's what I painted for Colonel Blok."

It was a caricature of Adolf Hitler, his eyes popping and his mouth open in an indignant cry as he was squeezed by the iron fist.

Michael was speechless. Wheels were spinning in his brain, but they found no traction. SS Colonel Jerek Blok, a

Nazi loyalist, had paid Frankewitz to paint a rather ludicrous caricature of the Reich's *Führer?* It made no sense! This was the kind of disrespect that granted a person an appointment with a noose, and it had been authorized by a Hitler fanatic. The bullet holes, the cracked glass, the caricature, the iron fist . . . what was it all about?

"I asked no questions." Frankewitz stood up from his chair. "I didn't want to know. All I wanted was to get home alive. Blok told me they might need me again, to do some more work. He told me it was a special project, and that if I let anyone else know about it the Gestapo would find out and come visit me." He smoothed the wrinkles in his silk robe, his fingers nervous again. "I don't know why I told Werner. I knew he was working for the other side." Frankewitz watched the rain streaming down the windows, his gaunt face streaked with shadows. "I think . . . I did it because . . . of the way Blok looked at me. As if I were a dog that could do tricks. It was in his eyes: he loathed me, but he needed me. And perhaps he didn't kill me because he thought he might need me again. I'm a human being, not a beast. Do you understand that?"

Michael nodded.

"That's all I know. I can't help you any more." Frankewitz's breathing had gotten hoarse again. He found another match and relit his cigarette, which had gone cold. "Do you have any money?" he asked.

"No, I don't." He had a wallet, given to him by his hosts, but there was no money in it. He stared at Frankewitz's long white fingers, then he took off his kid gloves and said, "Here. These are worth something."

Frankewitz took them without hesitation. Blue smoke wafted from his lips. "Thank you. You're a true gentleman. There aren't many of us left in the world."

"You'd better destroy that." Michael motioned toward the Hitler cartoon. He moved to the door and paused to add a final note. "You didn't have to tell me these things. I appreciate it. But one thing I have to tell *you:* I can't say that you're safe, knowing what you do."

Frankewitz waved his cigarette holder, leaving a scrawl of smoke in the air. "Is anyone safe in Berlin?" he asked.

For that question Michael had no answer. He began to unlatch the door; the dank room with its narrow, grimy windows had started to suffocate him.

"Will you come visit me again?" Frankewitz had finished his cigarette, and he crushed it in a green onyx ashtray.

"No."

"For the best, I suppose. I hope you find what it is you're looking for."

"Thank you. I do, too." Michael slipped the final lock, left the apartment, and closed the door behind him. Immediately he heard Theo von Frankewitz relocking the door on the other side; it was a frantic sound, the noise of an animal scurrying in a cage. Frankewitz coughed a few times, his lungs clogged with fluid, and then Michael walked down the corridor to the stairs and descended to the rain-swept street.

Wilhelm pulled the Mercedes smoothly to the curb, and Michael got in. Then the driver started them off again, heading west through the rain.

"You found out what you needed to know?" Mouse asked when Michael volunteered no information.

"It's a beginning," he answered. Hitler being crushed by an iron fist. Bullet holes on green-painted metal. Dr. Hildebrand, the researcher of gas warfare. A warehouse, on a landing strip where the air smelled of the sea. A beginning, yes: the entrance to a maze. And the invasion of Europe, poised to take place when the spring's wild tides eased. The first week of June, Michael thought. Hundreds of thousands of lives in the balance. Live free, he thought, and smiled grimly. The heavy yoke of responsibility had settled around his shoulders. "Where are we going?" he asked Wilhelm after another few minutes.

"To check you in, sir. You're a new member of the Brimstone Club."

Michael started to ask what that was, but Wilhelm's attention was on his driving and the rain was slashing down again. Michael stared at his own gloveless hands, while the questions turned in his mind and the torrent clawed at the windows.

5

"There it is, sir," Wilhelm said, and both Michael and Mouse saw it through the whirring windshield wipers.

Before them, veiled in the rain and the low-lying mist, a turreted castle rose from an island in the Havel River. Wilhelm had been following a paved road through Berlin's Grunewald Forest for almost fifteen minutes, and now the pavement ended at the river's edge. But the road continued: a wooden pontoon bridge that led over the dark water to the castle's massive granite archway. Entry to the pontoon bridge was blocked by a yellow barricade, and as Wilhelm slowed the car a young man in a maroon uniform, wearing dark blue gloves and carrying an umbrella, stepped out of a small stone checkpoint station. Wilhelm rolled down the window and announced, "The Baron von Fange," and the young man nodded crisply and returned to his station. Michael could see through a window into the structure, and he watched the young man dialing a telephone. The phone wires crossed the river and went into the castle. In another moment the man reappeared, lifted the barricade, and waved Wilhelm through. The Mercedes crossed the pontoon bridge.

"This is the Reichkronen Hotel," Wilhelm explained as they neared the archway. "The castle was built in 1733. The Nazis took it over in 1939. It's for dignitaries and guests of the Reich."

"Oh, my God," Mouse whispered as the immense castle loomed above them. He'd seen it before, of course, but never so close. And never had he dreamed he'd be about to enter it. The Reichkronen was reserved for Nazi party leaders, foreign diplomats, high-ranking officers, dukes, earls, and barons—*real* barons, that is. As the castle grew and its archway awaited like a gray-lipped mouth, Mouse felt very small. His stomach churned. "I don't . . . I don't think I can go in there," he said.

He had no choice. The Mercedes moved through the archway into a large courtyard. A wide set of granite stairs fluted upward to the double front doors, above which were the gilt letters Reichkronen and a swastika. Four young blond-haired men in maroon uniforms emerged from the doors and hurried down the stairs as Wilhelm braked the Mercedes.

"I can't . . . I can't . . ." Mouse was saying, feeling as if the breath were being squeezed out of him.

Wilhelm speared him with an icy stare. "A good servant," he said quietly, "does *not* let his master down." And then the door was opened for Mouse, an umbrella was held over his head, and he stood dazed as Wilhelm got out and came around to unlock the trunk.

Michael waited for his door to be opened, as befitting a baron. He stepped out of the car and into the protection of an umbrella. His stomach was tight, too, as were the muscles at the back of his neck. But this was no place for hesitation, and if he was going to survive this masquerade, he had to play his part to the hilt. He forced down the alarm of nerves and started up the steps at a brisk clip so the young man with the umbrella would have difficulty keeping up with him. Mouse followed a few paces behind, feeling smaller with every step. Wilhelm and the other two men brought the bags.

Michael walked into the lobby of the Reichkronen, entering the Nazi sanctum. It was a huge chamber, where pools of light from low lamps spilled over dark brown leather furniture and Persian rugs sparkled with golden threads. Above his head was a massive, ornate chandelier where perhaps fifty candles burned. Flames roared from logs in a white marble hearth that could serve as a garage for a Tiger tank; centered over the hearth was a large framed painting of Adolf Hitler, with gilded eagles on either side. Chamber music was playing: a quartet of string musicians, performing a Beethoven piece. And seated in the overstuffed leather chairs and sofas were German officers, most of them with drinks in hand, either engaged in conversation or listening to the music. Other people, among them a number of women, stood in groups, chatting politely. Michael looked around, getting the full impact of the monstrous place, and he heard Mouse give a soft, terrified moan just behind him.

And then, a woman's voice, as beautiful as a cello: "Frederick!" The voice was familiar. Michael started to turn in its direction, and he heard the woman say, "Frederick! My darling!"

She rushed at him, and her arms went around him. He smelled her scent: cinnamon and leather. She clasped him tightly, her blond curls against his cheek. And then she looked him in the face with eyes the color of champagne, and her crimson lips sought his mouth.

He let them find it. She tasted like a crisp white Moselle. Her body was pressed hard against his, and as the kiss went on Michael put his arms around her body and darted his tongue out to tease her lips. He felt her shiver, wanting to pull away but unable to, and he slowly caressed his tongue back and forth across her mouth. She suddenly seized his tongue with her mouth and sucked on it with a force that almost tore it from its roots. Her teeth clamped down on his tongue, trapping it with none-too-gentle pressure. This was the civilized way to make war, Michael thought. He squeezed her tighter, and she squeezed him with a crush that made his backbone pop. They stood like that for a moment, locked mouth to mouth and teeth to tongue.

"*Ahem.*" A man cleared his throat. "So *this* is the lucky Baron von Fange."

The woman released Michael's tongue and pulled her head back. Crimson spots seethed in her cheeks, and her beautiful pale brown eyes glittered with anger beneath thick blond brows. But there was a joyous smile on her mouth, and she said with a rush of excitement, "Yes, Harry! Isn't he beautiful?"

Michael turned his head to the right, and stared at Harry Sandler, who stood perhaps three feet from him.

The big-game hunter, the man who had engineered the murder of the Countess Margritta in Cairo almost two years before, grunted skeptically. "Wild beasts are beautiful, Chesna. Especially when their heads are on my wall. I'm afraid I don't share your taste, but . . . it's a pleasure to finally meet you, Baron." Sandler thrust out a large hand,

and the golden hawk that perched on his leather-trimmed left shoulder spread its wings for balance.

Michael stared at the hand for a few seconds. He could see it gripped around a telephone, ordering Margritta's murder. He could see it tapping out a radio code to his Nazi masters. He could see it squeezing the trigger of a rifle and sending a bullet through a lion's skull. Michael took the hand and shook it, keeping a polite smile on his face though his eyes had gone hard. Sandler increased the pressure, trapping Michael's knuckles. "Chesna's been boring me to death with stories about you," Sandler said, his ruddy face grinning. His German was very good. He had dark brown eyes that shed no warmth, and the pressure of his grip on Michael's hand continued to mount. Michael's knuckles throbbed. "Thank God you're here, so she won't have to tell me any more."

"Perhaps I'll bore you to death with stories of my own," Michael said, his smile broader; he made sure he showed no indication of the fact that his hand was about to break. He stared into Harry Sandler's eyes, and he felt a message pass between them: survival of the fittest. His knuckles were jammed together, caught in that bear claw of a hand. One more ounce of pressure, and the bones would crack. Michael smiled, and felt sweat crawl down under his arms. He was, for the moment at least, at the mercy of a killer.

Sandler, showing his square white teeth, released Michael's hand. Blood stung as it rushed through the cramping fingers. "As I said, a pleasure."

The woman, who wore a dark blue dress that fit her lean body as if it had been poured on, had blond hair that fell in curly ringlets around her shoulders. Her face, with its high, sharp cheekbones and full-lipped mouth, was as striking as a glimpse of the sun through storm clouds. She took Michael's arm. "Frederick, I hope you won't mind that I've been boasting about you. I've told Harry the secret."

"Oh? Have you?" What next?

"Harry says he'll give the bride away. Isn't that right?"

Sandler's smile slipped a notch, which didn't matter much since it was false to begin with. "I have to tell you, Baron: you're in for the fight of your life."

"Am I?" Michael felt as if the floor had turned to ice, and he was trying to keep from stepping through a thin spot.

"You're damned right. If you weren't around, Chesna would be marrying *me*. So I'm going to do my best to dethrone you."

The woman laughed. "Oh, my! What a delight! To be fought over by two handsome men!" She glanced at Wilhelm and Mouse, who stood a few feet away. Mouse's face was tinged with gray, his shoulders slumped under the immense weight of the Reichkronen. The luggage had already disappeared, whisked into an elevator by the bellboys. "You may go to your quarters now," she said, with the air of someone who was used to giving orders and being obeyed. Wilhelm gave Mouse a firm nudge toward a door marked *Treppe*— Stairs—but Mouse only went a few paces before he looked at Michael, his expression a mixture of panic and bewilderment. Michael nodded, and the little man followed Wilhelm to the stairway.

"Good servants are so hard to find," Chesna said, oozing arrogance. "Shall we go to the lounge?" She motioned toward a candlelit enclave on the other side of the lobby, and Michael allowed her to guide him. Sandler walked a few paces behind them, and Michael could sense the man was sizing him up. Of course the woman named Chesna was the agent Michael knew as Echo; but who was she? And how could she mingle so freely with the Reich's bluebloods? They were almost to the lounge when a pretty young dark-haired girl stepped in their path and said shyly, "Excuse me . . . but I've seen all your pictures. I think you're wonderful. Might I have your autograph?"

"Of course!" Chesna took the pen and pad the girl offered. "What's your name?"

"Charlotta."

Michael watched as Chesna wrote, in large and dramatic letters: *To Charlotta, All My Best, Chesna van Dorne.* She ended with a flourish and handed the pad back to Charlotta with a dazzling smile. "There you are. I have a new film coming out next month. I hope you'll look for it."

"Oh, I will! Thank you!" The girl, obviously thrilled, took

her autograph back to where she'd been sitting, on a sofa between two middle-aged Nazi officers.

In the lounge, which was decorated with framed symbols of German infantry and armor divisions, they chose a secluded table. Michael took off his topcoat and hung it on a wall hook nearby. When the waiter came, Chesna ordered a Riesling, Michael asked for the same, and Sandler ordered a whiskey and soda and a platter of chopped meat. The waiter seemed to be used to the request, and he left without comment.

"Harry, must you carry that bird everywhere?" Chesna asked teasingly.

"Not quite everywhere. But Blondi's my good-luck charm." He smiled, looking at Michael. The golden hawk—a beautiful creature—stared at Michael, too, and he realized that both the hawk and its master had the same cold eyes. Its talons gripped the patch of leather on the shoulder of Sandler's expensively tailored tweed jacket. "Do you know anything about birds of prey, Baron?"

"I know enough to avoid them."

Sandler laughed politely. He had a square-jawed, crudely handsome face with a crooked boxer's nose. His reddish hair was cropped short on the sides and back, and a small flame-colored wisp of hair fell over his creased forehead. Everything about him exuded haughty confidence and power. He wore a red-striped necktie and a pale blue shirt, and on his lapel there was a small gold swastika. "Smart man," he said. "I captured Blondi in Africa. It's taken me three years to train her. Of course she's not tame, just obedient." He took a leather glove from inside his coat and worked it onto his left hand. "She's lovely, isn't she? Did you know that I could give her a signal and she'd rip your face to shreds within five seconds or so?"

"That's a comforting thought," Michael said. His testicles felt as if they'd drawn up.

"I trained her on British prisoners of war," Sandler went on, taking a step into no-man's-land. "Smeared some mouse guts on their faces, and Blondi did the rest. Here, girl." He gave a low, trilling whistle, and offered Blondi the back of his glove. The hawk immediately stepped from Sandler's shoulder onto the glove, its talons clenching down. "I find nobility in savagery," Sandler said as he admired the golden hawk. "Maybe that's why I want Chesna to marry me."

"Oh, Harry!" She smiled at Michael; the smile had a warning in it. "I never know whether to kiss him or slap him."

Michael still hadn't gotten past the remark about the British POWs. He smiled, too, but his face felt in danger of cracking. "I hope you'll save the kisses for *me*."

"I've been in love with Chesna ever since I met her. It was on the set of . . . what movie was that, Chesna?"

"*The Flame of Destiny.* Heinreid brought you for a visit."

"Right. I suppose you're a fan, too, Baron?"

"Her number-one fan," Michael said, and he placed his hand on top of hers and squeezed it. A film actress, he'd realized she must be. And a highly successful one, at that. He recalled reading something about *The Flame of Destiny;* it had been a Nazi propaganda film, made in 1938. One of those movies full of Nazi banners, gleeful crowds cheering for Hitler, and idyllic landscapes of Germany.

Their glasses of white wine, the whiskey and soda, and the platter of raw chopped meat arrived. Sandler took a swig of his drink and then began to feed Blondi pieces of the bloody meat. The hawk gobbled them down. Michael smelled the coppery aroma of the blood, and his own mouth watered.

"So, when's the happy day?" Sandler asked, the fingers of his right hand smeared with crimson.

"The first week of June," Chesna answered. "We haven't set the exact day yet, have we, Frederick?"

"No, not yet."

"Happy for *you,* I might say. A tragedy for me." Sandler watched a hunk of meat go into Blondi's hooked beak. "Baron, do you *do* anything? Besides watch over the family estate, I mean?"

"I manage the vineyards. Also the gardens. We raise tulips." That had all been part of his biography.

"Ah, tulips." Sandler smiled, his gaze on the hawk. "Well, that must keep you very busy. Royalty is a wonderful occupation, isn't it?"

315

"If you can stand the hours."

Sandler stared at him; something glittered like a knife's edge—anger? jealousy?—down in the dark brown, soulless eyes. He pushed the platter of meat a few inches toward Michael. "Here," he said. "Why don't you feed Blondi."

"Harry," Chesna told him, "I don't think we need to—"

"All right." Michael picked up a piece of meat. Sandler slowly moved his gloved hand forward, so Blondi's beak was within Michael's reach. Michael started to offer Blondi the bloody food.

"Careful," Sandler said quietly. "She likes fingers. And then how would you pick your tulips?"

Michael paused. Blondi stared fixedly at the meat between his fingers. He could feel Chesna van Dorne tense beside him. Sandler was waiting, expecting the rich and idle tulip baron to back down. Michael had no choice but to continue the movement his hand had already begun. As his fingers neared Blondi's beak, the hawk began to make a soft, menacing hissing noise.

"Uh-oh!" Sandler said. "She smells something about you she doesn't like."

It was the odor of the wolf, caught in his pores. Michael hesitated, with the meat about four inches from Blondi's beak. The hissing noise was getting higher and harsher, like steam from a scalding kettle.

"I think you're really upsetting her. Shhhh, girl." Sandler pulled his hand and the hawk away from Michael, and blew gently on the back of Blondi's neck. Gradually the hissing noise subsided. But Blondi's gaze was still riveted on Michael, and he could sense the hawk wanted to leap from its leather perch and flail its talons at him. Like master, like hawk, he thought; there was no love lost at this table.

"Well," Michael said, "it's a shame to let good beef go to waste." He put the meat into his mouth, chewed, and swallowed. Chesna gave a horrified gasp. Sandler just sat, stunned and disbelieving. Michael sipped casually at his wine and dabbed his lips with a white napkin. "One of my favorite dishes is steak tartare," he explained. "This is almost the same thing, isn't it?"

Sandler's trance broke. "You'd better watch your groomto-be," he told Chesna. "He seems to enjoy the taste of blood." Sandler stood up; for the moment, their game was over. "I have business to attend to, so I'll say goodbye for now. Baron, I hope we'll have a chance to talk later. Of course you'll be attending the Brimstone Club?"

"I wouldn't miss it."

"If you can eat raw meat, you should love the Brimstone Club. I'll look forward to our next meeting." He started to shake Michael's hand again, then looked at his own blood-smeared fingers. "You'll pardon me if I don't shake hands?"

"No pardon necessary." His knuckles weren't ready for another pressure contest, anyway. Sandler, the hawk latched to his gloved left hand, gave Chesna a brief bow and then strode away out of the lounge.

"Charming," Michael said. "I've met nicer snakes."

Chesna looked at him; she was indeed a good actress, because her face retained the dreamy expression of a happy lover while her eyes were chilly. "We're being watched," she said. "If you ever try to stick your tongue down my throat again, I'll bite it off. Is that clear, darling?"

"Does that mean I'll get another chance?"

"It means that our arrangement of betrothal is fiction, not to be confused with reality. It was the best way to explain your presence and get you into this hotel."

Michael shrugged, rather enjoying needling this composed blond Nordic celebrity. "I'm just trying to play my part."

"You leave the acting to me. Just go where I tell you to go, do what I tell you to do, and speak when you're spoken to. Don't volunteer any information, and for God's sake don't try to match egos with Harry Sandler." She gave him a distasteful frown. "And what was that about the raw meat? Don't you think that was going a bit too far?"

"Maybe so, but it got that bastard out of here, didn't it?"

Chesna van Dorne sipped her wine but didn't answer. She had to admit that he was right. Sandler had been upstaged, and the big-game hunter wasn't one to take that lightly. Still . . . it *had* been amusing, in a bizarre way. She glanced at the man over the rim of her glass. Definitely not the tulip-plucking type, she decided. Without all the grime, the shaggy hair, and the beard, he was very handsome. But his eyes disturbed her in a way she couldn't define. They looked . . . yes, she decided; they looked like the eyes of a dangerous animal, and reminded her of the pale green eyes of a timber wolf that had frightened her when she was twelve years old and visiting the Berlin Zoo. The wolf had stared at her with those cold clear eyes, and even though bars separated them, Chesna had shivered and clung hard to her father's hand. She'd known what the wolf was thinking: *I want to eat you.*

"I want to eat something," Michael said. The raw meat had sharpened his appetite. "Is there a restaurant here?"

"Yes, but we can order room service." Chesna finished her wine. "We've got a lot to talk about." He was staring at her, and she avoided his gaze. She summoned their waiter, signed the check, and then took Michael's arm and led him out of the lounge like a thoroughbred dog on a leash. Once they were in the lobby and striding toward the row of gilt-doored elevators, Chesna turned on her magnificent smile like a klieg light.

As they neared the elevators, a man's husky voice said, "Miss van Dorne?"

Chesna stopped and turned, her smile aglow, ready to charm another autograph seeker.

The man was huge: a living bunker, standing about six-feet-three and at least two hundred and sixty pounds, with thick shoulders and arms. He wore an SS aide's uniform and a gray peaked cap, and his face was pale and emotionless. "I was told to give you this," he said as he offered Chesna a small white envelope.

Chesna took it, her hand that of a child's compared to the man's. The envelope bore her name.

Michael's heart lurched. Standing before him was the man called Boots, who had kicked and stomped Gaby's uncle to death in the barn at Bazancourt.

"I'm to return a reply," Boots said. His hair was cropped close to the skull, and his eyes were pale blue and heavy-lidded; the eyes of a man who saw everyone else in the world as frail constructions of flesh and bone. As Chesna tore open the envelope and read it Michael glanced at the SS aide's thickly soled jackboots. They reflected the candles of the chandelier on their glossy surface, and Michael wondered if they were the same boots that had knocked Gervaise's teeth from his head. He felt the man watching him, and he looked up into the dull blue eyes. Boots nodded curtly, no recognition in his gaze.

"Tell him I . . . *we'd* be delighted," Chesna told him, and Boots strode away toward a group of officers at the center of the lobby.

The elevator came. "Six," Chesna told the elderly operator. As they ascended she said to Michael, "We've just been invited to dine with Colonel Jerek Blok."

6

Chesna unlocked the white door and turned the ornate brass knob. The smell of fresh roses and lavender rushed at Michael as he crossed the threshold.

The living room, a majesty of white furniture, had a twenty-foot ceiling and a fireplace with green marble tiles. French doors led out to a terrace, which overlooked the river and the forest beyond. Resting atop a white Steinway piano was a large crystal vase that held roses and sprigs of lavender. On the wall above the fireplace was a framed painting of a steely-eyed Adolf Hitler.

"Cozy," Michael said.

Chesna locked the door. "Your bedroom is through there." She nodded toward a corridor.

Michael went through it and looked around the spacious bedroom with its dark oak furniture and paintings of various Luftwaffe airplanes. His luggage was neatly arrayed in a closet. He returned to the living room. "I'm impressed," he said, which was an understatement. He laid his topcoat down on the sofa and walked to one of the high windows. Rain was still falling, tapping on the glass, and mist covered the forest below. "Do you pay for this, or do your friends?"

"I do. And it's not inexpensive." She went to the onyx-topped bar, got a glass from a shelf, and opened a bottle of spring water. "I'm wealthy," she added.

"All from acting?"

"I've starred in ten films since 1936. Haven't you heard of me?"

"I've heard of Echo," he said. "Not Chesna van Dorne." He opened the French doors and inhaled the misty, pine-scented air. "How is it that an American became a German film star?"

"Talent. Plus I was in the right place at the right time." She drank her spring water and put the glass aside. " 'Chesna' comes from 'Chesapeake.' I was born on my father's yacht, in Chesapeake Bay. My father was German, my mother was from Maryland. I've lived in both countries."

"And why did you choose Maryland over Germany?" he asked pointedly.

"My allegiance, you mean?" She smiled faintly. "Well, I'm not a believer in that man over the fireplace. Neither was my father. He killed himself in 1934, when his business failed."

Michael started to say *I'm sorry,* but there was no need. Chesna had simply made a statement. "Yet you make films for the Nazis?"

"I make films to make money. Also, how better to cultivate their good graces? Because of what I do and who I am, I can get into places that many others can't. I overhear a lot of gossip, and sometimes I even see maps. You'd be amazed how a general can brag when his tongue's loosened by champagne. I'm Germany's Golden Girl. My face is even on some of the propaganda posters." She lifted her brows. "You see?"

Michael nodded. There was much more to be learned about Chesna van Dorne; was she, like her screen characters, also a fabrication? In any case, she was a beautiful woman, and she held Michael's life in her hands. "Where's my friend?"

"Your valet, you mean? In the servants' wing." She motioned toward a white telephone. "You can reach him by dialing our room number plus 'nine.' We can order room service for you, too, if you're hungry."

"I am. I'd like a steak." He saw her look sharply at him. "Rare," he told her.

"I'd like you to know something," Chesna said, after a pause. She walked to the windows and peered out at the river, her face painted with stormy light. "Even if the invasion is successful—and the odds are against it—the Allies will never reach Berlin before the Russians. Of course the Nazis are expecting an invasion, but they don't know exactly when or where it will come. They're planning on throwing the Allies back into the sea so they can turn all their strength to the Russian Front. But it won't help them, and by that time the Russian Front will be the border of Germany. So this is my last assignment; when we've completed our mission, I'm getting out with you."

"And my friend. Mouse."

"Yes," she agreed. "Him, too."

As the lycanthrope and the film star discussed their future, a gunmetal-gray staff car with an SS pennant drove through the hotel's courtyard a hundred and forty feet below. The car crossed the pontoon bridge and headed along the paved forest road that had brought Michael and Mouse to the Reichkronen. It entered Berlin and began to wind its way southeast toward the factories and dirty air of the Neukolln district. Black clouds were sliding in from the east, and thunder boomed like distant bomb blasts. The car reached a block of grimy row houses and the driver stopped in the street, heedless of other traffic. No horns blew; the SS pennant silenced all complaint.

A hulking man in an aide's uniform, a gray peaked cap, and polished jackboots got out, and he went around to the other side and opened the door. The rear seat's passenger, a rail-thin figure in uniform, a brimmed cap, and a long dark green overcoat, stepped out of the car, and he stalked into a particular row house with the larger man following at his heels. The gunmetal-gray car stayed exactly where it was. This wouldn't take very long.

On the second floor a burly fist knocked at a door marked with a tarnished number "5."

321

Inside the apartment there was the sound of coughing. "Yes? Who is it?"

The officer in the dark green overcoat nodded.

Boots lifted his right foot and kicked the door. It broke with a shriek of splitting wood, but the locks kept it from flying open. The door's stubbornness made Boots's face turn crimson with rage; he kicked it again, and a third time. "Stop it!" the man inside shouted. "Please, stop it!"

The fourth kick caved the door in. Theo von Frankewitz stood there in his blue silk robe, his eyes bulging with terror. He backed away, stumbled over a table, and fell to the floor. Boots entered the apartment, his metal-studded soles clacking. Frightened people had opened their doors and were peering out, and the officer in the overcoat shouted, "Back in your holes!" Their doors slammed, and locks clicked shut.

Frankewitz was on his hands and knees, scuttling across the floor. He jammed himself into a corner, his hands up in a gesture of supplication. "Please don't hurt me!" he shrieked. "Please don't!" His cigarette holder, the cigarette still smoldering, lay on the floor, and Boots crushed it underfoot as he approached the whimpering man.

Boots stopped, standing over him like a fleshy mountain.

Tears were crawling down Frankewitz's cheeks. He was trying to press himself into the wall of his apartment. "What do you want?" he said, choking, coughing, and crying at the same time. He looked at the SS officer. "What do you want? I did the work for you!"

"So you did. And very well indeed." The officer, his face narrow and pinched, walked into the room and glanced around distastefully. "This place smells. Don't you ever open your windows?"

"They . . . they . . . they won't open." Frankewitz's nose was running, and he snuffled and moaned at the same time.

"No matter." The officer waved a thin-fingered hand impatiently. "I've come to do some housecleaning. The project's finished, and I won't be needing your talents again."

Frankewitz understood what that meant. His face grew

322

distorted. "No . . . I'm begging you, for the love of God . . . I did the work for you . . . I did the—"

The officer nodded again, a signal to Boots. The huge man kicked Frankewitz in the chest, and there was a wet cracking noise as the breastbone broke. Frankewitz howled. "Stop that caterwauling!" the officer commanded. Boots picked up a throw pillow from the sea-green sofa, ripped it open, and pulled out a handful of cotton stuffing. He grasped Frankewitz's hair and jammed the stuffing into the man's gasping mouth. Frankewitz writhed, trying to claw at Boots's eyes, but Boots easily dodged the fingers; he kicked Frankewitz in the ribs and staved him in like a brine-soaked barrel. The screaming was muffled, and now it didn't bother Blok so much.

Boots kicked Frankewitz in the face, burst his nose open, and dislocated the jaw. The artist's left eye swelled shut, and a purple bruise in the shape of a boot sole rose on his face. Frankewitz began, in desperation and madness, to try to claw his way through the wall. Boots stomped his spine, and Frankewitz contorted like a crushed caterpillar.

It was chilly in the damp little room. Blok, a man with a low tolerance for discomfort, walked over to the small fireplace grate, where a few meager flames danced amid the ashes. He stood close to the grate and tried to warm his hands; they were almost always cold. He had promised Boots he could have Frankewitz. Blok's initial plan had been to dispatch the artist with a bullet, now that the project was done and Frankewitz wouldn't be called on to do any retouching, but Boots had to be exercised like any large animal. It was like letting a trained Doberman go through its paces.

Boots broke Frankewitz's left arm with a kick to the shoulder. Frankewitz had ceased his struggling, which disappointed Boots. The artist lay limply as Boots continued to stomp him.

It would be over soon, Blok thought. Then they could get back to the Reichkronen and out of this miserable—

Wait.

Blok had been staring at a small red eye of flame, there in the grate, as a piece of paper curled and burned. Frankewitz had just recently torn something up and cast it into the grate, and not all of it had been consumed. In fact, Blok could see a bit of what had been drawn on the paper: it looked like a man's face, with a sweep of dark hair hanging down over the forehead. A single bulging, cartoonish eye remained; the other had been burned away.

It was a familiar drawing. Too familiar.

Blok's heart started to pound. He reached down into the ashes and pulled out the fragment of paper. Yes. A face. *His* face. The lower part of it had been burned, but the sharp bridge of the nose was familiar, too. Blok's throat was dry. He rummaged in the ashes, found another unburned bit of paper. This one had what appeared to be a representation of iron armor on it, fastened with rivets.

"Stop it," Blok whispered.

Another kick was delivered. Frankewitz made no noise.

"Stop it!" Blok shouted, standing upright. Boots restrained the next kick, which would have shattered Frankewitz's skull, and stepped back from the body.

Blok knelt beside Frankewitz, grasped the man's hair, and lifted his head off the floor. The artist's face had become a work of surrealism, rendered in shades of blue and crimson. Bloody cotton hung from the split lips and red streams ran from the smashed nostrils, but Blok could hear the faint rumbling of Frankewitz's lungs. The man was hanging on to life. "What's this?" Blok held the fragments of paper before Frankewitz's face. "Answer me! What's this?" He realized Frankewitz couldn't answer, so he put the paper on the floor—avoiding the blood—and started pulling the cotton out of the man's mouth. It was a messy labor, and Blok scowled with disgust. "Hold his head up and get his eyes open!" he told Boots.

The aide gripped Frankewitz's hair and tried to force the eyelids open. One eye had been destroyed, jammed deeply into the socket. The other eye was bloodshot, and protruded as if in mockery of the cartoon eye on the piece of paper Blok held. "Look at this!" Blok demanded. "Can you hear me?"

Frankewitz moaned softly, a wet gurgling in his lungs.

"This is a copy of the work you did for *me*, isn't it?" Blok

324

held the paper in front of the man's face. "Why did you draw this?" It wasn't likely that Frankewitz had drawn it for his own amusement, and that brought another question to Blok's thin lips: "Who saw it?"

Frankewitz coughed, drooling blood. His good eye moved in the socket and found the fragment of char-edged paper.

"You drew the picture," Blok went on, speaking as if to a retarded child. "Why did you draw the picture, Theo? What were you going to do with it?"

Frankewitz just stared, but he was still breathing.

They weren't going to get anywhere this way. "Damn it to hell!" Blok said as he stood up and crossed the room to the telephone. He picked up the receiver, carefully wiped the mouthpiece with his sleeve, and dialed a four-digit number. "This is Colonel Jerek Blok," he told the operator. "Get me medical. Hurry!" He examined the paper again as he waited. There was no doubt; Frankewitz had repeated the drawing from memory, then tried to burn it. That fact made alarms go off in Blok's brain. Who else had seen this drawing? Blok had to know, and the only way to find out was to keep Frankewitz alive. "I need an ambulance!" he told the Gestapo medical officer who came to the phone. He gave the man the address. "Get over here as fast as you can!" he said, almost shouting, and hung up. Then Blok returned to Frankewitz, to make sure the man was still breathing. If the information died with this pansy-balled street artist, Blok's own throat would be kissed by a noose. "Don't die!" he told Frankewitz. "Do you hear me, you bastard? Don't die!"

Boots said, "Sir? If I'd known you didn't want me to kill him, I wouldn't have kicked him so hard."

"Never mind! Just go outside and wait for the ambulance!" After Boots had clumped out, Blok turned his attention to the canvases over by the easel and began to go through them, tossing them aside in his fearful search for any more such drawings as on the scraps of paper clenched in his hand. He found none, but that didn't ease him. He damned his decision not to execute Frankewitz long before now, but there had always been the possibility that more work was needed and one artist in on the project was enough. On the floor, Frankewitz had a fit of coughing, and spewed blood. "Shut up!" Blok snapped. "You're not going to die! We have ways to keep you alive! Then we'll kill you later, so shut up!"

Frankewitz complied with the colonel's command and slipped into unconsciousness.

The Gestapo's surgeons would put him back together, Blok mused. They would lace his bones with wires, sew together the gashes, and screw his joints into the sockets. Then he would look more like Frankenstein than Frankewitz, but drugs would grease his tongue and make him speak: why he'd drawn this picture, and who had seen it. They had come too far with Iron Fist to let it be ruined by this battered meat on the floor.

Blok sat down on the sea-green sofa, its arms protected with lace coverlets, and in a few minutes he heard the klaxon horn of the ambulance approaching. Blok reasoned that the gods of Valhalla were smiling on him, because Frankewitz was still breathing.

7

"A toast!" Harry Sandler lifted his wineglass. "To Stalin's coffin!"

"Stalin's coffin!" someone else echoed, and the toast was drunk. Michael Gallatin, stitting at the long dining table across from Sandler, drank without hesitation.

It was eight o'clock, and Michael was in the suite of SS Colonel Jerek Blok, amid Chesna van Dorne, twenty Nazi officers, German dignitaries, and their female companions. He wore a black tuxedo, a white shirt, and a white bow tie, and to his right Chesna wore a low-cut, long black dress with pearls covering the creamy swell of her breasts. The officers were in their crisp dress uniforms, and even Sandler had put away his tweeds in favor of a formal gray suit. He had also left his bird in his room, a fact which seemed to relieve many of the other guests as well as Michael.

"To Churchill's tombstone!" the gray-haired major sitting a few seats down from Chesna proposed, and all—including Michael—drank merrily. Michael scanned the table, examining the faces of the dinner guests. Their host and his lead-footed aide were absent, but a young captain had seated everyone and gotten the party going. After another few rounds of toasts, in honor of drowned U-boat men, the valiant dead of Stalingrad, and the fried corpses of Hamburg, white-jacketed waiters began to roll in the dinner on silver carts. The main event was roast boar with an apple in its mouth, which Michael noted with some pleasure was set in front of Harry Sandler. The hunter had evidently shot the beast in the forest's hunting preserve just yesterday, and as he cut slabs of greasy meat and slid them onto platters it was clear Sandler knew how to handle a carving knife as well as a rifle.

Michael ate sparingly, the meat too full of fat for him, and listened to the conversations on all sides. Such optimism that the Russians would be thrown back and the English would come crawling to Hitler's feet with a peace treaty was worthy of a gypsy and a crystal ball. The voices and laughter were loud, the wine kept flowing and the waiters kept bringing food, and unreality was so thick in the air Harry Sandler might have carved it. This was the food these Nazis were used to eating, and their bellies looked full.

Michael and Chesna had talked most of the afternoon. She knew nothing about Iron Fist. Neither did she know anything of Dr. Gustav Hildebrand's activities, or what went on at Hildebrand's Norway island. Of course she knew that Hildebrand advocated gas warfare—that was a common fact—but Hitler evidently remembered his own sniff of mustard gas in the Great War and didn't care to open that particular Pandora's box. Or, at least, not just yet. Did the Nazis have a stockpile of gas bombs and shells? Michael had inquired. Chesna wasn't sure of the exact tonnage, but she felt sure that somewhere the Reich had at least fifty thousand tons of weapons, kept ready in case Hitler changed his mind. Michael pointed out the fact that gas shells could be used to disrupt the invasion, but Chesna disagreed. It would take thousands of shells and bombs to stop the invasion, she said. Also, gas of the kind Dr. Hildebrand's father had helped develop—distilled mustard during the Great War, Tabun and Sarin in the late 1930s—might easily blow back on the defenders in the tricky coastal winds. So, Chesna told him, a gas attack on the Allies might backfire on the German troops instead. That had to be a possibility the high command had already considered, and she didn't think one Rommel—who was in charge of the Atlantic Wall's defenses—would allow. Anyway, she said, the Allies had control of the air now, and would certainly shoot down any German bombers that approached the invasion beaches.

Which left them where they'd begun, pondering the meaning of a phrase and a caricature of Adolf Hitler.

"You're not eating. What's wrong? Isn't it raw enough for you?"

Michael looked up from his deliberations and stared across the table into Sandler's face. It had grown more ruddy from all the toasts, and now Sandler wore a slack-lipped smile. "It's all right," Michael said, and forced the greasy meat into his mouth. He envied Mouse, eating a bowl of beef soup and a liverwurst sandwich in the servants' wing. "Where's your good-luck charm?"

"Blondi? Oh, not so far. My suite's next door. You know, I don't think she likes you very much."

"What a shame."

Sandler was about to reply—a gimcrack witticism, no doubt—but his attention was distracted by the red-haired young woman who sat next to him. They began to talk, and Michael heard Sandler say something about Kenya. Well, it took a bore to kill a boar.

At that moment the dining-room door opened, and Jerek Blok stalked in with Boots following behind. Instantly a chorus of cheers and applause rose up and one of the dinner guests proposed a toast to Blok. The SS colonel plucked a wineglass from a passing tray, smiled, and drank to his own long life. Then Michael watched as Blok, a tall, thin man with a sallow face, wearing a dress uniform studded with medals, made the rounds of the table, stopping to shake hands and slap backs. Boots followed him, a fleshy shadow.

Blok came to Chesna's chair. "Ah, my dear girl!" he said, and bent down to kiss her cheek. "How are you? You look lovely! Your new film is almost out, yes?" Chesna said it was imminent. "And it'll be a tremendous smash and give us all a boost, won't it? Of course it will." His gray-eyed gaze—the eyes of a lizard, Michael thought—found Baron von Fange. "Ah, and here's the lucky man!" He approached Michael, held out his hand, and Michael rose to shake it. Boots stood behind Blok, staring at the baron. "Von Fange, isn't it?" Blok asked. His handshake was loose and damp. He had a long, narrow nose and a pointed chin. His close-cropped brown hair swirled with gray at temples and forehead. "I met a Von Fange in Dortmund last year. Was that a member of your family?"

"I wouldn't be surprised. My father and uncles travel all over Germany."

"Yes, I met a Von Fange." Blok nodded. He released Michael's hand, leaving it feeling as if Michael had gripped something oily. Blok had bad teeth; the front lower teeth were all silver. "I can't remember his first name, though. What's your father's name?"

"Leopold."

"That's a noble name! No, I can't quite recall." Blok was still smiling, but it was an empty smile. "And tell me this: why isn't a strapping young man like you part of the SS? With your heritage, I could easily get you an officer's commission."

"He picks tulips," Sandler said. His voice was getting a little slurred, and he held his wineglass out to be refilled.

"The Von Fange family has cultivated tulips for over fifty years," Chesna spoke up, offering information from the German social registry. "Plus they own very fine vineyards and bottle their private labels. And thank you for bringing that to Colonel Blok's attention, Harry."

"Tulips, eh?" Blok's smile had grown a bit cooler. Michael could see him thinking: perhaps this wasn't SS material after all. "Well, Baron, you must be a very special man to have swept Chesna off her feet like this. And such a secret

329

she was keeping from her friends! Trust an actress to be an actress, yes?" He directed his silver smile at Chesna. "My best wishes to you both," he said, and moved on to greet the man who sat at Michael's left.

Michael continued picking at his meal. Boots left the dining room, and Michael heard someone ask Blok about his new aide. "He's a new model," Blok said as he took his chair at the head of the table. "Made of Krupp steel. Has machine guns in his kneecaps and a grenade launcher in his ass." There was laughter, and Blok basked in it. "No, Boots was until recently working on an antipartisan detail in France. I'd assigned him to a friend of mine: Harzer. Poor fool got his head blown off—excuse me, ladies. Anyway, I took Boots back into my command a couple of weeks ago." He lifted his filled wineglass. "A toast. To the Brimstone Club!"

"The Brimstone Club!" returned the refrain, and the toast was drunk.

The feast went on, through courses of baked salmon, sweetbreads in cognac, quail stuffed with chopped German sausage, and then rich brandied cake and raspberries in iced pink champagne. Michael's stomach felt swollen, though he'd eaten with discretion; Chesna had hardly eaten at all, but most of the others had filled their faces as if tomorrow was Judgment Day. Michael thought of a time, long ago, when winter winds were raging and the starving pack had gathered around Franco's severed leg. All this fat, grease, and running suet didn't fit the wolf's diet.

When dinner ended, cognac and cigars were offered. Most of the guests left the table, drifting into the suite's other huge, marble-floored rooms. Michael stood beside Chesna on the long balcony, a snifter of warm cognac in his hand, and watched searchlights probe the low clouds over Berlin. Chesna put her arm around him and leaned her head on his shoulder, and they were left alone. He said, in the soft murmuring of an enraptured lover, "What are my chances of getting in later?"

"*What?*" She almost pulled away from him.

"Getting in *here,*" he explained. "I'd like to take a look around Blok's suite."

"Not very good. All the doors have alarms. If you don't have the proper key, all hell would break loose."

"Can you get me a key?"

"No. Too risky."

He thought for a moment, watching the ballet of search-lights. "What about the balcony doors?" he asked. He'd already noticed there were no locks on them. Locks were hardly necessary when they were on the castle's seventh floor, more than a hundred and sixty feet above the ground. The nearest balcony—to the right, belonging to Harry Sandler's suite—was over forty feet away.

Chesna looked into his face. "You've got to be joking."

"Our suite is on the floor below, isn't it?" He strolled to the stone railing and peered down. A little more than twenty feet below was another terrace, but it wasn't part of Chesna's suite. Their quarters were around the castle's corner, facing the south, while Blok's terrace faced almost directly east. He searched the castle's wall: the massive, weather-worn stones were full of cracks and chinks, and here and there were ornate embellishments of eagles, geometric designs, and the grotesque faces of gargoyles. A thin ledge encircled every level of the castle, but much of the ledge on the seventh floor had crumbled away. Still, there were abundant hand- and footholds. If he was very, very careful.

The height made his stomach clench, but it was jumping from airplanes that he most dreaded, not height itself. He said, "I can get in through the balcony doors."

"You can get yourself killed any number of ways in Berlin. If you like, you can tell Blok who you really are and he'll put a bullet through your brain, so you won't have to commit suicide."

"I'm serious," Michael said, and Chesna saw that he was. She started to tell him that he was utterly insane, but suddenly a young giggling blond girl came out onto the balcony, followed closely by a Nazi officer old enough to be her father. "Darling, darling," the German goat crooned, "tell me what you want." Michael pulled Chesna against him and guided her toward the balcony's far corner. The wind blew into their faces, bringing the smell of mist and pine. "I might not have another opportunity," he said, in a

lover's moist and quiet tone. He began to slide his hand
down her elegant back, and Chesna didn't pull away because
the German goat and his nymphet were watching. "I've had
some mountaineering experience." It had been a course in
cliff climbing, before he'd gone to North Africa: the art of
making a hairline crack and a nub of rock support a hundred
and eighty pounds, the same skill he'd used at the Paris
Opéra. He glanced over the railing again, then thought better
of it. No use stretching his courage before he needed it. "I
can do it," he said, and then he smelled Chesna's womanly
scent, her beautiful face so close to his. Searchlights danced
over Berlin like a ghostly ballet. On impulse Michael pulled
Chesna against him, and kissed her lips.

She resisted, but only for a second because she also knew
they were being watched. She put her arms around him, felt
the muscles of his shoulders move under his tuxedo jacket,
and then felt his hand caress the base of her spine, where
the dimples were. Michael tasted her lips: honey-sweet, with
perhaps a dash of pepper. Warm lips, and growing warmer.
She put a hand against his chest; the hand made an effort to
push him back but the arm didn't agree. Defeated, the hand
slipped away. Michael deepened the kiss, and found Chesna
accepting what he offered.

"*That's* what I want," Michael heard the old goat's nymphet say.

Another officer looked out through the balcony doors.
"Almost time!" he announced, and hurried away. The goat
and nymphet left, the girl still giggling. Michael broke the
kiss, and Chesna gasped for breath. His lips tingled. "Almost time for what?" he asked her.

"The Brimstone Club's meeting. Once a month, down in
the auditorium." She actually—it was ridiculous—felt a little
dizzy. The altitude, she thought it must be. Her lips felt as if
they were on fire. "We'd better hurry if we're going to find
good seats." She took his hand, and he followed her off the
balcony.

They descended in a crowded elevator, along with other
dinner guests. Michael assumed the Brimstone Club was one
of those mystic leagues the Nazis prided themselves on, in a
country of orders, fellowships, and secret societies. In any

case he was about to find out. He noted that Chesna had a very tight grip on his hand, though her expression remained cheerful. The actress at her craft.

The auditorium, on the castle's first floor in the section behind the lobby, was filling up with people. Fifty or so Brimstone Club members had already found their chairs. A red velvet curtain obscured the stage, and multicolored electric lanterns hung from the rafters. Nazi officers had come dressed in their finery, and most everyone else wore formal attire. Whatever the Brimstone Club was, Michael mused as he walked with Chesna along the aisle, it was reserved for the Reich's gentry.

"Chesna! Over here! Please, sit with us!" Jerek Blok rose from his chair and waved them over. Boots, who might have taken up two chairs, was not in attendance, but Blok sat with a group of his dinner guests. "Move down!" he told them, and they instantly obeyed. "Please, sit beside me." He motioned to the seat next to him. Chesna took it, and Michael sat on the aisle seat. Blok put his hand on Chesna's and grinned broadly. "Ah, it's a wonderful night! Springtime! You can feel it in the air, can't you?"

"Yes, you can," Chesna agreed, her smile pleasant but her voice tense.

"We're so glad to have you with us, Baron," Blok told him. "Of course you know all the membership fees go toward the War Fund."

Michael nodded. Blok began talking to a woman sitting in front of him. Sandler, Michael saw, was sitting up on the front row with a woman on either side of him, talking animatedly. Tales of Africa, Michael thought.

Within fifteen minutes, between seventy and eighty people had entered the auditorium. The lanterns began to dim, and the doors were closed to shut out the uninvited. A hush fell over the audience. What the hell was this all about? Michael wondered. Chesna was still gripping his hand, and her fingernails were beginning to dig into his skin.

A man in a white tuxedo came out through the curtains, to polite applause. He thanked the membership for attending the monthly meeting, and for being so generous with their contributions. He went on, about the fighting spirit of the

Reich, and how the valiant youth of Germany would crush the Russians and send them fleeing back to their holes. The applause was more scattered, and some of the officers actually groaned in derision. The man—a master of ceremonies, Michael reasoned—continued, undaunted, about the shining future of the Thousand-Year Reich and how Germany would yet have three capitals: Berlin, Moscow, and London. Today's blood, he said in a booming voice, would be tomorrow's victory garlands, so we'll fight on! And on! And on!

"And now," he said with a flourish, "let the entertainment begin!"

The lanterns had gone out. The curtains opened, the stage illuminated by footlights, and the master of ceremonies hurried off.

Another man sat in a chair, reading a newspaper and smoking a cigar, at stage center.

Michael almost bolted to his feet.

It was Winston Churchill. Totally naked, the cigar clamped in his bulldog teeth and a tattered *London Times* in his pudgy hands.

Laughter swelled. The music of a brass band, hidden behind the stage, oompahed a comic tune. Winston Churchill sat smoking and reading, his pallid legs crossed and his etiquette hanging down. As the audience laughed and applauded, a girl wearing nothing but high black leather boots and carrying a cat-o'-nine-tails strutted out on stage. She wore a square smudge of charcoal on her upper lip: a Hitlerian mustache. Michael, his senses reeling, recognized the girl as Charlotta, the autograph seeker. There was nothing shy about her now, her breasts bobbing as she advanced toward Churchill, and he suddenly looked up and let out a shrill, piercing scream. The scream made everyone laugh harder. Churchill fell to his knees, his naked and flabby behind offered to the audience, and held up his hands for mercy.

"You pig!" the girl shouted. "You filthy, murdering swine! Here's your mercy!" She swung the whip and the lashes cracked across Churchill's shoulder, raising red welts on his white flesh. The man howled in pain and groveled at her feet. She began to whip his back and buttocks, cursing him like a blue-tongued sailor as the band oompahed merrily and the audience convulsed with laughter. Reality and unreality mixed; Michael realized the man was of course not the prime minister of England, just an actor who eerily resembled him, but the cat-o'-nine-tails wasn't a fiction. Neither was the girl's rage. "This is for Hamburg!" she shouted. "And Dortmund! And Marienburg! And Berlin! And—" She went on, a recitation of cities the Allied bombers had hit, and as the whip began to fling drops of blood the audience erupted in a paroxysm of cheering. Blok leaped to his feet, clapping his hands above his head. Others were standing, too, shouting gleefully as the whipping continued and the false Churchill shivered at the girl's feet. Blood streamed down the man's back, but he made no effort to rise or escape the whip. "Bonn!" the girl raged as the whip struck. "Schweinfurt!" Sweat glistened on her shoulders and between her breasts, her body trembling with the effort, moisture smearing the charcoal mustache. The whip continued to fall, and now the man's back and buttocks were crisscrossed with red. Finally the man shuddered and lay sobbing, and the female Hitler whipped him across his back one last time and then put a booted foot on his neck in triumph. She gave the audience a Nazi salute and received a bounty of cheering and applause. The curtains closed.

"Wonderful! Wonderful!" Blok said, sitting down again. A light sheen of perspiration had collected on his forehead, and he dabbed it off with a white handkerchief. "You see what entertainment your money buys, Baron?"

"Yes," Michael answered; forcing a smile was the most difficult thing he'd ever done in his life. "I do see."

The curtains opened again. Two men were shoveling glittering fragments from a wheelbarrow, scattering them over the stage. Michael realized they were covering the floor with broken glass. They finished their job, rolled the wheelbarrow away, and then a Nazi soldier pushed a thin girl with long brown hair onto the stage. She wore a dirty, patched dress made of potato sacks, and her bare feet crunched the glass shards. The girl stood in the glass, her head slumped and her hair obscuring her face. Pinned to her potato-sack dress was a yellow Star of David. A violinist in a black tuxedo appeared from the left side of the stage, wedged his instrument against his throat, and began to fiddle a lively tune.

The girl, against all human reason and dignity, began to dance on the broken glass like a windup toy.

The audience laughed and clapped, as if in appreciation of an animal act. "Bravo!" the officer sitting in front of Michael shouted. Michael would have blown the bastard's brains out if he'd had his derringer. This savagery surpassed anything he'd experienced in the Russian forest; this, truly, was a gathering of beasts. It was all he could do to keep from leaping to his feet and shouting for the girl to stop, but Chesna felt his body tremble and she looked at him. She saw the revulsion in his eyes, and something else there, too, that frightened her to the marrow of her bones. "Do nothing!" she whispered.

Under Michael's tuxedo jacket and crisp white shirt, wolf hair had emerged along his spine. The hairs scurried across his flesh.

Chesna squeezed his hand. Her own eyes were dead, her emotions switched off like an electric light. On stage, the violinist was playing faster and the thin girl was dancing faster, leaving bloody footprints on the boards. This was almost beyond Michael's power to endure; it was the brutalization of the innocent, and it made his soul writhe. He felt hair crawling on the backs of his arms, on his shoulder blades, on his thighs. The change was calling him, and to embrace it in this auditorium would be a disaster. He closed his eyes, thought of the verdant forest, the white palace, the song of the wolves: civilization, a long way from here. The violinist was playing frantically now, and the audience was clapping in rhythm. Sweat burned Michael's face. He could smell the musky animal perfume rising from his flesh.

It took a massive effort of will to hold back the wild winds. They came very close to engulfing him but he fought them, his eyes tightly closed and the wolf hair rippling across his chest. A band of hair rose on the back of his right hand, which clenched the armrest on the aisle, but Chesna didn't see it. And then the change passed like a freight train on dark tracks, the wolf hair itching madly as it retreated into his pores.

The violinist played a flurry of notes at satanic speed, and Michael could hear the sound of the girl's feet sliding on the glass. The music reached its zenith and ceased, to cheering and more shouts of "Bravo! Bravo!" He opened his eyes; they were wet with rage and revulsion. The Nazi soldier led the girl offstage. She moved like a sleepwalker, trapped in an unending nightmare. The violinist bowed, smiling broadly, another man with a broom came out to sweep up the bloody glass, and the curtains closed.

"Excellent!" Blok said, to no one in particular. "This is the best presentation yet!"

Attractive naked women appeared, rolling kegs of beer and iced mugs on carts along the aisles. They stopped to draw beer into the mugs and pass them to thirsty Brimstone Club members. The audience began to grow raucous, some of them breaking into obscene songs. Grinning faces gleamed with sweat, and beer sloshed as mugs were cracked together in vile toasts.

"How long does this go on?" Michael asked Chesna.

"Hours. I've known it to go on all night."

One more minute was too long, as far as he was concerned. He touched his pocket, and felt the key to their room that Chesna had given him. Blok was talking to the man next to him, explaining something with a hammering of his fist. An iron fist? Michael wondered.

The curtains opened again. At the center of the stage was a bed, its sheet a Russian flag. On that bed, her wrists and ankles tied to the bedposts, lay a dark-haired woman, nude, who might have been Slavic. Two naked, muscular men wearing Nazi helmets and jackboots goosestepped out from either side of the stage, to loud applause and excited laughter. Their weapons were raised for an assault, and the woman on the bed cringed but couldn't escape.

Michael had reached his limit. He stood up, turned his back on the stage, and walked quickly up the aisle and out of the auditorium.

"Where's the baron going?" Blok asked. "It's the shank of the evening!"

"I . . . don't think he's feeling well," Chesna told him. "He ate too much."

"Oh. Weak-stomached, eh?" He grasped her hand to keep her from bolting, too, and his silver teeth flashed. "Well, I'll keep you company, won't I?"

Chesna started to pull away, but Blok's grip tightened. She'd never walked out of a Brimstone Club meeting; she'd always been a loyal part of the group, and to walk out now— even following the baron—might cause suspicion. She forced her muscles to relax, and her actress's smile surfaced. "I'd love a beer," she said, and Blok motioned to one of the naked waitresses. Onstage, there was a scream, followed by the audience's shouts of approval.

Michael unlocked the suite door and went directly to the balcony, where he breathed in fresh air and fought down his churning stomach. It took a minute or two for his head to clear; his brain felt infected with corruption. He looked at the ledge that ran from the balcony along the castle's wall. Eight inches wide, at the most. Sculpted eagles and gargoyle faces were set in the cracked gray stones. But if he misstepped, or lost his handhold . . .

No matter. If he was going, it had to be now.

He eased over the terrace balustrade, set one foot on the ledge, and grasped the eye sockets of a gargoyle. His other foot found the ledge, too. He waited a few seconds, until he had his center of balance, and then he carefully moved along the ledge, a hundred and forty feet above Hitler's earth.

8

The ledge was still slick with rain. The wind had turned chill, and gusts plucked at Michael's hair and tugged his tuxedo jacket. He kept going, inch by inch, his chest pressed against the castle's mountainous wall and his shoes scraping along the ledge. The balcony of the next suite was perhaps thirty feet away, and then there was another eight feet or so to the southeast corner. Michael moved carefully onward, not thinking of anything but the next step, the next finger grip.

He grasped an eagle that suddenly cracked and crumbled, the fragments falling into the darkness. He squeezed himself against the wall with his forefinger and thumb hooked into a half-inch-wide fracture until he regained his balance. Then he went on, fingers searching for fissures in the ancient stones, his shoes testing the firmness of the ledge before each step. He thought of a fly, crawling along the side of a massive, square cake. One step followed the next. Something cracked. Careful, careful, he told himself. The ledge held, and in another moment Michael reached the next balcony and stepped over the balustrade. Curtains were closed over the terrace doors, but light streamed through a large window just on the other side of the terrace. The ledge went underneath that window. He would have to pass it to reach the corner, where a pattern of gargoyle faces and geometric figures ascended to the next level. Michael walked across the terrace, took a deep breath, and stepped over the railing onto the ledge again. He was wet under his arms, and sweat dampened the small of his back. He kept going, relying on the ledge and not on handholds as he passed the window; it was a spacious bedroom, clothes scattered on the bed but no one in the room. Michael made it past the glass, noting with some displeasure that he'd left his palm prints on it, and the corner was within reach.

He stood clinging to the southeast edge of the Reichkronen, wind slashing into his face and searchlights sweeping back and forth across the clouds. Now he would have to leave the safety of this ledge and climb up to the next level, using the sculpted stones as a ladder. Thunder rumbled in the sky, and he looked up, examining the gargoyle faces and geometric figures, judging where to put his fingers and toes. The wind was an enemy to balance, but that couldn't be helped. Go on, he told himself, because this corner was the kind of place that sapped courage. He reached up, got his fingers latched on a sculpted triangle, and began to pull himself up. One shoe tip went into a gargoyle's eye, the other found an eagle's wing. He climbed the carved stones, the wind swirling around him.

Twelve feet above the sixth-floor ledge, he put his fingers into the eyes of a gaping, demonic face and a pigeon burst out of the mouth in a flurry of feathers. Michael stayed where he was for a moment, his heart hammering and pigeon feathers whirling around him. His fingers were scraped and raw, but he was only eight feet below the seventh-floor ledge. He kept climbing over the sculpted stones, got one knee up on the ledge, and pulled himself carefully to his feet. The ledge made a cracking noise and a few bits of masonry tumbled down, but he was still standing on something more or less solid. The next balcony belonged to Harry Sandler's suite, and he reached it with relative ease. He quickly crossed the terrace, slipped over it on the opposite side— and faced a ledge between it and Blok's terrace that had all but crumbled to pieces. Only chunks of stone remained, with gaping holes between them. The largest ledgeless space was about five feet, but from Michael's precarious perspective it easily looked twice that distance. He would have to cling to the wall to get over it.

Michael eased along the decayed ledge, balancing on his toes, his fingers finding cracks in the stones. As he settled his weight forward, a piece of the ledge suddenly broke beneath his right foot. Legs splayed and his chest hugging the wall, he tightened his grip on fissures in the stones. His shoulders throbbed with the effort, and he heard the breath whistle between his teeth. Go on! he urged himself. Don't stop, damn it! He listened to the inner voice, its heat thawing the ice that had begun to form in his knee joint. He went on, step after wary step, and he came to the place where there was no ledge.

"He asked for my advice, and I gave it to him," came a voice from below Michael. Someone talking on a sixth-floor terrace. "I said those troops were green as new apples, and if he put them in that caldron, they'd be chewed to pieces."

"But of course he didn't listen." Another man's voice.

"He laughed at me! Actually laughed! He said he certainly knew his troops better than I did, and he'd ask for my opinion when he wanted it. And now we all know the result, don't we? Eight thousand men trapped by the Russians, and four thousand more marching to prison camps. I tell you, it makes you sick to think of this damned waste!"

Michael didn't feel well himself, thinking of how he'd have

to cling to the wall to get across that hole. As the two officers talked on the lower balcony, he stretched out as far as he could, hooked his raw fingers into cracks, and tensed his shoulders. Now! he thought, and before he could hesitate he swung out over the ledgeless gap, his shoulder muscles bunching under his shirt and his fingers and wrists as taut as pitons. He hung for a few seconds, trying to get his right foot up on the next fragment of ledge. A piece of masonry cracked off and fell, smaller pebbles of stone following it down into the dark.

"It's murder," the first officer was saying, his voice getting more strident. "Absolute murder. Young men by the thousands, being torn to shreds. I know, I've seen the reports. And when the people of Germany find out about this, there'll be hell to pay."

Michael couldn't get his foot up on the ledge, because the stone kept crumbling away. Sweat was on his face. His wrists and shoulders were cramping. Another chunk of masonry fell, and hit the castle's wall on the way down.

"My God, what was that?" the second officer asked. "Something just fell, over there."

"Where?"

Come on, come on! Michael told himself, and swore at his clumsiness. He got the toe of his right shoe wedged on a small piece of ledge that, mercifully, didn't fall. Some of the pressure eased on his fingers and wrists. But small bits of stone were still crumbling, the pebbles making little clicking noises as they ricocheted off the stones below.

"There! You see? I knew I heard it!"

In another few seconds the two men were going to lean over their balcony's railing, look up, and see him battling for balance. Michael slid his right foot forward, made room for the toe of his left shoe on the fragment of ledge, and then heaved with his straining shoulders and stretched so that his right foot found a stronger place to rest. Blok's terrace was within reach. He unhooked his right hand, gripped the balustrade, and quickly pulled himself over onto the sturdy surface. He rested a moment, breathing hard, his shoulder and forearm muscles slowly unkinking.

"This whole damn place must be falling apart," the first

officer said. "Just like the Reich, eh? Hell, I wouldn't be surprised if this balcony fell under our feet."

There was silence. Michael heard one of the men nervously clear his throat, and the next sound was that of the balcony door opening and closing.

Michael turned the knobs of the French doors and entered Jerek Blok's suite.

He knew where the dining room was, and the kitchen beyond that. In that area he didn't care to wander, since some of the waiters and kitchen staff might be around. He crossed the high-ceilinged living room, passing a black marble fireplace above which the requisite painting of Hitler hung, and reached another closed door. He tried the gleaming brass knob, and the door yielded to him. There were no lights in the room, but he could see well enough: shelves of books, a massive oak desk, a couple of black leather chairs, and a couch. This must be Blok's permanent office when he visited the Reichkronen. Michael closed the door behind him, walked across the thick Persian carpet—probably stolen from the house of a Russian nobleman, he thought grimly—and to the desk. On it was a green-shaded lamp, which he switched on to continue his search. On one wall was a large framed photograph of Blok, standing under a stone arch. Beyond him were wooden structures and coils of barbed wire, and a brick chimney puffing black smoke. On the stone arch was carved FALKENHAUSEN. The concentration camp, near Berlin, where Blok had served as commandant. It was the photograph of a man proud of his child.

Michael turned his attention to the desk. The blotter was clean; Blok evidently was the soul of neatness. He tried the top drawer: locked. So were all the other drawers. The desk had a black leather chair with a silver SS embedded in its backrest, and leaning against it in the desk's well was a black valise. Michael picked it up. The valise bore the silver SS insignia and the Gothic initials JGB. He put the valise atop the desk and unzipped it, reaching inside. His hand found a folder and drew it out.

Within the folder were various sheets of white paper—Blok's official SS stationery—on which numbers were typed. The numbers were arranged in columns, designating amounts of money. Budget sheets, Michael reasoned. Beside the numbers were initials: perhaps the initials of people, items, or a code of some kind. In any case he had no time to try to decipher them. His overall impression was that a large amount of money had been spent on something, and either Blok or a secretary had written down everything to the last deutsche mark.

Something else was in the folder, too: a square brown envelope.

Michael unclasped it and slid its contents out under the lamp.

There were three black-and-white photographs. Michael flinched, but then leaned forward and forced himself to study them closely.

The first photograph showed the face of a dead man. What was left of the face, that is. The left cheek had collapsed into a ragged-edged crater, holes covered the forehead, the nose had rotted into a gaping hole, and teeth showed through the tattered lips. More holes, each one about an inch in diameter, were scattered over the chin and the exposed throat. All that remained of the right ear was a nub of flesh, as if someone had burned it off with a blowtorch. The man's eyes stared blankly, and it took Michael a few seconds to realize that his eyelids were gone. At the bottom of the photograph, just below the corpse's ravaged throat, was a slate. And on that slate was chalked, in German: *2/19/44, Test Subject 307, Skarpa*.

The second photograph was a profile of what might have been a woman's face. There was a little dark, curly hair clinging to the skull. But most of the flesh was gone, and the wounds were so hideous and deep that the sinus passages and the root of the tongue were exposed. The eye was a white, melted mass, like a lump of candle wax. Across the corpse's cratered shoulder was a slate: *2/22/44, Test Subject 345, Skarpa*.

Michael felt prickles of cold sweat on the back of his neck. He looked at the third picture.

Whether this human being had been man, woman, or child was impossible to tell. Nothing remained of the face but wet

343

craters held together by strands of glistening tissue. In that gruesome ruin the teeth were clenched, as if biting back a final scream. Holes pocked the throat and shoulders, and the slateboard read *2/24/44, Test Subject 359, Skarpa*.

Skarpa, Michael thought. The Norwegian island where Dr. Gustav Hildebrand kept a second home. Obviously Hildebrand had been entertaining guests. Michael steeled himself, and looked at the photographs again. Test subjects. Nameless numbers; probably Russian prisoners. But—dear God!—what had done this kind of damage to human flesh? Even a flamethrower gave a cleaner death. Sulfuric acid was the only thing he could think of that might have wreaked such horror, yet the tattered edges of the flesh showed no sign of being burned, by either chemicals or flame. He was certainly no expert on corrosives, but he doubted that even sulfuric acid could have such a savage effect. Test subjects, he thought. Testing what? Some new chemical that Hildebrand had developed? Something so hideous that it could only be tested on a barren island off the coast of Norway? And what might this have to do with Iron Fist, and a caricature of a strangled Hitler?

Questions without answers. But of one thing Michael Gallatin was certain: he had to find those answers, before the Allied invasion a little more than a month away.

He returned the photographs to the envelope, then the envelope and papers to the folder, the folder to the valise, the valise zippered and replaced exactly where he'd found it. He spent a few more minutes looking around the office, but nothing else caught his interest. Then he switched off the lamp, crossed the room, and headed for the front door. He was almost there when he heard a key slip into the latch. He stopped abruptly, spinning around and striding quickly for the terrace doors. He was barely out onto the balcony when the door opened. A girl's breathy, excited voice said, "Oh, this looks like heaven!"

"The colonel enjoys luxury," came the husky reply. The door shut, and was relocked. Michael stood with his back against the castle wall and darted a glance through the glass of the French doors. Boots had found a female companion, evidently bringing her up to Blok's suite to try to impress her out of her dress. The next step, if Michael knew anything about seduction, was to bring her out to the balcony and lean her over the edge to give her a tingle. In that case this would not be the best place to stand.

Michael quickly stepped over the balustrade onto the treacherously gapped ledge. He slipped his raw fingers into chinks, held tight, and started back the way he'd come. The masonry cracked and crumbled under his weight, but he got across the gaps and reached the balcony to Sandler's suite. Behind him he heard the girl say, "It's so *high,* isn't it?"

Michael opened the terrace doors and slipped through them, closing them softly at his back. The suite was a mirror image of Blok's, except the fireplace was made of red stones and the painting above it was a different vision of the *Führer*. The place was quiet; Sandler must still be brimstoning. Michael walked toward the door, and saw standing near it a cage in which the golden hawk perched. Blondi wore no headmask, the hawk's dark eyes staring fixedly at him.

"Hello, you little bitch," Michael said, and tapped noisily on the cage. The hawk shivered with anger, feathers ruffling at the back of its neck, and began to make that hissing sound. "I ought to eat you and spit your bones out on the floor," Michael said. The hawk crouched over, its body quivering like a lightning rod in a storm. "Well, maybe next time." He reached for the doorknob.

He heard a faint, almost musical *ping*. Something clattered. Michael looked toward the hawk's cage, and saw counterweights descending from the ceiling. A small chain was playing out. Michael realized he'd just snapped a trip wire between him and the door, and he had no more time for further deliberation because the counterweights pulled the cage's door up and the golden hawk lunged out at him, its talons already shredding the air.

9

As Michael was balancing on the hotel's ledge, Jerek Blok wiped tears of laughter from his eyes. Onstage, the spectacle involved a female midget and a burly Slav who obviously had been the idiot in some godforsaken Russian village. The man's physical equipment, however, was huge, and he grinned at the Nazi laughter as if he understood the joke. Blok looked at his pocket watch; he was getting sated on debauchery, and after a while all asses—no matter how big or small—looked the same. He leaned toward Chesna and touched her knee in a gesture that was far from fatherly. "Your baron must not have a sense of humor."

"He wasn't feeling well." As for that matter, neither was she. Her face hurt from all the false smiles.

"Come on, enough beer-hall entertainment." He stood up and grasped her elbow. "I'll buy you a bottle of champagne in the lounge."

Chesna was overjoyed to be able to make a graceful exit. The show was far from finished—there were cruder, audience participation events yet to come—but the Brimstone Club had never been anything for her but a way to meet people. She allowed Colonel Blok to escort her to the lounge, thinking that the baron might at this moment be either on his way in or out of Blok's suite. So far, there'd been no shriek of a plummeting body. The man—whatever his real name might be—was crazy, but he hadn't lived this long in a dangerous profession by being careless. They sat down at a table, and Blok ordered a magnum of champagne and checked his pocket watch again. He asked the waiter to bring a telephone to the table.

"Business?" Chesna inquired. "So late?"

"I fear so." Blok closed his pocket watch and put it away in his neat uniform. "I want to hear all about the baron, Chesna: where you met him, what you know of him. As long

346

as I've known you, I've never thought you were the type of woman to be foolish.''

"Foolish?" She lifted her blond brows. "How do you mean?"

"These dukes, earls, and barons are cheap currency. You see them every day, holding court and dressed up like department-store dummies. Any man with a drop of royal blood pawns himself off as gold these days, when he's really pig iron. You can't be too careful." He wagged a warning finger at her. The waiter came with the telephone and proceeded to plug its prongs into the proper socket. "Harry and I were talking this afternoon," Blok went on. "He thinks the baron might be—how shall I say this?—interested in more than true love.''

She waited for him to continue; her heart was beating harder. Blok's pinched nose had picked up a scent.

"You say you've only known the baron a short time, yes? And already you're planning marriage? Well, let me get to my point, Chesna: you're a beautiful and wealthy woman, with a great reputation in the Reich. Even Hitler loves your films, and God knows the *Führer's* favorite film subject is himself. But have you ever considered the possibility that the baron simply wants to marry you for your money and prestige?''

"I have," she answered. Too quickly, she thought. "The baron loves me for myself.''

"But how can you be sure, without giving it time? It's not as if you're about to vanish from the face of the earth, is it? Why not give it through the summer?" He picked up the telephone, and Chesna watched him dial a number. She knew what number it was, and she felt her blood chill. "Colonel Blok," he said, identifying himself to the operator. "Medical, please." He spoke again to Chesna: "Three months. What could it hurt? I have to tell you, neither I nor Harry like the man. He's got a lean and hungry look. Something about him doesn't ring true. Pardon me." He returned his attention to the telephone again. "Yes, Blok here. How was the operation? . . . Good. Then he'll recover? . . . Enough to talk, yes? . . . And when might that be? . . . Twenty-four hours is too long! Twelve at the most!" He was speaking in his haughty colonel's voice, and he winked at Chesna. "Listen to me, Arthur! I want Frankewitz—"

Chesna thought she gasped aloud. She wasn't sure. What felt like a band of steel closed around her throat.

"—able to answer questions within twelve hours. Yes? End of conversation." He hung up and pushed the telephone away as if it were something distasteful. "Now, we were talking about the baron. Three months. We can find out everything there is to know about him." He shrugged. "After all, that's my specialty."

Chesna thought she might scream. She was afraid she'd gone as pallid as a corpse, but if Blok noticed he didn't say anything.

"Ah, here's our champagne!" Blok waited, drumming his spidery fingers on the tabletop, as the waiter poured flutes for them both. "To good health!" he toasted, and Chesna had to use all her skills to keep her hand from trembling as she lifted her glass.

And, as champagne bubbles tickled her nose, the counterweights fell, the chain rattled along its distance, the cage's door slid up, and Blondi came out at Michael Gallatin.

The talons raked air where his face had been a second before, because Michael had ducked low and Blondi's momentum carried her over him. She twisted in midair, her wings beating, and swooped upon him as he backpedaled, his arms up to protect his face. Michael feinted to the right and dodged to the left with a wolf's speed, and as Blondi flashed past him two talons ripped into his right shoulder and sprayed bits of black cloth. She turned again and let out an enraged shriek. Michael backed away, frantically looking for anything to defend himself with. Blondi spun around the room in a tight circle, then suddenly reversed direction and darted at his face, her wings widespread.

Michael dropped to the floor. Blondi shot over him, tried to stop, and skidded along the arm of a black leather sofa, clawing deep furrows in the cowhide. Michael rolled away, got to his knees, and saw an open doorway in front of him: a blue-tiled bathroom. He heard the beating of golden wings behind him, sensed claws about to dig into the back of his skull. He flung himself forward, rolling head over heels, and through the open door into the bathroom. As he spun around on the blue-tiled floor, he saw Blondi streaking after him. He grasped the edge of the door, slammed it shut, and heard a satisfying *thunk* as the hawk hit it. There was a silence. Dead? Michael wondered. Or just stunned? His answer came a few seconds later: the sound of frenzied clawing as Blondi attacked the door.

Michael stood up and gauged the boundaries of his prison. There was a sink, an oval mirror, a toilet, and a narrow closet. No windows, and no other door. He checked the closet but found nothing of use. Blondi was at work, tearing furrows on the other side of the bathroom door. To get out of Sandler's suite, he had to get out of this room and past the hawk. Sandler might return at any moment; there was no time to wait for the hawk to exhaust herself, and little chance that she'd lose interest. Michael knew she could smell the wolf on him, and it was driving her crazy. Sandler evidently didn't trust the Reichkronen's security system; the thin trip wire he'd managed to wrap around the doorknob as he'd gone out for the evening was a nasty surprise for the curious. Once a hunter, always a hunter.

Michael cursed himself for not being more alert. The grisly photographs had been on his mind. But what he'd found out tonight would be worthless if he couldn't get out. Blondi attacked the door again, her fury waxing. He looked at his reflection in the mirror and saw the ripped seam of his jacket. Some of the shirt was gone too, but his flesh was unscathed. So far. Michael gripped the edges of the mirror and lifted it off its mounting brackets. Then he turned it around, so the mirrored glass was aimed away from him. He lifted the mirror up over his face, like a shield, and then he went to the door. Blondi's talons must have been an inch deep in the wood by now. Michael held the mirror up with one hand, and then took a breath and with the other hand turned the knob and wrenched the door open.

The hawk shrieked and retreated. It had seen its own reflection. Michael protected his face with the mirror and backed carefully toward the terrace doors. He couldn't risk running into Sandler in the hallway; he'd have to get back to Chesna's suite the same way he'd come. Surely Boots and his prize had stopped dawdling by now and had left the balcony. Michael heard the whooshing sound of Blondi's powerful wings, coming at him. The hawk stopped short of its mirrored reflection and clawed wildly at the glass. Its strength almost knocked the mirror away from him, and he fastened his fingers around the edges. Blondi flew away and darted back again, unconcerned with Michael's fingers but concentrating on killing the hawk that had dared to invade her territory. Again the talons scratched at the glass. Blondi made a high skreeling sound, flew a circle around the room, and attacked the mirror once more as Michael backed toward the terrace. This time Blondi hit the mirror a glancing blow, and the force of it staggered Michael. His heel caught on the leg of a low coffee table; he lost his balance and fell. The mirror slipped and shattered against the fireplace stones with the sound of a pistol shot.

Blondi flew just below the ceiling, making tight circles around the crystal chandelier. Michael got to his knees; the terrace doors were about twelve feet away. And then Blondi made one final circle and swooped down at him, talons outstretched to tear into his unprotected eyes.

He had no time to think. The hawk was coming in a blur of deadly gold.

It reached him, wings outspread. The talons drove downward, and the hooked beak started to stab for the soft glittering orbs.

Michael's right hand flashed up, and he heard the seam rip at his armpit. In the next second there was a burst of golden feathers where the hawk had been. He felt Blondi's talons grip his forearm, tearing through the jacket and shirt to find the skin—and then the bloody, mangled thing spun away like a tattered leaf and whacked against the wall, puffing more feathers. Blondi slid down to the floor, leaving smears of gore against the paint. The bloody mass that had been a bird of prey twitched a few times, then was still.

Michael looked at his hand. Black hair seethed and rippled over the powerful claw of a wolf, and the curved nails were wet with Blondi's blood and entrails. The forearm muscles bulged under his sleeve, straining the seam. The hairs had advanced almost up to his shoulder, and he could feel his bones starting to warp and change.

No, he thought. Not here.

He stood up, on human legs. It took him a moment to stop the change before it overwhelmed him, because the odor of blood and violence had flamed his nerves. The curved nails withdrew, with little pricklings of pain. The hair retreated, making his flesh itch. And then it was over, and he was human again except for a taste of musky wildness in his mouth.

He hurried out to the terrace. Boots and the girl had disappeared into Blok's suite. Michael wished there was something he could do to cover his tracks, but the damage was done; he stepped over the balustrade, got onto the ledge, and made his way to the southeast corner, where he descended to the level below by using the carved gargoyle faces and geometric figures again. In another eight or nine minutes he stepped onto the balcony of Chesna's suite, and went inside, closing the terrace doors behind him.

Now he felt as if he could breathe again. But where was Chesna? Still at the Brimstone Club's gathering, of course. Maybe he ought to make another appearance as well—but not in a hawk-clawed tuxedo jacket. He went into the bathroom and scrubbed all traces of blood from beneath the fingernails of his right hand, then changed into a fresh white shirt and put on a dark gray suit jacket with black velvet lapels. He wore his white bow tie again, since that had survived the blood spattering. His shoes were scuffed, but they'd have to do. He checked himself quickly in a mirror, making sure he hadn't missed a spot of crimson or a golden feather, and then he left the room and took an elevator to the lobby.

The Brimstone Club's meeting was apparently over, because the lobby teemed with Nazi officers and their companions. Laughter boomed out from beer-sotted throats. Michael searched for Chesna in the crowd—and felt a hand grasp his shoulder.

He turned, and found himself face-to-face with Harry Sandler.

"Been lookin' for you. All over," Sandler said; his eyes

were bloodshot, his mouth wet and slack. "Where'd you go?" Beer had finished the job wine had begun.

"For a walk," Michael answered. "I wasn't feeling well. Have you seen Chesna?"

"Yeah. She's been lookin' for you, too. Asked me to help. Good show, wasn't it?"

"Where's Chesna?" Michael repeated. He pulled loose from Sandler's hand.

"Last I saw, she was in the courtyard. Out there." He nodded toward the entrance. "Thought you'd decided to go back home and pick some more tulips. Come on, I'll take you to her." Sandler motioned him to follow, and the big-game hunter began staggering and weaving across the lobby.

Michael hesitated. Sandler stopped. "Come on, Baron. She's lookin' for her loverboy."

He followed Sandler, through the crowd toward the Reich-kronen entrance. How the matter of the disemboweled hawk was going to be handled, he didn't know. Chesna was an intelligent, charming woman; she'd think of something. He was glad Mouse hadn't seen any of that hideous "entertainment," because it might have snapped the little man's last threads. One thing was clear to Michael: somehow, they had to find out what Gustav Hildebrand was working on. And, if possible, they had to get to Skarpa. But Norway was a long way from Berlin, and Berlin held enough danger on its own. Michael followed Harry Sandler down the steps, where the hunter almost lost his balance and broke his neck, which would have taken care of a task Michael planned to complete very shortly. They crossed the courtyard, the stones holding puddles of rainwater.

"Where is she?" Michael asked, walking beside Sandler.

"This way." He pointed toward the dark trail of the river. "There's a garden. Maybe you can tell me what kind of flowers are in it. Right?"

Michael heard something in the man's voice. A hardness, beneath the drunken slurring. His steps slowed. It occurred to him that Sandler was walking faster, keeping his balance on the uneven stones. Sandler wasn't as drunk as he pretended to be. Now what was this all a—

Sandler said, "Here he is," in a quiet, sober voice.

A man stepped out from behind a section of broken stone wall. He wore black gloves and a long gray coat.

There was a sound behind Michael: a boot sole, scraping stone. Michael whirled around and saw another man in a gray coat almost upon him. The man took two long strides, and the hand he'd already lifted came down. The blackjack he gripped in his fist hit Michael Gallatin on the side of the head and drove him to his knees.

"Hurry!" Sandler urged. "Get him up, damn it!"

A black car pulled up. Michael, adrift in a haze of pain, heard a door open. No, not a door. Heavier. The trunk lid? He was lifted up, and his scuffed shoes dragged across the stones. He let his body slump; it had all happened so fast, the gears of his brain had been knocked loose. The two men dragged him toward the car trunk. *"Hurry!"* Sandler hissed. Michael was lifted up, and he realized they were going to fold him up like a piece of luggage and throw him in the musty-smelling trunk. Oh no, he decided. Can't let them do that, oh no. He tensed his muscles then and drove his right elbow sharply backward. It hit something bony, and he heard one of the men curse. A fist struck him hard in the kidneys, and an arm gripped him around the throat from behind. Michael fought them, trying to get loose. If he could just get his feet on the ground, he thought dazedly, he'd be all—

He heard the whistle of air, and knew the blackjack was falling again.

It hit the back of his skull, making black explosions burst across the white landscape of a ghost world.

Musty smell. Sound of a coffin lid slamming shut. No. Trunk lid. My head . . . my head . . .

He heard the sound of a well-tuned engine. The car was moving.

Michael tried to lift his head, and when he did, an iron fist of pain closed around him, and dragged him under.

EIGHT

Youth's Last Flower

On a morning in the summer of Mikhail's fourteenth year, as the sun warmed the earth and the forest bloomed green as young dreams, a black wolf ran.

He knew the tricks now: Wiktor and Nikita had taught him. You propelled your body with the back legs, braked and turned with the front. You were always alert to the surface under your paws: soft dirt, mud, rocks, sand. All those called for different touches, different tensions of the body. Sometimes you kept your muscles tight as new springs, sometimes relaxed like old bands of rubber. But— and this was a very important lesson, Wiktor had said sternly—you remained constantly *aware*. That was a word Wiktor used many times, beating it into Mikhail's impatient brain like a bent nail. *Aware*. Of your own body, the keen rumbling of the lungs, the pumping of the blood, the movement of muscles and sinews, and the rhythm of four legs. Of the sun in the sky, and the direction you were traveling. Of your surroundings, and how to get home again. Of not only the world in front of you, but what was happening to right, left, behind, above, and below. Of the scent trails of small game and the sounds of animals fleeing your own scent. Aware of all these things and many more. Mikhail had never realized that being a wolf was such hard work.

But it was becoming second nature. The pain of transformation had lessened, though Wiktor had told him it would never entirely go away. Pain, as Mikhail understood it, was a fact of life. Still, the pain of change paled before the utter, exuberant thrill that Mikhail felt whenever his body bounded on all fours through the forest, his muscles rippling beneath his flesh and the sensation of power beyond anything he'd ever known. He was still a small wolf, but Wiktor said he'd grow. He was a fast learner, Wiktor said. He had a good head on his shoulders. In these burning days of summer Mikhail spent most of his time in the shape of a wolf, feeling naked and pale as a maggot when he wore his boy skin. He slept very little; every day and night there were new explorations to make, new things to see from eyes that missed nothing. Objects that had been matter-of-factly familiar to his human vision were a revelation to his wolf's gaze: rain was a shower of shimmering colors, the tracks of small animals in high grass were edged with the faint blue of body heat, the wind itself seemed to be a complex living thing that brought news of other lives and deaths from across the forest.

And the moon. Oh, the moon!

The wolf's eye saw it differently. An endlessly fascinating silver hole in the night, sometimes edged with bright blue, sometimes crimson, sometimes a hue that was beyond description. The moonlight fell in silver spears, lighting the forest like a cathedral. It was the most beautiful glow Mikhail had ever seen, and in that awesome beauty the wolves—even three-legged Franco—gathered on high rocks and sang. The songs were paeans of mingled joy and sadness: We are alive, the songs said, and we wish to live forever. But life is a passing thing, as the moon passes across the sky, and all the eyes of wolves and men must grow dim, and close.

But we'll sing, while there's such a light as this!

Mikhail ran for the thrill of running. Sometimes, when he returned to human form after hours spent on four legs, he had trouble balancing on two. They were weak, white stalks, and you couldn't get them to go fast enough. Speed was what entranced Mikhail; the ability of movement, of cutting left and right and having a tail that acted like a rudder keeping your balance in turns. Wiktor said he was becoming too enraptured with his wolf's body, and neglecting his studies. It wasn't only the changing of shape that made the miracle, Wiktor told him; it was the brain in the wolf's skull that could follow a scent of an injured stag on the wind and recite Shakespeare at the same time.

He burst through the underbrush and found a pond in a

hollow rimmed with rocks. The fragrance of the cool water on such a hot, dusty day was a beckoning perfume. There were still some things a human boy could do better than a wolf, and one of them was swimming. He rolled in the soft grass for the mighty pleasure of it. Then he lay on his side, panting, and let the change come over him. How this worked exactly was still a mystery to him: it began by imagining himself as a boy, just as he imagined himself a wolf when he desired to change in the other direction. The more complete and detailed he saw himself in his mind's eye, the faster and smoother the change. It was a matter of concentration, of training the mind. Of course there were problems; sometimes an arm or leg refused to obey, and once his head had balked. All this led to much merriment for the other members of the pack, but considerable discomfort for Mikhail. But with practice he was getting better. As Wiktor told him, Rome wasn't built in a day.

Mikhail leaped into the water, and it closed over his head. He came up spouting, and then he arched his white body and dove into the depths. As he stroked along the rocky bottom, he remembered how and where he'd first learned to swim: as a child, under the tutelage of his mother, in a huge indoor pool in St. Petersburg. Had that been him, really? A pampered, shy youth who wore shirts with high starched collars and took piano lessons? That seemed like a foreign world now, and all the people who had inhabited it had almost faded away. Nothing was real, except this life and the forest.

He shot up to the surface, and as he shook the water from his hair he heard her laugh.

Startled, he looked around and saw her. She was sitting on a rock, her long hair the color of spun gold in the sunlight. Alekza was as naked as he, but her body was infinitely more interesting. "Oh look!" she said teasingly. "What a minnow I've found!"

Mikhail treaded water. "What are you doing out here?"

"What are you doing in *there?*"

"Swimming," he answered. "What does it look like?"

"It looks silly. Cool, but silly."

She couldn't swim, he thought. Had she followed him

from the white palace? "It *is* cool," he told her. "Especially after you run." He could tell that Alekza had been running; her body was moist with a fine sheen of sweat.

Alekza carefully eased down on the rock, reached forward, and cupped a hand into the water. She lifted it to her mouth and lapped it like an animal, then poured the rest of it over the golden down between her thighs. "Oh yes," she said, and smiled at him. "It is cool, isn't it?"

Mikhail was beginning to feel much warmer. He swam away from her, but it was a small pond. He swam in circles, pretending that he didn't even notice as she stretched out against the rock and offered her body to the sun. And, of course, to his gaze. He averted his face. What was wrong with him? Lately, through the spring and now into the summer, Alekza had been much on his mind. Her blond hair, her ice-blue eyes when she was in her human form, her blond fur and proud tail when she was wolfen. The mystery between her thighs pulled at him. He'd had dreams . . . no, no, those were indecent.

"You have a beautiful back," she told him. Her voice was soft; there was something pliable in it. "It looks so strong."

He swam a little faster. Maybe to make the muscles of his back tense, maybe not.

"When you come out," Alekza said, "I'll dry you off."

Mikhail's penis had already guessed at how that was to be accomplished and grown hard as the rock Alekza perched on. He kept swimming as Alekza sunned herself and waited.

He could stay in the pond until she got tired and went back home, he thought. She was an animal: that's what Renati said about her. But, as Mikhail's swimming began to slow and his heart pounded with an unknown passion, he knew his time with Alekza would be soon, if not today. She wanted him, wanted what he had. And he was curious; there were lessons Wiktor could not teach. Alekza was waiting, and the sun was hot. Its glare off the water made him feel dizzy. He made two more circles, turning the situation over in his mind. A vital part of him had already made its decision.

He pulled himself out of the water, feeling a mixture of longing and fear as he watched Alekza stand up, her breasts drawing tight as she looked at what he offered. She came down off the rock, and he stood in the grass and waited.

She took his hand, guided him into the shade, and there he lay down on a bed of moss. She knelt beside him. Alekza was beautiful, though up close Mikhail could see that lines had deepened around her eyes and at the corners of her mouth. The wolf's life was hard, and Alekza was no longer a maiden. But her ice-blue eyes promised pleasures beyond his dreams, and she leaned forward and pressed her lips against his. He had a lot to learn about the art of love; his first lesson had begun.

Alekza made good her promise to dry him off, using her tongue. She began at the south and crawled ever so slowly northward, licking dry his legs, slowly lapping the water that beaded on his shivering skin.

She came to his blood-gorged center, and there she displayed the true quality of an animal: the love of fresh meat. Alekza engulfed him, as Mikhail moaned and sank his fingers into her hair. Like an animal also, she was fond of using her teeth, and she bit and licked up and down as pressure rapidly built in his loins. He heard a roaring in his head, and luminous streaks leaped through his brain like summer lightning. Alekza's warm mouth held him, her fingers squeezing at the base of his testicles. He felt his body convulse, a movement that was beyond his control, and for a number of seconds his muscles tensed as if they were about to rip through the flesh. The lightning in his brain danced, striking his nerves and flaming them. He groaned: a bestial sound.

Alekza released her grip on him and watched the seed fountain from Mikhail's body. He convulsed a second time, and delivered another hot white explosion. She smiled, proud of her power over this young flesh; then, as Mikhail's banner began to droop, she continued her journey of the tongue across his stomach, over his chest, and playing circles around and around on his skin. Goose bumps seethed in the wake of her passage. Mikhail began to harden again, and as his mind cleared from its initial delirium he realized now that there was more to be learned than the monks had ever dreamed.

Their mouths met, and lingered. Alekza bit at his tongue

and lips, she grasped his hands and placed them on her breasts, and then she sat astride his thighs and eased herself down on him. They were connected, a pulse clenched within moist heat. Alekza's hips began a slow rhythm that gradually increased in power and intensity, her eyes staring into his and her face and breasts glistening with sweat. Mikhail was a fast student; he rocked deeper into her, meeting her movements, and as their thrusts became harder and more urgent, Alekza threw back her head, her golden hair cascading around her shoulders, and cried out with joy.

He felt her shudder, her eyes closed and her lips making soft moaning noises. She offered her breasts to his kisses, her hips moving in tight, hard circles, and then Mikhail was overcome by that uncontrollable convulsion again. As his muscles tensed and the blood roared through his veins, a bounty of his essence exploded into Alekza's warm wetness. He felt stretched, his bones throbbing with swampy heat. The sky might have crashed down on his face like blue glass, and he wouldn't have cared. He drifted in an unknown land, but one thing he was certain of: he liked this place, very much. And he wanted to go back again as soon as he could manage the journey.

He was ready again faster than he would have thought. Body to body, he and Alekza rolled over the bed of moss, out of the shade and into the sunlight. Now she was underneath him, her legs up over his hips, and she laughed at his eagerness as he plunged deep again. This was better than swimming; he couldn't find the bottom of Alekza's pond. The sun beat down on them, its heat making their flesh wet and melding them together. It burned away the last vestiges of Mikhail's shyness, as well, and he met her thrusts with steady power. Her thighs were pressed against his sides, her mouth urging at his tongue, his back arching as he stroked in her depths.

As their bodies moved again through tension toward release, it happened without warning. Blond hair scurried over Alekza's stomach, over her thighs and arms. She gasped, her eyes dazed with pleasure, and Mikhail caught her wild, pungent odor. That smell triggered the wolf in him, and black hair rippled over his back, underneath her clenching fingers. Alekza contorted and began to change, her gritted teeth lengthening into fangs, her beautiful face taking on another form of beauty. Mikhail, still embraced within her, let himself go, too; black hair emerged over his shoulders, his arms, buttocks, and legs. Their bodies writhed in a mingling of passion and pain, and they turned and angled so the body that was becoming a black wolf was mounting the emergent blond wolf from behind. And in the instant before the change became complete, Mikhail shuddered as his seed entered Alekza. The pleasure overwhelmed him, and he threw back his head and howled. Alekza joined his singing, their voices combining in harmony, breaking apart and combining again: another kind of lovemaking.

Mikhail pulled out of her. The spirit was still willing, but the black-haired testicles were drained. Alekza rolled in the grass, then jumped up and ran in circles, snapping at her tail. Mikhail tried to run, too, but his legs gave way and he lay in the sun with his tongue hanging out. Alekza nuzzled him, rolled him over, and licked his belly. He basked in the attention, his eyes heavy-lidded, and he thought that there would never be another day like this one.

As the sun began to sink and the sky turned red, Alekza picked up the scent of a rabbit in the breeze. She and Mikhail started following it, racing each other through the woods to see who could track down the rabbit first, and as they ran they bounded back and forth over each other, happy as any lovers on earth.

2

This was a golden time. As autumn passed into winter, Mikhail's continued dalliances with Alekza resulted in the swelling of her belly. Wiktor demanded more and more of Mikhail's time as the days shortened and the frost bloomed; the lessons had advanced, and now involved higher mathematics, theories of civilization, religion, and philosophy. But

Mikhail, amazingly even to himself, found his mind craving knowledge just as his body craved Alekza. A double doorway had been opened: one to the mysteries of sex, one to the questions of life. Mikhail sat without fidgeting as Wiktor pushed him to think; and not only to think, but to make up his own mind about things. In their discussion of religion, Wiktor raised a question that had no answer: "What is the lycanthrope, in the eye of God? A cursed beast, or a child of miracle?"

The winter was a rare animal: a comparatively mild few months in which there were only three blizzards and hunting was almost always easy. It passed, and spring came again, and the pack counted itself blessed. Renati came with news one morning in May: two travelers—a man and a woman— in a wagon on the forest road. Their horse would be good meat, and they might bring the travelers into the fold. Wiktor agreed; the pack, now numbering only five members, could stand some new blood.

It was done with military precision. Nikita and Mikhail stalked the wagon on either side of the road while Renati followed behind and Wiktor went ahead to choose the place of ambush. The signal was given: Wiktor's strong voice, calling out as the wagon rumbled along beneath the dense pines. At once Nikita and Mikhail struck from both sides, leaping from the underbrush, and Renati bounded in from the rear. Wiktor jumped out of his hiding place, making the horse scream and leap in its traces. Mikhail saw the panic-stricken faces of the travelers; the man was bearded and thin, the woman dressed in a peasant's sackcloth. Nikita went for the man, biting into the forearm and dragging him off the wagon. Mikhail started to strike for the woman's shoulder, as Wiktor had instructed him, but he paused with his fangs bared and the saliva drooling. He remembered his own agony, and he couldn't bear to put another human being through that torment. The woman screamed, her hands up before her face. And then Renati leaped up onto the wagon, sank her fangs into the woman's shoulder, and knocked her to the ground. Wiktor sprang for the horse's throat, hanging on as the horse began to run. The animal didn't get very far before Wiktor brought it down, but Wiktor came out of the encounter covered with scrapes and ugly blue bruises.

In the depths of the white palace, the man died during his rite of passage. The woman survived, at least in body. Her mind, however, did not. She spent all her time huddled up in a corner, her back against the wall, sobbing and praying. No one could get her to speak anything but gibberish, not even to say her name or where she was from. She prayed night and day for death, until finally Wiktor gave her what she asked for, and put her out of her misery. On that day the pack hardly spoke to each other; Mikhail went running far away and back, and one word kept repeating itself over and over in his mind: *monster*.

Alekza gave birth, at the zenith of summer. Mikhail watched the infant emerge, and when Alekza asked eagerly, "Is it a boy? Is it a boy?" Renati mopped her brow and answered, "Yes. A fine, healthy son."

The infant lived through its first week. Alekza named him Petyr, after an uncle she remembered from her childhood. Petyr had strong lungs, and Mikhail liked to sing along with him. Even Franco—whose heart had been softened as he learned to get about on three legs—was entranced by the child, but it was Wiktor who spent the most time near the newborn, watching with his amber eyes as Petyr suckled. Alekza giggled like a schoolgirl as she held the infant, but everyone knew what Wiktor was looking for: the first signs of the war between wolf and human in the child's body. Either it would survive that war, and the body would make a truce between its natures, or it would not. Another week passed, then a month; Petyr still survived, still squalled and suckled.

Winds lashed the forest. A rainstorm was coming; the pack could smell its sweetness. But this was the night of the summer's last train, on its way east to be caged until next season. Both Nikita and Mikhail had come to see the train as a living thing, as night after night they raced it along the tracks, beginning in human form and trying to cross in front of it as wolves before it roared into the eastern tunnel. They both were getting faster, but it seemed that the train was getting faster, too. Possibly a new engineer, Nikita had said.

This man doesn't know the meaning of brakes. Mikhail agreed; the train had begun to come out of the western tunnel like a hell-bent demon, racing to reach home before the dawn light turned its heart to iron. Twice Nikita had completed the change and almost made the leap that would carry him through the beam of the train's cyclopean eye, but the train had picked up speed with a gout of black smoke and a rain of cinders and at the last second Nikita's nerve had faltered. The red lamp on the train's last car swung as if in mockery, and the light glowed in Nikita's eyes until it faded away in the long tunnel.

As the pines and oaks swayed on either side of the ravine and all the world seemed in tumultuous motion, Mikhail and Nikita waited in the dark for the summer's last train. Both of them were naked, having run from the white palace as wolves. They sat on the edge of the tracks, near the western tunnel's opening, and every so often Nikita would reach out and touch the rails, expecting to feel a trembling. "He's late," Nikita said. "He'll be going faster than ever, trying to make up the time."

Mikhail nodded thoughtfully and chewed on a weed. He looked up, watching the clouds move like plates of metal in the sky. Then he touched the rails; they were silent. "Maybe he broke down."

"Maybe he did," Nikita agreed. Then, frowning: "No, no! It's the final run! They'll get that train home tonight if they have to push it!" He tore up a clump of grass and, getting impatient, watched it fly before the wind. "The train will be here," he said.

They were silent for a few moments, listening to the noise of the trees. Mikhail asked, "Do you think he'll live?"

That question had never been very far from all their minds. Nikita shrugged. "I don't know. He seems healthy enough, but . . . it's hard to tell." He felt the rail again; no train. "You must have something strong inside you. Something very special."

"Like what?" That puzzled Mikhail, because he'd never thought of himself as any different from the rest of the pack.

"Well, look how many times I've tried to father a child. Or Franco. Or even Wiktor. My God, you'd think Wiktor could pop them out right and left. But the babies usually died within a few days, and those that lasted any longer were in such pain it was a horror to behold. Now here you are— fifteen years old—and you father a child who's lasted a month and seems all right. And the way you endured your own change, too; you just held on, long after the rest of us had given you up. Oh, Renati says she always knew you'd live, but she thought of the Garden every time she looked at you. Franco was betting scraps of food that you'd die within a week—and now he thanks God every day that you didn't!" He tilted his head slightly, listening for the sound of wheels. "Wiktor knows," he said.

"Knows what?"

"He knows what I do. What we *all* do. You're different, somehow. Stronger. Smarter. Why do you think Wiktor spends so much time going through those books with you?"

"He enjoys teaching."

"Oh, is that what he's told you?" Nikita grunted. "Well, why didn't he want to teach *me?* Or Franco, or Alekza? Or any of the others? Did he think we had rocks in our heads?" He answered his question himself: "No. He spends his time teaching you because he thinks you're worth the effort. And why is that? Because you *want* to know." He nodded when Mikhail scoffed. "It's true! I've heard Wiktor say it: he believes there's a future for you."

"A future? There's a future for all of us, isn't there?"

"That's not what I mean. A future beyond this." He made an expansive gesture that enfolded the forest. "Where we are now."

"You mean . . ." Mikhail leaned forward. *"Leave* here?"

"That's right. Or, at least, that's what Wiktor believes. He thinks that someday you might leave the forest, and that you could even take care of yourself out there."

"Alone? Without the *pack?"*

Nikita nodded. "Yes. Alone."

It was too incredible to consider. How could any member of the pack survive, alone? No, no; it was unthinkable! Mikhail was going to stay here forever, with the pack. There would always be a pack. Wouldn't there? "If I left the forest, who would take care of Alekza and Petyr?"

367

"That I don't know. But Alekza has what she's been living for: a boy child. The way she smiles . . . well, she doesn't even look like the same person anymore. Alekza wouldn't survive out there"—he jerked a finger toward the west—"and Wiktor knows it. Alekza knows it, too. She'll live out the rest of her life here. And so will I, Wiktor, Franco, and Renati. We're old, hairy relics, aren't we?" He grinned broadly, but there was a little sadness in his smile. His grin faded. "Who knows about Petyr? Who knows if he'll even live another week, or what his mind will be like when he gets older? He might be like that woman who cried in the corner all day long. Or . . ." He glanced at Mikhail. "Or he might be like you. Who knows?" Nikita cocked his head again, listening. His eyes narrowed. He put a finger on the rail, and Mikhail saw him smile faintly. "The train's coming. Fast, too. He's running late!"

Mikhail touched the rail and felt the distant train's power vibrating in it. Drops of rain began to fall, pocking up little puffs of dust from along the tracks. Nikita stood up and moved into the shelter of some trees next to the tunnel opening. Mikhail went with him, and they crouched down like sprinters ready for bursts of speed. The rain was falling harder. In another moment it was coming down in sheets, and the rails were drenched. Also, the ground was rapidly turning to mud. Mikhail didn't like this; their footing would be unstable. He pushed his wet hair out of his eyes. Now they could hear the thunder of the train, fast approaching. Mikhail said, "I don't think we should go tonight."

"Why not? Because of a little rain?" Nikita shook his head, his body tensed for the race. "I've run in rain worse than this!"

"The ground . . . there's too much mud."

"I'm not afraid!" Nikita snapped. "Oh, I've had dreams about that red lamp on the last car! Winking at me like Satan's eye! I'm going to beat the train tonight! I feel it, Mikhail! I can do it if I run just a little faster! Just a little bit—"

The train's headlamp exploded from the tunnel, the long black engine and the boxcars following. The new engineer had no fear of wet tracks. Rain and wind gusted into Mikhail's face, and he yelled, "No!" and reached for Nikita but Nikita was already gone, a white blur running alongside the rails. Mikhail sprinted after him, trying to stop him; the rain and wind were too strong, the train going too fast. His feet slid in the mud, and he almost fell against the speeding train. He could hear the rain hissing off the hot engine like a chorus of snakes. He kept going, trying to run Nikita down, and he saw that Nikita's footprints in the mud were changing to the paws of a wolf.

Nikita was contorted forward, almost running on all fours. His body was no longer white. Rain whirled around him—and then Mikhail lost his balance, falling forward and sliding in the mud. Rain crashed down on his shoulders and mud blinded him. He tried to scramble up, fell again, and lay there as the train roared along its track and into the eastern tunnel. It vanished, leaving a scrawl of red light on the tunnel's rock; then that, too, was gone.

Mikhail sat up in the downpour, rain streaming over his face. "Nikita!" he shouted. Neither human nor wolf replied. Mikhail stood up and began walking through the mud toward the eastern tunnel. "Nikita! Where are you?"

He couldn't see Nikita. The rain was still slamming down. Whirling cinders hissed out long before they touched the ground. The air smelled of scorched iron and wet heat.

"Nikita?" There was no sign of him on this side of the tracks. He made it! Mikhail thought, and felt a burst of joy. He made it! He made—

Something lay over on the other side of the tracks. A shapeless, trembling form.

Steam rose from the rails. On the tunnel's floor, cinders still glowed. And about eight feet from its entrance, lying sprawled in the weeds, was Nikita.

The wolf had leaped in front of the train, but the train had won. Its cowcatcher had torn Nikita's hindquarters away. His back legs were gone, and what remained of Nikita made Mikhail gasp and fall to his knees. He couldn't help it; he was sick, and that mingled with the blood washing along the railroad tracks.

Nikita made a noise: a soft, terrible moan.

Mikhail lifted his face to the sky, and let the rain beat it.

He heard Nikita's moan again, ending in a whimper. He forced himself to look at his friend, and saw Nikita's eyes staring back at him, the noble head twisted like a frail flower on a dark stalk. The mouth opened, and emitted that awful noise again. The eyes were dimmed, but they fixed on Mikhail and held him, and he read their message.

Kill me.

Nikita's body trembled in agony. The front legs tried to pull the rest of the ruined body away from the tracks, but there was no power left in them. The head thrashed, then fell back into the mud. With a mighty effort, Nikita lifted his head and stared once more, imploringly, at the boy who sat on his knees in the downpour.

Nikita was dying, of course. But not fast enough. Not nearly fast enough.

Mikhail lowered his face and stared into the mud. Pieces of Nikita's body, stippled with wolf hair and human flesh, lay around him like tattered pieces of a magnificent puzzle. Mikhail heard Nikita groan and closed his eyes; in his mind he saw a dying deer beside the tracks, and Nikita's hands gripping the animal's skull. He remembered the sharp twist Nikita had given the deer's neck, followed by a noise of cracking bones. It had been an act of mercy, pure and simple. And it was no less than what Nikita now asked for.

Mikhail stood up, staggered and almost went down again. He felt dreamlike, floating; in this sea of rain there were no edges. Nikita shivered and stared at him and waited. At last Mikhail moved. The mud caught his feet, but he pulled free and he knelt down beside his friend.

Nikita lifted his head, offering his neck.

Mikhail grasped the sides of the wolf's skull. Nikita's eyes closed, and the low moan continued in his throat.

We could fix him, Mikhail thought. I don't have to kill him. We could fix him. Wiktor would know how. We fixed Franco, didn't we?

But in his heart he knew this was far worse than Franco's mangled leg. Nikita was near death, and he was only asking for deliverance from pain. It had all happened so quickly: the downpour, the train, the steaming tracks . . . so quickly, so quickly.

370

Mikhail's hands gripped tighter. He was shaking as hard as Nikita. He would have to do this right the first time. A dark haze was falling over his vision, and his eyes were filling up with rain. It would have to be done mercifully. Mikhail braced himself. One of Nikita's forelegs lifted up, and the paw rested against Mikhail's arm.

"I'm sorry," Mikhail whispered. He took a breath, and twisted as sharply as he could. He heard the cracking noise, and Nikita's body twitched. Then Mikhail crawled frantically away through the rain and mud. He burrowed into the weeds and high grass, and curled up there as the torrent continued to beat down on him. When he dared to look at Nikita again, he saw the motionless, cleaved torso of a wolf with one human arm and hand. Mikhail sat on his haunches, his knees pulled up to his chin, and rocked himself. He stared at the carcass with its white-fleshed arm. It would have to be moved off the tracks, before the vultures found it in the morning. It would have to be buried deep.

Nikita was gone. To where? Mikhail wondered. And Wiktor's question came to him: what is the lycanthrope, in the eye of God?

He felt something fall away from him. Perhaps it was youth's last flower. What lay beneath it felt hard-edged and raw, like a seething wound. To get through this life, he thought, a man needed a heart that was plated with metal and pumped cinders. He would have to grow one, if he was going to survive.

He stayed beside Nikita's body until the rain ceased. The wind had gone, and the woods were peaceful. Then Mikhail ran home, through the dripping dark, to take Wiktor the news.

3

Petyr was crying. It was the dead of winter, the wind howled outside the white palace, and Wiktor crouched over the child, now seven months old, as Petyr lay on a bed of dried grass. A small fire flickered nearby; the child was swaddled in deerskin and a blanket Renati had made from the travelers' clothes. Petyr's crying was a shrill quaver, but cold was not the child's complaint. Wiktor, whose beard had started to show streaks of white amid the gray, touched Petyr's forehead. The child's skin was burning. Wiktor looked up at the others. "It's begun," he said, his voice grim.

Alekza, too, started to cry. Wiktor snapped, "Hush that!" and Alekza crawled away to be by herself.

"What can we do?" Mikhail asked, but he already knew the answer: nothing. Petyr was about to go through the trial of agony, and no one could help the child through that passage. Mikhail leaned over Petyr, his fingers busy at the blanket, folding it closer simply because his fingers wanted something to do. Petyr's face was flushed, the ice-blue eyes rimmed with red. A small amount of dark hair was scattered over the child's scalp. Alekza's eyes, Mikhail thought. My hair. And within that frail body, the first battle of a long war was beginning.

"He's strong," Franco said. "He'll make it." But his voice had no conviction. How could an infant survive such pain? Franco stood up, on his single leg, and used his pinewood staff to guide himself to his sleeping pallet.

Wiktor, Renati, and Mikhail slept in a circle around the child. Alekza came back, and slept touching Mikhail. Petyr's crying swelled and ebbed, became hoarse and still continued. So did the wail of the wind, beyond the walls.

As the days went on, Petyr's pain increased. They could tell, by the way he shivered and writhed, by the way he clenched his fists and seemed to be striking the air. They huddled around him; Petyr was hotter than the fire. Sometimes he screamed with silence, his mouth open and his eyes squeezed tightly shut. Other times his voice filled the chamber, and it was a sound that ripped Mikhail's heart and made Alekza weep. In periods when the worst of the pain seemed to ebb, Alekza tried to feed Petyr bloody meat she'd already chewed into a soft paste; he accepted most of it, but he was getting weaker, shriveling up like an old man before their eyes. Still, Petyr clung to life. When the child's crying would become so terrible that Mikhail thought God must surely end this suffering, the pain would break for perhaps three or four hours. Then it would come back, and the screaming would start again. Mikhail knew Alekza was nearing a crisis as well; her eyes looked like hollowed-out holes, and her hands trembled so much she could hardly guide food into her own mouth. She, too, was becoming older by the day.

After a long and exhausting hunt, Mikhail was awakened one night by a hideous gasping sound. He sat up, started to move toward Petyr, but Wiktor pushed him aside in his haste to get to the baby. Renati said, "What is it? What's wrong?" and Franco hobbled on his stick into the light. Alekza just stared, her eyes blank pools of shock. Wiktor knelt beside the child, and his face was ashen. The baby was silent. "He's swallowed his tongue," Wiktor said. "Mikhail, hold him from thrashing!"

Mikhail gripped Petyr's body; it was like touching a hot coal. "Hold him steady!" Wiktor shouted as he forced open the mouth and tried to hook the tongue with his finger. He couldn't get it out. Petyr's face had taken on a tinge of blue, and the lungs were heaving. The little hands clutched at the air. Wiktor's finger explored the child's mouth, found the tongue, and then he got a second finger clamped around it. He pulled; the tongue was caught in Petyr's throat. "Get it out!" Renati yelled. "Wiktor, get it out!"

Wiktor pulled again, harder. There was a popping noise as the tongue unjammed, but Petyr's face was still turning blue. The lungs hitched, couldn't draw in air. Sweat sparkled on Wiktor's face, though his breath came out in a gray plume. He lifted Petyr up, held the baby by the heels, and whacked him on the back with the flat of his hand. Mikhail winced at the sound of the blow. Petyr still made no noise. Again Wiktor struck him on the back, harder. And a third time. There was a whoosh of rushing air, and a plume of it exploded from the child's mouth. It was followed by a wail of pain and fury that made the storm's voice sound feeble. Alekza held her arms out to take the baby. Wiktor gave him to her. She rocked the child, grateful tears creeping down her cheeks, and she lifted one of his little hands and pressed it against her lips.

She pulled her head back, her eyes wide.

Dark hairs had risen from the white infant flesh. The body in her arms was already contorting, and Petyr opened his mouth to make a mewling noise. Alekza looked up at Mikhail, then at Wiktor; he sat on his haunches, his chin resting on his clasped hands, and his amber eyes glinted in the firelight as he watched.

Petyr's face was changing, the muzzle beginning to form, the eyes sinking back into the dark-haired skull. Mikhail heard Renati gasp beside him, a sound of wonder. Petyr's ears lengthened, edged with soft white hairs. The fingers of both hands and the toes of both feet were retracting, becoming claws with small hooked nails. Little popping noises chimed the shifting of bones and joints, and Petyr made grunting noises, but his crying seemed to be done. The change took perhaps a minute. Wiktor said quietly, "Put him down."

Alekza obeyed. The blue-eyed wolf pup, its sinewy body covered with fine black hairs, struggled to stand on all fours. Petyr made it up, fell, struggled to stand, and then fell again. Mikhail started to help him, but Wiktor said, "No. Let him do it on his own."

Petyr found his legs and was able to stand, the little body shivering, the blue eyes blinking with amazement. The stub of a tail wriggled, and the wolfen ears twitched. He took one step, then a second; his hind legs tangled and he went down once more. Petyr gave a short *whuff* of frustration, steam curling from his nostrils. Wiktor leaned forward, held out a finger, and ticked it back and forth in front of Petyr's muzzle. The blue eyes followed it—and then Petyr's head lunged out, the jaws opened, and clamped down on Wiktor's finger.

Wiktor worked his finger out of the pup's jaws and held it up. A little drop of blood had appeared. "Congratulations," he said to Mikhail and Alekza. "Your son has a new tooth."

Petyr, at least for the time being, had given up the battle with gravity. He squirmed across the floor, sniffing at the stones. A roach burst from a crack under Petyr's nose and ran for its life, and Petyr gave a high *yip* of surprise, then continued his explorations.

"He'll turn back, won't he?" Alekza asked Wiktor. *"Won't* he?"

"We'll see," Wiktor told her, and that was all he could offer.

About halfway across the chamber Petyr stubbed his nose on a stone's edge. He began yelping with pain, and as he rolled on the floor his body started changing back to human form again. The fine dark hair retreated into the flesh, the muzzle flattened into a nose—one of the nostrils bloody—and the paws became hands and feet. The yelping was now a steady, full-throated cry, and Alekza rushed to the baby and picked him up. She rocked him and cooed to him, and finally Petyr hiccuped a few times and ceased crying. He remained a human infant.

"Well," Wiktor said after a pause, "if our new addition survives the winter, he should be very interesting to watch."

"He'll survive," Alekza promised. The glint of life had returned to her eyes. "I'll make him survive."

Wiktor admired his bitten finger. "My dear, I doubt if you'll ever be able to *make* him do anything." He glanced at Mikhail, and smiled slightly. "You've done well, son," he said, and motioned Alekza and the baby back into the fire's warmth.

Son, Mikhail realized he'd said. *Son.* No man had ever called him son before, and something about that sounded like music. He would sleep that night, listening to Alekza crooning to Petyr, and he would dream of a tall, lean man in a military uniform who stood with a woman Mikhail had all but forgotten, and that man would have Wiktor's face.

4

At winter's end Petyr was still alive. He accepted whatever food Alekza gave him, and though he had the habit of changing to a wolf pup without warning and driving the rest of the pack crazy with his constant yapping, he stayed mostly within human bounds. By summer he had all his teeth, and Wiktor kept his fingers away from the baby's mouth.

Some nights, Mikhail sat on the ravine's edge and watched the train go past. He began counting the seconds off as it roared from the western tunnel into the eastern. Last year, he'd run the race halfheartedly with Nikita. It had never really mattered to him how fast he could change. He knew he was fairly quick about it, but he'd always lagged behind Nikita. Now, though, Nikita's bones lay in the Garden, and the train—an invincible thing—breathed its black breath and shone its gleaming eye through the night. Mikhail had often wondered what the crew had thought when they'd found blood and bits of black-haired flesh on the cowcatcher. *We hit an animal,* they'd probably thought if they considered it at all. *An animal. Something that shouldn't have been in our way.*

Toward the middle of summer, Mikhail began to lope along with the train as it burst from the tunnel. He wasn't racing it, just stretching his legs. The engine always left him in a whirl of sour black smoke, and cinders scorched his skin. And on those nights, after the train had disappeared into the tunnel, Mikhail crossed the tracks to where Nikita had died, and he sat in the weeds and thought, *I could do it, if I wanted to. I could.*

Maybe.

He would have to get a fast start. The tricky part was staying on your feet as your arms and legs changed. The way the backbone bowed your body over ruined your bal-

376

ance. And all the time your nerves and joints were shrieking, and if you tripped over your own paws, you could go into the side of the train, and a hundred other terrible things could happen. No, it wasn't worth the risk.

Mikhail always left telling himself he wouldn't come back. But he knew it was a lie. The idea of speed, of testing himself against the beast that had killed Nikita, lured him. He began to run faster, alongside the train; but still not racing it, not yet. His balance still wasn't good enough, and he fell every time he tried to change from human to wolf while running. It was a problem of timing, of keeping your footing until the front legs could come down and match the speed of the hind legs. Mikhail kept trying, and kept falling.

Renati returned from a hunt one afternoon with startling news: to the northwest, less than five miles from the white palace, men had started cutting down trees. They'd already made a clearing, and were building shacks out of raw timbers. A road was being plowed through the brush. The men had many wagons, saws, and axes. Renati said she'd crept in close, in her wolf form, to watch them working; one of the men had seen her, she said, and pointed her out to the others before she could get back into the woods. What did it mean? she asked Wiktor.

The beginning of a logging camp, he thought. Under no circumstances, he told the pack, were any of them to go near the place again, in either human or wolf form. The men would probably work through the summer and leave. It was best to let them alone.

But from that point on, Mikhail noted that Wiktor became silent and brooding. He forbade anyone to hunt except at night. He was nervous, and paced back and forth in the chamber long after everyone else had settled down to rest. Soon, when the wind was right, Mikhail and the others could recline in the sun outside the white palace and hear the distant sound of axes and saws at work, gnawing the forest away.

And the day came.

Franco and Renati went out to hunt, as a crescent moon hung in the sky and the woods thrummed with the sound of crickets. Little more than an hour had passed before the noise of distant gunshots silenced the insects and echoed through the corridors of the white palace.

Mikhail counted four shots as he stood up from Alekza's side. Petyr played with a rabbit bone on the floor. Wiktor dropped the book of Latin he'd been reading to Mikhail and rose to his feet. Two more shots were fired, and the sounds made Mikhail flinch; he remembered very well the noise of gunfire, and what a bullet could do.

As the last shot faded a howling began: Franco's hoarse voice, panicked and calling for help.

"Stay with Petyr," Wiktor told Alekza, and as he strode toward the stone stairway he was already changing. Mikhail followed, and the two wolves left the white palace streaking through the darkness toward Franco's wail. They had gone not quite a mile when they smelled the gunsmoke and the odor of men: a bitter, frightened sweat smell. Lanterns glowed in the woods, and the men were calling to each other. Franco had begun making a high, frantic *yipping* noise, an aural beacon that led Wiktor and Mikhail directly to him. They found him crouched on a bluff, amid dense underbrush, and before them lay a circle of tents around a campfire. Wiktor rammed his shoulder into Franco's ribs to shut him up, and Franco lay on his belly in a submissive posture, his eyes glittering with terror—not of Wiktor, but of what now occurred in the firelit clearing.

Two men with rifles slung around their shoulders dragged something out of the woods and into the light. There were six other men, all armed with either pistols or rifles and carrying lanterns. They gathered around the form that sprawled in the dust, and thrust out their lanterns over it.

Mikhail felt Wiktor shiver. His own lungs seemed full of icy needles. There on the ground was the carcass of a wolf with russet fur, pierced by three bullet holes. Renati's blood looked black in the lamplight. And there, for all to see, was a dead wolf with one human arm and a human leg.

My God, Mikhail thought. Now they know.

One of the loggers began to pray—a coarse, ranting Russian voice—and as he reached the end of his prayer he put the barrel of his rifle against Renati's skull and blew it apart.

"We heard the men," Franco said when they'd gotten

back to the chamber. He was shaking, and sweat gleamed on his skin. "They were laughing and talking around their fire. Making so much noise you'd have to be deaf not to hear them."

"You were stupid to go there!" Wiktor raged, spraying spittle. "Damn it to hell, they killed Renati!"

"She wanted to get closer," Franco went on dazedly. "I tried to turn her back, but . . . she wanted to see them. Wanted to get right up and hear what they were saying." He shook his head, fighting shock. "We stood at the edge of the clearing . . . so close we could hear their hearts beat. And I think . . . something about them, so close, hypnotized her. Like seeing creatures from another world. Even when one of the men looked up and saw her, she still didn't move. I think . . ." He blinked slowly, his brain gears sluggish. "I think . . . that for just one minute . . . she *forgot* she was a wolf."

"They'll leave now, won't they?" Alekza asked hopefully, holding the squirming child. "They'll go away, back to where they came from." No one answered her. "Won't they?"

"Pah!" Wiktor spat into the fire. "Who knows what they'll do? Men are crazy!" He wiped his mouth with the back of his hand. "Maybe they'll go. Maybe seeing Renati scared the shit out of them, and they're already packing up. Damn it, they *know* about us now! There's nothing more dangerous than a frightened Russian with a rifle!" He glanced quickly at Mikhail, then at the child in Alekza's arms. "Maybe they'll go," Wiktor said, "but I won't count on it. From now on, we keep a constant watch up in the tower. I'll go first. Mikhail, will you take the second watch?" Mikhail nodded. "We'll have to divide it among us into six-hour shifts," Wiktor continued. He looked around at Alekza, Petyr, Franco, and Mikhail: the surviving members of the pack. He didn't have to speak; his expression spoke for him, and Mikhail could read it. The pack was dying. Wiktor's gaze wandered around the chamber, as if in search for the lost ones. "Renati's dead," he whispered, and Mikhail saw tears bloom in his eyes. "I loved her," Wiktor said, to no one in particular. And then he gathered the folds of his deerskin robe about himself, abruptly turned away, and went up the stairs.

Three days passed. The sound of saws and axes at work had ceased. On the fourth night after Renati's death, Wiktor and Mikhail crept to the bluff that had overlooked the circle of tents. The tents were gone, and the campfire was cold. The stench of men was gone as well. Wiktor and Mikhail went northwest, following the swath of stumps, to find the loggers' main camp. It, too, had been cleared out. The shacks were empty, the wagons gone. But the road they'd cut into the forest remained, like a brown scar on the earth. There was no trace of Renati's carcass; the men had taken her with them, and what would happen when the eyes of the outside world saw the body of a wolf with a human arm and leg? The road pointed the way to the white palace. From Wiktor's throat came a low groaning noise, and Mikhail understood what he meant: *God help us*.

The summer moved on, a trail of scorching days. The loggers didn't return, and no other wagons cut ruts on the forest road. Mikhail began to go out to the ravine at night again, and watched the train roar past. Its engineer seemed to be going even faster than before. He wondered if the man had heard about Renati, and the stories that would surely follow: in those woods live monsters.

He raced the train a few times, always pulling up short when his body began to change from human to wolf and his balance was in jeopardy. The iron wheels hissed at him, and left him behind.

The summer ended, the forest turned to gold and crimson, the sun's rays slanted across the earth and the morning mist turned chill and lingered, and the soldiers came.

They arrived with the first frost. There were twenty-two of them, in four horse-drawn wagons, and Wiktor and Mikhail crouched in the underbrush and watched them setting up camp in the logging shacks. All of the soldiers had rifles and some carried pistols, too. One of the wagons was full of supplies, and along with crates marked *Danger! Explosives!* there was a bulky-looking gun mounted on wheels. Instantly a man who must have been in charge posted sentries around the camp, and the soldiers began to dig trenches and put sharpened wooden stakes at the bottom of them. They unrolled nets and hung them in the trees, with trip wires going in all directions. Of course they left their smell on all the traps, so those nets and wires were easily avoided—but then half of the soldiers took two wagons and went along the logging road to the place where the tents had been set up, and there they set up their own tents, dug new trenches, and strung up more nets. They took the crates of explosives and the wheeled gun off their wagon, and when they test-fired the gun it sounded like the end of the world and slashed thin pines down like the work of a dozen axes.

"A machine gun," Wiktor said when they were back in the white palace. "They brought a machine gun! To kill *us!*" He shook his head incredulously, his beard full of white. "My God, they must think there are hundreds of us in here!"

"I say we get out while we can," Franco urged. "Right now, before those bastards come hunting for us!"

"And where are we going to go, with winter coming? Maybe dig holes and live in them? We couldn't survive without shelter!"

"We can't survive where we are! They're going to start searching the woods, and sooner or later they'll find us!"

"So what shall we do?" Wiktor asked quietly, the firelight ruddy on his face. "Go to the soldiers and tell them we're not to be feared? That we're human beings, just like they are?" He smiled bitterly. "You go first, Franco, and we'll see how they treat you." Franco scowled and hobbled away on his staff, much more proficient on three legs than he was on one. Wiktor sat on his haunches and thought. Mikhail could tell what was going through the man's mind: hunting was going to be much more difficult with the soldiers and their traps out in the woods; Franco was right, sooner or later the soldiers would find them; and what the soldiers might do to them when they were captured was unthinkable. Mikhail looked at Alekza, who held the child close. The soldiers would either kill us or cage us, Mikhail thought. Death would be preferable to iron bars.

"The bastards chased me away from one home," Wiktor said. "They won't chase me from a second. I'm staying here, no matter what." He stood up, his decision made. "The rest of you can try to find somewhere else, if you like. Maybe you can use one of those caves where we hunted the berserker, but I'll be damned if I'll crouch and shiver in a cave like a beast. No. This is my home."

There was a long silence. Alekza broke it, her voice thin and grasping false hope: "Maybe they'll get tired of looking for us and leave. They won't stay very long, not with winter almost here. They'll be gone with the first snow."

"Yes!" Franco agreed. "They won't stay when the weather turns cold, that's for sure!"

It was the first time the pack had ever longed for the icy breath of winter. One good snowfall would clear the soldiers out. But, though the air turned cold, the sky remained clear. Dead leaves fell from the trees, and from the underbrush Wiktor and Mikhail watched the soldiers as they roamed the woods, tight knots of men with rifles aimed in all directions. Once a group of them passed within a hundred yards of the white palace. They dug more trenches, put sharpened stakes at the bottom of them, and covered the trenches over with dirt and leaves. Wolf traps, Wiktor told Mikhail. The snares were of no consequence, but the soldiers were searching in expanding circles, and one terrible day Mikhail and Wiktor watched in agonized silence as the men stumbled upon the Garden. Hands and bayonets went to work, digging up the graves that had been repaired after the berserker's death. And as those hands pulled the wolf and human bones from the earth, Mikhail lowered his head and turned away, unable to bear the sight.

Snow dusted the forest. The northern wind promised brutality, but still the soldiers remained.

October waned. The sky darkened, burdened with clouds. And on one morning, as Mikhail returned from hunting with a freshly killed rabbit in his jaws, he found the enemy less than fifty yards from the white palace.

There were two of them, both carrying rifles. Mikhail darted into the brush and crouched, watching the soldiers approach. The men were talking to each other, something about Moscow; their voices were nervous, and their fingers clutched the triggers. Mikhail let the rabbit slide from his mouth. Please stop, he told the soldiers in his mind. Please go back. Please . . .

They didn't. Their boots crushed the foliage down, and every step took them closer to Wiktor, Franco, Alekza, and the child. Mikhail's muscles tensed, his heart pounding. Please go back.

The soldiers stopped. One of them lit a cigarette, cupping the match from the wind. "We've gone too far," he said to the other man. "We'd better get back, or Novikov'll skin us."

"That bastard's crazy," the second man observed, leaning on his rifle. "I say we set the whole damned woods on fire, and be done with it. Why the hell does he want to set up a new camp in this mess?" He looked around at the forest, with the awe and fear that told Mikhail the man was a city dweller. "Burn it to the ground and go home, that's what I say."

The first man blew plumes of smoke from his nostrils. "That's why we're not officers, Stefan," he said. "We're too smart to wear stars. I'll tell you, if I have to dig another damned trench, I'm going to let Novikov know where he can stick his—" He stopped, smoke whirling past his head, and stared through the trees. "What's that?" he asked, his voice hushed.

"What's what?" Stefan looked around.

"There." The first man took two more steps forward and pointed. "Right there. See it?"

Mikhail closed his eyes.

"It's a building," the first man said. "See? There's a minaret."

"My God, you're right!" Stefan agreed. He instantly picked up his rifle and cocked it.

The noise made Mikhail open his eyes again. The two soldiers stood not fifteen feet from him. "We'd better tell Novikov about this," Stefan said. "I'll be damned if I'm going any closer." He turned away, hurriedly striding through the woods. The first man flicked his cigarette butt aside and followed his companion.

Mikhail rose up from his crouch. He could not let them get back to their camp. Could not; *must* not. He thought of bones being wrenched from the Garden like fragile roots, of Renati's skull being blown to pieces, of what these men would do to Alekza and Petyr once they returned with their guns and explosives.

Rage burned in him, and a low growl started in his throat. The soldiers were crashing through the woods, almost running. Blood was still in Mikhail's mouth from the dead rabbit; his body darted after the soldiers, a black streak through the gray forest. He ran silently, with the tight grace of a killer. And even as he closed on the two men and judged the point to begin his leap, he knew a simple fact: a wolf's tears were no different from a human's.

He sprang up and forward, his hind legs like iron springs, and he landed on the cigarette smoker's back before the man even knew he was there.

Mikhail drove the man down, into the dead leaves, and clamped his jaws on the back of his neck. He wrenched the head violently left and right, heard the sound of bones splintering. The man thrashed, but it was the death throes of nerves and muscle. Mikhail finished breaking his neck, and the man died without a sound.

There was a shuddered gasp. Mikhail looked up, his green eyes glittering.

Stefan had turned, and was lifting his rifle.

Mikhail saw the soldier's finger tightening on the trigger. An instant before the bullet left the rifle Mikhail leaped aside, diving into the underbrush, and Russian lead kicked up a gout of Russian dust. A second shot rang out, the bullet passing over Mikhail's shoulder and thunking into an oak tree. Mikhail swerved left and right, sliding to a sudden halt on a carpet of dead leaves, and heard the soldier running. The man bellowed for help, and Mikhail went after him like silent judgment.

The soldier tripped over his own boots, scrambled up, and kept going. "Help me! Help me!" he screamed, and spun around to fire a shot at what he thought was coming up behind him. Mikhail, however, was circling around to cut him off from his camp. The soldier kept running and screaming, dead leaves in his hair, and Mikhail burst out of the underbrush and started to leap but in the next second there was no need to waste the energy.

The ground opened under the soldier's feet, and the man went down into the dirt and leaves. His screaming stopped, on a strangled note. Mikhail stood carefully on the trench's edge and looked down. The soldier's body twitched, even with seven or eight sharpened stakes piercing him. The smell of blood was very strong, and that coupled with Mikhail's rage, caused him to spin around and around, snapping at his tail.

In another moment he heard shouts: more soldiers, rapidly approaching. Mikhail turned and sped back to where the first man lay dead. He gripped the corpse's neck between his jaws and struggled to haul the body into the brush. The body was heavy, and the flesh tore; it was a messy job. From the corner of his eye he saw a flash of white; Wiktor came to his side and helped him drag the corpse into the darkness beneath a thick stand of pines. Then Wiktor snapped at Mikhail's muzzle, a signal for him to retreat. Mikhail hesitated, but Wiktor roughly shoved him with a shoulder and he obeyed. Wiktor crouched down in the leaves, listening to the sounds of the soldiers. There were eight of them, and as four pulled the dead man off the stakes the other four began to stalk through the forest, their rifles cocked and ready.

The beasts had come, as Wiktor had always known they someday would. The beasts had come, and they would not be denied their bloody flesh.

Wiktor stood up, a ghost amid the trees, and ran back to the white palace with the foul scent of the beasts in his nostrils.

5

A hand gripped Mikhail's shoulder, rousing him from a
restless two hours of sleep, and a finger pressed against his
lips.

"Quiet," Wiktor said, crouching next to him. "Just listen." He glanced at Alekza, who was already awake and
clutching Petyr close, then back to Mikhail.

"What is it? What's happening?" Franco stood up, with
the help of his staff.

"The soldiers are coming," Wiktor answered, and Franco's face blanched. "I saw them from the tower. Fifteen or
sixteen of them, maybe more." He'd seen them in the deep
blue predawn light, darting from tree to tree, thinking they
were invisible. Wiktor had heard the squeak of wheels;
they'd brought their machine gun with them.

"What are we going to do?" Franco's voice quavered on
the edge of panic. "We've got to get out while we can!"

Wiktor looked at the low-burning fire, then slowly nodded.
"All right," he said. "We'll go."

"Go?" Mikhail asked. "To where? This is our home!"

"Forget that!" Franco told him. "We'll have no chance if
they catch us down here."

"He's right," Wiktor agreed. "We'll hide in the forest.
Maybe we can come back after the soldiers clear out." The
way he said it told them all he didn't believe it; once the
soldiers found the pack's den, they might move in themselves before the first snow. Wiktor stood up. "We can't
stay here any longer."

Franco didn't hesitate. He cast aside his staff, and gray
hair began to scurry over his flesh. Within a minute he was
changed, his body balanced on three legs. Mikhail would
have changed, too, but Petyr still wore human skin and so
Alekza couldn't change either. He elected to remain human.
Wiktor's face and skull began the transformation; he threw

off his robe, sleek white hair emerging from his chest, shoulders, and back. Franco was already going up the stone stairs. Mikhail grasped Alekza's hand and pulled her and the child after him.

Fully changed, Wiktor took the lead. They followed him through the winding passageways, past the high vaulted windows where the trees had broken through—and suddenly they saw the dawn sky light up. Not with the sun, which was still a red slash across the horizon, but with a sparkling, sizzling ball of white fire that rose from the forest and arced down, bathing everything with garish, incandescent light. The ball of fire fell in the palace's courtyard, and two more rose up from the woods and fell after it. The third one smashed the remaining stained glass from a window and came into the palace itself, sputtering and glowing like a miniature sun.

Wiktor barked at the others to keep moving. Mikhail lifted his hand to shield his eyes from the blinding glare, his other hand locked on Alekza's. Franco ran on his three legs just behind Wiktor. Beyond the windows, darkness had turned to false, cold white daylight. Something about this was dreamlike to Mikhail, as if he moved through the corridors of a nightmare on sluggish legs. The glaring light cast grotesque, distorted shadows on the walls, merging those of human and wolf into new life-forms.

Mikhail's sense of unreality remained even when the soldier—a faceless shape—appeared in the corridor before them, lifted his rifle, and fired.

Wiktor was already leaping for the man, but Mikhail heard Wiktor grunt and knew the bullet had hit its target. Wiktor drove the soldier down under his weight, and as the man screamed Wiktor tore his throat out with one savage twist.

"They're here! Over here!" another soldier shouted. "A dozen of them!" The noise of boots echoed on the stones. A second rifle fired, and sparks leaped off the wall just above Franco's head. Wiktor turned, slamming into Franco to back him up the way they'd just come. Mikhail saw perhaps eight or nine soldiers in the corridor ahead; escape through that route was impossible. Wiktor was barking, his voice hoarse with pain, some of the soldiers were shouting, and Petyr wailed in Alekza's arms. Two more shots rang out, both of the bullets ricocheting off the walls. Mikhail turned and ran, pulling Alekza with him. And then he came around the bend of a passage and stopped short, face-to-face with three soldiers.

They gaped at him, surprised to see a human being. But the first man regained his wits and trained his rifle barrel at Mikhail's chest.

Mikhail heard himself growl. He reached out, a blur of motion, grasped the barrel, and uptilted it as the gun fired. He felt the hot streak of the bullet as it kissed his shoulder. His other arm lunged forward, and it was only when his hooked claws sank into the man's eyes that he realized his hand had changed. It had happened in an instant, a miracle of mind over body, and as he tore the man's eyes out the soldier screamed and staggered back into his companions. The third man fled, bellowing for help, but the second soldier began firing his rifle wildly, without aiming. Bullets shrieked off the walls and ceiling. A shape jumped past Mikhail; it had three legs, and it plowed headlong into the soldier's belly. The man fought Franco, but it was Franco's legs that were crippled, not his fangs. He tattered the soldier's face and got a grip on the throat. Mikhail was on his knees, his body contorting, and he shook off his deerskin robe and let the change take him.

There was a flash of metal. The soldier drove his arm down, and the knife he'd drawn sank into the back of Franco's neck. Franco shuddered, but he didn't release the man's throat. The man pulled the knife out, struck again and again. Franco crunched down, crushing the soldier's windpipe. The knife sank into Franco's neck up to the hilt, and bloody spray burst from Franco's nostrils.

Two more soldiers appeared in the whirl of gunsmoke, fire sparking from their rifle barrels. A hammer blow hit Mikhail in the side, stealing his breath. Another bullet clipped his ear. Franco howled as a bullet struck him, but he propelled himself forward, the knife still in his neck, and sank his fangs into the leg of one of the soldiers. The other man shot Franco at point-blank range, but still Franco clawed and bit in a frenzy. Wiktor suddenly bounded out of the smoke, dark blood streaming from his shoulder, and he slammed into the second man, knocking him to the floor. Mikhail was fully changed now, the smell of blood and violence igniting his rage. He leaped upon the man Franco had attacked, and together he and Franco made quick work of him. Then Mikhail swerved and lunged onto Wiktor's combatant, his fangs finding the throat and tearing it out.

"*Mikhail.*"

It had been a soft groan.

He turned, and saw Alekza on her knees. Petyr was squalling, and she held him tightly. Her eyes looked glassy. A thin creeper of blood oozed from the corner of her mouth. Her knees were in a puddle of it. "*Mikhail,*" she whispered again, and offered the child to him.

He couldn't take Petyr. He needed hands, not paws.

"*Please,*" she begged.

But Mikhail couldn't answer, either. The wolf's tongue could form no words of human love, or need, or sorrow.

Alekza's ice-blue eyes rolled back into her head. She fell forward, still holding the child, and Mikhail realized that Petyr's skull was going to smash on the stones.

He leaped over a dead soldier and slid underneath the child, cushioning Petyr's fall with his body.

He heard more soldiers coming through the smoky corridor. Wiktor barked: a sound that urged him to follow. Mikhail stayed where he was, his mind dazed, his joints and muscles full of frost.

Wiktor bit Mikhail's wounded ear, and tugged at him. The soldiers were almost upon them, and Wiktor could hear the squeak of wheels: the machine gun.

Franco staggered forward, gripping Mikhail's tail between his teeth and jerking backward, almost ripping the tail off. The pain charged through Mikhail's nerves. Petyr was still wailing, the soldiers were coming with their machine gun, and Alekza lay motionlessly on the stones. Wiktor and Franco kept pulling at Mikhail, urging him to get up. There was nothing more he could do, for either Alekza or his son. Mikhail raised up and snapped at Wiktor, driving him back, and then he eased carefully out from underneath Petyr so the child slid to the floor. He stood up, the taste of blood bitter in his mouth.

The shapes of men stood in the smoke. There was the sound of metal scraping metal: a firing bolt being drawn back.

Franco lifted his head, awkwardly because of the knife in his neck, and howled. The noise echoed along the passageway, and stilled the finger that reached for the machine gun's trigger. And then Franco hobbled in the direction of the soldiers, his body tensing for a leap. He flung himself into the whirling smoke, his jaws gaping wide to tear whatever flesh his fangs might find. The machine gun chattered, and the bullets cut Franco in half.

Wiktor turned in the opposite direction and ran along the corridor, jumping over the dead soldiers. The machine gun was still speaking, bullets ricocheting off the walls like hornets. Mikhail saw Alekza's body shake as another bullet hit her, and a slug whined off the stones beside Petyr. It was Mikhail's choice; he could either die here or try to get out. He whirled around and followed the white wolf.

As soon as he sprinted away, he heard the machine gun cease firing. Petyr was still crying. One of the men shouted, "Hold your fire! There's a child in there!"

Mikhail didn't stop. Petyr's fate, whatever it might be, was beyond his control. But the machine gun didn't fire again, and the rifles were silent. Maybe there was mercy in the Russian heart, after all. Mikhail didn't look back; he kept going, right behind Wiktor, his mind already turning away from the present to the future.

Wiktor found a narrow ascending staircase and went up, leaving drops of blood on the stones. Mikhail added his own blood to them. They got through a glassless window on the upper level, slid down the sloping roof, and crashed into the thicket beneath. Then they were running side by side into the forest, and when they'd gotten a safe distance, they both stood panting in the chill dawn light, the dead leaves beneath them spattered with drops of red. Wiktor burrowed into the leaves and lay there, half hidden, as he rasped with pain. Mikhail wandered in dazed circles until he fell, his strength gone. He began to lick his wounded side, but his tongue

390

found no bullet; the slug had pierced the flesh and gone through at an angle, missing the ribs and internal organs. Still, Mikhail was losing a lot of blood. He crawled beneath the shelter of a pine tree and there he drifted into unconsciousness.

When he awakened, the wind had picked up, swirling through the treetops. The day had passed; the sun was almost gone. Mikhail saw Wiktor, the white wolf burrowed in the leaves. He got up on all fours, staggered to Wiktor, and nudged him. At first he thought Wiktor was dead, because he was so terribly still, but then Wiktor groaned and rose up, a crust of dried blood around his mouth and his eyes dull and lost.

Hunger gnawed in Mikhail's belly, but he felt too drained to hunt. He staggered in one direction and then another, unable to decide what it was he should do. So he just stood in position, his head drooping and his side damp with blood again.

From the distance there was a hollow booming noise. Mikhail's ears twitched. The sound repeated itself. He realized it was coming from the southeast, where the white palace was.

Wiktor walked through the forest and up a small, rocky ridge. He stood motionless, staring at something, and after a while Mikhail gathered his strength and climbed up the ridge to stand beside him.

Dark smoke was rising, whirling in the wind. A red center of flames burned. As Wiktor and Mikhail watched, there was a third explosion. They could see chunks of stone flying into the sky, and they both knew what was happening: the soldiers were blowing the white palace to pieces.

Two more blasts shot banners of fire into the falling dark. Mikhail saw the turreted tower—where his kite had been caught, long ago—crumple and go down. A larger explosion bloomed, and out of that blast flew what appeared to be fiery bats. They were caught in the wind, whirling around and around in fierce maelstroms, and in another moment Mikhail and Wiktor could smell the scorch and char of mindless destruction. Fiery bats spun over the forest, and began to fall.

Some of them drifted down around the two wolves. Neither one had to look to see what they were. The burning pages were written in Latin, German, and Russian. Many of them held the remnants of colored illustrations, rendered by a master's hand. For a moment it snowed black flakes of civilization's dreams, and then the wind swept them up and away, and there was nothing left.

Night claimed the world. The fires grew wild in the wind, and began to feed on trees. The two wolves stood atop their ridge of rocks. The flames gleamed redly in two sets of eyes: one that had seen the true nature of the beast, and hated that sight; and another that stared in dull submission, glazed with final tragedy. The flames leaped and danced, a mockery of happiness, and green pines shriveled to brown before their touch. Mikhail nudged Wiktor: it was time to go, to wherever they were going, but Wiktor didn't move. Only much later, when they could both feel the advancing heat, did Wiktor make a noise: a deep, terrible groaning sound, the sound of defeat. Mikhail climbed down the ridge and barked for Wiktor to follow. Finally Wiktor turned away from the flames and came down, too, his body shivering and his head slung low.

It was as true for wolves as it was for humans, Mikhail thought as they wound their way through the forest. Life was for the living. Alekza, Franco, Nikita . . . all the others, gone. And what of Petyr? Did his bones lie in the ruins of the white palace, or had the soldiers taken him? What would happen to Petyr, out in the wilderness? Mikhail realized he would probably never know, and maybe that was for the best. It struck him, quite suddenly, that he was a murderer. He had killed human beings, broken their necks and ripped out their throats and . . . God help him . . . it had been *easy*.

And the worst thing was that there had been pleasure in the killing.

Though the books were in ashes, their voices remained in Mikhail's mind. He heard one of those voices now, from Shakespeare's *Richard II*:

With Cain go wander through the shade of night,
And never show thy head by day nor light.

Lords, I protest, my soul is full of woe,
That blood should sprinkle me to make me grow.

He went on into the forest, with Wiktor following, as the
wind continued to whirl and the trees burned at their backs.

––––––– 6 –––––––

When the snow came, Mikhail and Wiktor had been living
for more than ten days in one of the caves where Wiktor had
hunted the berserker. There was room for two wolves, but
not two humans. The wind grew bitter, raging from the
north, and returning to human form would be suicide. Wiktor was lethargic, and slept day and night. Mikhail hunted
for them both, grasping whatever he could from the forest's
plate.

True winter sank its icy roots. Mikhail traveled to the
soldiers' camp and found it empty. There was no trace of
Petyr. The snow had filled in the wagon ruts and stolen all
scent of men. Mikhail bypassed the large area of burned
trees and the scorched ruin of stones where the white palace
had been, and returned to the cave.

On clear nights, when the blue-rimmed moon shone down
and the sky was ablaze with stars, Mikhail sang. His song
was all pain and longing now; the joy had been seared out of
him. Wiktor remained in the cave, a ball of white fur, and
his ears twitched occasionally at the black wolf's song, but
Mikhail sang alone. His voice echoed over the forest, carried
by the roaming wind. There was no answer.

Over the weeks and months that followed, Mikhail felt
himself drifting further and further away from humanity. He
had no need of that frail white body; four legs, claws, and
fangs suited him now. Shakespeare, Socrates, higher mathematics, the languages of German, English, and Latin, history, and the theories of religion: they belonged to another
world. In the realm to which Mikhail now belonged, the

subject was survival. To fail those lessons meant death.

The winter broke. Blizzards turned to rainstorms, and fresh green appeared across the forest. Mikhail returned from hunting one morning to find a naked old man with a white beard, sitting on his haunches on a pile of rocks at the highest point above the chasm. Wiktor squinted in the hard sunshine, his face wrinkled and pale, but he took his portion of the dead muskrat and ate it raw. He watched the sun climbing into the sky, his amber eyes devoid of light. His head tilted to one side, as if he'd heard a familiar sound. "Renati?" he called, his voice fragile. "Renati?"

Mikhail lay down on his belly nearby, the chasm below them, chewing his food and trying to shut out the quavering voice. After a while, Wiktor put his hands to his face and wept, and Mikhail felt his heart shatter.

Wiktor looked up, and seemed to see the black wolf for the first time. "Who are you?" he asked. "*What* are you?"

Mikhail kept eating. He knew what he was.

"Renati?" Wiktor called again. "Ah, there you are." Mikhail saw Wiktor smile faintly, addressing thin air. "Renati, he thinks he's a wolf. He thinks he's going to stay here forever, and run on four legs. He's forgotten what the miracle really is, Renati: that he's human, inside that skin. And after I'm dust and gone where you are he thinks he'll still be here, catching muskrats for his dinner." He laughed a little bit, sharing a joke with a ghost. "To think what I put in his head, hour after hour!" His feeble fingers picked at the dark scar on his shoulder and pressed against the hard outline of the bullet that was still lodged there. Then he turned his attention to the black wolf. "Change back," he said.

Mikhail licked muskrat bones and paid him no mind.

"Change back," Wiktor repeated. "You're not a wolf. Change back."

Mikhail grasped the small skull, burst it open between his jaws, and ate the brains.

"Renati wants you to change back, too," Wiktor told him. "Hear her? She's speaking to you."

Mikhail heard the wind, and the voice of an insane man. He finished his meal and licked his paws.

"My God," Wiktor said softly. "I'm going crazy as hell."
He stood up, peering down into the chasm. "But I'm not
crazy enough to think I'm really a wolf. I'm a man. You are,
too, Mikhail. Change back. Please."

Mikhail didn't. He lay on his belly, watching crows circle
overhead, and he wished he could have a bite of one. He
didn't care for Wiktor's odor; it reminded him too much of
shadowy shapes with rifles.

Wiktor sighed, his head bowed. He slowly and carefully
began to climb down the rocks, his body creaking at the
joints. Mikhail got up, and followed him to keep him from
falling. "I don't need your help!" Wiktor shouted. "I'm a
man, I don't need your help!" He continued down the rocks
to the cave, crawled into it, and lay curled up, staring at
nothing. Mikhail crouched on the ledge in front of the cave,
the breeze ruffling his fur. He watched the crows circling
around like black kites, and his mouth watered.

The springtime sun made the forest bloom. Wiktor did not
return to his wolf form, and Mikhail did not return to human
flesh. Wiktor grew more feeble. On chilly nights, Mikhail
entered the cave and lay next to him, warming the old man
with his body heat, but Wiktor's sleep was fragile. He was
constantly tormented by nightmares, and he sat up shouting
for Renati, or Nikita, or another of the lost ones. On warm
days he perched up on the rocks above the chasm and stared
toward the hazy western horizon.

"You should go to England," Wiktor told the black wolf.
"That's right. England." He nodded. "They're civilized in
England. They don't kill their children." He shivered; even
on the warmest day, his flesh was as cold as parchment.
"Do you hear me, Mikhail?" he asked, and the wolf lifted
his head and stared at him but did not answer.

"Renati?" Wiktor spoke to the air. "I was wrong. We
lived as wolves, but we're not wolves. We were human
beings, and we belonged to that world. I was wrong to keep
us here. Wrong. And every time I look at him"—he motioned toward the black wolf—"I know I was wrong. It's too
late for me. But it isn't for him. He could go, if he wanted
to. He *should* go." He worked his skinny fingers together,
as if tying and then untangling a problem. "I was afraid of

the human world. I was afraid of pain. You were, too, weren't you, Renati? I think we all were. We could have gone, if we'd chosen. We could have learned to survive in that wilderness." He lifted his hand toward the west, toward the unseen villages and towns and cities beyond the horizon. "Oh, that's a terrible place," he said softly. "But it's where Mikhail belongs. Not here. Not anymore." He looked at the black wolf. "Renati says you have to go."

Mikhail didn't budge; he dozed in the heat, but he could hear what Wiktor was saying. His tail twitched a fly away, an involuntary reaction.

"I don't need you," Wiktor said, irritation in his voice. "Do you think you're keeping me alive? Ha! I can catch with my bare hands what your jaws would miss a hundred times over! You think this is loyalty? It's stupidity! Change back. Son, do you hear me?"

The black wolf's green eyes opened, then drifted shut again.

"You're an idiot," Wiktor decided. "I wasted my time on an idiot. Oh, Renati, why did you bring him into the fold? He has a life before him, and he wants to throw away the miracle. I was wrong . . . so very wrong." He stood up, still muttering, and began to climb down to the cave again. At once Mikhail was up and following him, watching the old man's footing. Wiktor railed at him, as he always did, but Mikhail went with him anyway.

The days passed. Summer was on the rise. Almost every day Wiktor went up to the rocks and talked to Renati, and Mikhail lay nearby, half listening, half dozing. On one of those days the sound of a distant train whistle drifted to them. Mikhail lifted his head and listened. The train's engineer was trying to scare an animal off the tracks. It might be worth a trip there tonight, to see if the train had hit anything. He laid his head back down, the sun warm on his spine.

"I have another lesson for you, Mikhail," Wiktor said softly, after the train's whistle had faded. "Maybe the most important lesson. Live free. That's all. Live free, even if your body is chained. Live free, *here.*" He touched his skull, with a palsied hand. "This is the place where no man can chain you. This is the place where there are no walls.

And maybe that's the hardest lesson to learn, Mikhail. All freedom has its price, but freedom of the mind is priceless." He squinted up at the sun, and Mikhail lifted his head and watched him. There was something different in Wiktor's voice. Something final. It frightened him, as he'd not been frightened since the soldiers had come. "You have to leave here," Wiktor said. "You're a human being, and you belong in that world. Renati agrees with me. You're staying here because of an old man who talks to ghosts." He turned his head toward the black wolf, and Wiktor's amber eyes glinted. "I don't want you to stay here, Mikhail. Your life is waiting for you, out there. Do you understand?"

Mikhail didn't move.

"I want you to go," Wiktor said. "Today. I want you to go into that world as a man. As a *miracle*." He stood up, and immediately Mikhail did, too. "If you don't go into that world . . . of what use were the things I taught you?" White hair rippled over his shoulders, over his chest, stomach, and arms. His beard twined around his throat, and his face began to change. "I was a good teacher, wasn't I?" he asked, his voice deepening toward a growl. "I love you, son," he said. "Don't fail me."

His spine contorted. He came down on all fours, the white hairs scurrying over his frail body, and he blinked at the sun. His hind legs tensed, and Mikhail realized what he was about to do.

Mikhail leaped forward.

And so did the white wolf.

Wiktor went into the air, still changing. He fell, his body slowly twisting, toward the rocks at the chasm's bottom.

Mikhail tried to shout; it came out as a high, anguished yelp, but what he'd tried to shout was: *"Father!"*

Wiktor made no sound. Mikhail looked away, his eyes squeezed shut, and did not see the white wolf reach the rocks.

A full moon rose. Mikhail crouched above the chasm and stared fixedly at it. Every so often he shivered, though the air was sultry. He tried to sing, but nothing would come out. The forest was a silent place, and Mikhail was alone.

Hunger, a beast that knew no sorrow, gnawed at his belly.

The train tracks, he thought; his brain was sluggish, unused to thinking. The train tracks. The train might have hit something today. There might be meat on the rails.

He went through the forest to the ravine, down through the weeds and dense vines to the tracks. Dazedly he began to search along them but there was no scent of blood. He would go back to the cave, he decided; that was his home now. Maybe he could find a mouse or a rabbit on the way.

He heard a distant thunder.

He lifted his paw, touched a rail, and felt the vibration. In a moment the train would burst out of the western tunnel, and it would roar along the ravine and into the eastern tunnel. The red lamp on the last car would swing back and forth, back and forth. Mikhail stared at the place where Nikita had died. There were ghosts in his mind, and he heard them speaking. One of them whispered, *Don't fail me*.

It came to him, very suddenly. He might beat the train, this time. If he really wanted to. He might beat the train by beginning the race as a wolf, and ending as a man.

And if he wasn't fast enough . . . well, did it matter? This was a forest of ghosts; why not join them, and sing new songs?

The train was coming. Mikhail walked to the entrance of the western tunnel and sat down beside the rails. Fireflies glowed in the warm air, insects chirred, a soft breeze blew, and Mikhail's muscles moved under his black-haired flesh.

Your life is waiting for you, out there, he thought. *Don't fail me*.

He smelled the acrid odor of steam. A light glinted in the tunnel. The thunder grew into the growl of a beast.

And then, in a glare of light and a rain of red cinders, the train exploded from the tunnel and raced toward the east.

Mikhail got up—too slow! too slow! he thought—and ran. Already the engine was outpacing him, its iron wheels grinding less than three feet beside him. Faster! he told himself, and both sets of legs obeyed. He slung his body low, the train's turbulence whipping at him. His legs pumped against the earth, his heart pounding. Faster. Faster still. He was gaining on the engine . . . was level with it . . . was passing it. Cinders burned his back and spun past his face. He kept going, could smell his hair being scorched. And then he was past the engine by six feet . . . eight feet . . . ten feet. Faster! Faster! Freed of the train's wind, he surged forward, a body designed for speed and endurance. He could see the dark hole of the western tunnel. Not going to make it, he thought, but he cast that thought quickly aside before it hobbled him. He was past the engine by twenty feet, and then he began to change.

His skull and face started first, his four legs still hurtling him forward. The black hair on his shoulders and back retreated into the smoothing flesh. He felt pain at his backbone, the spine beginning to lengthen. His body was enveloped in agony, but still he kept running. His pace was slowing, his legs changing, losing their hair, his backbone straightening. The engine was gaining on him, and the eastern tunnel was in front of him. He staggered, caught his balance. Cinders hissed on the white flesh of his shoulders. His paws were changing, losing their traction as fingers and toes emerged. It was now or never.

Mikhail, half human and half wolf, lunged in front of the engine and leaped for the other side.

The headlamp's glare caught him in midair, and seemed to freeze him there for a precious second. The eye of God, Mikhail thought. He felt the hot breath of the engine, heard its crushing wheels, the cowcatcher about to slam into him and rip him to shreds.

He ducked his head into his chest, his eyes closed and his body braced for impact. He hurtled head over heels through the headlamp's glare, over the cowcatcher, and into the weeds. He landed on his back, the breath blasting from his lungs. The engine's heat washed over him, a fierce wind ruffled his hair, and cinders bit his bare chest. He sat up in time to see the red lamp swinging back and forth as the last car went into the tunnel.

And the train was gone.

Every bone in his body felt as if it had been wrenched from its socket. His back and ribs were bruised. His legs were sore, and his feet were cut. But he was in one piece, and he had crossed the tracks.

He sat there for a while, breathing hard, sweat glistening

on his body. He didn't know if he could stand up or not; he couldn't remember what walking on two legs felt like.

His throat moved. He tried to make words. They emerged, with an effort. "I'm alive," he said, and the sound of his own voice—deeper than he remembered—was a shock.

Mikhail had never felt so naked. His first impulse was to change back, but he stopped himself. Maybe later, he thought. Not just yet. He lay in the weeds, gathering his strength and letting his mind wander. What lay beyond the forest? he wondered. What was out there, in that world that Wiktor said he belonged to? It must be a monstrous place, full of danger. It must be a wilderness where savagery knew no bounds. He was afraid of that world, afraid of what he would find in it . . . and afraid, as well, of what he might find in himself.

Your life is waiting for you, out there.

Mikhail sat up, and stared along the tracks that led west.

Don't fail me.

England—Shakespeare's land—lay in that direction. A civilized land, Wiktor had said.

Mikhail stood up. His knees buckled, and he went down again.

The second try was better. The third one got him up. He had forgotten he was so tall. He looked up at the full moon. It was the same moon, but not nearly so beautiful as in the wolf's sight. Moonlight glinted on the rails, and if there were ghosts here, they were singing.

Mikhail took the first, tentative step. His legs were clumsy things. How he had ever walked on them before?

He would learn again. Wiktor had been right; there was no life for him here. But he loved this place, and leaving it would be hard. It was the world of his youth; another, more brutal world awaited.

Don't fail me, he thought.

He took the second step. Then the third. He still had difficulty, but he was walking.

Mikhail Gallatinov went on, a naked, pale figure in the summer moonlight, and he entered the western tunnel on two legs, as a man.

NINE

The Devil's Kingdom

"Herr Sandler's waiting," the man said. Michael saw

1

Michael heard the train whistle. Was it retreating on the tracks, coming back at him for another race? If so, he knew it would beat him this time. His bones ached, and his head felt like a blister on the edge of bursting. The train's whistle faded. He tried to look back over his shoulder, through the darkness, but could see nothing. Where was the moon? It had been there a moment before, hadn't it?

There was a soft tapping sound. Then again. "Baron? Are you awake, sir?"

A man's voice, speaking in German. Michael's eyes opened. He was staring up at a ceiling of dark, varnished wood.

"Baron? May I come in, please?" The tapping was insistent this time. A doorknob turned, and a narrow door opened. Michael lifted his head, his temples throbbing. "Ah! You're awake!" the man said with a pleasant smile. He was thin and bald, with a neatly trimmed blond mustache. He wore a pin-striped suit and a red velvet vest. Scarlet light glowed around him, as if he were standing on the rim of a blast furnace. "Herr Sandler wishes you to join him for breakfast."

Michael sat up slowly. His head pounded like hell's anvil, and what was that clacking racket? He remembered the blackjack; its blows must've unhinged his sense of balance as well as his hearing, because the entire room seemed to be gently rocking back and forth.

"Breakfast will be served in fifteen minutes," the man said, a cheerful announcement. "Would you prefer apple or grapefruit juice?"

"What is this place?" He realized he was on a bed. His

shirt collar was open, his white bow tie unknotted, his shoes unlaced and on the floor. They looked as if they'd been freshly polished. The room—a cramped little chamber—held a brown leather chair and a table on which rested a white bowlful of water. Where the window should have been was a square of metal bolted down. He heard the train's whistle again: a high, piercing note from somewhere far ahead. Well, he knew where he was now, and why the room was rocking, but where was the train headed?

"Herr Sandler's waiting," the man said. Michael saw movement behind him. In the corridor, where a curtained window let in a little crack of scarlet light, stood a Nazi soldier with a pistol.

What the hell was going on? Michael wondered. He decided it was prudent to play along. "I'll have apple juice," he said, and put his feet on the floor. He stood up carefully, testing his balance. His legs held him.

"Very good, sir." The man—obviously a butler—started to leave.

"One moment," Michael said. "I also want a pot of coffee. Black, no sugar. And three eggs; do you have those?"

"Yes, sir."

"Good. I want three eggs, still in their shells."

The man's expression indicated he didn't register the request. "I beg your pardon?"

"Three eggs. Raw. In their shells. Is that clear?"

"Uh . . . yes, sir. Very clear." He backed out the door, and closed it firmly.

Michael went to the square of metal and tried to hook his fingers underneath it. The thing wouldn't budge, its bolts driven deep. He found a pull cord and yanked it, turning on a small light globe at the ceiling. A closet held his gray coat with the black velvet lapels, but no other clothes. He looked around. It was a Spartan room, a moving prison cell. Certainly the soldier outside the door was guarding him; were there more soldiers aboard? How far from Berlin were they? Where were Chesna and Mouse? He didn't even know how much time had elapsed since the ambush, but he doubted that he'd been unconscious for more than a few hours. So if the sun was coming up, the Brimstone Club gathering had been last night. Had Sandler found what was left of his hawk? And if Michael was on his way to a Gestapo interrogation as a spy, then why had the butler still referred to him as "Baron"?

Questions, questions. None of them answerable yet. Michael walked two paces to the table, cupped water in his hands, and put it to his face. A clean white towel was folded next to the bowl, and he used it to dry his face. Then he cupped more water in his hands and lapped up a few swallows. A mirror hung on the wall nearby. Michael looked at his reflection. The whites of his eyes were a little bloodshot, but he bore no marks of the blackjack blows. With careful fingers he found the lumps on his skull, one just above his left temple and the other on the back of his head. The blows, either one of which could have killed him, had been delivered with restraint. Which meant Sandler—or someone else—wanted him alive.

His vision was still hazy. He would have to shake off the grogginess and do it fast because he had no idea what lay ahead of him. Back in the Reichkronen's courtyard he'd made the error of letting his instincts falter. He should've picked up the fact that Sandler's drunkenness was a sham, and he should have heard the man coming up behind him long before he did. Well, the lesson was learned. He would not underestimate Harry Sandler again.

He buttoned his collar and tied his white bow tie. No use going to breakfast looking unpresentable. He thought of the photographs he'd found in Colonel Jerek Blok's suite, the ravaged faces of victims of some horrible testing program on Skarpa Island. How much did Sandler know about Dr. Hildebrand's new project? Or about Iron Fist, and Frankewitz's labors to paint bullet holes on green metal. It was time to find out.

Michael took the coat from the closet, put it on, checked his tie again in the mirror, and then took a deep, head-clearing breath and opened the door.

The soldier who'd been waiting outside instantly drew his Luger from its holster. He aimed it at Michael's face.

Michael smiled tightly and lifted his hands. He waggled his fingers. "Nothing up my sleeves," he said.

"Move." The soldier motioned to his left with the gun, and Michael went along the swaying corridor with the soldier a few paces behind. The car held several other rooms that looked to be about the size of the one Michael had occupied. It wasn't a prison train, Michael realized; it was too clean, the wooden walls polished and brass fixtures gleaming. Still, there was a musty scent in the air: the lingering aromas of sweat and fear. Whatever went on in this train, it wasn't healthy.

A second soldier, also armed with a Luger, was waiting at the entrance to the next car. Michael was motioned to keep going, and he pushed through a doorway and found himself in luxury's lap.

It was a beautiful dining car, with walls and ceiling of dark rosewood and a red and gold Persian carpet on the floor. A brass chandelier hung from above, and along the walls were brass carriage lamps. Beneath the chandelier was a table covered with white linen, where Michael's host sat.

"Ah! Good morning, Baron!" Harry Sandler stood up, smiling broadly. He appeared well rested and wore a red silk robe with his initials in Gothic script over his heart. "Please, join me!"

Michael glanced back over his shoulder. One of the soldiers had entered, and stood beside the door, Luger in hand. Michael walked to the breakfast table and sat down across from Sandler, where a place setting of dark blue china was arranged for him. Sandler returned to his seat. "I hope you slept well. Some people have difficulty sleeping on trains."

"After the first couple of bumps, I slept like a baby," Michael said.

Sandler laughed. "Oh, that's great! You've kept your sense of humor. Very refreshing, Baron."

Michael unrolled his napkin. He had plastic eating utensils, whereas Sandler's were sterling silver.

"You never know how people will respond," Sandler went on. "Sometimes the scenes are . . . well . . . unpleasant."

"I'm shocked!" Michael said, with mock dismay. "Hit on the head in the middle of the night, shoved into a car's trunk, dragged away God knows where to wake up on a moving train? Some people would call that *unpleasant?*"

"I fear it's so. There's no accounting for taste, is there?" He laughed again, but his eyes were cold. "Ah! Here's Hugo, with our coffee!" The butler who had come to Michael's room emerged from a door that must've led to a kitchen, and he brought two small silver pots and two cups on a tray. "This is my train," Sandler said as Hugo poured the coffee for them. "A gift from the Reich. Beautiful, isn't it?"

Michael glanced around. He'd already noticed that the windows were covered with metal shutters. "Yes, it is. But do you have an aversion to light?"

"Not at all! As a matter of fact, we need some morning sun, don't we? Hugo, open these two." He motioned to the windows on either side of their table. Hugo produced a key from his vest, inserted it into a lock beneath one window, and turned it. There was a soft click as the lock disengaged, and then Hugo opened the shutters with a hand crank. Dawn light streamed through the window. Hugo unlocked the second window and cranked the shutters open the same way, then he pocketed his key and went back to the kitchen. Michael sipped his coffee—black and without sugar, just as he'd requested—and gazed out one of the windows. The train was moving through a forest, and the harsh sunlight glinted through the trees. "There," Sandler said. "That's better, isn't it? This is a very interesting train, as I think you'll find. My private car is the one at the rear, just behind where you woke up. Then there are three more cars between this one and the locomotive. A magnificent piece of machinery. Do you know much about trains?"

"I've had a little experience with them."

"What's fascinating to me about a train is that you can create your own world inside one. This train, for instance: anyone seeing it from the outside would see simply what appeared to be an ordinary freight hauler. They wouldn't think twice about it. But inside . . . well, it's *my* world, Baron. I love the sound of the wheels on the rails, the power of the locomotive. It's like riding inside a great, beautiful beast. Don't you agree?"

"Yes, I would." Michael sipped again at his coffee. "I've always thought of a train as being . . . oh . . . like a huge iron fist."

"Really? That's interesting. Yes, I can see that." He nodded. There was no change in his relaxed, pleasant expression. No response to the phrase, Michael thought. Did he know anything about Iron Fist, or not? "You surprise me, Baron," Sandler said. "I assumed you'd be . . . shall we say . . . *nervous?* Or perhaps you're just a good actor. Yes, I think that's probably it. Well, you're a long way from your tulip gardens now, Baron. And I'm afraid you won't be leaving this train alive."

Michael slowly lowered his coffee cup to the table. Sandler was watching him carefully, waiting for a response: a cry of anguish, tears, pleading. Michael stared at him for a few seconds, then reached for his silver pot and poured himself more coffee.

A frown flickered over Sandler's face. "You think I'm joking, don't you? This is far from a joke, my friend. I'm going to kill you: whether your death will be fast or slow is up to you."

The sound of the train's wheels suddenly changed. Michael looked out the window. They were passing over a bridge that crossed a wide, dark green river. Another startling sight caught his attention. The towers and turrets of a large building were visible above the trees, perhaps a half mile away. There was no doubt about it; it was the Reichkronen.

"Yes, there's the hotel," Sandler said, correctly judging the baron's response. "We've been circling Berlin for the past three hours. We'll continue to circle until the hunt's ended."

"The *hunt?*"

"Exactly." Sandler's smile returned; he was in the driver's seat again. "I'm going to hunt you, along the length of the train. If you can get to the locomotive and pull the whistle's cord three times before I find you, your death will be a quick bullet to the brain. If, however, I trap you before you get there, then . . ." He shrugged. "Hunter's choice," he said.

"You're out of your damned mind."

"Oh, that's the spirit!" Sandler clapped his hands together. "Let's get some emotion out of you! Come on, can't you work up a few tears? Maybe beg a little? Would it help if I told you I skinned the last man I hunted here? He was an enemy of Himmler's, so I gave him the skin. I do believe he mounted it."

Hugo came from the kitchen, rolling a tray that held their breakfasts. He put a platter of steak in front of Sandler, then a dish before Michael on which rested the three raw eggs. "You fascinate me, Baron!" the big-game hunter said, with a grin. "I don't know what to make of you!"

Michael's heartbeat had picked up and his throat was a little dry, but he was far from panic. He looked out the window, watching row houses and factories speed past. "I doubt if Chesna would like the fact that I've been kidnapped," he said frostily. "Or have you kidnapped *her*, too?"

"Of course not. She's still at the Reichkronen, and so's your valet. Chesna doesn't know anything about this, and she never will." He picked up a sharp knife and began to carve his steak. The inside of the meat was almost red, blood oozing into his platter. "At this moment the police are dragging the river for your body. Two people have come forward and said they'd seen you wandering along the riverbank after you left the Brimstone Club. You, unfortunately, seemed to have had a bit too much to drink. You were staggering around, and you refused to go back to the hotel." Sandler chewed a piece of steak and washed it down with coffee. "That riverbank can be very treacherous, Baron. You shouldn't have gone there alone."

"I'm sure someone saw me leave with you."

"In that crowd? I don't think so. Anyway, it doesn't matter. I received Colonel Blok's permission to take you; he doesn't want you marrying Chesna any more than I do."

So that was it, Michael realized. This had nothing to do with his mission, or the fact that he was a British secret agent. Sandler and Blok wanted Baron von Fange to disappear. It also was clear that Sandler didn't know about his hawk's fate; he probably hadn't had a chance to return to the hotel, and wouldn't go back until this ludicrous "hunt" was finished. Of course Chesna wouldn't believe the story about Michael being drunk. She'd know something was up; what would she do? He couldn't think about that right now, though. His primary concern was the smiling man who sat across the table from him, chewing on bloody meat. "I love Chesna," Michael said. "Chesna loves me. Doesn't that make a difference?" He let a little weakness creep into his voice; no use making Sandler *too* cautious.

"Oh, screw that! Chesna doesn't love *you!*" He speared another piece of meat on his fork and ate it. "Maybe she's infatuated. Maybe she likes your company—though I have no idea why. Anyway, Chesna sometimes lets her heart rule her head. She's a fantastic woman: beautiful, talented, well bred. And a daredevil, too. Did you know she flies her own plane? She did aerial stunts in one of those movies she made. She's a champion swimmer, and I can tell you she fires a rifle better than a lot of men I've met. She's tough up here"—he touched his skull—"but she's got the heart of a woman. She's been involved in ill-advised love affairs before, but she's never talked marriage. I'm a little disappointed; I always thought she was a better judge of character."

"Meaning you don't like the fact that Chesna chose me instead of you?"

"Chesna's choices are not always wise," Sandler said. "Sometimes she has to be led to the right decision. So Colonel Blok and I have decided you're out of the picture, permanently."

"What makes you think she'll marry you, even if I'm dead?"

"I'm working on it. Besides, it would be a great propaganda piece for the Reich. Two Americans who've chosen to live under the Nazi banner. And Chesna's a star, too. Our pictures would be in newspapers and magazines around the world. You see?"

Michael did see. Not only was Sandler a traitor and a murderer, he had a colossal ego. Even if Michael hadn't wanted to kill him before, this would have sealed it. He picked up his plastic spoon, broke the shell of the first egg,

410

lifted it to his mouth, and downed it. Sandler laughed. "Raw meat and raw eggs. Baron, you must've been raised in a barn!"

Michael ate the second egg the same way. Hugo returned, with carafes of apple juice for Michael and Sandler. The big-game hunter drank down his glass, but Michael paused with his glass right at his lips. He smelled a faint, slightly bitter odor. A poison of some kind? No, the odor wasn't that bitter. But there was a drug in the juice. A sedative, he reasoned. Something to make him sluggish. He put the glass aside and reached for his coffee again. "What's wrong?" Sandler asked. "Don't you like apples?"

"It smells a little wormy." He cracked the third egg's shell, and slid the yolk into his mouth, bursting it between his teeth. He swallowed, wanting to get the rich protein into his system as quickly as possible, then he washed it down with coffee. The tracks were turning to the northeast, beginning to circle around Berlin again.

"Aren't you going to beg?" Sandler leaned forward. "Just a little bit?"

"Would it do any good?"

Sandler hesitated, then shook his head. His eyes were dark and cautious, and Michael knew he'd sensed something he hadn't expected. Michael decided to probe once more: "So I don't have much of a chance, do I? Like a roach under an iron fist?"

"Oh, you have a chance. A small one." Again, there was no recognition of the phrase in Sandler's face. Whatever Iron Fist was, Harry Sandler knew nothing about it. "To die a quick death, that is. Just get to the locomotive before I find you. I'll be armed, of course. I've brought along my favorite rifle. You, unfortunately, will be unarmed. But you'll have a ten-minute head start. You're going to be taken back to your room for a while. Then you'll hear an alarm buzzer go off. That'll be your signal to start running." He carved another bite of steak, then slid the knife into the rest of it. "There's no use to try to hide in your room, or hold the door shut. I'll just find you that much faster. And if you think you can jump off the train, you're mistaken. There are soldiers aboard who'll be stationed between each car. And

411

the windows . . . well, you can forget those." He motioned to Hugo, who'd been standing nearby waiting to clear away the plates. Hugo began to crank down the window shutters again. Slowly the sunlight was sealed off. "Let's make this a sporting contest, all right?" Sandler urged. "You do your part, and I'll do mine."

The last shutter closed. Hugo brought the key from his vest to lock them, and in the folds of his coat Michael saw a pistol in a holster.

"Don't think about trying to get Hugo's gun," Sandler said, tracking Michael's gaze. "He spent eight months on the Russian Front, and he's an expert shot. Any questions about the ground rules?"

"No."

"You really do amaze me, Baron. I have to say I thought you'd be on your knees by now. It just goes to show: you never know what's inside a man, do you?" His grin was all teeth. "Hugo, will you return the baron to his quarters please?"

"Yes, sir." The pistol emerged from his holster and was pointed at Michael.

When the door to his room was closed, Michael found the chamber altered. The mirror, the table, the white bowl, and the towel were missing. Also the single hanger was gone from the closet. Michael had been looking forward to using shards of the mirror, pieces of the bowl, and the hanger to slash his way out of this. The light globe remained, however, and Michael looked up at it. The globe was out of reach, though he felt sure he could devise some way to burst it to pieces. He sat down on the bed to think, the train gently swaying and the wheels clattering on the rails. Did he really need weapons to beat Harry Sandler at his own game? He didn't think so. He could change into a wolf and be ready to go once the alarm buzzer sounded.

But he didn't change. He already had the edge in instincts and perception. All changing would do was lose him his clothes. He could walk on two legs and think like a wolf, and still beat Sandler. The only problem was that Sandler knew the train better than he. Michael would have to find a place suitable to set up an ambush, and then . . .

412

Then the heavy weight of the Countess Margritta would be lifted from him. Then he could write *finis* to that sorry episode of his life, and turn away from the compulsion of revenge.

He would beat Harry Sandler as a man, he decided. With hands instead of claws.

He waited.

Perhaps two hours passed, in which Michael lay down and rested. He was totally calm now, mentally and physically prepared.

The alarm buzzer went off, a jarring note. It lasted for maybe ten seconds, and by the time it had ended Michael was out the door and on his way toward the locomotive.

—————— 2 ——————

The soldier at the connection of cars shoved Michael along with the point of his pistol, and Michael went through the door into the opulent car where breakfast had been served. The soldier stayed behind, and the door hissed shut at Michael's back.

The metal shutters were all drawn. The chandelier lights burned low, as did the carriage lamps. Michael began walking through the car, but he stopped at the white linen-covered table.

The plates had not been cleared away. And there, in the remains of Sandler's steak, was the knife, stuck upright, the handle offered.

Michael stared at the knife. This was an interesting situation; why was the knife still there? One answer: Sandler expected him to take it. And what would happen if he did? Michael carefully placed a finger on the knife handle, felt all around it with a gentle touch, and found what he was seeking. A thin, almost invisible filament of wire was twined around the handle. It went up, hidden in the dimness of the room, to the chandelier overhead. Michael inspected the light fixture. Hidden in the ornamentation was a small brass pistol, and the filament was attached to its cocked trigger. He judged the angle of the barrel, realizing that if he'd pulled the knife from the steak the trigger would've tripped and a bullet would have gone through his left shoulder. Michael smiled grimly. So that was why he'd been left in his room for two hours. During that time Sandler and his train crew had been busy rigging up devices such as this. A ten-minute head start indeed, Michael thought. This game might've been over very quickly.

He decided to give Sandler something to think about, perhaps slow him down a little. He stepped aside, out of the pistol's line of fire, and kicked a leg out from underneath the table. As the table fell, the filament snapped and the pistol went off with a loud, sharp *crack*. The bullet blew splinters from the rosewood wall. Michael picked up the knife, and was amused anew; it had only a useless stub of a blade. He took the pistol from the chandelier, but he already knew what he would find. There had been only one bullet in the cylinder.

So much for that. He let the pistol fall to the carpet and went on through the car. But his steps were slower now, more wary. He looked for trip wires stretched along the floor, realizing at the same time that a trip wire might be waiting to brush through his hair. He paused at the door to the kitchen, his hand near the knob. Surely Sandler would expect him to try this door, to get at the utensils that might lie beyond it. The doorknob had been recently polished, and it shone like a promise. Too easy, Michael thought. Turning that knob might pull the trigger of a gun set up to blast him through the wood. He drew his hand away, retreated from the door, and kept going. Another soldier stood guard in the next connection between cars, his heavy-lidded eyes showing no emotion. Michael wondered how many of Sandler's victims had even gotten past the first car. But he couldn't congratulate himself yet; there were three more cars between here and the locomotive.

Michael went through the door into the next car. There was a central aisle along its length, and rows of seats on either side of the aisle. The windows were sealed with metal shutters, but two chandeliers spaced equidistantly at the ceiling glowed with false cheer. The car swayed gently back and forth as the train followed a curve, and the whistle blew a brief warning note. Michael knelt down, looking along the aisle at knee level. If a trip wire was there, he couldn't see it. He was aware that Sandler would be after him by now, and at any moment the hunter might burst through the door at his back. Michael couldn't wait; he stood up and slowly began walking down the aisle, his hands up in the air in front of him and his eyes watching for the glint of a wire at his knees or ankles.

There was no wire, either above or below. Michael had begun to sweat a little bit; surely there was something in this car, waiting for him to blunder into it. Or was it empty of traps, and this simply a mind snare? He approached the second chandelier, about twenty feet from the next car. He looked up as he neared the chandelier, his eyes searching the brass arms for a concealed weapon; there was none.

His left foot sank about a quarter inch into the carpet, and he heard the small, soft click of a latch disengaging.

He had stepped on a pressure pad. He felt the cold wind of death on the back of his neck.

In an instant Michael had reached up, grasped the chandelier, and pulled his knees up to his chest. The shotgun that was hidden at the floor to his left boomed, the lead pellets passing across the aisle where his knees had been two seconds before and slamming into the seats on his right. In another heartbeat the shotgun's second barrel fired, demolishing the seats. Shards of wood and pieces of shredded fabric whirled in the concussion.

Michael lowered his feet to the floor and let go of the chandelier. Blue gunsmoke drifted around him. One glance at the wrecked seats told him what the shotgun would've done to his knees. Crippled, he'd have writhed on the floor until Sandler arrived.

He heard the *whoosh* of the door opening at the far end of the car. He looked back. Sandler, wearing a khaki hunter's outfit, lifted his rifle, took aim, and fired.

Michael was already diving to the floor. The bullet sang over his left shoulder and thunked off a shuttered window.

Before Sandler could fix his aim again. Michael leaped up in a blur of motion and crashed headlong through the door at his end of the car. A soldier was there, as Michael had expected. The man had a pistol in his hand, and reached down to grasp the back of Michael's coat and pull him to his feet.

Michael didn't wait for the man to haul him up; he sprang up under his own power, slamming the top of his head against the soldier's chin. The man staggered back, his eyes wide and blurred with pain. Michael grasped the man's wrist, keeping the gun turned aside, and struck with the flat of his hand upward against the sharp Germanic nose. The soldier's nose shattered, the nostrils spraying blood, and Michael grabbed hold of the Luger and slung the man away from him like a sack of straw. He whirled around, looking through the door's small glass inset. Sandler was more than halfway down the aisle. Michael lifted the Luger to fire through the glass and saw Sandler stop in his tracks. The rifle barrel was coming up. Both guns went off at the same instant.

Splinters of wood exploded around Michael, just as fragments of glass flew at Harry Sandler. What felt like a burning brand kissed Michael's right thigh, and the shock knocked him to his knees. The door's glass inset was gone, and there was a hole in the wood the size of a man's fist where Sandler's bullet had passed through. Michael fired again through the door, and was answered a few seconds later by another rifle slug that threw a shower of splinters and hit the wall over Michael's head. This was a dangerous place to stay. Michael got up in a crouch, one hand pressed to the spreading crimson stain at his right thigh, and backed through the next door into the car ahead.

The clattering roar of the train wheels made him turn. The car he stood in had no floor; it was just a metal-shuttered shell, and Michael stood on the edge looking down at the speeding blur of the railroad tracks. Above his head an iron pipe attached to the ceiling went the length of the car, sixty feet or so. There was no way to the other side except hand over hand on the pipe. He looked toward the bullet-pocked door he'd just come through. Sandler was waiting, biding his time. Maybe one of the Luger slugs had hit him, or maybe the glass had blown into his face. It occurred to Michael that his best chance to get off this madman's leviathan was to continue to the locomotive and gain control of the throttle. If Sandler was gravely wounded, the soldiers would probably pick up the hunt. In any case he couldn't wait here very much longer; the rifle bullet had nicked a groove in his thigh, and he was losing a lot of blood. In another few minutes his strength would be a memory. He pushed the Luger down into his waistband and jumped over the rushing rails, locking his hands around the iron pipe. His body swung back and forth, warm blood creeping down his right leg. He started along the pipe, reaching out as far as he could with one hand before he let the other one loose.

Michael had made it past the midpoint when he heard, over the thunder of the wheels, the staccato bark of a high-powered rifle. The bullet hit the ceiling about six inches to the left of the pipe. Michael twisted his head, saw Sandler in the doorway behind him, chambering another round. Sandler was grinning, his face streaked with crimson rivulets from glass slashes. He lifted the rifle and took aim at Michael's head.

Michael held on with one hand and wrenched the Luger from his waistband. He saw Sandler's finger on the trigger, and he knew he'd never get a shot off in time.

"Drop it!" Sandler bellowed over the noise. "Drop it, you son of a bitch, or I'll blow your damned head off!"

Michael paused. He was calculating in inches and fractions of seconds. No, he decided; Sandler's next bullet would hit its mark before the Luger could fire.

"I said drop the gun! *Now!*" Sandler's grin had become a twisted rictus, and blood dripped from his chin.

Michael's fingers opened. The Luger fell onto the rails, and was gone.

"I got you, didn't I?" Sandler shouted, looking at the dark stain on Michael's thigh. "I knew I got you! You thought you were *smart,* didn't you?" He wiped his forearm across his face and stared at the crimson that smeared it. "You made me bleed, you son of a bitch!" he said, and Michael saw him blink dazedly. Glass shards glittered in the hunter's face. "You're a real card, Baron! I thought for sure the knife would get you! And the shotgun . . . that usually finishes the hunt! No one's ever made it this far before!"

Michael grasped the pipe with both hands. He was thinking furiously, cold sweat on his face. "You haven't got me yet," he said.

"The hell I don't! One squeeze of this trigger and I've got a new trophy!"

"You haven't *caught* me," Michael went on. "You call yourself a hunter?" He laughed harshly. "There's another car to go, isn't there? I can make it through whatever you've got in there . . . wounded leg and all!" He saw new interest—the thrill of the challenge—flare in Sandler's eyes. "You can shoot me right now, but I'll fall to the rails. You won't take me alive . . . and isn't that what it's all about?"

It was the hunter's turn to laugh. He lowered his rifle and licked blood from his lips. "You've got guts, Baron! I never would've expected such guts from a tulip sniffer! Well, we've both drawn blood, eh? So we'll call the first round even. But you won't make it through the next car, Baron; that I promise you."

"I say I will."

Sandler grinned fiercely. "We'll see. Go on. I'll give you sixty seconds."

Michael took what he could get. He continued along the pipe. Sandler shouted, "Next time, you're meat!" Michael reached a small platform in front of the next door and swung himself down onto it. The soldier who guarded the entrance to the final car stepped back, out of Michael's reach, and motioned him on with a gesture of his gun. Michael glanced back, saw Sandler sliding the rifle strap around his shoulder in preparation for crossing the pipe. The final car awaited, and Michael entered it.

The door closed behind him. Its glass inset was painted black. Not a trace of light entered the car; it was as dark as the blackest night. Michael looked for shapes before him—furniture, light fixtures, anything to tell him what lay ahead—but could make out nothing. He held his hands out in front of his face and stepped forward. Another step. Then a third. Still no obstructions. The wound at his thigh was a dull throb, the blood oozing down his leg. He took a fourth step, and something bit his fingers.

He pulled his hands back, his fingers stinging. Razors or broken glass, he thought. He reached out again, to his left, felt empty space. Two steps forward and a third to the left grazed his hand against more razors. Michael's blood had gone cold. It was a maze, he realized. The maze's walls were covered with broken razors.

He quickly took his coat off and wrapped it around his hands. Then he started forward again, deeper into the absolute dark. His senses quested; he sniffed the air, smelled engine oil, the bitter scent of burning coal in the locomotive, his own coppery blood. His heart was pounding, his eyes straining to make out shapes in the blackness. His hands touched another wall of razors, directly in front of him. He found a razor-studded wall to his left as well; the maze was leading him to the right, and he had no choice but to follow the passageway. It turned sharply to the left again, suddenly ceasing in a dead end. Michael knew he'd missed a corridor somewhere, and he'd have to backtrack. As he searched for the way out, the razors shredding the coat around his hands, he heard the door open and close at the entrance to the car: Sandler had arrived.

"Like my little maze, Baron?" Sandler asked. "I hope you're not afraid of the dark."

Michael knew better than to answer. Sandler would key in on the sound of his voice. He felt along the walls, wincing as a razor came through the fabric and sliced his fingers. There it was! A narrow corridor—or, at least, what appeared to be a corridor. He moved into it and kept going with his hands up in front of him.

"I can't figure you out, Baron!" Sandler said. The voice had moved; Sandler was coming through the maze. "I thought you'd break by now! Or maybe you *have* broken, and you're lying huddled in a corner. Is that right?"

Michael came to another wall. The corridor turned to the right at an angle that grazed blades through his shirt and across the flesh of his shoulder.

"I know you're terrified. Who wouldn't be? You know, for me that's the most thrilling part of the hunt: the terror in the eyes of an animal when it realizes there's no way out. Oh, did I tell you I know the way through this maze? I built it, you see. The razors are a nice touch, don't you think?"

Keep talking, Michael thought. The sound told him that Sandler was to his left, perhaps fifteen or twenty feet behind him. Michael went on, easing his way between the razors.

"I know you must be cut to pieces by now," Sandler said. "You should be wearing leather gloves, like I am. One must always be prepared, Baron; that's the mark of a true hunter."

A wall blocked Michael's way. He searched left and right for another passage. Sandler's voice was getting closer.

"If you surrender, I'll make it easy on you. All you have to say are three words: 'I give up.' I'll make your death a quick one. Is that agreeable to you?"

Michael's hands found the wall's edge, to his left. The coat was in tatters around his fingers, the cloth damp with blood. He could feel his strength leaving him, his muscles weakening. His wounded leg was going numb. But the doorway out of this car had to be just ahead, no more than another fifteen feet. Its glass inset would also be painted black, he reasoned. So finding the door would be difficult. He moved along the left-slanting corridor, the car swaying as the train rounded a curve. The corridor straightened out. The smell of burning coal was stronger. The door must be close, he thought. Not much farther to go now . . .

He took two more steps, and heard the metallic *ping* of a trip wire snapping.

Even as Michael flung himself forward to the floor, a row of flashbulbs exploded in his face. The light seared his eyes, made blue pinwheels whirl in his brain. He lay dazed, his balance and equilibrium destroyed, his eyes prickling with pain as if they, too, had been sliced.

"Oh, you almost got out, didn't you?" Sandler's voice came from about twelve feet behind and to the right. "Just wait for me, Baron. I'll be there shortly."

Michael's eyes were full of blue fire. He crawled out of the middle of the corridor, and lay with his back pressed up against a blade-covered wall. Sandler was striding toward him; he could hear the man's boots on the floorboards. He knew the hunter would expect to find him totally helpless, writhing in pain with his hands clawing at his eyes. He turned his body so his arms were unhindered, and he pulled his hands out of the shredded coat.

"Say something, Baron," Sandler urged. "So I can find you and put you out of your misery."

Michael remained silent, lying on his side. He listened to the noise of Sandler's footsteps, getting closer. Come on, damn you! Michael seethed. Come on, I'm waiting!

"Baron? The hunt's ended, I think." Michael heard the bolt click back on Sandler's rifle.

He smelled the man's minty after-shave. And then he heard the squeak of polished leather, the soft groan of a floorboard, and he knew Sandler's boots were within reach.

Michael grasped out with both hands, trusting his sense of hearing. His fingers found Sandler's ankles, in the middle of the corridor, and locked tight. He shoved forward and up with all the strength of his back and shoulders.

Sandler had no time to cry out. He fell, his torso twisting. The rifle went off, the bullet thunking into the ceiling, and he crashed against one of the razor-studded walls.

Then the hunter screamed.

As Sandler hit the floor, thrashing in pain, Michael leaped upon him. His hands closed on the hunter's throat and began to squeeze. Sandler choked—and then a wooden object slammed into the side of Michael's jaw and the rifle's butt knocked Michael's grip loose. Michael held the hunter's shirt. Sandler was trying to scramble away from him, and again the rifle butt struck Michael, this time across the collarbone. Michael fell backward, his vision still blinded by blue whorls, and he felt the wall's razors bite into his shoulders. The rifle went off once more, the spark of fire leaping from its barrel but the bullet going wild. Michael flung himself onto Sandler again, and drove him against the razors. Again Sandler screamed in pain, and terror was mingled in the cry as well. Michael got hold of the rifle, hung on to it as Sandler fought wildly. Leather-gloved fingers jabbed for Michael's eyes, grabbed his hair, and wrenched it. Michael struck his fist into the hunter's body, and heard a *whoosh* as the air exploded from the man's lungs.

They fought on their knees in the corridor, the car swaying and the razors at their backs. The rifle was between them, both men trying to use it as leverage to get to their feet. It was a silent struggle, with death awaiting the loser. Michael got one foot under him. He was about to haul himself up when Sandler's fist struck him hard in the solar plexus and knocked him down again. Sandler got his knee up, and it cracked Michael under the chin. The rifle pressed down across Michael's throat with all of Sandler's weight behind it. Michael struggled but he couldn't push the hunter off. He reached up, grasped Sandler's head, and shoved the man's face against the razored wall beside him. Sandler howled with agony, and the weight was gone from atop Michael.

Sandler scrambled to his feet, the rifle still in his grip. Michael reached out, snagged one of his ankles, and made him reel into the opposite wall. Sandler had had enough of his maze; he wrenched his foot out of Michael's grasp and staggered along the corridor, stumbling against the walls and bellowing with pain as the razors slashed him. Michael heard him fumbling with a doorknob, trying to get it open with a blood-slick hand, and at once he was on his feet going after the hunter.

Sandler threw his shoulder against the door. It burst open, flooding the corridor with harsh sunlight. The razors—hundreds of them on either side—glinted in the glare, and some of them were smeared with crimson. Michael was blinded anew, but he could see well enough to make out Sandler's silhouette framed in the doorway. He lunged forward and crashed into the hunter, the force of the blow taking them both through the doorway and onto the car's open-air platform.

Sandler, his face slashed to bloody ribbons and his eyes blinded by the sun, screamed, "Kill him! Kill him!" to the soldier who'd been standing guard on the platform. The man was momentarily stunned by the sight of the two gore-splattered figures who'd exploded from the car, and his Luger was still holstered. His hand went to the holster flap and unsnapped it, then he gripped the gun and started to pull it out.

Squinting in the glare, Michael saw the soldier as a dark

shape against a field of fire. He kicked the man in the groin before the Luger's barrel could find him, and as the soldier bent over, Michael brought his knee up into the man's face and knocked him backward over the platform's iron railing. The Luger fired into the air as the soldier vanished.

"Help me!" Sandler was on his knees on the platform, screaming to anyone who could hear. But the noise of the wheels silenced his voice. Michael put his foot down on Sandler's rifle, then visored his hand over his eyes to cut the glare: ahead of the platform was the coal tender and the locomotive, the stack spouting a plume of black smoke. Sandler was crouched over, blood dripping from his face, crimson splotches all over his khaki jacket. "Help me!" he shouted, but his voice was feeble. He shivered and moaned, rocking himself back and forth.

"I'm going to kill you," Michael said, in English. Sandler's rocking abruptly stopped. He kept his head lowered, drops of blood tapping to the metal. "I want you to think about a name: Margritta Phillipe. Do you remember her?"

Sandler didn't reply. The train was moving through a green forest once more, outside the boundaries of Berlin. From where Michael and the hunter were, neither the train's engineer nor the fire stoker could see them. Michael prodded Sandler's side with the toe of his shoe. "The Countess Margritta. In Cairo." He felt drained, all used up, and his knees were in jeopardy of buckling. "I hope to God you remember her, because you had her murdered."

Sandler finally looked up, his face lacerated, his eyes swollen into slits. "Who are you?" he rasped, speaking English.

"I was Margritta's friend. Stand up."

"You're . . . not German, are you?"

"Stand up," Michael repeated. He kept his weight on the rifle, but he'd decided against using it. He was going to break Sandler's neck with his bare hands and throw him off the train like a garbage sack. "On your feet. I want you looking at me when I kill you."

"Please . . ." Sandler moaned. His nostrils drooled blood. "Please . . . don't kill me. I've got money. I'll pay you a lot of money."

"That doesn't interest me. Get *up!*"

"I can't. Can't stand up." Sandler shivered again, his body crouched forward. "My legs . . . I think my legs are broken."

Michael felt a hot flare of rage course through him. How many men—and women—had Harry Sandler broken for the twisted cause of Nazi Germany? Had their cries for mercy been listened to? Michael thought not. Sandler was anxious to pay a price; so he would. Michael reached down, grasped the back of the hunter's khaki jacket, and started to haul him to his feet.

And in doing so, Michael put his hand into a final snare.

Because Sandler—shamming again, just as he'd shammed his drunkenness—suddenly uncoiled, his teeth gritted with fury, and the blade of the knife he'd drawn from inside his right boot glinted with yellow sunlight.

The knife came up in a vicious blur, its point aimed at the center of Michael Gallatin's stomach.

Less than two inches from penetration, the blade was checked. A hand seized Sandler's wrist, clamping tight. Sandler stared at that hand, his slitted eyes stunned.

The hand was not quite human, but neither was it fully an animal's claw. It was streaked with black hair, the fingers beginning to contort and retract into talons. Sandler gasped, and looked up into the man's face.

The baron's facial bones were shifting, the nose and mouth extending into a dark-haired muzzle. The mouth strained open, making room for the fangs as they slid, dripping saliva from amid the human teeth. Sandler was struck senseless; the knife clattered to the platform. He smelled an animalish reek, the odors of sweat and wolf hair. He opened his mouth to scream.

Michael, his spine already bending, thrust his face forward and sank his fangs into the hunter's throat. With a quick, savage twist of his head, he ripped out flesh and veins and crushed Sandler's windpipe. He pulled his head back, leaving a gaping hole where Sandler's throat had been. The man's eyes blinked and his face twitched, the nerves and muscles losing control. The scent of carnage overwhelmed Michael; he struck again, his fangs winnowing into the scarlet tissue, his head thrashing back and forth as he chewed all the way to the hunter's spinal cord. His fangs crunched on the spine, burst it open, and kept gnawing past the splintered edges. When Michael pulled back from Sandler this time, the hunter's head hung to the body by strands of tough muscle and connective tissue. A moan came from the windpipe's hole, as Sandler's lungs stuttered. Michael, his shirt ripping apart at the seams and his trousers drooping around his lower body, put a foot against the hunter's chest and shoved.

What was left of Harry Sandler toppled backward, and slithered off the speeding train.

Michael spat out a mouthful of flesh and lay on his side, his body between its two poles. He knew he had yet to get to the locomotive and slow the train; a wolf's paws couldn't control levers. He held himself back from a complete change, the wild winds whirling in his mind and the muscles rippling beneath the dark-haired flesh under a human's clothes. His toes ached in the stiff shoes, and his shoulders longed to burst free. Not yet! Michael thought. Not yet! He began to come back, over the primeval distance his body had already traveled, and in perhaps half a minute he sat up, his human skin slick with sweat and his wounded leg full of frost.

He grasped the rifle; there was a bullet in the chamber. Then he stood up, his brain and muscles sluggish, and climbed the ladder to the walkway that went across the top of the coal tender. He crouched to the locomotive, saw the engineer and fire stoker at work beneath the engine's overhang, and then he eased down the ladder into the locomotive.

When the two men saw him, they instantly lifted their hands in surrender; they were drivers, not fighters. "Off the train," Michael said, speaking in German again. He motioned with the rifle. *"Now."* The fire stoker jumped, rolling down a bluff into the woods. The engineer hesitated, his eyes wide with fear, until Michael pressed the rifle barrel to his throat. Then, preferring a shock to the bones instead of a bullet through the neck, the engineer leaped from the locomotive.

Michael grasped the red-handled throttle and cut the engine's speed. He leaned out and saw the bridge over the Havel River approaching. In the distance stood the towers of the Reichkronen. Here was as good a place as any. He throttled down and climbed up onto the top of the coal tender once more. The locomotive neared the bridge, its wheels grinding a slower rhythm. A steam valve was screaming, but Michael had no time to worry about that. The train was still going to cross the bridge at a good clip. He stood up, one hand clasped to his wounded thigh. The railroad bridge narrowed, and dark green water beckoned him. He spat out another piece of skin; Sandler's flesh was caught in his teeth. He hoped the river was deep under the bridge. If not, he'd soon be kissing mud.

Michael took a deep breath, and jumped.

3

The morning sun was warm and placid on Chesna's face, but inside a storm raged. She stood on the grassy riverbank in front of the Reichkronen, watching the rowboats slowly move with the current, then against it. They had been dragging the river for over four hours, but Chesna knew the nets would only find mud and river grass. Wherever the baron was, it was not at the bottom of the Havel.

"I tell you, it's a lie," Mouse said, standing next to Chesna. He was speaking quietly, because the search for the Baron von Fange had attracted a throng of onlookers. "Why would he have come down here, alone? And, besides, he wouldn't have gotten drunk. Damn it, I knew I shouldn't have let him out of my sight." The little man scowled and fretted. "Somebody had to take care of the fool!"

Chesna's tawny eyes watched the progress of the rowboats, the soft breeze stirring her golden hair. She wore a black dress: her trademark color, not her mourning suit. Soldiers had searched the banks several miles downriver, in case the body had washed up in the shallows. It was of no use, she thought. This was a sham; but whose sham, and why? One possibility had occurred to her, and sent shocks of alarm through her nerves: he'd been caught while exploring Jerek Blok's suite and taken away for questioning. If that were so, Colonel Blok hadn't given anything away when he'd told Chesna earlier this morning that the police had been summoned to start dragging the river. Other thoughts gnawed at her: if the baron broke under torture, he might tell everything he knew. Her own neck, and the necks of others in her finely tuned anti-Nazi organization, might be destined for piano-wire nooses. So should she stay here and continue to play the role of worry-wrought fiancée, or get out while she could? And there was the matter of Blok and Frankewitz, as well; the colonel had told a Gestapo doctor he wanted Theo von Frankewitz able to answer questions within twelve hours. That time limit was ticking away.

The river nets were not going to find Baron von Fange. Perhaps he was already snared in a net, and perhaps a net was about to enshroud her and her friends, too. I've got to get out, she decided. Make up some excuse. Get to the airport and my plane and try to make it to Switzerland . . .

Mouse glanced over his shoulder and inwardly quaked. Coming toward them were Colonel Blok and the monstrous man who wore polished jackboots. He felt like a pigeon about to be plucked and boiled in oil. But he knew the truth now: his friend—the baron, ha!—had been right. It was Hitler who had killed Mouse's wife and family, and it was men like Jerek Blok who were Hitler's weapons. Mouse slid his hand into the pocket of his perfectly creased gray trousers and touched the Iron Cross there. It had sharp edges.

"Chesna?" Blok called. The sun glinted off his silver teeth. "Any results?"

"No." She tried to keep the wariness out of her voice. "They haven't found so much as a shoe."

Blok, wearing a crisp black SS uniform, positioned himself on Chesna's other side, and Boots stood like a mountain behind Mouse. The colonel shook his head. "They won't find him, I'm afraid. The current's very strong here. If he went in anywhere near this point, he might be miles downriver by now. Or snagged on an underwater log, or caught between rocks, or . . ." He noted that Chesna looked pallid. "I'm sorry, my dear. I didn't mean to be so vivid."

She nodded. Mouse could hear the huge man breathing like a bellows behind him, and drops of sweat fell from his underarms. Chesna said, "I haven't seen Harry this morning. I would've thought he'd be interested in all this."

"I called his room just a few minutes ago," Blok said. "I told him what must've happened to the baron." Blok squinted in the glare off the gently rippling water. "Harry isn't feeling too well. Sore throat, he said. I think he's planning on sleeping most of the day . . . but he did tell me to convey his condolences."

"I don't think we know the baron's dead yet, do we?" Chesna asked coldly.

"No, we don't," Blok agreed. "But two witnesses said they saw him stumbling along the riverbank, and—"

"Yes, yes, I know all that! But they didn't see him fall into the river, did they?"

"One of them thought he heard a splash," Blok reminded her. He reached out and touched Chesna's elbow, but she pulled away. His fingers lingered in midair for a few seconds, then he dropped his hand. "I know you . . . had strong feelings for the man, Chesna. I'm sure you're quite upset as well," he said to Mouse. "But facts are facts, aren't they? If the baron didn't fall into the river and drown, then where is—"

"We've got something!" shouted one of the men in a rowboat, about forty yards offshore. He and his companion began to pull mightily at their dredge. "It's heavy, whatever it is!"

"The net's probably caught on a sunken log," Blok said to Chesna. "I'm afraid the current carried the baron's body far down—"

The net broke the surface. In its folds was a human body, dark with clinging mud.

Blok's mouth hung open.

"We've got him!" the man in the rowboat shouted, and Chesna felt her heart swell. "My God!" came the man's voice. "He's *alive!*" The two men struggled to pull the human body up over the rowboat's side, and the muddy figure splashed in the water and heaved itself in.

Blok took three steps forward. Water and mud swirled around his boots. "Impossible!" he gasped. "It's . . . utterly *impossible!*"

The onlookers, who'd been expecting a soggy corpse, if anything, surged closer as the rowboat angled toward the riverbank. The man who'd just been hauled from a wet grave pushed aside the folds of the net to get his legs free. *"Impossible!"* Chesna heard Colonel Blok whisper; he glanced back at Boots, his face white as cheese. Mouse gave a joyful cry when he saw the black hair and green eyes of the man in the rowboat, and he ran out into the water in his creased trousers to help pull the craft to shore.

As the boat keel bit solid earth, Michael Gallatin stepped out. His shoes squeaked, and mud clung to what used to be a white shirt. He still wore his bow tie.

"Good God!" Mouse said, stretching to put his arm around the man's shoulders. "We thought we'd lost you!"

Michael nodded. His lips were gray, and he was shivering. The water had been quite chilly.

Chesna couldn't move. But then she remembered herself, and rushed forward to throw her arms around the baron. He winced, supporting his weight on one leg, and he clasped his muddy arms to her back. "You're alive, you're alive!" Chesna said. "Oh, thank God you're alive!" She summoned tears, and they trickled down her cheeks.

Michael inhaled Chesna's fresh aroma. The chill of the river had kept him from passing out during the long swim, but now the weakness was catching up with him. The last hundred yards, then a short underwater swim to get himself tangled in the dredging net, had been brutal agony. Someone stood behind Chesna; Michael looked into the eyes of Colonel Jerek Blok.

"Well, well," the colonel said with a brittle smile. "Returned from the dead, have you? Boots, I do believe we've just witnessed a miracle. How did the angels roll away your stone, Baron?"

Chesna snapped, "Leave him alone! Can't you see he's exhausted?"

"Oh yes, I can see he's exhausted. What I *can't* see is why he isn't dead! Baron, I'd say you were underwater for almost six hours. Have you grown gills?"

"Not quite," Michael answered. His wounded thigh was numb, but the bleeding had ceased. "I had this." He lifted his right hand. In it was a hollow reed, about three feet long. "I'm afraid I was careless. I had too much to drink last night, and I went for a walk. I must've slipped. Anyway, I fell in and the current took me." He wiped mud from his cheek with his forearm. "It's amazing how you can sober up when you realize you're about to drown. Something trapped my leg. A log, I think. Gave me a nasty slash on the thigh. You see?"

"Go on," Blok commanded.

"I couldn't get loose. And the way I was held under, I couldn't lift my head to the surface. Luckily I was lying near some reeds. I uprooted one, bit off the end, and breathed through it."

"Very lucky, indeed," Blok said. "Did you learn that trick in commando school, Baron?"

Michael looked shocked. "No, Colonel. Boy Scouts."

"And you've been underwater for almost six hours? Breathing through a damned *reed?*"

"This 'damned reed,' as you put it, is going home with me. I may gild it and have it mounted. One never knows one's limits until life is put to the test. Isn't that right?"

Blok started to reply, then thought better of it. He glanced around at the people who had come forward. "Welcome back to the living, Baron," he said, his eyes cold. "You'd best take a shower. You smell very fishy." He turned and stalked away, followed by Boots, but then stopped abruptly and addressed the baron again. "You'd better hold on to your reed, sir. Miracles are few and far between."

"Oh, don't worry," Michael said; he couldn't turn down the opportunity. "I'll hold on to it with an iron fist."

Blok stood very still, ramrod stiff. Michael felt Chesna's arms tighten around him. Her heart was pounding. "Thank you for your concern, Colonel," Michael said.

Still, Blok didn't move. Michael knew those two words were wheeling in the man's brain. Was it a figure of speech, or a taunt? They stared at each other for a few seconds, like two beasts of prey. If Michael was a wolf, Jerek Blok was a silver-toothed panther. And then the silence broke, and Blok smiled faintly and nodded. "Good health to you, Baron," he said, and walked up the riverbank toward the Reichkronen. Boots glared at Michael for perhaps three seconds longer—enough to convey the message that war had been declared—and then followed the colonel.

Two German officers, one wearing a magnifying monocle, came forward and offered to help Michael to his suite. Supported between them, Michael limped up the riverbank with Chesna and Mouse behind him. In the hotel lobby the flustered and red-faced manager appeared to say how sorry he was for the baron's misfortune, and that a wall would be put up along the riverbank to prevent such future calamities; he suggested the services of the hotel physician, but Michael declined. Would a bottle of the hotel's finest brandy help to soothe the baron's injuries? The baron said he thought that would be a perfect balm.

As soon as the door of Chesna's suite closed and the German officers were gone, Michael eased his muddy body down onto a white chaise longue. "Where were you?" Chesna demanded.

"And don't give us that six-hours-in-the-river crap, either!" Mouse said. He poured himself a shot of hundred-year-old brandy, then took a glass to Michael. "What the hell happened to you?"

Michael drank down the brandy. It was like inhaling fire. "I took a train ride," he said. "As Harry Sandler's guest. Sandler's dead. I'm alive. That's it." He undid his bow tie and began to strip off his tattered shirt. Red razor slashes streaked his shoulders and back. "Colonel Blok assumed Sandler would kill me. Imagine his surprise."

"Why would Sandler want to kill *you?* He doesn't know who you really are!"

"Sandler wants—*wanted*—to marry you. So he tried his best to get me out of the way. Blok went along with it. Nice friends you have, Chesna."

"Blok may not be my friend very much longer. The Gestapo has Theo von Frankewitz."

431

Michael listened intently as Chesna told him about the phone call Blok had made. In light of that fact, his remark about "iron fist" seemed rather reckless. Frankewitz would sing like a bird once the Gestapo went to work on him. And though Frankewitz did not know Michael's name, his artist's eye—however bruised and bloodshot—would remember Michael's face. That description would be enough to bring Jerek Blok and the Gestapo down on all of them.

Michael stood up. "We've got to leave here as soon as we can."

"And go where? Out of Germany?" Mouse asked hopefully.

"For you, yes. For me, I'm afraid not." He looked at Chesna. "I have to get to Norway. To Skarpa Island. I believe Dr. Hildebrand's invented a new type of weapon, and he's testing it there on prisoners of war. What that weapon has to do with Iron Fist I don't know, but I'm going to find out. Can you get me there?"

"I don't know. I'll need time to arrange the connections."

"How much time?"

She shook her head. "It's difficult to say. A week, at the least. The fastest route to Norway would be by plane. There'll be fuel stops to arrange. Plus food and supplies for us. Then, from the coast of Norway, we'd have to use a boat to get to Skarpa. A place like that is going to be under tight security: offshore mines, a coastal radar station, and God only knows what else."

"You misunderstand me," Michael said. "You won't be going to Norway. You'll be getting yourself and Mouse out of the country. Once Blok realizes I'm a British agent, he'll figure out that your best performances have not been in films."

"You need a pilot," Chesna replied. "I've been flying my own plane since I was nineteen. I have ten years of experience. Trying to find another pilot to take you to Norway would be impossible."

Michael recalled Sandler mentioning that Chesna had flown her own stunts during one of her films. A daredevil, he'd called her; Michael was inclined to think that Chesna van Dorne was one of the most fascinating women he'd ever met—and certainly one of the most beautiful. She was the kind of woman who didn't need a man to direct her, or to praise the insecurity out of her. She *had* no insecurities, as far as Michael could see. No wonder Sandler had wanted her so badly; the hunter had felt the urge to tame Chesna. To survive this long as a secret agent in the midst of the enemy camp, Chesna had to be someone special indeed.

"You need a pilot," Chesna repeated, and Michael had to agree. "I'll fly you to Norway. I can arrange to find someone with a boat. From there, you're on your own."

"What about me?" Mouse asked. "Hell, I don't want to go to Norway!"

"I'll put you in the pipeline," Chesna told him. "The route to Spain," she clarified, when he continued to look puzzled. "When you get there, my friends will help you find a way to England."

"All right. Fine with me. The sooner I get out of this viper's nest, the better I'll feel."

"Then we'd best get packed and out of here right now." Chesna went to her room to start packing, and Michael went to the bathroom and got the mud off his face and out of his hair. He took off his trousers and looked at the wound across his thigh; the bullet had grazed cleanly, cutting no muscles, but it had left a scarlet-edged groove in the flesh. He knew what had to be done. "Mouse?" he called. "Bring me the brandy." He looked at his hands, the fingers and palms crisscrossed with razor cuts. Some of them were deep, and would require burning attention as well. Mouse brought him the decanter, and made a face when he saw the bullet wound. "Get the bottom sheet off my bed," Michael instructed. "Tear a couple of strips out of it, will you?" Mouse hurried away.

Michael first washed his hands in brandy: a task that made him wince with pain. He would smell like a drunkard, but the wounds had to be cleansed. He washed the cuts on his shoulders, then turned his attention to his grooved thigh. He poured some brandy on a washcloth and pressed the wet cloth against the wound before he had too much time to think about it.

He had need of a second washcloth, and this one he jammed between his teeth. Then he poured the rest of the golden fire over the red-edged wound.

"Yes, that's what I want from Frankewitz," Jerek Blok was saying into the telephone in his suite. "A description. Is Captain Halder there? He's a good man; he knows how to get answers. Tell Captain Halder that I want the information *now*." He snorted with exasperation. "Well, what do I care about Frankewitz's condition? I said I want the information now. This moment. I'll stay on the line." He heard the door open and looked up as Boots entered. "Yes?" Blok urged.

"Herr Sandler's train hasn't passed through the rail yard yet. It's over ten minutes late." Boots had been downstairs on another telephone, speaking to the rail master at the Berlin yards.

"Sandler told me he was putting the baron on the train. Yet the train's still on the rails somewhere and Baron von Fange comes up out of the river like a damned toad frog! What do you make of it, Boots?"

"I don't know, sir. As you said, it's impossible."

Blok grunted and shook his head. "Breathing through a hollow reed! The man's got nerve, I'll say that for him! Boots, I'm getting a very bad feeling about this." Someone came on the line. "I'm waiting to hear from Captain Halder!" he said. "This is Colonel Jerek Blok, that's who this is! Now get off the phone!" Red splotches had surfaced on Blok's pale cheeks. He drummed his fingers, reached for a fountain pen and a sheet of pale blue notepaper with the hotel's name on it. Boots stood at ease, hands clasped before him, waiting for the colonel's next command.

"Halder?" Blok said after another pause. "Do you have what I need?" He listened. "I don't care if the man's dying! Did you get the information? All right, tell me what you have." He picked up the pen and held its point poised. Then he began to write: *Well-dressed man. Tall. Slim. Blond-haired. Brown eyes.* "What? Repeat that," Blok said. He wrote: *A true gentleman.* "What's that supposed to mean? Yes, I know you're not a mind reader. Listen, Halder: go back to him and go over this once again. Make sure he's not lying. Tell him . . . oh, tell him we can inject him with something that'll keep him alive if we're sure he's being truthful. Wait just a moment." He put his hand over the receiver and looked at Boots. "Do you have the key to Sandler's suite?"

"Yes, sir." Boots brought the key from his shirt pocket.

"Give it to me." Blok took the key. He had promised Sandler he would feed Blondi her morning chunk of raw meat; he was one of the few people that Blondi seemed to abide, other than her master. At least she wouldn't fly at him when the door was unlocked and the cage opened on its trip wire. "All right, Halder," Blok went on. "Get back to him and go over it one more time, then call me. I'm at the Reichkronen." He gave Halder the telephone number, then hung up. He tore the blue sheet of notepaper off its pad. *Blond-haired. Brown eyes.* If that was true, it certainly didn't match the baron's description. What had he been thinking? he asked himself. That the baron—and possibly Chesna, too—was somehow mixed up in this? Ridiculous! But the baron's mention of "iron fist" had almost made him shit in his pants. Of course it was just a phrase. A common phrase anyone might use. But the baron . . . there was something not right about him. And now this situation with Sandler's train off schedule, and the baron coming up out of the river. Of course the baron had been taken to Sandler's train. *Hadn't* he?

"I've got to feed that damned bird," Blok said. The bloody meat was kept in a refrigerator in Sandler's kitchen. "Stay here and listen for the phone," he told Boots, and then he left his suite and strode to the door down the hall.

4

Chesna's chauffeur had brought the Mercedes from the Reichkronen's garage to the courtyard, and as Wilhelm and Mouse loaded the suitcases into the trunk, Chesna and Michael paused in the lobby to say their goodbyes to the manager.

"I'm so sorry about that dreadful accident," the florid-faced man said with a ceremonious wringing of his hands. "I do hope you'll return to the Reichkronen for another visit, Baron?"

"I'll look forward to it." Michael was clean and freshly shaved, and he wore a dark blue pin-striped suit with a white shirt and a gray-striped necktie. "Besides, the accident was my own fault. I'm afraid I . . . uh . . . was a little too relaxed to go roaming along the riverbank."

"Well, thank God for your presence of mind! I trust the brandy was satisfactory?"

"Oh, yes. It was fine, thank you." In Chesna's suite the maid would find a washcloth that looked as if it had been bitten almost in two, and a strip of the bed's bottom sheet now bandaged Michael's thigh.

"Fräulein van Dorne, I wish you and the baron the best of luck," the manager said with a crisp bow. Chesna thanked him, and slid a generous amount of appreciation into the man's palm.

Chesna and Michael walked through the lobby, arm in arm. Their plans were set: not for a honeymoon excursion, but for a flight to Norway. Michael felt pressure gnawing at him. Today was April 24, and Chesna had said they would need a week at the least to get their fuel stops and security precautions arranged through her anti-Nazi network. With the Allied invasion of Europe set for the first week of June, time might become a critical factor.

They were almost to the front entrance when Michael

heard the thump of heavy footsteps coming up behind them. His muscles tensed, and Chesna felt the tension ripple through his body. A hand grasped his shoulder, stopping him about ten feet short of the doorway.

Michael looked up, into the bland, square face of Boots. The huge man released Michael's shoulder. "My apologies, Baron, *Fräulein*," he said. "But Colonel Blok would like to have a word with you, please."

Blok strolled up, smiling, his hands in his pockets. "Ah, good! Boots caught you before you could get away! I had no idea you were leaving. I only found out when I tried to call your room, Chesna."

"We just decided about an hour ago." There was no hint of nervousness in her voice; a true professional, Michael thought.

"Really? Well, I can't say I'm surprised. Because of the incident, I mean." His gray, lizard eyes moved to Michael and then, heavy-lidded, returned to Chesna. "But surely you didn't plan on leaving before saying goodbye to me? I've always thought of myself as part of your family, Chesna." His smile broadened. "An uncle, perhaps, who meddles more than he ought to. Yes?" He withdrew his right hand from his pocket. Held between the thumb and first finger was a golden feather. Michael recognized it, and his stomach clenched. Blok, still smiling, fanned himself with the hawk's feather. "I'd consider it an honor to take you both to lunch. Surely you weren't thinking of leaving before you ate, were you?" The feather twitched back and forth, like a cat's whiskers.

Chesna stood her ground, though her heart was pounding and she smelled disaster. "My car's packed. We really should be going."

"I've never known you to pass up a leisurely lunch, Chesna. Perhaps the baron's habits have rubbed off on you?"

Michael took the initiative. He held his hand out. "Colonel Blok, it was very good meeting you. I hope you'll attend our wedding?"

Blok grasped Michael's hand and shook it. "Oh, yes,"

the colonel said. "Two events I never miss are weddings and funerals."

Michael and Chesna went through the doorway and started down the granite stairs. The colonel and Boots followed. Mouse was waiting, holding the Mercedes's door open for Chesna, and Wilhelm was putting the last suitcase into the trunk.

Blok's trying to stall us, Michael thought. Why? The colonel had obviously found Blondi's carcass and other signs of an intruder in Sandler's suite. If he was going to make an arrest, why hadn't he done so already? Michael walked Chesna around to her side of the Mercedes; Blok followed right behind them. Michael felt Chesna tremble. She also knew the game had taken a dangerous turn.

Chesna was about to slide into the car when Blok reached past Michael and took her elbow. She looked at the colonel, the sun on her face.

"For old times' sake," Blok said, and he leaned forward and kissed her lightly on the cheek.

"Until later, Jerek," Chesna answered, regaining some of her composure. She got into the car and Mouse closed the door, then went around to open the door for Michael. Blok followed on his heels while Boots stood a few yards away.

"It's been a pleasure, Baron," Blok said. Michael got into the Mercedes, but Blok held the door. Wilhelm was sliding behind the wheel and putting the key into the ignition. "I hope you and Chesna will enjoy the future you've chosen." He glanced up toward the courtyard entrance. Michael had already heard it: the low growl of a vehicle approaching across the pontoon bridge. "Oh, this I forgot!" Blok smiled, his silver teeth gleaming. "Sandler's servant got control of the train. They found Sandler's body, too. The poor man; an animal had already gotten to him. Now explain this to me, Baron: how could someone like you, a pampered civilian with no combat experience, have killed Harry Sandler? Unless, of course, you're not who you seem to be?" His hand went to the inside of his black SS jacket, as a truck carrying a dozen Nazi soldiers entered the courtyard portal.

Michael had no time to play the offended baron; he shoved his foot into the pit of the colonel's stomach and knocked

438

him backward to the paving stones. As Blok fell, a pistol was already in his hand. Mouse saw the glint of the Luger's barrel, aiming at the baron. Something inside him roared, and he stepped into the line of fire and kicked at Blok's gun hand.

There was a sharp *crack!* as the pistol went off, and in the next instant Blok's hand had been knocked open and the Luger spun away.

Boots was coming. Michael raised up out of the car, grabbed Mouse, and hauled him in. "Go!" he shouted at Wilhelm, and the chauffeur sank his foot to the floorboard. As the Mercedes lunged forward, Michael slammed his door shut and a hobnailed boot knocked a dent in its metal the size of a dinner plate.

"Get the gun! Get the gun!" Blok was yelling as he scrambled to his feet. Boots ran for the Luger and scooped it up.

As Wilhelm tore the Mercedes across the courtyard, a bullet hit the rear windshield and showered Michael, Chesna, and Mouse with glass. "Stop them!" Blok commanded the soldiers. "Stop that car!" More shots were fired. The left rear tire blew. The front windshield shattered. And then the Mercedes was crossing the pontoon bridge, its engine screaming and steam spouting from a bullet hole in the hood. Michael looked back, saw several of the soldiers running after them as the truck turned around in the courtyard. Rifles and submachine guns fired, and the Mercedes shuddered under the blows. The car reached the opposite bank, but the right rear tire exploded and now flames were licking up around the hood. "The engine's going to blow!" Wilhelm shouted as he watched the oil-gauge needle plummet and the temperature-gauge needle riot past the red line. The rear end was slewing back and forth, and he could hold the wheel no longer. The Mercedes went off the road and into the forest, angling down an incline and crashing through thick underbrush. Wilhelm fought the brakes, and the Mercedes grazed past an oak tree and came to rest amid a stand of evergreens.

"Everyone out!" Wilhelm told them. He opened the driver's door, grasped its arm rest, and popped a latch beneath it. The door's leather interior covering fell away, exposing a compartment that held a submachine gun and three ammunition clips. As Michael got out of the car and pulled Mouse along with him, Chesna opened a compartment beneath the rear seat that yielded a Luger. "This way!" Wilhelm said, motioning them farther down the incline into thicker tangles of vegetation. They started into it, Chesna leading the way, and about forty seconds later the Mercedes exploded, raining pieces of metal and glass through the trees. Michael smelled blood. He looked at his hands and found a thick smear of red on the fingers of his right hand. And then he looked back over his shoulder, and saw that Mouse had fallen to his knees.

Blok's shot, Michael realized. Just below Mouse's heart, the shirt was soaked with crimson. Mouse's face was pallid, and glistened with sweat.

Michael knelt beside him. "Can you stand up?" He heard his voice quaver.

Mouse made a gasping noise, his eyes damp. "I don't know," he said. "I'll try." He did, and got all the way up before his knees caved in. Michael caught him before he fell, and supported him.

"What's wrong?" Chesna had stopped and come back to them. "Is he—" She silenced, because she saw the blood on the little man's shirt.

"They're coming!" Wilhelm said. "They're right behind us!" He held the submachine gun at hip level and clicked off the safety as his gaze scanned the woods. They could hear the voices of the soldiers, getting closer.

"Oh no." Mouse blinked. "Oh no, I've messed myself up. Some valet I turned out to be, huh?"

"We'll have to leave him!" Wilhelm said. "Come on!"

"I'm not leaving my friend."

"Don't be a fool!" Wilhelm looked at Chesna. "I'm going, whether he comes along or not." He turned and sprinted into the forest, away from the advancing soldiers.

Chesna peered up the incline. She could see four or five soldiers coming down through the brush. "Whatever you're going to do," she told Michael, "you'd better do it fast."

He did. He picked Mouse up across his shoulders in a

fireman's carry, and he and Chesna hurried into the shadows of the trees. "This way! Over here!" they heard one of the soldiers shouting to his companions. A burst of submachine gun fire came from ahead, followed by a number of rifle shots. There was a shout: "We've got one of them!"

Chesna crouched against a tree trunk, and Michael stood behind her. She pointed, but Michael's eyes had already seen: in a clearing just ahead, two soldiers with rifles stood over Wilhelm's writhing body. Chesna lifted her pistol, took careful aim, and squeezed the trigger. Her target staggered back, a hole at his heart, and fell. The second soldier fired wildly into the trees and started to run for cover. Chesna, her face grim, shot the man in the hip and crippled him. As he fell, her next bullet went through his throat. Then she was on her feet, a professional killer in a sleek black dress, and she ran to Wilhelm's side. Michael followed, quickly making the same judgment as Chesna: Wilhelm had been shot in the stomach and the chest, and there was no hope for him. The man moaned and writhed, his eyes squeezed shut with agony.

"I'm sorry," Chesna whispered, and she placed the Luger's barrel against Wilhelm's skull, shielded her face with her other hand, and delivered the mercy bullet.

She picked up the submachine gun and pushed the Luger down into Michael's waistband. Its heat scorched his belly. Chesna's tawny eyes were wet and rimmed with red, but her face was calm and composed. One of her black high heels had broken, and she kicked the shoe off and threw its partner into the woods. "Let's go," she said tersely, and started off. Michael, with Mouse across his shoulders, kept pace with her though his thigh wound had opened again. His exhaustion was held at bay only by the realization of what would happen to them once they fell into the Gestapo's embrace. Any hope of finding the meaning of Iron Fist and communicating that secret to the Allies would be lost.

There was a movement on the left: the glint of sunlight on a belt buckle. Chesna whirled and sprayed a burst of fire at the soldier, who dropped to his belly in the leaves. "Over here!" the soldier shouted, and fired two bullets that thunked into the trees as Chesna and Michael changed direction and ran. Something came flying through the woods at them, hit a tree trunk at their backs, and bounced off. Three seconds later there was a ringing blast that knifed their eardrums, the concussion sending leaves flying. Dense white smoke billowed up. A smoke grenade, Michael realized, marking their position for the other soldiers. Chesna kept going, shielding her face as they tore through a tangle of thorns. Michael heard shouts from behind them, on their left and right. A bullet whizzed past his head like an enraged hornet. Chesna, her face streaked with thorn slashes, stopped in her tracks in underbrush near the edge of the road. Two more trucks had pulled off, and were disgorging their cargo of soldiers. Chesna motioned for Michael to back up, then she guided him in another direction. They struggled up a hillside through dense green foliage, then down again into a ravine.

Three soldiers appeared at the top, silhouetted against the sun. Chesna fired her weapon, knocked two of the men down, and the third fled. Another smoke grenade exploded on their right, the acrid white smoke flooding across the ravine. The hounds were closing in, Michael thought. He could sense them running from shadow to shadow, salivating as their gun sights trained in. Chesna ran along the bottom of the ravine, bruising her feet on stones but neither pausing nor registering pain. Michael was right behind her, the smoke swirling around them. Mouse was still breathing, but the back of Michael's neck was damp with blood. The hollow *crump* of a third smoke grenade went off amid the trees to their left. Above the forest, dark banners of crows circled and screamed.

Figures were darting down the hillside and into the smoke. Chesna caught sight of them, and her quick spray of bullets drove them back. A rifle slug ricocheted off an edge of rock beside her, and stone splinters jabbed her arm. She looked around, her face glistening with sweat and her eyes wild; Michael saw in them the fear of a trapped animal. She ran on, crouched low, and he followed on cramping legs.

The ravine ended, and yielded to forest once more. Amid the trees a stream snaked between mossy banks. A bend of the road lay ahead, and beneath it was a stone culvert through which the steam rushed, its opening all but clogged by mud and vegetation. Michael glanced back and saw soldiers emerging from the smoky ravine. Other figures were coming down the hillside, taking cover behind the trees. Chesna was already on her knees, starting to push herself into the muddy culvert. "Come on!" she urged him. "Hurry!"

It was a tight squeeze. And, looking at it, Michael knew he could never get himself and Mouse through there before the soldiers reached them. His decision was made in an instant; as Chesna lay on her stomach and winnowed into the culvert, Michael turned away and ran out of the stream bed into the woods. Chesna kept going, through the slime, and the mud and underbrush closed behind her.

A rifle bullet sliced a pine branch over Michael's head. He zigzagged between the trees, until a smoke grenade exploded almost in front of him and turned him aside. These hunters, he thought grimly, knew their work. His lungs were laboring, his strength sweating away. He tore through a green thicket, the sunlight lying around him in golden bars. He struggled up a hillside and down again—and then his feet slipped on a carpet of dead brown leaves and he and Mouse slid into a tangled nightmare of blue-black thorns that snagged their clothes and flesh.

Michael thrashed to get loose. He saw soldiers coming, from all sides. He looked at Mouse, and saw blood creeping from the little man's mouth.

"Please . . . please," Mouse was gasping. "Please . . . don't let them torture me. . . ."

Michael got his hands free and pulled the Luger from his waistband. He shot the first soldier he aimed at, and the others hit the ground. His next two shots went wild through the trees but the fourth clanged off a Nazi helmet. Michael took aim at a white face and squeezed the trigger. Nothing happened; the Luger's magazine was empty.

Submachine-gun fire kicked through the thorns, showering Michael and Mouse with dirt. A voice shouted, "Don't kill them, you idiots!" It was Jerek Blok, crouched somewhere up on the hillside. Then: "Throw out your gun, Baron!

We're all around you! One word from me and you'll be cut to pieces!"

Michael felt dazed, his body on the verge of collapse. He looked again at Mouse, and damned himself for pulling his friend into this deadly vortex. Mouse's eyes were pleading, and Michael recognized the eyes of Nikita, as the injured wolf lay on the railroad tracks a long, long time ago.

"I'm waiting, Baron!" Blok called.

"Don't . . . let them torture me," Mouse whispered. "I couldn't stand it. I'd tell them everything, and I . . . wouldn't be able to help it." His thorn-scarred hand clutched at Michael's arm, and a faint smile played across his mouth. "You know . . . I just realized . . . you never told me your real name."

"It's Michael."

"Michael," Mouse repeated. "Like the angel, huh?"

Perhaps a dark angel, Michael thought. An angel to whom killing was second nature. It occurred to him, quite suddenly, that a werewolf never died of old age; and neither would the man Michael had known as Mouse.

"Baron! Five seconds and we start shooting!"

The Gestapo would find a way to keep Mouse alive, Michael knew. They'd pump him full of drugs, and then they'd torture him to death. It would be an ugly way to die. Michael knew the same fate awaited him; but he was no stranger to pain, and if there was one chance that he might be able to get away and continue his mission, he had to take it.

So be it. Michael tossed the Luger out, and it clattered to the ground.

He put his hands to the sides of Mouse's head and took the little man's weight on top of him. Tears sprang to his eyes, burning trails down his thorn-scratched cheeks. An angel, he thought bitterly. Oh yes. A damned angel.

"Will you . . . take care of me?" Mouse asked softly, beginning to fall into delirium.

"Yes," Michael answered. "I will."

A moment later Blok's voice again: "Crawl out into the open! Both of you!"

One figure emerged from the thorns. Dusty, bleeding, and

exhausted, Michael lay on his hands and knees as six soldiers with rifles and submachine guns circled him. Blok came striding up, with Boots following. "Where's the other one?" He looked into the thorns, could see the motionless body lying in the coils. "Get him out!" he told two of the soldiers, and they waded into the tangle. "On your feet," Blok said to Michael. "Baron, did you hear me?"

Michael slowly stood up, and stared defiantly into Jerek Blok's eyes.

"Where did the bitch go?" the colonel asked.

Michael didn't answer. He flinched, listening to the sound of Mouse's clothes ripping on the thorns as the soldiers dragged him out.

"Where did the bitch go?" Blok placed the barrel of his Luger underneath Michael's left eye.

"Stop the bullshit," Michael replied, speaking in Russian. He saw the blood drain out of Blok's face. "You won't kill me."

"What did he say?" The colonel looked around for an interpreter. "That was Russian, wasn't it? What did he say?"

"I said," Michael continued in his native tongue, "that you suck donkey cocks and whistle out your ass."

"What the hell did he *say*?" Blok demanded. He glared at Boots. "You spent time on the Russian Front! What did he say?"

"I . . . uh . . . think he said . . . that he owns a donkey and a rooster that sings."

"Is he trying to be funny, or is he insane?"

Michael released a guttural bark, and Blok stepped back two paces. And then Michael looked to his side, at Mouse's corpse. One of the soldiers was trying to get Mouse's closed right fist open. The fingers wouldn't give. Suddenly Boots strode forward, lifted a foot, and smashed it down on the hand. Bones cracked like matchsticks, and Michael stood in shock as Boots crunched his weight down on the hand. When the huge man raised his foot again, the fingers were splayed and broken. There in the palm was a Cross of Iron.

Boots leaned over, started to reach for the medal.

Michael said, in German, "If you touch that, I'll kill you."

The man's voice—sure and steady—made Boots pause. He blinked uncertainly, his hand outstretched to grasp a dead man's last possession. Michael stared at him, smelling the heat of wildness burning in his veins. He was close to the change . . . very, very close. If he wanted it, it was right there within easy reach. . . .

Blok's pistol, held at the colonel's side, came up in a savage arc and thudded into Michael's testicles. Michael gasped in agony and dropped to his knees.

"Now, now, Baron," Blok chided. "Threats are beneath royalty, don't you agree?" He nodded at Boots, who plucked up the Iron Cross into his own fist. "Baron, we're going to get to know each other very well indeed. You may learn to sing in a higher register before I'm done with you. Haul him up, please," he told two soldiers, and the men pulled Michael to his feet. Pain throbbed in Michael's groin, doubling him over; even as a wolf, he wouldn't get very far before he crumpled into an exhausted heap. Now was not the time, or the place. He let the wild call drift away from him, like a fading echo.

"Come on, we've got a distance to travel." Blok walked up the hillside, and the soldiers shoved Michael ahead of them. Other soldiers walked on either side of him, their guns ready. Boots followed at a distance, the Iron Cross in his hand, and a few more soldiers began to drag Mouse's body up toward the road. Michael did not look at Mouse again; the little man was gone, and he would not have to face the torture that awaited.

Blok looked up at the blue sky, and his silver teeth gleamed brightly as he smiled. "Ah, it's a beautiful day, isn't it?" he said, to no one in particular. He would leave a detachment of troops to continue searching for her, and he had no doubt that the bitch would be found soon. She couldn't have gotten very far. After all, she was only a woman. His heart was hurting for being such a fool, but he looked forward to having Chesna in his hands. He had considered himself her agreeable uncle when he'd thought she was a loyal Nazi; now, however, a traitor of Chesna's magnitude merited treatment that was less familial and more familiar. But what a scandal! This must be kept from the newspapers, at all costs! And, also, from the prying eyes and ears of Himmler. So, a question: where to take the baron for interrogation?

Ah, yes! Blok thought. Of course!

He watched as the baron was shoved into the rear of a truck and made to lie down on his back with his hands pinned under him. A soldier sat next to him, with a rifle barrel pressed against his throat.

Blok walked over to confer with the truck driver as other soldiers continued their search in the forest for Germany's Golden Girl.

5

Michael smelled his destination before he saw it. He was still lying on his back on the truck's metal bed, his arms pinned underneath him, with armed soldiers sitting all around. The cargo bay had been covered with gray canvas, shutting off all but a crack of sunlight. His sense of direction was impaired, though he knew they weren't heading into the city; the road was far too rough for the civilian wheels of Berlin. No, this road had been tortured by its share of truck tires and heavy vehicles, and his back muscles gripped with pain every time a rut shook vibrations through the floor.

A strong smell seeped in through the canvas. The soldiers had noticed it as well; some of them shifted nervously and whispered to each other. The odor was getting stronger. He had smelled something akin to it, in North Africa, when he'd come upon a group of British soldiers who'd been hit by a flamethrower. Once the sickly-sweet smell of charred human flesh got up your nostrils, you never forgot it. This smell had burning wood in it, too. Pine wood, Michael thought. Something that burned very hot and fast.

One of the soldiers got up and lurched to the rear of the truck, to be sick. Michael heard two others whispering and caught a word: "Falkenhausen."

His destination was known. Falkenhausen concentration camp. Blok's child.

The smell drifted away. The wind had changed, Michael thought. But what in the name of God had been burning? The truck stopped, and stayed motionless for a moment or two. Over the low grumble of the engine he heard hammers at work. And then the truck continued on about a hundred yards or so, stopped again, and a strident voice shouted, "Bring out the prisoner!"

The canvas was whipped back. Michael was hauled out of the truck, into harsh sunlight, and he stood before a German major of the Waffen SS, a thick-bodied man wearing a black uniform that bulged at the seams. The man had a fleshy, ruddy face with eyes that were as white and hard as diamonds, but with none of their luster. He wore a black, flat-brimmed cap, and his brown hair was cropped to the scalp. Around his girth was a holster that bore a Walther pistol and a baton of ebony rubber: a bone-bruiser.

Michael glanced around. Saw wooden barracks, gray stone walls, dense green treetops beyond them. A new barracks building was going up, and prisoners in striped uniforms were hammering the joints together as guards with submachine guns stood in the shadows. Thick coils of barbed wire formed inner walls, and at the corners of the outer stone walls stood wooden guard towers. He saw an entrance gate, also of wood, and above it the stone arch he'd seen in the framed photograph in Blok's suite. A dark haze hung in the air, slowly drifting over the forest. He caught the scent again: burning flesh.

"Eyes *front!*" the Nazi major shouted, and grasped Michael's chin to jerk his head around.

A soldier jabbed a rifle into his spine. Another soldier wrenched his coat off, then tore his shirt away so hard the pearl buttons flew into the air. Michael's belt was removed, and his pants lowered. His underwear was pulled down. The rifle jabbed him again, in the kidneys. Michael knew what they wanted him to do, but he stared fixedly into the major's colorless eyes and kept both feet on the ground.

"Remove your shoes and socks," the man said.

"Does this mean we're engaged?" Michael asked.

The baton came out of the holster. Its tip pressed against Michael's chin. "Remove your shoes and socks," the major repeated.

Michael caught movement to his left. He glanced in that direction and saw Blok and Boots approaching.

"Eyes *front!*" the major commanded, and swung the baton a short, brutal blow against Michael's wounded thigh. Pain exploded through his leg as the gash burst open again, oozing scarlet, and Michael fell to his knees in the chalky dust. A rifle barrel looked him in the face.

"Baron," Blok said, "I'm afraid you're in our kingdom now. Will you obey Major Krolle, please?"

Michael hesitated, pain pounding in his thigh and beads of sweat on his face. A booted foot was planted on his back and drove him down into the dust. Boots leaned his weight on Michael's spine, making Michael grit his teeth.

"You really do want to cooperate, Baron," Blok went on. Then, to Krolle, "He's a Russian. You know how stubborn those sons of bitches can be."

"We cure stubbornness here," Krolle said, and while Boots held Michael down, two soldiers took off his shoes and socks. Now he was totally naked, and his wrists were clasped behind him with iron manacles. He was hauled to his feet, then shoved in the direction the soldiers wanted him to go. He offered no resistance; it would only lead to broken bones, and he was still exhausted from his battle with Sandler and the flight through the forest. There was no time to mourn Mouse, or to bewail his own predicament; these men meant to torture every shred of information out of him. It was to his advantage, though, that they thought he was an agent of the Soviet Union, because his presence would keep their attention on the East and away from the West.

It was a large camp. Distressingly large, Michael thought. Everywhere stood barracks buildings, most of green-painted wood, and hundreds of tree stumps testified to the fact that Falkenhausen had been carved out of the forest. Michael saw pallid, emaciated faces watching him through narrow windows with hinged shutters. Groups of skinny, bald prisoners passed, herded by guards with submachine guns and rubber batons. Michael noted that almost all the prisoners wore yellow Stars of David pinned to their clothes. His nudity seemed commonplace, and drew no attention. Off in the distance, perhaps two hundred yards, was a camp within the camp, more barracks enclosed by coils of barbed wire. Michael could see what looked like three or four hundred prisoners standing in rows on a dusty parade ground, while a loudspeaker droned on about the Thousand-Year Reich. He saw, in the distance on his left, a squat building of gray stones; from its two chimneys arose columns of dark smoke that drifted toward the forest. He heard the groan and rumble of heavy machinery, though he couldn't see where the noise was coming from. A change in the wind brought another odor to his nostrils: not the burned flesh smell this time, but a reek of unwashed, sweating humanity. In that smell there were notes of decay, corruption, excrement, and blood. Whatever was going on here, he thought as he watched the columns of smoke belch from the chimneys, had more to do with erasure than confinement.

Three trucks came along the road from the direction of the gray stone building, and Michael was ordered to halt. He stood at the roadside, a rifle barrel against his skull, while the trucks approached. Krolle flagged them down and took Blok and Boots around to the back of the first truck. Michael watched them as Krolle spoke to Blok and the major's ruddy face beamed with excitement. "The quality is excellent," Michael heard Krolle say. "In the entire system Falkenhausen's product stands out as the zenith." Krolle ordered a soldier to remove one of the pinewood boxes stacked in the rear of the truck. The soldier began to pry its nails open with his knife. "You'll see I'm continuing the standards of quality you so strongly demanded, Colonel," Krolle went on, and Michael saw Blok nod and smile, pleased with the ass-kissing.

The box's last nail was popped open, and Krolle reached in. "You see? I defy any other camp to match this quality."

Krolle was holding a handful of long, reddish-brown hair. A woman's hair, Michael realized. It was naturally curly. Krolle grinned at Blok, then reached deeper into the box. This time he came up with thick, pale blond locks. "Ah, isn't this one lovely!" Krolle asked. "This will make a grand wig, worth its weight in gold. I'm pleased to tell you our production is up thirty-seven percent. Not a trace of lice in the whole lot. The new delousing spray is a godsend.''

"I'll tell Dr. Hildebrand how well it works," Blok said. He looked into the box, reached down, and brought out a handful of gleaming coppery-colored hair. "Oh, that's just magnificent!''

Michael watched the hair fall from Blok's fingers. It caught the sunlight, and its beauty almost broke Michael's heart. The hair of a woman prisoner, he thought. Where was her body? He caught a hint of the burned smell, and his stomach lurched.

These men—these monsters—could not be allowed to live. He would be damned by God if he knew these things and did not tear the throats out of the men who stood before him, smiling and talking about wigs and production schedules. The cargo bays of all three trucks were loaded with pinewood boxes; loaded with hair, shaved off skulls like fleece off slaughtered lambs.

He could not let these men live.

He took a step forward, brushing past the rifle barrel. "Halt!" the soldier shouted. Krolle, Blok, and Boots turned to look at him, hair still drifting down into the box. "Halt!" the soldier commanded, and drove the barrel into Michael's rib cage.

Such pain was nothing. Michael kept going, his wrists manacled behind him. He stared into the colorless eyes of Major Krolle, and he saw the man flinch and step backward. He felt the fangs aching to slide from his jaws, his facial muscles rippling to give them room.

"Halt, damn you!" The soldier hit him on the back of the head with his rifle barrel, and Michael staggered but kept his balance. He was striding toward the three men, and Boots stepped between him and Colonel Blok. Another soldier, armed with a submachine gun, rushed at Michael and slammed him in the stomach with the gun butt. Michael doubled over and gasped in pain, and the soldier lifted his weapon to strike him across the skull.

The prisoner struck first, bringing his naked knee up into the man's groin with a force that lifted him off his feet and

sent him crashing to the ground. An arm locked around
Michael's throat from behind, squeezing his windpipe. Another man drove a fist into his chest, making his heart
stutter. "Hold him! Hold the bastard!" Krolle barked as
Michael kept thrashing wildly. Krolle lifted the baton and
brought it down on Michael's shoulder. A second blow
dropped him, and a third left him lying in the dust, his lungs
rasping as pain throbbed through his blackening shoulder
and bruised stomach. He hung on the edge of unconsciousness, fighting against the change. Black hair was about to
burst from his pores; he could smell the wildness in his skin,
taste its musky power in his mouth. If he changed here, lying
in the dust, he would be cut open and examined by German
knives. Every part of him—from organs to teeth—would be
tagged and immersed in bottles full of formaldehyde to be
studied by Nazi doctors. He wanted to live, to kill these
men, and so he battled against the change and forced it back
down.

Perhaps a few black wolf hairs had emerged from his
body—on his chest, the insides of his thighs, and his throat—
but they rippled away so fast that no one noticed them, and
even if one of the soldiers had seen, he would've thought his
eyes were playing tricks. Michael lay on his belly, very close
to passing out. He heard Blok say, "Baron, I think you're in
for a very rough visit with us."

Soldiers grasped beneath Michael's arms, pulled him up,
and began to drag him through the dust as he fell into
darkness.

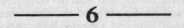

6

"Can you hear me?"

Someone speaking, from the far end of a tunnel. Whose
voice?

"Baron? Can you hear me?"

Darkness upon darkness. Don't answer! he thought. If

you don't answer, whoever's speaking will go away and let you rest!

A light switched on. The light was very bright; Michael could see it through his eyelids. "He's awake," he heard the voice say to someone else in the room. "You see how his pulse has increased? Oh, he knows we're here, all right." It was Blok's voice, he realized. A hand grasped his chin and shook his face. "Come on, come on. Open your eyes, Baron."

He wouldn't. "Give him a drink of water," Blok said, and immediately a bucket of cold water was flung into Michael's face.

He sputtered, his body involuntarily shivering with the chill, and his eyes opened. The light—a spot lamp of brutal wattage, drawn up close to his face—made him squeeze his eyelids shut again.

"Baron?" Blok said. "If you refuse to open your eyes, we'll cut your eyelids off."

There was no doubt they would. He obeyed, squinting in the glare.

"Good! Now we can get some business done!" Blok pulled up a chair on casters beside the prisoner and sat down. Michael could make out others in the room: a tall man holding a dripping bucket, another figure—this one thick and fleshy—in a black SS uniform that bulged at the seams. Major Krolle, of course. "Before we begin," Blok said quietly, "I'll tell you that you are a man whom hope has abandoned. There is no escape from this room. Beyond these walls, there are more walls." He leaned forward, into the light, and his silver teeth glittered. "You have no friends here, and no one is coming to save you. We are going to destroy you—either quickly, or slowly: that is the sole choice within your power to make. Do you understand? Nod, please."

Michael was busy trying to figure out how he was bound. He was lying, stark naked, on a metal table that was shaped like an X, his arms outstretched over his head and his legs apart. Tight leather straps secured his wrists and ankles. The table was tilted up and forward, so that Michael was very close to an upright position. He tested the straps; they wouldn't give even a quarter of an inch.

"Bauman?" Blok said. "Bring me some more water, please." The man with the bucket—an aide to Major Krolle, Michael assumed—answered "Yes sir" and walked across the room. An iron bolt slid back, and there was a quick glimpse of gray light as a heavy door opened and closed. Blok turned his attention to the prisoner again. "What is your name and nationality?"

Michael was silent. His heart pounded; he was sure Blok could see it. His shoulder hurt like hell, though it probably wasn't fractured. He felt like a wrapping of bruises around a barbed-wire skeleton. Blok expected an answer, and Michael decided to give him one: "Richard Hamlet. I'm British."

"Oh, you're British, are you? A Tommy who speaks perfect Russian? I don't think so. If you're so very British, say something in English for me."

He didn't respond.

Blok sighed deeply, and shook his head. "I think I prefer you as a baron. All right, let's say for the sake of speculation that you're an agent for the Red Army. Probably dropped into Germany on an assassination or sabotage mission. Your contact was Chesna van Dorne. How and where did you meet her?"

Had they caught Chesna? Michael wondered. There was no answer to that question in the eyes of his inquisitor.

"What was your mission?" Blok asked.

Michael stared straight ahead, a pulse beating at his temple.

"Why did Chesna bring you to the Reichkronen?"

Still no response.

"How were you planning on getting out of the country after your mission was completed?" No answer. Blok leaned a little closer. "Have you ever heard of a man named Theo von Frankewitz?"

Michael kept his face emotionless.

"Von Frankewitz seemed to know *you*," Blok continued. "Oh, he tried to shield you at first, but we gave him some interesting drugs. Before he died, he told us the exact description of a man who visited him at his apartment. He told us he showed this man a drawing. The man he described is you, Baron. Now tell me, please: what interest would a Russian secret agent have in a decrepit sidewalk artist like Frankewitz?'' He prodded Michael's bruised shoulder with his forefinger. ''Don't think you're being brave, Baron. You're being very stupid. We can shoot you full of drugs to loosen your tongue, but unfortunately those don't work very well unless you're in . . . shall we say . . . a weakened condition. Therefore we must satisfy that requirement. It's your choice, Baron: how shall we do this?''

Michael didn't answer. He knew what was ahead, and he was readying himself for it.

''I see,'' Blok said. He stood up, and moved away from the prisoner. ''Major Krolle? At your pleasure, please.''

Krolle stalked forward, lifted the rubber baton, and went to work.

Sometime later, cold water was thrown into Michael's face again and revived him to the devil's kingdom. He coughed and sputtered, his nostrils clogged with blood. His right eye was swollen shut, and the entire right side of his face felt weighted with bruises. His lower lip was gashed open, leaking a thread of crimson that trickled down his chin to his chest.

''This really is pointless, Baron.'' Colonel Blok was sitting in his chair again, next to Michael. On a tray in front of him was a plate of sausages and sauerkraut and a crystal goblet of white wine. Blok had a napkin tucked in his collar and was eating his dinner with a silver knife and fork. ''You know I can kill you anytime I please.''

Michael snorted blood from his nostrils. His nose might be broken. His tongue found a loose molar.

''Major Krolle wants to kill you now and be done with it,'' Blok went on. He chewed a bite of sausage and dabbed his lips with the napkin. ''I think you'll come to your senses before very much longer. Where are you from, Baron? Moscow? Leningrad? What military district?''

''I'm . . .'' His voice was a hoarse croak. He tried again. ''I'm a British citizen.''

''Oh, don't start that again!'' Blok cautioned. He took a

sip of wine. "Baron, who directed you to Theo von Franke-witz? Was it Chesna?"

Michael didn't answer. His vision blurred in and out, his brains rattling from the beating.

"This is what I believe," the colonel said. "That Chesna was in the business of selling German military secrets. I don't know how she learned about Frankewitz, but let's speculate that she is involved in a network of traitors. She was helping you with your mission—whatever that was—and she decided to intrigue you with some information that she thought you might take back to your Russian masters. Dogs do have masters, don't they? Well, perhaps Chesna thought you might pay for this information. Did you?"

No response. Michael stared past the blinding spot lamp.

"Chesna brought you to the Reichkronen to assassinate someone, didn't she?" Blok cut a sausage open, and grease drooled out. "All those officers there . . . possibly you were going to blow the entire place to pieces. But tell me: why did you go into Sandler's suite? You did kill his hawk, didn't you?" When Michael didn't answer, Blok smiled thinly. "No harm done. I despised that damned bird. But when I found all those feathers and that mess in Sandler's suite, I knew it had to be your doing—especially after that little drama on the riverbank. I knew you must have had commando training, to have gotten off Sandler's train. He's hunted over a dozen men on that train, and some of them were ex-officers who'd fallen from grace; so you see, I knew no tulip-growing 'baron' could have beaten Sandler. But he gave you a run, didn't he?" He poked his knife at the blood-crusted bullet gash on Michael's thigh. "Now, about Frankewitz: who else knows about the drawing he showed you?"

"You'll have to ask Chesna," Michael said, probing to see if she'd been captured.

"Yes, I will. Count on it. But for right now, I'm asking you. Who else knows about that drawing?"

They didn't have her, Michael thought. Or maybe it was just a faint hope. The security of that drawing was paramount to Blok. Blok finished his sausage and drank his wine, waiting for the Russian secret agent to answer. Finally he

456

stood up and pushed his chair back. "Major Krolle?" he said, and motioned the man forward.

Krolle came out of the darkness. The rubber baton was upraised, and Michael's bruised muscles tensed. He wasn't ready for another beating yet; he had to stall for time. He said, "I know all about Iron Fist."

The baton started to fall, aimed at Michael's face.

Before it could smash down, a hand grasped Krolle's wrist and checked its descent. "One moment," Blok told him. The colonel stared fixedly at Michael. "A phrase," he said. "Two words you got out of Frankewitz. They meant nothing to him, and they mean nothing to you."

It was time for a shot in the dark. "The Allies might think differently."

There was a silence in the room, as if mere mention of the Allies had the power to freeze flesh and blood. Blok continued to stare at Michael, his face betraying no emotion. And then Blok spoke: "Major Krolle, would you leave the room, please? Bauman, you, too." He waited until the major and his aide had left, then began to walk back and forth across the stone floor, his hands behind him and his body crooked slightly forward. He suddenly stopped. "You're bluffing. You don't know a damned thing about Iron Fist."

"I know you're in charge of security for the project," Michael said, choosing his words carefully. "I presume you didn't take me to Gestapo headquarters in Berlin because you don't want your superiors to find out there's been a security leak."

"There has been no leak. Besides, I don't know what project you're talking about."

"Oh yes, you do. I'm afraid it's no secret any longer."

Blok approached Michael and leaned over him. "Really? Then tell me, Baron: what is Iron Fist?" His breath smelled of sausage and sauerkraut.

The moment of truth had arrived. Michael knew very well that one sentence might spell judgment for him. He said, "Dr. Hildebrand's created something quite a bit more potent than delousing spray, hasn't he?"

A muscle clenched in Blok's bony jaw. Other than that, the man didn't move.

"Yes, I did get into Sandler's suite," Michael went on. "But before I did, I got into yours. I found your satchel, and those photographs of Hildebrand's test subjects. Prisoners of war, I suspect. Where are you shipping them from? Here? Other camps?"

Blok's eyes narrowed.

"Let's speculate, shall we?" Michael asked. "You're shipping POWs from a number of camps. They go to Hildebrand's workshop on Skarpa Island." Blok's face had turned a shade gray. "Oh . . . I think I'd like a sip of wine, please," he said. "To wet my throat."

"I'll *cut* your throat, you Slav son of a bitch!" Blok hissed.

"I don't think so. A sip of wine, please?"

Blok remained motionless. Finally a cold smile crept across his mouth. "As you wish, Baron." He took the goblet of white wine from the tray and held it to Michael's mouth, allowing him one swallow before he drew it away. "Go on with this fanciful conjecture."

Michael licked his swollen lower lip, the wine stinging it. "The prisoners are subjected to Hildebrand's tests. Over three hundred of them so far, as I recall. I assume you speak regularly with Hildebrand. You were probably using those pictures to show your superiors how the project's coming along. Am I correct?"

"You know, this room is very strange." Blok looked around. "You can hear the dead talking in it."

"You might want to kill me, but you won't. You and I both know how important Iron Fist is." Another shot in the dark that hit its target; Blok stared at him again. "My friends in Moscow would be thrilled to pass that information along to the Allies."

What Michael was hinting at took root. Blok said, "And who else knows about this?" His voice was reedy, and there might have been a quaver in it.

"Chesna's not the only one." He decided to lead Blok by the pinched nostrils. "She was with you while I was in your suite."

That sank in. Blok's expression was stricken for a second

458

as he realized that someone on the Reichkronen staff must be a traitor. "Who gave you the key?"

"I never knew. The key was delivered to Chesna's suite during the Brimstone Club's meeting. I returned it by dropping it into a flower pot on the second floor." So far, so good, he thought. It would never occur to Blok that Michael had descended the castle wall. He cocked his head to one side. His heart was beating hard, and he knew he was playing a dangerous charade but he had to buy time. "You know, I think you're right about this room. You *can* hear the voice of a dead colonel."

"Mock me if you wish, Baron." Blok smiled tightly, whorls of red in his cheeks. "But a few injections of truth serum and you'll tell me everything."

"I think you'll find I'm a little tougher than Frankewitz was. Besides, I can't tell you what I don't know. The key was delivered, and I returned it in an envelope along with the film."

"*Film?* What film?" The quaver was more pronounced.

"Well, I wouldn't have gone into your suite unprepared, would I? Of course I had a camera. Also furnished by Chesna's friend. I took pictures of the photographs in your satchel. Plus those other papers, the ones that looked like pages from an accounting book."

Blok was silent, but Michael could tell what he must be thinking: that secrets under his responsibility were out, possibly headed by courier to the Soviet Union, and the Reichkronen was a nest of traitors. "You're a liar," Blok said. "If these things were true, you wouldn't be volunteering them so freely."

"I don't want to die. Neither do I care to be tortured. Anyway, the information's already been passed. There isn't anything you can do about it now."

"Oh, I disagree. Very strongly." Blok reached onto his tray, and his hand gripped the fork. He stood beside Michael, his face blotched with red. "I'll tear the Reichkronen to the ground and execute everyone from the plumbers to the manager, if that's what is necessary. You, my dear Baron, will tell me all about how and where you met Chesna, what your escape route was going to be, and so much more.

459

And you're right: I won't kill you." He jabbed the fork's tines into the flesh of Michael's left arm and drew it out. "You do have a certain value, after all." Again the fork jabbed down, piercing Michael's shoulder. Michael flinched, sweat on his face. The fork was withdrawn. "I'm going to consume you," Blok said, and drove the tines into Michael's chest just below the throat, "like a piece of meat. I'll chew you up, digest what I need, and spit out the rest." He pulled the fork out, the tines tipped with blood. "You might know about Iron Fist—and about Dr. Hildebrand and Skarpa Island—but you don't know how Iron Fist is going to be used. No one knows where the fortress is but myself, Dr. Hildebrand, and a few others whose loyalty is unquestioned. Therefore, your Russian friends don't know either, and they can't pass the information to the British and Americans, can they?" He jabbed the fork into Michael's left cheek, then he drew it out and tasted Michael's blood. "This," Blok said, "is only the first course." He snapped off the spot lamp.

Michael heard him cross the room. The heavy door opened. "Bauman," the colonel said, "take this trash to a cell."

He had been holding his breath; now he let it go in a hiss between his teeth. For the time being, at least, there would be no more torture. Bauman entered, along with three other soldiers. Michael's wrists and ankles were unstrapped, and he was pulled up off the X-shaped table and guided by gunpoint along a stone-floored corridor. "Go on, you swine!" Bauman—a slim young man with round-lensed spectacles and a long, gaunt face—growled as he shoved Michael forward. On either side of the hallway were three-foot-high wooden doors with iron latches, set at floor level. In the doors were small square insets that could be slid back for, Michael assumed, either air or the passing in of food and water. The place smelled damp and ancient, with suggestions of sodden hay, human excrement, sweat, and unwashed flesh. A kennel for wild dogs, Michael thought. He heard the animalish moans and mutterings of his fellow prisoners.

"Stop," Bauman commanded. He held himself stiff-backed and looked at Michael with disinterest. "Get on your knees."

Michael hesitated. Two rifles jabbed his back. He bent down, and one of the soldiers drew the iron bolt back with a rusty shriek. Something scurried beyond the door.

Bauman opened it. A hot, sickening wave of stale air rolled out into Michael's face. In the kennel's rank darkness he could make out five or six skinny human bodies, perhaps others crouched up against the walls. The floor was covered with filthy hay, and the ceiling was only five feet off the floor.

"Go in," Bauman said.

"Mercy of God! Mercy of God!" an emaciated, bald-headed man with bulging eyes cried out, and lurched toward the door on his knees, his hands upraised and running sores all over his sunken chest. He stopped, shivering, and looked hopefully at Bauman, his eyes blinking in the gloom.

"I *said*, go in," the Nazi repeated. Two seconds after he'd spoken, one of the soldiers kicked Michael in the ribs with his booted foot, and the others shoved him into the hellish cubicle and slammed the door shut. The iron latch scraped into its socket. "Mercy of God! Mercy of God!" the prisoner kept shouting, until a gruff voice from the rear of the cell silenced him by saying, "Shut up, Metzger! No one's listening to you!"

7

As he lay on the filth-clotted hay in the foul darkness with the other prisoners mumbling and moaning in their sleep, Michael felt a sadness creep over him like a silken shroud.

Life was a precious thing; what was it about men who hated it so much? He thought of the dark smoke belching from the chimneys and tainting the air with the smell of burning flesh. He thought of pinewood boxes full of hair, and how someone—a mother, a father—in a kinder world had combed that hair, and stroked it, and kissed the forehead it fell upon. Now it was gone to the wig makers, and the body up in smoke. More than humans were being destroyed here; whole worlds were being charred to white ash. And for what? *Lebensraum*—Hitler's vaunted "elbow room"— and Iron Crosses? He thought of Mouse, lying dead in the thorns, the little man's neck broken by a quick and merciful twist. His heart clutched: perhaps killing was his nature, but it was far from his pleasure. Mouse had been a good friend. What better epitaph was there? To mourn a single human being in such a death-torn land seemed like standing in a flaming house and blowing out a candle. He sheered his mind away from the memory of Boots crushing the dead hand and plucking the medal from it. His eyes were wet, and he realized he could lose his senses in this hellhole.

Something Blok had said. What was it? Michael tried to concentrate past the carnage. Something Blok had said about a fortress. Yes, that was it. Blok's words: *No one knows where the fortress is but myself, Dr. Hildebrand, and a few others. . . .*

The fortress. What fortress had he meant? Skarpa Island? Michael didn't think so; it had been simple enough for Chesna to find out that Hildebrand had a home and work-shop on Skarpa. That fact wasn't a closely guarded secret. So what other fortress could Blok have meant, and what might that have to do with how Iron Fist was going to be used?

Bullet holes on glass and green-painted metal, Michael thought. Olive-green-painted metal. Why that particular hue?

He was pondering that when fingers touched his face.

He jumped, taken by surprise, and grabbed the slim wrist of a crouching figure outlined in dim blue. There was a muffled gasp; the figure thrashed to pull away, but Michael held firm.

Another figure, this one larger and also silhouetted in blue in Michael's night vision, uncoiled from the gloom to his right. An arm shot out. At the end of it was a fist, which cracked against Michael's skull and made his ears ring. A second blow grazed his forehead as he ducked beneath it, crouching on his knees. They were trying to kill him, he thought. A surge of panic rose within him. Were they that hungry that they wanted raw human flesh? He let go of the first figure, which scurried to the safety of a far corner, and concentrated on the larger, stronger one. A third blow was swung; Michael chopped at the open elbow and heard a satisfying grunt of pain. He saw the outline of a head and faint facial features. He slammed his fist into the face. A bulbous nose exploded.

"Guards!" a man shouted in French. "Guards! Help us!"

"Mercy of God! Mercy of God!" the shrieker began again at the top of his lungs.

"Stop that, you fools!" This man's language was German with a thick Danish accent. "You'll use up all the air!"

A pair of sinewy arms twined around Michael's chest. He rocked his head back and smashed his skull against another man's face. The arms lost their strength. The large figure with the burst nose was still full of fight. A fist hit Michael's bruised shoulder and drove a cry of pain from him. Then fingers were on his throat, the weight of a body pressing down on him. Michael brought the palm of his hand up in a short, vicious blow against the tip of the man's bearded chin and heard the crack of his teeth hitting together, possibly catching part of the tongue between them. The man groaned but kept squeezing Michael's throat, fingers digging for the windpipe.

A piercing scream overwhelmed all the other frantic voices. It was the scream of a young girl, and it rose to a hysterical crescendo.

The kennel door's small inset slid back. The brass nozzle of a fire hose was pushed through.

"Watch out!" the Dane warned. "They're going to—"

A high-pressure flood of water shot from the nozzle and hit the prisoners, its velocity flinging Michael and his combatant away from each other. Michael was driven against a wall, the water battering his flesh. The girl's scream became a strangled coughing. The shrieker had been silenced, his frail body hammered by the deluge. In another few seconds the water stopped, the fire hose was withdrawn, and the door's inset slid back into place. It was all over but the moaning.

"You! The new one!" It was the same gruff voice that had told Metzger to shut up, except now the man was speaking around a badly bitten tongue. His language was coarse Russian. "You touch the girl again and I'll break your neck, understand?"

"I don't want to hurt her," Michael answered in his native language. "I thought I was being attacked."

The other man didn't reply for a moment. Metzger was sobbing, and someone else was trying to soothe him. Water trickled down the walls and pooled on the floor, and the air reeked of sweat and steam. "She's out of her mind," the Russian told Michael. "About fourteen years old, is my guess. No telling how many times she's been raped. Some-where along the line, somebody put out her eyes with a hot iron."

"I'm sorry."

"Why?" the Russian asked. "Did you do it?" He snorted blood from his broken nose. "Gave me a hell of a knock, you son of a bitch. What's your name?"

"Gallatinov," he answered.

"I'm Lazaris. The bastards got me at Kirovograd. I was a fighter pilot. How about you?"

"I'm just a soldier," Michael said. "They got me in Berlin."

"*Berlin?*" Lazaris laughed and snorted more blood. "Ha! That's a good one! Well, our comrades will be marching through Berlin soon enough. They'll set fire to the whole damned city and drink a toast to Hitler's bones. I hope they catch that bastard. Couldn't you see him dancing on a meat hook in Red Square?"

"It's a possibility."

"Never. Hitler won't be taken alive, that's for sure. You hungry?"

"Yes." It was the first time he'd thought of food since he'd been thrown in this hole.

"Here. Hold your hand out and you'll get a feast."

Michael did. Lazaris found his hand in the dark, gripped it with wiry fingers, and put something into the palm. Michael sniffed it: a small clump of hard bread that smelled bitter with mold. In a place like this one didn't turn down handouts. He ate the bread, chewing it slowly.

"Where are you from, Gallatinov?"

"Leningrad." He swallowed the bread, and his tongue searched his teeth for crumbs.

"I'm from Rostov originally. But I've lived all over Russia." That was the beginning of Lazaris's recitation of his life history. He was thirty-one years of age, and his father was an "engineering specialist" with the Soviet air force—which meant, basically, that his father was head of a team of mechanics. Lazaris went on about his wife and three sons—all of them safe in Moscow—and how he'd flown more than forty missions in his Yak-1 fighter and shot down twelve Luftwaffe aircraft. "I was working on my thirteenth," Lazaris said wistfully, "when two more dropped out of the clouds right on top of me. They shot poor *Warhammer* to pieces, and I hit the silk. I landed less than a hundred yards from an enemy machine-gun nest." Michael couldn't see the man's face in the dark, but he saw the blue-outlined shoulders shrug. "I'm courageous in the sky. On land not so much so. And here I am."

"*Warhammer*," Michael repeated. "That was your plane?"

"Yes, I named her. Painted her name on the fuselage, too. Plus a swastika for every kill. Ah, she was a fine, beautiful beast." He sighed. "You know, I never saw her come down. That's for the best, I think. Sometimes I like to believe she's still up there, flying circles over Russia. All the pilots in my squadron named their planes. Do you think that's childish?"

"Whatever helps keep a man alive is not childish."

"My thoughts, exactly. The Americans do the same thing. Oh, you ought to see *their* planes! Painted up like Volga floozies—especially their long-distance bombers—but they can fight like Cossacks. What our air force could have done with machines like those!"

Lazaris had been shipped from camp to camp, he told Michael, and had been in Falkenhausen for what he thought must be six or seven months. He'd only been thrown into this kennel recently—maybe two weeks, he thought, though

465

it was hard to tell the passage of time in a place like this. Why he was in here was anyone's guess, but he missed seeing the sky.

"That building with the chimneys," Michael ventured. "What goes on in there?"

Lazaris didn't answer. Michael could hear the sound of the man's fingers, scratching his beard. "I do miss the sky," Lazaris said after a while. "The clouds, the blue freedom of it. If I could see one bird, my whole day was happy. But not many birds fly over Falkenhausen." He lapsed into silence. Metzger was sobbing again, a terrible, broken sound. "Someone sing to him," Lazaris told the others, speaking a crude but serviceable German. "He likes being sung to."

No one sang. Michael sat on the sodden hay with his knees drawn up to his chest. Someone groaned softly, followed by a diarrheic bubbling noise. From across the cell, which couldn't be more than eight feet or so, Michael heard the whimpering of the blind girl. He could see six figures, silhouetted in faint blue. He lifted a hand and touched the ceiling. Not a crack of light entered the kennel. He felt as if the ceiling were moving, and the walls, too, the entire cell constricting to smash them into bones and juices. It was an illusion, of course, but never in his life had he longed so much for a breath of fresh air and the sight of a forest. Steady, he told himself. Steady. He knew he could withstand more pain and hardship than the normal human being, because those things had been integral parts of his life. But this confinement was torture to his soul, and he knew he could break in a place like this. Steady. There was no telling when he might see the sun again, and he had to keep control of himself. Control was the wolf's theme. Without control, a wolf had no chance for survival. He could not—must not—give up hope, even here in this den of hopelessness. He'd been successful in diverting Blok's attention to the fictitious nest of traitors at the Reichkronen, but how long would that last? Sooner or later the torture would begin once more, and when it did—

Steady, he thought. Don't think about that. It will happen when it happens, and not before.

He was thirsty. He licked the wet wall behind him and caught enough moisture on his tongue for a satisfying sip.

"Lazaris?" Michael asked, sometime later.

"What is it?"

"If you could get out of here, is there a weak point somewhere in the camp? A place where the wall might be climbed?"

Lazaris grunted. "You must be joking."

"I'm not. Surely the guards change, the gate opens to let trucks in and out, a tunnel can be dug. Isn't there an escape committee here? Hasn't anyone tried to get out?"

"No," Lazaris said. "People here are fortunate to be able to *walk,* much less run, climb, or dig. There's no escape committee. There's no thought of escape, because it's impossible. Now put that out of your mind before you go insane."

"There's got to be a way out," Michael persisted. He heard desperation in his voice. "How many prisoners are here?"

"I don't know for sure. Possibly forty thousand or so in the men's camp. Maybe another twenty thousand in the women's camp. Of course they're always coming and going. The train pulls in with a new load every day."

Michael was stunned. Sixty thousand prisoners, by a conservative estimate. "And how many guards?"

"Hard to tell. Seven or eight hundred, maybe a thousand."

"The guards are outnumbered six to *one?* And still no one's tried to escape?"

"Gallatinov," the Russian said wearily, as if speaking to a troublesome child, "I don't know of anyone who can outrun a machine-gun bullet. Or who would care to try. The guards have dogs, too: Dobermans. I've seen what their teeth can do to human flesh, and I'll tell you it isn't pretty. If, by some astounding miracle, a prisoner was to get out of Falkenhausen, where would that wretch go? We're in the heart of Germany. From here, all roads lead to Berlin." He crawled away a few feet and rested his back against the wall. "For you and me, the war is over," he said quietly. "Let it go."

"The hell I will," Michael told him, and he screamed inside.

The passage of time was hard to judge. It might have been an hour or two later that Michael noted the prisoners were getting restless. Soon afterward he heard the sound of the door to the next kennel being unbolted. The prisoners were up on their knees, shivering in expectation. Then their own kennel door was unbolted and swung open to let in the excruciating light.

A small, black loaf of bread, shot through with veins of green mold, was thrown in among them. The prisoners fell upon it, tearing chunks out of it. "Bring your sponge!" one of the soldiers who stood in the corridor said.

Lazaris crawled forward, a gray sponge in his hand. He had at one time been a husky man, but the flesh had shrunken over his large bones. Dark brown hair spilled down his shoulders, his beard clotted with hay and filth. His facial flesh had drawn tight over his jutting cheekbones, and his eyes were dark holes in the pallid skin. His nose, a formidable beak that might've made Cyrano tip his hat, was crusted with blood around the nostrils, courtesy of Michael's fist. He glanced at Michael as he crawled past, and Michael shrank back. Lazaris had the eyes of a dead man.

The Russian immersed the sponge in a bucket of dirty water. Then he withdrew it, swollen with liquid. The bucket was pulled away, the kennel's door slammed shut—a brutal sound—and the iron latch slid back into place. The next kennel down the corridor was opened.

"Dinnertime," Lazaris said as he crawled past Michael again. "Everyone gets a drink from the sponge. Hey, you bastards! Leave something for my comrade!" There was the noise of a quick and decisive struggle, and then Lazaris nudged Michael's arm. "Here." He put a damp bit of bread in Michael's hand. "That damned Frenchman always tries to get more than his share. You've got to be fast around here if you want something better than a crust."

Michael sat with his back against the rough stones and chewed on the bread. He stared at nothing. His eyes stung. Tears crept from them and trickled down his cheeks, but who they were for he did not know.

468

8

The iron bolt shrieked back.

At once Michael was on his haunches, roused from a nightmare of chimneys whose black smoke covered the earth. The door opened. "Send the girl out!" one of the three soldiers who stood there commanded.

"Please," Lazaris said, his voice husky from sleep. "Please let her alone. Hasn't she suffered e—"

"Send the girl *out!*" the man repeated.

The girl had awakened, and was shivering in a corner. She made a soft whimpering noise, like a trapped rabbit.

Michael had reached the end of what he would bear. He crouched in front of the doorway, his green eyes glittering above the darkness of his fresh beard. "If you want her so badly," he said in German, "then come in and take her."

A rifle bolt was cocked. The barrel thrust in at him. "Out of the way, you vermin."

"Gallatinov!" Lazaris pulled at him. "Are you crazy?"

Michael remained where he was. "Come in, you sons of bitches. Three against one. What are you waiting for?" He shouted it: "Come on!"

None of the Germans accepted his invitation. They wouldn't shoot him, Michael reasoned, because they knew Blok and Krolle hadn't finished with him. One of the soldiers gathered saliva in his mouth and spat at Michael, and then the door was slammed shut and latched again.

"Now you've done it!" Lazaris fretted. "God knows what you've awakened!"

Michael spun around and grasped the other man's beard. "You listen to me," he said. "If you want to forget you're a man, that's fine with me, but I'm not going to lie here and moan for the rest of my life! You protected the girl when you thought I was after her; why won't you protect her from those bastards?"

469

"Because"—Lazaris worked Michael's hand off his beard—"you're only one, and they are legion."

The door was unlocked again. "Mercy of God!" Metzger shrieked. The door opened. Now six soldiers stood in the corridor.

"You!" The beam of a hand torch found Michael's face. "Come out of there!" It was Bauman's voice.

Michael didn't move.

"You won't like it if we have to drag you out," Bauman promised.

"Neither will the Kraut who tries to drag me."

A Luger emerged from Bauman's holster. "Do it," he told the other soldiers. They hesitated. "Do it, I said!" Bauman thundered, and he gave the nearest man a kick in the pants.

The first soldier crouched and started into the kennel. He reached out to grasp Michael's arm, and Michael smashed a handful of filthy hay into the man's face and followed that with a blow to the jaw that cracked like a gunshot. A second man hurtled through the door, and a third right behind him. Michael warded off a punch, then struck into the second soldier's throat with the flat of his hand. The third man caught Michael's jaw with a glancing blow, and a fourth soldier lunged upon him and hooked an arm around his throat. The girl began to scream, a high thin shriek that had years of terror behind it.

The sound—so much like the voice of a wolf, calling in the night—galvanized Michael. He drove his elbows backward into the rib cage of the man who was throttling him. The soldier grunted with pain and his grip loosened, and Michael thrashed free. A fist struck his bruised shoulder, and another hammered at his skull. He shook off a body with such force that the man was slammed against the wall. A knee thudded into his back, and fingers raked his eyes. There was a shrill cry of pain, and suddenly the soldier who was trying to gouge his eyes out flailed at the emaciated figure that had leaped upon him. Metzger's teeth had sunk into the soldier's cheek, and he was ripping the flesh like a maddened terrier.

Michael kicked out, and caught another soldier on the

point of the chin. The man was hurled through the door and clipped Bauman's legs. Bauman lifted a whistle to his mouth and began to blow quick, shrill notes. A fist swung past Michael's head, thunking into a Germanic face; with a hoarse roar Lazaris swung again, and this time burst the man's upper lip open in a spray of crimson. Then Lazaris grasped the hair of a guard whose SS cap had spun away, and slammed his forehead against the man's skull with a noise like an ax blade meeting timber.

A blackjack rose up like a cobra's head. Michael grabbed the wrist before the soldier could strike, and drove his fist into the man's armpit. He heard a rush of air behind him. Before he could twist around, a rifle butt hit him in the center of the back, between his shoulder blades, knocking the breath from his lungs. The blackjack crunched down on his arm, just above the elbow, and froze it with pain. A fist struck him on the back of the head, stunning him, and though he kept fighting wildly, he knew he was all but used up.

"Bring him out!" Bauman shouted as other soldiers came to his assistance. "Come on, hurry it up!"

The blackjack wielder began to beat at Lazaris and Metzger, driving them back against the wall. Two of the soldiers grabbed the blind girl and started hauling her out. Michael was thrown onto the corridor floor, where Bauman put a boot on his throat. The rest of the guards, most of them bruised and bleeding, scrambled out of the kennel.

Michael heard a submachine gun being cocked. He looked up, his vision misted with pain, and saw a guard pointing his Schmeisser into the kennel. "No!" Michael croaked, Bauman's foot pressed to his neck.

The gun fired, two short bursts amid the remaining five prisoners. Spent cartridges clattered to the stones.

"Stop that!" Bauman shouted, and uptilted the Schmeisser with the barrel of his pistol. Another quick burst pocked the stone wall and rained fragments and dust around them. "No firing without a direct order!" he raged, his eyes wild behind his glasses. "Do you understand me?"

"Yes, sir," the guard replied, thoroughly cowed, and he clicked the safety on his smoking gun and lowered it to his side.

Bauman's face had turned scarlet. He removed his foot from Michael's neck. "You know every round of ammunition has to be accounted for!" he shouted at the gunner. "I'll be filling out reports for a week with all that damned firing!" He motioned disdainfully to the kennel. "Close that up! And you men, get this trash on his feet!" He started striding along the corridor, and Michael was made to follow, his head pounding and his knees threatening to give way.

He was returned to the room with the X-shaped metal table. A light bulb burned overhead. "Strap him down," Bauman said. Michael began to fight again, dreading the bite of those straps, but he was exhausted and the issue was quickly settled. The straps were pulled tight. "Leave us," Bauman told the soldiers. When they were gone, he removed his glasses and slowly cleaned the lenses with a handkerchief. Michael noted that his hands were shaking.

Bauman put his glasses back on. His face was haggard, dark circles under his eyes. "What's your real name?" he asked.

Michael remained silent, some of the fog clearing out of his mind but his back and shoulders still hurting like hell.

"I mean what they call you in Britain," Bauman went on. "You'd better talk quick, my friend! There's no telling when Krolle might come around, and he's aching to use that baton on you!"

Michael was puzzled. Bauman's tone of voice had changed; it was urgent, not superior. A trick, he thought it must be. Of course it was!

"Chesna van Dorne hasn't been captured yet." Bauman lifted the table so Michael was almost upright, and locked it in place. "Her friends—our friends—are helping her hide. She's also working on the arrangements."

"Arrangements?" His throat felt bruised from the pressure of Bauman's boot. "What arrangements?"

"To get you out of here. And also to find a plane and set up the fuel stops. You were planning on going to Norway, correct?"

Michael was shocked speechless. It had to be a trick! My God! he thought. Chesna's been captured, and she's told everything!

472

"Listen to me very carefully." Bauman stared into Michael's eyes. A pulse beat rapidly at the German's temple. "I am here because I had a choice. Either fieldwork, which meant risking getting my ass shot off or being hung up from the balls by the Russians, or working here in this . . . this slaughterhouse. In the field I could do nothing for our friends; here I can at least communicate with them, and do what I can to help certain prisoners. Incidentally, if your intent was to get everyone in your cell murdered, you came very close to accomplishing it."

That explained the dramatics with the machine gun, Michael thought. Bauman was trying to keep the others from being killed. No, no! Blok or Krolle had set him up to this! This was all stage play!

"My task," Bauman said, "is to keep you alive until the arrangements are worked out. I don't know how long that will be. I'll get a radio code that will tell me how your escape's going to be managed. God help us, because prisoners only leave Falkenhausen as bags of fertilizer. I've made a suggestion; we'll see if Chesna thinks it's worthwhile."

"What suggestion?" he asked warily.

"Falkenhausen was built to keep prisoners in. The camp is understaffed and the guards are used to docility. Which is why you were very stupid just now. Don't do anything to call attention to yourself!" He paced back and forth as he talked. "Just play the brain-dead prisoner, and you might survive a week!"

"All right," Michael said, "let's pretend I believe you. How would I get out?"

"The guards—and Krolle, too—have gotten lazy. There are no uprisings here, no escape attempts, nothing to upset the day-to-day routine. The guards don't expect anyone to try to break out, simply because it would be impossible. But"—he stopped pacing—"neither do they expect anyone to try to break *in*. And that may be a distinct possibility."

"Break in? To a concentration camp? That's crazy!"

"Yes, Krolle and the guards would think so, too. As I said, Falkenhausen was built to keep prisoners in, but maybe not to keep a rescue team *out*."

A faint ember of hope sparked within Michael. If this man

was acting, he deserved star billing with Chesna. But Michael didn't let himself believe it yet; it would be utter foolishness to go along with this, and perhaps spill precious secrets in the process.

"I know this is difficult for you. If I were in your position, I'd be skeptical as well. You're probably thinking I'm trying to lead you into a trap of some kind. Maybe nothing I can say will make you believe otherwise, but this you *must* believe: it's my job to keep you alive, and that's what I'm going to do. Just do what you're told, and do it without hesitation."

"It's a huge camp," Michael said. "If a rescue team did get through the gate, how are they going to find me?"

"I'll take care of that."

"And what if the team fails?"

"In that case," Bauman said, "it's my responsibility to see that you die without revealing any secrets."

This hit a true note. If the rescue effort failed, that solution was what Michael would expect. My God! he thought. Do I dare trust this man?

"The guards are waiting outside. Some of them have loose lips, and they tell everything to Krolle. So I'll have to beat you, to make this look real." He began to wrap the handkerchief around the knuckles of his right fist. "I'll have to draw blood. My apologies." He drew the handkerchief tight. "When we finish here, you'll be returned to your cell. Again, I beg you: don't put up any resistance. We want the guards and Major Krolle to believe you're broken. Understand?"

Michael didn't reply. His mind was too busy, trying to sort all this out.

"All right," Bauman said. He raised his fist. "I'll try to get this over as quickly as I can."

He punched with the spare economy of a boxer. It didn't take very long for the handkerchief to become spattered with scarlet. Bauman gave Michael no body blows; he wanted all the damage—as superficial as it was—to be on display. By the time he was finished, Michael was bleeding from a gash above his left eye and a split lower lip, his face mottled with blue bruises.

Bauman opened the door and called the guards in, the

bloodstained handkerchief still bound around his swollen knuckles. Michael, almost unconscious, was unstrapped and dragged back to his kennel. He was thrown inside, on the damp hay, and the door was sealed.

"Gallatinov!" Lazaris shook him back to his senses. "I thought they would've killed you, for sure!"

"They . . . did . . . their worst." Michael tried to sit up, but his head felt like a lump of lead. He was lying against another body. A cool, unbreathing body. "Who is that?" Michael asked, and Lazaris told him. The bursts of machine-gun bullets had delivered the mercy of God. The Frenchman was also hit, and he lay huddled up and breathing heavily with slugs in his chest and stomach. Lazaris, the Dane, and the other prisoner—a German who moaned and cried without pause—had all escaped injury but for stone splinter cuts. The fourteen-year-old girl had not returned to the kennel.

She didn't come back. Sometime during the next eight hours—or at least Michael judged it to be so, though his sense of time had all but vanished—the Frenchman hitched a final breath and died. The guards brought another small loaf of black bread and allowed another dip of the sponge in their bucket, but they left the corpses among the living.

Michael slept a lot, rebuilding his strength. His thigh wound began to crust over, and so did the gash above his left eye: more signs of time's passage. He lay on the kennel floor and stretched, working the blood back into his stiff muscles. He closed his mind to the walls and ceiling and concentrated on visions of green forest and grasslands sweeping toward the blue horizon. He learned the routine: the guards brought bread and water once every day, and every third day a bucket of gray gruel that Lazaris sopped the sponge in. It was slow starvation, but Michael made sure he got every bit of bread, water, and gruel that he could scoop up and squeeze out.

The corpses swelled and began to reek of decay.

What was Blok up to? Michael wondered. Possibly going over the histories of the Reichkronen employees, trying to uncover a traitor who wasn't there? Possibly trying to find the fictitious camera and film? Or leading the search for Chesna? He knew that a resumption of torture was imminent; this time it would be with instruments instead of fists and Krolle's rubber baton. Michael wasn't sure he could survive it. When his torturers came for him again, he would let the change take him, he decided. He would tear out as many of their throats as he could before their bullets cut him to pieces, and that would be the end of it.

But what about Iron Fist, and the forthcoming invasion? The gruel bucket had come twice; he'd been in this filthy hole for at least seven days. The Allied command had to be warned about Iron Fist. Whatever it was, it was deadly enough to make delaying D day imperative. If the soldiers who hit the landing beaches were exposed to the corrosive substance that had caused those wounds in the photographs, then the invasion would be a massacre.

He awakened from a restless sleep, in which skeletons in green fatigues lay in huge piles on the shores of France, to hear the sound of thunder.

"Ah, listen to that music!" Lazaris said. "Isn't it lovely?"

Not thunder, Michael realized. The sound of bombs.

"They're hitting Berlin again. The Americans in their B-seventeens." Lazaris's breathing had quickened with excitement. Michael knew the Russian was imagining himself up there with the swarms of heavy bombers, in the turbulent sky. "Sounds like some of their bombs are falling short. The woods'll be on fire; it usually happens that way."

The camp air-raid siren had begun to wail. The thunder was louder, and Michael could feel the vibration of the kennel's stones.

"Lots of bombs coming down," Lazaris said. "They never hit the camp, though. The Americans know where we are, and they've got those new bomb sights. Now there's an aircraft for you, Gallatinov. If we'd had Forts instead of those lousy Tupolevs, we'd have knocked the Krauts to hell back in forty-two."

It took a moment for what Lazaris had said to sink in. "What?" Michael asked.

"I said, if we'd had B-seventeens instead of those damned Tu—"

"No, you said 'Forts.' "

"Oh. Right. Flying Fortresses. B-seventeens. They call

them that because they're so hard to shoot down. But the Krauts get their share." He crawled toward Michael a few feet. "Sometimes you can see the air battles if the sky's clear enough. Not the planes, of course, because they're too high, but their contrails. One day we had a real scare. A Fortress with two burning engines passed right over the camp, couldn't have been a hundred feet off the ground. You could hear it crash, maybe a mile or so away. A little lower and it would've come down on our heads."

Flying Fortress, Michael thought. *Fortress*. Long-range American bombers, based in England. The Yanks painted their bombers a drab olive green: the same shade as the metal pieces Theo von Frankewitz had decorated with false bullet holes. Blok had said, *No one knows where the fortress is but myself, Dr. Hildebrand, and a few others*. Frankewitz had done his work in a hangar on an unknown airfield. Was it possible, then, that the "fortress" Blok had been talking about was not a place, but a B-17 bomber?

It hit him then, full force. He said, "The American bomber crews give names to their planes, don't they?"

"Yes. They paint the names on the aircraft nose, and usually other art, too. Like I said, they paint their planes up like floozies—but get them in the air, and they fly like angels."

"Iron Fist," Michael said.

"What?"

"Iron Fist," he repeated. "That might be the name of a Flying Fortress, mightn't it?"

"Could be, I suppose. Why?"

Michael didn't answer. He was thinking about the drawing Frankewitz had shown him: an iron fist, squeezing a caricature of Adolf Hitler. The kind of picture that no German in his right mind would display. But certainly the kind of art that might be proudly displayed on the nose of a Flying Fortress.

"Sweet music," Lazaris whispered, listening to the distant blasts.

The Nazis knew the invasion was coming, Michael thought. They didn't know where, or exactly when, but they'd probably narrowed it down to the end of May or beginning of June, when the Channel's tides were less capricious. It stood to reason that whatever Hildebrand was developing would be ready for use by then. Perhaps the weapon itself was not called "Iron Fist," but "Iron Fist" was the means of putting that weapon into action.

The Allies, with their fighter planes and long-distance bombers, owned the sky over Hitler's Reich. Hundreds of bombing missions had been flown over the cities of Nazi-occupied Europe. In all those missions how many Flying Fortresses had been shot down by German fighters or anti-aircraft guns? And of those, how many had made crash landings, shot to pieces and with engines aflame? The real question was: how many intact Flying Fortresses had the Nazis gotten hold of?

At least one, Michael thought. Perhaps the bomber that had passed over Falkenhausen and come down in the forest. Maybe it had been Blok's idea to salvage that aircraft, and that was why he'd been promoted from commandant of Falkenhausen to head of security for the Iron Fist project.

He let his mind wander, toward fearsome possibilities. How difficult would it be to make a damaged B-17 airworthy again? It depended, of course, on the damage; parts could be scavenged from other wrecks all over Europe. Maybe a downed Fortress—Iron Fist—was being reconstructed at that airfield where Frankewitz had done his paintings. But why bullet holes? Michael wondered. What was the point of making a reconstructed bomber look as if it had been riddled with—

Yes, Michael thought. Of course.

Camouflage.

On D-Day, the invasion beaches would be protected by Allied fighters. No Luftwaffe plane would be able to get through—but an American Flying Fortress might. Especially one that was battle-scarred, and limping back to its base in England.

And once that aircraft got over its target, it could drop its bombs—containing Hildebrand's new discovery—onto the heads of thousands of young soldiers.

But Michael realized there were holes in his conjecture: why go to all that effort when Nazi artillery cannons could simply fire Hildebrand's new weapon amid the invasion troops? And if that weapon was indeed a gas of some kind, how could the Nazis be sure the winds wouldn't blow it back in their faces? No, the Germans might be desperate, but they were far from being stupid. How, then, if Michael was right, was the Fortress going to be used?

He had to get out of here. Had to get to Norway and put more pieces of this puzzle together. He doubted if the B-17 would be hangared in Norway; that was too far from the possible invasion sites. But Hildebrand and his new weapon were there, and Michael had to find out exactly what it was.

The bombing had ceased. The camp's air-raid siren began to whine down.

"Good hunting to you," Lazaris wished the flyers, and in his voice there was a tormented longing.

Michael lay down, trying to find sleep again. He kept seeing the grisly photographs of Hildebrand's test subjects in his mind. Whatever could do that to human flesh had to be destroyed.

The swollen corpses of Metzger and the Frenchman gurgled and popped, releasing the gases of decay. Michael heard the faint scratching of a rat in the wall next to him, trying to find its way to the smell. Let him come, Michael thought. The rat would be fast, a canny survivor, but Michael knew he was faster. Protein was protein. Let him come.

9

The gruel bucket was brought again, marking Michael's tenth day of captivity. The guards retched at the odor of the corpses and slammed the kennel door as soon as they could. Sometime later Michael was drifting in the twilight of sleep when he heard the latch sliding back. The door opened again. Two guards with rifles stood in the corridor, and one of them pressed a handkerchief over his mouth and nose and said, "Bring the dead men out."

Lazaris and the others hesitated, waiting to see if Michael would comply. A third figure peered into the kennel and shone a flashlight on Michael's pallid face. "Come on, hurry!" Bauman ordered. "We haven't got all night!"

Michael heard the tension in Bauman's voice. What was going on? Bauman slid his Luger out of his holster and pointed it into the kennel. "I won't say it again. *Out*."

Michael and Lazaris grasped Metzger's bony corpse and hauled it out of the kennel while the Dane and the German brought the second corpse out. Michael's knees groaned when he stood up, and the Dane fell to the stones and lay there until a rifle barrel prodded him up. "All right," Bauman said. "All of you, march."

They carried the corpses along the corridor. "Halt!" Bauman ordered when they reached a metal door. One of the guards unbolted it and pushed it open.

Michael knew that however old he lived to be, he would never forget that moment. Fresh, cool air drifted in through the doorway; maybe there was a trace of burning flesh in it, but it was sweet perfume compared to the kennel's stale rankness. The camp was quiet, midnight stars afire in the sky. A truck was parked outside, and Bauman directed the prisoners to it with their baggage of corpses. "Get them inside!" he said, tension still thick in his voice. "Hurry!"

The back of the truck was already loaded with over a dozen naked bodies, male and female. It was difficult to tell, because all the corpses had shaved heads, and the breasts of the females had flattened like dead flowers. The flies were very bad. "Come on, move!" Bauman said, and shoved Michael forward.

And then Bauman turned, with the grace of a motion he'd played out a hundred times in his mind in preparation for this moment. The knife slid down into his left hand from the inside of his sleeve, and he took a step toward the nearest guard, plunging the blade into the man's heart. The guard cried out and staggered back, scarlet spreading over his uniform. The second guard said, "What in the name of—"

Bauman stabbed him in the stomach, pulled the blade out and stabbed again. The first guard had crumpled to his knees, his face bleached, and he was trying to get his pistol out of his holster. Michael let go of Metzger's corpse and grabbed the man's wrist as the pistol came out. He smashed his fist into the man's face, but the guard's finger twitched on the trigger and the gun went off, startlingly loud in the silence. The bullet fired into the sky. Michael hit him again, as hard as he could, and as the guard crumpled he took the pistol away.

The Nazi who was grappling with Bauman shouted, "Help me! Someone, help—"

Bauman shot him through the mouth, and the man pitched backward into the dust.

In the distance dogs were barking. Dobermans, Michael thought. "You!" Bauman pointed at Lazaris, who stood staring in shock. "Get that rifle! Go on, you fool!"

Lazaris scooped it up. And aimed it at Bauman. Michael pushed the barrel aside. "No," he said. "He's on our side."

"I'll be damned! What's going on?"

"Stop that jabbering!" Bauman slid the bloody knife into his belt. He glanced at the luminous hands of his wristwatch. "We've got three minutes to reach the gate! Get in the truck, all of you!" Michael heard a shrill whistle blowing somewhere: an alarm signal.

The Dane scrambled into the back, over the corpses. Lazaris did the same, but the German prisoner fell to his knees and began to sob and moan. "Leave him!" Bauman said, and motioned Michael into the truck cab. Bauman got behind the wheel, turned the ignition key, and the engine sputtered and rumbled to life. He drove away from the stone building full of kennels, and toward Falkenhausen's front gate, dust pluming behind the rear tires. "Those shots will stir up a hornet's nest. Hang on." He swerved the truck between two wooden buildings and pressed his foot on the accelerator. Michael saw the chimneys to their left, spouting red sparks as more bodies were charred. And then three soldiers, one of them with a submachine gun, stood in the path of their headlights, waving the truck down. "We're going through," Bauman said tersely.

The guards leaped aside, shouting for the truck to halt. More whistles began to shriek. A burst of bullets whacked into the rear of the truck, making the steering wheel shudder in Bauman's grip. Rifle fire cracked: Lazaris was at work. Searchlights on towers in this section of the huge camp began to come on, their beams sweeping back and forth along the dirt roads and across the buildings. Bauman checked his watch again. "It should start to happen in a few seconds."

Before Michael could ask what he meant, there was a hollow *boom* to their right. Another blast followed almost immediately, this time behind them and on the left. A third explosion was so close Michael could see the gout of fire. "Our friends brought mortars to create a diversion," Bauman said. "They're firing them from the woods." Another series of blasts echoed over the camp. Michael heard scattered rifle fire. The guards were firing at shadows, maybe even at each other. He hoped they, in this instance, had true aim.

A searchlight's glaring white beam found them. Bauman cursed and swerved the truck onto another road to get away from the light, but it stuck close. A high, piercing steam whistle began: the camp's emergency alarm. "Now Krolle's in the act," Bauman said, his knuckles white on the wheel. "Those bastards on the towers have radios. They're pinpointing our posi—"

A guard stepped into the road ahead of them, planted his feet, and pulled back the bolt on his Schmeisser.

Michael saw the weapon fire in a low, sweeping arc. The two front tires exploded almost in unison, and the truck lurched as the engine and radiator were pierced. The guard, still firing, dove for cover as the truck careened past him in a storm of dust, and the front fender scraped sparks off a stone wall before Bauman could get control again. The windshield was cracked, and filmed with oil. Bauman kept driving, his head out the window and the flattened front tires plowing grooves in the road. About fifty yards farther and the engine made a noise like tin cans in a grinder, then died. "That's it for the truck!" Bauman was already throwing his door open. The truck halted, right in the middle of the road, and Michael and the German scrambled out. "Come on!" Bauman shouted to Lazaris and the Dane. They clambered out from the corpses, looking corpselike themselves. "The gate's this way, about a hundred yards!'' Bauman motioned ahead and started running. Michael, his naked body shivering with the effort, kept a few strides behind. Lazaris stumbled, fell, got up, and followed on spindly legs. "Wait! Please wait for me!" the Dane shouted as he lagged behind. Michael looked back, just as a searchlight hit the Dane. "Keep going!" Bauman yelled. The next sound was machine-gun fire, and the Dane was silent.

"Bastards! You filthy bastards!" Lazaris stopped in the road and aimed his rifle as the light swung upon him. Bullets marched across the ground in front of him as Lazaris squeezed off shot after shot. Glass exploded, and the light went out.

Bauman suddenly pulled up short, face-to-face with three guards who'd emerged from between two barracks buildings. "It's me! Fritz Bauman!" he shouted before they could lift their weapons. Michael hit the ground on his stomach. "The prisoners are rioting in Section E!" Bauman shouted. "They're tearing the place apart! For God's sake, get over there!" The soldiers ran on, and disappeared around the corner of another barracks. Then Bauman and Michael continued toward the gate, and as they came out from a cluster of wooden buildings there it was in front of them, across a dangerous area of open ground. The tower searchlights were aimed into the camp, sweeping back and forth. Mortar shells were still exploding in the center of Falkenhausen. "Down!" Bauman told Michael, and they lay on the ground against the wall of one of the wooden buildings as a searchlight crept past. He checked his watch once more. "Damn, it! They're late! Where the hell are they?"

A figure started to stumble past them. Michael reached out, grasped the man's ankles, and tripped him into the dust before a searchlight caught him. Lazaris said, "What are you trying to do, you bastard? Break my neck?"

A motorcycle with a sidecar suddenly roared across the open ground, and its driver skidded to a stop in front of a green-painted building near the gate. Almost at once a door opened and out rushed a stocky figure wearing combat boots, a Nazi helmet, and a red silk robe, two pistols in the holster around his thick waist. Major Krolle, awakened from his beauty sleep, wedged himself into the sidecar and motioned for the driver to go. Dust spat from the motorcycle's rear tire as the driver obeyed, and Michael realized Krolle was going to pass within a few feet of their position. Bauman was already lifting his pistol. Michael said, *"No,"* and reached for Lazaris's rifle. He stood up, his mind aflame with the image of hair drifting into a pinewood box, and as the motorcycle got within range he stepped out from the wall's protection and swung the rifle like a club.

As the rifle connected with the driver's skull and broke the man's neck like a stick of kindling, Falkenhausen's main gate exploded in a blast of flame and a whirlwind of burning timbers.

The concussion knocked Michael to the ground, and passed in a hot wave. The driverless motorcycle veered sharply to the left, spun in a circle, and crashed against a wooden wall before Krolle even knew he was in danger. The motorcycle pitched over on its side, the engine still running, and Krolle flopped out of the sidecar, his helmet knocked off and his ears ringing from the blast.

From the ruins of the gate emerged a camouflage-painted truck with armor shields protecting the tires. As it roared into the camp, the brown canvas covering its cargo bay was whipped back, exposing a .50-caliber machine gun on a swivel mounting. The machine gunner angled his weapon up and shot the nearest searchlight out, then turned its fire on the next one. Three other men in the rear of the truck aimed rifles at the tower guards and began to shoot. "Let's go!" Bauman yelled, getting to his feet. Michael was on his haunches, watching Krolle struggling to get up; the holster had slipped down and tangled around his legs. Michael said, "Take my friend and get to the truck." He stood up.

"What? Are you crazy? They're here for you!"

"Do it." Michael saw the rifle on the ground, its butt broken off. Krolle was whimpering, trying to pull one of the Lugers from its holster. "Don't wait for me." He walked to Major Krolle, grabbed the holster, and flung it away. Krolle gasped, blood running from a gash across his forehead and his eyes dazed. *"Go!"* Michael shouted to Bauman, and he and the Russian ran toward the truck.

Krolle moaned, finally recognizing the man who stood before him. There was a whistle around Krolle's thick neck, and he put it to his mouth but he didn't have wind enough to blow.

Michael heard the clatter of bullets against armor plate. He looked back and saw that Lazaris and Bauman had reached the truck and climbed inside. The machine gunner was still firing at the tower guards, but now slugs were striking the truck as well. More soldiers were coming, alerted by the blast and blaze. A rifle bullet ricocheted off one of the truck's tire shields, and the machine gunner swiveled his weapon and shot down the soldier who'd fired it. The kitchen was heating up; it was time to get out. The truck was put into reverse, and withdrew through the flame-edged aperture where the gate had been.

At his feet, Krolle was trying to crawl away. "Help me," he croaked. "Someone . . ." But he could not be heard over the shouts and the firing of guns and the wailing emergency siren, a sound that must've reached Berlin. Michael said, "Major?" and the man looked at him. Krolle's face distorted into a rictus of sheer horror.

Michael's mouth was opening, the muscles rippling in his jaws. Making room for the fangs that slid, dripping saliva, from their sockets. Dark bands of hair rose over the naked flesh, and his fingers and toes began to hook into claws.

Krolle scrambled up, slipped, got up again with a strangled yelp and ran. Not toward the gate, because the monstrous figure blocked his way, but in the opposite direction, into the depths of Falkenhausen. Michael, his spine contorting and his joints cracking, followed like the shadow of death.

The major fell to his knees beside a barracks and tried to get his bulk into the crawl space beneath. Failing that, he struggled up once more and staggered on, calling for help in a voice that did not carry. A wooden building was on fire perhaps three hundred yards away, hit by a mortar shell. Its red light capered in the sky. The searchlights were still probing, their paths interweaving, and guards shot at each other in the confusion.

There was no confusion in the mind of the wolf. He knew his task, and he would relish this one.

Krolle looked back over his shoulder and saw the thing's green eyes. He gave a bleat of fear, his robe dusty and undone, and his well-fed, white belly hanging out. He kept running, trying to call for help between gasps of air. He dared to look again and saw the monster gaining on him with a steady, powerful loping stride—and then Krolle's ankles hit a low pinewood barrier, and with a scream he pitched over it and slid facedown a steep dirt incline.

Michael leaped nimbly across the barricade—set there to keep trucks from tumbling over—and stood on the edge of the incline, peering at what lay before him. In his wolf's body his heart hammered with a fearsome rhythm as he saw the beast's banquet laid out at the bottom of the pit.

How many corpses were strewn there was impossible to say. Three thousand? Five thousand? He didn't know. The steep-walled pit was about fifty yards from side to side, and the naked dead lay tangled in obscene, bony piles, thrown one on top of another so deep that he couldn't see the pit's floor. In that gray, hideous, unfathomable mass of rib cages, emaciated arms and legs, bald skulls and hollowed eyes, one figure in a red robe struggled toward the pit's opposite side, crawling across the bridges of decaying flesh.

Michael held his position on the edge, his claws gripping the soft dirt. The firelight leaped, painting the huge mass grave with hell's radiance. His mind was numbed; there was so much death. Reality seemed warped, a bad dream from which he must surely soon awaken. This was the fingerprint of true evil, beyond which all fictions paled.

Michael lifted his head to heaven, and screamed.

It came out as a hoarse, ragged wolf's wail. In the pit Krolle heard it, and looked back. Sweat glistened on his face, flies swarming around him. "Stay away from me!" he shouted to the monster on the pit's edge. His voice cracked, and madness broke through. "Stay away from—"

A corpse shifted beneath him with a noise like a whisper. Its movement caused other bodies to part, and Krolle lost his balance. He clawed at a broken shoulder, trying to grip a pair of legs with his sweaty hands, but flesh rippled under his fingers and he went down amid the dead. The corpses rose and fell like sea waves, and Krolle thrashed to stay at the surface. He opened his mouth to scream; flies rushed into it, and were sucked down his throat. Flies blinded him, and winnowed into his ears. He clawed at rotting flesh, his boots finding no purchase. His head went under, corpses shifting around him like waking sleepers. Taken one by one, the bodies weighed about as much as the shovels that had pitched them down here; together, in their twisted linkage of arms and legs, they closed over Krolle's head and crushed him down into the suffocating depths. He was borne to the bottom, where a slender arm hooked around his throat and flies struggled in his windpipe.

Krolle was gone. The corpses kept shifting, all across the pit, making room for another. Michael, his green eyes burning with tears of horror, turned away from the dead, and ran toward the living.

He scared the yellow piss out of two Dobermans that were being held on leashes by their masters, and then he streaked past them and across the open ground near where the wrecked motorcycle lay. A truckful of soldiers was about to drive through the broken gate, in pursuit of the rescue team. Michael changed their plans by leaping up over the truck's tailgate into the rear, and the soldiers yelled and jumped out as if they'd grown wings. The driver, intimidated by the sight of a thin and obviously hungry wolf snapping at his face on the other side of the windshield, immediately lost control and the truck slammed into Falkenhausen's stone wall.

But the wolf was no longer perched on the hood. Michael bounded through the blown-open gate, and out into freedom. He cut across the dirt road and entered the forest, his nose sniffing. Engine oil, gunpowder, and . . . ah, yes . . . the rank odor of a Russian fighter pilot.

He kept to the brush on the road's edge, following the scents. The smell of blood: someone had been wounded. About a mile away from Falkenhausen the truck had turned off the main road onto one that was little more than a . . . well, than a wolf's trail. The rescue team had been prepared; what looked—and smelled—like a second truck had come out of this trail and roared away to leave tire treads for the pursuers, while the original vehicle had entered the dense forest. Michael followed Lazaris's reek, through the silent sylvan glades.

He followed the twisting trail for almost eight miles, and then he heard the voices and saw the glint of flashlights. He crouched amid the pines and watched. In a clearing before him, shielded from aerial observation by a camouflage net overhead, were the armored truck and two civilian cars. Workers were dismantling the truck, rapidly removing the armor and taking the machine gun off its mount. At the same time others were hurriedly painting the truck white with a Red Cross on the cab doors. The cargo-bay area was being transformed into an ambulance, with tiers of stretcher beds. The machine gun was wrapped in burlap, put into a wooden box lined with rubber, lowered into a trench. Then shovels went to work, covering the weapon.

A tent had been set up, and from it protruded a radio antenna. Michael was flattered. They'd gone to a hell of a lot of effort for him, not to mention risking their lives.

"I tried to get him to come, damn it!" Bauman suddenly walked out of the tent. "I think he went crazy! How was I to know he was about to snap?"

"You should have *made* him come! God only knows what they'll do to him now!" A second figure stalked out, following Bauman. Michael knew that voice, and when he sniffed the air he caught her fragrance: cinnamon and leather. Chesna wore a black jumpsuit, a holster and pistol around her waist, her blond hair hidden beneath a black cap and her face daubed with charcoal. "All this work, and he's still in there! And instead of him, you bring *this* thing!" She motioned angrily at Lazaris, who emerged from the tent placidly chewing on a biscuit. "My God, what are we going to *do?*"

A wolf could smile, in its own way.

Two minutes later a sentry heard a twig snap. He froze, questing for movement in the dark. Was there someone standing by that pine tree, or not? He lifted his rifle. "Halt. Who's there?"

"A friend," Michael said. He dropped the twig he'd just broken and came out with his hands upraised. The sight of a naked, bruised man emerging from the forest made the sentry shout, "Hey! Someone come over here! Hurry!"

"What's all that damned noise!" Chesna said as she, Bauman, and a couple of others rushed to the sentry's assistance. Flashlights were turned on, and they caught Michael Gallatin in their crossfire.

Chesna stopped abruptly, the breath shocked out of her.

Bauman whispered, "How the *hell* . . ."

"No time for formalities." Michael's voice was raspy and weak. The change, and the eight-mile run, had tapped the last of his reserves. Already the figures around him were blurring in and out of focus. He could let himself go now. He was free. "I'm . . . about to pass out," he said. "I hope . . . someone will . . . catch me?" His knees buckled.

Chesna did.

TEN

Destiny

His first impression upon awakening was of green and golden light: the sun, shining through dense foliage. He thought of the forest of his youth, the kingdom of Wiktor and the family. But that was long ago, and Michael Gallatin lay not on a pallet of hay but on a bed of white linen. The ceiling above him was white, the walls pale green. He heard the song of robins and turned his head toward a window on his right. He could see a network of interlocking tree branches and slices of blue sky between them.

His mind, even with all the beauty, found the emaciated corpses in the mass grave. That was the kind of thing that, once viewed, opened your eyes forever to the reality of human evil. He wanted to weep, to cleanse himself of that sight, but his eyes wouldn't let the tears go. Why weep when the tortures were already done? No, the time for tears had passed. It was time now for cold reflection, and a gathering of strength.

His body hurt like hell. Even his brain felt bruised. He lifted up the sheet and saw he was still naked. His flesh resembled a patchwork quilt, rendered in shades of black and blue. His wounded thigh had been stitched up and painted with iodine. Various other cuts and punctures on his body—including the stab wounds inflicted by Blok's dinner fork—had been treated with disinfectant. The kennel filth had been scrubbed off him, and Michael figured that whoever had done the job was deserving of a medal. He touched his hair and found that it had been washed, too; his scalp stung, probably from an astringent lice-killing shampoo. His beard had been shaved off, but there was a fresh rough

493

stubble on his face that made him wonder how long he'd lain in an exhausted slumber.

One thing he knew for certain: he was famished. He could see the slats of his ribs, and his arms and legs had gotten thin, the muscles wasted. On a small table beside his bed there was a silver bell. Michael picked it up and rang it to see what would happen.

In less than ten seconds the door flew open. Chesna van Dorne came in, her face radiant and scrubbed of its commando charcoal, her tawny eyes bright, and her hair in golden curls around her shoulders. She was a beautiful vision, Michael thought. He was hardly distracted by her shapeless gray jumpsuit and the Walther pistol in its holster around her waist. Following behind her was a gray-haired man with horn-rimmed glasses, dressed in dark blue trousers and a white shirt with his sleeves rolled up. He carried a black medical bag, which he set on the table beside the bed and unsnapped.

"How are you feeling?" Chesna asked, standing by the door. Her expression was one of businesslike concern.

"Alive. Barely." His voice was a husky whisper. Speaking was an effort. He tried to sit up, but the man—obviously a doctor—pressed his hand against his chest and eased him back down, which was about as difficult as restraining a sickly child.

"This is Dr. Stronberg," Chesna explained. "He's been taking care of you."

"And testing the limits of medical science at the same time, I might add." Stronberg had a voice like gravel in a cement mixer. He sat on the edge of the bed, produced a stethoscope from his bag, and listened to the patient's heartbeat. "Breathe deeply." Michael did. "Again. Once more. Now hold your breath. Let it out slowly." He grunted and took the instrument's ear cups out. "You're wheezing a bit. Low-grade infection in the lungs, I think." A thermometer slid under Michael's tongue. "You're fortunate you keep yourself in such good condition. Otherwise twelve days in Falkenhausen on bread and water might have left you with much worse than exhaustion and congested lungs."

"Twelve *days?*" Michael said, and reached for the thermometer.

Stronberg grasped his wrist and pushed it aside. "Leave that alone. Yes, twelve days. Of course you have other ailments as well: a mild case of shock, a broken nose, a severely bruised shoulder, a bruise on your back from a blow that almost ruptured your kidneys, and your thigh wound was close to contracting gangrene. Lucky for you, it was caught in time. I had to clip some tissue, though; you won't be using that leg for a while."

My God! Michael thought, and he shivered at the idea of losing his leg to a knife and bone saw.

"There's been blood in your urine," Stronberg went on, "but I don't think your kidneys are permanently damaged. I had to insert a catheter and drain off some fluid." He removed the thermometer and checked its reading. "Low fever," he said. "At least you've cooled off since yesterday."

"How long have I been here?"

"Three days," Chesna said. "Dr. Stronberg wanted you to rest."

Michael could taste bitterness in his mouth. Drugs, he thought. Antibiotic and tranquilizer, most likely. The doctor was already preparing another syringe. "No more of that," Michael said.

"Don't be an idiot." Stronberg grasped his arm. "Your system's been exposed to such filth and germs you're fortunate you don't have typhus, diphtheria, and bubonic plague." He jabbed the needle in.

There wasn't much he could do about it. "Who cleaned me?"

"I hosed you down, if that's what you mean," Chesna told him.

"Thank you."

She shrugged. "I didn't want you infecting my people."

"They did a fine job. I'm indebted." He remembered the smell of blood on the forest trail. "Who got hit?"

"Eisner. He took a bullet through the hand." She frowned. "Wait a minute. How did you know anyone was hit?"

Michael hesitated. How indeed? he thought. "I . . . didn't know, for certain," he said. "A lot of bullets were flying."

"Yes." Chesna was watching him carefully. "We're lucky we didn't lose anyone. Now maybe you can tell me why you refused to come out with Bauman, and then wandered into camp more than eight miles from Falkenhausen. What did you do, *run* that distance? And how did you find us?"

"Lazaris," Michael said, stalling while he thought up a good answer. "My friend. Is he all right?"

Chesna nodded. "He brought an army of lice with him. We had to shave him bald, but he said he'd kill anyone who touched his beard. He's in even worse shape than you, but he'll live." She raised her blond brows. "You were about to tell me how you found us?"

Michael remembered hearing Chesna and Bauman arguing that night as they came out of the tent. "I think I went a little crazy," he explained. "I went after Major Krolle. I don't recall much of what happened."

"Did you kill him?"

"He . . . was taken care of," Michael said.

"Go on."

"I took Krolle's motorcycle. That's how I got through the gate. A bullet must've punctured the gas tank, because I only got a few miles before the engine stopped. Then I started walking through the woods. I saw your flashlights, and I came in." Flimsy as hell, he thought, but that's all he could come up with.

Chesna was silent for a moment, staring at him. Then she said, "We had a man watching the road. He saw no motorcycle."

"I didn't use the road. I went through the forest."

"And you just happened to find our camp? In all the woods? You stumbled onto our camp when none of the Nazis could track us down?"

"I guess I did. I got there, didn't I?" He smiled wanly. "Call it destiny."

"I think," Chesna said, "that you've been breathing through another hollow reed." She came a little closer to the bed as Stronberg prepared a second injection. "If I didn't know you were on our side, Baron, I might have grave

496

misgivings about you. To beat Harry Sandler at his own game is one thing; to travel, in your condition, over eight miles through the forest at night and find our camp—which was very well hidden, I might add—is something quite different."

"I'm good at what I do. That's why I'm here." He winced as the second needle broke the skin.

She shook her head. "No one is *that* good, Baron. There's something about you . . . something very strange."

"Well, we can debate this all day, if you like." He let feigned exasperation creep into his voice. Chesna's eyes were sharp, and they saw his evasion. "Have you got the plane ready?"

"It's ready, whenever I want it." She decided to let this matter go, for now. But this man was hiding something, and she wanted to know what it was.

"Good. When can we leave?"

"There'll be no traveling for you," Stronberg said firmly. He snapped his bag closed. "Not for two weeks, at least. Your body's been starved and brutalized. A normal man, one without your commando training, would be a basket case by now."

"Doctor," Michael said, "thank you for your attention and care. Now would you please leave?"

"He's right," Chesna added. "You're too weak to go anywhere. As far as you're concerned, the mission is over."

"Is that why you got me out? To tell me I'm an invalid?"

"No. To keep you from spilling your guts. Since you were imprisoned, Colonel Blok has closed down the Reichkronen. From what I hear, he's been questioning all the employees and going over their records. He's having the place searched room by room. We got you out of Falkenhausen because Bauman let us know Blok was about to start torturing you the following morning. Four more hours and a catheter would have been an impossibility."

"Oh. I see." In that light the loss of a leg was a minor inconvenience.

Dr. Stronberg was about to retreat to the door. But he paused and said, "That's an interesting birthmark you have. I've never seen anything quite like it."

"Birthmark?" Michael asked. "What birthmark?"

Stronberg looked puzzled. "Under your left arm, of course."

Michael lifted his arm, and had a shock of surprise. From the armpit to his hip were streaks of sleek, black hair. Wolf hair, he realized. With all the stress to his mind and body, he had not fully changed back since leaving Falkenhausen.

"Fascinating," Stronberg said. He leaned closer to look at the streaks. "That's one for a dermatologist's journal."

"I'm sure it is." Michael lowered his arm and clasped it to his side.

Stronberg walked past Chesna to the door. "We'll start you on solids tomorrow. Some meat with your broth."

"I don't want any damned broth. I want a steak. Very rare."

"Your stomach's not ready for that," Stronberg said, and he left the room.

"What day is this?" Michael asked Chesna after the doctor had gone. "The date?"

"May seventh." Chesna walked to a window and peered out at the forest, her face washed with afternoon light. "In answer to your next question, we're in the house of a friend, about forty miles northwest of Berlin. The nearest village is a small hamlet called Rossow, eleven miles to the west. So we're safe here, and you can rest easy."

"I don't want to rest. I've got a mission to finish." Even as he said it, he felt whatever Stronberg had given him beginning to work. His tongue was numb, and he was getting drowsy again.

"We received a radio code from London four days ago." Chesna turned from the window to look at him. "The invasion's been scheduled for the fifth of June. I've radioed back the message that our assignment is incomplete, and that the invasion may be in jeopardy. I'm still waiting for a reply."

"I think I know what Iron Fist is," Michael said, and he began to tell her about his Flying Fortress theory. She listened intently, with no evidence that she agreed or disagreed: a poker face. "I don't think the plane's hangared in Norway," he told her, "because that's too far from the invasion beaches. But Hildebrand knows where the plane is. We've got to get to Skarpa . . ." His vision was fogging up, the taste of medicine thick in his mouth, ". . . and find out what Hildebrand's developed."

"You can't go anywhere. Not in the shape you're in. It would be better if I chose a team myself and flew them up."

"No! Listen to me . . . your friends may be good at breaking into a prison camp . . . but Skarpa's going to be a hell of a lot tougher. You need a professional for the job."

"Like yourself?"

"Right. I can be ready to go in six days."

"Dr. Stronberg said two weeks."

"I don't give a damn what he said!" He felt a flush of anger. "Stronberg doesn't know me. I can be ready in six days . . . providing I get some meat."

Chesna smiled faintly. "I believe you're serious."

"I am. And no more tranquilizers or whatever it is that Stronberg's stuck into me. Understand?"

She paused, thinking it over. Then: "I'll tell him."

"One more thing. Have you . . . thought about the possibility that . . . we may run into fighter planes between here and Skarpa?"

"Yes. I'm willing to take that risk."

"If you get shot, I don't care to . . . go down in flames. You'll need a copilot. Do you have one?"

Chesna shook her head.

"Talk to Lazaris," Michael said. "You might . . . find him very interesting."

"That *beast?* He's a flier?"

"Just talk to him." Michael's eyelids were getting heavy. It was hard to fight against the twilight. Better to rest, he thought. Rest, and fight again tomorrow.

Chesna stayed beside the bed until he was asleep. Her face softened, and she reached out to touch his hair but he shifted his position and she pulled her hand back. When she'd realized he and Mouse had been captured, she'd almost gone crazy with worry, and not because she feared he would spill secrets. Seeing him emerge from the forest—filthy and mottled with bruises, his face hollowed by hunger and the ordeal of captivity—had almost made her faint. But how had he tracked them through the woods? *How?*

Who are you? she mentally asked the sleeping man. Lazaris had inquired how his friend "Gallatinov" was doing. Was the man British, or Russian? Or some other, more arcane nationality? Even in his drained condition, he was a handsome man—but there was something lonely about him. Something lost. All her life, she'd been brought up on the taste of silver spoons; this was a man who knew the taste of dirt. There was a cardinal rule in the secret service; do not become emotionally involved. To break that rule might lead to untold suffering and death. But she was tired—so very tired—of being an actress. And living life without emotion was like playing a part for the critics instead of the audience: there was no joy in it, only stagecraft.

The baron—Gallatinov, or whatever his name might be— shivered in his sleep. She saw the flesh of his arms rise in goose bumps. She remembered washing him, not with a hose but with a scrub brush as he lay unconscious in a tub of warm water. She had scrubbed the lice from his scalp, his chest, beneath his arms, and in his pubic hair. She had shaved him and washed his hair, and she had done all that because no one else would. That was her job, but her job did not require that her heart ache as she'd cleaned the grime from the lines in his face.

Chesna pulled the sheet up around his neck. His eyes opened—a glint of green—but the drugs were strong, and he went under again. She wished him a good sleep, beyond this world of nightmares, and closed the door quietly when she left.

2

Less than eighteen hours after he'd first awakened, Michael Gallatin was on his feet. He relieved himself in a bedpan. His urine was still blushed with blood, but there was no pain. His thigh throbbed, though his legs were sturdy. He paced the room, testing himself, and found he walked with a limp. Without painkillers and tranquilizers in his system, his nerves felt raw, but his mind was clear. It had turned toward Norway, and what he had to do to get himself ready.

He lay on the pinewood floor and slowly stretched his muscles. Deep pain gnawed at him as he worked. Back on the floor, legs up, crunch head toward knees. Stomach to the floor, lift chin and legs at the same time. Slow push-ups that made his shoulder and back muscles scream. Sit on the floor, knees bent, and ever so slowly lower the back almost to the floor, linger past the point of agony, and come up again. A light sheen of sweat glowed on Michael's skin. Blood pumped through his veins and gorged his muscles, and his heart reached a hard rhythm. Six days, he thought as he breathed raggedly. I'll be ready.

A woman with gray-streaked brown hair brought his dinner: strained vegetables and a hash of finely chopped beef. "Baby food," Michael told her, but he ate every bit. Dr. Stronberg returned to check him again. His fever was down, and the wheezing in his lungs had decreased. He had, however, popped three stitches. Stronberg warned him to stay in bed and rest, and that was the end of the visit.

A night later, another helping of ghastly beef hash in his stomach, Michael stood in the darkness and eased his window open. He slipped out, into the silent forest, and stood beneath an elm tree as he changed from man to wolf. The rest of his stitches popped open, but the thigh wound didn't bleed. It was another scar to add to his collection. He loped on all fours through the woods, breathing the fragrant, clean air. A squirrel caught his attention, and he was on it before it could reach its tree. His mouth watered as he consumed the meat and fluids, then he spat out the bones and hair and continued on his jaunt. At a farmhouse perhaps two miles from the cottage, a dog barked and howled at Michael's scent. Michael sprayed a fence post, just to let the dog know its place.

He sat atop a grassy knoll and stared at the stars. On such a beautiful night as this, the question had to be asked: what is the lycanthrope, in the eye of God?

He thought he might know the answer to that now, after

the sight of the mass grave at Falkenhausen, after the death of Mouse and the memory of an Iron Cross being plucked from his broken fingers. After his time in this land of torment and hatred, he thought he knew; and if not, the answer would do for now.

The lycanthrope was God's avenger.

There was so much work to be done. Michael knew Chesna had courage—and plenty of it—but her chances of getting on and off Skarpa Island without him were slim. He had to be sharp and strong to face what was ahead for them.

But he was weaker than he'd thought. The change had sapped his strength, and he lay with his head on his paws under the clear starlight. He slept, and dreamed of a wolf who dreamed he was a man who dreamed he was a wolf who dreamed.

The sun was coming up when he awakened. The land was green and lovely, but it hid a black heart. He got up off his belly and started back the way he'd come, following his own scent. He neared the house and was about to change to human form again when he heard, above the song of the dawn birds, the faint noise of radio static. He tracked it, and about fifty yards from the house found a shack covered with camouflage netting. An antenna was mounted on the roof. Michael crouched in the brush and listened as the radio static ended. There were three musical tones, followed one after the other. Then Chesna's voice, speaking German: "I read you. Go ahead."

A man's voice, transmitted from a great distance, answered. "The concert is set. Beethoven, as planned. Your tickets must be purchased as soon as possible. Out." Then the crackle of dead air.

"That's it," Chesna said, to someone in the shack. A moment later Bauman emerged and climbed a stepladder to the roof, where he removed the antenna. Chesna came out, dark circles beneath her eyes indicating a troubled sleep, and began to stride through the forest toward the house. Michael silently kept pace with her, keeping to the green shadows. He sniffed her fragrance, and he remembered their first kiss in the lobby of the Reichkronen. He was feeling stronger now; all of him was feeling stronger. A few more days of rest, and a few more nights of hunting the meat and blood he needed, and—

He took another step, and that was when the quail hidden in the brush shrieked and leaped out from beneath his paw.

Chesna whirled toward the sound. Her hand was already gripping the Luger and drawing it from her holster. She saw him; he watched her eyes widen with the shock as she took aim and squeezed the trigger.

The gun spoke, and a chunk of bark flew from the tree next to Michael's head. She fired a second time, but the black wolf was no longer there. Michael had turned and plunged into the dense foliage, the bullet whining over his back. "Fritz! Fritz!" Chesna shouted for Bauman as Michael winnowed through the underbrush and ran. "A wolf!" he heard her say as Bauman came running up. "It was right there, looking at me! God, I've never seen one so close!"

"A *wolf?*" Bauman's voice was incredulous. "There are no wolves around here!"

Michael circled through the woods back in the direction of the house. His heart was pounding; the two bullets had missed him by fractions of inches. He lay in the brush and changed as quickly as he could, his bones aching as they rejointed and his fangs sliding into his jaws with wet clicking sounds. The gunshots would have already roused everyone in the house. He stood up, newly fleshed, slipped in through his window, and closed it behind him. He heard other voices outside, calling to ask what had happened. Then he got into bed, pulled the sheet up to his throat, and was lying there when Chesna entered minutes later.

"I thought you'd be awake," she said. She was still a little nervous, and he could smell the gunsmoke on her skin. "You heard the shots?"

"Yes. What's going on?" He sat up, pretending alarm.

"I almost got chewed up by a wolf. Out there, damned close to the house. The thing was staring at me, and it had . . ." Her voice trailed off.

"It had what?" Michael prompted.

"It had black hair and green eyes," she said, in a quiet voice.

"I thought all wolves were gray."

"No." She stared into his face, as if truly seeing him for the first time. "They're not."

"I heard two shots. Did you hit him?"

"I don't know. Maybe. Of course, it could've been a bitch."

"Well, thank God it didn't get you." He smelled breakfast cooking: sausages and pancakes. Her intense stare was making him jittery. "If it was as hungry as I am, you're very lucky it didn't take a bite out of you."

"I guess I am." *What am I thinking?* Chesna asked herself. *That this man has black hair and green eyes, and so did the wolf? And what of that? I must be losing my mind, to even think such a thing!* "Fritz . . . says there are no wolves in this area."

"Ask him if he'd like to go for a walk in the woods tonight, and find out." He smiled tightly. "I know *I* wouldn't."

Chesna realized she was standing with her back against the wall. What had been wheeling through her mind was utterly ridiculous, she knew, but still . . . no, no! That was crazy! Such things were the stuff of medieval fireside tales, when the winter wind blew cold and howled in the night. This was the modern world! "I'd like to know your name," she said at last. "Lazaris calls you Gallatinov."

"I was born Mikhail Gallatinov. I changed my name to Michael Gallatin when I became a British citizen."

"Michael," Chesna repeated, trying out the sound of it. "I just received a radio message. The invasion is still set for June fifth, barring bad weather in the Channel. Our mission stands: we're to find Iron Fist and destroy it."

"I'll be ready."

His color looked better this morning, as if he'd gotten some exercise. *Or perhaps a vigorous dream?* she wondered. "I believe you will be," she said. "Lazaris is doing better, too. We had a long talk yesterday. He knows a lot about airplanes. If we have engine trouble on the way, he might be useful."

"I'd like to see him. Can I have some clothes?"

"I'll ask Dr. Stronberg if you're up to getting out of bed."

Michael grunted. "Tell him I want some of those pancakes, too."

504

She sniffed the air, and found their scent. "You must have a very good sense of smell."

"Yes, I do."

Chesna was silent. Again, those thoughts—insane thoughts—crept through her mind. She brushed them aside. "The cook's making oatmeal for you and Lazaris. You're not ready for heavy food yet."

"I could've starved on gruel in Falkenhausen, if that's what you and the good doctor want."

"It's not. Dr. Stronberg just wants your system to recuperate." She walked to the door, then paused there. She stared into his green eyes and felt the hairs stir at the back of her neck. They were the eyes of the wolf, she thought. No, of course that was absolutely impossible! "I'll check on you later," she said, and went out.

A frown settled over Michael's features. The bullets had been a close call. He had been almost able to read Chesna's thoughts; of course she wouldn't come to the correct conclusion, but he'd have to watch his step around her from now on. He scratched his rough beard and then looked at his hands. There was dark German earth under his fingernails.

Michael's breakfast—watery oatmeal—was delivered in a few minutes. Stronberg entered a little later and pronounced his fever all but gone. The doctor railed, however, about the broken stitches. Michael said he was up to doing some mild calisthenics, so he ought to be allowed clothes to walk around in. Stronberg at first flatly refused, then said he'd think about it. Before an hour passed, a gray-green jumpsuit, underwear, socks, and canvas shoes were brought to Michael's room by the same woman who prepared the meals. An added encouragement was a bowl of water, a cake of shaving soap, and a straight razor, with which Michael removed his stubble.

Freshly shaved and dressed, Michael left his room and roamed through the house. He found Lazaris in a room down the corridor, the Russian slick-bald but still heavily bearded, his proud prow of a nose made even more huge because of his gleaming dome. Lazaris was still pallid and somewhat less than energetic, but there were faint spots of color in his cheeks and his dark brown eyes had a glint in them. Lazaris said he was being treated very well, but his request for a bottle of vodka and a pack of cigarettes had been refused. "Hey, Gallatinov!" he said as Michael started to leave. "I'm glad I didn't know you were such an important spy! It might have made me a little nervous!"

"Are you nervous now?"

"You mean, just because I'm in a nest of spies? Gallatinov, I'm so scared my shit comes out yellow. If the Nazis ever found this place, we'd all dance in piano-wire neckties!"

"They won't. And we won't."

"Yes, maybe our wolf will protect us. Did you hear about that?"

Michael nodded.

"So," Lazaris said, "you want to go to Norway. Some damned island off the southwest coast. Right? Goldilocks told me all about it."

"That's right."

"And you need a copilot. Goldilocks says she's got a transport plane. She won't say what kind, which makes me think it's not exactly one of the latest models." He lifted a finger. "Which means, Comrade Gallatinov, that it's not going to be a fast plane, and neither is it going to have a very high ceiling. I've told Goldilocks this, and I'll tell you: if we run into fighter planes, we've had it. No transport plane can outrun a Messerschmitt."

"I know that. I'm sure she does, too. Does all this mean you'll do the job, or not?"

Lazaris blinked, as if amazed that the question should even be asked. "I belong in the sky," he said. "Of course I'll do it."

Michael had never doubted that the Russian would. He left Lazaris and went in search of Chesna. He found her alone in the rear parlor, studying maps of Germany and Norway. She showed him the route they were going to fly, and where the three fuel and supply stops were. They would travel only in darkness, she said, and the trip would take them four nights. She showed him where they were going to land in Norway. "It's a strip of flatland between two mountains, actually," she said. "Our agent with the boat is here." With the point of her pencil, she touched the dot of a coastal village named Uskedahl. "There's Skarpa." She touched the small, rugged land mass—a circular brown scab, Michael thought—that lay about thirty miles down the coast from Uskedahl and eight or nine miles offshore. "This is where we're likely to run into patrol boats." She made a circle just to the east of Skarpa. "Mines, too, I'd guess."

"Skarpa doesn't look like the place for a summer vacation, does it?"

"Hardly. There'll still be snow on the ground up there, and the nights will be cold. We'll have to take winter clothing. Summer comes late in Norway."

"I don't mind cold weather."

She looked up at him, and found herself staring into his green eyes. Wolf's eyes, she thought. "There's not very much that gets to you, is there?"

"No. I won't let it."

"Is it that simple? You turn yourself off and on, depending on the circumstances?"

Her face was close to his. Her aroma was a scent of heaven. Less than six inches, and their lips would meet. "I thought we were talking about Skarpa," Michael said.

"We were. Now we're talking about you." She held his gaze for a few seconds longer, and then she looked away and began to fold the maps. "Do you have a home?" she asked.

"Yes."

"No, I don't mean a house. I mean a home." She looked at him again, her tawny eyes dark with questions. "A place where you belong. A home of the heart."

He thought about it. "I'm not sure." His heart belonged in the forest of Russia, a long way from his stone manse in Wales. "I think there is—or used to be—but I can't go back to it. Who ever can, really?" She didn't answer. "What about you?"

Chesna made sure the maps were folded crease to crease, and then slid them into a brown leather map case. "I have no home," she said. "I love Germany, but it's the love for a sick friend, who will soon die." She stared out a window, at the trees and golden light. "I remember America. Those cities . . . they can take your breath away. And all that space, like a vast cathedral. You know, someone from California visited me before the war. He said he'd seen all my pictures. He asked me if I might like to go to Hollywood." She smiled faintly, lost in a memory. "My face, he said, would be seen all over the world. He said I ought to come home, and work in the country where I was born. Of course, that was before the world changed."

"It hasn't changed enough for them to stop making motion pictures in Hollywood."

"*I've* changed," she said. "I've killed human beings. Some of them deserved a bullet, others were simply in the path of them. I have . . . seen terrible things. And sometimes . . . I wish that more than anything, I could go back, and be innocent again. But once your home of the heart is burned to ashes, who can build it back for you?"

For that question he had no answer. The sunlight shone through the window into her hair, making it glint like spun gold. His fingers ached to lose themselves in it. He reached out, started to touch her hair, and then she sighed and snapped the map case shut, and Michael closed his hand and drew it back.

"I'm sorry," Chesna said. She took the map case to a hollowed-out book and slipped it into a shelf. "I didn't mean to ramble on like that."

"It's all right." He was feeling a little fatigued again. No sense pushing himself when it wasn't necessary. "I'm going back to my room."

She nodded. "You should rest while you can." She motioned to the parlor's shelves of books. "A lot of reading material in here, if you like. Dr. Strönberg has a nice collection of nonfiction and mythology."

So this was the doctor's house, Michael thought. "No, thank you. If you'll excuse me?" She said of course, and Michael left the parlor.

Chesna was about to turn away from the shelves when a book spine's faded title caught her eye. It was wedged between a tome on the Norse gods and another on the history of the Black Forest region, and its title was *Völkerkunde von Deutschland:* Folktales of Germany.

She wasn't going to take that book from its shelf, open it,

and look at its page of contents. She had more important things to do, like getting the winter clothing together and making sure they'd have enough food. She wasn't going to touch that book.

But she did. She took it down, opened it, and scanned the contents.

And there it was. Right there, along with chapters on bridge trolls, eight-foot-tall woodsmen, and cave-dwelling goblins.

Das Werewulf.

Chesna shut the book so hard Dr. Stronberg heard the pop in his study and jumped in his chair. Utterly ridiculous! Chesna thought as she returned the volume to its slot. She strode to the doorway. But before she got there, her strides began to slow. And she stopped, about three feet from the door.

The nagging, gnawing question that would not be banished returned to her again: how had the baron—Michael—found his way to their camp through the black woods?

Such a thing was impossible. Wasn't it?

She walked back to the bookshelves. Her hand found the volume and lingered there. If she read that chapter, she thought, would it be admitting that she might possibly believe it could be true? No, of course not! she decided. It was harmless curiosity, and only that. There were no such things as werewolves, just as there were no bridge trolls or phantom woodsmen.

What would it hurt, to read about a myth?

She took the book down.

3

Michael roamed the dark.

His hunting was better than the night before. He came into a clearing and faced a trio of deer—a stag and a pair of does. They bolted immediately, but one of the does was lame and could not shake the wolf that was rapidly gaining on her. Michael saw she was in pain; the lame leg had been broken, and grown back at a crooked angle. With a burst of speed he hurtled after her and brought her down. The struggle was over in a matter of seconds, and thus was nature served.

He ate her heart, a delicious meal. There was no savagery in this; it was the way of life and death. The stag and the remaining doe stood on a hilltop for a moment, watching the wolf feast, and then they vanished into the night. Michael ate his fill. It was a shame to waste the rest of the meat, so he dragged her beneath a dense stand of pines and sprayed a territorial circle around her, in case the farmer's dog wandered this way. Tomorrow night she'd still be worthy.

The blood and juices energized him. He felt alive again, his muscles vibrant. But he had gore all over his muzzle and belly, and something had to be done about that before he returned to the open window. He loped through the forest, sniffing the air, and in a while he caught the scent of water. Soon he could hear the stream, rushing over rocks. He wallowed in the chilly water, rolling in it to get all the blood off. He licked his paws clean, making sure no blood remained on the nails. Then he lapped to quench his thirst, and started back to the house.

He changed in the woods and stood up on two white legs. He walked silently to the house, his feet cushioned on May grass, and slid through the window into his bedroom.

He smelled her at once. Cinnamon and leather. And there she was, edged in dark blue, sitting in a chair in the corner.

He could hear her heart pounding as he stood before her. Perhaps it was as loud as his own.

"How long have you been here?" he asked.

"An hour." She was making a valiant effort to keep her voice steady. "Maybe a little longer." This time her voice betrayed her.

"You waited all that time for me? I'm flattered."

"I . . . thought I'd look in on you." She cleared her throat, as if only incidentally getting around to the next question. "Michael, where have you been?"

"Just out. Walking. I didn't want to use the front door. I thought I might wake everybody in the hou—"

"It's past three in the morning," Chesna interrupted. "Why are you naked?"

"I never wear clothes past midnight. It's against my religion."

She stood up. "Don't try to be amusing! There's nothing at all amusing about this! My God! Are *you* out of your mind, or am I? When I saw you gone . . . and the window open, I didn't know what to think!"

Michael eased the window shut. "What did you think?"

"That . . . you're a . . . I don't know, it's just too insane!"

He turned to face her. "That I'm a what?" he asked quietly.

Chesna started to say the word. It jammed in her throat. "How . . . did you find the camp that night?" she managed to say. "In the dark. In a forest that was totally unfamiliar. After you'd spent twelve days on starvation rations. *How?* Tell me, Michael. How?"

"I did tell you."

"No, you didn't. You pretended to tell me, and I let it go. Maybe because there was no possible rational explanation for it. And now I come into your room, I find your window open and your bed empty. You slide back in, naked, and try to laugh it off."

Michael shrugged. "What better to do, when you're caught with your pants down?"

"You haven't answered me. Where have you been?"

He spoke calmly and carefully, measuring his words. "I needed some exercise. Dr. Stronberg seems to think that I'm not ready for anything more strenuous than a match of chess—which, by the way, I beat him at today, two out of three. Anyhow, I went out last night and walked, and I did the same tonight. I chose not to wear clothes because it's a fine warm night and I wanted the feel of the air on my skin. Is that such a terrible thing?"

Chesna didn't reply for a moment. Then: "You went out walking, even after I told you about the wolf?"

"With all the game in the forest around here, a wolf won't attack a human."

"All *what* game, Michael?" she asked.

He thought fast. "Oh, didn't I tell you? I saw two deer from my window this afternoon."

"No, you didn't tell me." She stood very still, close enough to the door so she could reach it in a hurry. "The wolf I saw . . . had green eyes. Just like yours. And black hair. Dr. Stronberg has lived here for almost thirty-five years, and he'd never heard of a wolf in these woods. Fritz was born in a village less than fifty kilometers north of here, and he's never known of any wolves in the area either. Isn't that very strange?"

"Wolves migrate. Or so I've heard." He smiled in the darkness, but his face was tense. "A wolf with green eyes, huh? Chesna, what are you getting at?"

The moment of truth, Chesna thought. What *was* she getting at? That this man before her—this British secret agent who had been born a Russian—was a bizarre hybrid of human and beast? That he was a living example of the creature she'd read about in a book on folklore? A man who could transform his body into the shape of a wolf and run on all fours? Maybe Michael Gallatin was eccentric, and perhaps he had a keen sense of smell and an even keener sense of direction, but . . . a *werewolf*?

"Tell me what you're thinking," Michael said as he walked closer to her. A floorboard creaked softly under his weight. Her aroma lured him. She took a step backward. He stopped. "You're not afraid of me, are you?"

"Should I be?" A quaver in her voice.

"No," he said. "I won't hurt you." He walked toward her again, and this time she didn't retreat.

He reached her. She could see his green eyes, even in the gloom. They were hungry eyes, and they awakened a hunger within her. "Why did you come to my room tonight?" Michael asked, his face close to hers.

"I . . . said I . . . wanted to look in on—"

"No," he interrupted gently. "That's not the real reason, is it?"

She hesitated, her heart hammering, and as Michael slipped his arms around her she shook her head.

Their lips met, and melded. Chesna thought she must truly

be losing her mind, because she imagined she tasted a hint of blood on his tongue. But the coppery tang was gone in an instant, and she grasped his back and pressed her body against his with mounting fever. His erection was already large, and its pulse throbbed in her fingers as she caressed him. Michael slowly unbuttoned her nightgown, their kisses deep and urgent, and then he stroked his tongue between her breasts and gently, teasingly, licked up from her breasts to her throat. She felt goose bumps erupt over her skin, a sensation that made her gasp with pleasure. Man or beast, he was what she needed.

The nightgown drifted down around her ankles. She stepped out of its folds, and Michael picked her up in his arms and carried her to the bed.

On that white plateau their bodies entwined. Heat met heat, and pressed deep. Her damp softness gripped him, her fingers clenched to his shoulders and his hips moving in slow circles that rose and fell with graceful strength. Michael lay on his back, Chesna astride him, and together they made the bedsprings speak. He arched his spine, lifting her as she held him deep inside, and at the height of his arch their bodies shuddered in unison, a sweet hot pulsing that brought a cry from Chesna and a soft gasp from Michael.

They lay together, Chesna's head cradled against Michael's shoulder, and talked in hushed voices. For a short time, at least, the war was somewhere far away. Maybe she would go to America, Chesna said. She had never seen California, and perhaps that was the place to begin anew. Did he have anyone special waiting for him in England? she asked, and he said no one. But that was his home, he told her, and that's where he would return when their mission was done.

Chesna traced his eyebrows with her finger, and laughed quietly.

"What's so funny?" he asked.

"Oh . . . nothing. It's just . . . well, you would never believe what I was thinking when I saw you coming through the window."

"I'd like to know."

"It's crazy, really. I think my imagination's been running

wild, ever since that wolf scared the daylights out of me."
She turned her attention to the hair on his chest. "But . . . I
thought—don't laugh now—that you might be a . . ." She
forced the word out. ". . . werewolf."

"I am," he said, and looked into her eyes.

"Oh, you are?" She smiled. "Well, I always suspected
you were more of a beast than a baron."

He made a growling sound, deep in his throat, and his
mouth found hers.

This time their lovemaking was more tender, but no less
passionate. Michael's tongue lavished her breasts, and
played with joyful abandon across the fields of her body.
Chesna clung to him, arms and legs, as he eased into her.
She urged him deeper, and like a gentleman he met her
request. They lay facing each other, merged iron to silk, and
they moved in slow thrusts and circles like dancers to music.
Their bodies trembled and strained, glowing with the moisture of effort. Chesna moaned as Michael balanced above
her and teased her soft folds until she was near the point of
release, then he plunged into her and she thought she might
sob with the sheer ecstasy of it. She shivered, whispering
his name, and his rhythm took her to the edge of delight and
then over it, as if she'd leaped from a cliff and was falling
through a sky that shimmered with iridescent colors. Michael's sure strokes did not falter, until he felt the hot
clenching followed by an eruption that seemed to stretch his
spine and muscles almost to the point of pain. He remained
part of Chesna, nestled between her thighs, as they kissed
and whispered and the world turned lazily around their bed.

The following morning Dr. Stronberg pronounced Michael
well on the way to recovery. His fever was gone, and the
bruises on his body had almost faded. Lazaris, also, was
stronger and able to walk around the house on stiff legs. Dr.
Stronberg turned his attention, however, to Chesna, who
appeared not to have gotten much sleep the night before.
She assured the doctor that she was feeling fine, and would
make sure she got at least eight hours of sleep tonight.

After nightfall a brown car left the house. Dr. Stronberg
and Chesna were in the front and Michael and Lazaris, both
wearing their baggy gray-green jumpsuits, sat in the back.

Stronberg drove northeast on a narrow country road. The trip took about twenty minutes, then Stronberg stopped at the boundary of a wide field and switched his headlights on and off twice. A lantern signaled back, at the field's opposite side. Stronberg drove toward it and pulled the car beneath the shelter of some trees.

Camouflage netting had been draped over a framework of timbers. The man with the lantern was joined by two other men, all in the simple clothing of farmers, who lifted an edge of the netting and motioned their visitors in.

"This is it," Chesna said, and Michael saw the airplane in the lanterns' yellow glow.

Lazaris laughed. "Saint Peter's ghost!" he said, speaking a mixture of crude German and Russian. "That's not a plane, it's a deathtrap!"

Michael was inclined to agree. The tri-engined transport aircraft, painted dark gray, was large enough to hold seven or eight passengers, but its airworthiness was suspect. The machine was covered with bullet-hole patches, its wing-engine cowlings looked as if they'd been attacked with sledgehammers, and one of its wheel struts was badly warped.

"It's a Junkers Ju-fifty-two," Lazaris said. "That model was built in 1934." He looked under the aircraft and ran his fingers along a rusted seam. He muttered with disgust as he found a hole as big as his fist. "The damned thing's falling apart!" he said to Chesna. "Did you get this from the garbage pile?"

"Of course," she answered. "If it was perfect, the Luftwaffe would still be using it."

"It *will* fly, won't it?" Michael asked.

"It will. The engines are a little rough, but they'll get us to Norway."

"The real question," Lazaris said, "is will it fly with *people* in it?" He found another rust-edged hole. "The cockpit floor looks as if it's about to fall through!" He went to the port wing engine, reached up, and put his hand past the propeller into the machinery. His fingers emerged slimed with dirty oil and grease. "Oh, this is wonderful! You could grow wheat on the dirt in this engine! Goldilocks, are you trying to commit suicide?''

"No," she said tersely. "And I've asked you to stop calling me that."

"Well, I thought you must like fairy tales. Especially now, since I've seen this wreck you call an aircraft." Lazaris took a lantern from one of the men, walked around to the fuselage door, and ducked low to enter the plane.

"This is the best I could do," Chesna told Michael. "It might not be in the best condition"—they heard Lazaris laugh harshly as he shone the lantern around in the cockpit—"but it'll get us where we need to go. Regardless of what your friend thinks."

They had to travel more than seven hundred miles, Michael thought. Part of that journey would be over the bitterly cold North Sea. If the airplane developed engine trouble over the water . . . "Does it at least have a life raft?" he asked.

"It does. I patched the holes in it myself."

Lazaris emerged, swearing, from the Junkers. "It's all rust and loose bolts!" he fumed. "If you sneeze too hard in there, you'll blow the cockpit glass out! I doubt if the damned thing can do over a hundred knots, even with a tail wind!"

"No one's twisting your arm to go with us." Chesna took the lantern from him and returned it to its owner. "But we're leaving on the twelfth. The night after tomorow. Our clothing and supplies should be ready by then. We'll have three fuel and security stops between here and Uskedahl. With luck we should reach our landing strip on the morning of the sixteenth."

"With luck"—Lazaris placed one finger against a nostril and blew his nose—"this damned plane won't lose its wings south of Denmark." He turned to regard the Junkers again, his hands on his hips. "I'd say this poor creature must've tangled with a Russian fighter pilot. Yes, that's what I'd say." He looked at Michael, then at Chesna. "I'll go with you. Anything to get German dirt off my feet."

Back at Dr. Stronberg's house, Chesna and Michael lay together in bed as the wind rose outside and swirled through the trees. There was no need for talking; their bodies communicated with an eloquence that was at first fierce, then gentle.

Chesna slept in Michael's arms. He listened to the roving wind, his mind on Skarpa and Iron Fist. He didn't know what they would find on that island, but the memory of the grisly photographs in Blok's satchel was leeched to his brain. The weapon that made such hideous wounds had to be found and destroyed, not just for the sake of the Allied invasion, but for the sake of those who had already passed through the Nazis' trials of torture. With such a weapon in the hands of Hitler, the entire world might yet be branded with a swastika.

Sleep called him and took him away. In his nightmares soldiers goosestepped through the shadow of Big Ben, Hitler wore a coat of black wolf fur, and Wiktor's voice whispered, *Don't fail me.*

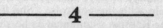

4

Airborne, the Junkers was more of an eagle than it appeared, but the plane shuddered in rough air and the wing engines smoked and shot bluish-white sparks. "Drinking oil and fuel like a fiend!" Lazaris fretted as he sat in the copilot's seat and watched the gauges. "We'll be walking within two hours!"

"Just so we can reach our first fuel point," Chesna said calmly, her hands on the controls. Conversation was difficult, due to the hoarse roar of the engines. Michael, sitting at a cramped navigator's table behind the cockpit, checked the maps; their initial stop—a hidden airfield operated by the German Resistance—lay just south of Denmark. The second stop, tomorrow night, would be at a partisan field on the northern tip of Denmark, and their final fueling point lay within Norway. The distances looked huge.

"Never make it, Goldilocks," Lazaris said. The Junkers

trembled in a sudden seizure, and loose bolts rattled like machine-gun fire. "I saw those parachutes back there." He jerked a thumb toward the cargo bay, where their packets of food, canteens, winter clothes, submachine guns, and ammunition were stored. "They're made for babies. If you expect me to jump out of this crate wearing one of those, you're insane." As he talked, his eyes scanned the darkness, searching for the telltale blue sputters of Nazi night-fighter engines. He knew, however, that they would be hard to see, and by the time you saw, one of the bullets would be on their way. He cringed at the thought of what heavy machine guns would do to this flimsy cockpit, and so he kept talking to hide his fear, though neither Chesna nor Michael was listening. "I'd have a better chance of surviving if I jumped for a haystack."

Little more than two hours later, the starboard engine began to miss. Chesna watched the needles of the fuel gauges settle toward zero. The Junkers's nose kept wanting to sink, as if even the plane itself was in a hurry to get back on the ground. Chesna's wrists ached with the effort of holding the Junkers steady, and before long she had to ask Lazaris to help with the controls. "She flies like a battleship," was the Russian's comment as he steered toward the map coordinates that Michael gave him.

An arrow of fire appeared on the ground: friendly flames, pointing toward their first landing strip. Lazaris took the Junkers in, circling down over the arrow, and when the wheels bit the earth, there was a collective sigh from the cockpit.

Over the next eighteen hours the Junkers was refueled and the engines oiled as Lazaris took charge of the ground crew—most of them farmers, who'd never been within a hundred yards of an airplane. Lazaris got hold of some tools and, under the protection of a camouflage net, he probed into the starboard engine with grimy relish. He made a dozen small corrections, muttering and cursing all the while.

When midnight came again they were in the air, crossing from Germany into Denmark. One's darkness was the same as the other's. Lazaris again took the controls when Chesna got tired, and blasted bawdy Russian drinking songs against the incessant rough music of the engines. Chesna hushed him by pointing to a streak of blue, passing about five thousand feet overhead. The night fighter—probably a new model Heinkel or Dornier, she told them, judging from its speed—was gone to the west within seconds, but the sighting of such a predator took away Lazaris's desire to sing.

On the ground in Denmark they were treated to a banquet of fresh potatoes and blood sausage, a meal that particularly satisfied Michael. Their hosts were again poor farmers, who had obviously been preparing the feast as if for the arrival of royalty. Lazaris's bald dome caught the attention of a little boy, who kept wanting to feel it. The family's dog sniffed nervously around Michael, and one of the women present was thrilled because she recognized Chesna from a picture in a dog-eared magazine about German film stars.

Stars of another kind greeted them as they flew over the North Sea on the following night. A meteor shower shot bolts of red and gold through the darkness, and Michael smiled as he listened to Lazaris laugh like a child.

When they landed, they stepped out of the plane into the chill of Norway. Chesna broke out their parkas, which they slipped on over their gray-green commando outfits. A British agent who introduced himself as Craddock was among the Norwegian partisans who met them, and they were escorted by reindeer sled to a stone cottage where another feast was laid out. Craddock—a sincere young man who smoked a pipe and whose right ear had been shot off by a German rifle bullet—told them the weather was closing in farther north, and they could expect snow before they reached Uskedahl. The broadest woman Michael had ever seen—obviously the older daughter of their host family—sat close beside Lazaris, watching him intently as he chewed on an offering of salt-dried caribou meat. She had tears in her eyes when they left the next night, on the final leg of their journey, and Lazaris clutched a white rabbit's foot that had somehow gotten into his parka.

These were only a small fraction of the millions of human beings whom Hitler had decided were not quite a step above beasts.

The Junkers's engines whined in the thin, cold air. The

morning of May 16 came with snow that whirled out of the darkness against the cockpit windshield. The airplane pitched and yawed, buffeted by stong winds over the jagged mountain peaks. Both Lazaris and Chesna gripped the steering yokes as the Junkers rose and fell hundreds of feet. Michael could do nothing but strap himself in and hold on to the table, sweat trickling under his arms and his stomach lurching. The Junkers shuddered violently, and they all heard the frame creak like bass violin notes.

"Ice on the wings," Chesna said tersely as she scanned the gauges. "Oil pressure's dropping on the port-side engine. The temperature's coming up fast."

"Oil leak. We've ripped a seam." Lazaris's voice was all business. The Junkers vibrated again, as if they were running over a cobblestone road. He reached to the control panel and cut back the power on the left wing engine, but before he could get his fingers off the lever there was a heart-stopping *boom* and flames spat from around the engine cowling. The propeller seized up and froze.

"Now we'll find out what she's made of," Lazaris said, through gritted teeth, as the altimeter began to fall.

The Junkers's nose descended. Lazaris pulled it up again, his gloved hands clenched on the yoke. Chesna added her strength to his, but the plane had a mind of its own. "I can't hold it!" she said, and Lazaris told her, "You'll have to." She did, putting her back and shoulders into it. Michael unbuckled his seat straps and leaned over Chesna, gripping the yoke with her. He could feel the immense, trembling strain the aircraft was under, and as wind sideswiped the plane and slewed it to the left he was slammed up against the cockpit bulkhead.

"Strap in!" Lazaris shouted. "You'll break your neck!" Michael leaned forward again, helping Chesna hold the plane's nose as steady as they could. Lazaris glanced at the port wing engine, saw streamers of red fire flowing back from the blistered cowling. Burning fuel, he realized. If the wing's fuel tank blew . . .

The Junkers slewed to the side again, a violent twist that made the frame moan. Lazaris heard the sound of rending metal, and he realized with a start of pure horror that the cockpit floor had split open right under his legs.

"Let me have her!" he said, and he pushed the yoke forward and nosed the Junkers into a screaming dive.

Michael saw the altimeter needle spinning crazily. He couldn't see anything beyond the windshield and the snow, but he knew the mountains were there and so did Chesna. The aircraft fell, the fuselage moaning and straining like a body in torment. Lazaris watched the port wing engine. The fires were going out, extinguished by the wind. When the last flicker of flame had gone, he wrenched back on the yoke as the muscles in his shoulders popped. The Junkers was slow in responding. His wrists and forearms were in agony. Chesna grasped the yoke and pulled back on it, too. Then Michael added his power, and the Junkers vibrated and groaned but obeyed. The altimeter needle leveled off at just below two thousand feet.

"There!" Chesna pointed to the right, at a point of fire through the snow. She turned the plane toward it and continued to let the altitude slowly fall.

Another point of fire sparked. Then a third. "That's the airstrip," Chesna said as the altimeter needle crawled down the gauge. A fourth fire began to burn. Oilcans, flaming on either side of the landing field. "We're going in." She pulled back on the throttles, her hand shaking, and Michael quickly strapped himself into his seat.

As they approached the flame-lit field, Chesna straightened the wings and cut the remaining two engines. The Junkers, an ungainly bird, glided in with the noise of snow hissing on the hot cowlings. The tires hit earth. Bounced. Hit again, a smaller bounce. And then Chesna was standing on the brake, and the Junkers was leaving a plume of snow and steam behind it as it rolled across the field.

The airplane slowed, and with a rush and gurgle of leaking hydraulic fluid the tires crunched to a halt.

Lazaris peered down between his legs, where he saw a crack of snow about six inches wide. He was the first out of the airplane. As Chesna and Michael emerged, Lazaris was walking in dazed circles, reacquainting his feet with solid earth. The Junkers's engines steamed and crackled, having the last words.

As Michael and Chesna were unloading the supplies, a battered, white-painted truck pulled up beside the Junkers. Several men got off and began to unroll a huge white tarpaulin. Their leader was a red-bearded man who gave his name as Hurks, and proceeded to help load the knapsacks, submachine guns, ammunition, and grenades into the truck. As Hurks worked, the other men labored to get the tarpaulin over the Junkers.

"We almost went down!" Lazaris told Hurks as he gripped his rabbit's foot. "That storm almost knocked our damned wings off!"

Hurks looked at him blankly. "What storm? This is springtime." Then he returned to work, and Lazaris stood there getting snow in his beard.

There was a groan and clatter of weakened bolts snapping. Michael and Chesna turned toward the airplane, and Lazaris gasped with horror. The flame-blackened port wing engine hung off its mount for a few seconds, then the last few bolts broke and the entire engine crashed to the ground.

"Welcome to Norway," Hurks told them. "Hurry it up!" he shouted to the men over the wind's shrill wail. "Get that thing covered!" The men worked fast, spreading the tarpaulin over the Junkers and staking it down with white ropes. Then, with the passengers and the other Norwegians in the truck, Hurks got behind the wheel and drove them away from the landing strip toward the seacoast, about twenty-five miles to the southwest.

The sun silvered the sky to the east as they drove through the narrow, muddy streets of Uskedahl. It was a fishing village, the houses made of gray wood and stones. Thin creepers of smoke curled from chimneys, and Michael smelled the aromas of strong coffee and bacon fat. Down where the rocks met the slate-colored sea, a small fleet of boats chugged out on the dawn tide, nets rigged up and ready. A pack of skinny dogs barked and yipped at the wheels of the truck, and here and there Michael noted a figure watching through half-drawn shutters.

Chesna elbowed him in the ribs and motioned out toward

the harbor. A big Blohm und Voss flying boat, a swastika painted on its tail, was skimming the smooth surface about two hundred yards offshore. It made two slow circles of the fishing fleet, then gained altitude and vanished into the low-lying clouds. The message was understood: the Nazi masters were watching.

Hurks stopped the truck in front of a stone house. "You get off here," he told Michael, Chesna, and Lazaris. "We'll take care of your goodies."

Neither Chesna nor Michael liked the idea of leaving the guns and ammunition with a man they didn't know, but neither did they wish to risk the weapons being found if the village was inspected by the crewmen of that flying boat. Reluctantly they got off the truck. "You go in there." Hurks pointed toward the house. Its door glistened with a shellac of dried seal blubber. "Rest. Eat. Wait." He put the truck into gear and drove away through the mud.

Michael opened the door and entered. His hair brushed a little waterfall of silver bells nailed at the top of the threshold, and they jingled as merrily as Christmas Eve. The bells caught in Chesna's hair, too, and they dragged over Lazaris's stubbled scalp. The inside of the house was gloomy and smelled of fish and dried mud. Nets hung from the walls, and here and there a crooked picture clipped from a magazine was stuck on a nail. A small fire glowed at the center of a cast-iron stove.

"Hello?" Michael called. "Anyone here?"

Springs squalled. On an old brown sofa was a large mound of dirty clothes. The mound had begun to quiver, and as the new arrivals watched they saw it sit up, the sofa's springs straining.

"Saint Peter's ghost!" Lazaris breathed. "What is *that?*"

Whatever it was, it reached for a bottle of vodka on the floor beside it. A large brown hand uncorked the bottle, lifted it, and there was the sound of liquid gurgling down a gullet. Then a belch. The mound struggled to stand, and rose up to well over six feet.

"Welcome!" The voice was husky and slurred. A woman's voice. "Welcome!" She came toward them, into the stove's ruddy light. The floorboards creaked under her, and

Michael was surprised they didn't collapse altogether. The woman had to be two hundred and fifty pounds, if an ounce, and perhaps six feet two inches tall. She approached them, a wobbling mountain on legs. "Welcome!" she said once more, either deficient in sense or language. Her broad, wrinkled face grinned, displaying a mouth that held three teeth. She had the almond-shaped eyes of an Eskimo, yet her eyes—set in nests of wrinkles—were pale blue. Her skin was coppery brown, and her lank, straight hair—cropped as if beneath an oversized bowl—was a brassy orange: the commingling, Michael realized, of generations of Eskimo and Nordic genes, battling for dominance. She was quite an extraordinary-looking woman, standing there grinning and wrapped in folds of multicolored blankets. Michael judged her to be in her late forties or early fifties, given the wrinkles in her face and the gray amid the orange hair.

She offered the vodka bottle. "Welcome?" she asked, a gold pin stuck in one of her nostrils.

"Welcome!" Lazaris said as he snatched the bottle from her hand and swallowed the clear fire. He paused to make a respectful whistling noise, then went back to his guzzling. Michael pried the bottle out of his fingers and returned it to the woman, who licked the neck's rim and took another slug.

"What's your name?" Chesna asked, speaking German. The woman shook her head. "Your name?" Chesna tried her luck at Norwegian, though she knew very little of the language. She pressed a hand against her breastbone. "Chesna." Pointed at Michael. "Michael." Then at the happy Russian. "Lazaris."

"Ah!" The woman nodded gleefully. She pointed between her massive thighs. "Kitty!" she said. "Welcome!"

"A man could get in a hell of a lot of trouble around here," Lazaris observed sagely.

The cabin, if not exactly clean, was at least warm. Michael took off his parka and hung it on a wall hook while Chesna tried to communicate with the huge, rather tipsy Eskinordic. The best she could do was understand that the woman lived here, and that there were plenty of bottles of vodka.

The door opened, and the bells chimed. Hurks closed the

door behind him. "Well!" he said as he peeled off his heavy coat. "I see you've met Kitty!"

Kitty grinned at him, drank the rest of the bottle, and flopped down on the sofa with a splintering crash.

"She's a bit hard on the furniture," Hurks admitted, "but she's pleasant enough. Who's in charge among you?"

"I am," Chesna said.

"All right." Hurks spoke to Kitty in a singsong dialect that sounded to Michael like a mixture of grunts and clicks. Kitty nodded, her grin gone, and stared at Chesna. "I've told her who you are," Hurks said. "She's been expecting you."

"*She* has?" Chesna shook her head. "I don't understand."

"Kitty's going to take you to Skarpa Island," Hurks explained. He went to a cupboard and brought out a box of shortbread biscuits.

"*What?*" Chesna glanced at the woman, who was smiling with her eyes closed and the empty bottle clutched against her belly. "She's . . . she's a *drunk!*"

"So? We're all drunks up here nowadays." He took a beat-up coffeepot from a table, shook it to slosh the liquid around, and then set it atop the stove. "Kitty knows the water, and she knows Skarpa Island, too. Me, I don't know a damned thing about boats. I can't even swim. Which would be beside the point, I suppose, if you bumped a mine."

"You're saying that if we want to get to Skarpa, we have to put our lives in *her* hands?"

"That's it," Hurks said.

"Skarpa!" Kitty's eyes opened. Her voice was a low, guttural growl. "Skarpa dirty bad! Pa*too!*" She spat on the floor. "Nazee boys! Pa*too!*" Another wad of spit hit the stained planks.

"Besides," Hurks went on, "it's Kitty's boat. She used to be the best fisherman for a hundred miles around. She says she used to be able to hear the fish sing, and when she learned their songs and sang back, they swam into her nets by the ton."

"I'm not interested in singing fish," Chesna said coolly. "I'm interested in patrol boats, searchlights, and mines."

"Oh, Kitty knows where those are, too." He brought tin

cups down from their hooks. "Kitty used to live on Skarpa Island, before the Nazis came. She and her husband and six sons."

There was a clink as the empty vodka bottle was tossed aside. It landed in the corner, near three others. Kitty dug into the folds of the sofa, and her hand emerged gripping a fresh bottle. She pulled the cork out with her remaining teeth, tipped the bottle, and drank.

"What happened to her family?" Michael asked.

"The Nazis . . . shall we say . . . recruited them to help build that big son-of-a-bitch chemical plant. They also recruited every other able-bodied person from Kitty's village. And Kitty herself, of course, since she's strong as an ox. They also built an airfield and flew in slave labor. Anyway, the Nazis executed everyone who did the work. Kitty's got two bullets in her. They hurt her sometimes when the weather turns really cold." He touched the pot. "Coffee will have to be black, I'm afraid. We're out of cream and sugar." He began to pour coffee for them; it came out thick and sludgy. "Kitty lay with the corpses for three or four days. She's not exactly sure how long it was. When she decided she wasn't going to die, she got up and found a rowboat. I met her in forty-two, when my ship went down with a torpedo in the guts. I was a merchant marine seaman, and thank God I got to a raft." He gave the first cup to Chesna, then offered her some shortbread.

"What did the Nazis do with the bodies?" Chesna took the coffee and a biscuit.

Hurks asked Kitty, again using that grunt-click language. Kitty replied in a quiet, drunken voice. "They left them for the wolves," Hurks said. He offered the box to Michael. "Biscuit?"

Along with the muscular coffee and the shortbread, Hurks produced a packet of dried, leathery mutton that Michael found tasty, but Chesna and Lazaris had difficulty swallowing. "We'll have a good pot of stew tonight," Hurks promised. "Squid, onions, and potatoes. Very tasty, with a lot of salt and pepper."

"I won't eat a squid!" Lazaris said as he shrugged off his parka and sat down at a table, his coffee cup before him. He shuddered. "Damn things look like a cock after a night in a Moscow whorehouse!" He reached for his cup. "No, I'll just eat the onions and pota—"

There was a movement, very fast, behind him. He saw the glint of a blade, and Kitty's huge bulk falling over him like an avalanche.

"Don't move!" Hurks shouted—and then the blade was thrust down, before either Michael or Chesna could get to the Russian's aid.

The knife, its wickedly hooked blade used for skinning seals, slammed into the scarred tabletop, between Lazari's outstretched second and third fingers. It missed the flesh, but Lazaris jerked his hand to his chest and squalled like a cat with a burning tail.

His scream was followed by another: a scream of hoarse, drunken laughter. Kitty wrenched the knife out of the table-top and did a merry dance around the room like a massive and deadly whirligig.

"She's mad!" Lazaris hollered, checking his fingers. "Absolutely mad!"

"I'm sorry," Hurks apologized after Kitty had sheathed her knife and fallen onto the sofa again. "When she drinks . . . she has this little game she likes to play. But she always misses. Most of the time, that is." He held up his left hand; part of the third finger was severed up to the knuckle.

"Well, for God's sake get that knife away from her!" Lazaris shouted, but Kitty was already folded up around it, swigging down more vodka.

Michael and Chesna stuffed their hands into the pockets of their jumpsuits. "It's important we get to Skarpa as soon as possible," Michael said. "When can we go?"

Hurks posed the question to Kitty. She thought about it for a moment, her brow knitted. She got up and waddled outside. When she returned, her feet covered with mud, she grinned and answered.

"Tomorrow night," Hurks translated. "She says there'll be a blow tonight, and fog follows wind."

"By tomorrow night I might be down to the stumps!" Lazaris buried his hands in his pockets until Kitty returned to the sofa, then he dared to withdraw them and to finish his

527

meal. "You know," he ventured after Kitty had begun to snore, "there's something we all ought to be thinking about. If we get on that island, do whatever it is you heroic types are supposed to do, and get off with all our body parts, then what? In case you haven't noticed, our Junkers has lived up to its name. I couldn't put that engine back on, even with a crane. And anyway, it's burned to a crisp. So how do we get out of here?"

The question was not one that Michael hadn't already considered. He looked at Chesna, and saw she had no answer for it either.

"That's what I thought," Lazaris muttered.

But Michael couldn't let that problem contaminate his mind right now. Skarpa had to be reached and Dr. Hildebrand dealt with first, then they'd find a way out. He hoped. Norway would not be a pleasant place to spend the summer with the Nazis hunting them down. Hurks got the vodka bottle away from Kitty and passed it around. Michael allowed himself one fiery sip, and then he stretched out on the floor—his hands wedged in his pockets—and was asleep in just over a minute.

5

Kitty's boat slid through the mist, its engine growling softly. The water hissed as it parted before the figurehead, a wooden gargoyle with a trident, and a shielded lantern illuminated the interior of the wheelhouse in dim green.

Kitty's hands—broad and coarse—were delicate on the wheel. Michael stood beside her, watching through the dripping windshield. Kitty had been drunk for most of the day, but as soon as the sun had begun to set she put aside the vodka and washed her face in icy water. It was past two o'clock on the morning of the nineteenth, and Kitty had pulled the forty-foot, weather-beaten relic out of its harbor slip about three hours before. Now, here in the wheelhouse, she was silent and brooding, with no trace of the grinning, drunken woman who'd greeted them in Uskedahl. She was all deadly business.

She had been right about the blow on the night of the seventeenth. A fierce wind had rushed down from the mountains and screamed over Uskedahl until dawn, but the houses were built for such caprices and there was no damage except to the nerves. She was correct, as well, about the fog that had crept over Uskedahl and the bay, blanketing everything in white silence. How she could steer in this soup he didn't know, but every so often she cocked her head and seemed to be listening; surely not for the singing of fishes, but for the sound of the water itself, telling her something it was not in his power to understand. She made minor corrections of the wheel from time to time, as gently as nudging an infant.

Kitty suddenly reached out and grabbed Michael's parka, pulling him closer and pointing. He couldn't see anything but fog, though he nodded. She grunted with satisfaction, let him go, and steered in that direction.

There had been a strange incident at the dock. As they'd been loading their gear onto the boat, Michael had found himself face-to-face with Kitty sniffing at his chest. She had sniffed his face and hair, then had drawn back and stared at him with those blue Nordic eyes. She smells the wolf in me, Michael thought. Kitty had spoken to Hurks, who had translated for her: "She wants to know what land you come from."

"I was born in Russia," Michael had said.

She spoke through Hurks, pointing at Lazaris: "*He* stinks like a Russian. You have a perfume like Norway."

"I'll take that as a compliment," Michael answered.

And then Kitty got very close to him, staring intensely into his eyes. Michael stood his ground. She spoke again, this time almost in a whisper. "Kitty says you're different," Hurks translated. "She thinks you're a man of destiny. That's a high praise."

"Tell her thank you."

Hurks did. Kitty nodded, and moved away toward the wheelhouse.

A man of destiny, Michael thought as he stood beside her

and she steered deeper into the fog. He hoped his destiny—and that of Chesna and Lazaris as well—wasn't a grave on Skarpa Island. Hurks had stayed in Uskedahl, a stranger to travel by water since the U-boat torpedoing of his freighter. Lazaris was no lion of the sea either, but fortunately the water was glassy and the boat's progress smooth, so Lazaris had only heaved twice over the side. Perhaps it was nerves, or perhaps it was the reek of fish that clung to the boat like a miasma.

Chesna entered the wheelhouse, the hood of her parka up over her head and her hands in black woolen gloves. Kitty kept staring straight ahead, guiding the boat toward a point the others couldn't see. Chesna offered Michael a drink from the thermos of strong black coffee they'd brought, and he accepted it. "How's Lazaris?" Michael asked.

"Conscious," she answered. Lazaris was down in the cramped little cabin, which Michael had noted was even smaller than the kennel at Falkenhausen. She peered out at the fog. "Where are we?"

"Hell if I know. Kitty seems to, though, and I guess that's what matters." He returned the thermos to Chesna. Kitty turned the wheel a few degrees to starboard, and then she reached down to the greasy throttles and cut the engines. "Go," Kitty told him, and pointed forward. Obviously she wanted Michael to watch for something. He took a flashlight from a corroded metal locker and left the wheelhouse with Chesna following.

On the bow Michael stood over the figurehead and probed with the light. Tendrils of fog wafted through the beam. The boat drifted, and waves lapped at the boards. There came the noise of boots on the deck. "Hey!" Lazaris called, his voice as tight as new wire. "What happened to the engines? Are we sinking?"

"Quiet," Michael said. Lazaris came forward, guiding himself along the rusted railing. Michael slowly swung the flashlight beam from right to left and back again. "What are you looking for?" Lazaris whispered. "Land?" Michael shook his head, because he really had no idea. And then the flashlight hit a faint, ill-defined object off on the starboard side. It looked like the rotten piling of a dock, with gray fungus growing all over it. Kitty had seen it, too, and she guided the bow toward it.

In another moment they all could see it, perhaps more clearly than they'd wished.

A single piling had been sunk into the muck. Bound to that piling by rotting ropes was a skeleton, immersed up to its sunken chest. A bit of scalp and gray hair remained on the skull. Twined around the skeleton's neck was a noose of heavy wire, and attached to the wire was a metal sign with faded German words: ATTENTION! ENTRY FORBIDDEN!

In the light, small red crabs scuttled in the skeleton's eye sockets and peered out between the broken teeth.

Kitty corrected the wheel. The boat drifted past the grisly signpost and left it in darkness. She started the engine again, throttling it to a low mutter. Not twenty yards from the piling and skeleton, the flashlight beam picked out a floating gray ball, covered with kelp and ugly spikes.

"That's a mine!" Lazaris yelped. "A mine!" he shouted at the wheelhouse, and pointed. "Boom boom!"

Kitty knew where it was. She veered to port, and the mine rolled in the boat's wake. Michael's stomach knotted. Chesna leaned forward, gripping the port-side railing, and Lazaris watched for more mines on the starboard side. "One over here!" Chesna called. It bobbed and lazily turned, encrusted with barnacles. The boat slid past it. Michael spotted the next one, almost dead ahead. Lazaris scrambled back to the wheelhouse, and returned with another flashlight. Kitty kept the boat at a slow, constant glide, weaving among the mines that now appeared on all sides. Lazaris thought his beard would turn white as he watched a mine, its spines covered with kelp, drift over the crest of a swell almost in their path. "Turn, damn it! Turn!" he hollered, motioning to port. The boat obeyed, but Lazaris heard the mine scrape across the hull like fingernails on a blackboard. He cringed, waiting for the blast, but the mine disappeared in their wake and they went on.

The last of the mines floated away on the starboard side, and then the water was free of them. Kitty rapped on the windshield, and when she had their attention, she put a finger to her lips and then drew it across her throat in a slashing gesture. The meaning was clear.

In a few minutes a searchlight appeared through the fog, sweeping around and around atop its tower on Skarpa Island. The island itself was still invisible, but soon Michael could hear a slow, steady thumping noise like a huge heartbeat. The noise of heavy machinery at work in the chemical plant. He switched off his flashlight, and so did Lazaris. They were getting close to shore. Kitty turned the boat, staying just outside the searchlight's range. She suddenly cut the engine, and the boat whispered through the swells. Michael and Chesna heard another, more powerful engine growling somewhere in the fog. A patrol boat, circling the island. The noise grew distant and faded, and Kitty throttled up with a careful hand.

The searchlight skimmed past them, dangerously close. Michael saw the glint of smaller lights through the murk: what looked like bulbs on outside catwalks and ladders, and the dark shape of a huge chimney that rose into the mist. The heartbeat thump was much louder now, and Michael could make out the hazy forms of buildings. Kitty was guiding them along Skarpa's rugged coastline. Soon they left the lights and the sound of machinery behind, and Kitty veered the boat into a small, crescent-shaped harbor.

She knew this harbor, and took them straight to the crumbling remains of a seawall. She killed the engine, letting the boat drift across silvery water at the base of the wall. Michael switched his light on and made out a barnacle-crusted dock just ahead. The rotting prow of a long-sunken boat jutted up from the water like a strange snout, and hundreds of red crabs clung to it.

Kitty emerged from the wheelhouse. She called out something that sounded like "Copahay ting! Timesho!" She motioned to the dock, and Michael jumped from the boat onto a platform of creaking, sodden timbers. Chesna flung him a rope, which he used to tie the boat to a piling. A second rope, thrown from Kitty, completed the task. They had arrived.

Stone steps led up from the dock and seawall. Beyond them, Michael saw by the flashlight beam, was a cluster of dark, dilapidated houses. Kitty's village, now occupied only by ghosts.

Chesna, Michael, and Lazaris checked their submachine guns and strapped them on. Their supplies—rations of fresh water, dried beef, chocolate bars, ammo clips, and four grenades apiece—were in backpacks. Michael, in his previous examination of their supplies, had also noted something else wrapped up in a little packet of waxed paper: a cyanide capsule, similar to the one he'd popped into his mouth on the roof of the Paris Opéra. He hadn't needed it then, and he would die by a bullet rather than use one here on Skarpa.

Their equipment ready, they followed Kitty up the ancient steps into the dead village. She probed ahead with the flashlight she'd taken from Lazaris, the beam revealing a rutted main road and houses covered with wet mold as white as ash. Many of the roofs had collapsed, the windows without glass. Still, the village was not entirely dead. Michael could smell them, and he knew they were close by.

"Welcome," Kitty said, and motioned them into one of the sturdier-looking houses. Whether this one had been her home, Michael didn't know, but it had become a home again. As they crossed the threshold, Kitty's light speared through the mist and caught two skinny wolves, one yellow and one gray. The gray one leaped for an open window and was gone in an instant, but the yellow wolf wheeled on the intruders and showed its teeth.

Michael heard the bolt of a submachine gun going back. He grabbed Lazaris's arm before the Russian could fire, and said, "No."

The wolf backed toward the window, its head held high and fire in its eyes. Then it abruptly turned, lunged up into the window frame and out of the house.

Lazaris released the breath he'd been holding. "Did you see those things? They'll tear us to pieces! Why the hell didn't you let me shoot?"

"Because," Michael said calmly, "a burst of bullets would bring the Nazis here about as fast as you could reload. The wolves won't hurt you."

"Nazee boys nasty," Kitty said as she shone the flashlight around. "Wold not much so. Nazee boys make dead, wold yum dead.'' She shrugged her massive shoulders. ''Such done.''

This house, wolf droppings on the floor and all, would be their headquarters. Most likely, Michael reasoned, the German soldiers who guarded Hildebrand's chemical plant were as fearful of the wolves as Lazaris was, and wouldn't come here. Michael let the others start unpacking their gear, and then he said, ''I'm going out to do some scouting. I'll be back as soon as I can.''

''I'm going with you.'' Chesna started to shrug her backpack on again.

''No. I can move faster alone. You wait here.''

''I didn't come with you to—''

''Argue,'' Michael finished for her, ''and that's not why we're here. I want to get in closer to the plant and take a look around. Better one scout than two or three. Right?''

Chesna hesitated, but his voice was firm and he was staring holes through her. ''All right,'' she agreed. ''But for God's sake, stay low!''

''I plan on it.''

Outside, Michael strode briskly along the road and away from the village. Woods and sharp-edged boulders began about seventy yards east of the last house and ascended toward Skarpa's heights. He knelt down, waiting to make sure Chesna hadn't followed him, and after a couple of minutes he unstrapped his gun, took off his backpack and his parka. He began to undress, his skin rippling in the chill. Naked, he found a secure niche to wedge his backpack, clothes, and Schmeisser into, and then he sat on his haunches and began the change.

As a wolf, he realized the scent of the food in his pack would draw Skarpa's wolves like a dinner bell. One way to fix that. He urinated all over the rocks around his cache, and if that smell wouldn't keep the wolves back, they were welcome to his dried beef. Then he stretched, getting blood into his muscles, and he began to lope nimbly over the rocks above Wolftown.

After he crested the ridge, it was a half-mile jaunt through dense forest before he smelled the reek of men. The thumping noise was louder; he was going in the right direction.

Other aromas crowded into his senses: the bitter smell of exhaust from the plant's chimney, the smell of wet steam, hares, and other small animals quivering in the woods at his passage, and . . . the musky perfume of a young female.

He heard the soft cracking of a twig off to his left, and when he glanced that way, he caught just the quickest glimpse of yellow. She was keeping pace with him, probably made a little nervous with curiosity and his own male aroma. He wondered if she'd witnessed his change. If so, she'd have interesting tales to tell her pack.

The bitter smell got worse, and so did the man-reek. The yellow she-wolf began to lay behind, intimidated by the nearness of humans. After a moment she stopped, and Michael heard her make a high-pitched *yip yip yip*. He understood the message: Don't go any closer. He wouldn't have cared to if he'd had a choice about it, but he kept going. About fifteen yards later he came out of the woods and there was Hildebrand's creation, rising like a dirty mountain beyond a chain-link fence topped with barbed wire.

Smoke chugged from a massive chimney of gray stones. Around it were concrete buildings, connected by catwalks and pipes that snaked through the place like one of Harry Sandler's mazes. The thumping heartbeat noise was coming from somewhere at the center of the complex, and lights shone through the shutters of windows. Alleys wound between the buildings; as Michael watched, on his belly at the edge of the woods, a truck turned a corner and grumbled away like a fat beetle into another alley. He saw several figures up on the catwalks. Two workmen twisted a large red flywheel, and then a third checked what looked like a panel of pressure gauges and signaled an okay sign. Work was going on here around the clock.

Michael got up and slinked along the fence. Soon he made another discovery: an airfield, complete with hangars, a fuel tank, and fueling trucks. On the field, lined up in an orderly row, were three night fighers—a Dornier Do-217 and two Heinkel HE-219s, all with nose radar prongs—and a wicked-looking Messerschmitt Bf-109 day fighter. Overshadowing everything on the field was a huge Messerschmitt Me-323 transport aircraft, its wingspan over a hundred and eighty feet and its length almost a hundred feet. The Nazis were obviously doing some serious business here. For now, though, there was no activity on the airfield. Beyond the field the cliffs of Skarpa fell to the sea.

Michael returned to the forest's edge and chose his spot. He began to dig a hole beneath the fence; for this task, a wolf's paws were superior to human hands. Still, the ground was full of small rocks and it was strenuous work. But the hole grew, and when it was large enough, Michael pressed his belly to the earth and clawed himself under the fence. He stood up, on all fours, and glanced around. No soldiers in sight. He ran into the nearest alley, heading toward the heartbeat with a shadow's silence.

He smelled and heard the truck coming before it turned into the alley behind him, and he leaped around a corner and flung himself flat before the headlights found him. The truck passed; in its backwash, Michael caught a sour odor of sweat and fear: a zoolike smell he associated instantly with Falkenhausen. He got up and followed the truck at a respectful distance.

The truck paused before a long building with shuttered windows. A corrugated metal gate was drawn up from within, and harsh light spilled out. The truck pulled into the portal, and a few seconds later the corrugated metal began to clatter down again. It fell, sealing off the light.

Michael's gaze found a ladder, running up the building's side to a catwalk about twenty feet above. The catwalk continued along the center of the roof. There was no time for deliberation. He found a group of oilcans nearby and crouched behind them. When the change was done and his white skin tingled with the cold, he stood up, ran to the metal-runged ladder, and quickly scaled it, something that a man's hands and feet could do but a wolf's paws could not. The catwalk went on to the next structure, but on this building's roof there was an entry door. Michael tried it, and the knob turned. He opened the door, found himself in a stairwell, and started down.

He emerged into a workshop of some kind, with a conveyor belt and hoists just below the roof. There were stacks of crates and oil drums, and a couple of heavy load-pulling machines standing about. Michael could hear voices; all the activity was down at the other end of the long building. He carefully wound his way through the equipment, and instantly crouched down behind a rack full of copper tubing when he heard an irritated voice say, "This man can't work! My God, look at those hands! Palsied like an old woman! I said bring me men who can use saws and hammers!"

Michael knew that voice. He looked out from his hiding place, and saw Colonel Jerek Blok.

The hulking Boots stood beside his master. Blok was shouting into the face of a German officer who had flushed crimson, and to their left stood a skinny man in the baggy gray uniform of a POW. The prisoner's hands were not only palsied, they were gnarled by malnutrition. Beyond those four men stood seven other prisoners, five men and two women. On a large table were bottles of nails, an assortment of hammers and saws, and nearby a pile of timbers. The truck, flanked by two soldiers with rifles, was positioned near the metal gate.

"Oh, take this wretch back to his hole!" Blok gave the prisoner a disdainful shove. "We'll have to use what we've got!" As the officer pushed the POW back to the truck, Blok put his hands on his hips and addressed the others. "I trust you are all well and eager to work. Yes?" He smiled, and his silver teeth threw a spark of light. There was no response from the prisoners, their faces pale and emotionless. "You gentlemen—and ladies—have been selected from the others because your records indicate a familiarity with carpentry. We are therefore going to do some woodcraft this morning. Twenty-four crates, built to the specifications as follows." He withdrew a piece of paper from his pocket and unfolded it. "Thirty-two inches in length, sixteen inches in height, sixteen inches in width. There will be no deviations from this formula. These crates will be lined with rubber. The points of all nails will be blunted once they are hammered in. All rough edges will be sanded to a uniform smoothness. The lids will be double-hinged and padlocked instead of nailed shut." He gave the list to Boots, who went about nailing it up on a bulletin board for all to see. "Moreover,"

Blok continued, "these crates will be inspected at the end of sixteen hours. Any not passing my inspection will be broken and its creator made to begin anew. Questions?" He waited. Of course there were none. "Thank you for your attention," he said, and strode toward the metal gate with Boots right behind him.

The gate was being drawn up by the two guards, and the truck driver was backing it out with the officer and the palsied POW aboard. Blok did not attempt to hitch a ride on the truck, but he and Boots followed it out and then the metal gate was closed again. One of the guards shouted, "Get to work, you lazy shits!" to the prisoners, and the other strolled over to a woman and poked at her behind with the barrel of his rifle. A frail-looking man with gray hair and wire-rimmed glasses took the first step toward the worktable, then a younger man followed. When all the prisoners were moving—sluggishly, their minds and bodies beaten—the two guards sat down at a table and began to play cards.

Michael slipped back to the stairwell the way he'd come, ascended to the roof and then to the ladder again. On the ground he crouched behind the oilcans once more and grew a warm coat. His joints throbbed with the stress of so many changes within such a short time, and his muscles were sore, but he was ready to run again. He came out from his hiding place and sniffed the air. Through the multitude of scents he found the lemony tang of Jerek Blok's hair pomade, and that was the trail he followed.

He turned a corner and saw Blok and Boots walking briskly just ahead. He followed them, slinking low. Twenty-four crates, Michael thought. Lined with rubber. What would go into those crates? It had occurred to him that the crates were about the size needed to hold a small shell, rocket, or bomb. The big transport plane out on the runway must be here to carry the loaded crates to wherever Iron Fist was hangared.

Michael's blood pounded in his veins. He had the killing desire. Taking Blok and Boots would be a simple matter, here in this alley, though both men wore holsters and pistols. It would be a balm to the soul to tear Boots's throat out and spit in his face. But he held himself back; his mission was to find out where Iron Fist was, and what kind of horror Dr. Hildebrand had created. First the mission, then he would feed his desire.

He followed the men to a two-storied concrete blockhouse near the center of the plant. Again, the windows were shuttered. Michael watched as Blok and Boots climbed a metal staircase and went through a second-floor doorway. The door closed behind them. Michael crouched down, waiting to see if they'd come out, but the minutes ticked past and they did not. It would be dawn in two hours. It was time to get back to Wolftown.

Michael returned to the place where he'd dug his way in. This time he dug the hole deeper so a human body might crawl under. Dirt flew from beneath his claws, and then he eased beneath the fence and ran into the woods.

The yellow wolf, who thought herself crafty, came out of the underbrush and followed off to the side. Michael outdistanced her, wanting to reach his equipment and change before she could get too close.

On two legs, dressed and with his backpack on and the Schmeisser strapped to his shoulder, Michael sprinted along the road back through Wolftown. Chesna rose up from where she'd been hiding behind a wall of crumbling stones, her machine gun aimed at the approaching figure. It was Michael, she saw in another moment. He had dirt all over his face.

"I've found a way in," he told her. "Let's go."

6

The journey from Wolftown to the plant was harder on human legs than on wolfen, Michael soon learned. As he, Chesna, and Lazaris went through the woods, he heard noises all around them. The yellow wolf had brought her companions. Kitty had remained behind, to watch the boat, and also because her bulk would have slowed their progress to a crawl. Lazaris jumped at every sound—real or imagined—but Michael made sure the Russian kept the safety on his weapon and his finger off the trigger.

Michael went under the fence first. Lazaris followed, muttering beneath his breath at how he'd been born a stupid fool and did not wish to die as one. Then Chesna crawled under, her mind turning over the question of how Michael had dug such a hole without a shovel. In the shelter of an alley they stopped to remove extra ammo clips and two grenades from their packs. The clips went into the pockets of their parkas while the grenades were latched to the Schmeissers' straps. Then they went on, staying close to the wall, with Michael in the lead.

He guided them toward the building where the prisoners were working. The two guards would be easy to overcome, and information about the plant could be gotten from the guards and the prisoners. Still, he took nothing for granted; each step was a careful one, and each turn a challenge. Near their target building Michael heard the noise of footsteps approaching and motioned Chesna and Lazaris down. He knelt, at an alley corner, and waited. One soldier was about to round the corner. As soon as Michael saw the man's knees, he came up off the ground in a burst of power and drove his gun butt against the soldier's chin. The man was lifted off his feet by the blow, and fell on his back to the pavement. He twitched a few times, then lay still. They dragged him into a recessed doorway and left him there folded up like a package after Lazaris had removed the soldier's knife and cut his throat with it. Lazaris's eyes glittered with blood lust, and he slipped the knife under his parka.

A knife was also being used in Wolftown. Kitty used her hooked, blubber-slicing blade to cut hunks of dried beef into bite-sized pieces. As she put one into her mouth and chewed on it, she heard a wolf howl somewhere in the village.

It was a high, piercing call that echoed over the harbor and ended in a series of quick, staccato barks. She did not like that sound. She picked up a flashlight and, armed with her knife, went out into the misty chill. There was no sound but the waves lapping against the seawall. Kitty stood there for a moment, slowly looking from left to right. The wolf made another noise: a series of harsh yips. Kitty left the house, walking toward the dock. Her boots squished in the dark mud that held her family's bones. When she reached the dock, she switched on the flashlight, and there she found it.

A dark gray rubber boat, tied up beside her own craft. There were three sets of oars in it.

Kitty's knife pierced the rubber in a dozen places. The boat gurgled as it crumpled and sank. Then she half ran, half careened on her stumpy legs toward her house again. As she went through the door, she smelled their sausage-and-beer sweat, and she halted in the presence of more dangerous beasts.

One of the black-clad Nazee boys motioned with his rifle and spoke his gibberish. How could a human tongue make such a noise? Kitty wondered. The other two soldiers also held rifles on her, their faces daubed with black camouflage paint. The Nazee boys had known they were here, she realized. They had come prepared for a slaughter.

She would give them one. She grinned, her blue Nordic eyes glittering, and she said, "Welcome!" as she lifted her knife and lunged forward.

Michael, Lazaris, and Chesna had reached the workshop building's roof. They went along the catwalk and down through the stairwell. "Watch where you point that thing!" Michael whispered to Lazaris as the barrel of the Russian's weapon wandered. He led them through the jumble of equipment, and in another moment they could see the two soldiers, engrossed in their card game. The prisoners were working on the crates, sawing and hammering, proud of their carpentry skills even under the Nazi thumb.

"Wait," Michael told Chesna and Lazaris, and then he crept closer to the guards. One of the prisoners dropped a nail, reached down to get it, and at floor level saw a man crawling on his belly. The prisoner gave a soft, stunned gasp, and another glanced over in Michael's direction.

"Four aces!" the guard with a winning hand crowed as he spread his cards out on the table. "Beat me!"

"As you wish," Michael said, rising up behind the man and slamming him over the head with the butt of his Schmeisser. The guard moaned and toppled, scattering cards. The second man reached for his rifle, which leaned against the wall, but he froze when the Schmeisser's business end kissed his throat. "On the floor," Michael said. "Get on your knees, hands cupped behind your head."

The soldier complied. Very quickly.

Chesna and Lazaris emerged, and Lazaris prodded the unconscious man's ribs with the toe of his boot. When the soldier groaned softly, he gave him a kick that made him pass out again.

"Don't kill me!" the man on his knees begged. "Please! I'm just a nobody!"

"We'll make you a no-head in a minute!" Lazaris said as he pressed the knife blade to the man's quivering Adam's apple.

"He can't answer questions through a cut throat," Chesna told the Russian. She put the barrel of her gun against the soldier's forehead and pulled back the cocking bolt. The soldier's eyes widened, wet with terror.

"I think we have his attention." Michael glanced over at the prisoners, who had stopped working and were mesmerized with surprise and bewilderment. "What's going into those crates?" he asked the guard.

"I don't know."

"You lying bastard!" Lazaris put some pressure on the blade, and the man yelped as a trickle of warm blood ran down his throat.

"Bombs! Hundred-pound bombs! That's all I know!"

"Twenty-four of them? A bomb for each crate?"

"Yes! Yes! Please don't kill me!"

"They're being packed up for transport? In the Messerschmitt out on the field?"

The man nodded as his uniform's collar reddened.

"Transported to where?" Michael persisted.

"I don't know." More pressure from the blade. The man gasped. "I swear I don't know!"

Michael believed him. "What's inside the bombs?"

"High explosives. What's inside any bomb?"

"Don't get cute," Chesna warned, her voice crisp and deadly. "Just answer the questions."

"That fool doesn't know. He's just a guard."

They looked to see who'd spoken. It was the frail prisoner who had gray hair and wore wire-rimmed glasses. He came a few steps closer and spoke in what sounded like a heavy Hungarian accent. "It's a gas of some kind. That's what's inside the bombs. I've been here for over six months, and I've seen what it can do."

"I have, too," Michael said. "It burns the flesh."

The man smiled faintly, a bitter smile. "Burns the flesh," he repeated. "Oh, it does more than burn the flesh, my friend. It eats the flesh, like a cancer. I know. I've had to burn some of the bodies. My wife among them." He blinked, his eyes heavy-lidded. "But she's in a better place than this. They torture me every day, by forcing me to live." He looked at the hammer he held, and then dropped it to the concrete. He wiped his hand on his trouser leg.

"Where are the bombs stored?" Michael asked him.

"That I don't know. Somewhere deeper in the plant. There's a white building next to the big chimney. Some of the others say that's where the gas is made."

"The others?" Chesna asked. "How many prisoners are there?"

"Eighty-four. No, no. Wait." He thought about it. "Danelka died two nights ago. Eighty-three. When I first came here, there were over four hundred, but . . ." He shrugged his thin shoulders, and his eyes found Michael's. "Have you come to save us?"

Michael didn't know what to say. He decided the truth was best. "No."

"Ah." The prisoner nodded. "Then it's the gas, is it? You're here because of that? Well, that's good. We're already dead. If that stuff ever gets out of here, I shudder to—"

Something whammed against the corrugated-metal gate.

Michael's heart kicked, and Lazaris jumped so hard the blade bit deeper into the soldier's throat. Chesna removed her gun barrel from the man's forehead, leaving a white circle where it had been pressed, and aimed the weapon toward the gate.

Again, something hit the metal. A rifle butt or billy club, Michael thought. A voice followed: "Hey, Reinhart! Open up!"

The soldier croaked, "He's calling me."

"No, he's not," the gray-haired prisoner said. "He's Karlsen. Reinhart is on the floor."

"Reinhart!" the soldier outside shouted. "Open up, damn you! We know you've got the pretty one in there!"

The female prisoner who'd been poked with the rifle, her black hair framing a face as pale as a cameo, picked up a ballpeen hammer. Her knuckles bleached around the handle.

"Come on, be a sport!" It was a different voice. "Why hog her all for yourselves?"

"Tell them to go away," Chesna ordered. Her eyes were flinty, but her voice held a nervous edge.

"No," Michael said. "They'll come in the way we did. On your feet." Karlsen got up. "To the gate. Move." He followed the Nazi, and so did Chesna. Michael pressed his gun into the man's spine. "Tell them to wait a minute."

"Wait a minute!" Karlsen shouted.

"That's better!" one of the men outside said. "You bastards thought you were going to sneak one by us, didn't you?"

The gate was hoisted by a chain-and-pulley device, operated with a flywheel. Michael stepped to one side. "Pull the gate up. Slowly." Chesna got out of the way, too, and Karlsen started turning the flywheel. The gate began to fold upward.

And at that moment Reinhart, who'd been shamming for the past two minutes, suddenly sat up at Lazaris's feet. He clutched at his two broken ribs and reached up for the wall beside their card table. Lazaris gave a shout and stabbed downward with the knife, sinking it into Reinhart's shoulder, but he was powerless to prevent what happened next.

Reinhart's fist punched a red button attached to electrical cords on the wall, and a siren shrieked somewhere on the building's roof.

The gate was a quarter of the way up when the alarm began. Michael could see four pairs of legs. Without hesitation he clicked off the safety on his gun and sprayed bullets below the gate, chopping down two soldiers who screamed and writhed in agony. Karlsen released the flywheel and tried to scramble beneath the corrugated metal as it clattered down again, but a burst from Chesna's gun ripped him open and the gate clunked on his butt.

Lazaris repeatedly stabbed down on Reinhart, fierce strength behind the blows. The German crumpled, his face a mass of torn flesh, but the siren kept going. A black-haired figure swept past him. The woman raised her hammer and broke the alarm button to fragments. Still, a switch had been triggered and the siren would not be silenced.

"Get out while you can!" the gray-haired prisoner shouted. *"Go!"*

There was no time to deliberate. That siren would bring every soldier in the plant down on them. Michael ran for the stairwell, with Chesna a few paces behind and Lazaris bringing up the rear. They came out onto the roof, and already two soldiers were running along the catwalk toward them. Michael fired, and so did Chesna. The bullets sparked off the catwalk railing, but the soldiers flung themselves flat. Rifles cracked, the slugs zipping past their heads. Michael saw another pair of soldiers, coming across the catwalk from the building behind them. One of them fired a shot that snagged Chesna's parka, and puffed goose down into the air.

Michael readied a grenade, then paused while the fuse sizzled and the soldiers got closer. A bullet sang off the railing beside him. He flung the grenade at the two men who were coming up from behind, and three seconds later there was a blast of white fire and two shredded figures twitching on the catwalk. Lazaris wheeled toward the other pair in front of them and fired short bursts that knocked sparks off the slate roof. Michael saw three more soldiers advancing over the catwalk behind them. Chesna's gun rattled, and the soldiers crouched down as slugs ricocheted off the railings.

The rooftop was turning into a hornet's nest. A bullet struck the slates to Michael's left and spun like a burning

545

cigarette butt less than five inches past his face. Chesna suddenly cried out and went down. "I'm hit!" she said, her teeth gritted with pain and anger. "Damn it!" She was clutching her right ankle, blood on her fingers.

Lazaris sprayed bullets first in one direction, then another. A soldier screamed and fell over the railing to the pavement twenty feet below. Michael bent down to help Chesna to her feet, and as he did he felt a bullet pluck at his parka. They had no choice; they had to get back down the stairwell before they were cut to pieces in the cross fire.

He hauled Chesna up. She fired at the soldiers behind them, even as Michael pulled her to the stairwell door. A bullet hit the catwalk railing beside Lazaris and metal splinters pierced his jaw and cheek. He retreated, spraying bullets across the roof. As they got into the stairwell, slugs marched across the door and knocked it off its hinges. Michael felt a searing sting of pain in his left hand, and he realized a bullet had just gone through his palm. His hand went numb, the fingers twitching involuntarily. He kept hold of Chesna, and they all backed down the stairwell to the workshop. Two Germans entered at the top of the stairs, and Lazaris cut them down before they could aim their weapons. The bodies slid over each other down the steps. More soldiers crawled into the stairwell, and a few seconds later a grenade was flung and exploded with a *whump* of fire and concussion. But Michael, Chesna, and Lazaris were already in the workshop, where the prisoners had taken cover amid the equipment and oil drums. Soldiers scurried down to the bottom of the smoky stairwell and fired into the workshop. Michael looked over his shoulder toward the metal gate. More Germans were trying to wrench it up by hand from the other side, their fingers curled under the edge. As they struggled, other soldiers fired bullets through the gap at floor level. Michael released Chesna, who fell to her knees, her face glistening with the sweat of pain, and popped a fresh ammo clip into his gun. His hand was streaming blood, the wound a perfect puncture. He shot beneath the gate, and the Germans scrambled away from it.

The siren had stopped its shrieking. Over the noise of gunshots a strident voice rang out: "Cease fire! Cease fire!" The shooting dwindled, and halted.

Michael crouched down, behind a half-track load puller, and Chesna and Lazaris knelt in the shelter of oil drums. Michael heard the fearful moaning of some of the prisoners, and the clicks of guns being reloaded. A haze of blue smoke drifted through the workshop, carrying the pungent odor of gunpowder.

A moment later a voice amplified through a loudspeaker came from beyond the metal gate: "Baron? It's time you and Chesna threw out your weapons. It's over."

Michael glanced toward Chesna, and their eyes met. It was Jerek Blok's voice. How did he know?

"Baron?" Blok continued. "You're not a stupid man. Certainly not. You know by now that this building is surrounded, and there's no possible way you can get out. We will take you, one way or the other." He paused, letting them think it over. Then: "Chesna, dear? Surely you understand your situation. Throw out your weapons, and we'll have a nice talk."

Chesna examined the blue-edged hole in her ankle. Her thick woolen sock was wet with blood, and the pain was excruciating. A cracked bone, she thought. She fully understood the situation.

"What are we going to *do?*" Lazaris asked, with a note of panic. Blood trickled down into his beard from the splinter wounds.

Chesna got her backpack off and unsnapped it.

"Baron, you amaze me!" Blok said. "I'd like to know how that escape from Falkenhausen was engineered. You have my deepest respect."

Michael saw Chesna reach into her pack. Her hand came out with a square of waxed paper.

The cyanide capsule.

"No!" Lazaris grasped her arm. "There's another way."

She shook her head, pulling free. "You know there's not," she said, and began to unwrap the packet.

Michael crawled across the floor to her. "Chesna! We can shoot our way out! And we've still got grenades!"

"My ankle's broken. How am I going to get out of here? Crawl?"

He gripped her wrist, preventing her from putting the capsule on her tongue. "I'll carry you."

She smiled faintly, her eyes dark with pain. "Yes," she said. "I believe you would." She touched his cheek, and ran her fingers across his mouth. "But it wouldn't do any good, would it? No. I'm not going to be caged and tortured like an animal. I know too much. I'd be sentencing a dozen others to—"

Something clattered across the floor about fifteen feet away. Michael looked toward it, his heart pounding, and saw that one of the soldiers in the stairwell had just thrown a grenade.

It went off, before any of them could move.

Flame sputtered from the fuse. There was a *pop!* and a bright flash, then chalky-white smoke began to pour from it. Except it was not smoke, Michael realized in another two seconds. It had a sickly-sweet, orangelike odor: the smell of chemicals.

A second gas grenade popped, near the first one. Chesna, her eyes already stinging and watering, lifting the cyanide pill to her mouth. Michael couldn't bear it. For better or worse he swiped the capsule out of her hand.

The chemical smoke settled over them like the folds of a shroud. Lazaris hacked and coughed, struggled to his feet with tears blinding him, and flailed into the vapors. Michael felt as if his lungs were swelling up; he couldn't draw a breath. He heard Chesna cough and gasp, and she clung to him as he tried to pick her up. But his air was gone, and the smoke was so dense that direction was destroyed. One of Hildebrand's inventions, Michael thought and then, blinded and weeping, he fell to his knees. He heard the prisoners coughing, being overcome as well. A figure appeared through the smoke before him: a soldier wearing a gas mask. The man aimed his rifle at Michael's head.

Chesna slumped beside him, her body hitching. Michael

fell over her, struggled to rise again, but his strength was stolen. Whatever the chemical was, it was potent. And then, with the reek of rotten oranges in his nostrils, Michael Gallatin blacked out.

——— 7 ———

They awakened in a cell, with a barred window overlooking the airfield. Michael, his wounded hand bound with bandages, peered out into silvery daylight and saw the big transport Messerschmitt still there. The bombs hadn't been loaded yet.

All their equipment and their parkas had been stripped away. Chesna's ankle was bandaged as well, and when she peeled the bandages away for an inspection, she found that the wound had been cleaned and the bullet removed. The effects of the gas grenades remained; all of them kept spitting up watery mucus, and found a bucket placed in the cell for just that purpose. Michael had a killer headache, and all Lazaris could do was lie on one of the thin-mattressed cots and stare at the ceiling like a drunkard after a vodka binge.

Michael paced the cell, stopping every so often to look through the wooden door's barred inset. The corridor was deserted. "Hey!" he shouted. "Bring us some food and water!" A guard came a moment later, glared at Michael with pale blue eyes, and went away again.

Within an hour two guards brought them a meal of thick, pasty oatmeal porridge and a canteen of water. When that had been consumed, the same two soldiers wielding submachine guns appeared once more and ordered the captives out of their cell.

Michael supported Chesna as she limped along the corridor. Lazaris stumbled, his head fogged and his knees as soft as taffy. The guards took them out of the building, a stone stockade on the edge of the airfield, and down an alley into the plant. A few moments later they were entering another, larger building not far from where they'd been captured.

"No, no!" they heard a high, boyish voice shout. "Dribble the ball! Don't run with it! *Dribble!*"

They had walked into a gymnasium, with a floor of polished oak boards. There were rows of bleachers and frosted glass windows. A knot of emaciated prisoners were struggling for possession of a basketball as guards with rifles looked on. A whistle blew, deafening in the enclosure. "No!" The boyish voice cracked with exasperation. "That's a foul on the blue team! The ball belongs to the red team now."

The prisoners wore armbands of blue or red. They stumbled and staggered, stick figures in baggy gray uniforms, toward the goal at the other side of the court. "Dribble the ball, Vladimir! Don't you have any sense?" The man who was shouting stood at the edge of the court. He wore dark slacks, a striped referee's shirt, had a long mane of blond hair hanging halfway down his back, and stood almost seven feet tall. "Get the ball, Tiomkin!" he shouted, and stomped his foot. "You missed an easy shot!"

This had gone from the crazy to the insane, Michael thought. And there was Jerek Blok, standing up in the bleachers and motioning them over. Boots was sitting a few rows above his master, perched like a glowering bulldog. "Hello!" the seven-foot-tall, blond-maned man said, speaking to Chesna. He smiled, showing horselike teeth. He wore round glasses, and Michael judged him to be no older than twenty-three. He had dark brown, shining, childlike eyes. "Are you the people who caused all that noise this morning?"

"Yes, they are, Gustav," Blok answered.

"Oh." Dr. Gustav Hildebrand's smile switched off, and his eyes turned sullen. "You woke me up."

Hildebrand might be a chemical warfare genius, Michael thought, but that fact didn't prevent him from being a simpleton. The towering young man turned away from them and shouted to the prisoners, "Don't stop! Keep playing!"

The prisoners stumbled and staggered to the opposite goal, some of them falling over their own feet.

"Sit down here." Blok gestured to the bleacher beside him. "Chesna, will you sit beside me, please?" She obeyed, nudged by a gun barrel. Michael took the next place, and Lazaris, as puzzled by this display as by anything in his life, eased down beside him. The two guards stood a few paces away. "Hello, Chesna." Blok reached out and grasped her hand. "I'm so glad to see you a—"

Chesna spat in his face.

Blok showed his silver teeth. Boots had risen to his feet, but Blok said, "No, no. It's all right," and the huge man sat down again. Blok withdrew a handkerchief from his pocket and wiped the spit from his cheek. "Such spirit," he said quietly. "You're a true German, Chesna. You just refuse to believe it."

"I am a true German," she agreed coldly, "but I'll never be the kind of German you are."

Blok left his handkerchief out, in case it was needed again. "The difference between winning and losing is a vast chasm. You are speaking from the bottom of that chasm. Oh, that was a good shot!" He clapped his hands in appreciation, and Boots did, too. Hildebrand gave a glowing smile. "I taught him to do that!" the mad doctor announced.

The game went on, the prisoners halfheartedly grappling for the ball. One of them fell, winded, and Hildebrand shouted, "Get up! Get up! You're the center, you have to play!"

"Please . . . I can't . . ."

"Get up." Hildebrand's voice was less boyish, and brimmed with menace. "This minute. You're going to keep playing until I say the game is over."

"No . . . I can't get up. . . ."

A rifle was cocked. The prisoner got up. The game went on.

"Gustav—Dr. Hildebrand—loves basketball," Blok explained. "He read about it in an American magazine. I can't fathom the game myself. I'm a soccer fan. But each to his own. Yes?"

"Dr. Hildebrand certainly seems to rule the game with an iron fist," Michael said.

"Oh, don't start that again!" Blok's face took on a shade

of crimson. "Haven't you gotten tired of barking up that trail yet?"

"No, I haven't found the trail's end." Michael decided it was time for the big guns. "The only thing I don't know," he said, almost casually, "is where the Fortress is hangared. Iron Fist: that's the name of a B-seventeen bomber, isn't it?"

"Baron, you continually amaze me!" Blok smiled, but his eyes were wary. "You never rest, do you?"

"I'd like to know," Michael urged. "Iron Fist. Where is it?"

Blok was silent for a moment, watching the hapless prisoners run from one side of the court to the other, Hildebrand shouting at their errors and misplays. "Near Rotterdam," he said. "On a Luftwaffe airfield."

Rotterdam, Michael thought. Not France after all, but German-occupied Holland. Almost a thousand miles south of Skarpa Island. He felt a little sick, knowing that what he'd suspected was true.

"That said, I'll add this," Blok continued. "You and your friends—and that bearded gentleman down there I haven't been introduced to and neither do I wish to be—will remain here on Skarpa until the project is concluded. I think you'll find Skarpa a more difficult nut to crack than Falkenhausen. Oh, by the way, Chesna: turnabout is fair play, don't you agree? Your friends got to Bauman, my friends got to one of the gentlemen who met your plane near Uskedahl." He gave her a brief, bone-chilling smile. "As a matter of fact, I've been on Skarpa for a week, tidying up affairs and waiting for you. Baron, I knew where you would go when you got out of Falkenhausen. It was just a question of how long it would take you to get here." He winced at a collision between two prisoners, and the basketball bounced away down the court. "Our radar watched you weave through the mine field. That was nice work."

Kitty! Michael thought. What had happened to her?

"I think you'll find the stockade more roomy than your quarters at Falkenhausen, though," the colonel said. "You'll get a nice fresh sea breeze, too."

"And where will you be? Getting a suntan up on the roof?"

"Not quite." A flicker of silver. "Baron, I'll be getting prepared to destroy the Allied invasion of Europe."

It was said so offhandedly that Michael, though his throat felt constricted, had to answer in kind. "Really? Is that your weekend job?"

"It will take much less than a weekend, I think. The invasion will be destroyed approximately six hours after it begins. The British and American troops will be drowning each other trying to swim back to their ships, and the commanders will go mad with panic. It will be the greatest disaster in history—for the Reich's enemies, of course—and a triumph for Germany. And all that, Baron, will happen without our soldiers having to fire a shot of our precious ammunition."

Michael grunted. "All because of Iron Fist? And Hildebrand's corrosive gas? Twenty-four one-hundred-pound bombs won't stop thousand of soldiers. As a matter of fact, your troops are more likely to get gas blown back in their faces. So tell me: what asylum were you recently released from?"

Blok stared at him. A muscle twitched in the side of his face. "Oh, no!" He giggled, a terrible sound. "Oh, my dear Baron! Chesna! Neither of you know, do you? You think bombs are going to be dropped on *this* side of the Channel?" His laughter spiraled upward.

Michael and Chesna looked at each other. A horror, like a knot of snakes, began to writhe in Michael's stomach.

"You see, we don't know where the invasion is going to be. There are a dozen possibilities." He laughed again, and dabbed his eyes with the handkerchief. "Oh, my! What a surprise! But you see, it doesn't matter where the invasion is. If it happens this year, it's going to happen within the next two to four weeks. When it begins," Blok said, "we're going to drop those twenty-four bombs on London."

"My God," Michael whispered, and he saw clearly.

No German bomber could pierce England's aerial defenses. The Royal Air Force was too strong, too experienced since the Battle of Britain. No German bomber could get anywhere even remotely close to London.

But an American B-17 Flying Fortress could. Especially one that appeared to be a cripple, shot full of holes and returning from a bombing mission over Germany. In fact, the Royal Air Force might even give the struggling craft an escort. How would the British fighter pilots know that the bullet holes and battle damage had been painted on by a Berlin street artist?

"Those twenty-four bombs," Blok said, "have a center of liquid carnagene within a shell of high explosives. Carnagene is the name of the gas Gustav's created, and it's quite an accomplishment. He'd have to show you the equations and the chemical notations; I don't understand them. All I know is that when the gas is inhaled, it triggers the body's own bacteria: the microbes that cause the decay of dead tissue. The microbes, in a sense, become carnivorous. Within seven to twelve minutes the flesh begins to be . . . shall we say . . . eaten from the inside out. Stomach, heart, lungs, arteries . . . everything."

Michael didn't speak. He had seen the photographs, and he believed it.

One of the prisoners had collapsed, and did not move. "Get up." Hildebrand prodded at the man's ribs with his sneaker. "Come on! Get up, I said!" The prisoner remained motionless. Hildebrand looked up at Blok. "He's broken! Bring me a new one!"

"Do it," Blok told the nearest guard, and the soldier hurried out of the gymnasium.

"The red team will have to go on with four players!" Hildebrand blew his whistle. "Keep playing!"

"That's a fine example of the master race," Michael said, still stunned. "He's too dumb to know he's an idiot."

"In some ways he is an idiot, I'm afraid," the colonel agreed. "But in the field of chemical warfare, Gustav Hildebrand is a genius, surpassing his father. Take carnagene, for instance; it's fantastically concentrated. What's contained in those twenty-four bombs is enough to kill, at a rough estimate, thirty thousand people, depending on the prevailing winds and rainfall."

Chesna had roused herself, fighting off the same shock that had hit Michael. "Why London?" she asked. "Why don't you just drop your bombs on the invasion fleet?"

"Because, dear Chesna, bombing ships is an unprofitable undertaking. The targets are small, the Channel winds unpredictable, and carnagene doesn't get along well with sodium. As in salt water." He patted her hand before she could jerk it away. "Don't you be concerned. We know what we're doing."

Michael knew, as well. "You want to hit London so word can be communicated to the invasion troops. When the soldiers hear about what that gas does, they'll be paralyzed with terror."

"Exactly. They'll all swim home like good little fishies, and leave us alone."

A panic amid the landing troops would end all chances for success. There was no way the soldiers wouldn't hear about the attack on London, if not over the BBC then over the scuttlebutt network. Michael said, "Why only twenty-four bombs? Why not fifty?"

"The B-seventeen we have can only hold that many. It's enough for the purpose. Anyway"—he shrugged—"the next batch of carnagene isn't refined yet. It's a long, expensive process, and one mistake can destroy many months of labor. We'll have some ready, though, in time to perfume your comrades from the East."

The twenty-four bombs contained all the carnagene that was ready for use, Michael realized. But it was more than enough to destroy D-Day and strengthen Hitler's grip on the throat of Europe.

"By the way, we do have a target in London," Blok said. "The bombs will fall along Parliament Street to Trafalgar Square. Perhaps we can even get Churchill, as he smokes one of those disgusting cigars."

Another prisoner fell to his knees. Hildebrand grasped the man's white hair. "I told you to pass the ball to Matthias, didn't I? I didn't say for you to shoot!"

"We won't see each other again," Blok told his unwilling guests. "I will have other projects, after this one. You see, this is a feather in my cap." He gave a silver smile. "Chesna,

555

you have broken my heart.'' His smile faded as he placed a long thin finger beneath her chin. She twisted away from him. ''But you're a wonderful actress,'' he said, ''and I'll always love the woman in your films. Guards, will you take them back to their cell now?''

The two soldiers came forward. Lazaris stood up, dazed. Michael helped Chesna to her feet, and she gasped with pain as some weight settled on her injured ankle. ''Goodbye, Baron,'' Blok said as Boots stared impassively. ''I trust you have a good relationship with the commandant of the next prison camp you're in.''

As they walked along the edge of the court, Dr. Hildebrand blew his whistle to stop the game. He grinned at Chesna and followed her a few steps. ''Chemistry is the future, you know,'' he said. ''It's power, and essences, and the heart of creation. You're full of it.''

''You're full of it, too,'' she told him, and with Michael's help she limped away. She had seen the future, and it was demented.

Once that cell door shut on them, they were finished. So, too, were thirty thousand or more of London's citizens, and possibly the prime minister himself. Finished also was the invasion of Europe. It would all be ended when the cell door shut.

This was in Michael's mind as he supported Chesna. Lazaris walked a few paces ahead, the soldiers a few paces behind. They were going through the alley, toward the stockade. Michael could not let that door shut on him again. No matter what. He said, in English, ''Stumble and fall.''

Chesna obeyed at once, moaning and grasping her ankle. Michael bent to help her as the two soldiers yammered for him to get her up. ''Can you take one?'' he asked, again in English. She nodded. It would be a desperation move, but they were damned desperate. He pulled Chesna up—then suddenly twisted his body and flung her at the nearest guard. Her fingernails went for his eyes.

Michael grabbed the other soldier's rifle and uptilted it. Pain shot through his wounded hand, but he grappled for the gun. The soldier almost got it away from him, until Michael drove his knee into the man's groin. As the soldier gasped and doubled over, Michael wrenched the rifle away and clubbed him across the back of the neck with it.

Lazaris blinked, his mind still sluggish from the gas grenades. He saw Chesna clawing at the soldier's eyes, and the man trying to hold her off. He took an uncertain step forward. A rifle fired, and a bullet cracked off the pavement between him and Chesna. He stopped, looked up, and saw another soldier on a catwalk above.

Michael shot at the soldier, but it was a wild shot and his hand had gone dead again. The other guard bellowed and thrust Chesna aside. She cried out and fell, catching her bad ankle beneath her. "Run!" she shouted to Michael. *"Go!"* The half-blinded guard, his eyes bloodshot and watering, swung his rifle in Michael's direction. A bullet whined past Michael's head, fired from the catwalk. A Gallatinov ran.

Behind him the guard wiped his eyes and saw the fleeing man through a haze. He lifted his weapon and took aim. He squeezed the trigger.

Before the bullet could leave the barrel, a body slammed into his back. The guard staggered and went down, the rifle firing into the air. Lazaris landed on top of him and fought to get the gun away.

The soldier on the catwalk tracked his prey with his own rifle. He shot.

Something smashed against the side of Michael's head. A fist, he thought. An iron fist. No, something hot. Something on fire. He took three more strides and fell, his momentum skidding him across the pavement on his belly and crashing him into an area of trash cans and broken crates. His head was aflame, he thought. Where was the rifle? Gone, spun out of his grasp. He pressed his hand against his right temple, feeling warm wetness. His brain felt soggy, as if the shock had liquefied it. Got to get up, he urged himself. Got to run. Got to . . .

As he pulled himself to his knees, a second bullet clanged against a can only a few feet away. He got up, his head pounding with fiery agony, and he staggered through the alley toward where he thought the fence must be. The fence. Got to crawl under it. He rounded a corner, and almost directly into the path of an oncoming truck. It shrieked to a halt, but Michael hugged the wall and started running again, the smell of burned rubber in his nostrils. He turned another corner, lost his balance, and slammed into the wall. He fell, darkness beginning to call him, and he crawled into a narrow doorway and lay there shivering with pain.

He had been shot. He knew that much. The bullet had grazed his head, and taken flesh and hair with it. Where was Chesna? Where was Alekza, and Renati? No, no; that was another, better world. Where was Lazaris? Was the Russian safe, with Wiktor? He shook his head; his mind was clouding, keeping secrets from him. The train was late! I'll make it, Nikita! Watch me!

His skin stung and itched. The air smelled bad. What was that bitter stench? His skin . . . what was happening to his skin? He looked at his hands. They were changing, the fingers becoming claws. The bandage slipped off and fell. The bones of his spine creaked and shifted. New pain shot through his joints, but compared to the agony of his head that pain was almost pleasure.

Chesna! He almost shouted it. Where was she? He couldn't leave her. No, no! Wiktor! Wiktor would take care of Chesna. Wouldn't he?

His body thrashed against the confinement of strange things that bound his legs. Something split along his black-haired back, and he flung that off, too. The things that fell aside had a terrible smell to them. A man-smell.

His muscles clicked and popped. He had to get out of this awful place, before the monsters found him. He was in an alien world, and nothing made sense. The fence. Beyond it was freedom, and that was what he craved.

But he was leaving someone behind. No, not only one. Two. A name came to him, and he opened his mouth to shout, but the song was harsh and ragged and made no sense. He shook away heavy objects that hung by strings to his hind paws, and he ran to find the way out.

He picked up his own scent trail. Three monsters with pale, hideous faces saw him, and one of them shrieked with terror; even a wolf could understand that emotion. Another of the figures lifted a stick, and flame shot out of it. Michael spun away from them, a hot breeze ruffling the hair at the back of his neck, and he ran on.

His scent led him to the hole beneath the fence. Why was the man-smell here, too? he wondered. They were familiar aromas; whose were they? But the forest beckoned him, and promised safety. He was hurting badly. He needed rest. A place to curl up, and lick his wounds.

He crawled under the fence, and without looking back at the world he was departing, he leaped into the arms of the forest.

8

The yellow she-wolf came to sniff his scent while he was curled up in a nest of rocks. He had been licking at his wounded paw. His skull was filled with a terrible pain that waxed and waned, and his vision misted around the edges. But he could see her, even in the blue twilight. She stood on a rock about seventy feet above him and watched him as he suffered. A dark brown wolf joined her after a while, then a gray one with a single eye. The other two wolves came and went, but the yellow female remained vigilant.

Sometime later—and when this was he didn't know, because time had become dreamlike—he smelled the human reek. Four of them, he thought. Maybe more. Passing by his hiding place. In another moment he heard the scrape of their boots on the stones. They went on, searching for . . .

Searching for what? he asked himself. Food? Shelter? He didn't know, but the men—the white-fleshed monsters—frightened him, and he determined to stay away from them.

An explosion roused him from a feverish sleep. He stared, his green eyes dull, at flames rising into the darkness. The boat, he thought. They'd found it, down in the harbor. The thought doubled back on itself, and puzzled him. How had he known that? he wondered. Whose boat was it, and what use did a wolf have for a boat?

His curiosity made him get up and slowly, painfully, descend over the rocks to the harbor. The yellow wolf followed on one side, and on the other a small pale brown wolf that yipped nervously all the way down to the village. Wolftown, he thought as he looked at the houses. That was a good name for it, because he could smell his own kind here. Fire crackled beyond the seawall, and the figures of men walked through the smoke. He stood near the corner of a stone house, watching monsters roam the earth. One of them called to another: "Any sign of him, Thyssen?"

"No, Sergeant!" another one shouted back. "Not a trace! We found the commando team and the woman, though. Over that way." He pointed.

"Well, if he tries to hide here, the damned wolves will finish him off!" The sergeant strode in one direction with a group of men, and Thyssen went in another.

Who were they talking about? he wondered as the flames reflected in his green eyes. And . . . why did he understand their language? This was a puzzle, to be thought out when the throbbing in his skull had ceased. Right now he needed water and a place to sleep. He lapped from a muddy pool of snowmelt, then he chose a house and entered it through the open front door. He lay down in a corner, curling his body up for warmth, placed his muzzle on his paws, and closed his eyes.

Later, a floorboard's creak awakened him. He looked up into the glare of a flashlight, and he heard a voice say, "Jesus, that one's been in a fight!" He stood up, his tail to the wall, and bared his fangs at the intruders, his heart pounding with fear. "Easy, easy," one of the monsters whispered. "Put a bullet in it, Langner!"

"Not me! I don't want a wounded wolf jumping at my throat!" Langner backed out, and in another few seconds so did the man with the light. "He's not here!" Langner called to someone else outside. "Too many wolves around for my taste. I'm getting out."

The black wolf with a blood-crusted skull settled back into his corner again, and slept.

He had a strange dream. His body was changing, becoming white and monstrous. His claws, his fangs, and his coat of sleek black hair all went away. Naked, he crawled into a world of terrors. And he was just about to rise up on his fleshy legs—an unthinkable act—when the nightmare jarred him to his senses.

Gray dawn and hunger. They linked together. He got up and went in search of food. His head was still hurting, but not so much now. His muscles felt deeply bruised, and his steps were uncertain. But he would live, if he could find meat. He sniffed a death scent; the kill was nearby, somewhere in Wolftown.

The scent drew him into another house, and there he found them.

The corpses of four humans. One was a massive, orange-haired female. The other three were males, dressed in black with black-smeared faces. He sat on his haunches, and studied their positions. The female, her body punctured by at least a half-dozen holes, had her hands clenched around the throat of one of the males. Another male lay in a corner like a broken doll, his mouth open in a final gasp. The third man lay on his back near an overturned table, the carved-horn handle of a knife protruding from his heart.

The black wolf stared at that knife. He had seen it before. Somewhere. He saw, as if from a vision, a human hand on a table, and the blade of that knife slamming down between the fingers. It was a mystery, too deep for him, and he let it go.

He began with the male crumpled in the corner. The facial flesh was soft, and so was the tongue. He was feasting when he smelled the musk of another wolf, and then came the low, warning growl. He whirled around, his muzzle red, but the dark brown wolf was already bounding forward to attack, claws flailing at the air.

The black wolf spun to one side, but his legs were still unsure and he lost his balance, crashing over the upturned table. The brown animal snapped at a foreleg and barely missed catching it between powerful jaws. Another wolf, this one a ruddy amber hue, came through a window into the room and lunged at the black with fangs bared.

He knew death was imminent. Once they caught him between them, they would tear him to pieces. They were strangers to him, just as he was to them, and he knew this was a struggle for territory. He snapped at the amber wolf—a young female—with such ferocity that she scrambled backward. But the brown one, a husky male, was not so easily intimidated; a claw flashed out, and red streaks appeared across a black-haired rib cage. Fangs snapped, lunging and parrying like the weapons of swordsmen. The two wolves collided, chest to chest, trying to overwhelm the other with brute strength.

He saw his chance, and shredded the brown wolf's left ear. The animal yelped and backed off, feinted to one side, and then moved in again, eyes murderous with rage. Their bodies collided once more, with a force that knocked the breath out of both of them. They grappled wildly, each trying to grip the other's throat as they battled back and forth across the room, a deadly ballet of teeth and claws.

A brown-haired, muscular shoulder whammed into the right side of his skull, blinding him with fresh agony. He cried out in pain—a high quavering yelp—and fell back into the corner. The breath rumbled in his lungs, and he snorted blood. The brown wolf, almost grinning with the excitement of combat, started to jump at him to finish the job.

A rough series of quick, throaty barks froze the brown wolf on the edge of attack.

The yellow female had entered the house through the door. Right behind her was the one-eyed gray, an old male. The female darted forward, nudging the brown one in the side. She licked his bloody ear, and then shoved him aside with her shoulder.

The black wolf waited, his muscles trembling. Again, the pain in his skull was savage. He wanted to let them know he wasn't about to give up his life without further struggle; he shouted—the equivalent of "Come on!"—and his guttural bark made the yellow female's ears twitch. She sat on her haunches and watched him, perhaps a spark of respect in her eyes as the black wolf announced his intention to survive.

She stared at him for a long time. The old gray and the brown male licked her coat. The small, pale brown male entered and yipped nervously until she silenced him with a cuff to the muzzle. Then she turned, a regal motion, and with a flip of her tail she went to the knife-stuck corpse and began to tear at it.

Five wolves, he thought. Five. That number bothered him. It was a dark number, and it smelled of fire. Five. In his mind he saw a beach, and soldiers struggling to shore through the waves. Over them loomed the shadow of a huge crow, flying inexorably toward the west. The crow had glass eyes, and on its beak were arcane scratchings. No, no, he realized. Letters. Something painted there. Iron—

The heady aromas of blood and fresh meat distracted him. The others were feeding. The yellow female lifted her head and grunted at him. The message said there was enough for all.

He ate, and let the mysteries drift away. But when the brown male and the amber female began to rip at the huge orange-haired corpse on the floor, he shuddered and went outside, where he was violently ill.

That night the stars came out. The others began to sing, their bellies swollen. He joined them—tentatively at first, because he didn't know their rhythms, then full-voiced as they accepted his song and swirled his into their own. He was one of them now, though the brown wolf still growled and sniffed disdainfully at him.

Another day dawned, and passed. Time was a trick of the mind. It had no meaning, here in the womb of Wolftown. He gave the others names: Golda, the yellow leader, older than she appeared; Ratkiller, the dark brown male whose principal pleasure was chasing rodents through the houses; One-eye, a beautiful singer; Yipper, the whelp of the litter and not quite right in the mind; and Amber, a dreamer who sat for hours gazing from the rocks. And, as he soon learned, Amber's four pups, sired by Ratkiller.

A quick shower of snowflakes fell one night. Amber danced in their midst, and snapped at them as Ratkiller and Yipper ran circles around her. The snowflakes melted as soon as they touched the warm ground. It was a sign of summer on the way.

The following morning he sat up on the rocks while Golda honored him by licking the crusted blood away from his skull wound. It was a language of the tongue, and it said he was welcome to mount her. Desire stirred in him; she had a lovely tail. And as he roused himself to please her, he heard the drone of engines.

He looked up. A huge crow was rising into the air. No, not a crow, he realized. Crows didn't have engines. An aircraft, with an immense wing span. The rising of the plane in the silver morning air made his flesh crawl. It was a horrible thing, and as it turned southward he made a soft groaning noise deep in his throat. It had to be stopped. In its belly was a cargo of death. It had to be stopped! He looked at Golda and saw she didn't understand. Why didn't she? Why was it only he who understood? He propelled himself off the rocks and raced down to the harbor as the transport aircraft began to grow distant. He clambered up onto the sea-wall, where he stood moaning until the plane was lost to sight.

I've failed, he thought. But exactly what it was that he had failed at made his head hurt, and he had to let it go.

But his nightmares seized him, and those he could not escape.

He was human, in the nightmares. A young human, with no sense of the world. He was running across a field where yellow flowers budded, and in his hand was a taut string. At the end of that string, floating up into the blue, was a white kite that danced and spun in the high currents. A human female called him, a name he couldn't exactly understand. And as he was watching the kite sail higher and higher the shadow of the glass-eyed crow fell over him, and one of its whirling propellers chewed the kite into a thousand fragments that blew away like dust. The airplane was olive green, and riddled with bullet holes. As the severed string fell to earth, so did a mist. It swirled around him, and he breathed it. His flesh began to melt, to fall in bloody tatters, and he pitched to his knees as holes opened in his hands and arms. The woman, once beautiful, staggered across the field toward him, and as she reached him, her arms outstretched, he saw a bleeding cavity where her face had been.

In the stark daylight of reality he sat on the dock and stared at the burned hulk of a boat. Five, he thought. What was it about the number that terrified him so?

The days passed, a ritual of eating, sleeping, and basking in the warming sun. The corpses, hollowed-out and bony, gave up their last meal. He reclined on his haunches and regarded the knife, stuck there in a cage of bones. It had a hooked blade. He had seen that knife, in another place. Being driven down between a pair of human fingers. Kitty's game, he thought. Yes. But who was Kitty?

An airplane, its green metal pocked with painted holes. The face of a man with silver teeth: a devil's face. A city with a huge clock tower, and a wide river meandering to the sea. A beautiful woman, with blond hair and tawny eyes. Five of six. Five of six. All shadows. His head hurt. He was a wolf; what did he know, or care, of such things?

The knife beckoned him. He reached for it as Golda watched with lazy interest. His paw touched the handle. Of course he couldn't pull the knife out. What had made him believe he could?

He began to pay attention to the rising and falling of the sun and the passage of days. He noted the days were lengthening. The five of six. Whatever that was, it was fast approaching, and that thought made him shiver and moan. He ceased singing with the others, because there was no song in him. The five of six dominated his mind and would not let him rest. Hollow-eyed, he faced another dawn, and he went to stare at the knife in the stripped skeleton as if it were a relic from a lost world.

The five of six was almost upon him. He could sense it, ticking nearer. There was no way to stop its approach, and that realization chewed his insides. But why did it not bother any of the others? Why was he the only one who suffered?

Because he was different, he realized. Where had he come from? At whose nipples had he suckled? How had he gotten here, in Wolftown, as the five of six neared with every breath he drew?

He was with Golda, basking in the warming breeze near the seawall as the stars blazed in the heavens, when they heard Yipper give a long, quavering note from up in the rocks. Neither of them liked that sound; there was alarm in it. Then Yipper began a series of fast, harsh barks, relaying a warning to Wolftown. At once the black wolf and Golda were up off their bellies, hearing the noise that made Yipper shriek with pain.

Gunfire. Golda only knew it meant death. The black wolf knew it was the noise of a Schmeisser submachine gun.

Yipper's shrieking stopped abruptly as another burst rattled. Ratkiller took up the alarm, and Amber spread it. The black wolf and Golda ran deeper into Wolftown, and soon they smelled the hated scent of men. There were four of them, coming down the rocks into the village and sweeping their lights before them. They fired at everything that moved, or that they thought might have moved. The black wolf caught another odor, and recognized it: schnapps. At least one of the men, perhaps the others, too, was drunk.

In another moment he heard their slurred voices: "I'll make you a wolfskin coat, Hans! Yes, I will! I'll make you the most beautiful damned coat you've ever seen!"

"No, you won't! You'll make it for yourself, you son of a bitch!"

There was rough laughter. A burst of bullets whacked into the side of a house. "Come on out, you hairy shits! Come out, and let's play!"

"I want a *big* one! That little thing up on the rocks won't even make a decent *hat!*"

They had killed Yipper. Drunken Nazis with submachine guns, hunting wolves out of sheer boredom. The black wolf knew this, without knowing how he knew. Four soldiers, from the garrison that guarded the chemical plant. Shadows stirred in his mind; things moved, and sleeping memories began to awaken. His skull throbbed—not with pain, but with the power of recollection. Iron Fist. The Flying Fortress. The five of six.

The fifth of the sixth month, he realized. The fifth of June. D Day.

He was a wolf. Wasn't he? Of course! He had black hair and claws and fangs. He was a wolf, and the hunters were almost upon him and Golda.

A light streaked past them, then came back. They were caught in its glare. "Look at those two! Damn, what coats! Black and yellow!" A submachine gun chattered, and bullets marched across the ground beside Golda. She panicked, turned, and fled. The black wolf raced after her. She went into the house where the skeletons lay.

"Don't lose them, Hans! They'll make fine coats!" The soldiers were running, too, as fast as their unsteady legs could manage. "They're in there! That house!"

Golda backed against the wall, terror in her eyes. The black wolf smelled the soldiers outside. "Get around to the rear!" one of them shouted. "We'll catch them between us!" Golda leaped for the window as bullets whacked into the frame and splinters flew. She fell back to the floor, spun madly in a whirl of yellow. The black wolf started out through the door, but a light blinded him and he retreated as bullets knocked holes in the wall above his head.

"Now we've got them!" a coarse voice crowed. "Max, go in there and clean them out!"

"Not me, you bastard! *You* go first!"

"Ah, you gutless shit! All right, I will! Erwin, you and Johannes watch the windows." There was a clicking noise. The black wolf knew a fresh ammo clip was being loaded into the gun. "I'm going in!"

Golda again tried to get out through the window. Splinters stung her as another burst fired, and she dropped back with blood on her muzzle.

"Stop that shooting!" the coarse voice commanded. "I'll get them both myself!" The soldier strode toward the house, following his light, the courage of schnapps in his veins.

The black wolf knew he and Golda were doomed. There was no way out. In a moment the soldier would be at the doorway, and his light would catch them. No way out, and what would fangs and claws be against four men with sub-machine guns?

He looked at the knife.

His paw touched the handle.

Don't fail me, he thought. Wiktor had said that, a long time ago.

His claws struggled to close around the handle. The soldier's light was almost into the room.

Wiktor. Mouse. Chesna. Lazaris. Blok. Names and faces whirled through the mind of the black wolf, like sparks escaping a bonfire.

Michael Gallatin.

I am not a wolf, he thought, as a blaze of memory leaped in his brain. I am a—

His paw changed. Streaks of white flesh appeared. The black hair retreated, and his bones and sinews rejointed with wet whispering sounds.

His fingers closed around the knife handle and drew it out of the skeleton. Golda gave a stunned grunt, as if the air had been knocked from her.

The soldier stopped on the threshold. "Now I'll show you who your master is!" he said, and glanced back at Max. "You see? It takes a brave man to walk into a wolf's den!"

"Two more steps, coward!" Max taunted.

The soldier probed with the light. He saw skeletons, and the yellow wolf. Ha! The beast was trembling. But where was the black bastard? He took the two final steps, his gun ready to blow its brains out.

And as the soldier entered, Michael stepped out from his hiding place beside the doorway and drove Kitty's hooked blade into the pit of the man's throat with all the strength he could summon.

The German, strangling on blood, dropped the Schmeisser and the light to clutch at his severed windpipe. Michael scooped up the submachine gun, planted a foot against the man's belly, and shoved him backward through the doorway. Then he fired at the other man's light, and there was a scream as the bullets mangled flesh.

"What was that? Who screamed?" one of the men at the rear of the house hollered. "Max? Hans?"

Michael walked out the door, his knee joints aching and his spine stretching. He stood at the corner of the house and took aim just above the two flashlights. One of them weaved toward him. He sprayed fire at the Nazis. Both lights exploded and the bodies crumpled.

That was the end of it.

Michael heard a noise behind him. He turned, an oily sweat leaking from his pores.

Golda stood there, only a few feet away. She stared at him, her body rigid. Then she showed her fangs, snarled, and ran away into the darkness.

Michael understood. He did not belong to her world.

He knew who he was now, and what he had to do. The transport plane had already taken the bombs of carnagene away, but there were other crows on the field: the night fighters. Those each had a range of about a thousand miles. If they could find out exactly where Iron Fist was hangared, and . . .

And if it wasn't too late. What was the date? He had no way of knowing. He hurried to find clothes that might fit him from the four dead men. He had to settle for the shirt and jacket from one soldier, the trousers from another, and the boots from a third. All of the clothes were damp with blood, but that couldn't be helped. He stuffed his pockets with ammo clips. A gray woolen cap, free of bloodstains, lay on the ground. He put it on, and his fingers found the gash and the scabbed crust on the right side of his head. A fraction of an inch more, and the bullet would have smashed his skull.

Michael strapped the submachine gun around his shoulder and started along the road to the rocky slope. The fifth of June, he thought. Had it passed already? How many days and nights had he been here, believing himself a wolf? Everything was still dreamlike. He quickened his pace. The first task was getting into the plant; the second was getting to the stockade and freeing Chesna and Lazaris. Then he would know if he had failed or not, and whether tattered bodies lay in the streets of London because of it.

He heard a howl, a floating quaver, behind him. Golda's voice. He didn't look back.

On two legs he climbed toward his destiny.

9

They had made a meager effort to fill up the hole he'd dug under the fence, but it was obvious their shovels had been lazy. It took him a few minutes to scoop the loose dirt out, and he winnowed under again. The thumping heartbeat of the plant was in operation again, light bulbs glowing on the catwalks overhead. He went through the alleys, threading his way toward the edge of the airfield, where the stockade was. A soldier came around a corner and strolled in his direction. "Hey! Got a smoke?" the man asked.

"Sure." Michael let him get close and dug in a pocket for cigarettes that weren't there. "What time is it?"

The German checked his wristwatch. "Twelve-forty-two." He looked at Michael and frowned. "You need a shave. If the captain sees you like that, he'll kick your—" He saw the blood, and bullet holes stitched across the jacket. Michael saw his eyes widen.

He hit the German in the stomach with the gun butt, then cracked him across the skull and dragged his body to a group of empty chemical drums. He took the watch, heaved the body into a drum, and put the lid on it. Then he was on his way again, almost running. Forty-two minutes after midnight, he thought. But of what day?

The stockade building's entrance was unguarded, but a single soldier sat at a desk just inside the door, his boots propped up and his eyes shut. Michael kicked the chair out from under him and slammed him against the wall, and the soldier returned to dreamland. Michael took a set of keys from a wall hook behind the desk and went along the corridor between several cells. He smiled grimly; the log-sawing snore of a certain bearded Russian reverberated in the hallway.

As Michael tried various keys in the lock of Lazaris's prison, he heard a gasp of surprise. He looked at the cell two doors down and across the corridor, and behind the barred inset Chesna, her eyes brimming with tears in her dirty, haggard face, tried to speak but couldn't form words. Finally they burst out: "Where the *hell* have you been?"

"Lying low," he said, and went to her cell door. He found the right key, and the latch popped. As soon as Michael had pulled the door open, Chesna was in his arms. He held her as she trembled; he could feel her ribs and her clothes were grimy, but at least she hadn't been beaten. She gave a single, heartbreaking sob, and then she struggled to gather her dignity. "It's all right," he said, and kissed her lips. "We're going to get out of here."

"Well, get *me* out of here first, you bastard!" Lazaris shouted from his cell. "Damn it, we thought you'd left us to rot!" His hair was a crow's-nest stubble, his eyes glaring and wild. Chesna took the submachine gun and watched the corridor as Michael found the proper key and freed Lazaris.

The Russian emerged smelling of something more pungent than roses. "My God!" he said. "We didn't know if you'd gotten away or not! We thought they might have killed you!"

"They gave it a good shot." He glanced at the wristwatch. It was creeping up on one o'clock. "What's the date?"

"Hell if I know!" Lazaris answered.

But Chesna had kept count of their twice-daily feedings. "It's too late, Michael," she said. "You've been gone for fifteen days."

He stared at her, uncomprehending.

"Today is the sixth of June," she went on. "It's too late."

Too late. The words had teeth.

"Yesterday was D day," Chesna said. She felt a little light-headed, and had to grasp hold of his shoulder. For the last twenty-four hours particularly, her nerves had been worn to a frazzle. "It's all over by now."

"No!" He shook his head, refusing to believe it. "You're wrong! I couldn't have been a . . . couldn't have been gone that long!"

"I'm not wrong." She held his wrist and looked at the watch. "It's been the sixth of June for one hour and two minutes."

"We've got to find out what's going on. There must be a radio room here somewhere."

"There is," Lazaris said. "It's in a building over by the fuel tanks." He explained to Michael that he had been forced to work along with some other slave laborers to unclog an overflowing cesspool near the soldiers' barracks, which accounted for the reek of his clothes. While up to his waist in shit, he'd been able to gather information about the plant from his fellow laborers. Hildebrand, for instance, lived in his lab, which was at the center of the plant near the chimney. The huge fuel tanks held oil to heat the buildings during the long winter months. The slave laborers were kept in another barracks not far from the soldiers' quarters. And, Lazaris said, there was an armory in case of partisan attack, but exactly where that was he didn't know.

"Can you get in that man's clothes?" Michael asked Lazaris, once they were back to where the guard lay sprawled. Lazaris said he'd give it a try. Chesna went through the desk, and found a Luger and bullets. In another few moments Lazaris was in a Nazi uniform, the shirt taut at his shoulders and the trousers drooping around his legs. He pulled the belt to its last notch. At least the guard's flat-brimmed cap fit. Lazaris still wore the boots that had been issued to him when they'd left Germany, though they were encrusted with indelicacies.

They started toward the radio room, Chesna still hobbling but able to walk on her own. Michael saw the radio tower, two lights blinking on it to alert low-flying aircraft, and steered them in that direction. After fifteen minutes of dodging through the alleys, they reached a small stone structure that was, again, unguarded. The door was locked. One of Lazaris's shitty boots kicked compliance into it. Michael found a light switch, and there was the radio under a clear plastic cover atop a desk. Chesna had had more experience with German radios than he, so he stood aside as she turned it on, the dials illuminating with dim green, and began to search the frequencies. Static crackled from the tinny speaker. Then a faint voice, in German, talking about a diesel engine that needed overhauling: a ship at sea. Chesna came upon a Norwegian voice discussing the king-mackerel catch, possibly a code being transmitted to England. Another change of frequencies brought orchestral music into the room—a funeral dirge.

"If the invasion happened, it ought to be all over the airwaves," Michael said. "What's going on?"

Chesna shook her head, and kept searching. She found a news report from Oslo; the crisp German announcer talked about a new shipment of iron ore that had just sailed for the glory of the Reich and that a line for milk rations would be formed at six o'clock in front of Government Hall. The weather would continue unsettled, with a seventy-percent chance of rainstorms. Now back to the soothing music of Gerhardus Kaathoven. . . .

"So where's the invasion?" Lazaris scratched his beard. "If it was supposed to happen on the fifth—"

"Maybe it didn't," Michael said. He looked at Chesna. "Maybe it was canceled, or postponed."

"There'd have to be a damned good reason to postpone something of that magnitude."

"Maybe there was. Who knows what it might be? But I don't think the invasion's happened yet. If it had begun on the morning of the fifth, you'd hear something about it on every frequency by now."

Chesna knew he was correct. The airwaves should be burning up right now, with news reports and messages to and from various partisan groups. Instead, it was simply another morning of funeral dirges and milk lines.

It was clear to Michael what had to be done. "Lazaris, can you fly one of those night fighters out on the strip?"

"I can fly anything with wings. I'd suggest the Dornier two-seventeen, though. It's got a thousand-mile range if the fuel tanks are loaded, and it's a quick little bitch. Where are we going?"

"First to wake up Dr. Hildebrand. Then to find out exactly where Iron Fist is being hangared. How long would it take us to fly from here to Rotterdam? That's almost a thousand miles."

He frowned. "You'd be cutting it damned close, even if the tanks are brimmed." He thought about it. "The Dornier's maximum speed is over three hundred. You might be able to sustain two-fifty, on a long flight. Depending on the winds . . . I'd say five hours, give or take."

There were too many if's, Michael thought, but what else could they do? They began a search of the building. In another room, full of filing cabinets, he found a map of Hildebrand Industries Skarpa Chemical Installation thumbtacked to the wall next to a portrait of Adolf Hitler. A red X indicated the radio room's location, and the other buildings were marked "Workshop," "Mess Hall," "Testing Chamber," "Armory," "Barracks Number One," and so on. The development lab was about a hundred yards from their present position, and the armory was way over on the opposite side of the plant from the airfield. Michael folded the map and put it in a bloodstained pocket for later reference.

The development lab, a long white building with a thicket of pipes connecting it to a series of smaller structures, stood near the central chimney. Lights glowed through narrow windows of frosted glass; the doctor was at work. Atop the lab building's roof stood a large tank, but whether it held chemicals, fuel, or water Michael didn't know. The front door was barred, and locked from the inside, but a metal-runged ladder ascended to the roof and that was the path they took. On the roof a skylight had been opened. Michael leaned over its edge, with Lazaris holding on to his legs, and peered in.

Three men in white coats and white gloves worked at a series of long tables, where microscopes, racks of test tubes, and other equipment were set up. Four large, sealed vats, like pressure cookers, stood at one end of the lab, and it was from them that the pulsing heartbeat noise came. Michael assumed it was the noise of an electric engine, stirring whatever was in the devil's brew. About twenty feet off the floor a catwalk ran the length of the lab, passing within a few feet of the skylight and going to a panel of pressure gauges near the chemical vats.

One of the three men was almost seven feet tall and wore a white cap over blond hair that flowed down his back. He was engrossed in studying a group of microscope slides.

Michael pulled himself away from the skylight. The pulse made the roof throb. "I want you both to get back to the airfield," he told them. Chesna started to protest, but he put a finger to her lips. "Just listen. Lazaris, if that Dornier isn't fueled up, you and Chesna will have to do it. I remember seeing a fuel truck on the field. Can you handle it?"

"I used to fuel *Warhammer* myself. I was my own ground crew." He shrugged. "There won't be much difference. But there might be guards watching the planes."

"I know. After I finish here, I'm going to try to create a diversion. You'll know it when it happens." He looked at his watch. It was thirty-two minutes after one. He took the watch off and gave it to Chesna. "I'll be at the field in thirty minutes," he promised. "When the fireworks start, you'll have a chance to top the Dornier's tanks off."

"I'm staying with you," Chesna said.

"Lazaris can use your help more than I. No arguing. Just get to the field."

Chesna was professional enough to know that she was wasting time. She and Lazaris hurried back across the roof to the ladder, and Michael strapped the submachine gun around his shoulder. He eased himself over the skylight edge and caught hold of an iron pipe that snaked across the lab ceiling. Hand over hand, he guided himself toward the catwalk and stepped over its railing.

He crouched down and watched the three men. Hildebrand called one of them over and showed him something on the slide. Then Hildebrand shouted and slammed his fist on the table, and the other man nodded docilely, his shoulders slumped in submission. The work was not going well, Michael thought. What a pity.

A droplet of moisture plunked to the catwalk next to him. He looked up. Set at intervals along the iron pipe were spray nozzles, and one of them was leaking. He held out his palm and caught a few drops, then sniffed at them. The odor of brine. He licked his palm. Salt water. From the tank on the roof, he realized. Plain seawater, probably. Why was there a storage tank of seawater on the lab roof?

He remembered something that Blok had said: *Carnagene doesn't get along well with sodium. As in salt water.* Perhaps salt water destroyed carnagene. If that were so, Hildebrand had set up a system so that if any of the gas escaped into the lab, nozzles would deliver a saltwater spray. The system's controls had to be within easy reach of anyone working below. Michael stood up and walked to the control panel near the vats. There was a row of red switches, all at the ON position. He began to flip them all off. The heartbeat noise faltered and began to die.

A beaker crashed to the floor. One of the men shrieked. It was Hildebrand. "You fool!" he shouted. "Turn the aerators back on!"

"No one move." Michael walked back toward them, the

Schmeisser's barrel upraised. "Dr. Hildebrand, we're going to have a little talk."

"Please! The switches! Turn them on!"

"I want to know where Iron Fist is. How far from Rotterdam?"

One of the others suddenly bolted in the direction of the front door, but Michael shot him down before he could take three strides. The man fell, crimson spreading over his white coat.

The noise echoed within the lab. Someone would have heard it. Time was growing short. He trained the smoking gun barrel on Hildebrand. "Iron Fist. Where is it?"

"The . . ." Hildebrand swallowed thickly, staring up into the Schmeisser's eye. "The Luftwaffe airfield at Wassenaar. On the coast, sixteen miles northwest of Rotterdam." He glanced at the vats. "Please . . . I'm begging you! Turn the aerators back on!"

"And what will happen if I don't? Will the carnagene be destroyed?"

"No! It'll—"

Michael heard the sound of metal buckling.

"It'll explode in its raw form!" Hildebrand shouted, his voice choked with panic.

Michael looked at the sealed vats. The lids were bulging, and pressure blisters had appeared along the seams. My God! he realized. The stuff was swelling within the vats like yeast!

The other lab technician suddenly picked up a chair and ran toward a window. He smashed the glass with it and screamed, "Help! Someone help—"

Michael's gun silenced him. Hildebrand lifted his arms. "Hit the switches! I'm begging you!"

The vats were buckling outward. Michael started toward the control panel, and at the same time Hildebrand ran to the broken window and began to try to squeeze his long body through it. "Guards!" he yelled. "Guards!"

Michael stopped, ten feet shy of the switches, and turned his weapon on the architect of evil.

The bullets shattered Hildebrand's legs. He fell, writhing

in agony, to the floor. Michael put another clip in the Schmeisser and started to finish the man off.

One of the vats split open along its seam with a blast of popping rivets. A flood of thick yellow liquid streamed out, spewing across the floor. A siren began to shriek, overwhelming Gustav Hildebrand's screams. A second vat burst open, like a swollen tumor, and another yellow tide rolled across the floor. Michael stood, transfixed with horror and fascination, as the liquid coursed below the catwalk, its sludgy weight shoving chairs and tables before it. In the yellow swamp of chemicals were streaks of foamy dark brown that sizzled like grease in a frying pan. The third vat exploded with such force that the lid crashed against the ceiling, and the sludge drooled over the rim as Michael retreated toward the skylight.

The chemicals—at this stage an unrefined muck instead of a gas—surged across the floor. Hildebrand was crawling desperately for a red flywheel on the wall; the saltwater-tank release, Michael realized. Hildebrand looked back and gibbered with horror as he saw the flood almost upon him. He reached up, straining to grasp the flywheel. His fingers locked around it, and wrenched it a quarter turn.

Michael could hear the water coursing through the pipes, but in the next instant the raw carnagene rushed over Gustav Hildebrand and he screamed in its acidic embrace. He writhed like a salted snail, his hair and face dripping with carnagene. He began to claw at his own eyes, his voice a wail of agony, and blisters rose and burst on the white flesh of his hands.

The nozzels erupted their saltwater spray. Where the drops fell, the chemicals hissed and melted. But it was of no consequence to Hildebrand, who was a mass of seething red blisters thrashing in the mire. Hildebrand sat up on his knees, the flesh falling from his face in strands, and opened his mouth in a silent, terrible scream.

Michael took aim, squeezed the trigger, and blew most of Hildebrand's chest away. The body slithered down, smoke rising from the ruined lungs.

Michael strapped the Schmeisser around his shoulder again, climbed up on the catwalk railing, and leaped.

He grabbed hold of a pipe at the ceiling and clambered along it to within reach of the skylight. Then, his shoulder muscles cramping, he pulled himself up to the roof. He looked back down again; the carnagene was evaporating under the seawater shower, and Hildebrand lay like a jellyfish that had washed up in the wake of a storm.

Michael stood up and ran for the ladder. Two soldiers were climbing up. "The carnagene's gotten out!" Michael shouted, in a display of terror even Chesna might have admired. The soldiers leaped off the ladder. There were three more Germans, trying to break the door open. "The gas is out!" one of the soldiers cried with genuine horror, and all of them scattered, yelling it at the top of their lungs while the siren continued to shriek.

Michael checked the map and ran toward the armory. Everywhere he saw a soldier, he hollered about the carnagene being loose. In another few minutes he could hear shouts from all over the plant. The effects of the carnagene were well known, even by the common guards. Sirens were coming to life from every direction. By the time he got to the armory, he found that a half-dozen soldiers had already broken into the building and were making off with gas masks and respirators. "The carnagene's out!" a wild-eyed German told him. "Everyone in Section C is already dead!" He put his mask on and stumbled away, breathing from his oxygen cylinder. Michael entered the armory, broke open a crate of concussion grenades and then a crate of .50-caliber aircraft machine-gun bullets. "You!" an officer shouted, coming into the room. "What do you think you're—"

Michael shot him down and continued his work. He placed the crate of grenades atop the crate of bullets, dragged over a second crate of grenades, and broke that open, too. Then he yanked the pins on two of them, dropped them back in with their brethren, and fled.

Over on the airfield, Lazaris and Chesna crouched near the fuel truck as the sirens wailed. A guard lay about twenty feet away, shot through the chest by a Luger bullet. The truck's pump chugged, delivering aircraft-engine fuel through a canvas hose into the right wing tank of the Dornier night fighter. Both wing tanks, Lazaris had found, were about three-quarters full, but this would be their only opportunity to fuel and it would be a long flight. He held the nozzle in place, the octane flowing under his hands, while Chesna watched for any more guards. Thirty yards away was a corrugated-metal hut that served as a briefing room for pilots, and after Chesna had broken its door open she'd found a reward inside: maps of Norway, Denmark, Holland, and Germany showing the exact location of the Luftwaffe's airfields.

The sky lit up. There was a mighty boom that Chesna first thought was thunder. Something big had just blown up. She could hear the noise of firing, what sounded like hundreds of bullets going off. There were more explosions, and she saw flames and the orange streaks of tracer bullets rising into the night over on the opposite side of the plant. A hot wind rolled across the field, bringing a burning smell.

"Damn!" Lazaris said. "When that son of a bitch says *diversion,* he means it!"

She looked at the watch. Where was he? "Come on," she whispered. "Please come on."

Within fifteen minutes, over the continuing noises of destruction, she heard someone running. She flattened down on the concrete, her Luger ready for a shot. And then his voice came to her: "Don't shoot! It's me!"

"Thank God!" She stood up. "What blew?"

"The armory." His cap was gone, his shirt almost torn off by the concussion's winds that had caught him just as he'd flung himself into an alley. "Lazaris! How much longer?"

"Three minutes! I want to run the tanks over!"

In three minutes it was finished. Michael sent the fuel truck on a collision course into the Messerschmitt Bf-109, wrecking a wing, then he and Chesna got into the Dornier while Lazaris buckled himself into the pilot's seat. "All right!" Lazaris said as he cracked his knuckles. "Now we'll find out what a Russian can do with a German fighter plane!"

The props roared, and the Dornier left the ground in a burst of speed.

Lazaris circled the plane over Skarpa's fiery center. "Hold on!" he shouted. "We're going to finish the job!" He pressed a switch that started the machine guns charging, and then he dropped them into a shrieking dive that jammed them back in their seats.

He went for the huge fuel tanks. The third strafing pass sparked a red cinder that suddenly bloomed into a white-orange fireball. Turbulence bucked the Dornier as Lazaris zoomed for altitude. "Ah!" he said with a broad grin. "Now I'm home again!"

Lazaris circled one last time over the island, like a vulture over a bed of coals, and then he turned the plane toward Holland.

—————— **10** ——————

Jerek Blok had always assumed that on the day it finally happened, he would be so cool, ice wouldn't melt in his hands. But now, at seven-forty-eight on the morning of June 6, both his hands were trembling.

The radio operator in the airfield's gray concrete control building was slowly dialing through the frequencies. Voices drifted in and out through a storm of static; not all of them were German, evidence that British and American troops had already seized some radio transmitters.

Through the pre-dawn hours, there'd been scattered reports of parachutes descending over Normandy. Several airfields reported being bombed and strafed by Allied planes, and just before five o'clock in the morning, two fighter planes had screamed out of a rain shower and marched bullets through the building where Blok now stood, bursting out every window and killing a signals officer. Dried blood streaked the wall behind him. One of the three Messerschmitts on the field had been shot up beyond repair, and another had a riddled fuselage. The nearby storage warehouse, where Theo von Frankewitz had been confined, had also been badly damaged. But, thank the fates, the hangar had been unscathed.

As the sun rose in a cloud-plated sky and a strong salt breeze blew inland from the English Channel, the fragmented radio reports told the tale: the Allied invasion of Europe had begun.

"I want a drink," Blok said to Boots, and the hulking aide opened a thermos of brandy and gave it to him. Blok uptilted it, the harsh liquor making his eyes water. Then he listened, his heart pounding, as the radio operator found more voices in the cyclone of war. The Allies were swarming ashore, it appeared, in a dozen places. Off the Normandy beaches lay a truly fearsome armada: hundreds of troop transports, destroyers, cruisers, and battleships, all flying either Stars and Stripes or Union Jacks. The sky was claimed by hundreds of Allied Mustang, Thunderbolt, Lightning, and Spitfire fighter planes, strafing German strongholds while the big Lancaster and Flying Fortress bombers flew deeper into the heart of the Reich.

Blok took another drink.

The day of his destiny, and that of Nazi Germany, had arrived.

He looked at the other six men in the room, among them Captain van Hoven and Lieutenant Schrader, who had been trained to serve as the B-17's pilot and copilot. Blok said, "We go."

Van Hoven, his craggy face resolute, walked on shattered glass to a lever on the wall and without hesitation pulled it downward. From atop the building a shrill bell began to ring. Van Hoven and Schrader, along with their bombardier and navigator, ran toward the large reinforced concrete hangar about fifty yards away as other men—the ground crew and the B-17's gunners—came out of a barracks behind the hangar.

Blok put the thermos aside, and he and Boots left the building and strode across the pavement. Since leaving Skarpa Island, Blok had lived in a Dutch mansion about four miles from the airfield, where he could oversee the loading of the carnagene bombs and the final training of the crew. Then there had been drills at all hours of the night and day; he would find out now if the drills had been worthwhile.

The crewmen had entered the hangar through a side door,

and now, as Blok and Boots approached, the hangar's main doors were winched open. When they were halfway open, a low muttering echoed out across the pavement. The noise rapidly grew, through a snarl to a roar. The hangar doors continued to part, and as they opened the uncaged monster began to emerge.

The glass dome of the bombardier's position was marred with cracks that looked real even within a distance of a few feet. Painted bullet holes, the edges grayish blue to simulate bare metal, punctured the olive-green skin beneath the drawing of Hitler squeezed in an iron-mailed fist. The words "Iron Fist," in English, completed the B-17's nose art. The huge aircraft slid from the hangar, its four propellers whirling. The glass of the belly turret gun and the top turret were painted to look as if they had been almost completely shattered. False bullet holes pocked the sides of the plane in random patterns, and had been painted on the looming tail fin. All the pieces had been put together, using the cannibalized parts of several crashed B-17s, after Frankewitz had done the artwork. United States Army Air Force insignia completed the deception.

Of all the B-17's gun positions, only two—the waist's swivel machine guns—were manned and loaded. But no firing would be necessary, because this was in essence a suicide flight. The Allied planes would let Iron Fist pass to its target, but coming home again was a different question. Van Hoven and Schrader both understood the honor of piloting this mission, and their families would be well provided for. But the waist positions, with their wide rectangular openings through which the machine guns were swiveled to follow targets, would look more convincing if . . .

Well, that was a task yet to be completed.

Once free of the hangar, Van Hoven braked Iron Fist to a halt. Blok and Boots, holding their caps down in the windstorm of the props, walked toward the main entry door on the plane's right side.

A movement caught Blok's eye. He looked up. An aircraft was circling the field. He had a few seconds of horror, expecting another strafing attack, until he saw it was a

Dornier night fighter. What was the fool doing? He didn't have permission to land here!

One of the waist gunners unlatched the door for them, and they entered the plane. As Boots crouched forward, along a narrow walkway through the aircraft's waist, Jerek Blok drew his Luger and fired two shots into the head of the starboard waist gunner, then blew the port-side gunner's brains out as well. He went about the task of positioning the bodies in the rectangular openings so their blood would stream down the sides of the plane and they would be in full view.

An authentic touch, he thought.

In the cockpit Van Hoven released the brakes and started them rolling once more along the runway to their takeoff point. There they stopped again, while pilot and copilot checked their gauges and instruments. In the bomb bay behind them, Boots was performing his own function: removing the rubber safety caps from the nose fuses of the twenty-four dark green bombs, and carefully giving each fuse a quarter twist with a wrench to arm them.

His final work done, Blok left Iron Fist and went out to wait for Boots by the side of the runway. The magnificently camouflaged aircraft trembled, like an arrow about to be shot into flight. When the carnagene exploded in the streets of London, the messages of disaster would go to the commanders of that armada off the Normandy shore, and then trickle down to the soldiers. By nightfall there would be mass panic and retreat. Oh, what glory for the Reich! The *Führer* himself would dance with—

Blok's throat clutched. The Dornier was landing.

And, worse, the stupid fool of a pilot was speeding along the runway right for Iron Fist!

Blok ran in front of the B-17, waving his arms wildly. The Dornier, burning rubber as its brakes locked, cut its speed but still came on, blocking the runway. "Get out of the way, you idiot!" Blok shouted, and drew his Luger again. "You damned fool, get off the runway!" Behind him the engines of Iron Fist were revving to a thunderous roar. Blok's cap whirled off his head, and went into one of the props where it was shredded to dust. The air shimmered with oily heat as the B-17's engines built power. Blok held his Luger at arm's length as the Dornier rolled toward him. The pilot was insane! German or not, the man had to be forced off the run—

Through the Dornier's windshield he saw that the co-pilot had golden hair.

The pilot was bearded. He recognized both their faces: Chesna van Dorne and the man who'd been with her and the baron. He had no idea how they'd gotten here, but he knew why they'd come and that must not be allowed.

With a shout of rage, Blok began firing the Luger.

A bullet cracked the windshield in front of Chesna's face. A second ricocheted off the fuselage, and a third punched through the glass and hit Lazaris in the collarbone. The Russian cried out in pain, glass fragments flying around Michael, who sat behind the cockpit. As Blok kept firing at the windshield, Michael reached for the entry hatch's handle and turned it. He leaped out onto the runway's pavement and sprinted beneath the Dornier's wing toward Colonel Blok, the propellers of the night fighter and the B-17 whirling up roaring windstorms.

He was on the man before Blok knew he was there. Blok gasped, tried to get a shot off into Michael's face, but Michael grabbed his wrist and uptilted the Luger's barrel as the bullet fired. They grappled between the propellers, Blok trying to dig his fingers into Michael's eyes. Michael struck his fist into Blok's jaw, snapping the man's head back. Blok held on to the Luger, and Michael held on to the colonel's wrist. Blok shifted his weight violently in an effort to throw Michael into the Dornier's prop, but Michael had read the move seconds before it came and he was ready to resist it. Blok shouted something—a curse, lost in the engine noise— and chopped the flat of his free hand at Michael's nose. Michael was able to dodge the full power of it, but the blow hit the side of his head and stunned him. Still, he gripped on to Blok's wrist, bending the arm back at the elbow in an effort to snap it. Blok's trigger finger spasmed with the pain, and two bullets left the Luger. They pierced one of the B-17's engine cowlings, almost overhead, and the black smoke of burning oil bloomed from the wounds.

Michael and Blok battled between the propellers, the wind

screaming around them, threatening to throw them both into the spinning blades. In Iron Fist's cockpit, Van Hoven saw the trails of burning oil from one of the four engines. He released the brakes, and the aircraft began to lurch forward. Boots, still working in the bomb bay, looked up as he realized they were moving and roared, "What the hell are you doing?"

Blok slammed his elbow into Michael's chin and wrenched the Luger free. He lifted it to blow the false baron's skull apart. He grinned in triumph: his last grin, a fleeting triumph.

Because in the next second Michael hurtled forward in a burst of power, catching Blok at the knees and lifting him up and backward. The Luger's bullet passed over Michael's back, but the blades of Iron Fist's propeller bit true.

They carved Jerek Blok into red streamers of blood and bone from the waist up, as Michael gripped the legs and dove to the pavement beneath the props. In an eyeblink, there was nothing left of Blok but those legs, and a mist of blood staining the concrete. Silver teeth clinked down, and that was all.

Michael rolled beneath the blades, Blok's disembodied legs still twitching where they lay. In the bomber's cockpit, Van Hoven veered Iron Fist off the runway into the grass to avoid the Dornier, and as he passed the black night fighter he failed to note the figure that was following.

The bomber was picking up speed, moving back onto the pavement. Michael Gallatin reached up, past the bleeding body that lay over the rectangular gunport, and locked his hands around the machine-gun barrel. In the next second the B-17 was hurtling forward, and Michael lifted his feet up and winnowed into the plane, shoving the dead man aside with his shoulder.

Iron Fist reached the runway's end and nosed up. Its wheels left the ground, and Van Hoven turned the plane— one of its engines leaving a scrawl of black smoke—toward England.

Two minutes later the Dornier followed. Chesna had taken the controls as Lazaris pressed his hand to his broken collarbone and fought off unconsciousness. She looked at the fuel gauges; the needles had fallen past their red lines, and the warning lights of both wing tanks were blinking. She powered the plane after the trail of smoke as the wind shrilled through the windshield cracks in front of her face.

The B-17 climbed to about five thousand feet before it leveled off over the gray Channel. In the waist section, as wind whipped through the gun ports, Michael looked out at the smoking engine. The prop had ceased turning, and small sputters of fire shot from the blackened cowling. The damage wouldn't stop Iron Fist; in fact, it only made the masquerade more convincing. He searched the dead men for weapons, but found nothing. And as he stood up from his search he felt the B-17 pick up speed and there was a *whoosh* as something flew past the starboard gun portal.

Michael peered out. It was the Dornier. Chesna circled, about five hundred feet above. Fire! he thought. Shoot the bastard down! But she didn't, and he knew why. She feared hitting him. The die was cast. If Iron Fist was to be stopped, it was up to him.

He would have to kill the pilot and co-pilot, with his bare hands if necessary. Every passing second took them closer to England. He looked around for a weapon. The machine guns were loaded with belts of ammunition, but they were bolted to their mounts. The plane's interior had been stripped bare except for a red fire extinguisher.

He was about to go forward when he saw another plane through the portal. No, two more. They were diving on the Dornier. His blood went cold. They were British Spitfire fighters, and he saw the bright orange streaks of their tracer bullets as they opened fire on Chesna. Blok's camouflage was successful; the Spitfires' pilots thought they were protecting a crippled American Fortress.

In the Dornier Chesna jinked the plane violently to one side as tracers zipped past. She wobbled the wings and flashed the landing lights, but of course the Spitfires didn't turn away. They came in for the kill. Chesna felt the plane shudder and heard bullets crash into the port-side wing. And then the alarm buzzers went off, and that was the end of the fuel. She dove for the sea, a Spitfire on her tail. It sent a stream of bullets into the Dornier's fuselage, and they ricocheted off the metal ribs of the plane like a storm of hailstones. The Dornier was almost down on the water. She said, "Hang on!" to Lazaris, and wrenched the yoke back to lift the nose an instant before the plane smacked down. There was a bone-jerking impact, the seat belt cutting into Chesna's body as she was thrown forward. Her head slammed against the yoke, knocking her almost senseless. She tasted blood in her mouth, her tongue bitten. The Dornier was floating, and the Spitfires circled overhead and flew off after the Fortress.

Good shooting, she thought grimly.

Lazaris got his seat belt off while Chesna unsnapped her own. Water was flooding into the cockpit. Chesna stood up, her ribs throbbing with pain, and went back to the rack where a life raft was stored. The escape hatch was nearby, and together she and Lazaris forced it open.

Michael saw the orange life raft bloom on the Channel's surface. A British destroyer was already moving toward the downed Dornier. The two Spitfires circled Iron Fist, then took up positions on either side and slightly behind. Escorting us home, Michael thought. He leaned out the starboard portal, into the wail of the wind, and frantically waved his arms. The Spitfire on that side wobbled its wings in a sign of greeting. Damn it! Michael raged as he pulled back in. He smelled blood, and saw it all over his hands. It had come from the corpse that had been leaning out of the plane. Blood had streamed down the bomber's side.

He leaned out again, smeared more blood on his hands, and began to paint a Nazi swastika on the olive-green metal.

There was no response from the Spitfires. They held their position.

Desperate, Michael knew he had only one remaining option.

He found the safety on the starboard waist gun. He unlatched it and trained the barrel on the slow-flying Spitfire. Then he squeezed the trigger.

Bullets ripped holes along the plane's side. Michael saw the amazed expression of the pilot, staring right at him. He swung the gun back and kept shooting, and an instant later the Spitfire's engine belched smoke and fire. The aircraft dove away, still under the pilot's control but heading for the drink.

Sorry, old chap, Michael thought.

He went to the opposite portal and started to open fire

with the gun there, but the second Spitfire zoomed to a higher altitude, its pilot having seen what had happened to his companion. Michael gave a few bursts to drive home his point, but the bullets—thankfully—missed by a wide margin.

"What was that damned noise?" Van Hoven shouted in the cockpit. He looked at Schrader and then at Boots, whose face had become pallid at the reality of riding in this death plane to London. "It sounded like one of our own guns!" Van Hoven looked out the glass, and gasped with horror as he saw the flaming Spitfire gliding toward the sea. The second Spitfire buzzed them like an angered hornet.

Boots knew the colonel had killed the gunners. That was part of the plan, though the guns had been loaded to lure the crewmen into believing they would be alive when they crossed the Channel. So who was back there manning the machine gun?

Boots left the cockpit, moving through the bomb bay where the carnagene was armed and ready.

Michael kept firing as the Spitfire circled them, the gun shuddering in his hands. And then he got what he wanted: the Spitfire's wing gun sparked. Bullets thunked into the side of Iron Fist and threw sparks around Michael. He returned the fire as the British plane turned in a swift circle. The bastard was mad now, ready to shoot first and ask questions la—

Michael heard the clatter of hobnails on metal.

He looked to his left, and saw Boots coming at him along the walkway. The huge man stopped suddenly, his face a rictus of shock and rage at seeing Michael manning the machine gun, and then he came on with murder in his eyes.

Michael swiveled the gun to the left to shoot him down, but its barrel clunked against the rim of the opening and would go no further.

Boots hurtled forward. He kicked out, and before Michael could protect himself the big boot smacked into his stomach and sent him reeling backward along the walkway. He fell and skidded, the breath knocked out of him.

The Spitfire delivered another barrage, and as Boots reached Michael, machine-gun bullets tore through Iron Fist's skin and ricocheted around them. Michael kicked into the man's right knee. Boots howled with pain and staggered back as Van Hoven put Iron Fist into a shallow dive to escape the enraged Spitfire pilot. Boots went down, clutching his knee, as Michael gasped for breath.

On its next pass the Spitfire sent bursts of bullets into Iron Fist's bomb bay. One of those bullets ricocheted off a metal spar and glanced away to hit a carnagene bomb's fuse. The fuse sputtered, and smoke began to fill the compartment.

As Boots tried to haul himself up, Michael hit him on the point of the chin with an uppercut that snapped his head back. But Boots was as strong as an ox, and in the next second he heaved himself up and crashed headlong into Michael, throwing them both back against a metal-ribbed bulkhead. Michael hammered his fists down on Boots's cropped skull, and Boots punched into Michael's bruised stomach. Spitfire bullets ripped through the bulkhead beside them, showering them with orange sparks. Iron Fist shuddered, an engine smoking on its starboard wing.

In the cockpit Van Hoven leveled the plane off at one thousand feet. The Spitfire kept flashing back and forth, determined to bring them down. Schrader shouted, "There!" and pointed. The hazy landmass of England lay within sight, but now a third engine was smoking and beginning to miss. Van Hoven throttled forward, giving the bomber all the power it could handle. Iron Fist headed toward England at two hundred and ten miles per hour, Channel whitecaps breaking in its wake.

A fist cracked against the side of Michael's jaw, and Boots drove a knee into his groin. As Michael crumpled, Boots grasped his throat and lifted him, slamming his skull into the metal overhead. Stunned, Michael knew he had to change but he couldn't get a grip on the thought. He was lifted again, and again his skull hit the overhead. As Boots started to lift him a third time, Michael cracked his forehead against Boots's face, crunching the man's nose. Boots dropped him and staggered back, blood streaming from his nostrils. But before Michael could set himself for another attack, Boots swung a kick at his ribs. Michael dodged the blow, catching most of its impact on his right shoulder, and the breath hissed between his gritted teeth.

The Spitfire came head-on at Iron Fist. The wing guns sparked, and in the next instant the cockpit was full of flying glass and flames. Van Hoven slumped forward, his chest punctured by a half-dozen bullets, and Schrader writhed with a broken arm. One of Iron Fist's engines exploded, sending shrapnel tearing through the cockpit. The bombardier cried out, blinded by metal fragments. The aircraft sank lower toward the waves, flames gnawing in the ruined cockpit and across the starboard wing.

Boots limped toward Michael, who tried desperately to shake off the pain. Reaching down, Boots gripped his collar and hauled him up, then slammed a fist into his face. Michael fell back against the bulkhead, blood all over his mouth.

Boots drew his fist back, to smash into Michael's face again.

Before the blow could be delivered, Michael twisted to one side and his hands found the red cylinder of the fire extinguisher. He tore it loose from its straps and swung it around as Boots's fist came at his face. The man's fist was stopped short by the cylinder, and his knuckles broke like matchsticks. Michael punched the cylinder into Boots's stomach like a battering ram. The breath whooshed from the huge man, and Michael struck upward with the cylinder into Boots's jaw. He heard the satisfying crunch of the jawbone breaking. Boots, his eyes glazed with pain and his lips split open, grappled with Michael for the cylinder. A knee drove into Michael's side, and as he sagged to his knees Boots wrenched the cylinder away from him.

Boots lifted the fire extinguisher, intending to smash Michael's brains out with it. Michael tensed to lunge at him before the cylinder could slam down.

Over the shriek of the wind Michael heard the chatter of the Spitfire's guns. Fiery tracers came through the plane's side and ricocheted off the bulkheads. He saw three holes, each the size of a fist, open across Boots's broad chest. And in the next instant a bullet clanged against the fire extinguisher, and it went off with a blast like a miniature bomb.

Michael flung himself flat as pieces of metal clattered in all directions. Chemical foam hissed on the bulkheads. He looked up, and saw Boots standing there holding on to a machine-gun mount with one arm.

Boots's other arm lay a few feet away, the hand still

twitching. He looked at it, blinking with dumb amazement. He released his grip, and staggered toward his arm.

When Boots moved, his intestines began to slide from the gaping wound in his side. Pieces of red metal glistened in the hole, and his clothes were drenched with chemical foam. Another wound had been torn open on the side of his throat, the blood streaming down from the severed veins like a crimson fountain. With each step Boots diminished. He stopped, staring down at his hand and arm, and then turned his head to look at Michael.

He stood there, dead on his feet, until Michael got up, walked to him, and knocked him over with a finger.

Boots crashed down, and lay still.

Michael felt near passing out, but one glance out the portal and the realization that the sea was less than three hundred feet below cleared his head. He stepped over Boots's grisly bulk and went toward the cockpit.

In the bomb bay he recoiled at the smoke and the hissing noise. One of the carnagene bombs was about to detonate. He went on, finding the navigator desperately trying to fly the plane as the pilot lay dead and the copilot was severely wounded. Iron Fist was dropping steadily, the Spitfire circling above. The coast of England was less than seven miles away. Michael said to the terrified navigator, "Put us down. *Now.*"

The man fumbled with the controls, chopping the power off and trying to get the nose up as Iron Fist—now truly a crippled bird—dropped another hundred feet. Michael braced himself against the pilot's seat. Iron Fist fell, plowing into the Channel with a surprisingly gentle bump, its force at last spent.

Waves washed over the wings. Michael didn't wait for the navigator. He went back through the bomb bay to the plane's waist and unlatched the entry door. There was no time to search for a life raft, and he doubted if one had survived that hail of bullets. He jumped into the Channel's chilly water, and swam away from the aircraft as fast as he could.

The Spitfire came down low, skimming the surface, passed over Michael, and headed toward the green land beyond.

Michael kept going, wanting to get as much distance as he could between him and the Fortress. He heard hot surfaces sizzling as the plane began to sink. Perhaps the navigator got out, perhaps not. Michael didn't pause. The salt water stung his wounds and kept him from passing out. Stroke after stroke, he left the airplane behind. When he had gotten a distance away, he heard a rush and gurgling and looked back to see the plane going down at the tail. Its nose reared up, and on it Michael could see Frankewitz's drawing of Hitler squeezed in an Iron Fist. If fish could appreciate art, they'd have a grand time.

Iron Fist began to disappear, sinking rapidly as water gushed into the waist gun portals. In another moment it was gone, and air bubbles rose and burst at the turbulent surface. Michael turned away and swam toward shore. He was weakening; he felt himself wanting to let go. Not yet, he told himself. One more stroke. One more, and one after that. Breaststrokes definitely were superior to dog paddling.

He heard the chugging of an engine. A patrol boat was coming toward him, two men with rifles on the bow. A Union Jack pennant whipped in the rigging.

He was home.

They picked him up, wrapped a blanket around him, and gave him a cup of tea as strong as wolf piss. Then they trained their rifles on him, until they could get to shore and turn him over to the authorities. The boat was about a mile from harbor when Michael heard a distant, muffled *whump*. He looked back, and saw a huge geyser of water shoot up from the surface. One or more of the carnagene bombs had exploded in their bomb bay at the bottom of the English Channel. The geyser settled back, the water thrashing for a moment, and that was the end of it.

But not quite.

Michael stepped out on a dock, a harbor village behind him, and scanned the Channel for a British destroyer that he knew must be arriving soon. He shook himself, and water droplets flew from his hair and clothes. He felt overcome with happiness, even standing at the point of Home Guard rifles.

So happy, in fact, that he felt like howling.

ELEVEN

Unforeseen Circumstances

1

His eyes were rimmed with red, his face chalky. It was a very bad sign.

"None of it survived, I'm afraid," Martin Bormann said. He cleared his throat. "Dr. Hildebrand is dead and . . . the project seems not to have borne fruit."

He waited for more of it, his hands clenched into fists on his desktop before him. On the wall behind him a portrait of Frederick the Great watched in judgment.

"We . . . don't think the aircraft ever reached London," Bormann went on. He glanced uneasily at the other man in the room, a gray-haired, stiff-backed field marshal. "That is to say, there's no evidence the carnagene was delivered to its target."

He said nothing. A pulse beat steadily at his temple. Through a gilt-edged window the shadows of June 6 were spreading over Berlin. Tacked up on another wall were maps of Normandy, showing beaches that the world would soon know under the code names Utah, Omaha, Gold, Juno, and Sword. Everywhere on those maps, red lines were pushing inland, and black lines marked the retreat—oh, what traitors! he thought as he looked at them—of German troops.

"The project was a failure," Bormann said. "Due to . . . unforeseen circumstances."

"No, it's not that," Hitler answered in a small, quiet voice. "It's that someone didn't believe strongly enough. Someone didn't have the necessary willpower. Bring me Blok." His voice was more strident. "Colonel Jerek Blok. That's who I'd like to see. At once."

"Colonel Blok is . . . no longer with us."

"The traitor!" Hitler almost rose from his desk. "What

595

did he do? Run and give himself up to the first British soldier he saw?"

"Colonel Blok is deceased," Bormann said.

"Yes, I would've committed suicide, too, if I'd botched things like he has!" Hitler stood. His face was flushed and moist looking. "I should've known not to give him any responsibility! He was a failure, pretending to be a success! The world is full of them!"

"At least Germany is, I fear," the field marshal said under his breath.

"When I think of the time and money spent on this project, I'm almost ill!" Hitler came out from behind his desk. "So Blok took his own life, did he? How was it done? A pill or a pistol?"

"A . . ." Bormann almost said *propeller*. But telling the *Führer* what had really happened would open a real can of worms. There would be the matter of the German Resistance—those foul pigs—and the secret agents who somehow destroyed all of the carnagene. And the distasteful matter of Chesna van Dorne, too. No, no! It was best to let the story stand as it was: that a fleet of bombers had hit Skarpa's tanks and armory, and the explosion had ruined the chemicals. The *Führer*, in these troublous times, had more to worry about than reality. "A pistol," he said.

"Well, it saved us a bullet, didn't it? But all that time and effort, wasted! We could have developed the solar cannon with that money! But no, no—Blok and his conspirators had to talk me out of it! I'm too trusting, that's the problem! Martin, I think the man might have been working for the British after all!"

Bormann shrugged. Sometimes it was better to let him believe as he would. He was easier to handle that way.

"My *Führer?*" The field marshal motioned to the Normandy maps. "If you might turn your attention to the current situation, please? You'll notice here, that the British and Canadians are moving toward Caen. Over here"—he touched another portion of the map—"the American troops are progressing toward Carentan. Our troop disposition is stretched too thin to contain both problems. Might I ask your opinion on which divisions to block this threat?"

Hitler said nothing. He stood staring not at the maps, on which life-and-death struggles were displayed, but at his collection of watercolors, in which imaginary wolves lurked.

"My *Führer?*" the field marshal urged. "What shall we do?"

A muscle twitched in Hitler's face. He turned away from the paintings, went to his desk, and opened its top drawer. He reached in, and his hand emerged with a knifelike letter opener.

He walked back to the paintings, his eyes glazed and his gait that of a sleepwalker, and he plunged the blade through the first one, ripping the farmhouse scene from top to bottom and with it the wolf that hid in a shadow. The blade pierced the second watercolor, the one of a mountain stream in which a wolf crouched behind a rock. "Lies," Hitler whispered, tearing the canvas. "Lies and deceptions."

"My *Führer?*" the field marshal asked, but there was no answer. Martin Bormann turned away and went to stand at a window overlooking the Thousand-Year Reich.

The blade tore through the third painting, in which a wolf hid amid a field of white eidelweiss. "Lies," the man said, his voice strained with tension. The blade went back and forth, and shreds of canvas fell around his polished shoes. "Lies, lies, lies."

In the distance an air-raid siren went off. Its howl reverberated over the broken city, hazed with dust and smoke from previous bombing raids. To the east lay oncoming night.

Hitler dropped the blade to the carpet. He clapped his hands over his ears.

A bomb flashed on the outskirts of the city. Bormann put his hands over his eyes to shield them from the glare. As Hitler stood trembling with the remnants of his visions underfoot, the German field marshal placed his hand over his mouth, for fear he might scream.

Big Ben chimed the eleventh hour. In another circumstance Michael Gallatin mused, that would be known as the wolf's hour. In this case, however, it was eleven o'clock on a sunny morning in the middle of June, and even a wolf wouldn't be brave enough to face London traffic.

He watched the traffic from a window over Downing Street, the cars moving alongside the Thames into the swirl of Trafalgar Square. He felt fresh and alive. It was always so when death was faced and beaten—at least for a time. He wore a dark blue suit, a white shirt, and a blue-printed tie, and under his clothes his ribs were laced with adhesive tape. His palm wound was still bandaged and his thigh gave him some trouble, but he was all right. He would run again, as fast as ever.

"What are you thinking?" she asked him, coming up behind.

"Oh, that it's a beautiful day and I'm glad to be out of the hospital. Days like this don't look so nice from a bed."

"I'd say that depends on the bed, wouldn't you?"

Michael turned to face her. Chesna looked refreshed, her face free of the lines that pain had put there. Well, perhaps a few remained; that was life. "Yes," he agreed. "I certainly would."

The office's door opened, and a large-boned, big-nosed man in the uniform of a Royal Air Force captain entered. Lazaris's hair was growing out, and he had kept his beard, though it was now neatly trimmed. He was as clean as soap, and he even smelled soapy. His left arm and shoulder were covered with plaster under his RAF jacket, a plaster patch mending the broken collarbone. "Hello!" he said, glad to see them. He smiled, and Chesna realized that in his own coarse way, Lazaris was very handsome. "I'm sorry I'm late."

"That's all right. Evidently we're not on military time." Their appointment had been scheduled for eleven o'clock sharp. "Speaking of military, have you enlisted in the RAF?"

"Well, I'm still an officer of the Russian air force," he replied, speaking his native tongue, "but I've been made an honorary captain, just yesterday. I went up in a Spitfire. Oh, that's a plane! If we'd only had Spitfires, we could have—" He smiled again, and let it go. "I'm going back, as soon as I can." He shrugged. "Like I say, in the sky I'm a lion. What about the both of you?"

"I'm home," Michael said. "For a long time. Chesna is going to California."

"Oh yes!" Lazaris tried English: "Cal-e-for-nye-ay?"

"That's the place," Chesna said.

"Verra gut! You be a verra beeg stir!"

"I'll settle for a small part. Even maybe as a stunt pilot."

"Pilot! Ya!" The mere mention of that word made a dreamlike expression surface on the Russian's face.

Michael slipped his hand into Chesna's and looked out at London. It was a beautiful city, made more beautiful by the fact that there would never again be Nazi planes in the sky over it. Bad weather had forced the postponement of D-Day from the fifth of June to the sixth; since that day, hundreds of thousands of Allied soldiers had gone ashore on the Normandy beaches, steadily pushing the Nazis back toward Germany. The war wasn't over yet, of course; there would be more trials and tribulations once the Nazis were pushed back into their own den. But the initial step had been taken. The invasion of Europe was a grand, if costly, success. It was only a matter of weeks now before Paris would be liberated, and Gaby's homeland set free.

Hitler's advance was ended. From this point on there would be a long retreat, the lurching German war machine caught between the crushing—dare he think it?—iron fists of America, Great Britain, and Russia.

As the sun fell upon his face, Michael thought of the path. Of McCarren and Gaby, the underground passages, Camille and Mouse, the rooftop battle at the Paris Opéra, the fight in the woods before Berlin, Mouse's ruined house and ruined life, the Iron Cross that meant nothing. He thought of the Reichkronen, and Harry Sandler's murder train, the kennels of Falkenhausen, and the long flight to Norway. Of Kitty, and a knife with a hooked blade.

There had been another path, too: he had been walking it since a boy chased a kite into a Russian forest. It had led him through a world of joy and sadness, tragedy and triumph, to this point in time, and beyond this point lay the future.

Man or beast? he wondered. He knew now which world he truly belonged to. By accepting his place in the world of men, he made the miracle true. He did not think he had failed Wiktor. In fact, he thought Wiktor might be proud of him, as a father is proud of a beloved son.

Live free, he thought. If that were at all possible in this world, he would try his best at it.

A buzzer went off on the receptionist's desk. She was a small, lantern-jawed woman with a carnation on her lapel. "He'll see you now," she told them, and got up to open the door into the inner sanctum.

The man within, bulldog stocky, got up from his desk and came forward to meet them. He had heard grand things about them, he said. Please sit down! He motioned them to three chairs. The medal ceremony, he said, would be a small, quiet affair. There was no use in alerting the press to such a sensitive undertaking. Did they agree to that? They did, of course.

"Would you mind if I smoked?" he asked Chesna, and when she said she wouldn't, he produced one of his long trademark cigars from a rosewood cigar case on his desk and lit it. "You must realize the service you've performed for England. For the world, actually. Incalculable service. You have friends in high places, and you'll all be well taken care of. Ah, while we're on the subject of friends!" He reached into a desk drawer and brought out an envelope sealed with wax. "This is from a friend of yours, Major Gallatin."

Michael took it. He recognized the seal on the blob of wax, and smiled faintly. The envelope went into his coat pocket.

The prime minister went on at length about the ramifications of the invasion and that by the end of summer the Nazis would be fighting on the borders of Germany. Their chemical warfare plans had been miserably dashed; not only in this Iron Fist affair, he said, but also because of Gustav Hildebrand's . . . ah . . . shall we say *dissolution?*

Michael studied his face. He had to ask a question. "Excuse me, sir?"

"Yes, Major?"

"Do you . . . just happen to have any relatives in Germany?"

"No," Churchill said. "Of course not. Why?"

"I . . . saw someone dressed up to resemble you."

"Ah, the cheeky bastards!" the prime minister growled, and puffed a gout of blue smoke.

When their audience with the prime minister was ended, they left the building and stood on Downing Street. A car with an RAF driver was waiting for Lazaris. He embraced Chesna, one-handedly, and then hugged his comrade.

"Gallatinov, you take care of Goldilocks, eh?" Lazaris smiled, but his eyes looked a little damp. "Around her you act like a gentleman . . . which means like an Englisher, not like a Russki!"

"I'll keep that in mind." He thought, however, that Lazaris was a fine gentleman, even for a Russki. "Where will you be?"

Lazaris looked up, at the cloudless blue. He smiled again, slyly, clapped Michael on the shoulder, and got into the waiting car like a member of the royal family. The RAF driver pulled them away from the curb, and Lazaris gave Michael a salute. Then the car merged with traffic, and was gone.

"Let's walk," Michael said. He took Chesna's hand and guided her toward Trafalgar Square. She was still limping a little, but her ankle was healing with no complications. He liked Chesna's company. He wanted to show her his home, and who knew what might come of that? Something lasting? No, probably not. They were both moving in different directions, but now linked by hands. For a time, at least . . . it could be sweet.

"Do you like animals?" he asked her.

"*What?*"

"I'm just curious."

"Well . . . dogs and cats, yes. What animals do you mean?"

"A little larger," he said, but did not elaborate. He didn't want to scare her before they left their London hotel. "I'd like for you to see my home, in Wales. Would you care to go?"

"With you?" She squeezed his hand. "When do we leave?"

"Soon. My house is very quiet. There we'll have plenty of time to talk."

Again, she was puzzled. "Talk? About what?"

"Oh . . . myths and folklore," he said.

Chesna laughed. Michael Gallatin was one of the most curious—and certainly unique—men she'd ever met. His nearness excited her. She said, "Will we only talk?"

Michael stopped, in the shadow of Lord Nelson, put his arms around Chesna van Dorne, and kissed her.

Their bodies pressed together. Citizens of London stopped to gawk, but neither Michael nor Chesna cared. Their lips merged together like liquid fire, and as the kiss went on Michael felt a tingling sensation.

He knew what it was. Black, sleek wolf hair was rippling up his backbone, under his clothes. He felt the hair rise over his back and shoulders, tingling in this moment of pure, intense passion and joy, and then his flesh itched as the hair began to recede.

Well, there was always more where that came from.

Michael kissed the corners of her lips. Her aroma, cinnamon and leather, was in his soul. He hailed a passing cab, and he and Chesna got in and headed for Piccadilly and their hotel.

On the way he took the envelope from his pocket, broke the waxed seal, and removed the letter. There were two words, written in a familiar handwriting: *Another mission?*

He returned the letter to the envelope and the envelope to his pocket. The man in him yearned for peace, but the wolf in him yearned for action. Which one would triumph? That he couldn't say.

Chesna leaned against him, her head on his shoulder. "Is that something you need to take care of?"

"No," Michael told her. "Not today."

A battle had been won, but the war went on.